THE
EDEN
PASSION

MARILYN
HARRIS

THE EDEN PASSION

Marilyn Harris

BALLANTINE BOOKS • NEW YORK

Library of Congress Catalog Card Number: 78-21602

ISBN 0-345-28537-9

This edition published by arrangement with
G. P. Putnam's Sons

Manufactured in the United States of America

First Ballantine Books Edition: April 1980

For my friends in England,
June and Bob Robinson,
Peter Ashen,
Emmie and Harry Cox,
Michael and Dorothy Taylor,
gratefully, for their
hospitality and assistance.

The steam whistle was already heard across the fields: already in mid-Atlantic the great steamers were crossing against wind and tide; privilege, patronage and the power of rank were already beginning to tremble and were afraid . . .

Yet we who have lived in the century, we who are full of its ideas, we who are swept along the full stream of it—we know not, we cannot see where it is carrying us . . .

—Sir Walter Besant
The Victorians

Eden Castle,
North Devon,
England

IN THE LATE afternoon of May 2, 1851, having left the mildness of spring behind in London, in a cold rain, Elizabeth looked up to see the gray silhouette of Eden Castle in the distance.

Beside them now rode only three riders on horseback. At Taunton that morning, the fourth had galloped ahead to inform the inhabitants of Eden Castle that the body of Edward Eden was coming home.

Approaching exhaustion, Elizabeth looked with sympathy at John. Not one word had they exchanged during the entire journey. Not once had he partaken of food or drink, and not once had he relinquished his control of the reins, although all the riders had offered repeatedly to spell him, as had Elizabeth herself.

But apparently there was a turmoil inside his young head that compelled him to keep silent. Looking up, she saw that he too had caught his first glimpse of Eden Castle.

She closed her eyes, unable to look at him any longer, unable as well to view the great hulk of that castle drawing nearer. Her one thought now was to have done with it and return immediately to London. All she was bringing home was a broken shell. The spirit and memory of Ed-

1

ward Eden still resided in London, in the hearts of those thousands of men and women and children who had followed the wagon to the extreme western edge of the city before they had commenced ιο fall back. She belonged with them, and although she hadn't the faintest idea how, she fully intended to continue his work and reopen the Common Kitchen, to feed, clothe and give shelter as best she could to anyone who came to her door in need.

Passing beneath the gatehouse arch now, Elizabeth looked up into the driving rain at the awesome facade of the castle. Grander than Buckingham, or so it seemed to her. Ahead she saw a small group of people moving down a flight of steps, all clothed in rain-wet black, a man and a woman as far as she could tell, while at the top of the stairs, inside the shelter of an arch, she saw an old woman clutching two children to her skirts.

Turning about, she looked ahead and saw that the guardsmen were leading them toward a black iron fence whch surrounded a small graveyard. The gate was open, and beyond she saw a scattering of marble stones, and there to the left, near the fence, she saw three gravediggers, their spades in their hands. Then the grave itself was visible.

Through the narrow gate, John guided the horses into a small clearing on the left and brought them to a halt. His head, rain-drenched, inclined slowly forward as though he were aware that his job was done. How she longed to somehow penetrate that terrible silence into which he had fallen.

She was aware of activity at the rear of the wagon, saw four guardsmen climbing aboard, each lifting one corner of the coffin and hoisting it down to earth.

As she swùng to the ground, she glanced back up at John. "Are you coming?" she asked, trying to stretch the stiffness out of her legs so that she might walk erect, like a lady.

Although that pale boyish face lifted and looked down on her, he gave no response.

Then Elizabeth felt her attention being drawn to the coffin being slowly lowered into earth. The rain, she noticed, made a peculiar sound on the coffin lid, as though it were hollow. And in that instant, a new sense of loss swept over her.

No words? She glanced quickly about in search of a priest. No one to tell the world about this man? Then, although she'd vowed not to break, she bent her head over and gave in to one small moan. It sounded out of place in that death yard, as though mourners and corpses alike must maintain the silence of the grave.

The coffin was lowered now. As the first clods of dirt struck the coffin lid, she turned slowly away and walked a distance beyond the mound of dirt.

What was the connection between the man himself and that almost obscene ritual which was taking place behind her? All at once, an unexpected memory from an earlier time rose up before her. She remembered Edward as she'd first seen him in the Common Cell at Newgate, recalled how he'd put his arm around her and warmed her with his own cloak. She remembered him in the banqueting hall in the house on Oxford Street, laughing, lifting the children into the air, carrying them on his shoulders. And she thought too of certain facts that again had nothing to do with what was going on behind her, of the reality of his seventeen Ragged Schools scattered throughout London which were still functioning, existing quite well now on contributions from charity and from the Union. She thought of the hundreds of abandoned children who had been fed and clothed and housed, and in certain instances, educated, like herself. She thought of the Common Kitchen, the door always open. She thought of his love and tenderness and kindness to all. She thought on all these things and more, and felt her heart fill, not with grief, but with gratitude that she had known such a man.

Then she could restrain herself no longer and wept openly for Edward Eden, for John, his son, and even for the men and women standing rigidly beside the grave.

She looked back at the place where the gravediggers were doing their job. Let them! The man himself had long ago escaped and now resided in thousands of human hearts. Try to contain him in mere earth and wood, she thought with a smile.

It could not be done. . . .

Harriet stood atop the stairs outside the Great Hall, in the cold drizzling rain, feeling nothing, seeing little, and completely aware that her awesome strength was fast running out. Behind her, she was aware of James huddled in the shelter of the arch with the two children. What in the name of God was the delay?

Annoyed, she glanced down at the wagon standing at the foot of the Great Hall steps, its wheels coated with mud from the graveyard. She saw the boy and the young woman in close huddle. Feeling sorry for both, Harriet had issued an invitation for them to take refuge around the fire in the servants' hall.

She had not expected such a simple and humane gesture to be a matter for discussion. But apparently it was. So still she waited, consuming what strength she had left in an attempt to keep her mind away from the fresh grave, the realization of the man they had just buried.

Edward. The name still hurt.

Then at last she saw the two moving toward the stairs, the young woman in the lead. "Milady," she called up in a curiously aggressive voice. "We thank you for your kind invitation." At that moment, Harriet saw the young boy move up close beside her. He must be about fifteen, Harriet thought, perhaps sixteen. His face bore a peculiar expression, resolution of some sort. She couldn't tell.

The young woman was speaking again. "I will not be staying, milady. I want to return to London right away."

Considering it settled, Harriet was in the process of retreating when she heard the woman speaking again, and looked back to see her climbing the stairs. Midway up, she stopped as though she did not want to come any closer. "I beg your pardon, milady," she said. "With your permission, the boy will stay."

Harriet turned slowly back. A peculiar request. She couldn't very well say no, for the boy was standing within earshot. "Of course," she murmured, "if he desires . . ."

The woman moved up another step, her face tense, as though she were trying very hard to say the right thing. "The boy here," she began, looking back over her shoulder, "is Mr. Eden's son."

The words came softly over the wind and rain. "Mr.

Eden's . . ." As Harriet tried to repeat what she thought she had heard, she found she couldn't.

The woman repeated it for her. "His son, milady. I have his paper back in London, his baptismal certificate. I'll send it right away if you wish . . ."

But at that moment Harriet was not thinking of baptismal records. Instead she gazed steadfastly down upon the boy who, with matching steadfastness, returned her gaze. She saw it now, although she did not want to admit to it, the similarity, the stance, the line of the jaw, the hair coloring, the eyes, especially the eyes. It might have been a young Edward staring up at her.

She looked away over the inner courtyard. My God, she couldn't turn him out. She owed Edward that much. But who was the mother? That poor thin woman on the steps before her?

As she looked back at the two waiting patiently at midstep, she tried to erase all traces of uneasiness from her face. "Of course, he's welcome," she said.

She continued to watch closely as the boy and the woman hurried back to the wagon, was still watching as the boy reached into the back and withdrew a small satchel. A moment later he fell into a close and loving embrace with the young woman.

Still Harriet stood watching, trying to conceal her agitation, to tell herself that it was nothing, that of course their solicitor would have to launch a discreet but thorough investigation, perhaps discover the identity of the mother. There was plenty of room in the servants' hall to accommodate a young boy.

Everything seemed to wait in the cold dusk as the boy watched the wagon pass through the gatehouse arch. Harriet saw him bow his head as though he'd offered a brief prayer. Then those eyes, Edward's eyes, were staring up at her. He appeared so alone, both boy and satchel dwarfed by the vast emptiness of the courtyard.

Clearly they couldn't stand like this all evening. Someone had to move. With an effort of will she pulled away from those intense young eyes and issued a command to one of the waiting stewards. "Take him to the servants'

hall," she called down. "And see that he has dry clothes
and something to eat."

The steward started toward the boy, his hand outstretched for the satchel. But at the last moment Harriet
saw the boy scoop up the luggage and start toward the
stairs.

As he came upward, her first impulse was to withdraw.
But she held her ground and was about to redirect him to
the servants' door when without warning a dazzling smile
broke across those young features.

He stood less than three feet from her. "If you don't
mind," he commenced in a voice remarkable for its
strength and clarity, "I prefer to reside in my father's
chambers. It's a waste of time, don't you think, to get settled in one place, only to have to move to another?"

Again she found that speech was beyond her, and she
did well to move to one side as he walked past her, beneath the arch, past James and the children into the Great
Hall.

He turned briefly back. "I know the way," he announced. "I need no assistance."

He proceeded on across the Great Hall, when suddenly
at mid-point he stopped. "If it wouldn't be too much trouble," he asked, "a fire would be pleasant. My father always said there was nothing worse than a May Devon
rain."

Harriet followed a few steps after him. She saw him
glance lightly up at the ceiling of the Great Hall, as though
he were searching his mind for something.

Apparently he found it, for the smile on his face broadened. "I believe my father told me that the fire well in
his chambers required a half a dozen good oak logs, approximately the length of a man's arm." He was silent a
moment, assessing her. "If the steward would be so kind
as to lay such a fire, I'd be most grateful."

There was not a trace of impudence on the young face,
only quiet conviction. Then he turned again and proceeded across the Great Hall, his head erect, shoulders
back.

Harriet watched him, noted the swing of his arms, the
way he carried his body, the angle of the head. Suddenly

and without warning she shivered, though not from cold now, but rather from the incredible sensation that true recognition was just beyond her, that if only she could remove certain veils from her eyes, the mystery of his identity would be solved.

She stepped quickly forward and asked in a voice remarkable for its fearful quality, "Who are you?"

Just a few steps short of the far doorway which led into the heart of the castle, the boy stopped. Slowly he turned, an expression of quizzical impatience on his face, as though he was certain this was old ground that had been gone over before to everyone's satisfaction. He placed his luggage on the floor by his feet, then stood erect. With visible and awesome pride he said, "My name is John Murrey Eden. My father was Edward Eden. I have come home."

She saw him pause again, as though to see if there would be further interrogation. And at last he disappeared into the darkened corridor.

Behind her, she heard James trying to articulate something, a protest, she assumed, though it came out as little more than sputtering. She glanced over her shoulder and saw her husband in a crouched position, clutching their children to him, as though they all were in imminent danger from an unidentified threat.

She looked back toward the empty doorway, and stood absolutely still, listening. There were a dozen passageways leading out from that corridor. It had taken her over a month to learn them all. Surely the boy would return in a moment and confess to being lost.

But he didn't. In fact, she heard his step on the staircase now, moving steadily upward in the proper direction toward Edward's third-floor chambers, as though he knew the interior of vast Eden Castle as intimately as he knew any place on earth.

In the event that someone followed after him—and he was certain they would—he left the door ajar and turned to confront his father's chamber.

Oh, and it *was* familiar. He'd not counted on remembering so much. Now he heard an odd rustling in his ear, as though his father were still here, telling him about Eden. He reached back through the door and lifted a small lamp from its position on the wall and took one tentative step forward. In spite of the shadows, every object in that Spartan interior seemed to be presenting itself to him for judgment.

Stepping toward the center, he realized critically that there was an absence of everything. No carpet, but merely cold stone floor. No cushions, only straight-backed wooden chairs. Not even lamps that he could see, save for the one he held in his hand, no tapestries softening the walls, no paintings to engage the eye or the mind. In less than a minute he completed the bleak inventory which he already knew by heart and sat slowly in a near chair.

Infuriated, he looked about, almost choking on the self-denial which emanated from those barren walls. Suffering from an incoherent blend of anger and fatigue, he strode toward the wardrobe and jerked it open and found precisely what he knew he would find, less than a dozen garments, worn, some not even cleansed.

Damn! Look! He pulled forth a jacket. A beggar wore better. And look! Another, with buttons missing. And now he commenced jerking the garments off their hooks and hurling them to the floor, his rage and bewilderment increasing, his breath catching in his throat, his eyes playing tricks on him in the dim light so that now and then as he touched a sleeve, he saw the man himself. And still he pulled forth the clothes, talking aloud now—"How would it have offended your soul to buy decent clothes? You looked after others, why not yourself?"—always punctuating the unanswered questions with curses of outrage, the pile of discarded garments ever-growing, some hurled halfway across the chamber until at last his hands found one remaining cloak, a dark gray with torn collar.

Breathing heavily from his exertion, John held it. Without warning he slipped to his knees and clasped the cloak to him and buried his face in it and smelled the scent of the man they had just buried in the graveyard behind the castle.

"Papa," he whispered, and clasped the cloak even

tighter in his arms, and for the first time gave in to his grief.

For several minutes he was aware of nothing but the loss of his father. Then gradually the sensation of someone standing in the door caused him to look quickly up where he found the wide sympathetic eyes of a young boy staring at him.

Grateful for the shadows which earlier had plagued him, John hurriedly wiped away the embarrassing tears and stood, dropping the gray cloak onto the pile of abandoned garments.

But before John could speak, the boy stepped into the room, eyeing the scattered garments. "You made a mess," he said, in so solemn a tone that, in spite of himself, John smiled.

"I did indeed," he agreed.

The boy stepped farther into the room, somberly surveying the walls and bare furnishings as John had done earlier. Still safe in shadows, John brushed away the last of his tears and determined to his own satisfaction the identity of his young visitor. This would be his cousin— his uncle, Lord Eden's son—the next heir to Eden Castle. From where John stood, he guessed the boy's age at about eight, saw his slight frame tightly encased in a slim black jacket, his skin pale, hair and eyes dark, as his scrutiny of the chamber continued.

"What's your name?" John called out to the boy, whose inspection had led him to the large table near the center of the room.

Still not looking at him, but concentrating now on the face he was drawing with the tip of his finger in the dust on the table, the boy replied, "Richard Grenville Powels Eden," then leaned sharply over to put eyes and nose on the dust face.

"That's quite a name," John said, watching him.

"Clara calls me Dick sometimes, but my mother doesn't like it."

"What should I call you?"

"Richard." For the first time the boy looked up. "Are you going to live here?"

John nodded. "It's my home."

"They're arguing about you downstairs."

Interested, John stepped forward. "What are they saying?"

The boy shrugged. "They don't know who you are." Suddenly his face brightened as with his fist he rubbed out the circle face he'd drawn on the table. "But I know. Your name is John Murrey Eden. Your father was my uncle Edward, and you have come home."

A grin passed between the two boys. With relief, it dawned on John that at least one had understood the message he'd been asked to repeat downstairs.

"Do you want me to help you unpack?" Richard asked now, his journey about the room taking him close to the pile of discarded garments. For a moment he seemed to stare down on them as though remembering his first sight of John kneeling. "I'm sorry about your father," he said quietly. "Clara said he was a good man."

"And who would Clara be?" John asked, following after him.

"Nursemaid," Richard replied. "She doesn't tend me as much as she does my sister," he added defensively.

Preoccupied, John looked toward the open door. It was only a matter of time before . . .

"Do you play marbles?" Richard asked, coming up alongside him.

Struggling in an attempt to keep his thoughts in order, John nodded, "On occasion."

"I have four blue cat's eyes," Richard boasted, grinning. "Do you want to see them?"

Without waiting for a reply, he began eagerly to dig down into his pocket, something in his manner which suggested to John that he was suffering from loneliness.

"Look!"

Before him on that outstretched palm John saw four glistening cat's eyes. "They're magic." The boy grinned.

"How so?"

"Aunt Jane said words over them. They always win."

Aunt Jane. There was a familiar name. His father's aunt . . .

"She's very old," Richard was saying, "but she's a good

witch. I'll take you up to see her after dinner if you wish."

John smiled. "I'd like that," and again he examined the marbles. "I'm afraid I wouldn't stand a chance against magic marbles."

Without hesitation Richard selected two marbles and placed them in John's hand. "There, now," he announced. "We're even."

The small but generous gesture had a peculiar effect on John. "Thank you."

Suddenly from the doorway came a voice. "Richard!" As one, both boys turned toward the woman standing there, lamp in hand.

"Mama." Richard smiled, going to her side with no real alarm. "We're going to play marbles tomorrow, and after dinner, I said I would take him to—"

Lovingly she reached out and drew him close. "Clara has been searching for you," she whispered. "Run along now. We'll talk later."

John sensed a good relationship between the two, love tempered with maternal caution.

Putting envy aside, John thanked Richard again for his gift of marbles and reassured him that if circumstances permitted, the game was on for the next day.

Then the boy was gone, leaving the two of them in the chamber, confronting each other over the glow of lamplight.

Lady Eden. Harriet. John had recognized her immediately in the graveyard, though he'd only seen her once before, years ago in the magistrate's office the morning of the hearing, when his father had made his idiocy public by ceding all claim to his own fortune. In all the intervening years, his father had never been able to give him one coherent reason for that moment of lunacy, and it had been on that day that their path had started downward.

"Lady Eden," he murmured, feeling the need to break the uncomfortable silence. But now he saw a transfixed quality on her face, as though she were not seeing him at all.

"My lady . . ." He smiled, trying to break the curious spell. "If my appearence offends you, I'm . . ."

Without warning, the hand holding the lamp wavered. The lady's face seemed to go bloodless. Quickly she lifted her head as though for breath. Then her eyes closed, and had John not stepped quickly forward and taken the lamp from her, lamp and all would have gone crashing to the floor as she collapsed.

For a moment he could only stare down on her. Was she ill?

"My . . . lady?"

He called a second time, then looked frantically over his shoulder in the hope that help had arrived. But there was no one there.

"My lady, I . . ."

He couldn't very well just leave her on the floor. He set the lamp on the table and tried to determine the manner in which to lift her. He noticed now the hem of her black gown, damp and mud-caked from his father's burial. Perhaps she possessed a delicate constitution that could not absorb the rituals of death.

He moved awkwardly about her. Where were those safe points where a woman could be lifted without . . . ?

Nothing to do, but do it. On that note of determination, he gently eased her over onto her back, stole a quick glance behind him to confirm the distance to the bed, then reached beneath her arms and commenced to drag her, her body extending in the process, her head fallen grotesquely forward, her hands flopping puppet fashion.

Breathless from his effort, he perched on the bed on his knees, looking down. She was so still, apparently unmindful of the rough transport, and so beautiful. In the awkward fashion in which he'd dragged her up onto the bed, her gown had become twisted, and now certain aspects of her body were being revealed to him in fascinating detail. One breast had slipped almost entirely free of its black binding.

Abruptly he closed his eyes against a most curious sensation. He scrambled backward off the bed and took refuge behind the large table. Over the flickering lamp, he saw her, still unmoved.

Suddenly he drew a shuddering breath and hurled himself toward the door in search of help.

He heard a soft moan behind him and looked back. She was stirring, her head turning gently from side to side. Well, he couldn't abandon her now that she was reviving. Anyway, he had a strong feeling that she had come with a message.

Then he must see her safely revived and receive her message. As he approached the edge of the bed, he stopped. Best to let her discover that naked breast first.

Her eyes were opened now, obviously trying to assess everything at once, her location, her position on the bed, and at last her half-naked front.

He heard her gasp, "Sweet Lord." She gave him an embarrassed glance, then turned away. When she turned back, black unfortunately covered everything, though he found the blush on her cheeks most becoming.

"I . . . apologize," she whispered. "I've only fainted once before in my entire life . . ."

"No apologies are necessary." He smiled. In an attempt to put her at ease, he added, "The day has been difficult —for all."

He was aware of her staring at him again. It was just that expression that had led to her recent faint, and he didn't want to go through that again. "Lady Eden, may I assist—"

"No," she murmured, stopping him with her hand. "I'm quite restored."

Beyond the lamp, the darkness in the room was now complete, though John continued to hear rain pelt against the windows, and thought, without warning, of his father lying in the coffin in cold earth.

"Lady Eden," he said, turning away from the table, "if you *are* restored, might I again request a fire? As I said, the day has left a chill that . . ."

Behind, he heard a rustling, as though she were on her feet. Then he heard her voice, less soft. "There will be no fire," and the sternness in her tone caused him to look back.

"I don't understand," he confessed.

She drew herself up as though to face an unpleasant

task. "It is our opinion," she began, "Lord Eden's and my own, that until we receive documentation of your true identity, we cannot offer you access to these chambers."

He'd expected as much. "Do *you* doubt my identity?" he demanded, returning to the table. "I've been told by many, including my father, that I bear a strong resemblance to him."

"What others say does not concern us," she replied with admirable strength. "There *is* a resemblance, and if the woman sends the necessary papers that will prove beyond any doubt that you are who you claim to be, then this castle and all its inhabitants will welcome you, and you will be given free access to your father's chambers."

He listened closely. "And if the papers arrive and there still are doubts?"

She started forward, one hand making minor adjustments to her person. "Then you will be welcome to stay in the servants' hall for as long as you make yourself useful."

"And for now?" he asked.

Still not looking at him, she moved safely past before she turned with her reply. "For now, you will gather up your satchel and follow me downstairs, where a steward is waiting to take you to the servants' hall."

He stared at her for a moment, confounded by how he should deal with her foolishness. "My lady . . ." He laughed, shaking his head and repeating the claim which he'd made countless times before. "I *am* John Murrey Eden. My father was—"

Something brought her to anger. "It's a matter of unimportance to us," she snapped, "the claims of your identity. As my husband pointed out, dozens of young men could present themselves to our gates within the next few years, all claiming a kinship with this family. We are well aware here of your father's spirit of abandon. We must protect ourselves, for our children's sake, if nothing else."

The meanness of her sentiment seemed to have a more devastating effect on her than it did on John. He saw her bow her head as though a new weakness had swept over her.

"Lady Eden, would you care to—"

He'd tried to offer her the comfort of a chair, but again she shook her head. "No, I don't intend to stay. If you will be so good as to gather your things and follow after . . ."

But John had no intention of following after her, not until he'd waged a respectable battle.

Now, in spite of her impatient waiting, he took the chair that he'd intended to offer to her and sat easily at the table. "I'm not surprised by Lord Eden's assessment of my father," he commenced, ignoring her startled expression at his disobedience. "My father always told me that he shared nothing but blood with his younger brother, that they had tried over the years to develop a brotherly relationship and that they both had failed."

Abruptly he leaned forward and clasped his hands upon the table. Without looking up, he asked, "You knew my father, didn't you?"

He'd not expected such a simple question to elicit such a terrifying lack of response.

"Of course you knew him," he went on, in spite of the taut silence. "He told me that he had met you on the occasion of your engagement to his brother. He spoke fondly of your beauty and generous spirit."

"Will . . . you please fetch your satchel?" Her voice sounded as though she were suffocating.

Still he persisted. "If you spent only ten minutes with my father, you knew him to be a gentleman."

Now he looked up into her eyes, amazed at the suffering he saw there. "I assure you," he concluded quietly, "bastards have not been sown all over London. After my mother, he sought no other woman."

In spite of the mask which had fallen over her features, he sensed new interest. "Is the . . . woman who brought you here your mother?" she asked.

"Elizabeth?" He laughed softly. "No, though she's a loving substitute."

"Then . . . who . . . ?"

"My mother is dead," he replied. "Shortly after I was born. I never knew her."

The information seemed to hang in the still room, as

though in search of a receiver. Then she spoke again. "I must ask you to fetch your satchel and follow after me."

Amazed, he stood. "To what end?" he demanded. "I assure you I am in my proper place."

She too seemed to be suffering from new agitation. "What is proper for you and what isn't is for us to decide. I want these chambers cleared—"

"You have no right—"

Both their voices were rising, their anger, if nothing else, drawing them together. "No right!" she echoed. "May I remind you that I am mistress here, you the intruder. Any and all discussion of what is right will emanate from me."

They were standing so close he could see nerves quivering around the corners of her eyes. Again, silence fell between them. Weary after the two-day journey from London, John unfortunately lapsed into a childlike stubborness. "What if I refuse to obey you?" he challenged.

Taken aback by such impudence, she responded in kind. "Then I shall summon two watchmen and have you bodily removed."

He met the threat. "Then I'm afraid that's what you must do, for I have no intention of leaving chambers that are rightfully mine."

He thought that he had called her bluff. But within the moment she marshaled new strength, moved through the opened door and merely lifted a hand, a magic hand apparently, for within the instant he heard heavy boots moving from the far end of the corridor, drawing nearer.

A moment later two burly watchmen appeared, no expression at all on their faces save an eagerness to do their mistress's bidding. In a voice so cold as to deny all female qualities, she commanded, "Escort him below."

Then the two were moving toward him, their immense shadows falling over his face. Well, he decided, might as well go with grace. But as the first coarse hand clamped itself on his shoulder, all pretense slipped from him and he shook off the hand, eager to do battle with them.

They too seemed surprised by such foolhardiness, and for a moment the confrontation held, he backing slowly away into the dead end of the room itself, the two giants stalking him.

"Come, pup." One smiled toothlessly. "These here is gintleman's chambers. Pups gits special kennels—"

"Don't harm him," she called out, something desperate in her tone, as though she regretted having set certain forces in motion.

But too late. As one Goliath reached out for him, the second merely stepped forward and most effectively blocked his escape route. He felt a massive arm go around his waist and lift him effortlessly off his feet.

Something vaulted within him. The smell of the two encapturing him, the look of brutal delight on their faces, and perhaps an awareness of his own helpless position, all these things conspired against him, and suddenly he commenced flailing, his fist moving down to his captor's groin and delivering an effective blow to that spongy area. Within the instant he heard the man wail and felt the viselike grip around his waist slacken, and in the next moment he was free and darted away from the pursuit of the second watchman, and in a blur caught a glimpse of the lady's face, her hand pressed to her mouth.

It was only a matter of time. He knew it and they knew it. Still he gave a good show for several minutes, inflicting minor pain on first one, then the other.

Then it was over. Outraged as though by a flea, the two giants drove him back into the far corner, effortlessly pinned his arms and delivered two blows, one to his midsection, which caused him to crumple forward, and one to his jaw, which sent him reeling backward into a painful collision with the stone wall.

For several moments those shadowy chambers whirled about him. Far off in the distance he heard a woman's scream, as though at last she'd undone herself as well as him. His last conscious thought as he slid down the wall was for his father.

"I'm home, Papa . . ."

Then there was only blackness and silence, except for that soft sobbing which seemed very close now and which interrupted itself only long enough to whisper a name.

"Edward . . ."

"I said not to harm him," she cried, cradling the young boy's head, despising the two gargoyle faces which stared down on her.

"He was a handful, milady," one muttered, still rubbing his side where apparently a sharp elbow had found its mark.

"What is your wish now, milady?" the second watchman asked.

Still she held the lifeless head. What *was* her wish? Without giving her thoughts a chance to take shape, she again bent low and with the hem of her dress tried to stanch the slight flow of blood slipping from the side of his mouth.

In the silence, with the two watchmen gaping down on her, she was aware that they were about to be joined by a third. Moments before she heard his actual footsteps, she sensed him.

Then he was upon them, causing a small congestion in the door as the two watchmen rushed to pay their respects.

"My lord . . ." They bowed in tandem.

"James," she murmured, moving out of the shadows. "He . . . resisted," she began and finished, feeling that it was an adequate explanation for the sprawled youth still lying in the corner.

But James, apparently confounded by it all, merely sidestepped the watchmen, and as though nothing had been said, asked, "What happened?"

She looked up at her husband, amazed, as she always was when she first caught sight of him after even a brief separation, that she was bound to this man for life.

"It's as I said," she repeated, helpless to alter the edge on her voice. "I explained our dilemma, asked him courteously to quit these chambers, and he . . . resisted."

Now on her husband's face she saw a surprising look of remorse. As though for his own edification, he stepped toward the boy and encircled him, a cautious examination. "It could be a young Edward . . ."

"Then why," she implored, "did you ask me to remove him to the servants' hall?"

"It was as much your judgment as mine," he countered defensively. "You said we needed proof and I agreed."

She couldn't even look at him now, not with Edward's face still before her only a short distance away. Refusing to have any further hand in it, she walked the distance to the windows and took comfort in the chill night. Finally she heard James address the watchmen. "As long as you've knocked him senseless, you might as well deliver him to the proper quarters."

As the watchmen lifted the boy and left the room, she was tempted to follow after them, but James was at her side. "Now, what happened?"

Again she moved to put distance between them. "It's as I said, James," she repeated herself for the third time. "I found him here, quite willing and eager to settle in. Richard was with him," she added.

Now James became peculiarly adamant. "I want Richard to have nothing to do with him."

Amused at his foolish sentiment, she smiled. "They are boys, James. It's natural that they should seek each other's company."

"Boys!" he exclaimed. "That was no boy I saw downstairs. He charged in here with the aggressiveness of a man. And neither was that a boy," he added, "I saw sprawled in the corner."

No, she thought, amazed that at last they agreed on something. Beneath the hem of her gown, her toe found the substance of the satchel. Strange, the fascination she felt suddenly for that crude rain-dampened luggage. "Well, it's done with for a while," she said with dispatch.

"And what brought about the blows?"

She looked at him, trying hard to be civil in the face of his denseness. "Obviously he felt that he belongs here."

"And what if he does?"

"Then of course he will be allowed to stay."

"In what capacity?"

Was the man totally dense? Didn't he realize that he was posing questions to which she had no answers? Still bewildered by the agitation she felt within her, she tried again to send him on his way. "Why don't we deal with each problem as it arises?" she counseled quietly. "For now, may I make a suggestion?"

"Please do."

At times his submissiveness was a joy. "Why don't you go immediately to your writing bureau and compose a letter to Mr. Morley Johnson in London. Tell him precisely what has happened and tell him that we desire a complete investigation."

"If you wish . . ."

"One thing more, James. Tell Mr. Johnson that we are most interested in the identity of the boy's mother."

Here James laughed. "That may prove too much of a search even for Morley Johnson," he commented. "He might be well advised to start among the prostitutes in St. James Park, or else with that piece of damaged goods who delivered the boy to us."

"No," she replied quickly. "The boy swears she is not his mother."

Surprised, James looked up. "You've already questioned him?"

"Briefly."

"And what did he say?"

Annoyance surfaced. "That the woman driving the wagon was not his mother," she repeated.

Still the denseness persisted. "Did he say who his mother was?"

"James, if he had said that, would I now be asking you to write to Morley Johnson?"

"All right," he said, lifting both his hands as though to stay her anger. As he started toward the door, he muttered, "I knew this would happen. Someone always had to pay for Edward's profligacy. It strikes me as unfair that it is the innocent who always have to do the paying."

"You've been asked to pay nothing yet," she said in an attempt to soothe. "Go ahead and write to Johnson. He'll know what to do."

From the door he looked back. "Aren't you coming?"

"No, you go along. I'll restore the chamber and join you shortly."

"What's to restore? The boy was only here for a—"

"James, please . . ." Over the lamplight she tried not to

see his face and failed. "Look about," she said, and as she gestured, she saw for the first time the strewn garments on the floor near the wardrobe. A little surprised, she looked again.

Now James saw them as well. "Why would he do that?" he puzzled, stepping back into the room. "Those are Edward's. Why would he . . . ?"

Suddenly, in her deep need for privacy she felt a residue of weakness sweep over her. The stone floor beneath her feet seemed to waver. She reached quickly out for the table and would have collapsed again had it not been for James.

He escorted her to a near chair, lightly scolding. "You must lie down. The day has been a strain on—"

"I'm fine," she murmured, and saw him still hovering over her, one hand stroking her shoulder as though she were a pet. "Please leave me," she whispered, too exhausted for anything but the truth.

"I won't," he announced in a witless display of husbandly concern. "This room is chill. Come. You need the warmth of a fire." He knelt before her, his voice falling very low. "Let me assist you to your chambers." One hand was now on her upper leg, a shy quality in his voice. "We'll send the maids to the kitchen. Then I'll warm you."

She bent slightly forward, as though a new weight had just fallen upon her. It had been weeks since he'd made such a request. She had hoped that he had found a cooperative serving maid or two to accommodate his needs.

"Did you hear me?" he whispered. Then, as though he sensed her unspoken objections, he reminded her, "I do have rights, you know."

She felt as though a huge animal were crouching at her feet. He *did* have rights and she her duty. Perhaps if she were fortunate he would impregnate her and she would be spared her duty for another year.

Now, as the recently mentioned whores in St. James Park surely struck bargains with their clients, Harriet struck a bargain with her husband. "Go and write to Mr. Johnson, and give me an interval of privacy. I'll meet you in my chambers in an hour."

Still incapable of looking at him, she waited for his reply. Even if he agreed, she'd have to hurry. Three brandies dulled the sensations, but she must consume them quickly for them to take effect.

"One hour," he whispered finally, both hands grasping her upper legs.

Then at last, as though aware that he must function on her terms or not at all, he left the room.

Now slowly she moved forward to face her true ordeal, the presence of the young boy with Edward's face, Edward's form and manner. Quickly she skirted the table, her eyes falling immediately on the abandoned satchel. For a moment, conscience stopped her. She had no right to examine its contents.

If he *were* Edward's son, perhaps the proof would be in that satchel. And perhaps the disproof as well. She wondered which she preferred. She slipped to her knees before the satchel. The single strap fell loose, and with both hands she drew open the luggage. It was too dark where she was kneeling, and hurriedly she rose and carried the satchel to the table, where the lamp was burning brightly.

Her hand moved down and drew forth a shirt, muslin, hand-sewn, a second shirt, identical to the first. Then came a pair of trousers, three belt loops torn, a light jacket, a nightshirt, a small collection of articles wrapped in white linen, and a soft brushed cap.

All? She tilted the bag toward the lamp and saw a gleam of white, and withdrew a large pamphlet of some sort. In the light of the lamp she read the title, *The Great Exhibition—London—1851—The Art Journal Illustrated Catalog of the Industries of All Nations.*

She placed the heavy catalog on the table beside the meager collection of garments and plunged her hand into the luggage a final time. Another book? Hurriedly she withdrew a small white leather Book of Common Prayer. In gold on the cover was stamped the name John Murrey Eden. Inside she found a simple inscription, "With loving devotion on the occasion of your baptism, from your godfather, Daniel Spade."

Daniel Spade. There was a familiar name. Edward's friend, the cause of poor Jennifer's illness.

Again she looked down at the inscription. Edward's sister Jennifer was to have been Mrs. Daniel Spade, but fate and fever intervened, leaving Daniel dead, Jennifer witless. She still spoke of him now and then as though he were due to arrive at any moment and take her away.

Harriet's perceptions of those distant events, her memory of the recent burial and of the young boy lying unconscious in the servants' hall, settled over her like a state of confused reverie. She let the Book of Common Prayer fall from her hand. True, a baptism had been mentioned, but there was no date, no parish registry, not even the name of the church.

Suddenly she resented that such a mystery had been thrust upon her. She'd been doing well enough, Edward safely lost to her, living out his days in London obscurity, his companions, even his financial straits, those of his own choosing.

She'd managed to create a tolerable half-life for herself here, mistress of Eden Castle, with senseless Jennifer for company, and occasionally she would climb the stairs to old Jane's fourth-floor apartment and the two would take tea together, and she'd listen to Jane grumble that her life persisted without point or purpose. The old woman was approaching ninety, the last living link to Edward and James's mother, the beautiful Marianne.

And best of all, Harriet had her two children, open and generous Richard, and lovely Mary, unformed as yet, but promising.

In this attitude of strength, she commenced placing the items back into the satchel. Surely the boy had more than this. Somewhere.

The satchel refilled, she laced the strap into place and was just starting toward the door, lamp and satchel in hand, when she turned back and caught sight of the scattered garments on the floor near the wardrobe. She'd send maids back. She had burgeoning responsibilities of her own.

Suddenly she shivered. She looked slowly over her shoulder as though the abandoned garments had spoken to her.

"Edward . . ." she mourned. Carefully she replaced the

lamp on the table, abandoned the satchel as well, and returned to the clothes scattered about before the wardrobe.

She knelt and reached out for a near garment, a worn black jacket. Tenderly she arranged it in her arms as though it were a child, rocked with it back and forth, chained to the strange ritual by longing, by loneliness, by guilt for Edward's child whom years ago she had conceived, carried, birthed and given away.

Acutely conscious of what she was doing, she continued to hold the jacket, pressing it closer. And for one blessed moment she had no other activity in view, no reason for being where she was, and no relationship to her surroundings.

He awakened on a hard cot in a low-ceilinged whitewashed cell with a circle of plain faces staring down upon him.

He closed his eyes briefly, one hand reaching up to his aching jaw, and worse than that, his aching pride. In his conquest of Eden, he'd planned to start on slightly higher ground.

No matter! He would not pass many days here. For now the subject of highest priority was those faces. The entire cell was filled, and beyond, he could see craning necks peering in at the doorway.

He turned toward the nearest face, that of an old man with red cheeks and white hair. He reminded John of his father's old coachman, John Murrey, his namesake. "Are you . . . the butler?" he asked tentatively.

Several of the maids snickered, their prim lace caps quivering. Even the old man's placid blue eyes smiled, as did his slightly too large mouth. "No, lad." He grinned. "Mr. Rexroat is upstairs, seeing to Lord Eden. My name is Dana. I've been a footman here for forty years. But swelling joints has slowed me a bit."

John looked with renewed interest on the man. Now, here was someone to talk to. As always, John had an insatiable desire to know all about every Eden who had preceded him. At last he stood, fully recovered, and glanced toward the old man. "My name is John Murrey Eden." He smiled, extending a ready hand.

But to his surprise, the old man seemed to draw back. "Come," John said, "take my hand. I assure you, you'll be the first today to do so."

Now apparently the old man found his tongue. "It ain't you, lad," he muttered. "It's just that . . . Well, we don't know who you are," he blurted, "or what to do with you." He looked directly at John. "You see, lad," he went on, "most of us here remember well your father." He paused. "A good man he was, who went through bad times." He cast a surveying eye over John. "If you ain't his flesh, then the Almighty's playing pranks."

John looked up. "Then what's the problem?"

"It's them, lad," the old man replied, casting his eyes upward. "They're the ones requiring the proof."

In an attempt to ease their bewilderment, John clamped a warm hand on Dana's shoulder. "I assure you, I *am* my father's son," he said with conviction. "Proof *will* be along. In the meantime, what are we to do with me?"

Dana appeared to be on the verge of framing a reply when John heard footsteps in the corridor outside the cell. Obviously the others heard them as well, for within the moment there was a pronounced rush on the door as all tried to flee at once, causing an impossible congestion.

Just beyond the door frame John saw a man in black cutaways with high stiff collar, sharply creased trousers and black boots.

"Mr. Rexroat," Dana whispered in John's ear.

John took a step forward. "Good evening," he said pleasantly enough and extended his hand, and withdrew it a moment later, unclasped.

Still the man stood in the doorway, those eyes unblinking. Then he stepped to one side and with a wave of his hand motioned for someone in the corridor to come forward. Within the instant a steward appeared, bearing John's satchel.

John glanced down at the satchel. In truth he'd forgotten about it. "Thank you," he said to Mr. Rexroat. "I'm afraid I didn't have time to retrieve—"

Then the man spoke, his voice as cold as his appearance. "I have just come from Lord Eden," he announced. "It is his desire that you work."

Work! John had had enough of that to last a lifetime. Both in the Ragged Schools and in the Common Kitchen, that's all he had done for the last few years. His father had thrived on it. Not John.

Still he stood as erect as Rexroat himself and met the challenge, because it would serve his purpose to do so. "I'm a good worker," he boasted. "Set me a task and it will be done as expertly as though you'd done it yourself."

A smile broke the iron facade of Mr. Rexroat's face. "We'll see," he said.

"You do that," John countered. "For the short duration of my stay down here"—and he gestured about the small cell—"I'll earn my keep."

"You won't be staying here," Rexroat responded, the smile broadening. "Odd-boys sleep in the cellar."

The cellar? Struggling to match the man's enjoyment, John invited, "Lead the way."

Apparently the cheery cooperation was more than Rexroat had bargained for. He lifted one hand, as though to dismiss the suggestion. "Dana will take you down," he pronounced haughtily. "I have other duties to attend to." Now for the first time he addressed the entire gathering. "I would advise the same course of action for all of you. Be off with you now," and with the wave of his hand he sent the congregation scurrying.

Now Rexroat was moving toward him again. "You have brought considerable confusion and consternation into this house," he pronounced firmly. "If it were left to me, you would be taken immediately to the constable in Exeter and charged with fraud. But Lord Eden, being a good Christian, has decided to treat you with . . . compassion. You are to be given shelter and food, which you will take with the lower servants in their hall, and you are never, under any circumstances, to venture up those stairs into the higher regions of the castle. Is that clear?"

"Couldn't be clearer if I'd said it myself." John smiled, amazed and a little pleased at how quickly he'd brought the man to the brink of anger.

"And there will be no fraternizing with the upper

servants either," the man added, his voice rising. "Your one and only domain will be the scullery and the stables. Is that clear?"

Stables! Although the last few years had been grim, he'd never had to clear horse dung before. Still he smiled. "I'll do your bidding in all ways."

Suddenly the man's facade dropped altogether. "I don't know who you think you are," he whispered fiercely.

Again John smiled. "Perhaps I didn't introduce myself. My name is John Murrey—"

"See to him, Dana," Rexroat muttered angrily. "Show him his territory and make it clear that he is not to depart it." In his retreat he cleared the door and sent his voice back. "He won't be with us for long, I can assure you of that."

Then he was gone and there were only two in the cell now. Almost reluctantly John glanced over his shoulder at Dana, standing a short distance away.

Wearily the old man shook his head. "You may find it hard to believe, lad, but Rexroat has no real power." He laughed softly and shook his head. "Nobody below stairs has no real power now."

Interested in spite of the bleak new feelings which had begun to settle over him, John asked quietly, "And where does the true power reside?"

Dana grinned. "Now, where do you think it would reside, lad? Who do you think is responsible for sending you down here?" Before John could reply, Dana supplied a ready answer. "Her ladyship, who else?"

Then he heard old Dana again, his tone apologetic. "Still, I'll have to deliver you to the cellar," he said softly. Then, as though to halt the gloom, he added, "But we both know it won't be forever, now, don't we, lad? Your friend, that young woman, will send your papers right enough. Then I personally will assist you back up to your father's chambers where you belong."

At last John turned, grateful for the reassurance. He was on the verge of expressing his gratitude when, just beyond the door, he thought he saw something white.

Apparently Dana saw it as well and moved past him. "Wait here," Dana whispered.

John watched as the old man made his way stealthily to the door, stopping short of the threshold. "Miss?" John heard him whisper, his tone of voice gentle.

Obviously he'd found someone, a timid someone who required special consideration. John listened carefully as the old man asked, "May I be of assistance, miss? The corridors are dark. And shouldn't you be at dinner now? It must be approaching nine. Her ladyship will be . . ."

Then the man disappeared, leaving John staring at the empty doorway. He tried to overhear. What now? he wondered. Another objection to his presence? Another challenge to his identity? He turned away from the invisible confrontation, resigning himself to another delay.

"Lad?" It was Dana again from the doorway. "You . . . have a visitor," he stammered.

"A visitor?" John repeated, his head reeling from the variety of manners to which he'd been treated since his arrival here only a few hours ago.

"Aye, lad." At that, Dana stepped back, and in the next minute an apparition in white appeared, a woman with dark hair streaked with gray which hung loose down her back, a soft fringe of curls about her face.

"Edward," she whispered, and was in his arms before he could protest or seek explanation.

"Oh, Edward, I knew it was you," she murmured close to his ear.

In his confusion he looked up and caught Dana's eye. The man was speaking volumes without saying a word. The message was clear. Apparently Dana felt it important that John return her embrace. Tentatively his hands lifted to her waist, then, finding that area too intimate, moved up to the safety of her shoulders.

Just when he thought he was doing very well, she drew back and he saw tears on her face. "Edward"—she smiled in spite of the tears—"I was so worried. Everyone told me that you were dead." There was a childlike quality in her voice. "But you aren't dead at all, are you?" she asked softly. "Though they have treated you shamefully, haven't they? Oh, I saw them right enough, those wicked men carrying you down here. Just like the time they carried you out of the banqueting hall on Mother's command." Her voice drifted, as though for an instant she'd lost touch with who she was and what she was saying.

In the interim, John again looked beseechingly at Dana. The man stepped forward, and in passing whispered, "It's Miss Jennifer, your aunt, your father's sister. She thinks . . . " .

It was clear what she thought, and John remembered her now. How often and how lovingly his father had spoken her name. In fact, John could not remember the name ever standing by itself. Always it had been preceded by "dearest," or "sweet."

Acutely aware of the role he must play where this woman was concerned, he opened his arms wide and summoned her back to him, anything to call a halt to her demented circling. "Dearest Jennifer . . ." He smiled.

Immediately the circling stopped. And once again John experienced the curious delight of holding a woman close, though the sensations were very different this time, no arousal, merely a feeling of pity, the feeling that at the very instant when everyone was denying his relationship to his father, he had *become* his father, at least as far as this woman was concerned.

For several moments she clung to him. Once or twice he heard her sigh. Then a smile broke on those pale features and she whispered, "We must hurry. Daniel is waiting for us."

Within the moment she was tugging at his hand. Gently he protested, "Wait, please . . ." Again he looked helplessly back toward Dana. Unfortunately the old man seemed to have gone temporarily blind with pity.

"Edward, please." she begged again. "Don't tease me. You've no idea how long I have searched for you. And Daniel *is* waiting."

With no choice, he allowed her to drag him forward a few feet, and might have gone all the way with her had he not at the last moment remembered Mr. Rexroat's strong command that he stay out of the upper regions of the castle.

"Wait, Jennifer," he begged, withdrawing his hand. He sat quickly on the edge of the cot and gently patted the place beside him, indicating that she was to follow suit. "Come. We've time," he said.

Her face at first seemed to register objection. But at the last moment she sat beside him, clasping his hand, pressing it to her cheek, then to her breast. "Oh, Edward," she sighed. "I become so frightened when I lose you. You must give me a daily schedule of all your activities so I'll always know where to find you."

In an attempt to soothe her, he laughed quietly. "Now, how would you lose me? One loses a pair of gloves, a book, not a—"

"Oh, it's quite easy to lose people in this place," she interrupted. She seemed to be looking around her, seeing clearly her surroundings. "What *are* you doing here, Edward?" she asked, dropping his hand. "This is the servants' hall. Papa doesn't like us to come down here. You know that."

Then the tugging was on again, joined now by new desperation. "Oh, come, Edward, please," she begged, "let's get out of here."

At that moment her voice seemed to break. Suddenly her hands flew up to her mouth as though to cancel out her last words. Her eyes, over her trembling hands, were wide and distended.

Unable to watch such a spectacle of confusion and fear, John knelt before her. "I am not Edward, Jennifer," he began softly. "I'm . . ."

He thought he saw a brief light of reason in her eyes, as though she'd grasped his words, had seen clearly the subtle differences between the one kneeling before her and the one recently buried in the graveyard.

Was it true recognition? He couldn't be certain, but suddenly she was pulling backward, her head shaking back and forth. "No," she protested, "not dead, not Edward . . ."

As she dragged herself across the cot, she almost fell off the other side. Dana moved forward first, both hands extended in assistance. But at the sight of those hands, she righted herself and ran to the far wall, increasing both distance and isolation.

"No, wait," John commanded. "Jennifer, please," he begged. "We only want to . . ."

But again she pushed back into the corner, her terror a thing of substance.

"Jennifer . . ."

But the woman who once had responded to the name of Jennifer was missing, and in her place was a husk filled with terror. He saw a thin stream of spittle running down her jaw.

Uncertain whether he should advance or retreat, hearing the continuous siren of her screams, he looked frantically back at Dana, only to find the man in close huddle in the doorway with several servants who obviously had been summoned by her screams. "Fetch her ladyship," he heard Dana shout over the din. He saw the message relayed to the back of the gaping servants, saw a lady's maid whisper something which seemed momentarily to defeat Dana.

Angrily John watched the inefficient little gathering. Something had to be done. Jennifer had dissolved into a frenzy of motion, pulling at her hair, then shaking her head angrily, animal fashion, as though mystified that the pain could not be altered.

Again John shouted at the gaping servants. "For God's sake, do something—"

At that moment the light of a solution seemed to blaze on Dana's face. "Get Aggie!" he commanded one of the stewards.

Within the instant, the man had fled.

John looked back toward Jennifer and prayed quickly for Aggie's arrival, whoever that might be. Jennifer's fingers had already succeeded in ripping her gown, her hands clawing at her throat now, leaving long red scratches. Briefly he lowered his head, feeling responsible for the disintegration. If someone didn't come soon . . .

Then behind him he heard movement and looked over his shoulder to see the servants parting and in spite of the dimness of the corridor he saw what appeared to be a giant moving toward him, a giant in skirts with an enormous expanse of white apron, coming still closer, a woman he saw now, though a monstrous woman, approaching seven feet was his guess. Her dark hair was pulled back into a rigid knot. There was something confident and solid about her as she stood in the doorway.

As she stepped into the room, John saw more clearly the field of her apron, blood-splotched, and saw in her massive hand a large butcher knife, still glistening with blood.

Then the mountainous woman started forward. As she passed by John, he noticed her bulbous nose, and he noticed too her ears, pendulous scarlet ears that showed up like large drops of sealing wax.

As she approached Jennifer, he saw her toss the butcher knife onto the cot, where it bounced once and left two red stains of fresh blood. Without a trace of a smile she stood directly before Jennifer and commanded, "Stop it!"

When the command seemed to make no difference, the giant woman shouted again, "I say, stop it!"

For the first time in several long minutes the ear-shattering screams ceased. Jennifer looked up at her as though weighing the wisdom or folly of disobeying that strong command.

A moment later the decision to disobey was clearly made, and as the screams started again, the woman stepped forward, grabbed Jennifer by the shoulders, guided her to the edge of the cot and sat her down. Apparently taken by surprise, Jennifer fell silent, though now the room was filled with the sound of her breathing.

John could not see her face, which he considered a blessing. He looked quickly up to see the old woman staring directly at him, the look of condemnation clear on her face.

"You the cause of this?" she demanded, pointing to the collapsed Jennifer.

John discovered that he could not answer the direct question. Was he the cause of it? In truth, no. In essence, perhaps yes. Vaguely he nodded.

"Well, if you was the cause, you could have been the cure," she snapped, wiping her bloodied hands on her apron. She seemed on the verge of saying more, when abruptly she focused her attention on Jennifer. With what appeared to be considerable effort, she got down on her knees and enclosed Jennifer's hands in her own. Her voice, when she spoke, took John by surprise. It was musical now, and soft. "Look at you, lassie." She smiled. "A fine picture to be presentin' to your brother. Why, I couldn't believe my ears, I couldn't. There I was, butchering me a nice side of beef, when I heard screams to wake the dead. Then someone come and said it's Miss Jennifer, having a terrible row with her brother, and I thought, now, why are those two quarreling, and since nobody would tell me, I said, Aggie, you'd better go find out. . . ."

The voice, the tone that implied that nothing unusual had occurred, seemed to be effective medicine. John had the feeling that everyone was listening carefully, as though to a master storyteller. From where he stood now, he saw Jennifer, not at peace, but certainly quiet. And when the woman posed a direct question. "Now, tell Aggie what happened?" he saw Jennifer lean forward and whisper something in her ear, the bond of trust between the two women impressive.

Then he saw Aggie struggling to her feet. Once up, her mouth started working again, this time the torrent of words aimed at John.

"Edward, I'm ashamed of you," she scolded, "upsetting yo'ir sister like that."

He leaned wearily against the wall, debating with himself whether to resist the old woman's madness or to join it.

In the next instant he had his answer, as sternly she summoned him forward. "Come! Right here!" she ordered, stabbing her finger at the floor.

When he was within easy reach of the old woman, she grabbed him, literally dragging him forward, until he stood directly before Jennifer where she sat on the edge of the cot.

Aggie waited before she spoke, as though to give him all the time he needed, as though to let him compare his humiliation with her grief. He bowed his head. No comparison was possible.

"Now," Aggie commenced with businesslike dispatch.

"You are to apologize, Edward, for making your sister cry."

A stray wisp of reason intervened. He heard a voice in his head protest, *"I am not Edward."*

"Apologize, Edward!" It was Aggie again, her blood-dried hand clamped on his shoulder.

"I'm . . . sorry," he muttered.

"Good," she concluded. As she stepped back, she commanded, "Help your sister to the door." She lifted her voice and shouted over the heads of the servants, "Esther! Helen!"

Within the moment, two maids appeared, their neat white aprons and lace caps in stark contrast to Aggie's soiled appearance. "Take Miss Jennifer to her chambers," she commanded. "See to her," she added.

Carefully John reached down for Jennifer's hand and lifted her to her feet. He felt totally dependent on the large woman hovering close behind them. It was up to her to give him every word, every movement. This she did, whispering now in his ear, "Tell her that you love her."

"I love you," John murmured.

"And tell her if she wishes, you and Daniel will be waiting for her here in about an hour . . ."

Baffled by this promise he could never keep, he looked over his shoulder, ready to protest.

But protest was useless, and as he felt her fingers digging into his back and heard her fiercely whisper, "Tell her!" he closed his eyes and made the promise to the floor.

Apparently the words were precisely what Jennifer wanted to hear. She grasped his arm. "I love you so much, Edward," she whispered. "Please always love me in return."

He did well to nod. Still baffled, he made his way back to the cot and sat heavily, aware that all eyes were now focused on him. He bowed his head into his hands.

In the next moment, he heard a man's voice, Dana's he suspected, scattering the servants again, and with his head down he heard retreating footsteps.

His jaw still ached, his belly was empty, he'd not

rested his head on a pillow for two days and two nights, and everyone he had met here had either denied his identity or conferred a false one upon him. For one bleak moment in that self-imposed blindness he himself seemed to lose track of who he was.

Hurriedly now he lifted his head. "Dana . . ." But the doorway was empty, as was the corridor beyond. Then he saw her in the far corner of the cell, that enormous black shadow with bloodstained apron, looking at him as though she were the watchdog. he the interloper.

"So!" she spoke at last, both hands planted on her mammoth hips, her stomach heaving from her recent exertion. "You're John Murrey Eden!"

This simple statement of fact, coming after such endless denials, sounded mocking. Still he nodded. "When I arrived here, yes," he conceded. "Now, I'm not so certain."

"Oh, you're him all right." She grinned. "No doubt about it. No one but flesh and blood of Mr. Edward could cause the ruckus you've caused tonight."

"It was not my intention—"

"It was never your father's intention either." She laughed, coming around the cot to his side.

He retreated a step. "And what am I to do when Jennifer returns?" he asked quietly.

She dismissed him with a wave of her hand. "Oh, she won't be back down tonight," she said confidently. "Those are good girls I sent with her. They'll fix the elixir that puts her to sleep."

"And come morning?"

Again she smiled, though it seemed a mean smile now. "From what I hear, come morning you'll be safely tucked away in the cellar." She leaned closer, covering him with her foul breath. "And odd-boys have been known to descend those dark stairs, never to return. So in a way, you might say that the problem will be self-solving."

He saw this for what it was, a mindless attempt to frighten him. "I've been in cellars before," he said.

"Not like this one, you ain't." She grinned. Then she threw back her head and laughed heartily. "Oh, a tough one you are, ain't you, lad," she said, coming still closer, until he felt that enormous arm go around him and draw him close, whether in an embrace or a stranglehold, he couldn't tell.

"It'd be my guess," she went on, "that you'll be needin' a friend 'fore you're done here, and you got one in old Agony Fletcher." She stepped farther back, arranging him at arm's length as though the better to view him. "My domain is the butcher's block in the kitchen court. and you can't mistake me 'cause the Lord made only one Agony, and if you ever lose me, just follow the blood drippings and you'll find me right enough."

At the end of this speech, John tried to repeat the strange name. "Agony . . ."

"Agony it is," she confirmed with pride. "Me mum gave it to me, she did, saying I was an agony to bring into this world and boxing me ears ever' time she looked at me so as I'd never forget it."

This seemed to provoke helpless laughter in the old woman, who now lifted the hem of her soiled apron and dabbed at her eyes. As John again caught sight of her damaged ears, he believed everything she'd told him.

Her laughter over, she seemed to be viewing him now with a mixture of compassion and curiosity. "Oh, you're a green one, you are," she mused. "Half-man, half-boy." Her eyes seemed to glaze briefly. "But your father's son, that's for certain. My Gawd, the dead do rise."

Embarrassed by the close scrutiny, he looked away. Apparently she saw his discomfort and moved to dispel it. "Are you hungry?" she asked.

He nodded.

"Well, for Gawd's sake, why didn't you say so?" she scolded. "Come," she ordered, and accompanying the verbal invitation was a gesture of such strength that John felt himself lifted instantly to his feet as she grabbed his hand and dragged him after her.

All the way down the endless corridor, she gave him a running commentary concerning the various rooms they were passing, and he tried to pay attention, feeling that a knowledge of his surroundings might be important.

"And that passageway there leads to the laundry, bakery, and brewery offices, and to the upper and lower servants' offices, and that there is the buttery and that the pantry, and that'un the lower servants' private rooms. And that'un there to the knife room, shoe room, mangling room and ironing room . . ."

John tried to look in all directions, down the endless passageways which led to more passageways. He could never learn them all.

Finally, "The kitchen," she announced with pride, and released him.

He stood motionless, surveying it all. It was an enormous room, high-ceilinged with heavy oak beams supported by eight heavier oak columns. There were two massive fireplaces on either side, both covered with grilles through which he could see flames. In the far corner he saw a rumpled couch, two easy chairs, and a small hook rug, clearly someone's corner of ease and comfort. On the rug before the fire he saw a black-and-white mongrel dog contentedly chewing a joint the size of a man's arm.

Without warning his stomach informed him again that he had not eaten in over forty-eight hours. He now looked up to see Aggie bustling about on the far side of the room, lifting a lid to a kettle, dipping a ladle into its contents and filling a large wooden bowl. At last she called to him, "Come! Eat!"

That was all he needed, and he commenced making his way through the clutter, his eyes fixed on the steaming bowl which she'd placed on a low bench, accompanied by a round of dark bread.

She stood back, smiling, as he slid along the bench, lifted the wooden spoon and filled his mouth with the rich tomato goodness of stew.

Three bowls later, the spoon at last slowed. He ran the tip of his tongue over the burned skin of his upper mouth, a small price to pay for such satiation. And for the first time he looked up to see Aggie sitting in one of the easy chairs, her legs spread, the dog resting his head on her lap, a small clay pipe clenched in her teeth, her eyes narrowed and focused on him.

He'd never seen a woman with a pipe before, and watched, fascinated. Still she stared at him as though see-

ing him for the first time. Under that relentless gaze he
ducked his head. He heard dimly in the distance the
voices of the other servants at dinner. With his head
down he felt an overpowering need to sleep. Also he felt
a terrible awareness of where he was. Two days earlier
he'd had a very different conclusion in mind for this night.

Now, as though keeping pace with his thoughts, he
heard Aggie ask quietly, "And where do you go from
here, lad?"

He shrugged. "To the cellar, I suppose, with the odd-
boys."

She inhaled deeply on the pipe. "What if proof of who
you are don't come?" she asked bluntly.

Still fighting exhaustion, he tried to address the question. "It will come," he said softly.

"That baggage you arrived with? She don't look none
too bright . . . "

Annoyed by the old woman's assault on Elizabeth, he
tried to defend her. "She's very kind and she—"

"Is she your mum?"

"No."

"Then who is?"

He shook his head, having no appetite for the subject.
"I don't know. All my father told me was that she died
when I was born."

"Convenient."

"It's the truth."

Slowly Aggie leaned back in her chair, her face red
from exposure to the heat. "Well, not to worry, lad. You
won't be exiled for long, I can promise you that. There's
too many upstairs that need you, no matter who you are.
They'll come and fetch you right enough and carry you
off for their own purposes."

He was on the verge of asking her to repeat herself
when he head footsteps in the far corridor and looked
up to see a half dozen stewards returning from their
dinner. The old footman, Dana, was in the lead and now
appeared pleased at the sight of John before an empty
bowl.

"So you've eaten." He smiled. "I was just coming
to—"

"Of course he's et," Aggie snapped, on her feet now, her gruffness laced into place. Roughly she thrust a lantern at old Dana and gave him a harsh command. "Take him down where he belongs 'fore Rexroat comes blowin' in here. I'm in no mood for his jawin', so take him down where he belongs. I'm sick to death of the sight of him."

Bewildered by her sudden change, John pushed away from the bench. He saw Dana waiting impatiently at the far door, lantern in hand, his face awash with pity, as though he dreaded the errand ahead of him.

Enough, then! On this resolve, John started toward the door, weary of delays. Apparently the subcellar was as low as one could go in Eden Castle. While it had not been his intention to start there, still there was something of a challenge in it. It might, in the end, make the climb out more interesting.

As he skirted the last table, he glanced in Aggie's direction. In that moment he altered his course and moved toward her side. Out of the corner of his eye he saw the other servants edging back. He touched her shoulder and kissed her lightly on the cheek. "Thank you," he whispered, aware of the shocked silence coming from behind him, acutely aware of old Aggie herself, who turned slowly toward him, a look of confusion on her face, as though twin instincts were waging a relentless war, on one side a clear impulse to smack him for such impudence, on the other a desire to hug him to her.

Obviously the battle was a standoff, with no clear victor. "Go on with you," she muttered, and again turned away.

He moved back through the servants and rejoined Dana at the door. Lifting his voice into a tone of false confidence, he said, "Lead the way, my friend."

Then they were moving again back down the endless corridors, Dana in the lead. To keep his mind off his destination, John counted the torches in their fixed standards; four, six, seven—where was Elizabeth now? Had she made it safely to Taunton? Would she stop there for the night?

Papa, tell me more of Eden. Is it beautiful?

At the end of the corridor they came to a wide reception room, two staircases leading off in opposite directions, one broad one which clearly led up and one narrow one which led down. Predictably Dana took the one leading down through a low door to a stone staircase, the descent steep, the only light now coming from the lantern.

John perceived a marked change in the temperature, a damp cold. Still they moved downward, until at last they came out into a stone chamber with one small passageway on the right and ahead what appeared to be a mountain of stones scattered in profusion, as though a cave-in had occurred, blocking the next staircase down.

Curious, John looked closely at the gray crumbling barrier. "Is that—?"

"Don't know," Dana snapped with unprecedented bluntness, and moved steadily forward into the narrow passageway on the right, lifting the lantern high to light the way.

Finally he stopped before a low door, "Here it is," he announced.

"Thank you, Dana." John smiled, stepping forward and pushing the low door open. He ducked his head and moved into the cell, felt the dirt floor beneath his feet and saw nothing but a mound of straw in the corner. In comparison, the small whitewashed cell had been paradise.

Still Dana held his position in the door, one hand covering his nose in defense against the odors of waste and decay which seemed to be increasing with the dampness. "Ain't fit for stock," he grumbled angrily. "let alone . . ."

At last John agreed. "No, but according to Aggie, it won't last too long." He moved toward the door to speed the old man on his way. "Get some sleep." He smiled. "Come morning, I'll need your assistance. I've never been an odd-boy before."

The old man looked at him affectionately. "At least your duties will take you into the light of day, sir."

Sir! He couldn't have said anything that would have pleased John more. "Then be off with you," he urged.

Finally the old man turned and lifted his hand in salute and disappeared down the passageway.

John watched the length of the corridor, and was still watching when the lantern light faded and left him in darkness. For a moment his heart accelerated. But in the silence he heard snores in the cell opposite him, and drawing comfort from the realization that he was not alone, he stepped back into his own narrow cell, felt along the floor until he found his satchel, then like a blind man felt farther with the toe for his boot until he felt the beginning of straw.

As he settled on the pallet, he reached for the satchel and withdrew his jacket, meager protection against the damp cold. Reaching farther, he felt for his two books, one the Book of Common Prayer, and the other the catalog of the Great Exhibition. Slowly he withdrew the one which would bring him the most comfort. How he'd looked forward to it, strolling the central promenade of the Great Exhibition with his father and Elizabeth, leading them ultimately to the wing where those magnificent black machines had been arranged.

He closed his eyes and let the catalog of the Great Exhibition fall limp in his lap, overcome by a sense of disappointment. How hard they had worked. How unfair of fate to deny . . .

But even before his mind had completed the thought, a new awareness moved in, too painful to deal with, the image of his father crushed beneath the machine, the sad journey back to the house in Bermondsey, Elizabeth's speechless grief, the funeral procession, all leading here to this pit.

His head was heavy with fatigue, and he made no effort to hold himself erect. He slipped down onto straw, the catalog still clasped in his hands.

His mind, equally as numb, made no attempt to make sense out of his surroundings. All he knew for certain in the last minutes before sleep came was that one day he'd close and bolt these mean cells, and if he had need of odd-boys, he'd move them up into the light of day.

When he was Lord of Eden, he'd do all this, and more.

Lord of Eden! Dear God, what a climb he had to make from here to there.

As he began to wonder about the nature of the climb, for some reason he felt inexpressibly sad. It wasn't that he lacked energy. He had that. Or determination. He had that in abundance. And ability as well.

Then why sad?

But sleep came, obscuring both the question and the need for an answer.

London, May 10, 1851

IN SPITE OF the fact that he was a halfhearted husband, Morley Johnson liked to awaken with his arm slung over his wife's swollen belly. On occasion, just as he was opening his eyes, he felt the baby kicking, pushing against Minnie's womb as though eager to get out. In quiet moments such as these, the baby, number seven, reminded Morley of himself. Both were trying to break out of encasements of one sort or another.

With his eyes opened, he lay in the predawn darkness. Beyond the pillow, he observed the small room filled with used furnishings. In the next room, the other six children were still asleep, noisome stairsteps commencing at two and leading to seven.

Morley rolled onto his back now, taking half the bedclothes with him. Oh, God, but he was sick to death of narrow beds, small rooms and the smell of cabbage filtering down into his law office below.

Still he counseled himself patience. An impatient man made mistakes, a valuable lesson he'd learned from his old mentor, Sir Claudius Potter. And in truth, Morley's rise thus far had been remarkable. In the miraculous time of thirty-eight years, he's shaken the dirt of his father's Hampshire farm from his boots forever, had walked to London, educated himself, served a tedious but valuable apprenticeship in the Temple, had applied for admittance to the bar, had passed the examinations on the fourth try, and now was entitled to put "Solicitor" after his name.

Rather enjoying the recall of his own accomplishments, he stretched luxuriously in bed, his toes touching the footboard, his long, lean frame uncurling for the first time after the night's sleep. His mind raced downstairs to his cluttered desk, to the urgent letter he'd received yesterday, delivered by special courier from Lord Eden. Apparently Morley was to play police inspector today, though the letter by and large had been incoherent. His lordship had mentioned the death of his brother, Edward, and the arrival on the doorsteps of Eden Castle of a young man who had claimed kinship with the family. Lord Eden had instructed Morley to launch a search for proof, if indeed proof existed, and to report back to him immediately when and if documentation was uncovered.

He stared up at the ceiling in the darkness. Where to start? Suffering momentary mental confusion concerning the future, he preferred to sink back into his noteworthy past. How fast events had moved the last few years! Morley admitted to the bar, Sir Claudius' death in the riding accident, then the crowning achievement, the humble letter he'd penned to Lord and Lady Eden, applying for the vacant post of solicitor to the vast, though abused Eden estates. He'd presented an effective case, pointing out that as Sir Claudius' clerk how intimately acquainted he was with all the Eden affairs, informing them of his own shiny bronze plaque, MORLEY JOHNSON, SOLICITOR, and begging for the privilege to serve that great family with humility and dedication.

In the next post, he'd received his reply. A trial association of twelve months. If at the end of that time all were pleased, the position would be his.

Now, with the year's trial over, with the Eden ledger books firmly in his command, Morley Johnson was, as they say, a man on his way. He had a rare talent, as great as if not greater than old Sir Claudius himself. To be true, he'd learned from that gentleman how to take in one sum from the estate agents and how to list another in the ledger books, pocketing the difference.

But to the best of his knowledge, certain daring refinements of the game had not even occurred to Sir Claudius. For example, in the past Morley had penned a simple note to Lord Eden. *Estate tax due. Selling Platt number Thirteen due east of Taunton to highest bidder.*

Perhaps his lordship had taken all of three minutes to glance at the note, had scribbled his initials and had returned it to Morley, whereupon the estate agent had been notified that a bidder by the name of Ross Gourland had put up the capital and the deed was to be transferred posthaste.

And who was Ross Gourland? Morley smiled. Who else? And who was Sidney Blackston? Who else? He was now the proud though anonymous possessor of two small estates on the outskirts of Taunton. Of course, he must move with care, but that he intended to do, constructing a good solid foundation on which a limitless structure might be built.

He stretched again, then snuggled close to his sleeping wife. Damn that protuberance! He loved to have her when she was half-asleep. Now one hand moved up to her swollen breasts. Carefully he worried loose the tie on her nightdress and eased the fabric down. As his lips closed around her nipple, she stirred.

"No, luv," she whispered sleepily. "Let me ease this un out 'fore you slip another in."

Damn! She was right. Still he had a hunger. And since he'd probably pass the entire day tramping through the slum areas of London in search of a bastard's mother, the least she could do was give him a moment's respite in this gray dawn.

"Turn over," he commanded, determined to take his comfort whether she liked it or not.

Again she protested, her eyes wide, as though aware of what he was asking. "No, luv, please. We ain't animals."

"Turn over!"

Reluctantly she did as she was told, dragged her bulbous body upward onto her hands and knees while he lifted her nightdress and mounted her.

It was over in less than five minutes. He felt reasonably better, and she certainly was none the worse for wear.

In fact, as she rolled back over, she giggled prettily, her mussed brown hair spread across the pillow. "Oh, you're dreadful, Morley." She smiled. "You really are."

As he climbed off the bed, he looked back down on her. She'd enjoyed it, he was certain, in spite of her protests. All women protested, he thought, as he commenced his toilet, undoubtedly considered it their duty to do so.

He lit the lamp near the washbasin and was constantly aware of her eyes on him, admiring eyes, of course.

"Where is it you're headed today for, luv?" she asked, still nestling in the bedclothes.

"On a search," he said, trimming his jaw whiskers in the wavy glass.

"You're not a detective," she protested. "You're a solicitor."

"When you serve the Eden family," he said to her reflection, "you play any role they ask you to play."

"What if the boy is who he says he is?" she asked sleepily.

"I'll have to find the mother before anyone can prove that, now, won't I?" He lifted the lamp from the table, thrust it toward the wardrobe and withdrew a plain black jacket, twice patched, and matching trousers.

At that moment the door to their bedchamber opened and three young faces appeared. One announced, "Mama, I've wet . . ." As she put her arm around the offender, Morley decided there would be no breakfast for him this morning. He'd stop at a coffeehouse along the way.

As the other three children appeared following the younger ones, the smell of soiled linen filled the room, and every place he looked he saw a small white ghost in a nightshirt.

Thank God for whatever wild-goose chase would take him out of this place. As he sidestepped small bodies, he saw Minnie's distressed face. "I'll fix your breakfast."

"Not now," he called back, moving eagerly toward the top of the stairs.

"It will only take a . . ."

But he didn't stop, and pretended not to hear as he hurried down the stairs and through his narrow office, retrieving the letter from Lord Eden from off his desk, then moving quickly out into the early-morning traffic of Holborn, relieved to shut the door on all domesticity.

He stood a moment, the push of traffic increasing about him. Then he unfolded the Eden letter and read it again, the tone strident for the normally placid Lord Eden. Clearly something had momentarily dragged his attention away from his hounds and horses.

And the object of this agitation? A young man, according to the letter, fifteen, sixteen, no one seemed to know for sure. Apparently he answered to the name of John Murrey Eden, and most important of all, he claimed to be the son of Edward Eden.

Morley stepped to one side in order to permit the passage of a large cart heaped with fresh fruit. As the peddler passed him by, he snagged a ripe red apple and was on the verge of fishing through his pockets for a halfpenny. But apparently the peddler hadn't noticed. So why should Morley call it to his attention?

Now blessed with free breakfast, he proceeded slowly down the pavement, munching on the fruit contentedly, still eyeing the letter from Eden. He really couldn't understand what all the fuss was about. The young man, whoever he was, posed no real threat to the Eden fortune. Ten bastards of Edward Eden could surface, and not one could lay a legitimate claim to any portion of the Eden inheritance. On that foolish July morning in 1848, when Edward Eden had given up all claim to his own fortune, he had rendered his line bereft as well.

True, the boy had a right to reside at Eden, and the Christian impulses of Lord and Lady Eden would assure him of clothes to wear and food to eat. But by the same token they could toss him out anytime they chose. At best he would never be anything but a peripheral family member.

His jaws, still munching the apple, suddenly ceased.

With the tip of his tongue he shifted the seeds from the core to the front of his mouth and spit them out. According to the letter, the young man in question had arrived bearing Edward Eden's body, in the company of a woman known only as Elizabeth.

Morley commenced walking again down the pavement, appalled by the size and challenge of the undertaking. In all of London, there probably were ten thousand Elizabeths. He looked again at the closing paragraph. Ah, a bonus! This Elizabeth, it seemed, had a maimed hand.

Then, with renewed purpose he turned the corner, heading toward Oxford Street. Perhaps there still was someone in the neighborhood who remembered Edward Eden and his Ragged School, someone, more importantly, named Elizabeth with a maimed hand.

As his speed increased, the thought of failure never entered his mind. Sooner or later he would uncover the boy's true identity, not that it mattered to him, but only because it seemed to be of such monumental importance to Lord and Lady Eden. He was at last beginning to understand that invaluable lesson which he'd learned at the knee of Sir Claudius Potter.

Keep your client contented, for their contentment leads to their apathy, and their apathy leads to your enrichment. . . .

⁂

Bermondsey, May 10, 1851

As ELIZABETH KNELT on the floor before the small trunk in the back room of the house in Bermondsey, she closed her eyes. The bright sun had begun to hurt them.

Of course she knew that the cause of discomfort was much more than mere sun. Commencing on the first of May with Edward's death, until now, May 10, she'd never closed her eyes for more than two hours at a time. The journey back from Eden after the funeral had been difficult.

But they finally had glimpsed the spires of London late last evening, and after prayers of thanksgiving, the four riders of Mr. Jack Willmot's had taken themselves off for reunions with their families.

Of course she had thanked them profusely. And after their departure she had lit the lamp and carried it into this small back room, Edward's room, and had spent the night lovingly going through his belongings, weeping for him anew at the sight of each worn object, and trying to keep her thought away from the riddle of her future.

Now she shifted positions upon the bare floor and gently lowered one of the shirtwaists into the open trunk. She still had a vivid sense of the man himself, which somehow, mysteriously, seemed to be growing stronger. Countless times throughout that long night she'd heard his voice, the weight of his foot on the front stoop, his laughter.

In a wave of new grief, she bent over the trunk. Both of them were gone now, John *and* Edward. How mildly hurt she'd been by John's decision to stay at Eden. Yet not surprised. Eden had been his dream for as long as she could remember.

Abruptly she leaned back and tried to ease a painful stitch out of her neck. Softly she crumpled to one side. In all the earth, was there any place of sorrow greater than here, any place more weighted with unreceived love? Lying prone on the floor, her maimed hand stroked the side of the trunk. She was weeping again, without a sound, recalling that first night in the Common Cell at Newgate when as a young prostitute she had crawled across the straw and offered herself to Edward. He'd touched her face with such gentleness, had lifted her ugly burned hand and had kissed it, *kissed it*.

From that moment to this, she had never left his shadow. Now shadows were all she had left. Even his grave was so far away. How pleasant it would have been to put flowers on it and keep it tended.

Sleep, please let me sleep, she prayed, and nestled her

head deeper into the crook of her arm. She was just in the process of losing consciousness when she heard what sounded like a step at the front door. She listened closely. The old house had a way of creaking. Homeless ghosts, according to Edward. Still she postponed sleep, wondering now if she'd remembered to bolt the door. When the three of them had been living here, she, Edward and John, she'd never thought of such things. With two men about, why should she?

Now, newly aware of her aloneness, she struggled to her feet and was just turning to the door when a man appeared before her.

"Miss?" he inquired politely, and apparently saw the fear in her eyes and moved back. "I just came to see . . ."

With a surge of relief she recognized him, the tall, broad frame and weathered face of Mr. Jack Willmot, the professional foreman for whom Edward and John had worked at the Crystal Palace, the man who ten days ago had brought her Edward's crushed body, who had stayed during that terrible night and had seen to the coffin, who had kindly lent his own wagon and team of horses and four of his best riders to accompany her on the journey to Eden.

"Mr. Willmot," she whispered, slipping into a near chair, still trying to draw deep breath.

"I'm sorry I frightened you, miss." He smiled, holding his position in the doorway. "When my men reported in last night, I though I'd come over and see . . ." He broke off speaking and seemed to be concentrating on the crumpled hat in his hands. "I . . . we . . . were worried when you didn't return right off. I was on the verge of sending out new riders . . ."

"It was a difficult journey," she murmured, and gestured through the door behind him to the front parlor. "Won't you sit down, Mr. Willmot?" she invited. "I was just getting ready to fix myself a cup of tea," she lied. "I'd be most grateful if you'd join me."

"I don't mean to put you to any trouble . . ."

"Oh, it's no trouble." She smiled. As she approached where he was standing just inside the door, she saw clearly the direction of his eyes falling on the small trunk.

"His?" he asked, a respectful tone in his voice, which pleased her.

She nodded. "Not much, I'm afraid. Somehow in the last few years of his life, Edward managed to give everything of value away."

"I'll never forget him," Mr. Willmot vowed, his voice breaking.

His sincerity moved her. "Nor will anyone who had the good fortune to know him," she agreed softly. How good it was to have someone with whom she could share her grief. Now she moved past him, lightly touching his arm. "Come, Mr. Willmot. There are comfortable chairs in the parlor, and I'm certain I can find a biscuit or two . . ."

Then she hurried into the small kitchen, filled the teakettle from the rain barrel outside the door and realized with newly sinking spirits that she had yet to start a fire in the old stove.

As though he'd heard both her thoughts and her distress, he appeared in the low-ceilinged kitchen and without a word disappeared into the woodshed and reemerged with kindling in his arms.

A short time later they were seated in the parlor, a tea tray between them. As Elizabeth poured, Jack Willmot opened the tin of biscuits which she'd found at the back of the cupboard, and for several moments still no words were spoken as they sipped the good hot brew.

"And the boy?" Willmot asked, as though picking up the thread of an abandoned conversation.

"He stayed at Eden, of course," Elizabeth replied, still seeing John as she'd last glimpsed him, standing alone in the inner courtyard of Eden Castle.

"Will he be . . . cared for?" Willmot asked quietly.

"Oh, I'm sure of it," Elizabeth reassured him. "His father has told him stories of Eden since he was a babe. It's always been his dream."

"Why didn't you stay?" he asked bluntly.

She looked up, surprised by both the bluntness and the question. "I don't belong there," she said simply.

"Why not?" he asked. "As Edward Eden's wife, I should think . . ."

She gaped at him, then lowered her head. "I was not Edward's wife."

The news seemed to have a peculiar effect on the large man. Without looking up, she sensed that he was sitting as motionless as she. With difficulty she lifted the tin of biscuits. "Please help yourself," she offered, trying to dispel the look of surprise from his face.

But Mr. Willmot was not interested in biscuits. "And . . . the boy?" he stammered.

". . . is Edward's son, not mine. Though I raised him," she added with pride.

She glanced to the left through the open door which led to Edward's room. The corner of the trunk was just visible from where she sat. Lovingly she eyed it and decided that as long as she inhabited this house, she would keep that room just as it was now, his bed linens still on the bed where he'd slept the night before his death, his presence, his soul everywhere.

She was aware of Willmot's eyes upon her, the silence between them heavy with unasked questions. Now she stood, longing to return to her new shrine. "I kept his house for him, Mr. Willmot, and raised his son and saw to all his needs . . ." She hesitated, then added, ". . . save one."

Apparently he was sensitive to her growing distress, and stood as though to take his leave. "I'm . . . sorry, miss," he apologized.

"Elizabeth," she said sharply. "My name is Elizabeth."

"Elizabeth," he repeated. "Perhaps I shouldn't have come . . ." He was backing away from her now, and at the same time fumbling in a pocket of his brown jacket. "I . . . we thought . . ." he stammered, "well, what we did was pass the hat." Abruptly he looked at her as though to reassure her. "It isn't charity, no," he repeated firmly. "There's not a rough-jack on that entire crew who hasn't shared bread with Edward Eden, or lifted a pint. So it isn't charity," he added. "Consider it partial payment of our debt to him—for what he gave us."

She watched carefully as he continued to fumble through his pocket. *For what he gave us.* She knew he wasn't talking about bread or pints. Again she felt her emotions perilously close to the surface.

She sat in a near chair and was aware of him stepping close again. "Here," he said, lifting her hand and placing a stack of notes in it.

"It's not much," he added, "slightly more than twenty pounds. But it will see to your needs for a while."

She looked down at the notes and knew that she had no choice but to remain silent.

In concern, he knelt before her, refilled her teacup and offered it to her. But she merely shook her head and was on the verge of trying to thank him when a knock sounded at the front door, a curious rap of strength in this room of grief. She looked up as though under attack, her eyes filled with tears. Within the instant, Jack Willmot was on his feet. "Shall I see . . . ?"

She nodded.

He took one step toward the door, then returned to her side and gathered the notes. "Put these in your pocket," he urged. "They were hard-earned and intended for you alone."

Passively she obeyed, viewing events around her now as an endurance test. From where she sat, she heard a man's voice coming from the stoop.

"Only a moment of your time. That's all. I'd be most grateful . . ."

She tried to stand and failed. As she sank back into the chair, she told Mr. Willmot to, "Let him in. It's clear he won't go away until you do."

Still reluctant, at last Jack Willmot stepped back from the door, and in the next minute a gentleman appeared, with rosy cheeks and plain clothes. His dark eyes darted over all aspects of the front parlor, then moved to Elizabeth, where they held fast.

No one spoke. Seldom had she been the object of such close scrutiny. His eyes left her face and moved down to her maimed hand. She thought she saw him smile, but she couldn't be certain. When he continued to stare at her hand, she felt a wave of old embarrassment and hurriedly hid it in her pocket, where her fingers found the pound notes which Mr. Willmot had given her.

Then the inspection was over and the gentleman bowed. "I'm sorry for this . . . intrusion, miss," he began. "Allow me to introduce myself. My name is Morley Johnson. I am solicitor to the Eden family."

Beyond the man's shoulder she saw Jack Willmot still waiting. In a way she wished he would leave. Perhaps the nature of the business was private. Sternly she scolded herself for her pride and invited, "Mr. Willmot, close the door please and take a seat . . ."

Assuming that the two men had met at the door, she dispensed with introductions and waited until both were settled, Mr. Willmot opposite her, Mr. Johnson in a straight-backed chair to her right.

She made an effort at ease. "Would you care for tea, Mr. Johnson?"

"No, don't bother, miss."

"The nature of your business, then, Mr. Johnson, if you will."

The tall man nodded, and he too seemed to sit more erect in his chair, as though ready to approach the heart of the matter. Only Jack Willmot sprawled comfortably opposite her with the ease of a witness.

Then Mr. Johnson was speaking again. "A few questions, miss. That's all. Did you remain at Eden for any period of time?"

A peculiar question. "No," she replied, "though I was invited, by her ladyship . . ."

"A most gracious lady."

"But I declined," Elizabeth added.

"Of course," Mr. Johnson murmured.

Silence. Jack Willmot shifted in his chair, crossed his legs and turned at an angle facing Johnson, as though suddenly interested in the conversation.

Elizabeth closed her eyes, her fatigue increasing.

"Miss?" It was Johnson again, leaning closer. "Some of the questions that I'm required to ask of you may be . . . awkward. I apologize in advance . . ."

"Ask what you like, Mr. Johnson," she replied.

"How long did you know Mr. Edward Eden?"

A harmless question. She was tempted to reply, "All my life," as before Edward Eden she'd had no life. But she didn't. Instead she counted up the years between 1836 and 1851. "About fifteen," she replied, and felt astonished at the figure. Had that been all? A mere fifteen?

"And you met him where?" Johnson persisted.

What now? It would be imprudent of her to say, "As a prostitute in the Common Cell at Newgate," so she lied. A small white one. "In his Ragged School on Oxford Street," she murmured, and looked away toward the small window on her left.

"You were a . . . pupil?"

"At first, yes," she said, looking back. "But I took to my books right enough and later I became a full volunteer, teaching the young ones . . ." Her voice fell as her mind darted back to those blissfully happy days.

Then Mr. Johnson was there again, his manner still apologetic. "Forgive me, miss." He smiled. "But if I may ask, what was your . . . relationship to Mr. Eden?"

Quickly she glanced at Jack Willmot. No white lie here, not when she'd spoken the truth earlier.

Apparently Jack Willmot saw her discomfort and turned to Johnson with a question of his own. "In what capacity are you here, Johnson, and where are your questions leading?"

As though annoyed by the intrusion, Johnson looked toward Willmot. "Forgive me, sir, but I was about to ask you the same question."

Elizabeth saw Jack Willmot's confidence falter. He seemed to look to her for an answer. And in spite of her weariness, she rallied. Jack Willmot had been far too kind to let him struggle thus. Now to Johnson she said, "Edward had been employed by Mr. Willmot. He was with him the night he died, and without his support I doubt if any of us would have survived from that night to now."

As though moved by her tribute, she saw Willmot lower his head.

Again a feeling of quiet stole over the room. And in tthat quiet she found the courage to answer Morley Johnson's last question. "The relationship I shared with Edward Eden," she commenced, "was a simple one. I kept his house, and in the later years, his books as well."

Johnson seemed to be listening with interest and at this

point withdrew from the inner pocket of his plain jacket a small notepad and point. While he was still in the process of recording something, he asked bluntly, "But you were not his . . . wife?"

"No."

"Did you share his bed?" Johnson asked, still not looking at her, apparently unaware of her embarrassment.

Again Willmot interrupted. "I protest, Johnson. I can't see what—"

"I'm not here to question you, Mr. Willmot," Johnson snapped, all traces of kindness gone from his voice. "Though I may in time," he added.

But still Willmot moved forward in his chair. "I don't give a damn who you've come to question. I'm saying that in certain areas, you've got no right—"

As Johnson turned in his chair to meet the angry challenge, Elizabeth sat up. "Please, Mr. Willmot," she soothed. Then to Johnson she said, "No, I never shared his bed."

He looked at her, clearly disbelieving. "If I may be so bold," he said. "What was your . . . profession . . . before you went into the Ragged School?"

She gazed at him without speaking. There was something arrogant in his manner now, which suggested that he already knew the answers to the questions he was asking.

"I was a prostitute, Mr. Johnson," she whispered, feeling battered.

He smiled at her. "And yet, you are asking me to believe that you never knew Edward Eden in a carnal way?"

"I didn't," she protested, leaving her chair, her anger dragging her to her feet in spite of her fatigue.

Within the instant Willmot was beside her, the full force of his fury aimed downward on the still-grinning Johnson. "I'm asking you to leave now, sir," he said, his voice taut, as though he were exerting massive self-control.

Sensing an ally, Elizabeth felt strength returning. "No," she said, settling back into the chair. "Let him ask all his questions now and never return."

Apparently Jack Willmot gave in to her judgment,

though he did not return to his chair, but instead took up a protective stance directly behind her.

"As I said," Johnson commenced again, a new conciliatory tone in his voice, "some of the questions might be awkward. But you must know that I'm acting under explicit instructions from Lord and Lady Eden."

Baffled, Elizabeth looked closely at him. "What possible interest would Lord and Lady Eden have in me?" she asked quietly.

"Oh, not you directly," Johnson hastened to explain. "It's the boy."

Suddenly everything became clear. Of course. John. Obviously Lord and Lady Eden thought that *she* was John's mother.

In a way relieved, she leaned back in the chair. "I'm not the boy's mother, Mr. Johnson," she said, "if that's what you want to know, though I raised him and feel a kinship with him as close as flesh."

He nodded as though at last he believed something she had said. "Then would you be so kind, miss, as to shed some light on his origins? Lord and Lady Eden will make it worth your while, I promise."

A flair of leftover anger surfaced. "I want nothing from Lord and Lady Eden," she said sharply, "and I can shed little light on the boy's . . . origins, as you put it."

"Well, he surely didn't appear like Moses in a basket." Johnson countered, laying his pad and point aside as though there were nothing worthwhile to write at the moment.

"No," she murmured, and tried to turn her mind to that distant day when Edward had reappeared after a prolonged absence, babe in arms. His son, or at least that's what he had told one and all.

"He'd been away . . ." she began hesitantly.

"Where?"

"I don't remember. All I know is that Daniel Spade was quite worried . . ."

"Spade?"

"Edward's good friend who ran the school."

Johnson nodded as though he too were putting pieces of the puzzle together. "And where is this Spade?"

"Dead," Elizabeth whispered, "of the fever. Many years ago."

"Go on." He reached for his notepad again.

"I can't go on, Mr. Johnson," she said. "I don't know the answers to the questions you're asking."

"Well, you must know more," he badgered. "You were there. Think!"

Behind her she was aware of Jack Willmot, ready at the first word from her to toss the man out. Yet in a way the puzzle fascinated Elizabeth as well, that mysterious and unidentified woman who had been the fortunate recipient of Edward's love.

She leaned forward and covered her face with her hands, trying to clear the cobwebs of fatigue and grief from her brain. Then suddenly she had an idea. "St. Dunstan's," she exclaimed. "The little parish church near Oxford Street. We took John there for baptism. Surely . . ."

But all the time she spoke, Johnson merely wagged his head. "Nothing," he broke in. "I was there first thing this morning. The entry is listed, to be sure. But it's a useless document, covered with scrolls and angels. According to that foolish parchment, God was his maker, both father and mother."

She detected the derision in his voice and hated it, his cynicism somehow soiling her memory of that glorious morning. Still she tried to speak civilly to him. "The priest said nothing?" she asked, remembering the kind old man well.

"In his dotage," Johnson muttered. "He remembered Mr. Eden more for his generous donations to the church than for the baptismal of his son. Try to remember," he urged. "After Mr. Eden's long absence, when he first appeared with the babe, did he say where he had come from?"

She shook her head. Then: "I do remember overhearing Edward talking to Daniel Spade," she said slowly.

Johnson sat up.

"He said something about . . . the Lakes."

"The Lakes?" Johnson parroted.

She nodded. "For some reason I had the feeling he'd come from there."

"The Lakes?" Johnson repeated. "Anything more?"

She shook her head. "We were all just glad to see him, Mr. Johnson. I don't think it would have mattered to any of us where he'd come from."

"The . . . Lakes," he repeated a third time.

Abruptly Johnson sat up as though burdened with another idea. "And you're certain," he asked, rising, "that the lad now at Eden and the babe which mysteriously appeared in Mr. Eden's arms are one and the same?"

To this foolish question she laughed softly. "Now, who else would it be?"

"Oh, substitution would be quite possible," Johnson interjected, "that babe disappearing and another taking its place."

"Mr. Johnson," she began, rising to face him, "I washed that babe when all of him fit easily into my two hands. I dressed him, cleansed him, cared for him every minute of every day until now . . ."

Strange, how the sensation of loneliness descended without warning. She'd been missing Edward. Now she longed for John. "No," she concluded in an attempt to banish the sensations. "The young man at Eden is the babe grown up, I'd swear to it. And I'd swear further that he *is* Edward Eden's son."

Johnson stared at her as though still not quite convinced. "Were there any distinguishing marks on the babe that we could look for in the young man?" he asked, closing his notepad as though expecting her usual unsatisfactory response.

"Distinguishing—"

"A birthmark," he interrupted, clearly annoyed by the fruitlessness of his search.

"No," she replied. "The babe was flawless, as is the young man." Then she remembered. "On his chest, there's a small scar."

His interest renewed, Johnson stepped closer. "A scar? What kind of—"

"Oh, it was raw and red-looking when Edward first brought him home. Like he had been cut."

Again the notepad was flipped open. "Did he say—"

She shook her head, recalling Edward's reluctance to talk about it. "He said nothing," she replied, "and it healed right enough, and lately when I scrubbed his back for him, I noticed that it was beginning to stretch out altogether. Like the letter B, it was."

"B?" Johnson repeated. He scribbled something more in his notepad, then again flipped it closed.

Now she saw him glance up at the still-impatient Jack Willmot. "Before I take my leave, sir," he commenced, as though on good behavior before that man of massive strength, "you say you employed Mr. Eden and his son for a period of time leading up to his death?"

Willmot nodded. "Aye, they were part of my crew at the Exhibition site. Worked with them both night and day on that undertaking."

Johnson seemed pleased by the man's apparent willingness to cooperate. "Then could you, sir, shed any light on the mystery at hand?"

"I'm not certain I understand what the mystery at hand is."

"We're seeking," Johnson began wearily, "documentation of the legitimacy of John Murrey Eden."

Willmot stepped forward, coming between Elizabeth and the man. "If Mr. Eden said the boy was his son," he pronounced in clear tones, "then it's a fact. The man's word was gold, sir. If you'd known him at all, you'd know that to be true."

In the face of this declaration, Johnson merely smiled. "Oh, I knew the man right enough, Mr. Willmot. But apparently I knew a different side of him. The Edward Eden I knew was the one I found repeatedly drunk and senseless in the Common Cell at Newgate after a night's brawling and wenching. That's the Edward Eden I knew, the same one charged once with attempted murder for attacking the night warden, the same Prince of Eden who cohorted with pimps and thieves and whores . . ."

Too late, he obviously caught himself up, cast an apologetic look at Elizabeth and now beat a hasty retreat to the door, with Jack Willmot following directly behind him.

There he stopped and looked back. "I thank you for your time," he said stiffly, "and I apologize for any offense . . ."

Willmot stepped closer.

But Johnson held his ground, his parting words something of a threat. "And I fear I must return, for Lord and Lady Eden are determined to get to the bottom of this mystery. If you think of anything that you feel might be pertinent to the subject, I'll leave my card."

He placed a small white card on the near table. "The sooner the mystery is solved," he said ominously, "the better for all concerned."

At that moment Elizabeth moved toward the door, a new fear pressing against her. "John," she began, "is John well? Will this in any way affect . . . ?" Suddenly the thought that John might be exposed to abuse was more than she could bear. Again the circumstances of the morning and her incredible fatigue took a tremendous toll. Fighting back tears, she asked again, "Is John—"

"Well," Johnson interrupted, "or so I hear. Of course he won't enjoy total access to the bosom of the family until we can prove his identity beyond a shadow of a—"

"Who else could it be?" she cried now, stepping closer to the door. "Tell them if there's any doubt just to open their eyes and *look!* They'll see Edward standing before them, in all aspects, Edward . . ." Striving to hold back her tears, she clutched at the open door and watched the man retreat down the steps.

Embarrassed, she knew she must make one last effort at control. But it was useless. The tears could not be stanched. The questions, Morley Johnson's insinuations, the thought of John alone, perhaps suffering, was too much. As she inclined her head forward, giving in to her grief, she was aware of Mr. Willmot's arm about her, supporting her into the back room, Edward's room, and placing her gently on the bed.

"Don't, please," he soothed, kneeling beside her.

She was grateful for his kindness and tried to thank him. But there was no more strength. She covered her face with her hands in an attempt to blot out his concerned expression, and had no choice but to weep herself dry.

Her last awareness was of Jack Willmot lifting her into his arms, holding her as though she were a child, as though confident that his strength would be equal to her disintegration.

Although doubtful at first, to her surprise, a few moments later a feeling of quiet stole over her. The light of noon sun gradually sank from her vision. And even though now and then she still felt racked by sobs, she saw the approaching darkness and welcomed it and bid it come closer.

What he'd done had been more for the memory of Edward Eden than for the young woman. Yet now, holding her close, he confessed quietly to himself that she moved him deeply.

Jack Willmot continued to cradle her until he felt her small frame go limp against his chest, then gently he lowered her to the pillow, wiped the residue of tears from her face and drew the light coverlet over her.

He stepped back, feeling awkward and out of place. Oh, not that he hadn't had plenty of experience with women. But nothing important, and certainly nothing lasting or permanent. As a professional foreman, his jobs took him everywhere. And he liked it that way and he definitely preferred male company, the simpler the better, like his crew on the Exhibition site. What a collection of navvies those had been. First-class, and top among them had been Edward Eden and his boy.

Again he felt an uncharacteristic moment of weakness, haunted, as he'd been every night since it had happened, by the remembered image of that power loom slipping the winch, the explosion, the sparks, the shouts of the men, the smoke clearing to reveal . . .

God! Would he ever rid his mind of it? Now, as though to move away from the remembered horror, he adjusted the coverlet over the sleeping Elizabeth and moved back to the door.

Briefly he paused at the door, staring down at the small opened trunk belonging to Edward Eden. Slowly he lowered the lid, as though to put the man and his memory behind him.

He'd leave her for now, but he'd be back. He had an appointment later this week with Mr. Thomas Brassey, and he suspected that the great contractor had a new job for him. If it was local, he'd take it. If not, he'd pass it by.

For a period of time he must remain in London, keep an eye on her, as it were, until she'd settled safely into a new life. That was the least he could do for her, for Edward Eden, for the boy. Also he had a feeling that the offensive solicitor would be back.

The thought enraged him, and he vowed at that moment to place a watch on the house. He was certain there would be no shortage of volunteers, and he'd pay them out of his own pocket.

He moved rapidly through the front parlor, stopping by the table and pocketing the small white card left by the solicitor. If she was forced to have any further dealings with Mr. Morley Johnson, he intended to be present.

In some amazement he stopped at the door. What had happened to his predictable personality of forty years, the hard-bitten foreman with the reputation for working men until they dropped, of braving foreign countries and foreign climes, of caring for nothing and no one save the successful execution of the job of the moment? What had happened to that iron man?

He chided himself for his own foolishness. Nothing had happened to him, nothing at all, though he closed the door softly behind him, checked the latch, tested the knob and started off down the narrow lane, feeling the difference in all aspects of his being.

Later that afternoon, Morley Johnson sat at his cluttered desk with the afternoon sun falling through the smudged windows, the raucous shouts of his children above causing a fine rain of plaster to filter down upon him and the smell of Minnie's dinner haddock causing his stomach to turn. He thought bleakly, "Fruitless! All of it!"

He leaned back in his chair and caught himself as the weakened left rear leg creaked ominously. My God! What had he gained for himself and his future this day? Exactly nothing except aching feet and an aching head from tramping through the slum of Bermondsey. Again he arranged the blank sheet of stationery before him, preparatory to writing to Lord and Lady Eden. Another fruitless gesture, for what did he have to tell them?

Abruptly he flipped open the notepad and studied his scribbled notes. For a moment his eyes blurred, his mind no longer thinking about clues. Interesting, the honesty with which she'd admitted to prostitution, yet in the next breath had asked him to believe that she had never, not once, accommodated Edward Eden.

He made a curious noise, half-grunt, half-chuckle. Did she take him for a fool? And who was that watchdog in constant attendance? No, Morley Johnson was wiser than that and knew a whore and whore's bully when he met them straight on.

Now again he leaned back in his chair with caution, fascinated by his present train of thought. With a wave of humor it occurred to him that perhaps he should contact that high-minded gentleman, Mr. William Gladstone, who, according to coffeehouse gossip, suffered two insatiable hungers; one, to wear the mantle of the Chancellor of the Exchequer, and two, to satisfy himself between the legs of every whore in London. Gossip further had it that he would achieve the latter long before he acquired the former. Together with his wife, Catherine, he'd founded the House of Charity for Prostitutes at Nine Rose Street, Soho. Again Morley smiled. Clearly Gladstone had his priorities in order. First he'd rape, then he'd redeem. For that matter, perhaps he'd already come in contact with the whore Elizabeth. She *was* fetching, in a soiled way.

Abruptly Morley bent forward and rested his head in his hands. *What would it be like to go where many men had gone before?*

Overhead, he heard his children racing back and forth through the narrow rooms. And looking up, he saw his office door ajar, a habitual custom at Minnie's request so that she could effortlessly call him if there was need.

Suddenly angry at the imprisonment and lack of privacy, he stood up with such force that the chair clattered backward. It was like working in a goddamned nursery or Common Kitchen with tradesmen tramping through at all hours of the day delivering cabbages and spuds.

In rising despair he went to the window and tried to see beyond the streaked coal dust to the street. He thought longingly of Sir Claudius Potter's elegant chambers in the Temple, the handsome marble mantelpiece, oriental carpet, vast mahogany desk, and most important, the small chamber at the rear containing a low comfortable couch where at any given hour of the day or night Sir Claudius might disappear, a ravishing beauty in tow, with the brief order that he was not to be disturbed.

Thinking on such remote delights, Morley grasped the sill and pressed his forehead against the window. Why not him? It had been the Eden fortune which had supplied Sir Claudius with those luxuries. Why not him as well?

By God, there was no reason in the world, and suddenly he slammed his fist down against the sill and turned to the desk with renewed purpose. He knew what to do. He would *not* be imprisoned in this smelly hole for the rest of his life, weighted down by children and an ever-pregnant wife. He knew precisely what Lord and Lady Eden wanted to hear, and he'd tell them, if not the truth, then a harmless deviation from it.

As the ideas came faster than he could deal with them, he reached for his pad to jot them down, to be fully developed later. At that moment, the bulbous Minnie appeared in the door, her face flushed from cooking heat. "Tea, luv." She smiled, one hand rubbing her protuberance in an obscene fashion.

"Get out!" Morley shouted, seized suddenly by incomprehensible anger at her ugliness.

"But, luv, all I said was—"

"Get out!" he shouted again, and started up from his desk as though to bodily assist her with her exit. He heard her waddling up the stairs, weeping softly. A wave of remorse swept over him. He'd have to mend bridges later, but that presented no problem. She was like the dough she kneaded each night—perfectly malleable to his touch.

But for now he had other goals in mind, greater ones, which hopefully would lead him out of this grim office and into chambers as elegant as Sir Claudius', with his own private nook for relaxation, for escape, for . . .

Why couldn't he rid the whore from his mind?

But she continued to cling like lint, and it was with the greatest of efforts that he forced his attention down onto his desk, and the letter to Lord and Lady Eden. As he'd taken great pains with that first letter he'd written years ago, so too this one must strike just the right tone, an earnest report bespeaking earnest effort, certainly to include mention of the scar on the babe's chest and perhaps suggesting an immediate inspection to see if the young boy's chest bore the same. Then too he would apprise them of his dead end at the Baptismal Registry, but counter that dead end with the new clue concerning the Lakes, even going so far as to suggest that, in spite of the hardship of leaving his family, he'd be more than willing to undertake a journey to said district in the hope that a personal investigation would yield more than a written one.

Then too, and with this thought his excitement vaulted, if her ladyship was still desirous of such an action, he'd be most willing to stop back by her ancestral home of Hadley Park in Shropshire, where after the death of her father, Lord Powels, an untrustworthy uncle had moved in and was apparently running the rich sheep and grazing land with an unrestrained hand. She had complained to him several times before that she longed for a first-hand account. Then he would supply her with one, and perhaps another firm block would be cemented into place in the relationship between Morley Johnson and the Edens.

Yes, by God, that last was a stroke of genius, binding one mission to another. And now with what eagerness he reached for his stationery, dipped his pen, shook it twice and commenced the letter which might, with luck, lead him out of this pit of stifling domesticity.

❧

Eden Castle,
June 1851

As HIS WIFE entered the small library, James looked up from Morley Johnson's interesting letter. Peculiar, he thought, lowering the pages. In daylight she looked alive. At night he'd swear he was mounting a corpse.

"Sorry to disturb you," he said.

"You didn't disturb me," she replied quietly, closing the door, then leaning against it. "I was told," she began, "that you wanted to see me."

He nodded and pushed back in his chair at the writing bureau. He felt mysteriously exhausted, as though the appearance of this "wife" had suddenly fatigued him. Wife, he thought, annoyed. Oh, she had borne him children and permitted him ascess to her bed. But she always carried with her that damnable air of a condemned and passive prisoner. He saw it now in the rigid manner in which she was standing at attention before him. He wondered briefly what he would have to require of her before that cold mask splintered and fell away.

Now, to his surprise, he found that he could no longer stand the sight of her, and merely tossed the letter toward her across the bureau and turned away.

"What—" she began.

"Read it for yourself," he snapped. "You may find it interesting."

Slowly he turned back in his chair. She was devouring the letter, her eyes skimming rapidly over the lines. Well, he was glad she found the letter of such interest. As for himself, it was his opinion that Morley Johnson had launched a fruitless first investigation, and was now proposing a very expensive and fruitless second investigation. What was the point? He knew that ultimately his wife would do with the boy what she wished, depending upon her whim of the day. The only paragraph of Morley Johnson's letter which had made any sense was the one in which he had pointed out that the boy, whoever he might be, posed no real threat to the Eden fortune. The Eden purse strings would remain firmly in James's hands, where he fully intended to keep them until it was time to hand them over to young Richard.

Still reading? "My God, Harriet, shall I read it for you?" The sound of his voice raised in irritation echoed around the quiet room. His annoyance mounting, he stood and lightly paced before the fireplace. His eyes lifted to his mother's portrait. Abruptly he stopped, his hands laced behind his back, his head tilted up at the sight of that breathtaking beauty.

Suddenly he turned away from the portrait of his mother and looked again at the cold fish who presently wore the mantle of Lady Eden. The contrast was too brutal, and even though he saw her now with the pages of the letter limp in her lap, he found again that he could not bear the sight of her, and moved rapidly toward the sideboard and the decanter of brandy.

"Would you care for brandy?" he asked over his shoulder, pouring a snifter, then pouring a second without waiting for her reply.

"No, thank you," she said.

He looked up, surprised. Did she only imbibe at night? "Are you certain?"

"I'm certain."

He shrugged, lifted the snifter and welcomed the strong liquid. It had a clearing effect on his head. He took the brandy back to the bureau, sat in the chair, and assuming that she had at last digested the contents of the letter, asked a direct question. "Your opinion?"

"I was . . . hoping," she began, "for more."

"As were we all," he conceded. "But I doubt if there's more to be learned—anywhere."

She bent her head to one side, rubbing her forehead as though to contain or soothe a pain. "Mr. Johnson mentions the Lakes . . ."

"A wild-goose chase, if you ask me."

"We don't know for certain."

"Yet what's to be gained?"

She sat up on the edge of the window seat, a look of surprise on her face. "His identity, of course," she snapped, that same air of patronization in her manner which she frequently adopted when talking with him.

He loathed it, had endured it for ten years and found in that moment a peculiar inability to endure more. "We know his identity," he said harshly, leaning across the desk. "We may not care for it, but I do believe we know it."

She gave him a look of such intensity that with relish he moved to enlighten her. "Oh, he's Edward's son," he said lightly. "I've never doubted that from the first moment I laid eyes on him. And his mother is the whore, the sickly-looking creature who dragged him out here and who deposited him on our doorstep." He leaned back in the chair now, pleased with her stunned expression. "It's my opinion that the two are in alliance together. He is to milk us for all he can, then share the cream with her."

Pleased with himself, he concluded with a smile. "But it won't work. Two weeks ago I gave Rexroat instructions to put him in the odd-boy cellar, and to work the skin off him." Again he smiled. "Of course, I haven't checked within the last few days, but the boy may very well be gone as of this moment, our problem solved."

Suddenly she was on her feet, confronting him. "You had no right—"

"No right?" He smiled, pleased by her anger.

"What if Johnson finds proof, legitimate proof—"

"He won't."

"There are clues to go on . . ."

"Nothing that amounts to anything."

"They are . . . unexplored," she cried, her contempt for him visible in every angle of her face. Then, as though unable to abide his presence, she started angrily toward the door, turning her back on him as though he were a mere servant.

"Wait!" he shouted as she reached the door.

For a moment he wasn't certain whether she'd obey him or not, the door opening, her gray silk skirts billowing with the speed of her departure.

Then she stopped, her back still to him, the brief flare of anger over. In a sense he was sorry to see it go, though now with morbid fascination he dwelt on her heaving shoulders, a discernible lowering of her head, as though at the last minute she had remembered her role, and remembered equally how easy it was to defeat him with her passivity.

"Close the door," he commanded. Slowly she obeyed him and turned at last to face him with what appeared to be supreme contempt.

For a moment he stared at her with matching contempt. He saw her arms relaxed at her side, a pose of pure strength which he found literally unendurable. To destroy it in any manner that was necessary was now his goal. The young boy and the letter long since forgotten, he started slowly out from behind the bureau, warning himself in advance not to strike her. In the past, how richly she had received his blows, smiling at him even as her eyes had filled with tears.

No, it must be more this time, and suddenly he felt the winds of inspiration blowing. The fastidious atmosphere of the small library faded as he drew near to her, blood racing at the close view of her contemptuous indifference. Decency was only a word then, as without speaking he grasped her by the shoulders and violently pushed her to a position near the wall beside the door. He felt her stiffen at his touch, her eyes closed, the only visible sign of her fear.

"James," she whispered, "this is a . . . public room."

"I know the nature of the room," he said with a calmness he did not feel. Now he stood before her, his own anger in control. He'd at least learned that lesson from her in ten miserable years of marriage, that the victor of any match was always the one in control. Absorbed by his projection of her weak and weeping, he calmly ordered, "Get to your knees, madam."

"James, I—"

"To your knees," he repeated, stepping forward, placing his hands on her shoulders and forcing her down.

After her intial protest she did as she was told, as though at last it had dawned on her that they were fighting the same battle.

She opened her eyes and looked up at him. Incredibly, when she spoke, her voice was as firm and filled with purpose as though they were sitting opposite each other at tea. "The steward said you wanted to see me. I assumed it was to discuss the letter, the future of the boy . . ."

Stepping closer, he smiled. "We can discuss the boy if you wish, and the letter." One hand moved down to the front of his trousers. "You've expressed yourself quite openly," he went on, monitoring her face closely. "Clearly you harbor the opinion that I possess neither the skill nor the intelligence to deal with such a complex problem."

"No . . ."

Though only whispered, the single word brought him incredible delight as for the first time he saw her eyes open wide in clear terror.

"No, what?" He smiled, the buttons on his trousers undone at last. Now he hunched his shoulders and plunged his hand deep into the opening. "Do you mean, no, I don't understand the problem, or no, I'm not equipped to deal with it? Which?"

"No, please . . ." she gasped, and her lips, dried, apparently refused to form any more words. For a moment her eyes locked rigidly on his hand.

With what enthusiasm he watched her, the iron facade beginning to crumble as clearly she preceived his intention. In a last moment of consideration, he thought that all she had to do was weep and perhaps beg. All she had to do to spare herself the humiliation was to apologize for providing him with ten long years of unrelieved misery, to look up at him and concede that he was master, not with mere words, for she'd mouthed those false phrases before. No, now he wanted to see it in her face. Not once in his entire life had anyone ever looked upon him with that degree of fear which bespoke true power. Wasn't he entitled to it once?

Of course he was, though what he saw in her face was not fear. Intimidated and angered, he moved forward, with a sense of no turning back.

Then suddenly she pushed him away, struggling to her feet, her arms moving upward as though for protection. Taken by surprise, James at first dared to hope that perhaps she was on the verge of weeping, begging. But instead he saw her move quickly to the door, as though nothing at all had happened, as though she were quite accustomed to imposing her will upon his, without explanation.

Enraged, he started after her, and was just in the process of turning her about when she looked directly at him, her face revealing her fear, but her voice as contained as ever.

"You seem to be suffering a point of confusion, James. I am your wife, not one of your—"

He tightened his grip on her arm. "You will do as I say."

"I think not."

Again he tried to push her to her knees, but she stepped to one side, grasping the doorknob, the incongruity of a smile on her face. "You know as well as I that all I must do is lift my voice in a single cry of alarm and every watchman within earshot will come to my aid."

"They are *my* watchmen," he shouted, his anger and frustration blending.

"Are they?"

"They take their commands from me."

"Shall we test them?"

He considered challenging her, then changed his mind. With trembling hands he restored himself and sank down into the chair behind the bureau, his sense of defeat still growing.

He watched as methodically she straightened herself. Then she gathered up the pages of the fallen letter and stood erect before him where he sat crumpled behind the bureau. Without looking at him, still concentrating on folding the letter, she spoke. "As you have suggested, James, I will attend to this. I fear that you are not yourself today and would recommend a long ride across the moors." At last she looked down on him, an expression filled with hate. "Tend to your hounds and horses. Leave everything else to me."

He had thought to answer, some obscene remark. But at the door she stopped. "I will take my leave now. I will respond to Morley Johnson myself. It is my wish that he make his journey, both to the Lakes as well as to Hadley Park."

Halfway out of the door, she stopped again. "Tend to yourself." She smiled. "You look quite undone."

And with that she was gone, closing the door behind her.

He sat for a moment, unmoving behind the bureau. The trembling started someplace deep inside him, a tidal wave of unspent rage cresting until at last it erupted, and leaning angrily forward, he grasped the near inkwell and hurled it against the closed door, hurled the quill after it, then the hourglass after that, then the blotter, each small and insignificant item striking with hollow reverberations against the closed door until at last the surface of the bureau was stripped, his childish rage spent and, exhausted, he crumpled upon the bureau, weeping.

Once outside the door, she saw the Great Hall in dim outline only, saw as through a mist two house stewards hurrying toward her, clearly summoned by the crashing of objects against the closed door behind her.

As the two approached, she drew herself up and knew that the tirade would not last long. It was a mere child inside the library, displaying a child's rage.

"My lady," murmured one of the stewards, gaping at the bombardment going on within the library. Then, as she had predicted, a silence fell.

"It's nothing," she soothed the two men, and without a word signaled to them both that no further inquiry was to be made.

Both good servants, they clearly understood and commenced a subtle retreat. Still she detained them, anxious to present a calm front. "A request, if you will," she began kindly. "Would one of you be so good as to go to the kitchen court and inform Mrs. Swan that I will be down in a quarter of an hour. If she'll have the books ready, I would appreciate it. And inform the servants that I will be in the house warden's office for three hours for the purpose of greeting them personally."

The stewards bobbed their heads, clearly appreciative of her ladyship's attention. The earlier disturbance coming from behind the library door forgotten, they bowed and started off in tandem across the Great Hall.

Then she was alone with an agony that could not be postponed much longer. She knew she possessed neither the strength nor the will to climb to the privacy of her third-floor chambers. Yet she also knew that she needed privacy as desperately as she'd ever needed it in her life. Thus she moved hurriedly along the outer corridor which skirted the Great Hall, heading toward the small cloakroom to the right of the central arch, a never-used chamber except on those occasions of large entertainments.

As she walked, the sickness continued to rise in her throat. She lifted her head and tried to draw a long breath. And just in time she reached out for the cloakroom door, jerked it violently open, slipped into its safe darkness and leaned over, vomiting.

It lasted for several moments, until there was nothing more to bring up, and still it continued in racking convulsions which left her eyes moist, her sides aching.

Shuddering, she leaned against the wall and closed her eyes. The one aspect of the incident that frightened her most was that she couldn't predict for certain what she would do if he made such a demand of her again.

Now she felt for the letter crumpled in her pocket and grasped it eagerly, as though seeing a lifeline. The young man. *Edward's son.* How she longed for a glimpse of that face.

She vowed then that before she slept that night, she would write to Morley Johnson. She still felt a strong compulsion to know the boy's true identity, though she hoped that the search would never end. Let Johnson search forever and find everything or find nothing. It mattered little. It was her firm intention to bring the boy up out of the grim odd-boy cellar, to cleanse him, to dress him as handsomely as possible, to assign him to her son as friend and companion, and to assign him to herself as well.

In the excitement of the moment, she remembered fragments of Johnson's letter, "*. . . the prostitute, Elizabeth . . . came from the Lakes . . . a distinguishing mark on his chest in the form of a scar, in shape resembling the letter B . . .*" In an instant of perception, she saw a clear image of Edward's face before her.

Astonishing, how strong she felt now. She felt surrounded by the very atmosphere of youth, so deeply familiar, and yet so legendary.

A quarter of an hour, she'd said. It had been that easily. Quickly she folded the letter from Morley Johnson and tucked it in her pocket.

Now with an excitement that she couldn't readily grasp, she hurried across the deserted Great Hall with a genuine sense of mission, smiling gently at the thought of how angry James would be tonight to see a young Edward seated at his table.

With immense relief John felt the rusted jagged metal cut through the bottom of his bare foot. For effect, he gave one sharp yell and grabbed the injured member, hopping about, doubly pleased to see his own blood oozing between his fingers.

At the end of the stables, he saw Samuel, the overseer, look up. pitchfork in hand. "What in the hell . . ." the old man shouted.

Now John feigned a collapse into the manure he'd heaped to one side. He twisted in the brown slime and groaned effectively, all the while keeping his eye on the thundering approach of the squat, square-built Samuel. As the man drew nearer, John closed his eyes as though suffering unbearable pain, although in truth he was praying silently, "Oh, God, let it work."

Since his arrival at Eden Castle, John had labored in a way that he'd not thought possible. Now his days commenced at a quarter past five, with the arrival of Samuel, the overseer, built like a block, with perpetually flaming cheeks and matching hair, when lantern in hand he'd rouse John from his pallet of straw in the odd-boy's cellar and lead him forth into the darkness of dawn.

Again he looked up, curious to see what was delaying Samuel, and saw the man still a distance away. Apparently the dictates of his kidneys took priority over his curiosity to see what fate had befallen his last odd-boy. Take your time, John thought. Give the blood a chance to flow.

In the interim, he again leaned back against the soiled straw and thought of that first morning, recalling the two minor shocks from which he had suffered. One, from the deep rumbling snores he'd heard all night coming from the cell across the way, he'd assumed that lying in darkness there was an army of odd-boys with whom he might share his plight. Hence his surprise that first morning when he'd seen a solitary figure stumbling up out of the night, a flat-faced, dull-eyed boy from Mortemouth named Maddon. Not that the boy had told him his name. Old Samuel had grunted introductions. In fact, if Maddon possessed the art of speech at all, he'd never once displayed the talent for John's benefit. Of course he could scream in an impressive manner. They all could attest to that after yesterday. But up until that tragic moment, poor Maddon had simply gone dumbly about his labors, exhibiting a passive acceptance.

Gingerly John examined his foot, the nerve endings beginning to throb most convincingly, the blood still flowing. With his free hand he reached out for a closer examination of the cooperative piece of metal; a piece of rusted banding of some sort, perhaps from an old wagon. No matter. It had accomplished the purpose.

As Samuel's piss continued to splatter into the hay, John closed his eyes and remembered the second shock of that first morning. He'd thought that the only way out from his cell would be back up the narrow twisting staircase and through Aggie's delicious kitchen court. And he'd felt certain that that surprise farewell kiss he'd given her would be good for some preferential treatment. And it would have been, if he only had been permitted to exit up the stairs and through the kitchen court.

But he wasn't. That first morning, Samuel had thrust a dark brown smelly smock and work trousers upon him, then had led the way in the opposite direction, lantern aloft, through a low narrow passageway designed for moles, not men, with poor dumb Maddon following behind, until at last they had emerged into the stableyard through an opening in the castle wall. As Samuel had dished up their morning ale, he'd informed John in clear terms that this and this alone was his access route both into and out of the castle.

"Odd-boys smell," Samuel had pronounced with a grin, and at that point John had not understood him. True understanding had come later that day. While he was still trying to keep down the vinegary ale, Samuel had thrust a brown rag filled with something lumpy into his hand and had announced "Luncheon." John had stuffed the brown rag into his smock in time to catch the heavy wheelbarrow which Samuel had pushed toward him. Similarly armed, Maddon had led the way to a small shed near the corner of the castle wall, where John was informed of his duties.

Starting here at the shed where the emptyings of all the chamber pots in the castle were kept, stretching that long line up the hill, past the stables, past the cow barns, and farther up past the sheep-shearing sheds, John's duty, all day and well into the night, was to fill the wheelbarrow with dung, human and animal, it mattered not, and empty each load on the muck mountain at a distance of about a quarter of a mile away, where fertilizers were made for the fields of oats and barley, a satanic place of smells and flies and cut off from the rest of the estate by a natural rise of land.

That first day, John had lost count of the number of times he and Maddon had made the hideous trip up the hill and down, trying to keep the unwieldy load in balance, for if it spilled, it meant picking it up without benefit of shovel, and John's had spilled several times, and by noon that day, in the hot sun with the putrid odors causing him to gag, he, along with Maddon, had partaken of lunch, and with dung-encrusted fingers he'd opened the brown rag to find two rolls encrusted with green mold which nonetheless he'd bitten into eagerly, then spit out, vomiting, as he'd found the yeasty interior crawling with maggots. With watering eyes and burning throat, he'd watched, amazed, as with infinite patience Maddon had picked his rolls free of maggots, then with a self-satisfied grin had popped them into his mouth.

Never, John had vowed sternly to himself. But on the third day, when the hunger pangs had joined the sharp pains caused by the poisonous odors, he had joined Maddon in picking his own rolls free of maggots, and with eyes closed he had shoved it all into his mouth and swallowed quickly.

But that had not been the worst of it. The worst of it came every day at midafternoon when the other workers took their tea break, and naturally, wanting diversion from their own mind-numbing and back-breaking labors, selected as their entertainment the two odd-boys, who would be ordered to climb upon the muck mountain, with bare feet and bare chests, smocks removed, and with their hands, work into the putrid slime the ingredients which were daily delivered in a small cart from Mortemouth, an equally smelly enrichment which consisted of sugar-bakers' scum, soap-boilers' ashes, hogs' hair, malt dust and horn shavings.

To the accompaniment of about seventy men laughing, John and Maddon were forced to strip down to their breeches, enter the fenced pen, dragging the cart between them like oxen, scatter the white chalk over the brown slippery muck, then, using their bare feet, work the mixture in. If they slipped and fell facedown, which they frequently did, the men cheered enthusiastically, and at the end of the "fun," the boys were placed in the back of the cart and dragged, stinking, to the large pig trough, where they were thrown into the stagnant brown water and emerged, sputtering, and in John's case, usually vomiting. He had vomited more the last eighteen days than he'd vomited in his entire life, his stomach churning constantly, his arms and face and back baked red from the sun.

How many times he had considered running away. But something had prevented him from doing this, the daily hope that word from London would arrive, that perhaps one day crossing the barnyard he'd spy old Dana or Aggie, and they'd remember him and take pity on him, or more fanciful yet, that Lady Eden would relent and lift him out of this horror. But nothing had come from any quarter, and the days had stretched on, and in a frightening way he'd accustomed himself to the odors, the slime of body waste, the humiliation, the bullying. He'd even grown accustomed to poor dumb Maddon's company, and in the last few days had grown as silent and as unresponding.

Then only yesterday, working too near the smith's fire, Maddon's smock had caught on fire. John, working at the far end of the stables, had heard his screams and had looked up in time to see the boy, his entire body engulfed in flames, dancing in a macabre jig about the anvil. The smithy had quickly thrown water on him and after a few minutes had doused the flames. And with what kindness had the group of men looked down on the poor boy, his arms blackened and still smoking, his eyes wide with pain. Carefully they had given him a large supply of ale and placed him in the back of a cart and had hauled him down to Mortemouth for his mother and the physician to attend to. And John had finished the day alone, his head churning with both revulsion and inspiration, nothing so permanently damaging as setting himself on fire, of course, but a moderate injury which would free him at least for a day or two from the inhuman burdens which had been placed upon him.

Hence, a few minutes earlier, he'd spied the rusted, razor-sharp banding, had arranged it carefully beneath a light covering of straw, had slipped off his boot, climbed up onto the manger, and taking careful aim, had jumped downward, directing his foot toward the invisible metal, and smiling in spite of the pain as he felt his foot sliced opened.

Now with old Samuel standing before him, buttoning up his cock, John again lay back against the pile of manure, waiting for the old man's kindness to waft over him, as it had descended over Maddon the previous day.

Instead, "You dumb bastard!" the man shouted down on him, still arranging his genitals inside the heavy soiled trousers. "What have you gone and done now?"

"It's my . . . foot, sir," John said in a gasp, as though the pain were increasing.

"I can see that," Samuel snapped.

"I was cleaning the manger, sir," he began, "and when I jumped down, I didn't see—"

"Where's your boot?" the man asked, his face a map of suspicion.

"I'd removed it, sir," John began. "A thorn was lodged—"

"Thorn, my ass," the man shouted down. "I ought to lodge me whip against your backside, that's what I ought to do."

For a moment John was intimidated by the old man's fearful mood, though he doubted seriously if he would really whip him. "No matter, sir," he said, releasing his foot, inspecting it for the first time, an impressive cut which laid bare the flesh on the bottom of his foot and stretched across his instep. And blood, he'd never seen such blood, his entire foot red and glistening, a small pool forming on the smelly straw.

First making certain that Samuel had seen it as well, he then reached for his abandoned boot and commenced to pull it over the injured foot, again wincing, though not for effect this time, closely monitoring the old man's re- action as he struggled to his feet and commenced limp- ing toward his abandoned shovel, a tremendous show of determination which he felt certain was bound to make a difference.

Finally it did. "What do you think you're doing?" the man yelled now.

Without looking at him, John bent over and lifted his shovel, no longer performing for effect, feeling a painful throbbing in his foot and up the side of his leg, feeling his boot beginning to grow damp and sticky with his own blood.

Still Samuel watched, permitting him to lift one shovel

full of manure, when suddenly John felt dizzy and lost his balance and fell again onto the manure, his eyes closed against the increasing discomfort.

Then Samuel was upon him, squatting down, still grumbling, but something soft and approachable in his sunbaked eyes. "Here now, lad," he scolded, tugging the boot off. "You're not Hercules, you know."

John lay quietly back, giving the man all the time he needed for his untutored examination. Then came the words for which John had staged the entire and rather extreme theatrical. "We can do without you for a day or two," he muttered. "Best get off this for a while, or it'll swell on you."

Soberly John watched as the old man shuffled off to the far end of the stable and returned with a thick brown bottle of something and a length of soiled cloth.

Apprehensively John drew back. "What is—"

"Never you mind," Samuel scolded. "Just hold yourself rigid and think on the day you was born." And with that he turned about and grasped John's leg as though he were a horse to be shod, uncorked the brown bottle with his teeth, and commenced pouring the liquid directly onto the cut.

Suddenly John came to life, one yell punctuating the silence of the barn, followed by a series of inarticulate curses as he felt his foot aflame, runners of pain now shooting up the length of his leg. His head first flattened in the manure, then lifted as new agony washed over him. Indulging in a wrestling match now with old Samuel, who continued to hold his leg between his own, he was forced to pinch his eyes shut and fall helplessly back, the burning at last beginning to recede.

"Good soldier," Samuel muttered at last, releasing the foot. Then he lifted the brown bottle and carefully replaced the cork. "Old Samuel's magic elixir." He grinned. "My own blend of lye and lime. You'll be right enough in a day or two."

Listlessly John raised halfway up, still gasping. The bleeding had stopped right enough, the cut itself gaping white and pink like a large opened toothless mouth. God, he'd not counted on the treatment being worse than the

injury. And as Samuel commenced to bind the entire foot
in the strip of muslin, John closed his eyes and still
smelled the acrid fumes.

"There!" the man pronounced at last, surveying his
handiwork with a look of pride.

At last John forced his attention down to his bound
foot. In spite of the heat, he began to shiver.

Now old Samuel grinned down on him. "You may
count the hours tonight, lad, but come morning, you'll
feel better."

John nodded and again reached for his boot. But Samuel interceded. "Wouldn't do that if I was you," he
warned. "There'll be some natural swelling. Give it room
to breathe."

"But I—"

"Off with you," the old man grumbled. "You'll be no
good to me for the rest of the day. Get to your cell and
stay off it, so you can work double tomorrow."

Apparently the man's tenderness had been depleted.
Now he looked down on John as though still in a mood
to whip him. "Be off with you," he shouted. "The sight of
you makes me sick."

Before he changed his mind, John scrambled to his
feet, grabbing his boot in the process, and started limping
toward the door. Still the man shouted after him, "Stupid,
that's what you are, you hear? That's why you'll never be
anything more than an odd-boy. Taking off your boot,"
he cried, scoffing, " 'cause of a thorn. Well, you'd best
learn to live with thorns, lad, 'cause that's all life has
in store for you."

As John beat a painful retreat, the harsh voice continued to fall like rocks upon his head. "And keep to
your cellar, you hear? Smelling like you do, decent folk
don't want you near them."

How could he not hear? As he reached the barn door,
he saw that others had heard as well, a grinning congregation of workers. Still he cut a torturous path across
the yard, leaving the jeering men behind, taking small
consolation in the realization that someone else would
have to climb the muck heap today and fight the flies

and feel the brown slime growing encrusted on arms and legs.

Then the pain in his foot became unbearable and he pushed weakly against the low door and slipped into the cool darkness of the underground tunnel.

He closed the door behind him and grasped the wall, blinded by the quick transition from sun to blackness. For a moment, alone, the facade cracked, and leaning over, he moaned and pressed his forehead against the mossy wall.

It didn't last long, the self-pity, the tears. He'd not cried like that since he was a child. Not that it had accomplished anything. But in that black passageway, certain things were clearer to him now than they had ever been before.

They *wanted* him to run away, wanted to rid themselves of his awkward presence. With kinship possible, they couldn't very well simply turn him out. So their plan was to drive him away in another manner.

He held still in the dark passage. How stupidly he'd almost played into their hands. For a moment, overcome with his new perceptions, he was tempted to go back to old Samuel and report to work as fit as ever.

But the persistent throbbing in his foot convinced him that perhaps it would be to his advantage to take the time which had been given to him. Using the narrow walls for support, he made his way slowly back to his cell, found his pallet of straw in the dark and fell onto it, too weary even to strip off the smelly heavy smock.

He lay for a moment on his back, and stared unseeing up into the dark. With his face still wet from recent tears, he rolled onto his side, homesick for Elizabeth, for his clean whitewashed room at the top of the stairs in the small house in Bermondsey, for just a small portion of kindness and grace, for his father . . .

Finally all memories slipped away. Then he would sleep for a while, and come dawn, he would rise willingly to cart the dung, to climb the muck heap, to spit the maggots out of his rolls, to perform any duty that was required of him, confident in his determination to survive.

Impatiently Harriet glanced about at the narrow house warden's office, the ledger books scattered on the desk before her, the line of servants still stretching out of the door. She craned her neck to one side in an attempt to see old Dana. Over a half hour ago she'd sent him to fetch the boy. Still no sign of his return.

Now she laced her mask firmly into place and gave the complainer of the moment a warm smile.

It was Esther, a fleshy serving maid who predictably was objecting to having to pay twopence when she exceeded her daily allotment of one quart of beer. "It ain't fair, my lady," the broad-faced girl whined, "comin' out of our wages . . ."

Gently Harriet disagreed. "It's most fair, Esther." She smiled. "And if you think about it, I'm sure you'll agree. A quart of beer should be more than enough per day. Anything beyond that is intemperance. And we all must pay for our intemperance. As for your wages, they are far higher than any you would receive this side of London."

As she launched forth into a mild sermon, she again twisted her head to one side, trying to see into the gloom of the corridor beyond. Where *was* Dana? How long did it take to fetch one boy from the stables?

". . . so I would advise, Esther, that you learn that all-important lesson of moderation. It would be better for your health as well as your purse."

Docilely the large woman bobbed her head and smiled gratefully. Before the next servant stepped forward, Harriet hastily restacked the various ledgers and handed them to Mrs. Swan. "All in order"—she smiled up at the woman—"as I knew they would be."

Mrs. Swan bowed and took the ledgers from her, her lined face mirroring the respect of those around her. "It's a joy to serve you, my lady," she murmured.

Harriet ignored the compliment and asked further, "Is Mr. Rexroat available?" She longed for a confrontation with the stern old man, who, on James's instructions, had banished the boy to the odd-boy cellar.

For a moment Mrs. Swan looked vaguely about, her prim lace-and-lavender cap sitting rigidly atop her gray hair. "I believe, my lady, that he is in attendance upstairs. I can summon him if you wish."

"No, don't bother," Harriet said hastily. Attendance upstairs. That would be James. Now she didn't want the additional delay. She'd see the old butler later and warn him for the future that he was to take all final orders from her, not Lord Eden. She'd thought she'd made it clear to him before, but apparently not.

Thus resolved, she was on the verge of summoning the next servant when suddenly, at the far edge of the line, she spied Dana, his face red with exertion.

Quickly she stood, trying to see beyond him, anxious to catch a glimpse of the boy. But as well as she could see, the old footman was alone.

"Come," she called, waving him forward, motioning for the line of servants to move back.

Slowly the old man pushed forward until he stood directly before her, his black jacket spotted with dust, the odor that of the stables.

"Well?" she demanded, a bit more stridently than she might have wished.

For a moment Dana seemed loath to speak. "I was told, my lady," he began, "that the lad was . . . injured."

His voice sounded far away. Harriet leaned forward. "I . . . beg your pardon?" she inquired.

"Injured, my lady," Dana repeated. "Don't know how or to what extent. Didn't stop to find out. I thought it best if I report back—"

Then she was moving, skirting the desk, ignoring the line of waiting servants, knowing full well that she'd let the mask slip, but unable to help herself. "Where is he?" she demanded.

Dana shrugged. "I imagine he's in his cell," he said. "You wait here and let me fetch him for you. I'm sure Mrs. Swan will—"

But Harriet was not in a waiting mood. *Injured!* "Take me to him," she commanded.

Without a word, he led the way the length of the passage and turned at last into the narrow stairwell which led to the buttery. As they crossed through the first cellar and again started down, she felt a discernible change in the air. It occurred to her that she'd never been here before. In those early days of her residency at Eden Castle, she'd explored only as far as the first cellar. This was totally new and disquieting territory.

She looked down now and saw that Dana had reached bottom and was standing in a massive stone chamber of some sort, the lamplight catching on a mountainous pile of rubble near the far wall, clearly an ancient cave-in.

Holding the lamp aloft, he made his way down a line of doors, stopping at last before one. "This is his," he announced, and stepped back as though certain she would command him to do so.

But she shook her head. "You go. He may be . . ." She had thought to stay sleeping. But as a wave of putrid odor filled her nostrils, she at last found her courage and moved forward into the dark cell.

With the lamplight only a step behind her, she saw a form crumpled on straw. More truly it resembled a lump of discarded garments carelessly heaped, though now in the faint illumination she saw the angle of an arm, the side of a cheek, eyes closed, the mussed fair hair heavily coated with something, his entire body as motionless as though . . .

"Is he . . . ?"

"Sleeping," came Dana's confident reply. Quickly the old man lowered the lamp and ran it the length of the boy's sprawled body, holding it low over one bandaged foot.

Slowly she knelt, her hand gently outreaching to the reproduction of that face she had loved. Carefully she brushed back the long strands of matted hair. "Is it . . . ?"

"Appears to be just a cut, my lady. He'll survive."

Oh, yes, she thought firmly, her hand stroking his brow now, her eyes feeding on his beauty, which shone through in spite of the grime. How stupid she had been on that evening several weeks ago when first she'd buried Edward, then had exiled his son, thus denying herself the only source of light she'd ever known.

Now she was keenly aware of Dana closely watching her. "No lasting damage, my lady," the man repeated. "He's a strong one, that one is, like his father."

Hearing it thus confirmed moved her deeply, as though all she'd ever needed was the confirmation from an old footman. Eager now to end the encounter before she revealed too much, she bent over, and with a hand that trembled she tried to rouse him.

"John?" she murmured, speaking his name hesitantly, for in truth another had almost slipped out.

"John? Can you hear me?"

He had been dreaming of a woman, not Elizabeth, some soft female presence whom he could not identify. Thus he was not surprised when, for an instant upon awakening, his dreams matched reality.

Slowly his eyes opened. Lying on his side, he could not at first find support for an upward movement. But within the moment he found the strength to scramble backward, certain that the voice had come to do him harm.

But apparently, seeing his apprehension, she leaned closer. "No, John, please," she whispered urgently. "You're quite safe, I promise."

His brain still sleep-fogged, he rubbed his eyes. And since for the last eighteen days he had been forced to account for every movement, accountability now seemed the order of the day. "I was sent here," he murmured, "by Samuel. With his permission. Ask him if you don't—"

Then the kneeling woman reached out for his hand. "You're finished with Samuel, John, I promise. He'll no longer dictate to you on any matter."

Still blinking, he looked first at the white, well-tended hand covering his own filthy one. Then slowly he looked up into her face. She seemed sincere, but her initial kindness on that first night had seemed sincere as well. "I don't . . . understand," he confessed.

Again she smiled. "A terrible mistake was made. You don't belong here. And I've come to take you upstairs."

Then it occurred to him. The papers from London had arrived, proof of who he was and his legitimacy in this household. "You've heard, then," he said, beginning to relax for the first time since she'd awakened him.

"Heard what?" she asked.

"From London, from Elizabeth."

But even as he spoke, she commenced shaking her head. "No," she murmured. "No word. Not yet."

"Then I don't understand," he said.

With new urgency she grasped both his hands and moved yet closer. "It doesn't matter, John," she soothed. "Once I thought it did, and there are others to whom it's a matter of great importance. But not to me." Her face shone with a most dazzling smile. "It's enough that you are here, and that the tragic blunder which sent you to this place will now be put right."

You sent me here, he thought grimly.

Still she talked on. "You are Edward's son," she pronounced quietly. "Of that I have no doubt. I wish for all our sakes, but most particularly yours, that we could identify your mother. And perhaps one day we can. But in the meantime, it is my wish that you take your rightful place upstairs with the family. Please, if you can, find it in your heart to forgive—all of us."

"No need," John said, now looking up for the first time at the dim figure holding the lamp. "Who . . . ?"

"It's me, sir. Dana."

John smiled, remembering his old friend. As for the lady, John watched her for a few moments, then decided to put her new largesse to the test. "Well, my lady, what now?" he demanded softly.

Then she stirred herself, lifted a hand to Dana for assistance, and rising, looked back down on John. "Can you walk?"

He nodded. "I walked in here."

"Then come"—she smiled—"and we'll walk out together."

"Our destination?"

"Where else?" She smiled. "Your father's chambers, though we must do something to those Spartan rooms." She seemed almost gay now. "Something tells me," she added playfully, "that you do not share your father's devotion to the plain life."

He returned her smile, impressed by her powers of perception, and dragged himself to his feet. "No, I appreciate comfort, particularly after these two weeks."

"And you shall have it," she promised. "As soon as you

are able, we shall scout the castle together. There are lovely furnishings in the unoccupied apartments. You shall select what you wish."

A splendid suggestion, he thought, and was in the process of saying so when in his eagerness he put his full weight on his injured foot, and the pain took him by surprise.

Dana stepped quickly forward and offered his arm. And she was there, too, reaching for the lamp so that the old man might give John his full support. "You need a physician," she said sternly, staring down at the blood-stained bandage.

"No," John protested, leaning heavily on Dana, wishing now that he'd not indulged in the theatrical of self-mutilation. Then, seeing the waves of sympathy wash across her face, he changed his mind and decided that a wounded animal was always a pitiable sight.

As she started toward the low door, John remembered his satchel filled with meager items, perhaps unimportant compared to the promises of riches to come, nonetheless his, and at the moment all he possessed. "Wait," he called out.

When she saw the cause for his delay, she returned to the straw pallet and began to fill the satchel, her hands lingering on the Book of Common Prayer as well as the catalog of the Great Exhibition.

"Were you . . . ?" she began. "Were you with your father when he . . . died?"

"I was," he replied, puzzled.

Still she held the Great Exhibition catalog, staring down on it. "Would it be asking too much," she said, still not looking at him, "when you're feeling better, of course, for you to tell me about him, your life in London, his . . . death?"

A large order, yet he'd be only too happy to oblige. "I'll be willing to tell you whatever I can, my lady," he promised.

Abruptly she looked up at him. "I wish you wouldn't call me that," she said.

"Call you . . . what?" he asked, bewildered.

"My lady . . . "

He cast a quick glance at Dana and saw what appeared to be embarrassment on that normally neutral face. "Then what am I to call you?" he asked.

Slowly she rose, bringing the satchel with her, then stooping again to retrieve the lamp. "My name is simple," she said to the floor.

Although he knew, still he asked, "And what is your name?"

"Harriet," she said, now looking at him, the glow of the lamp between them.

"Then . . . Harriet." He smiled, feeling self-conscious, and reached for the satchel in her hand.

Apparently the simple designation brought her pleasure, for she lifted the lamp higher and started toward the door.

Again John exchanged a quick look with Dana, the old man's eyes moving heavenward.

"It won't do," she said patly, watching their struggling approach. Then she issued a command. "Let him rest on the step, Dana, and run ahead and fetch two of the strongest stewards."

Immediately John tried to protest. "No, it isn't necessary—"

"It *is* necessary," she countered.

Finally John permitted Dana to ease him down on a low step. With his head down, he listened to the old man take the stairs two at a time, and at last far above him he heard the upper cellar door open, then close, then silence.

Still he sat with his head down, feeling foolish. How his father had been able to talk—to everyone. And at last, summoning a degree of courage, he glanced quickly up to see her standing a distance away, holding the lamp close to the piled stones near the far wall.

"I'm surprised that it has never been excavated," he said, referring to the cave-in, recalling his father's account of the tragic day when *his* father had abandoned his smuggling activities after the cave-in which had claimed the life of his beloved manservant.

Now she looked slowly back at him. "Excavated?" she repeated, clearly at a loss to understand.

He found it difficult to believe that he knew more about

Eden than she did. He was on the verge of explaining further when suddenly she moved away from the fallen stones.

"Your father told you a great deal about Eden?" she questioned.

"Everything."

She drew closer now, as though the better to see, yet conversely she lowered the lamp and placed it on the stone floor, casting both of them into shadows. "Did he . . . miss his home?" she asked timidly.

Again he nodded. "I think so. In his own way."

"Why didn't he return, then?"

Gently John hedged. "His work was in London, and his friends. He loved the city, though I could never understand why."

"You didn't?"

He shook his head, pleased that they were at least exchanging words. "No," he said, then immediately altered his statement. "Oh, some of it was pleasant enough. It was nice before we . . ." He paused, not absolutely certain how he should describe that grim July morning when his father had given his fortune away. ". . . when we were living on Oxford Street," he concluded. "It was comfortable."

"Did he teach in his school?" she asked.

"No," John replied. "He was kept busy simply raising funds, seeing to repairs . . ."

"And Daniel Spade helped him?"

He looked up, surprised that she knew that familiar name. "Helped?" He smiled. "It was Daniel's school." Stirred to new interest, he leaned forward. "Did you know Daniel Spade?"

Quickly she shook her head. "I only heard your father speak of him, with love and devotion."

"Did you know my father well?" he asked, and was in no way prepared for her reaction, a slow retreat until at last she took refuge near the pile of fallen stone, her face lost in shadows.

He tried to peer through the darkness in an attempt to glean a hint concerning her new mood. And unable to see, he rose at last, concerned, and limping, gained her side, amazed to find her seated on one of the near boulders, her face buried in her hands.

He held still, awed by such a ready display of grief. "My lady," he commenced, then corrected himself. "Harriet, are you . . . ill?"

Still there was no response, and he found something strangely moving in her bowed despair. "Please," he whispered, reaching out and lightly touching her shoulder. "Let me . . ."

Then her face lifted, and at that close proximity he saw tears. He wasn't certain who reached out first, but before he could say how it had happened, her arms were about his waist, drawing him close.

At first he felt embarrassment at the sudden and unexpected intimacy, and could only think on himself, how pleasurable it was to feel her arms tightening about him, yet how unappealing he must be in his wretched odd-boy garments, and most mysterious of all, how much he wanted to be clean and brushed for her.

At last, sadly, he felt her arms go limp about his waist, and as she looked up, he saw again how beautiful she was.

As he was cataloging the dimensions of her features, he heard steps on the stairs. She apparently heard them as well and moved quickly away. With what incredible speed they both took up their initial positions, he slumped on the steps, his injured foot extended, while she retrieved the lamp, wiped the telltale moisture from her cheeks and stood as though at attention.

He watched her for as long as he dared, hearing the footsteps growing louder. How much of her life must have been spent in secret warfare, the private face at odds with the public one.

There his thoughts were forced to stop, as behind him he sensed the arrival of three, Dana in the company of two strapping stewards.

"Make an armchair," she commanded. "And take Mr. Eden to his father's chambers on the third floor. Follow me."

In a rush of movement he saw the two stewards bend low and grasp each other's forearms, forming a taut, secure square. Then Dana was there, assisting him upon the human seat, helping him to find his balance on it.

Take Mr. Eden to his father's chambers.

As the feverish activity suddenly ceased, he looked down to find her staring directly at him. "Not a very fitting throne"—she smiled—"but I think we'll make a good enough entrance."

He smiled back at her. "Lead the way."

As they reached the top of the stairs and turned into the broad corridor which connected the various rooms of the kitchen court, they commenced to draw attention. As servants' heads continued to twist out of the narrow doorways, John looked ahead and heard Harriet issuing a spate of orders.

"Fetch hot water," she ordered, "tubs of it," she added, "and two pitchers of lavender water, and lye soap and clean linens. And send Peggy to me and prepare the bed in Mr. Eden's chamber. And fetch the physician from Mortemouth," she added, not altering her pace in the least though at each command a servant broke ranks and fled, apparently to do her bidding.

The sound of scurrying footsteps filled his ear. What fun, he thought, to speak so lightly and scatter so many!

Again she looked back at him, and the light in her eyes might have mirrored his own, as though both were children who knew they were behaving outrageously, yet had not the least compunction to alter their behavior.

"Are you faring well?" she called up to him.

"Never better." He smiled, though in truth his foot was throbbing, his buttocks were aching from the hard shifting seat, and the smell of manure was still accompanying him in an invisible cloud.

Yet with undisguised delight he took in those gaping servants' eyes, the same ones who had only a few weeks earlier borne silent witness to his banishment.

Then, just as he felt his festive mood increasing, he looked ahead to the end of the corridor and spied a familiar mountain in female form, the grand harridan herself, God's great example of an ugly woman.

"Ah, it's you, lad," cawed the screech-owl voice.

He looked down into the flat face of old Agony

Fletcher. For the first time the procession came to a halt, as though in the presence of a new power. He saw Harriet step toward Aggie, even that proud lady approaching the massive cook with a degree of respect.

Whatever words were exchanged, John couldn't hear. As the secret conversation stretched on, John began to take pity on the two stewards who laboriously had provided him with support.

Struggling down from the precarious elevation, he hopped to one side and was in the process of thanking them when suddenly Aggie's voice descended upon him. "You! There!"

Then he saw her bearing down on him, and to the amusement of all, though to his own humiliation, he felt her lift him into her arms as though he were an object without weight or substance, and without the least sign of stress commence to carry him down the corridor.

Adding to his humiliation was his brief glimpse of Harriet's maternal expression as he was borne unceremoniously past.

Curious, the degree of resentment the expression provoked in him. He'd liked it much better down in the cellar when she'd clung to him with a need that clearly was not maternal.

As he'd been unconscious the last time he'd been carried along this route, now he sat up as much as Aggie's iron grip would permit, and looked about with intense interest at the passing scene, the stone walls less cold now, softened with immense hanging tapestries, the wall fixtures no longer the crude torches which lined the servants' hall, but gleaming urns of polished brass which bathed the entire passageway in soft golden light.

Then, as though the castle itself were beckoning with its splendor, they left the grand passageway and entered the Great Hall. He saw it clearly now, all aspects of the grandeur, starting at the high complex saddle-topped ceiling, interlaced with ornate plasterwork, down to the vast paintings of Roman scenes and on down to the elegant wood carvings.

Long before he was ready, they had passed through the Great Hall and were now moving up the Grand Stair-

case. As they moved through the broad upper gallery, he
saw the scarlet carpet drop away and noticed the muted
shades of Persia, delicate mauves and blues, and the walls
were lined with awesome portraits, every Eden since the
beginning of time, or so he guessed. Also along this gallery he saw a number of heavy carved doors, all mysteriously closed.

His curiosity vaulting, he was on the verge of address-
ing a question to the silent lady who walked behind. But
at that moment a small army of black-clad serving maids
passed them by, their arms laden with pitchers and linens,
their steps indicating urgency. So for now he tabled all
questions, confident that there would be time later, and
gave all his attention over to his triumphant return.

As they gained the top of the stairs and started down
the third-floor corridor, John looked forward to his release. It did not serve a man's ego to be carried about,
infant fashion, in the arms of a woman.

But women seemed to be the plague of the day, as,
approaching his father's chambers, he saw the same army
of maids who had passed them in the corridor, joined now
by as many stewards, who apparently had climbed the
castle via a different route, easily thirty servants in all,
some at work spreading fresh linen on the bed, others
filling an enormous tub which sat in the center of the
room with pitcher after pitcher of steaming water, the
unmistakable fragrance of lavender greeting his nostrils,
and still others hanging drapes at the windows and others
lighting lamps.

Then at last Aggie lowered him to the floor near the
tub and commanded him to "Strip!"

All at once, every head, male and female, ceased their
labors and lifted in his direction.

"Wait a minute," he tried to protest.

"Ain't got no minutes to wait," Aggie exploded.

Apparently Harriet saw his mortification and moved
to ease it. "A moment, Aggie"—she smiled—"for decency's
sake."

Then gradually the room began to clear, the stewards
in groups of twos and threes casting a backward look over
the chamber before they bowed to Lady Eden.

Finally the room was empty with the exception of Aggie, Dana, Harriet, and of course himself, who once again was the object of Aggie's persistent attention.

"Now!" She grinned, and as he looked up he saw her heading toward him, her hands outstretched.

"I'm quite capable, Aggie, of—"

"You're capable of nothing," she snorted, "like all men. Come, now . . ." And again all protest was useless as she bullied him into a position near the tub and was just reaching down to lift the grimy smock when suddenly she stopped.

She glanced over her shoulder. "My lady"—she grinned—"are you sure you have an appetite for this?"

John looked in Harriet's direction and saw a blush creep up the side of her face. "With your permission, John," she began quietly, "may I stay for a moment?"

Even old Aggie seemed shocked. "He may act like a lad, my lady," she said, "but I assure you, he's more man than boy."

The disquiet on Harriet's face seemed to increase. "I want to see his chest," she whispered. "Then I shall leave him to you."

For a moment Aggie continued to stand between them. Then quickly she grabbed the hem of his smock and pulled it over his head.

Harriet was moving toward him, her eyes focused, not on his face, but on the area of his chest. Everything in the chamber seemed to wait on her careful scrutiny, as at last he saw one hand shyly lift.

Then contact. He felt her fingers on his chest, lightly tracing something. He tried to explain. "An old cut, that's all," he said.

When still she seemed disinclined to speak, he added, "It's getting smaller. Elizabeth says it will be almost invisible in a—"

"How?" The word was scarcely more than a whisper, and still her eyes had not lifted to him.

"I'm not certain," he said.

"You don't remember it?"

"My father said it was from a fall."

"It was deep once."

Again he nodded and looked down. Perhaps there was something about the ancient scar tissue that he'd failed to notice.

When she continued to study it, the tips of her fingers examining all aspects of it, he again felt embarrassment and looked beyond her to Aggie's broad face that seemed to wear an expression as bewildered as his own.

"Lads take tumbles, my lady," she said gruffly. "He'll have a matching one on his foot soon enough."

Then apparently the inspection was over. She stepped back, her eyes at last meeting his. "We were told that the infant that Edward claimed as his son bore a scar on his chest." She smiled self-consciously, as though belatedly aware of the intimacy. "I'm . . . sorry," she whispered. "I had to be as certain as possible."

"Are you convinced?" he asked.

"For now."

What did that mean? But before he had a chance to ask, she was moving toward the door. "We'll find your mother, John, I promise," she said. At the door she stopped and turned back. "And if not the woman herself, at least her identity." Again she smiled, the light from a near lamp catching on her face. "For now," she concluded, "welcome home."

He watched her leave with a strange longing. "Will you be back?" he called after her.

She was halfway out of the door before she answered. "As soon as you're ready. We'll have dinner here, together."

Then she was gone, and he was alone with Aggie staring at him, and Dana. There was a moment's pause during which time he tried to digest the vacuum caused by her absence.

Then Aggie was upon him, muttering something about the "foolishness of it all," and he gave himself over completely to the strength of her hands, and saw Dana in attendance, supporting him as she stripped off his soiled trousers and plunged him into the hot steaming water, injured foot and all.

For a moment everything went around in circles, the stinging so severe that tears came to his eyes. But he kept still because to cry out would be like a boy. And he wanted nothing more to do with boyhood.

In spite of the crush of duties which were pressing upon her, Harriet sat at her dressing table, with Peggy in hovering attendance, and looked down at her wrists as though she saw fetters. They were forged from nothing but her new and mysterious willingness to let everyone in the castle tend to themselves.

Now, as Peggy expertly brushed and looped her hair into a French knot, Harriet marveled again at her new attitude. Never before had she luxuriated in the pleasing vapors of a perfumed bath before dinner. And why had she selected this primrose-pink silk gown cut low in the bodice and delicately trimmed with Brussels lace? No reason except that it made her look and feel like a young girl.

"Which jewels, my lady?" Peggy asked, lifting the jewel case for her selection.

Harriet hesitated. Then, "None," she said and looked up, shocked by her own response. The blush was there in her reflected image for both to see.

Diplomatically Peggy closed the jewel case and murmured in tactful agreement, "The gown is sufficient. It needs nothing."

As Peggy tidied up the articles of toilet, Harriet moved away from the dressing table to the sideboard and the decanter of brandy. No, she must wait. Behind her she heard Peggy still at work. "Why don't you leave that until later?"

"Very well, my lady." Obedient to a fault, Peggy moved instantly to the door.

"One small request," Harriet called after her. "Would you please take a message to Lord Eden," she began, keeping her face turned away. "Tell him that I shall not be dining with him tonight."

And at last, blessedly, Peggy was gone. Harriet held her position by the sideboard. Abruptly she leaned softly against the wall. What had come over her? Look how her hands trembled, and there, her reflection in the glass, a woman with flushed cheeks. She was behaving as though she were sixteen. No, worse! Even at sixteen she'd not given in to these foolish sensations.

Now she glanced nervously about and indulged in the comfort of one small brandy. Feeling steadier at the first sip, she took the glass to a near chair and sat primly on the edge. She sipped again, and at last settled back into the arms of the chair, wondering bleakly when all of her ignored duties would catch up with her.

Well, no need to think on it. They would come soon enough. For now she was blessedly alone, groomed, for her evening appointment with . . .

Then he was before her, in her imagination, those earnest blue eyes following the movement of her fingers on his chest.

No! Angrily she sipped again in an attempt to dispel his image. Had she lost all sense? He was a mere boy.

Again she tipped the snifter and drained it and felt a lassitude extending to all parts of her body. How pleasant it was to sit and do nothing but wait for the summons to reenter his chamber.

He was a boy.

Then she would have to take certain steps. She would have to see to it that she was never alone with him. At all times she must contrive for others to be in the chamber with them, or at table, or walking the headlands, or riding the moors.

She held still, the storm subsiding. She had survived mightier storms and would survive this one. It had simply been the intersecting of certain circumstances, that was all, the boy's remarkable resemblance to Edward, the remembrance of that day.

Suddenly there was a knock at the door. "Wait," she called out, not wanting anyone to see her in this state.

Coming from the other side, she heard the voice of a steward. "Just come to inform you, my lady, that Aggie is ready to serve dinner in Mr. Eden's chambers. He's waiting."

She lifted her head and issued a terse command. "Fetch my children!"

She listened to his footsteps. The children would keep her safe. How pleased Richard would be. And male companionship would be good for Mary as well, take her away from Clara's indulgent affection.

Again the heavy storm was subsiding. How foolish she had been. Carefully she stood and walked the short distance to her wardrobe, where she reached inside and found the comfort of a black, high-necked, safe gown, bereft of hope.

She changed quickly, her eyes not once lifting to the glass, her fingers moving down one row of buttons and up another. Only when she tried to manipulate the buttons high up on her throat did she glance at her reflection. What an image that was! Her face appeared older, thinner, the hollows at her temples deeper.

Thus changed, she walked back to her chair and tested herself. It was Edward waiting for her, not in dream or fantasy, but truly Edward, younger, at the height of his powers, waiting to receive her, to run together through the high summer sun to the secret glen where, undetected, they would shed their clothes and catalog their respective beauty.

She held still in the chair. Nothing. All strength and dexterity was firmly in place. Now her foot would make no false step.

Relieved to be herself again, she went to the door, where she heard her children's chattering approach.

Slightly bewildered, she glanced down at the small half-moons of blood on the palm of her left hand where her fingernails had cut into the flesh, the nails themselves bent back to the quick.

Before now, John had thought that Elizabeth was the only female in the world who took cruel delight in a scrub brush and a cake of lye soap. But Elizabeth's touch had been a caress compared to Aggie's brutal scraping. And not a shred of modesty had the old woman exhibited, moving indomitably over all parts of his body, her only utterance a grunt now and then aimed at Dana to, "Shift him," and "Turn him to."

Now seated gingerly on the edge of the bed in a fine white nightshirt with lace trim, John gazed down on the physician, a plain middle-aged man with sober countenance who seemed more impressed by his surroundings than the state of the foot suspended between his hands. "A nagging but superficial wound," he'd pronounced, had applied a camphor plaster and was now in the process of wrapping it in soft clean muslin.

Then Aggie was there again, drawing the coverlet up about him, adjusting his pillows so that he might sit erect. Briefly, with Aggie still hovering over him, he experienced his first and profound sense of homecoming. No more temporary residence in the Ragged School of the moment, no more dismal cell at the top of the stairs of the house in Bermondsey. He had waited a long time for this particular dream, but now it had come true. He was in residence at Eden, a true Eden himself, welcomed at least by one into the bosom of the family.

Aggie stood back, still dropping pronouncements upon his head. "You need food now," she said. "Aggie's best, and you shall have it."

Before he could find out what "Aggie's best" was, he saw her lumber to the door and command a steward, "Go inform her ladyship that the lad is cleansed. Then follow behind to the kitchen. I'll have need of several hands."

As the steward left the room, John sat up, eager to see "her ladyship" again, but wishing that he did not have to greet her from this helpless, childlike position in bed.

Then, just as the last maid was making the final adjustments on an elegant bouquet of summer flowers, he heard a soft knock at the door.

It was Lady Eden, though he was in no way prepared for what first greeted his eyes, two children in nightshirts with loosely fitted gray dressing robes hanging tentlike about their small frames.

They stopped in the doorway, gaping and shy. He recognized Richard, the boy who had greeted him first on that grim night of his arrival at Eden. And the little girl standing beside him, her blond head bowed with the weight of timidity, was most probably his sister.

No, he hadn't expected this, and sat up a bit straighter and tried to catch a glimpse of the woman who still stood safely in shadows just beyond the door. Why the children?

He'd looked forward to a private meeting, alone with that gentle presence who had rescued him from the odd-boy cellar. And even before she stepped forward into the room, he discerned a change, something disagreeably hard in the manner in which she was using her children as though they were shields.

"My children, John," she began, sounding older. "They expressed a great desire to meet their cousin."

He liked that. Cousin. Kinship.

"You've met Richard, I believe," she went on, still standing by the door.

John nodded and dragged his attention away from her peculiar performance to the slight dark boy who was staring mercilessly at him. "Of course, I remember Richard. Good evening." He smiled at the boy, who seemed incapable of response. Peculiar. He remembered him that first night as being quite talkative.

"And that is Mary," she said, still bound to her position at the door.

At the mention of her name, the plump little girl seemed to press closer to her brother, her blond curly head down, one tiny thumb inserted into her mouth.

"Mary," John repeated, and wondered where the vitality in the room had gone. Now every moment seemed a tableau, with no one moving or speaking save for the barest essentials.

Then he saw Richard approaching the bed, his eyes fastened in clear fascination on the bandaged foot.

"How did you do it?" the boy asked.

"A piece of metal," John replied, "concealed in straw. It will work every time."

Richard looked up, apparently hearing the truth in the confession. "You did it . . . on purpose?"

"Of course." John smiled. "Wouldn't you, if you wanted to get out of a distasteful task?"

He heard Harriet laugh softly. "Good heavens, don't give him any ideas, John."

Then Richard was there again, stepping closer. "Didn't it hurt?" he asked.

"A little."

"Did you cry?"

"No, it didn't hurt that much."

"Herr Snyder said that a dog bit him once and it hurt so much that he cried."

"Herr Snyder?" John inquired, pleased that Richard seemed to be warming to him again. "And who is Herr Snyder," he asked, "and where did this vicious dog bite him?"

"He's my tutor and he bit him on the arm. He still bears the scar." Richard looked admiringly at the foot. "I don't have a scar anyplace," he mourned softly.

"You will." John laughed. "When I get out of this bed, come with me and I'll find you a scar."

He had spoken in jest, but the boy apparently took him seriously. "Will you really?" he asked.

"Of course I will. And we're due a marble game as well. I still have the two cat's eyes you gave me. Let me warn you, though. I'm an awesome opponent."

"I'll beat you." Richard grinned, pulling up on the bed until he was seated directly beside John, a clear ally.

John looked back at the two near the table. Harriet was smiling, one hand cupped about her daughter's head. John now turned his attention to the little girl.

"Mary?" he called from the bed. "There's room enough here for all. Why don't you join us?"

But no. The direct invitation seemed to make the little girl turn in on herself. Quickly she buried her face in the folds of her mother's black gown.

"She doesn't like people," Richard pronounced with brotherly authority.

"Why?" John asked, alternately monitoring all three, still possessed by the feeling that something was being tested.

Richard shrugged. "I've told her that Herr Snyder will make her stand up and recite her lessons."

"Do you stand up to recite?" John asked, finding comfort in the boy, who seemed the only one eager and willing to talk.

"Oh, yes," Richard boasted. "Herr Snyder says I'm quick. Do you do lessons?"

John hesitated. "I did once."

"Were you quick?"

John smiled. "Quick enough, I suppose." Out of the corner of his eye he saw Lady Eden approaching the foot of the bed. Still John focused all his attention on his bedmate. "What's your favorite subject?" he asked.

The boy thought a moment. "History"—he smiled—"and science. Do you know about Copernicus?"

Not expecting to be put on the spot in such a manner, John floundered.

Then suddenly Richard was possessed by an idea. "Mother?" he called out, scrambling to the foot of the bed. "May John attend my lessons? Herr Snyder would be pleased to have him, I know, and it would be so much fun, almost like a real schoolroom."

John sat up, ready to protest. While he'd enjoyed his schoolwork, he'd had enough of it to last a lifetime.

Unfortunately he saw that the idea held appeal for Lady Eden as well. "A good idea, Richard," she said. "Although I'm certain that Herr Snyder will want to test John. He may be well in advance of you. But yes," she concluded, looking directly at John. "I think your education should be continued. I'm certain your father would have wished it."

At that moment a knock sounded at the door and he saw Lady Eden turn as though relieved to be out from under the burden of this new silence. She called out, "Come—"

Upon the instant, a parade of stewards entered bearing silver trays with domed tops and an accompanying odor that was irresistible. A few minutes later Harriet stood beside the bed, a heaping platter in her hands.

It was a glorious sight, that still-smoking beefsteak, surely the largest he'd ever seen, wreathed with golden potatoes and tiny onions in a cream sauce, and at either end of the platter, two small bundles of asparagus, all the odors blending, the platter warm in his lap. He shook his head and remembered the maggot rolls. Of the two worlds at Eden, one was vastly superior. In all ways.

"Eat," she invited, handing him cutlery.

He looked up from the platter. "Alone? I had thought that we might—"

"I'm afraid I have no appetite," she said.

As he watched her move back to the table and pour a glass of wine, he was simultaneously aware of Mary creeping closer, apparently drawn to the food more than anything else. In a quiet gesture, John waved her closer and with a fork speared an onion, and using it as bait, drew the little girl up onto the bed, where she settled opposite her brother.

"Open wide," John whispered. Immediately she obeyed, and he guided the onion inside the mouth, whereupon the rosy lips clamped shut and commenced chewing contentedly.

Richard protested, "Mother, she's eating his dinner."

"It's all right," John soothed. "There's more than enough."

He looked up to see Lady Eden standing again at the foot of the bed, a scolding expression on her face.

"Please let her stay," John said. "I grew up with children. I've missed them."

He saw her expression turn to one of acquiescence. As he cut into the beefsteak, he invited Richard, "Help yourself."

But the boy declined, apparently not wanting to imitate his sister's childish behavior. Then for a few minutes the various faces around him faded in importance as he channeled his concentration down onto the platter.

The first awareness he had of his own piggishness was Richard's soft giggle. "Clara would box your ears for not chewing twenty-five times."

"And who is Clara?" John asked, not looking up, the words muffled through potatoes and beefsteak.

"She's the nursemaid," Richard replied.

"Then I'm glad she's not here," John mumbled.

In a miraculously short time the platter was cleaned and Harriet was offering to fill it again. Groaning, he declined and leaned back against the pillows, returning Mary's intense stare. The child was quite beautiful, overplump, resembling a cherub in a Renaissance painting.

Suddenly feeling indulged and indulgent, he moved the platter to one side, lifted the white napkin and draped it, clownlike, over his head. Predictably the soberness on her face broke and she giggled prettily.

"He's a ghost, Mary," Richard said, his voice filled with mock terror.

"I'm not either," John retorted, entering effortlessly into the spirit of play. How often his father had played with him and the other children in the Ragged School as well.

"Then what are you?" Richard demanded.

"I'm a . . ." He hesitated. ". . . a scarecrow," he shouted suddenly, and wildly flapped his arms, sending both children shrieking and laughing to the foot of the bed.

Just in time he saw Lady Eden remove the platter before the activity sent it crashing to the floor. How happy she looked.

Over the shrieks of the children, he was not at first aware of the new presence in the room. Not until he looked up, laughing, and saw Lady Eden turned rigidly about did his attention follow hers to the shadowy figure standing in the door, both arms braced, as though in support against the door frame.

Apparently the children had spotted him as well. Within the instant the sounds of laughter had ceased. Richard pressed closer to him and drew the coverlet up over both, as though for protection, while Mary nestled beneath his arm, her thumb moving to her mouth.

As for the figure in the door, he seemed content merely to stand in that peculiar posture of support, his identity a mystery until he heard Harriet whisper, "James . . . I sent a message with Peggy. She was to inform you that I was—"

"Occupied! Yes, I received it." As he started into the room, staggering slightly, John sat up, alarmed by all aspects of the man, his garments clearly mussed, his eyes dulled.

"I waited dinner for you, madam," he said, swaying back and forth on the balls of his feet. Drunk, he eyed the remains of food on the table. "I had no idea," he slurred, "that you were dining elsewhere."

"I have not dined, James," she said calmly, apparently detecting his state of inebriation and wanting to do nothing to aggravate him.

Incredibly, he pursued his investigation of the table,

lifting each domed top and allowing it to fall with a clatter. "Better than I got," he pouted.

As he drew near to where she was standing, John saw her retreat. "Help yourself," she soothed. "There's more than—"

But apparently his lordship was no longer interested in food, and now lifted his glazed eyes to the bed. Suddenly he smiled and raised his hand in mock salute. "Welcome home, Edward." He grinned. "The whores of London no longer hold appeal for you? Well, I warn you in advance, there's nothing here but dim-witted maids." He leaned closer, almost falling across the foot of the bed. "But I'd say that that portion of the female anatomy which holds the greatest interest for both of us is far removed from the area of the brain. At opposite ends of the pole, one might say. Right?"

Suddenly he crumpled against the bedpost, clinging with both hands, the amusement fading from his contorted face.

John sat with held breath, hugging both children to him.

"Ah," Lord Eden exclaimed now, spying the children. "I see you've met my babes." Again he grinned. "Miracles, they are," he said, "slipped from the womb of that frozen lady over there." Vaguely he pointed behind him in the general direction of Lady Eden. "Blocks of ice, Edward, is what I was expecting for progeny. A man could break his cock on that iceberg."

"Please, James . . ."

Embarrassed for all of them, John lowered his head. Apparently the whispered plea had summoned his uncle's attention, for suddenly he turned to her, and impervious to her sharp cry, grasped her by the arms and bodily pushed her forward, forcing her to stand in a position at the foot of the bed.

Seeing his mother abused, Richard objected softly. "Papa, please . . ."

But Lord Eden was in no mood for mercy. Appearing suddenly to sober, he moved into a position behind her and twisted her arms backward. Again John started forward, but she lifted her eyes, begging him, without words, to hold still.

"Look upon her, Edward, if you will," his uncle now commanded. "You wanted her once. Do you still desire her?"

Mortified both for himself and for her, John shook his head. "I am not Edward," he muttered.

But if his uncle heard, he gave no indication of it and continued to taunt her. "Look upon her," he ordered again. "You think you see a woman? Then your eyes deceive you. You see winter, that's what you see. It's easier to mount a corpse than it is to mount this lady, Edward," he went on.

John had never seen such silent suffering. "Please release her," he demanded.

"Release her?" Lord Eden exclaimed, laughing. "I've a better idea. Between us, let's thaw her. You've plenty of experience and I've a sudden hunger. What do you say? A welcoming-home present, brothers sharing and sharing alike."

All the time he talked, he was forcing her down upon the foot of the bed, her hands struggling against the progress of his fingers down the buttons of her gown.

John had seen enough. Quickly he released the children with a whisper, "Run!" He called after Richard, "Bring help." Then he was out of bed, hobbling toward the table, where he grabbed a serving knife. Trembling, he confronted his uncle with a command of his own. "Release her," he ordered, wondering if he'd have the courage to use the knife if the man didn't obey.

Half-kneeling over his terrified wife, his uncle at last turned to face him. "You're not . . . Edward," he stammered.

The man was pushing up from the bed, his glazed eyes searching John's face as though recognition were still dawning. "You're . . . the bastard," he pronounced. "The bastard's bastard," he added. "You don't belong here," he shouted. "I thought I'd given orders that you were to be—"

Fortunately for John, the man stumbled on the edge of the carpet, falling heavily against the table, giving John a moment's reprieve to gain the door and glance down the corridor. Empty.

"Please, sir," John begged, seeing his uncle on his feet and moving toward him.

"Bastard!" the man shouted, as though the delay had simply fanned his fury. As he drew nearer, his arms lifted, hands coming closer, aimed at John's throat.

The knife was still there, awaiting the command from the brain. But that command never came. Instead, as his uncle's hands closed about his throat, he felt his knees give way. He dropped the knife and was in the process of defending himself with bare hands when suddenly he heard a dull vibrating thud, saw his uncle's surprised face close at hand, saw his besotted eyes slip upward, then immediately he felt the entire weight of the man's body slump against him.

Quickly John rolled to one side and let the man fall halfway out of the door. Scrambling to his feet, he saw Harriet, her hands grasping a silver platter, still holding it at the ready as though eager to strike the fallen man again.

Slowly John looked down on the figure sprawled at his feet. Not a sign of life or movement. Apparently their thoughts were similar. "Is he . . . ?" she whispered, and could not finish.

John knelt for a closer look. "No," he murmured, returning his attention to Harriet.

For a moment the two of them stared at each other. Then suddenly she dropped the silver tray as though it had become hot.

"It's over," he said, and stepped forward to assist her with her belated terror. But abruptly her hand moved out, informing him that he was to hold his position. He watched as she turned back into the room and walked to the far window.

What now? he wondered bleakly. He looked down at the still body and caught sight of his own bare legs and was acutely aware of the foolish spectacle he must present. If it hadn't been for his uncle's brutal words and actions, there would have been an element of farce to the entire episode.

Now the mess had to be cleaned up, and he was just stooping to pick up the silver tray and the fallen knife when, coming from the far end of the corridor, he heard Richard's frantic chatter.

Hurriedly he lifted the tray and knife and deposited them on the table, where they no longer resembled weapons. If the woman standing at the window was aware that they would shortly be joined by others, she gave no indication of it. Obviously either through choice or necessity she was leaving it all up to him.

Then Richard was there, gaping down at his father's body, and following behind, John saw an enormous rosy-cheeked woman dressed in black, a fussy lace cap atop her head, her hand pressed against her mouth. "Gawd! What—"

John stepped forward, more or less in control. "I'm afraid he's had too much to drink," he said.

The large woman looked at him. "Is he—"

"Merely passed out," John soothed.

Richard chimed in now. "Clara didn't believe me at first," he said. "She accused me of telling tales, but I wasn't, was I?"

John smiled down on the boy. "No," he agreed, then tried to soften the horror of the evening. Blessedly he saw no sight of Mary. Obviously she had been left behind in safe hands. "Your father didn't mean anything he said or did tonight," he said kindly to the boy. "He'd just had too much dinner wine."

"Where's Mother?" Richard asked, craning his neck around the doorway. But Clara's sharp eyes had already found her. "My lady," she called out, as though sensing that her mistress might be in need of assistance.

John waited to see if that unresponding figure was recovered and capable of response. He looked as long as he dared, then to Clara he suggested, "Could you summon two watchmen to assist Lord Eden to his chambers? And it might be well if his manservant sat with him for awhile."

At first the woman looked at him as though uncertain of his legitimate voice of authority. Obviously Richard saw her hesitation and with admirable nine-year-old courage that displayed the seed of the future Lord Eden commanded her, "Fetch the watchmen. We can't leave him here. These are John's chambers, and he has a sore foot."

In spite of the non sequitur, the large woman turned immediately and lumbered off down the corridor.

Richard stepped gingerly over the body of his father and joined John on the other side. "He was dreadful, wasn't he?" he murmured.

"He wasn't himself," John said, his attention torn between the window and the door.

"Is Mother . . .?"

"Well." John smiled. "I think she would appreciate a moment alone, however."

The boy gazed tenderly toward the figure by the window, a clear look of longing on his face. "She never cries," he whispered.

"And she's not crying now," John soothed, feeling awkward talking about her when she must be overhearing everything.

At last John heard approaching footsteps. Clara appeared first, a look of pride on her face, as though the watchmen had failed to believe her, as she had failed to believe Richard.

"See, I told you," she announced, pointing a finger downward at the still man.

"Would you be so good as to assist him to his chambers?" John said, again taking the lead.

As with Clara, both men looked at him as though they too were questioning the weight of his authority.

Again Richard interceded. "He's my cousin," he announced proudly. "You'd better do what he says."

Their doubt banished, they took up positions on either side of his lordship and unceremoniously lifted him to his feet, suspending his weight between them, and with his head hanging limp, the little procession started laboriously down the corridor.

The three of them, Clara, Richard and John, watched until they disappeared. John was aware of Clara shaking her head, part censure, part pity, though Richard apparently had lost all interest, and was now in the process of returning to the chamber, clearly ready to take up the fun where they had left off.

Tactfully John suggested another course of action. "It's late, Richard," he said. "Why don't you run along with Clara now."

"She's a nursemaid," the boy replied, as though shocked by the suggestion.

"It's past your bedtime," the woman said cooperatively.

So eager was John to end the debate and clear his chambers, he made a rash promise. "Go with Clara now," he said to the boy. "Then come for me in the morning and I'll attend classes with you."

Richard seemed to require a moment to think on this. "Promise?" he asked shyly.

"I promise."

"Come along now," Clara urged, and at last the young boy obeyed, though he turned for a final word. "I'm glad you're here." He smiled at John.

"Thank you," John murmured, moved by the boy's expression of affection.

Then he stood alone, watching the two of them down the corridor. Finally he stepped inside the room and closed the door, his eyes going immediately to where she stood. Still unmoved, she resembled a slim black statue.

"My lady," he began tentatively, and stopped.

"May I . . ." he commenced again, thinking to offer her something, a chair, a glass of wine. But she moved with determination away from the area of the window, and gaining the safe center of the room, looked at him for the first time.

He'd never seen such an expression on a face before. "Please sit down," he suggested quietly from the window.

Suddenly she laughed. "Sit down!" she parroted, her hands a blur of nervous movement about her throat. "Good heavens, I've no time to sit," she went on. "I've at least a hundred chores to attend to. My correspondence for one, and I must look in on Jennifer before I retire and certain arrangements must be made for you."

As she burst into action, he could only gape, though he did manage a faltering, "For . . . me, my lady?"

"Of course, for you," she replied. "You will need a

tailor immediately. Shall I fetch one from Exeter? Or perhaps you have a favorite in London. If so, give me his name and I shall write to the gentleman."

"No," he muttered, bewildered by her performance. And he was certain it *was* a performance.

"Then I shall fetch one for you. I'm afraid those worn garments will never do."

As she babbled on about the poor quality of his wardrobe, he felt his bewilderment blend with anger. Did she know how silly she sounded?

Then, to his amazement, she was making fun of him. "Look at you." She smiled. "The little boy needs a new nightshirt, one which will at least cover those knees."

"It was not my choice, my lady," he muttered, tugging at the too-short nightshirt.

"Well, we'll fix it, I promise," she said, her voice resembling a mother speaking to a young child. "For tomorrow," she went on, her giddiness seeming to increase, "I'm afraid you'll have to wear your old garments to class. But after that I shall get you proper schoolboy clothes, matching Richard's would be nice, don't you think?"

"I'm not a schoolboy, my lady," he said, trying to rein in both his anger as well as his embarrassment.

"Oh, but you are," she said. "And you must attend to your studies immediately. Come morning, I shall inform Herr Snyder that he now has two pupils."

His suffering was acute, a blend of bewilderment and disappointment. What had come over her? Having recently been humiliated herself, did she possess that kind of character that compelled her to soothe her own hurt by inflicting it on others?

"My lady," he said sternly, trying to walk with dignity in spite of his bandaged foot, "I will attend class with Richard tomorrow because I promised him. After that, the choice will be my own. I've spent twelve years of my life with my head in books to satisfy my father. I see no need—"

But if she was shocked by his impudence, she gave no indication of it. Her manner was that of one accustomed to dealing with stubborn children. "You'll like Herr

Snyder, I know," she said. "He's a brilliant man, a grad-
uate of—"

"I'm not questioning his brilliance, my lady. I'm
merely—"

"There," she soothed, watching him hobble back to the
bed. "A good idea," she confirmed. "You need your rest."

Although he was headed in that direction, now he altered his course and veered to one of the chairs near the
table. He sat defiantly and poured himself a glass of
claret. "Not tired at all, my lady," he snapped, "though
the events of the evening have been . . . taxing."

He'd not intended to remind her in such a vicious
manner of her recent humiliation. But she'd driven him to
it. Now gulping the claret, he made a face at the strong
liquid and tried to hide his discomfort by again tugging
at the too-short nightshirt.

"Oh, John," she said, standing just beyond the table,
"if only you knew how silly you looked."

As his mortification and hurt blended, he responded
with the first words that came to mind. "Not half as silly
as you, my lady, a short time ago."

The silence crashed against him like a physical blow.
Regret, as deep and strong as any he'd ever felt, pressed
upon him, and though fearful of what he might find, he
turned to face her and saw new anguish in her eyes.

*What were they doing to each other? And more im-
portant, why?*

"My lady, I—"

But she was moving toward the door.

"Harriet, I'm sorry."

But apparently she wasn't interested in his apology. As
she closed the door behind her, he considered following
after her, begging her to return so that they might start
again. But he held his position in the chair and merely
stared at the closed door.

Suddenly in perplexed anger he stood and pressed his
full weight down upon his foot and welcomed the wave
of pain. What did she want of him? What role was he
supposed to play for her? And why the necessity to play
any role?

There the aimless thoughts stopped. Amazed, he looked

down and realized he'd been pacing, placing full weight on his foot and feeling nothing.

But there were other feelings, equally as painful and far more baffling. He glanced toward the foot of his bed. How effortlessly he still saw her, prone, helpless beneath the drunken man, his hands fumbling at the buttons of her gown.

Still he stood, eyes fixed on the bed, defenseless against the sensations which swept over him.

No! Quickly he felt his ardor dampened by a weight of shame. But because the sensations would not let him be, he substituted *her* image with the faintly remembered image of the prostitute named Rosa whom the rough-jacks had forced upon him in the dimly lit back room of the London pub. He'd only just touched her breasts when his father had intervened and put a stop to the fun.

Now he envisioned Rosa on the bed, her thick black hair done in two plaits with loose strands on either side. And he fell across the mussed bed linens, facedown, and clung to the opposite side until the mysterious upheaval crested and left him shuddering.

He closed his eyes. Beneath his body he felt a small spreading moisture. Would he always be plagued thus? Did all men suffer in similar fashion? Or was it just him, some private weakness that he could neither account for nor control?

Slowly he turned over on his back. He shouldn't have spoken to her as he had. He had no desire to add to her unhappiness. Yet she had provoked him into it, clearly baiting.

Now he cautioned himself that he must move with greater care in the future. His brief life as an odd-boy may have been dangerous and full of hazards. But all that appeared as nothing compared to the unseen hazards which he sensed about him in the upper corridors of Eden Castle.

London,
July 1851

ALTHOUGH MORLEY JOHNSON had been at work for over a month on the laborious preparations for his journey, at last everything was ready and all that detained him now was the weeping woman who stood on the pavement, her linsey-woolsey dress smelly with July perspiration.

God! With dwindling patience Morley sent his eyes heavenward, as though for divine intervention. As a new wave of inconsolable weeping dragged Minnie's head downward, Morley cast his eyes in a more appealing direction, to the elegant coach and four waiting just beyond the pavement, capable of taking him the length and breadth of England, if he so desired.

Morley Johnson with his own coach! He smiled in spite of the lamentation going on behind him. Securely tucked away in his pocket and of even greater importance than the coach and four was a letter of unlimited credit, made out in his name and bearing that most remarkable of all designations, the Eden seal. And tucked safely in the same pocket was the letter from Lady Eden which had started the wheels of this adventure rolling. Come about a month ago, it had, requesting that he make all the necessary arrangments for a journey to the Lakes, or wherever the clues might lead him, a journey of unlimited duration, to be concluded with a stop by Hadley Park for a firsthand account of how Lady Eden's childhood home was faring under the dubious hand of her old uncle.

He patted the inner pocket where the letters rested. Now he was aware of Minnie moving up close behind him as though to summon his attention. As he turned to face her, he smelled the sourness of regurgitated milk, the tiny babe in her arms nursing hungrily at her tit.

My God, when had that happened? Undoubtedly while he'd been admiring the coach, the witless woman had dragged out her shapeless breast and had given it to the infant. Adding to his embarrassment, Morley now saw the driver of the coach, a blank-faced knave named Gavin, look sideways, clearly amused by the maudlin scene on the pavement.

Hurriedly Morley stepped between his nursing wife and the sly amusement of the man sitting atop the coach. "Have you lost your senses?" he whispered. "Cover yourself. Now!"

Confronted with her husband's anger, Minnie pulled her breast, still dripping milk, from the babe's mouth and stuffed it back into the bodice of her dress.

The tears were at last subsiding. As again she dabbed at her eyes, he cast a glance over his silent brood, all staring wide-eyed at their distraught mother. "Look to her," he said sternly to the oldest ones. "And help her as much as you can. If you're all good, I'll bring you surprises. If not, I'll throw the surprises away and give you my belt."

Then he found that he could look upon them no longer. A feeling of excitement crept over him. Then leave! To that end, without even the courtesy of good-bye kisses, he swung himself rapidly up into the coach, enjoying immensely the instant elevation. As he looked back down on the pavement, he saw poor Minnie all but collapsed among the circle of weeping children.

As the coach picked up limited speed along Holborn, Morley looked eagerly out of the windows on both sides, hoping to catch a glimpse of a familiar face, someone who knew him and would look with admiration at his new status.

But he saw no one, and in the limited foot traffic on the pavement, not one face seemed interested, not one set of eyes looked admiringly up.

They were moving down New Oxford Street now. Tottenham Court Road would be the next turn, then Barnet and the Great North Road. He knew no one in those districts, and someone *must* admire him.

At that moment, above the rattle of the coach wheels, he had a brilliant idea. He sat still in the carriage seat for a moment. *The little whore, Edward Eden's whore, alone perhaps in the house in Bermondsey.*

He made a peculiar grunting sound. What a fitting way to commence this journey of liberation, freed for the first time in his life from domestic obligation!

"Driver!" he shouted, lowering the window. "Turn left here and make for the river."

He felt the horses slow as the coachman, bewildered, called back, "The Great North Road is to the right. What in the hell—"

"Do as I say, man," Morley shouted, "or else I'll sack you and find another driver before we leave London."

Apparently the threat was effective, for with some difficulty the driver angled the horses through the traffic and turned left on Charing Cross.

Morley shouted again. "It's a business stop, in Bermondsey. Turn left after you cross the bridge."

If the driver heard, he gave no indication of it, though he made no protest either. Relieved, Morley leaned back against the cushions. The carriage was moving at a good speed now, the rhythmic clatter seeming to keep pace with his accelerating pulse. How impressed that little prostitute would be as this grand coach drew up in front of her wretched house.

Incapable of thinking any more, he closed his eyes. Oh, God, how wonderful the world was and all creatures who inhabited it. How marvelous the thought that he did not have to return that night to that smelly flat on Holborn Street, and that dripping woman and those somber children. How magnanimous God had been to create whores. Why, there must be whores the length of England, and he intended to sample them all, as proper gentlemen did, whenever it suited his fancy.

❧
Bermondsey,
July 1851

THE THOUGHT WEAKENED her, and all her bravery was for naught, the thought that Edward should be here, or John, helping her to clean and straighten the long table in their kitchen, the house fragrant with the good smells of boiling spuds and joints, and in honor of the reopening of their Common Kitchen, a pot of furmenty bubbling on the back of the old stove, a lovely treat of wheat and raisins, sugar and spices.

She paused a moment in her labors in an attempt to deal with those persistent ghosts. Weakly she sat on one of the broad benches. For a moment she experienced new feelings of grief as acute as she'd ever felt, as though no time at all had passed.

Perhaps it was too soon. She'd tried to tell Jack Willmot that. But the man had simply outtalked her, had pointed out that she needed diversion and occupation as acutely as the poor residents of Bermondsey needed the Common Kitchen.

And he'd been right in all aspects. As long as she kept busy and did not dwell on the past, she had found survival, if not easy, at least possible.

She smiled now and ran the damp cloth over the table as it occurred to her that for these past difficult weeks she'd been surrounded by love in a way that was unprecedented in her life. Of course, she was smart enough to know that it was merely residual love for Edward, everyone viewing her as a living link with that great man. But what matter? And as Jack Willmot had pointed out, what better way to keep alive his memory than to reopen the Common Kitchen? Of course she hated being dependent upon Jack Willmot for funds. But what could she do? She knew no profession save one. And she could not now return to that constant humiliation.

Newly troubled by her sense of dependency, she eased around the end of the table near the window. Still bent over, she heard a noise, the rattling approach of a carriage. She lifted the near curtain and looked out. Jack Willmot had promised to stop in later in the day and assist her with final preparations. But it was morning, and Mr. Willmot would never travel in such a conveyance. She leaned closer to the window. Then who?

Then she saw who and recognized him immediately. What had brought him back here? She'd answered all his questions, at least all that she was capable of answering.

He was standing on the pavement now, saying something to the driver atop the high seat. Suddenly it occurred to her that perhaps she should run and bolt the front door and deny him entrance.

But halfway across the front parlor, another thought intervened. What if he had brought her news of some sort concerning John? What if the boy were ill and in need of her, or wanted simply to come home, having found Eden lacking?

Thus, instead of throwing the bolt, as she reached the door she flung it open, apparently taking Mr. Johnson by surprise.

"Miss . . ." He smiled, bobbing his head, then stood curiously to one side, as though eager not to block her vision of something at the pavement.

But she saw nothing at the pavement except the rather overlarge carriage and the driver who sat with suspect rigidity.

"Mr. Johnson, won't you come in?" she murmured, remembering her manners and trying to forget the unpleasantness of their last meeting.

He ducked his head through the low doorway and apparently detected the various good odors coming from the kitchen. He lifted his head, his long straight black hair cupping about his collar in the process. "Smells of my youth"—he smiled—"my mother's kitchen at harvest time."

She smiled, flattered, though still a bit nervous, and

watched as he fell into a close examination of the clean
well-ordered room, quite a change from the chaos of his
last visit. She managed a timid, "Please sit down, Mr.
Johnson. May I offer you something? Coffee? Tea?"

"No, no, I don't want to inconvenience you."

"It will be no inconvenience, I assure you."

"It's clear you are expecting guests."

"Guests!" She laughed at the generous description of
the wretched humanity who would be seated at the long
table in the kitchen that evening. "Not guests, Mr. Johnson," she corrected. "With the help of Edward's friends,
I'm reopening the Common Kitchen. The first serving will
be this evening."

He seemed perplexed. "Charity?"

She nodded.

He still seemed mystified. "I had no idea." He sat up
as though fascinated by the subject. "And where, may I
ask, was Mr. Eden getting his funds?"

"Oh, he worked, he did," she said proudly, "as did
John. It wasn't much. But we shared everything."

He looked at her now with intense interest. "And how
are *you* paying for such philanthropic acts?"

She was on the verge of informing him of Mr. Willmot's generous support when, without warning, she felt
his hand covering hers in an intimate touch, and looked
up to see a strange smile on his face.

"No need for deception with me," he murmured, moving closer to the edge of his seat. "Old ways die hard, I
know, though God has a reason for everything."

While she was still puzzling this, he stood and moved
to the side of her chair, his hand in the process stroking
her shoulder. "You've made a pleasant little den here,"
he went on, lifting his hand just as she was about to
draw away, finding the gesture intimate and repellent.
"Any man would pay handsomely to pass a few hours in
this comfortable retreat. How clever of you to locate here
in this remote spot in Bermondsey, where a gentleman's
friends are not likely to see his carriage and make a damaging report to an offended wife. May I ask," he said,
grinning from the far side of the room, "how many do
you . . . feed here in the course of a day?"

What was the matter with him? His manner had become extremely familiar, every word weighted with innuendo. In an attempt to answer his question, she said, "They come at night only."

"Of course."

"And I don't recall how many. As many as I can accommodate."

He was approaching Edward's door, closed now, the room itself tidied, though left for the most part exactly as it had been when he had inhabited it. Mr. Johnson looked back at her again, a look of admiration on his face. "You . . . must have remarkable stamina." He smiled.

"I don't understand," she murmured. "It's hard work, to be sure, but the rewards are great.'"

"I'm sure they are."

Before she could protest, he pushed open the door to Edward's room and peered in. As his rude inspection stretched on, she considered asking him to leave. "Mr. Johnson, I'm afraid that I—"

"Of course, of course," he said, turning away from Edward's room, though leaving the door ajar. "Business first." He smiled, returning to the chair and with a gesture inviting her to do the same.

Business! Then he did have something of importance to discuss with her. On that note of hope, she settled opposite him. "Does it concern John?" she asked, taken aback by the focus of his eyes, which seemed to be resting on her breasts.

"Yes, it concerns the boy," he said. "I have been authorized by Lord and Lady Eden to undertake an extensive journey for the purpose of trying to discover the true identity of the boy's mother."

Sweet Lord! With a sigh she turned away. Why was everyone so concerned with that ancient mystery?

"I am just now," he continued, "on my way out of London, in my own carriage, as you can see, and I thought it might be wise if I made a final stop here in the hope that during the intervening days since our last meeting perhaps you have remembered something that might seem innocent to you, but that could be of vast importance to a trained mind?"

No, she'd remembered nothing, and lowered her head in an attempt to swallow her disappointment. No message from John, apparently, though still she felt compelled to ask, "And how is he? John, I mean? Have you received news? Has he—"

He seemed annoyed by her digression. "The boy's present state is none of my concern," he said. "But his past is of vast concern to everyone at Eden." He leaned forward in his chair as though to force her attention to the matter at hand. "Do you remember anything?" he asked sternly.

Wearily she shook her head, wanting only to be rid of him. "No more than what I told you the last time you were here."

"You mentioned that on that day long ago, Mr. Eden had returned from the Lakes. You don't remember what part?"

"If he said, I never heard. He was ill . . ."

Suddenly the man leaned forward, as though at last she'd said something that interested him. "Ill? In what way ill?"

His demanding voice seemed to penetrate all aspects of the quiet room. Prudently she wondered how much she should reveal of Edward's addiction. It had been a sad chapter in his life, and he was gone, so why resurrect it?

But Mr. Johnson was there again, his face reflecting his interest. She'd had more than enough of him, and now, in an attempt to speed his exit, she confessed softly, "He was an opium eater," then amended her statement, "at that time in his life, he was. After his return with John as a babe, he ceased altogether. Never indulged again." She closed her eyes. "I remember nothing else, Mr. Johnson," she whispered. "I swear it. I'm sorry that again I can be of no service to you."

She was in the process of leaving her chair and heading toward the door. But as she passed him, he reached out and grabbed her hand and with unexpected force drew her close. "You've been of immense help." He smiled up at her. "There are several well-known opium cottages in the Lakes. You have narrowed my search considerably, and I'm grateful."

"I'm glad," she said, embarrassed, not wanting yet to struggle openly for possession of her hand, feeling certain that he would release it.

Her embarrassment increasing, she tried to back away. "It's getting late, Mr. Johnson," she said. "We both have duties to attend to. You must be on the road, and I must make certain preparations for the evening.

As the struggle of hands persisted, he stood and reached for her upper arm and drew her to him in a close embrace. "I'm afraid I haven't made myself clear," he whispered. "I've come this morning on both business and pleasure. The business is over, and I . . ."

Holding her fast about the waist with one hand, he reached up for her breast with the other, and at last his incredible intention became clear. Her first impulse was to laugh. Now she tried to push his hand away, and unwittingly parroted his words. "Nor have I made myself clear, Mr. Johnson," she said, still struggling. "I'm asking you to leave, and if you do so immediately, nothing will be said—"

"Oh, what a pretty lady." He grinned down on her. "And what an eloquent protest. Heightens the fun, eh, what, and warms the blood. No wonder you could please a man like Edward Eden."

Still his amusement increased, along with the activity of his hands. "What a charming switch," he whispered, growing quite breathless close to her ear. "I've seen many a lady behave like a whore. But you're the first whore I've ever seen to take on the airs of a lady."

"I am not a whore," she gasped, struggling futilely against his superior strength. Both his arms were around her now, pinning her hands at her sides, while she, with rage and fear increasing, tried to avoid his mouth, which was coming closer.

Still not quite able to believe her predicament, she tried reason for a final time. "Mr. Johnson, I beg you. Please release me. You're making a fool of yourself."

"Morley Johnson does not make a fool of himself," he pronounced angrily, "nor does he permit a whore to do so. I came prepared to pay like all your clients. Now I think I'll insist upon a free meal."

Suddenly he spun her about and twisted both arms behind her, a painful wrenching which caused her to moan. Fully conscious of her fate, she commenced a mighty struggle, her fear at last made manifest in a prolonged sirenlike scream as she felt him propel her forward across the room, half-shoving, half-lifting her, but moving her steadily toward Edward's bedchamber.

Between screams, she begged him to release her, a witless refrain, her mind racing ahead to the ordeal itself, the degradation and humiliation that she thought she'd put behind her years ago.

At that moment, with the bed drawing nearer, she summoned all the strength she could muster, whirled about and brought one knee up, a select blow, carefully aimed, which caused the man to buckle, releasing her altogether as both his hands were summoned to the area of his groin.

She struggled free, as shocked as he by the accuracy of her assault. She watched him a moment, bent over on himself, a sputtering sound escaping his lips. She looked down upon him with contemptuous indifference, confident that she had won, determined now to make it to the front door.

Unfortunately, absorbed prematurely in her victory, she was in no way prepared for the lightning-fast speed with which his hand shot forward, pulling himself up within the instant. Nor was she prepared for his other hand, which lifted high into the air over her head, curled itself into a fist and came hurtling down against the side of her face, a blow of such force that she felt her neck crack, the room and everything in it going suddenly dark.

As she felt herself being carried to the bed, her last conscious thought was one of sadness that there had been no message from John, that she'd let the man in, that living with Edward for all these years had made her weak and foolishly trusting.

For the most part it was a safe darkness and a safe silence, though it faltered once and she opened her eyes to a single shaft of sunlight streaming in through Edward's window. She felt a crushing weight on her body, a familiar thickness between her legs, her back moving rhythmically up and down on the bed, all old and readily identifiable sensations. And teeth were gnawing at her breast, causing great pain, but even that was familiar, as was the chafing deep inside her.

She was a whore again, back in St. James Park. And that realization caused the greatest pain. Tears filled her eyes. She whispered a name. "Edward . . ."

Then the obliging fist delivered another blow to the side of her head, then another, and yet another, and she went willingly into this new darkness, leaving behind her the realization of who she was and what she had once again become.

As Jack Willmot waited in Thomas Brassey's outer office, one thought and one thought alone brought him enormous pleasure. And that was the realization that little Elizabeth was at last safe, that largely through his efforts, she was in the process of leaving her grief and shame behind and turning her eyes to the future. In a way, Jack viewed it as having settled a debt with Edward Eden.

Now he looked up in anticipation as another gentleman left Thomas Brassey's inner office. Willmot had been sitting in the plain narrow chamber for over an hour, and during that time dozens of men had passed in and out of the inner sanctum. Something was afoot with the great contractor. Of that Willmot was certain. Brassey had built railroads on five continents and Jack Willmot had been his foreman on three. Whatever impossible task he had in mind, Jack would go with him.

The room was empty now, all the men having come and gone except himself. In the silent waiting, Jack found his thoughts going back to the house in Bermondsey. With his eyes closed, he could see her clearly, her small yet determined figure tackling any job, an impressive display of strength which on occasion faltered as, without warning, she would slip into a mood of grief.

Jack Willmot was an honest-enough man to admit to himself that she moved him, stirred him in a way that no other female in his entire life had stirred him. Also he was smart enough to understand the reasons and courageous enough to realize that little or nothing would ever come of it. She belonged to Edward Eden, would always belong to him, even in death.

No, it was best that Thomas Brassey was now on the verge of sending him God knew where. It was becoming increasingly difficult to remain in her presence simply in the capacity of friend and adviser. He would always see to her support, he'd promised her that, and he would certainly remain in London long enough to determine that the Common Kitchen was a success, that her female friends, the volunteers from Edward's Ragged Schools, would keep a close and watchful eye on her. And certainly between jobs, whenever fate brought him back to London, he would look in on her and savor her sweetness and take a portion of it with him back into the harshness of his all-male world. A professional foreman was not, by nature, suitable material for marriage.

At that moment, the office door opened. He glanced quickly in that direction, saw Brassey's familiar form, his arm around the shoulder of the departing gentleman.

"Within a fortnight," he heard Brassey call out. "And pack your warmest and say your good-byes. I can't even estimate the length of the . . ."

Then apparently his eye fell on Jack and a warm smile lit the craggy features. "Ah, Willmot." He smiled, hand extended. "Sorry to have kept you waiting."

As Willmot passed into his office, he was aware of Brassey lingering at the door for a word of farewell to the departing gentleman. In the interim, Jack studied the office, as remarkable as the man who inhabited it, a small room considering the scope of what it represented, a simple desk, well-cluttered, boasting a miniature of his wife and children, several easy chairs, well-worn, a sideboard with a single decanter of brandy and several mismatched glasses, no distinguishing characteristics in the entire room except for . . . that. His eyes lifted to the far wall, covered entirely by an enormous map of the world, flattened, thin red lines indicating Mr. Brassey's past accomplishments, an impressive crisscrossing which to the casual eye seemed effortlessly to link the entire world.

Willmot smiled and shook his head. From behind he heard a low though forceful voice. "It's enough to make a sane man weary, isn't it?"

Willmot laughed. "I suppose that's what keeps us safe, Mr. Brassey, a negotiable lack of good sense."

Brassey shared his humor and seemed to settle more comfortably into his chair, his attention now focused on Jack. "And you, Willmot?" he asked. "What have you been up to besides that glass monstrosity now sitting on the meadows of Hyde Park?"

For an instant Jack felt a twinge of hurt. He was very proud of the Crystal Palace and of the men who'd helped him to create it. Then at the last moment he saw a twinkle in Brassey's eye, and knew that no defense was necessary. "It was quite an undertaking," he replied.

"It was indeed," Brassey agreed, "a remarkable design. The Duke of Devonshire's gardener is to be commended, and I understand that Her Majesty is delighted." He leaned forward across the desk. "I looked for you at the grand opening last month to tender my congratulations, but unfortunately in the crowds I couldn't find you."

Willmot lowered his head and concentrated on smoothing the wrinkles from his cap. "I wasn't there, sir," he replied. "There had been an accident the night before . . ."

"So I heard," Brassey replied sympathetically. "It always hurts to lose a good man. You can't help but feel responsible. I've lost only a few, but one is too many."

Willmot nodded, grateful for his understanding. Then, as though Brassey sensed the painful nature of the subject, he moved away from it. "And what have you been up to since?" he asked, leaning back in his chair, one hand rubbing his chest.

"Very little, I'm afraid," Willmot replied. "There were certain affairs that I had to attend to."

"The dead man's?"

Willmot nodded. "He left a son, and a woman."

Again Brassey seemed to understand. In the interim, Jack saw her image, her slim shoulders, her sweetness.

Then into the silence he heard Brassey's voice again, still compassionate, though quietly warning. "Be careful, Jack, widows are God's great temptations."

"She's not a . . . widow, sir. They were never married." He looked up at the confession, expecting to see a degree of surprise on the face opposite him. But he saw nothing.

Then came a blunt question. "And now you've fallen in love with her?"

"No," Jack said, too quickly, hearing confirmation in his own protest. "Her heart is still quite occupied," he went on, "and will be, I suspect, for the rest of her life."

For several minutes there was only silence in the room and the ticking of a clock somewhere behind him and muted carriage wheels on the street below. Then "Poor Jack," he heard Brassey mourn. "I offer you my deepest sympathy and offer you an escape route as well, if you want it."

Grateful, Jack looked up. "I do indeed, sir. I've been in London long enough."

"Can you successfully leave her behind?"

To that direct question Jack gave a direct answer. "I must."

In a burst of energy Brassey reached for the pointer lying on the desk and strode rapidly to the map of the world. He lifted the stick to a broad area directly above North America. "Canada," he announced, smiling at Willmot. "Five hundred and thirty-nine miles from here" —and he moved the pointer to the Atlantic coast—"to here," and he slid the pointer to the American Great Lakes. He lowered the pointer and dragged it between his hands, confronting Willmot directly. "It has fallen our lot to connect the two," he said with a smile. "Would you say it's possible?"

"With you in command, sir, anything is possible. I'd say that you had proved that often enough in the past."

Brassey nodded, apparently pleased with his response. Still he questioned on. "It's an untrod wilderness," he warned. "Can English navvies survive such a wilderness?"

"No question about it, sir," he pronounced. "If they want a railway stretching between those two puddles of water, there is only one man in the world who can give it to them, and that's yourself."

He'd really not meant to be so effusive, but apparently his words had pleased Brassey, who looked on him now with the warmest of smiles, not a man who needed flattery, but perhaps a man who needed confirmation of his legendary abilities.

"I intend to employ eight crews," Brassy said, "of five hundred navvies each. I have need of eight foremen, with one good man to oversee the lot." He looked directly up at Willmot where he stood as though at attention opposite the desk. "I have signed all save the one good man."

Willmot grinned. "Correction, sir. You now have signed him."

"I'm grateful," Brassey murmured, standing, indicating the end of the meeting.

As Willmot stepped backward, he remembered one all-important point which as yet had not been discussed. "When do we leave, sir?" he asked.

"As soon as possible," Brassey said. "The first ships will leave from Portsmouth within the fortnight, with both men and materials." He caught up with Willmot and rested his arm on his shoulder. "I'd like for you to be with them."

Apparently Brassey spotted both his hesitancy and confusion. "Too soon?" he inquired thoughtfully.

Willmot drew a deep breath and continuously arranged his hat in his hands. At the door, Brassey looked closely at him. "You *are* in love, aren't you?"

"No," Willmot said. "It's just that she's . . . very young, and fate has never been too generous with her."

Then apparently Brassey saw that there was nothing more to say. He gave Willmot a final pat on the shoulder. "Do what you have to do," he said kindly. "If you change your mind, let me know as soon as possible."

Hearing this absurd statement provided Jack with needed strength. "Oh, I won't change my mind, sir," he promised. "I'll be in that wilderness with you."

Brassey nodded skeptically. "If first you can extricate yourself from this one."

Willmot stepped across the threshold. "A fortnight," he confirmed. "I'll be there."

The two men shook hands. In a few moments Willmot found himself on the street once more. *Canada.* Well, he'd wished for the end of the earth, and apparently he'd been granted his wish.

For a while he walked at random. The afternoon sun was hot, causing the pavement to shimmer. *Fierce winters. Can the men survive them?* He walked down several streets, then found himself in a public house, a pint of ale before him on the table.

In spite of the crowds around him, he felt alone. *A fortnight!* So soon. Was she ready? Was he ready to leave the warmth of that small house in Bermondsey? If Brassey was getting old, Willmot was getting old as well. All his life he'd thought that ultimately he'd settle down with a woman, perhaps have a brood of children and leave the far corners of the earth to the younger twigs.

Suddenly he lifted the pint and drained the ale to the bottom, annoyed by the confusion in his head. Old? He was scarcely forty, with all his powers and senses intact. But concerning domesticity? Had he lost his mind? Oh, yes, he could just see himself seated at a simple hearth, a babe on each knee, a woman, any woman screaming at him from the kitchen. It would be mostly a fitting-in of domestic jobs, talking about the cost of things, eating frugally and ultimately sleeping without touching her.

No, thank you! He'd take the red savages any day. And as though with the sense at last of being back on track, he slapped a coin on the table to cover the cost of the ale, again adjusted his hat and stepped out into the late-afternoon heat, his steps carrying him forward with purpose now.

His destination? The house in Bermondsey, where it was his intention to assist Elizabeth with her first night in the Common Kitchen and ultimately, before the evening came to an end, to say good-bye.

It was almost five o'clock when Jack Willmot turned the corner into the small lane in Bermondsey and looked ahead to see a crowd already gathered out front of the low-roofed cottage. With his hands shoved easily into his pockets, his resolution locked into place, he looked at the small gathering. Was there any news in the world more welcome than the news of a free meal?

Less than twenty yards away, he looked again, puzzled at a group of three old women, their tattered brown shawls covering their heads, one weeping. A strange reaction to the promise of free food.

Approaching the house, he was about to address them, asking them to be patient, that soon . . . Then he smelled it, the acrid odor of burned food, and worse, now saw a wisp of smoke creeping out of the window in the area of the kitchen.

Fear vaulted. "Elizabeth!" he shouted, and violently pushed open the front door, only to be driven back by clouds of smoke. Frantically waving his arms before him, he covered his nose with one hand and cried out again, "Elizabeth!"

At that moment the smoke cleared through the vacuum caused by the open door and he saw the outline of several men in the kitchen, heavy pieces of burlap wrapped about their arms, their faces covered with kerchiefs.

What in the . . . ? Again he rushed forward, flapping his arms until at last he gained the kitchen door, and though his eyes were tearing from the smoke, he saw the culprit, kettles scorched and still smoking, the grease from joints boiled over, adding to the flames which the men had just put out.

"Open the windows," Willmot shouted, "and prop open the back door."

The men moved into action, unwinding the heavy burlap from their arms, and a few seconds later, cleansing drafts of fresh air began to ease the smoke out. The mystery deepened as Willmot saw clearly the extent of the damage, the entire area around the stove blackened and scorched, the kitchen a ruin, cluttered with upturned chairs and broken pottery, mute evidence of the desperation with which the men had attacked the flames.

Carelessness was Willmot's first thought. How could she have been so careless? Then, looking about for her in order that he might deliver a lecture, and seeing only the men, he suddenly demanded, "Where is she? Where is Elizabeth?"

Both men looked down at the floor and seemed to concentrate on the watery black ashes. Why didn't they answer? He was in the process of demanding again when suddenly a third man appeared in the back door, his body tilted to one side against the weight of a bucket of water.

"A woman's with her, guv," this man muttered, apparently the only one with a tongue and voice. "In there, they is," he added, shifting the bucket. "She's the one that give the alarm. If it hadn't been for her . . ."

What was he trying to say? Willmot looked over his shoulder into the front parlor. Then he was moving again. "Elizabeth . . ."

At that moment the door which led to the small bedroom opened. Through the smoke he caught a glimpse of a familiar face, one of Elizabeth's friends, a volunteer from the Ragged School, a pleasant woman by the name of Matilda Clifford.

Now Willmot saw nothing pleasant on her face. She seemed willing only to open the door a crack, and then she clung to both the door and the frame.

Stepping close, he saw tears streaming down her face. "Mr. Willmot," she stammered.

"Where is she?" he demanded.

The woman held her ground and pressed the hem of her apron to her lips and offered him a tearful, scarcely coherent explanation. "I saw the the smoke, I did, sir, from the end of the lane. Elizabeth's a good cook, and I knew that . . ."

Then tears overcame her, though before she covered her face he thought he heard the words, "She's hurt bad, sir."

That was enough. Woman or no, he stepped forward and pushed her to one side, his eye falling curiously at first on the shafts of evening sun filtering down upon the bed, alive with millions of particles of dust and ash. And inevitably the beams of light led him to the bed, mussed beyond description, and the woman lying on it.

"Dear God," he whispered, feeling her suffering as acutely as though it were his own, her position on the bed easily identifiable, mute proof of the nature of her ordeal, her clothes ripped down the front, exposing bleeding breasts, teeth marks discernible, her legs spread, one small foot slipperless. But it was her face that seized him, yet made it more difficult for him to draw any closer, her mouth half-open, the lower lip cracked and bleeding, upper lip swollen until it no longer resembled a lip, her eyes shut in pools of dark bruises, one open laceration on her cheek, dripping blood, her arms spread limp at her sides, as though she'd been beaten into unconsciousness and had had no choice but to endure.

Suddenly he closed his eyes. He'd seen men with amputated limbs, he'd seen them impaled on spikes. He'd seen many atrocities. But he'd never seen anything as pitiable as that slim frail figure on the bed.

"Here, sit, sir." Matilda's voice came from behind. Apparently she'd recovered enough from her own shock to spy his and was now offering him a chair.

But to sit was the last impulse in his mind. Coming fast on the heels of horror was anger. "Who?" he demanded, whirling on the woman as though she had the answer and was withholding it from him.

"I don't know, sir," she said, backing away from his rage. "Like I said, I only just arrived to give her a hand with the old folks, and I saw the smoke . . ." Her eyes grew wide, as though certain he'd hold her responsible. "I was just trying to rouse her, sir, when you come in. She's not said nothing yet. I think she needs a physician, I do, sir. There was bad blows to her head. You can see for yourself . . ."

"Then go fetch one," he shouted, still trying to deal with his rage and anguish.

Immediately Matilda abandoned the chair, as though only too happy for an excuse to flee the room.

"And hurry!" Willmot called after her.

He followed the vibrations of her rapidly retreating footsteps across the front parlor, then shouted again at one of the gaping old women at the front door. "Fetch me a basin of clean water, and linen," he ordered. "Be quick!"

On that note of determination he moved rapidly back to the bed. Later there would be time for questions and answers, and perhaps even justice. Gently he straightened her legs, and with tenderness he drew the light coverlet up, stopping short of her lacerated breast. Seeing the damaged flesh close at hand, he again weakened.

He should have been here, he thought angrily. How stupid of him to have left her alone in this part of London, where it was common knowledge that there was no man in the household, only a young woman alone.

Now, where to start? Where was the greatest need, and greatest pain? Was it better to leave her safely unconscious, or should he try to rouse her? Unable to answer his own questions, he at last sat on the edge of the bed and lifted her into his arms, a sheltering cocoon come too late. He held her close and gave in to tears for her, for her ordeal, for his negligent absence.

Finally his grief dissolved into a gentle rocking motion, though still he held her close, one broad hand supporting her head, the other flattened against her back, her arms hanging limp on either side.

Then suddenly he noticed one not so limp, her hand lifting of its own accord, heard at the same time a soft moan, and quickly he released her to the pillow, where he saw her mouth uselessly working, the bruised lips trying to form words.

"Lie still, Elizabeth, please," he begged.

He saw the swollen eyes trying to open, heard her groan, and again he tried to offer comfort. "Be still, please. A physician is on his way."

Her hand was on his arm now, clinging with awesome strength. She was trying to say something, but he couldn't understand.

Where was the physician? Why was he taking so long?

Still there was incredible effort coming from the bed. She appeared to be trying to lift herself.

"Elizabeth, please . . ."

But at that moment, clearly audible words left her lips, a fear-ridden plea as moving as any he had ever heard.

"Don't . . . leave . . . me," she begged, and continued to pull at his arm, as though seeking the entrance into the security of his embrace.

"Sweet Lord," he whispered, overcome, and lifted her again and held her close, heard the beginning of deep grief-racked sobs.

He had never thought that such human anguish was possible. Still he held her, pressed her more strongly to him. And ultimately, with dread, with resignation, he said good-bye to Canada and Mr. Thomas Brassey. That wilderness would have to be spanned without him. The one here would keep him occupied for a while.

He bent closer over her and tried with all his strength to absorb a portion of her grief and suffering.

As well as she could remember, she had given in to only one moment of weakness, and that was when strong arms had offered her a belated shelter. Now, no more! There would be no more weakness, for there was no shelter that could be trusted.

Amazed at her capacity to survive, Elizabeth heard her heart beating and she tried to open her eyes and through one narrowed slit of vision saw the man bent over her.

Jack Willmot. She knew that much, though earlier, once, she'd mistaken him for Edward. Then suddenly, without warning, she felt a slipping, a sort of headlong plunging, as though the bed were tilting.

"Elizabeth?"

She heard someone calling her name.

"Elizabeth? Can you hear me?"

Of course she could hear him. A whore's hearing was always intact. As she looked up at him again, she saw to her amazement that his eyes were filled with tears. Why tears? No one had ever wept over her before.

"Who was it?" Willmot was demanding. "Who was it, Elizabeth? I beg you. Give me a name."

She looked up at him, annoyed by the request. What would he do with the name? Go after him, no doubt, and cause more trouble. Besides, good prostitutes did not reveal the names of their clients.

"Leave me . . ." she muttered, and felt a painful crack on her lower lip, felt something cool rolling down her chin. As her discomfort increased, it blended with annoyance. *Give me a name!* How sadly she'd misjudged Jack Willmot, having once thought him to be a man of intelligence. What would he do with the name of Morley Johnson? Report him to the local constable? A rape trial perhaps, pitting the Eden solicitor against a self-confessed whore?

"Leave . . ." she tried to whisper, and turned on her side and drew the coverlet up until it was almost covering her head. Why didn't he leave? What was there left to contemplate?

With her back to him, she closed her eyes, the better to endure his silent pity. She felt dull and began quietly to plot the future. No more excursions into the realm of charity. No more compassion, no more decency. What decency she had known in this life had been buried along with Edward Eden. And all residual traces had been beaten out of her by Morley Johnson. Apparently she'd been designed by nature for one purpose, and beyond that, her life had no value.

Morley Johnson had said something that had interested her. *A charming den, away from the prying eyes of business associates and wives, where carriages could come and go without fear of being recognized.*

A proper house, yes, that's what she'd have, a clean comfortable retreat. She could read and write and do figures now and keep her own books. And if she handled it properly, and she fully intended to handle it properly, she could have security in abundance.

"Elizabeth, please look at me."

There he was again. Aware now that he was bending over her in an attempt to see her face, she held still and feigned sleep.

A few moments later she opened one eye and no longer saw him leaning over her. Thank God. Now she closed her eyes and tried to relax into the pillow. Would this room serve best? she wondered, her mind still turning on the details of her future. It had been Edward's room. She'd wanted to keep it intact. But what foolishness, that! Edward was dead, and in a way the room had already been initiated. Yes, this chamber would work very well, convenient to the front parlor.

At last, in the tumult of her thoughts, her pain was beginning to recde. There would be no more beatings, of that she was certain, although in a way she'd invited it. She'd called him a fool, and while all men were, none liked to hear it from the lips of a whore.

Cleanliness first, she thought, and comfort in pleasant surroundings, gentlemen invited to partake of claret in the front parlor, and herself with a whole wardrobe of pretty dressing gowns which opened easily. And of course the necessary equipment to keep herself clean and unimpregnated. No birthings, please, to ruin her figure, no child whom she might laboriously raise, only to have him turn his back on her as John had done.

A small death there, but she dealt with it, as she continued to deal with her discomfort. It could all be borne. With what matter-of-factness she now contemplated recent events. In fact, how pleased she was to discover that she remembered hardly any details . . .

"Elizabeth?"

The voice took her by surprise. She thought he'd left long ago. What was he staying for? Annoyed, she turned onto her back and with amazement saw his face still streaming with tears, of exhaustion or distress, or both.

"Please," he begged, "tell me the name."

But she kept silent and with pleasure watched his misery, as from now on she intended to draw her greatest sustenance from the misery and dependence of all men.

Eden Castle,
October 1851

DISAPPOINTED!

He'd not counted on that. Yet, there was the truth of it.

Seated in the Great Hall, with little Mary on his lap, Richard on one side, his aunt Jennifer on the other, John was forced out of the habit of honesty to look around him and admit that he was disappointed.

He felt momentarily sad. How could a life so long dreamt of result in disappointment? He shifted Mary on his lap and quietly rested his chin atop her head and tried not to hear the torturous sounds coming from the quartet grouped around the pianoforte.

The habitual Sunday-evening musicale. Herr Snyder's idea, to torture all the inhabitants of Eden Castle every Sunday from five o'clock until seven with the most wretched sounds this side of hell.

In an attempt to block the dissonance from his ear, he looked discreetly about in an effort to see if others were suffering as he was. His nearest co-sufferer, Richard, had solved the problem simply enough. He saw the boy slumped down in his chair, his black jacket flared out in front to accommodate a slim green volume. From that angle, John could not see the title, but whatever it was, it was captivating the boy completely.

And John knew, without looking, that to his left, his poor senseless aunt Jennifer was not suffering in any profound way. Indeed, out of all the miserable inhabitants of the castle, Jennifer alone seemed to enjoy the Sunday-evening musicales.

As the quartet attempted and failed a spirited allegro, John looked beyond Jennifer and her nurse to the rotund and dogmatic Herr Snyder, Teutonic to the marrow of his bones. Still John rather liked him because for the most part the man ignored him. He'd taken all of Herr Snyder's initial examinations and apparently had passed with flying colors. Relieved of the "classroom," John was simply given free run of the library. And in a way, he enjoyed his freedom to explore the rich shelves on his own, renewing his acquaintance with certain familiar authors, recalling his father's insistence that he "fully understand" such men as Rousseau and Diderot.

And he greatly enjoyed making new discoveries, delving for the first time into practical, hard-minded books such as *A History of the East India Company,* a catalog of incredibly wealthy men and how they achieved their riches, this particular book reawakening fond memories of the many times he'd prowled the London docks with his father, watching the arrival of the giant clipper ships from India laden with tea and spices, silks and the smell of money.

He still remembered how fascinated he had been by the white-turbaned, dark-skinned, dark-eyed men who had stared down on them from the high decks, arrogant-looking men who seemed in possession of secrets that it would behoove John to learn.

India! Even the name sounded magical. How many times, in a boyish pout, he had threatened to stow away and sail with the white-turbaned men.

Now again India was providing him with a rich escape from the stifling routine of Eden Castle. If only he'd thought to bring the book with him. If only he'd had Richard's foresight.

Now he looked past Richard to the scattering of upper-level servants who were pressed into service as an audience; there, Mr. Rexroat. And beyond Rexroat, Clara, the children's nursemaid. He liked Clara very much. Her good-hearted nature reminded him of the volunteers in his father's Ragged School.

Beyond Clara were a few favored and trusted maids, plain Peggy, Lady Harriet's favorite, and old Gertrude, the harridan who looked after his great-aunt Jane, who never left her fourth-floor apartment and who, at ninety, seemed bent on outliving Methuselah.

That was all in one direction, and with a slow turning of his head he looked to his right, to the two seated a distance apart from the others, his attention focusing first on his uncle, slouched, legs extended, his eyes puffed and bloodshot. It was common knowledge in the castle that his drinking habit had increased, and also it was common knowledge that the two guards whose shadowy presence in the far arch John could just barely discern had strict orders from Lady Eden to follow his lordship at all times. According to Clara, who loved to gossip, the two watchmen had been instructed not to interfere in any way with his lordship's various habits and desires, but neither were they ever to let him out of their sight except at night, when he was safely locked into his chambers. And at the first display of drunken violence, they were to fall upon him immediately and by whatever means necesary restrain him.

Now staring at the crumpled man, John felt a surge of pity for him. Had he always been thus, or was something destroying him? Of course, John remembered all too well that alarming first night in his chambers when his uncle in a drunken rage had attacked Lady Harriet. Curious, his sympathy that night had been with *her*.

Her! At last, as though some instinct had warned him to postpone this scrutiny for as long as possible, his eyes finally rested on her, and in bewilderment he contemplated that female who in rapid and mysterious succession could cause him to feel annoyance and peace, anger and calm, humiliation and pride, hate and love.

Suddenly he shivered and tried to look away, but couldn't. If only she would treat him with a degree of consistency. On occasion, during walks along the headlands with the children, he'd found himself totally captivated by her warmth and beauty, her generosity of spirit, the expression of love which, without warning, would cover her face when she looked at him. And at other times, how painfully he'd endured her coldness and caprice, greeting her warmly, only to be slapped down with a command as frigid as though he were still an odd-boy.

Abruptly he closed his eyes and again rested his cheek atop Mary's silken head. And how, he wondered, would she appear before him tonight for their habitual visit to the fourth-floor wing to see Aunt Jane, another ritual as unbending as all the others, though this one was slightly more depressing, to witness firsthand the ravages of age.

With his eyes still closed, he allowed his mind and a portion of his heart to return to that other life. *Elizabeth.* How he missed her, that cheerful and predictable little sparrow who had raised him. He should have written to her months ago, simply to inquire as to her well-being. Perhaps after Christmas he would journey to London for the purpose of a visit.

Oh, God, would it never end, that cacophony coming from around the pianoforte? In the next instant he saw the bows go limp over the instruments, heard the blessed peace of silence, followed by a light scattering of applause.

Again he looked toward Lady Harriet and saw her in a close huddle with the old maid, Gertrude, Aunt Jennifer's keeper. Apparently arrangements were being made for the next step in the routine. Still looking in that direction, he saw his uncle leave the Great Hall, his step rapid, as though he could scarcely wait to reach the sideboard in the small library, where, amidst the decanters of brandy and claret he would start his evening's journey into oblivion.

John looked up now to see Clara standing before him. "I'll take her, sir." She smiled, indicating the still-napping Mary.

He nodded, only too happy to relinquish the small deadweight. "I'm afraid her musical appreciation is sadly lacking."

As the little girl settled, without losing a wink, into Clara's ample arms, the large woman leaned close with a whispered confidence. "Hers, as well as mine, sir."

John laughed and tried to stretch the tightness out of his arms and legs where Mary had been sleeping. Spying Richard, still seated, his nose in the book, he said, peeping his voice down, "He's solved the problem right enough."

"Not for long, he hasn't," Clara muttered. John looked up and followed the direction of her gaze to Lady Harriet, who had just dispatched Gertrude and who had now turned her attention on her errant son.

As she drew near, John thought again how beautiful she was, a grace and dignity to her bearing that he'd never seen before in any female.

Now she stopped a few feet away, not looking at anyone but her son. "Richard, I'm ashamed," she said, her voice bereft, as though the boy had inflicted a wound upon her. "These people rehearse long hours and travel a great distance, all the way from Exeter for our benefit and enjoyment. How must they feel to look out and see you reading a book? How hurt they must be."

So effective was her performance that for a moment even John felt sorry for the musicians.

"But I did not ask them to come, and they play abominably. I thought it best to pass the time in a constructive way," Richard replied, his voice strong.

She seemed to think on this for a moment, as though she knew she was engaged in a delicate battle of wills. "I respect your intent," she said, "but do not approve of your lack of consideration of others. I think it best if you pass the remainder of the evening in your chambers. And perhaps you'll be able to better think on the lesson without the distraction of supper."

Doubly clever, John thought, looking admiringly down on the boy, whose face now bore the look of one who had set a goal for himself and had achieved it. He'd just been excused from the tedious visit to Jane's fourth-floor chamber, which was undoubtedly what he wanted all along.

As the boy rose, apparently eager to see his punishment through, Harriet moved a step closer. Clearly the edict was hurting her more than it was him. "May I ask," she began, "the nature of the book which has led you to such unhappy circumstances?"

Only too willing to oblige, Richard held up the thin volume, one finger still inserted at the page where he'd left off. "Pascal, Mama," he said with suspect calm. *"Justice and the Reason of Effects."*

Then he was moving, apparently unaware of the faces, one in particular that gaped after him.

Clara was there apologizing. "He meant nothing by it, my lady," she murmured.

But there was no need for apology. "Oh, I'm aware of that." Harriet smiled, looking after her son with adoring eyes. "Pascal," she marveled softly. "What a glorious future he has ahead of him."

As soon as Richard had disappeared, she stirred herself out of her reflection and looked sternly about, as though having momentarily lost her direction. "Well, then," she said, her eye falling first on John, then moving down to Jennifer who still sat motionless in her chair.

"She's getting worse," Harriet murmured.

"Oh, I think not, my lady," Clara again soothed. "The music always has a strange effect on her. She's like a child, is all, and must be watched."

Harriet nodded. "Come along," she ordered. "I've sent Gertrude ahead. We'll take tea with Jane."

John cast a departing look toward Clara, then fell in behind the rapidly moving Harriet, clad in dark blue taffeta, amazed at how much taller he was than she. He couldn't remember such a difference in their heights only a few short months ago.

Once on the broad staircase, the traffic thinned. Ahead, Jennifer slowed her pace, which meant that they had to follow suit as well. In the ease of the reduced speed, he became aware of Harriet relaxing a bit. "Do you think I was too hard on Richard?" she asked suddenly.

John smiled. "You probably were harder on yourself." She looked quizzically at him.

"On those infrequent occasions," he went on, enjoying the ease with which they were walking and talking, "when my father felt it his duty to punish me, I'm certain that I didn't feel half the pain that he did."

He could feel her eyes on the side of his face, and was aware for the first time of her delicately flowered scent; it seemed to emanate from her hair. "And did he punish you often?" she asked.

He shook his head, amused at the remembrance of his father trying to act paternal. "No, although Elizabeth had a go at it many times."

Ahead, he heard soft humming, Jennifer trying to prolong the mood of the music. Apparently Harriet heard it as well, and now her thoughts turned in a different direction. "Do you share Richard's critical opinion of our Sunday-evening musicales?" she asked, stopping for a moment, as Jennifer had bent to examine something on the stairs.

Prudently he paused before answering. "Yes," he said truthfully, then added quickly, "I'm not a connoisseur, however. In the Ragged School, our exposure to music consisted of a polka every Thursday night."

She leaned back against the banister, apparently more than willing to give the women up ahead all the time they needed. "I've asked you two questions within the last five minutes"—she smiled—"and you've answered both with references to the past."

Surprised, he looked down on her. It was true, though he couldn't account for it.

"Do you miss London and all your friends?" she asked.

"No," he said. "And I have no friends there. My father did, lots of them. But they were his friends, not mine."

"Have you written to Elizabeth?"

"No," John replied, "and I should have. And will soon."

She nodded, and both walked in silence, heads down. How pleasant it was, he thought, and why couldn't they do it more often?

"Are you happy here, John?" she asked.

Again he counseled himself prudence. "It was a difficult beginning," he said, "and on occasion I find myself wanting . . ."

He hesitated, and she rushed in with unexpected urgency. "What?"

With effort he tried to catalog precisely what was in his head. "More leisure, I suppose," he said, aware how vague it sounded.

"More leisure? For what purpose?"

He smiled down on her. "To talk, as we are talking now."

All of her defenses seemed to dissolve. He saw a becoming blush on her face. "We talk," she said.

"Not very often."

They were beyond the third-floor landing now. The fixed lamps were few and far between, thus the passage was darker, requiring greater care. Ahead, Jennifer and Peggy seemed to be faring well. As for himself, he felt the gloom increasing, seeming to herald the dismal chambers they shortly would be entering. No one but Jane inhabited the fourth floor.

About midway up the last flight of stairs, Jennifer suddenly balked and sat on the steps, her face clearly flushed with the exertion of the climb. "Come, Edward." She smiled, extending a hand to John. "Sit beside me while I catch my breath. Daniel will wait."

Obviously the trance brought on by the music was over and she was back among her ghosts again. John glanced quickly at Harriet. She nodded, giving him permission to respond as his father. He wished she had said no.

He moved up the steps until he was seated beside Jennifer. "Only a short distance farther. Do you know where we're going?"

She looked at him and smiled. "Of course I know where we're going, Edward. Why do you insist upon treating me like a child?" Leaning still closer, she reached up and stroked his brow. "How handsome you are, Edward," she whispered. "And how much I love you."

Embarrassed, with the maid and Harriet closely watching, John ducked his head. "Come," he said sternly. "Surely you've caught your breath by now. Aunt Jane will be very disappointed if we don't appear soon."

As he reached for her hand, she pulled away and scrambled to the far side of the staircase. "I don't want to go," she whispered, "and you shouldn't either."

"Why?" he asked. "We come here every Sunday evening."

"But not tonight," she warned.

John tried reason and gentleness. "Do you have any idea how hurt old Jane will be?" He smiled. "You don't want to hurt her, I know . . ."

Suddenly she turned her face to the wall, though still she was pleading. "Don't go, Edward. Daniel said don't go."

Behind him he heard Harriet.

"She *is* worse."

John asked, "What shall we do?"

"I don't think we have much choice. We'll have to leave her. Perhaps when she sees us walking away, she'll come."

Now Harriet climbed to the landing and spoke softly to Peggy. "Stay with her until she's ready to leave. She'll be restless tonight. At the first opportunity, please notify Mrs. Swan."

Still standing at mid-step, John looked down at the trembling figure in white. She did appear genuinely frightened. But of what? They had made this walk every Sunday for the last several months.

"Are you coming, John?" It was Harriet calling to him from the top of the stairs.

"I'm coming," he called up, and bent over to touch Jennifer's shoulder. "You wait here, then," he soothed. "I'll be back shortly, and if you like, we'll go looking for Daniel."

Suddenly from down the corridor in the direction of Jane's chamber came a sharp scream. Harriet looked up, and John as well.

Then John was moving, taking the remaining steps two at a time, not waiting to see who was following. As he approached the closed door which led to Jane's apartment, he hesitated, and in that instant Harriet caught up with him, took the lead and flung open the door, both reaching the arch which led into the bedchamber simultaneously. Looking sharply down, they focused on the bed itself. Gertrude, the old maid, was standing at the bedside, her attention fixed on the bed, on Jane, motionless, her mouth and eyes locked in a frozen death mask.

"Oh, no," Harriet mourned softly, and turned away.

From the bedside came weeping, Gertrude doing her best to explain. "When I come in, my lady, she was right enough. I even plumped her pillow for her and said company was a-coming."

John listened, feeling awkward in the presence of death, and thought of Jennifer's warning. He went to

Harriet's side. "What may I do to be of service?" he asked kindly. "Would you care for me to fetch——"

"No," she said, walking away from him, approaching the death bed. "Gertrude can do what has to be done."

The old maid's tears were subsiding. "Of course, my lady," she murmured, apparently grateful that blame would not be placed. She dabbed at her eyes a final time and reached gingerly for the coverlet to hide the dead face.

"No, leave it," Harriet commanded. "Go tell Aggie and Mrs. Swan what has happened. Tell them to come up in one hour to prepare her for burial. And tell Aggie to summon the gravediggers. There's a small plot between her father and brother . . ."

As Harriet issued orders, John retired to a far corner near the window. An hour, he thought grimly. What would they do for an hour in the presence of the dead woman? And worse. Now it occurred to him that there would be a funeral to endure. He'd not been to the graveyard since that rainy May morning when they'd buried his father. He felt no compulsion to go there now.

A few minutes later the room fell quiet behind him, and he turned to see Harriet on her knees at the bedside. Abruptly she looked up. Her eyes were dry. He watched closely as she raised herself from her kneeling position and with tenderness lifted Jane's arms and crossed them upon her breasts. Her hand lingered a moment, caressing the dead woman's forehead. "I don't know why I feel so bereft," she murmured. "I've been expecting it for months, years even."

Without warning a smile crossed her face. "I don't know what I would have done without her in those bleak, early days of my life here."

Stirred to interest, he stepped away from the window. "Were they so bleak?"

The smile faded. "Just death," she said, "or a form of it."

"Why?"

She looked at him as though taken aback by the direct question. For a moment he thought she would answer.

"Harriet," he began, moving directly beside her, "there's no cause for us to stay here now. Why don't we——"

But she said, "No," said it harshly this time. Then in the next minute she assumed a manner which suggested that he was nothing more than a servant. "You go along," she ordered. "Death never holds much meaning for the young. What a tedious bore it all is when you're young."

He was on the verge of disagreeing, but she gave him no chance. "Go along with you," she said again. "I had thought that you might appreciate feeling closer to the family——"

"I do," he broke in hurriedly, annoyed that somehow he had failed her. Did she treat her own children thus, or merely him?

From the opposite side of the chamber, safe in shadow, she spoke again, not one tone of her voice resembling that other woman who had climbed the stairs with him. "Did you hear what I said?" she asked. "I told you to leave. I don't want you here. Just leave me alone."

Yes, leave, was what he counseled himself, and was in the process of doing so, casting a final look at the old woman dead on the bed.

Then, "I'm sorry," he heard Harriet whisper.

Embarrassed, he shrugged off her apology. "No need," he muttered. "But what you said is not true," he added. "I know about death. I was there when my father was killed. I held his head in my lap . . ."

Apparently he'd succeeded in moving both of them, for quickly she stepped forward and put her arms around him. "Don't, John, please . . ." she whispered.

Locked in that soft fragrant embrace, his father's death faded in importance and he closed his eyes and slipped his arm around her waist.

Apparently the enjoyment was mutual, for it was several moments before she separated herself from him.

He watched, fascinated, as she restored the handkerchief to her sleeve, all traces of her previous anger gone, her attention now focused self-consciously on the lace of her cuff. "We mustn't quarrel so often," she said quietly. "I have to stay here for a decent interval," she explained then, harking back to the cause of their harsh words. "I was brought up to believe that it's wrong to leave the deceased alone."

"Why?" he asked.

She smiled as though aware that what she was about to say was foolishness. "Satan may come for them if they're alone."

"And he won't come with company present?"

She blushed. "Satan has no power in the presence of love."

He stared at her, thoroughly enjoying her new mood. "Do you believe all that?" he asked.

She shook her head. "No, but all my old servants did, all Shropshire-born and full of Celtic madness."

"And what else did they tell you?"

"Oh, hundreds of tales." She laughed, lifting her head to the ceiling as though that was the source of her memory. What a graceful arch her neck made, like a swan's and how prettily her auburn hair pressed against the lace collar of her gown. "Let me see," she went on, "someone who loved the deceased must kiss the coins that weight the eyes, thus assuring the dead person that when the eyes open, the first glimpse will be of paradise."

"Will you kiss the coins?"

She lowered her head. "Of course. I loved Jane dearly. She was a fortress when I was in sore need of one." Again he heard that warm tone of intimacy, as though she were on the verge of sharing important secrets with him.

With the thought in mind of encouraging this impulse, he stepped closer until he was standing directly beside her. Simultaneously she moved toward the bed and the dead woman. "Thank you for staying with me," she said briskly, "and I'm grateful for the privacy of this moment. I've been wanting to talk with you."

"About what?" he inquired, not really caring as long as there was a remote possibility that at some point, under certain stress, she would put her arms around him again.

"I've received several letters of late from Morley Johnson," she began.

Lost in her beauty, he at first found little meaning in her words. Then he remembered, and with a sigh sat in a near chair. Perhaps the solicitor had managed to uncover something.

As he waited for her to continue, he prompted softly, "And?"

She shook her head. "And nothing, I'm afraid."

It was as he'd thought. Then why had she brought it up? "I suspect"—he smiled—"that Mr. Johnson is simply having a prolonged holiday for himself and spending Eden money in the process."

"It does seem to be taking him ever so long," she said. "He hasn't even mentioned stopping by Hadley Park yet. I'm almost as interested in that report as the other."

"Your home?" he asked, recognizing the name from earlier conversations.

"My childhood home, yes. Naturally I'm curious to learn what my uncle is doing with it. It was such a beautiful estate once." She looked at him. "I would like for you to see it sometime."

A pleasant invitation, a pleasant thought, traveling with her in the seclusion of a carriage. "Then call Mr. Johnson back"—he grinned—"and we'll go and do our own inspecting."

Apparently something he had said or the manner in which he had said it caught her interest, for she sat in the chair next to him, a light reprimand on her face. "You don't take any of it very seriously, do you?" she asked. "Have you no curiosity about your natural mother?"

He answered honestly, "None," then abridged his reply. "Oh, once I did. When I was very young. I quizzed my father constantly on who she was and where she was."

The interest on her face was intense, "And what did he say?"

John shrugged. "That she was beautiful, that she was a lady, that he had loved her very much, and that she had died giving me birth."

"And that was all?"

"That was all." He looked back at her. "What does it matter?" he demanded. "Do you still doubt my identity?" He pushed his hands deep into his pockets and walked to the center of the room. "There are people in this castle who address me by my father's name. Isn't that proof enough? And if Morley Johnson finds nothing, what will happen then? Will I be sent back to the odd-boy cellar?"

Quickly she stood. "No, never," she said. "I promise you that. It's just that I'm thinking of your future. Beyond Eden."

Beyond Eden! Now, there was a puzzle. All his life the only future which had held any meaning for him was Eden. Now that he was here, he found he could not think in terms of another future. "I don't understand," he said, aware of her hand on his arm.

"You're strong and capable," she said. "The entire world would open to you, if only we could . . ."

"Identify my mother," he said, completing the foolish statement for her.

But she only nodded, obviously unaware of her foolishness. "Whether you like it or not, John, you are a member of a society to whom parentage is very important."

He couldn't quite believe this turn of the conversation. Now he moved away from her hand. "Parentage never seemed to matter much to my father," he said over his shoulder.

"Oh, but you're wrong," she disagreed, following after him. "Edward's bastardy mattered a great deal to him. He suffered acutely because of it. But even there he was more fortunate than you. At least he knew—"

"And what of my future?" he asked, sensing that she was arguing him into a corner. "You brought the subject up. What do you envision for me?"

She shrugged. "A . . . profession. You're capable . . ."

"What kind of profession?"

"Anything you want. Anything that—"

"My father had none."

"He had his Ragged Schools, his social reform—"

John laughed aloud. "All those institutions as well as the dedication belonged to Daniel Spade. My father merely provided the funds." He broke off and stared at her. What was she trying to tell him? That parentage or no, his time here was limited?

Now he wanted to put an end to the conversation.

"Then I suggest we wait for word from Morley Johnson," he concluded, "for everything."

Still she was watching him, her eyes blank, as though her mind had momentarily abandoned her.

"Come." He smiled, trying to ease this new tension. "We must keep a close watch out for Satan. As you said, we owe old Jane that much."

She agreed, as though she too were eager to postpone a final decision. Just as she was settling beside him, there was a soft knock on the door, and a moment later Gertrude and Aggie appeared, their arms filled with the paraphernalia of death, a thick, multi-folded piece of muslin, clearly a winding sheet, an earthenware decanter exuding the heavy fragrance of oil of clove.

Now all three women gathered about the bed. John leaned forward in his chair, legs apart, and rested his elbow on his knees. Birth and death, the two truly great female rituals. He held still, wondering if he should leave.

When he heard Aggie announce, full-voiced, "Well, then, to work," and when he looked up to see her bodily lift Jane and prepare to strip the nightdress over that gray shriveled face, John decided that he'd seen enough, and he'd just cleared the arch when he heard Harriet calling after him. "Wait, John . . ."

Slowly he retraced his steps as far as the arch, where he halted, his eyes fixed on the grim deathbed ritual.

In the interim, Gertrude was speaking again. "My lady, Mr. Rexroat and the stewards are waiting outside," she said, keeping her voice down, as though fearful of disturbing the now naked cadaver cradled in Aggie's arms. "They want to know if they should raise the black banners."

He heard Harriet's whispered "Yes," and though he was aware of female voices forming a soft hum to one side, all of his attention was drawn forward by the sight of the ninety-year-old female corpse, her skin wrinkled into reptilianlike folds, the whole horrible specter taking on a gray pallor, and over all, a nauseating odor.

Stunned by the ugliness, he felt the need to turn away. But Harriet was there again, backoning him to come closer. When apparently she saw his hesitation and its cause, her face softened. "Merely the ravages of years, John."

The Aggie was there, her voice steady in spite of the rigorous scrubbing she was now giving to a dead leg. "He ain't probably never seen a naked female before, my lady, let alone a dead one."

Still he waited in silence, struggling to digest his feelings of embarrassment and horror.

"Have you, John?" Harriet asked.

He shook his head.

Aggie snickered. Harriet stepped closer. He was aware of her hand extended to him, something in it, urging him to take it. "Do her one last favor," she suggested softly. "She was very fond of your father and served him well when he needed defense."

At last he looked down and saw in her hand two heavy gold coins. "Kiss them"—she smiled—"and place them on her eyes. Surely your kiss will assure her of paradise."

Feeling foolish, but interested in satisfying her and fleeing the room, he took the coins from her hand, pressed each in turn to his lips, then laid them carefully on the still-wide-staring eyes.

"Oh, she's stiffening fast," Aggie muttered. "You all best clear now so I can get on with what I have to do."

Never had John received a command so eagerly. With the placement of the last coin, he'd made contact with the cold flesh. Now, after only a few broad strides, he found himself out in the corridor, where the number of servants had increased as news of the death had spread, all apparently drawn to the grim room, he alone trying to escape from it. As he pushed his way through the gaping faces, the servants stepped back, and as the traffic decreased near the end of the corridor, he looked eagerly toward the steps.

It occurred to him that the schedule for the evening would undoubtedly be canceled. Would there even be dinner? In spite of his queasiness at the sight of death, he felt hungry, and remembering the bowl of dried fruit in his chambers and the appealing thought of a closed door and an interval of privacy, he increased his speed, moving through the shadowy corridors, still struggling with the image of the dead woman and Harriet's insistence that he "come closer."

He would never understand her, he decided wearily, and didn't want to think about her anymore. Yet he did, and took her image with him all the way back to his chambers, where, closing the door, his eye fell on the enormous rosewood four-poster.

He was beginning to feel the old discomfort, a growing tension. Did it hurt her, he wondered, when a man entered a woman? He wouldn't want to hurt anyone, and how unfair the design if it brought pleasure to one and pain to the other.

Growing breathless from his thoughts, he approached the bed reverently, as though the image he'd projected there had become a reality. He clung to one of the posts, mortified by his ignorance and inexperience. He'd have to find out soon. He could not live much longer with the need. Nor could he go on pretending that the bedclothes were the dark-haired whore named Rosa.

Then what to do? Who could teach him, tell him what he needed to know? Who would reassure him that he was not a monster, but a mere man?

Harriet was never happier than when circumstances called for direct action. Given a crisis, she flourished.

She glanced toward the end of the corridor, hoping to catch a glimpse of John in the faltering state in which he'd left Jane's deathbed. But he was gone, clearly the young boy again, frightened by death, embarrassed by the naked body.

"My lady, you were saying?" It was Rexroat, dragging her attention back to the matter at hand.

"Yes," she murmured. Where had she left off? "Mourning banners are to be raised immediately," she commanded. "And have a messenger go down to Mortemouth. She may have friends there who would want to attend the service. And ask Herr Snyder to pen the obituary and instruct him to place a copy on my bureau for my inspection first thing in the morning."

"Very well, my lady," he said, bowing. "And when will services take place?"

Harriet thought a moment. She would have preferred the following day, but there was something indecent about too great a speed. "The day after tomorrow," she said at last. "That will give the coffinmakers time and the gravediggers as well. She will lie in state tonight and tomorrow. I want two guards posted around the clock at the door, and two stationed within the chamber. But no one who wants to see her is to be denied. Is that clear?"

"Perfectly, my lady."

"Then see to it. Aggie will inform you when she is ready. In the meantime, spread the word throughout the castle."

"I feel certain, my lady, that everyone has heard—"

"Lord Eden?"

Their eyes met in a moment of understanding. "No, my lady, but I don't believe he is in the castle."

Surprised, she looked up. "Where is he?"

"I believe I saw him passing through the gates, on foot, shortly after the musicale."

"Were the guards—"

"They were in attendance, my lady." He nodded firmly.

Good. What a burden he was becoming. Yet his course of self-destruction was clear.

"Well, then," she said finally, moving away from the distasteful subject. "See to everything."

He bobbed his head and backed away, a clear look of disapproval on his face. Well, let him snicker, she thought. Let them all snicker. It was her intention to tell the world of Jane's death, to inform them, between the lines, that in spite of the old woman's spotted and infamous past, the present Lady Eden had loved her dearly, had found in the strong-willed old woman an ally.

Renewed with purpose, she moved briskly down the corridor, one-half of her mind moving toward duty, and the other half reviewing recent events. She smiled at the passing stones beneath her feet. How brutal of her to have forced him into a close inspection of poor Jane. She'd never seen him so undone. He really was a boy. And how hostile he had been when she had mentioned his future. What precisely did he intend to do, live at Eden in useless luxury for the rest of his life? And his total lack of concern over his parentage, that too was a source of annoyance. And the mystery which loomed large over all—who *was* the mother? Who was the woman who obviously had offered Edward comfort and love only months after Harriet had rejected him?

For a moment the puzzle seemed to confound her anew, and suffering from a peculiar mix of envy and grief, she thought again on her own ancient secret.

Suddenly she drew herself sharply up. Though the corridor in all directions was empty, she thought she heard a sound coming from . . .

Careful, she warned herself, looking toward the end of the passage and his chambers. There still was a great deal that was dangerous about the young man. At times his resemblance to his father was almost more than she could bear.

There! She heard it again, a sound like . . .

Of course he was only a boy, and that fact must be kept constantly before her eyes.

Was it crying she heard? Moving slowly, she started toward his chamber door. A brief check. How would it hurt?

Thus resolved, she went the distance to his door and stopped, one hand upraised, ready to knock. Perhaps she shouldn't. But in spite of this last-minute warning, she knocked softly, and receiving no answer, pushed open the door and saw nothing at first in the large chamber, dimly lit by one lamp on the far table.

"John?" she whispered, spying now a figure stretched out, facedown on the bed. When still he didn't reply she thought he might be sleeping and thought how pleasant it would be to stare down at him, the exact replica of Edward.

Stealthily she moved across the room. "John?" she whispered again, drawing close enough to see that he wasn't sleeping at all. "Are you well?" she asked, longing to stroke back that single lock of fair hair which lay upon his brow.

"Not well." He smiled up at her.

Alarmed, she leaned closer, grateful for a legitimate

excuse to touch his brow. "You *are* warm. Perhaps I should summon the physician. It would only take—"

"No! I need no doctor." He broke off. "I'm sorry if I behaved badly upstairs," he muttered.

She disagreed. "I'm the one who should—"

"I've never seen anything so ugly in my life."

"Once," she began in an instructive manner, "Jane was quite a handsome woman. Did your father tell you about Jane Locke and William Pitch?"

"Of course."

"Everything?"

He looked at her as though not quite certain what she was driving at. "Everything," he repeated.

"Even that they were not . . . married?"

He smiled. "My father always said that it would have been disaster if they *had* been married," he said, revealing that he knew all.

Stirred to interest on Edward's thoughts on the matter, she leaned closer to the bed. "And what else did your father say?"

"On what given subject?" he asked. "To the best of my recollection, there was not a topic in the world on which my father, at one time or another, did not express a lengthy opinion." The smile faded. "You didn't know him very well, did you?"

Now it was her turn to smile, and she lowered her head, fearful that he might see more. "Not very well," she murmured to her clasped hands.

He seemed to sit up with greater interest, as though remembering something. He fluffed the pillow behind his back and relaxed into it. "As a matter of fact," he began, as though puzzled, "out of all the residents of Eden, my father told me less about you than anyone else."

With her eyes down, she repeated, "I didn't know him very well."

"Nor he you," John concurred. "I think he would have liked you very much."

She felt moved by this expression of approval.

"You don't love Uncle James, do you?"

Her first impulse was to reprimand him for his impudence. He had entered an area which was none of his concern. And yet how good it would be to confirm his statement, to no longer have to shoulder the unbearable weight of hate alone.

"Do you?" he prompted again, and before she had a chance to answer, he went on, clearly revealing vast areas of inexperience where matters of the heart were concerned. "I don't understand," he muttered, propping his knees up, his hands, Edward's hands resting lightly upon them. "How could old Jane and William Pitch enjoy such a scandalous though right love while you suffer from such a proper and wrong one?"

She stared at him and felt the need for a brief defense. "It isn't that it's so wrong . . ." she began, and never finished.

"Oh, isn't it?" he demanded. "I've seen enough to know that you don't love him, perhaps you have never loved him."

The mood, the new openness between them, their respective postures of relaxation, the flickering lamplight which offered both a shield of shadows, all these elements suddenly made it very easy for her to speak the truth. "No," she admitted quietly. "I feel no love for him. I never have."

The blunt admission seemed to take him off guard, as though he'd been expecting polite deception. "Then why did you marry him?"

She leaned back in the chair. "I had no choice."

"Nonsense! My father said we always have choices if we but know where to look for them."

"Yes," she conceded. "He said that to me as well."

"Then you *did* speak with him," he exclaimed.

"Of course I spoke with him." She laughed. "He was here during my engagement party . . . to James."

"And my father tried to talk you out of it, didn't he?"

Dear heaven, what were they doing? "Yes," she confirmed.

John nodded broadly. "Why didn't you listen to him?"

"Because he didn't know what he was talking about. Arrangements had been made," she concluded, "between my father and Lady Marianne that could not be—"

"What nonsense!" he exploded. "Arrangements! What

right had either of them to make arrangements for your life?"

For a moment it was Edward sitting on the bed scolding her. "It's the way things are done," she murmured.

"It's the way you permitted them to be done," he countered.

"No, I had no choice."

"I don't believe it."

"It's true."

She looked up and saw him looking at her, Edward looking at her. It was as though she'd been given a chance at life again.

"Have you ever truly loved a man?" The question was so softly spoken, so unexpected that again she had no choice but to answer truthfully. "Yes," she whispered. "Once."

"Who was he?"

"His identity is unimportant."

Apparently he agreed, for he did not press further in that direction. But there still was his abstract curiosity to be satisfied. "How did it make you feel?" he asked, leaning forward, "and how did you know that it was truly love?"

All the stagnant years which stretched between that moment and now faded. All the deception and loneliness, the lies and falseness disappeared as though they had never existed. "As though I couldn't quite draw enough breath," she mused, "as though my ears had suddenly gone deaf to all voices save one, my eyes blind to all faces save—"

"Did he touch you?" he asked, as though he were clinging to every word.

"Of course he touched me." She smiled, her embarrassment eased by his obvious inexperience.

"How?" he demanded.

"Really, John, I'm not certain . . ."

Suddenly he leaned forward and grasped her hand, his face as entreating as she'd ever seen it. "Please," he begged. "I know so little, and I don't know where to go to find out. My father told me a great deal, but in the area of . . . love, he was strangely reticent, or negligent." Again he held her hand and seemed to be trying to draw her closer. "But you could tell me," he said, simply. "How would it hurt?"

Her eyes had grown accustomed to the dim light, and she saw his face clearly, saw his urgency. "What do you . . . want to know?" she asked, a guarded concession.

"Everything!" he said, and at last drew her to the edge of the bed. "When this . . . gentleman touched you, how did he do it? Did you protest, or did you want to be touched?"

From some source deep within her came her reply. "There is no touch in heaven or on earth like the touch of a beloved."

He grinned, clearly pleased by her words. "Go on," he urged. "And when he kissed you, how did he do it?"

"With his lips." She smiled back at him. Still there was only the lightness of banter between them. She had no real objection to this curious classroom, though the lecture might be more safely delivered if she were not seated so close to him.

But as she started to rise, he tightened his grip on her hand. A bit surprised by his strength, she settled back again and vowed to leave at the first opportunity.

"Please go on," he begged.

"What was the question?" she asked, still puzzled by the silence.

"How did he kiss you?" he repeated. "Like this?" And without warning he leaned forward and brushed his closed lips lightly across her cheek.

She shook her head, amused by the feathery sensation, a child's kiss. He must have kissed the woman Elizabeth thus a thousand times.

"No," she said, the mood between them still clinical, still safely objective.

"Then how?"

Abruptly she laughed, a mixture of embarrassment and enjoyment. "I can't . . . just show you." She blushed.

"Then how am I to learn?" he asked, leaning back against the pillow, his face sunk into angles of dejection.

She watched him, still amused, though in a way feeling sorry for him. It had never occurred to her that the male of the species would need instruction in the art of manhood.

"Look at me," she urged softly, not at all certain what she was going to do when he did. And when apparently he refused, she edged closer to him and tenderly lifted his chin, forcing eye contact.

"One cannot simulate that deep affection," she began, "that on occasion develops and flowers between a man and a woman. And when it exists, truly exists, one needs no instruction in any aspect of lovemaking."

He was listening closely, his mood as somber as hers, his face stilled with attention. "Did you love him . . . in that way?" he asked.

She nodded, her hand now stroking his face, her fingertips on his lips, tracing the contours. He seemed scarcely to be breathing.

How would it hurt, Edward, to love your son?

"Oh, you are so like . . ." But she broke off, unable to finish.

How would it hurt not to be afraid of him, of the feelings which might arise between them?

"Harriet . . ." He too tried to speak, and failed.

How would it hurt to ease the loneliness of her existence in the warmth and youth of this boy?

"How . . . did he kiss you?" John whispered. "Please . . ."

She drew a deep breath. For a moment she relished the amazing tangle of human destinies that had robbed her of one man and sent her his duplicate.

How would it hurt? To whom were they responsible? For her there was only a weak and drunken husband. For him, a dead father and an unidentifiable mother.

In the last moment, she cast a searching eye over his face, receptive to any stray warning which she might find there. And finding nothing, she went the short distance to his lips, her eyes still open, and saw him meet her with admirable courage, neither faltering, not even at the initial contact, a smooth, cool, familial kiss, lips chastely closed.

She held it for less than five seconds, and was in the process of drawing back, when suddenly she felt his arms around her, no longer passive, no longer in need of instruction, and the last image she saw was Edward's face, his lips drawing closer.

Inside his embrace, she gave herself completely to his unexpected passion, a little amused that once she'd thought he'd needed instruction. He'd needed nothing except an invitation to act.

As the kiss continued, she felt his tongue probing deeper, meeting hers now, all her concentration focused on the dark moist interior of her mouth.

The thought that once she might have denied herself this affection was absurd. Behind her was a lifetime of denial. Now they both shared a secret, the realization that in each other was a harbor, a sheltering warmth when the demands of the world became too much for them. It occurred to her that unhappy people always had secrets. They were necessary for survival.

Finally, reluctantly she stopped it. The "instruction" of the kiss was over. Carefully, not wanting to cause offense, she separated herself from his arms and sat weakly on the edge of the bed, her lips still moist.

He did not object to the separation, as though he too knew they had moved too fast. She looked back at him, saw gratitude in his eyes, his hand still holding hers.

A very becoming smile broke the tension on his face. "Is that how he kissed you?"

She nodded, not certain whether or not she could manage words.

"Did he find you as beautiful as I do?"

But she could not keep her eyes away from him, and now as she looked up, she saw nothing boyish on his face. At the height of the kiss, a major portion of the boy had died, or been transformed. "Yes," she murmured in answer to his question. "He was the first—and last—to call me beautiful."

He shook his head as though unable to account for the blindness of the world. And in the next moment, when she felt him trying to draw her close again, she stood and regretfully withdrew her hand, not ashamed of what they had done, but simply feeling a need to move with greater caution.

Again he did not protest the separation. But as she was moving toward the foot of the bed, he summoned her attention. "Harriet?"

She looked back, still trying to quiet all those sensate points within her which had lain dormant for so long.

When he had her attention, he said a curious thing. "From now on," he began quietly, his knees arched, his arms resting easily upon them, "May we be . . . friends?"

She laughed. "We're friends now. We always have been."

"No," he disagreed. "Until tonight, I've had the feeling that you've not been certain who I am. One day you treat me like Richard, the next like a stranger, the next like a servant . . ."

"That's not true," she protested.

Suddenly he moved to the foot of the bed and stood before her, towering over her, both his hands holding her face, forcing her attention.

"It *is* true," he whispered, "and you know it."

She had no choice but to listen, to watch the fascinating way in which the lamplight caught on his features.

"But as I see it," he went on with confidence, "you have a son, and have no need of another. You have an army of servants, and I wouldn't be a very good one anyway."

At some point she had ceased taking an active interest in everything around her save his eyes, the strength of his hands holding her fast.

"But you have a profound need," he said tenderly, "for a friend, a companion, someone to walk with you and talk with you, someone to confide in, someone to soothe and comfort, and . . . protect you."

What an appealing prescription! Never in her entire life had she known the luxury of such a friend. "Very well"—she smiled—"though what if I become too dependent upon you?"

"It is not possible."

"What if one day you come to me and say, Harriet, I want to go out into the world?"

"My world is here, all that interests me."

"What if Elizabeth summons you?"

"Elizabeth has no cause to summon me. That part of my life is finished."

"What if I look up one day in need, and you're gone?"

"I won't be."

"What if . . . you fall in love with a young woman?"

"I *am* in love."

The simple declaration moved her, the earnest conviction in his eyes. With what ease she stepped into his arms, no passion now, but rather a simple and tenanted shelter, his hands lightly pressing her head to his chest, as though trying to demonstrate that he could be all things to her.

She closed her eyes, a little amazed at the realization that for the first time in years she had nothing to be afraid of, nothing to dread. What kindly providence had sent her this glorious gift, this reprieve from the tomb? How easily they had kissed, how effortlessly they had talked and touched, how simply they stood in a light embrace. No matter the womb from which he had slipped. He was hers now.

She lifted her lips and lightly kissed him. She mustn't stay any longer. And besides, there was no cause for haste. They had a lifetime before them.

Without a word she stepped away from his embrace and walked the distance to the door, thinking on all that had transpired. A miracle, really. Whether it had been old Jane's death, the sudden shrinking of all viable companionship, the silent castle, the abandoned schedule, the prison door of routine thrown open, now, in the darkness of this night, she sensed a new dawn.

"I breakfast alone in my chambers at a quarter past eight every morning," she said to the closed door. "Will you join me tomorrow?"

She knew the richness of the invitation, the reprieve she was offering him, the chance to escape from the children's dining room, from the children's world. But when she heard no immediate response, she turned and looked at him across the chamber. *Edward.*

He was standing where she had left him, his face reflecting the meaning of the invitation. "I'd like that very much." He smiled, and she thought how courtly he looked, how generous time would be with him, and what fun it would be to train her own lover.

How shy they both had become. "Then I'll see you in the morning," she concluded, and waited a moment for his response. But there was none.

As she hurried down the corridor toward her own chambers, she smiled, then laughed outright as she realized that the only goal in her life now was to look as beautiful as possible for breakfast.

❧

Christmas Eve, 1851

NOT GENERALLY INCLINED to listen to gossip of any sort, Clara Jenkins stood at the second-floor window of the nursery and looked down at the inner courtyard, covered with a light scattering of snow. The wagon was just entering the gate. The two had been gone the better part of the afternoon.

Sweet Lord, how the servants' dining room had twittered at lunch, for that matter had twittered at every meal for the last few weeks, the opinions equally divided, half approving, half condemning, as though it were their duty both to approve and condemn.

As for herself, Clara had taken no part in any of the silly debates. In twenty years she'd risen from serving girl to head of the nursery by keeping her mouth closed and shunning all participation in kitchen gossip.

Still, something was afoot, and while she was ill-equipped to say what, there was part of the proof below in the back of the wagon, her ladyship seated in a position of abandonment upon the bare boards, practically buried in freshly cut boughs of fir and pine, two enormous Yule logs dragging the ground, her red velvet hood thrown back revealing her scandalously loosened hair—she wore it in that fashion constantly now—as though she were a girl of sixteen instead of . . .

Behind her, Clara heard Mary playing with building blocks, stacking three atop each other, then knocking them over with glee. Richard was still closeted with Herr Snyder, who'd insisted on lessons in spite of the holidays.

She looked again toward the courtyard, the two of them kneeling in the wagon now, John playfully brushing the snow from her hair. She could hear their laughter as the wagon drew to a stop, the horses obedient under the skillful hands of old Dana, who alone had been chosen to accompany them into the woods in search of greenery for the Yuletide celebration that evening. She saw stewards and watchmen running from all directions to assist with the enormous logs, her ladyship leaning close over John's face, brushing snow with her gloved hand.

Well, what was so wrong in what she saw? she wondered. Since . . . When *had* it started? With the death of old Miss Jane Locke—that was it, the very week when the entire castle had erupted into a kind of joyful confusion. Of course the funeral itself had been proper enough, a fitting send-off for the old woman. But then all traces of mourning had vanished.

If Clara lived to be one hundred, she'd never witness firsthand so vast a change in any human being as the change which had taken place these last few weeks in her ladyship. She did look younger, girllike almost, her laughter ringing through the cold air, her hands reaching out for John, who moments before had jumped to ground and was just now offering her his support.

As he grasped her waist and swung her to earth, Clara felt a blush on her cheeks. How close he'd held her for just a moment.

This, then, was the source of the gossip coming from all parts of the servants' hall, this "intimacy" as Gertrude had called it, springing up between her ladyship and the young man. Of course they were intimate, Clara thought, still defending what she saw. Why shouldn't they be? Was there something in the world which prohibited aunts and nephews from being intimate? Her ladyship was naturally warmhearted. The young man was obviously a pleasant diversion from the tragic dissipation of Lord Eden, who scarcely left his chambers.

There! Look! How proudly they stood beside the two massive logs, supported upright by six stewards. And how long had it been since Eden had enjoyed the ritual of lighting a Yule log?

"Come, Mary. Look!" she urged, beckoning for the child to share the pleasing spectacle with her.

The little girl did not need a second invitation. Within the instant she abandoned her blocks and ran to the window, where Clara swung her up into her arms and pointed downward. "Look! Your mama and John. Look what they have brought you."

A high-pitched squeal left the child's lips. Whether it was excitement over the Yule logs or recognition of the two she loved so dearly, Clara had no idea. Then she was struggling for her freedom, clearly wanting to run to the courtyard herself and be a part of the festivities instead of merely looking down.

Clara saw her ladyship lift her eyes to the nursery window, as though she'd sensed her daughter's presence, and for a moment Clara stilled the struggling little girl with the suggestion, "Wave to your mother. Look! She's waving to you."

"Mama!" Mary called out through the glass, delighted that they were looking at her.

A change here as well, Clara thought, studying the rosy-cheeked child, who seemed to have blossomed in the new relaxed atmosphere of the castle. She seemed to be laughing constantly, either atop John's shoulders, which were always available for rides, or simply clasped securely in his arms.

"Let me go," Mary was insisting, and below Clara saw her ladyship nod her approval. Hurriedly Clara fetched the child's warm cape from the wardrobe and swung it over the tiny shoulders. "Careful on the steps," she warned her, "and mind your mother."

Then she was gone, the sound of her running sending back soft echoes in the corridor.

Returning quickly to her position by the window, Clara again caught herself smiling. The scene below was even more chaotic, as several stablemen had heard the excitement and had now run to join the fun.

Certainly there was nothing furtive or secretive in their mutual ease and affection. Look at them now, leaning in on each other in some fresh spasm of amusement, laughing openly, the stewards laughing with them, nothing hidden, their happiness visible for all to see and share.

Then, below her on the steps Clara caught sight of Mary, taking the steps one at a time until at last John spied her and rushed to her aid and lifted her, squealing, high into the air over his head, while her ladyship looked on.

And the look on that face brought tears to Clara's eyes. Never had she seen such a look of pure joy, as though the sight of John and her daughter sharing such bliss was almost more than she could bear.

When, a moment later, John lowered Mary into one arm, and drew her ladyship close beneath the other, and the three of them watched as the stewards carried the Yule logs up the steps of the Great Hall, Clara closed her eyes and dismissed all the foolish gossip and prepared herself for the tidal waves of happiness which shortly would fill her nursery.

As she turned away from the window, she decided with a smile that she knew what the trouble was.

It was simply a matter of adjustment. This old castle was so accustomed to gloom and misery and tragedy that happiness seemed out of place here.

Well, the castle and the gossipers had better adjust themselves soon enough, for it was Clara's unschooled opinion that happiness had at last come to Eden to stay.

London,
February 1852

SHE WAS NOT a prostitute.

Prostitutes were disorderly, and there was nothing about Elizabeth's present existence which could be called disorderly.

Now awaiting her last client of the evening, she sat relaxed in her easy chair by the window and looked about at the new items of minor luxury with which she had provided herself out of her increased income; the two new brass lamps which softly reflected the light from the fire, the gilt-edged mirror just over the sideboard, the soft rose carpet beneath her feet, and the latest, the little fur cape draped prettily over the opposite chair, too attractive to hide in the wardrobe, the gift, only last evening, from Lord Kimbrough.

Again she looked about, pleased. How different it was from her early days in St. James Park, when she had accommodated gentlemen for a shilling and a crust of bread.

She viewed it as a service and was now bringing much more to the art and taking much more away from it. Undeniably she had acquired a polish during her years with Edward, a soft cultivation and concern for others which meant that she could talk with her gentlemen, hear their problems, all about their cold wives and suffocating homes, could lend them a most compassionate and sympathetic ear. And apparently that alone was a rich commodity, as rich as what she gave them in bed.

The handsome rosewood clock on the mantel, a gift from the banker Mr. Soames, chimed a quarter past nine. He was late, her last client, Mr. G., but then he generally was. Only returned from Naples that day, or so his note had informed her, hand-delivered by special messenger about noon. He'd mentioned his wife being ill. She was sorry to hear that, being as fond of the wife as she was of the master.

She reached beside her to the near table and poured a small glass of sherry. Generally she did not take spirits before a client. She owed them that much. But she knew from experience that Mr. G., for whom she was waiting, would not require her services in bed. At least he never had. It seemed to suit him well enough just to sit and talk, to "breathe the peace," or so he'd put it. With the government, Mr. G. was, and high up, too.

In fact, her entire clientele pleased her, for no other reason than that they were gentlemen and treated her with kindness and dignity. Slowly she tipped the sherry one way, then the other in the fragile crystal glass, the prisms catching the light from the fire and magnifying it through the sherry. In a way she felt pride in what she was doing. How did it differ from what Edward had done, or Daniel for that matter? In their Ragged Schools, they had offered shelter and food, and in many cases like herself, an education to the poor and abandoned children of London. In her establishment she too offered shelter and food, and in certain cases, education to the rich and abandoned men of London. As Edward himself had been abandoned. Surely he would understand that, his ghost would understand, as on occasion she was still aware of his presence in the small house.

Suddenly she sat up, feeling restless. In a way, she wished that Mr. G. *would* take her to bed. She was lonelier than usual tonight and eager to play her game, when with her eyes closed she'd coax the gentleman of the moment into a giving mood and would replace him with an image of Edward.

Of course, it didn't always work. The gentleman had to be fairly whole himself before she could steal a bit of pleasure for herself. But there had been moments of enjoyment, small assaults on that monumental need brought on by her unreciprocated love for Edward Eden.

She closed her eyes. Beyond the window, she listened closely for carriage wheels. Now, where was he? She leaned close to the window and drew back the curtain. The street outside was dark and shadowy save for one gas lamp directly across the way. She leaned closer, spying a familiar figure, not Mr. G., but rather Jack Willmot's whore's bully.

She gazed solemnly at the shadowy figure, thinking on that piece of unfinished business. Poor Jack. She received weekly letters from him in Canada, plain, blunt letters which spoke of unbearable cold and red savages, though he claimed that Mr. Brassey's Grand Railway was going well. And the bluntest of all, the habitual closing paragraph, begging her, in the name of Edward's memory, to turn away from her "present activities," and reconsider his proposal of marriage, which was still in force.

Marriage! The word still astounded her, almost as much as her initial astonishment at the man who had mentioned it. Marriage! Oh, yes, she could just envision Jack Willmot married to Edward Eden's "whore," left alone for the better part of every year while he tramped around the world building railroads, waiting for letters to arrive containing the pittance on which she would have to live, supporting a brood of children as well.

Still angry, she turned away from the window and the shadowy presence of the whore's bully. Of course she'd rejected his patronizing proposal, and shortly he'd gone off to Canada, heartbroken, or so he'd claimed. And the very next night, the watch had commenced, the presence of a man on the pavement across the way, each standing four-hour shifts as well as she could determine, a round-the-clock vigil.

Now she found herself hoping that the bullies sent detailed reports to Canada about how well the lady was faring, how the carriages seemed to be getting more elegant, and that one of her most regular clients was the great man whom Jack Willmot had sent to her in the first place for the purposes of "rescuing her," that noble statesman, sure to be prime minister one day, Mr. William Gladstone.

Then she heard it, the rattling approach of a carriage, and moved quickly to the window. A few minutes later she saw the carriage door open, caught her first glimpse of his top hat and heavy cape.

A handsome figure of a man he was, she thought as now she saw him speaking words of consideration to his coachman. For some reason, she thought of Edward, his devotion to his driver, old John Murrey. What a bond of affection those two men had shared, Edward even naming his son after the old man. *John Murrey Eden.* What a weight of loneliness and mystery there was there. Not a word from the boy since she'd deposited him at Eden last May, not a hint concerning his well-being.

Now, as the first gentle knock sounded at the door, she ran to it and flung it open.

"Willie," she whispered. "How I've missed you," and dragged him by the gloved hand into the warmth of her parlor, confident that in his loneliness she could find relief from her own.

"Elizabeth . . ." He smiled and opened his arms, and she stepped into them, a paternal embrace, nothing more, though she enjoyed his fragrance and the feel of his soft fur collar against her cheek.

Still, he seemed more than content merely to look at her. "The last time I saw you," he began, his voice low and resonant, a speaker's voice now denying its power, like the man himself, "I said to myself, you're safe, Willie. She cannot become more beautiful or warm or loving than she is now." He shook his head sadly in spite of his generous words. "How mistaken I was," he concluded.

She laughed and denied his words. "I'm the same as always, though I was worried about you, afraid you wouldn't come."

Some disapproving expression crossed his face, and he went on talking as he shook off the heavy cape and removed his hat as well, depositing both with easy familiarity in a near chair. "A ministerial crisis," he muttered. "It seems as though Lord Russell's Whig administration is on the verge of sinking."

"And you were called back to salvage it?" she asked, taking his gloves, feeling a flair of pride that so great a man now stood in her front parlor.

He laughed heartily, a good sound, one which she

rarely heard from those lips. "Either salvage it or sink it," he said at the end of the laugh. "But here, let's not talk of politics. I've had my fill of that for a while." He reached behind him into the folds of the cape and withdrew a thick brown package and thrust it at her. "For you, dearest, from Florence, for your kindness in receiving me tonight and for all your comfort in the past."

"It wasn't necessary, Willie," she murmured. "I'm always pleased to—"

"I know, I know," he said, dismissing her sentiment. "Open it. It will give me pleasure."

She took the package and carried it to the comfortable arrangement of sofa and chairs near the window. "Help yourself," she invited, gesturing toward the sherry. His favorite.

As he poured himself a glass from the decanter, she sat in the chair, the package in her lap, and released the narrow gold cord and drew back the paper. It was a bolt of lace, pristine white, delicate petit point, exquisite. "Oh, Willie, how beautiful."

"Delivered with an ulterior motive." He smiled, settling in the chair opposite her. "I'll send London's finest dressmaker around to you tomorrow with strict instructions that she is to make you the most elegant gown in all of London. Then, when it is done, you must wear it only for me. Agreed?"

She nodded and took loving note of the man opposite her, tall, slim, his hair still thick and only slightly graying at the temples, his jaws adorned in the stylish bewhiskered fashion of the day. And the most remarkable feature of all, his eyes, so dark with a piercing gaze which he was now leveling at her with such intensity that she blushed.

"I have no need of dressmakers, Willie," she said, "not even London's finest. I'll make the gown myself and wear it only for you."

She leaned forward with the intention of taking his hand, a harmless gesture which he'd permitted in the past. But at that moment he reached for the sherry, refilled his glass and leaned back again in a conscious effort to lighten the mood. "And tell me of yourself, dearest," he said. "While the rest of the world serves out its sentence of suffering, you seem to go serenely on."

Go serenely on! Was that the impression she gave? Then she was more successful than she'd ever dreamt. She thought then that she might speak of herself. But she changed her mind. Gentlemen did not come here to listen to her speak of herself. "Tell me of Naples," she asked, ignoring his invitation to speak, sincerely enjoying his tales of the world. "And everything you saw between here and there. How limited England seems when compared with—"

He smiled as though he were a father indulging a pretty child. "Not limited, dearest. Never think that. Because it's familiar does not make it less. We are blessed to live in what may be the richest paradise on earth."

He sipped again at the sherry and looked about at the warm cozy room, his mind apparently running on two tracks at once. "How peaceful it is here," he murmured appreciatively, "how simple."

She smiled. To a man, all of her clients seemed to appreciate the simplicity and peace of her house.

Then he was back on track, his voice lifting. "You asked of Naples," he said harshly, looking at her as though she'd committed a minor offense.

"I've seen paintings," she said. "It appears so beautiful."

"God made it beautiful," he said. "Men are in the process of making it ugly."

It all no doubt came from his heart, but she knew him well enough to know that he was addicted to theatrical methods. So she merely settled back again, ready for a theatrical.

"What I saw of Naples," he went on, "you'll not find in paintings or picture books. Appalling." Again he shook his head. "With what false largess did King Ferdinand establish a constitution, and what a mockery of the word it is."

She was listening carefully, eager, as always, to learn as much as possible about the world beyond England. Therefore it was a few seconds later before she realized he'd stopped speaking, his eyes gazing intently at her.

"Elizabeth," he whispered, "would you . . . be so kind as to . . ."

It was only when she heard his changed voice that she remembered how remiss she'd been.

"Of course, Willie." She smiled. "I'm afraid I quite forgot. You should have spoken sooner."

But there was no response, and he sat absolutely motionless and watched intently as her hand moved down the front of her dressing gown. At last she drew the fabric to one side, revealing one bared breast.

As she tucked the material in on itself, she looked down. She'd taken great care with her toilet, knowing that the sight of her breasts brought him pleasure. She'd lightly dusted her flesh with powder, giving her skin a patina of white marble. Only one. That was how he preferred it at first.

"Now," she went on, feeling perfectly at ease, "you were speaking of Naples," knowing that he preferred to resume the conversation as though nothing at all out of the ordinary had occurred.

For a moment he didn't speak. He seemed incapable of lifting his vision beyond that one bared breast. She thought sadly, what a polite yet barbaric ravishment.

"Dear Willie, do go on," she urged.

After several moments he did, the words sounding as though they had been forged on the anvil of brutal self-discipline. "Naples," he began, his eyes never once lifting to her face, "is a sinking ship. Ferdinand promises liberty, but in practice he has arrested any and all who have tried to implement the constitution or have in any manner opposed his rule."

He spoke for several minutes. Then again, without warning, Naples was forgotten as softly he whispered, "Might I look upon . . . both?"

Again without a word she drew back the opposite side of her dressing gown, and decided to go a step further and unbuttoned the robe to the waist and gracefully shook herself free of the encumbrance, bared now from the waist up.

He sat braced in the chair, though now he seemed to wear a fixed expression. "Might I . . ." he began timidly.

"Might I . . . that is to say, would it be an offense if I were to . . . just a touch," he whispered.

The request was without precedent. Pleased, she sat still and watched, as though it were the most fascinating spectacle in the world, the shy progress of that one inquiring hand which moved like a wounded bird attempting flight, made the journey halfway, then seemed to falter, then found a source of new strength and landed at last with a feather touch of two fingers on the upper half of her left breast.

So engrossed was she in the subtle sensations that only now did she take note of his face, his eyes closed, mouth open, seated on the edge of his chair, in an attempt to shorten the extension of his arm.

She felt his fingers grow brave and brush across her nipple, only a passing touch, though within the instant they returned, his thumb now braced against the upper half of her breast, the finder fully exploring, back and forth.

There were limitations even to her female instincts, and a little amazed that this reluctant gentleman could have brought her to such a pitch, she reached one hand out. "Willie, please," she whispered. "Let me help you."

For just a moment they sat, connected in that distant manner. Then suddenly he stood with such force that the chair scraped backward. "No," he muttered, and took the distance to the far corner of the room in four strides and stopped near the wall.

She closed her eyes, feeling embarrassed. Glancing down, she caught a glimpse of her exposed breasts. How obscene they looked now, and hurriedly she drew the dressing gown up about her shoulders.

Nothing to do but wait. It would take him a while to recover. Carefully she poured herself a sip of sherry and turned and looked over her shoulder into the bedchamber, the lamp within casting a soft inviting glow over the coverlet. If her late-night visitor had been any one of her dozen or so other gentlemen, she would have been in that room now, healing, being healed.

She looked again at his bowed head. Feeling herself to be almost in control, she poured another glass of sherry and carried it to him, and saw, close at hand, the tears on his face.

"Oh, Willie," she whispered, moved by the sight. "I'm so . . . sorry," not certain what she was apologizing for, but feeling the need anyway.

Incredibly, he laughed, and reached for his handkerchief and commenced wiping his face. "What fools we are," he said, his voice muffled behind the barrier of white linen. "What a strange and humbling scene we've just played out," he concluded, refolding the handkerchief and placing it back into his pocket.

He spied the sherry in her hand. "Ah, balance," he exclaimed, and drained the glass in one swallow and placed it on the table before him. Then he turned the full weight of his eyes down on her, apparently restored except for his expression of sadness. "My dearest," he whispered. "Why do you endure me?"

It was an academic question, requiring no answer, and she gave none.

Then it came, as she knew it would, as it always did, the first soft reprimand. "I would be . . . remiss," he said, "if I failed to make inquiry about your soul."

She closed her eyes.

"I have promised my wife faithfully," he went on, "that I would try with all my might to turn you toward the Light, beg you to retrace this path of pain which you have set for yourself and join the others at the House of Charity."

At last she turned away. "I'm quite comfortable here, Willie," she said, unable to look at him.

He followed after her to the center of the room, his manner clinical. "May I ask," he began, "how many . . . are you seeing now?"

She looked up, mildly angry. "That's none of your concern."

"*You* are my concern," he said kindly. "The thought of men . . . abusing you . . ."

"They do not abuse me, Willie." She smiled, pushing aside the anger. "They are gentlemen all, like yourself."

Apparently the comparison registered. He bowed his head as though conceding her point, then commenced pulling on his gloves. Quickly he reached for his cape and swung it lightly over his shoulders. Then followed his top hat, and at last he stood before her fully garbed. Still he seemed to be mysteriously feeding on her face. "You must help me, Elizabeth," he said, "make me strong, prevent that final loss of all resolution and carry forward the little self-discipline I have."

She listened, not trusting herself to speak.

"All that I require," he went on, "is that you permit me to come here occasionally and enjoy your simple room, the beauty of your face and form, with soul intact. Is that asking too much?"

"You know it isn't, Willie."

"Well, then," he exclaimed, "I'll take my leave." At the door he stopped. She saw him place something on the table. "Next Thursday?" he asked, smiling back at her.

She nodded.

"And wear the lace for me. Would you do that? Please?"

Again she nodded.

He paused for a last long searching glance at her. Then he was gone, his boots sending back their echoes on the pavement.

She stood at the center of the room, enjoying the cold blast of wintry air which swept across the floor. She held still until she heard the carriage pull away from the pavement, the wheels rattling over the cobbles, diminishing at last as it turned the corner, heading toward the bridge and the respectable part of London.

She bowed her head, shivering, and hurried to close the door. She caught a fleeting glimpse of the whore's bully standing beneath the gas lamp. If only he knew how useless his watch was this night.

As she threw the bolt, she looked down on the table and saw a twenty-pound note. *Twenty pounds.* For what? Angered and confused, she left it on the table and moved hurriedly back into the room, where she extinguished the lamp and welcomed the semidarkness, the only light now coming from the bedchamber on her right.

Feeling weary, she made her way into the room, the need still great within her. She dreaded what she knew she would have to do in order to get through the night. This act alone made her feel unworthy. Such a self-enclosing ritual, giving nothing, sharing nothing. Still, with only fleeting regret and increasing loneliness she stripped off the dressing gown and drew forward the small trunk from the corner of the room, filled with Edward's possessions, his books and papers and clothes.

In sore need, she gathered an armful of his garments and pressed them to her and carried them to the bed, where with one hand she threw back the coverlet and slipped between the linens, burying her face in the shirts, a shuddering, empty embrace with unresponding fabric which nonetheless was capable of demeaning her, moving her, bringing her to fever pitch and ultimately lowering her indifferently into a semiconscious state which might, under certain limited circumstances, be called sleep.

❧

Shropshire, April 1852

WELL, IT HAD been his own Grand Tour, that's what it had been, a damn nuisance at times, and great sport at others.

Now, after nine months of rattling about the English countryside and most of Scotland as well, Morley Johnson was more than ready to return to London. In a curious way, he even missed dear Minnie and that smelly brood of children she'd thrust upon him.

He leaned back in the carriage, quite adept now at taking its bounces and rolls. One thing was certain. He was a changed man, more worldly, all of his rough edges polished, clearly capable of managing the vast Eden fortune. Yes, it had been a profitable nine months in that respect. He was indeed a man of the world.

Unfortunately in other respects it had been less profitable. He closed his eyes a moment to rest them from the burgeoning green Shropshire landscape beyond his window. Well, only this one last stop at Hadley Park, to perform watchdog duties for Lady Eden, then he'd give his new driver joyous orders to make for London.

Again he relaxed into the cushions, amazed at his own cleverness. He'd kept careful accounts throughout the entire journey, sending humble records back to Eden each month, accounting for every penny. Yet through skillful management, he was returning to London richer by close to four hundred pounds, a handsome start toward the purchase price of a new piece of Eden land.

On the seat beside him was a small hamper packed with a light repast. He reached for the lid and withdrew a round of good cheddar and a loaf of brown bread. Roughly he tore off a piece of each and commenced chewing contentedly, his eyes blinking rapidly as his mind turned in a thousand directions. What would he find at Hadley Park? What was he supposed to find? or even look for? And why had he not received any instructions or encouragement from Eden since Christmas?

Though his mouth was filled, he stopped chewing, baffled. In the first months of the journey, he'd received several dispatches from Lady Eden, urging him to ignore nothing, to pursue each clue concerning the identity of the boy's mother to its natural conclusion, "regardless of cost." Lovely words, those. He smiled and commenced chewing again.

He'd done precisely as he had been commanded to do, had pursued the first lead, months ago, to the Lakes, that wet chill area that had almost been the death of him, and he had located an old Beaker woman in Westmoreland named Mrs. Simpson who had recalled the "gentleman in question," had indeed cooked for him when he had been of a mind to eat, though mostly he "was content to drink his special elixir."

Opium. Morley had known that But to establish Edward Eden's use of opium had not been the point of the journey, and try as he would, Morley had been unable to unearth any female or even the remains of a female who might have consorted with Eden and borne him a child.

Then all that remained was this last foolish stop, though perhaps he'd better do the best he could to make up for his failure in the other matter.

He must make the Eden family, what was left of it, totally dependent upon him. Then when they were wholly vulnerable and least expecting it, he would thrust forward into their ripeness and make that monstrous wealth his own.

He sat up suddenly, amazed at how his dreams of wealth and power had set his sexual appetites whirling. He would have to find a woman tonight, one last fling before he confronted Minnie and the marital bed.

Dear God, what plainness there. Where would that boring woman fit into his grand scheme?

In an attempt to ease his sudden depression, he pulled up his cloak collar, shoved his hands into his pockets and focused, unseeing, on the horizon line a distance away.

The Mermaid Inn, Shropshire

USUALLY THERE WERE few sights in this life which brought Humphrey Hills as much pleasure as the rattling approach of a grand, road-dusty carriage, and the weary face of a gentleman with a rich purse and the inclination to spend it.

Now on this mild April evening, he looked out of the dining-room window of his flourishing public house, the Mermaid, and saw such a sight approaching slowly from the direction of Shrewsbury on the Wales Turnpike.

"Guests!" he shouted over his shoulder to the serving maids. "Step lively," he added, knowing they would, but feeling the need to shout it anyway.

Beyond the arch, he saw the beloved face of his

young clerk, Bobby. What a joy there! He softened his tone. "Guests, Bobby. See to them."

The young man nodded, his eyes reflecting and sending back Humphrey's love.

Pleased by this brief interlude, Humphrey leaned closer to the window for a better look, taking pride in his ability to place any carriage, any gentleman in his proper class.

Now, as the cumbersome conveyance rolled closer, he decided, regretfully, not titled. No coat of arms. Hired, most likely, out of London. And the driver appeared to be nothing more than a crude country boy.

Humphrey leaned closer, one hand massaging his bald head, his eyes a little blurry from too much brandy.

Another tradesman-turned-gentry, no doubt, a plain bastard who by some stroke of fate or fortune had acquired a pretty mountain of coin and now expected the world to fawn at his feet.

Well, he didn't like it and again he took up his customary position at his customary table, where he sat each night, drinking too much brandy and dwelling on the misery of his entire life.

Sadly he lifted his eyes to the handsome black iron gates across the road, the entrance to the grand estate known as Hadley Park. There, as he knew all too well, was the beginning of his grief-ridden life.

Quickly he averted his eyes long enough to pour another snifter of brandy. He sipped and realized with new regret that the grand world across the road had changed as well; Lord Powels dead, Lady Powels dead, Lady Harriet, who apparently had survived her crucible, as good as dead, at least to him. She'd disappeared shortly after her ordeal. Where, Humphrey had no idea, though he'd tried hard enough to find out. And with everyone dead or absent, the old uncle had moved in, a total recluse.

But it wasn't the uncle who occupied Humphrey's thoughts. As always, it was *her,* the missing Lady Harriet, and now he lifted his glass and wished her a plague of disasters, as acute as those which she had caused him to suffer.

With his eyes half-closed, Humphrey rested his head on the table, his mind still occupied with the graceless world in which he was forced to serve his penance as an innkeeper.

An innkeeper! He moaned audibly. Once he'd had such dreams. With his eyes closed and his brain beginning to melt under the effects of the brandy, he saw her again, Lady Harriet, that beautiful little girl from his childhood, riding her spirited pony to the very edge of the road and looking down upon him where he was cutting weeds.

He'd never seen such a vision. And how happy he'd been when she had come to the road the next day, and the next and the one after that, her loneliness as great as his own.

What harm had he done, what offense that warranted his father coming upon him in his cellar room, binding him to the bed, and with mindless anger delivering an untold number of lashes to his back with a horsewhip, all the time shouting down on him that he was to remember his place.

With his head down, he suffered a painful ringing in his ears, as though an invisible alarm had gone off, the mind of the fourteen-year-old boy still recoiling, trying its best and failing to protect itself against such pain.

And the next day, workers from the estate had commenced building the stone wall that still stood, the barrier which had separated him forever from his dream.

Beyond him in the entrance hall he heard voices, the familiar one of his clerk, Bobby, and another one, strident, demanding. Almost undone by old grief, he turned his head toward the distant, elegant Georgian lines of Hadley Park looming sideways in his vision, the entire rich yellow limestone estate bathed in the becoming pink light of dusk.

Suddenly his eyes fell on the fourth-floor window and he remembered the time, about sixteen years ago, that he'd kept a constant vigil on those attic windows.

Slowly he raised up, remembering clearly the grand scheme which, if only fate had been generous enough to let work, might have provided a very different conclusion to his miserable existence.

But no! As always fate had not shown the least inclination to generosity, and not only had the aborted plan cost him one thousand pounds, but he'd suffered new humiliation as well at the hands of one Mr. Edward Eden.

As the memories continued to march over him, he felt as battered as though he'd just been freshly assaulted. Was there to be no period in his entire life in which fate would say, "Now, Humphrey Hills, you may have it as you please. Set the pace, call the tune . . ."

Suddenly he raised up and shouted, "Bobby?"

A serving maid near the kitchen steps asked, "Shall I fetch him for you, Mr. Hills?"

"Is he still with the new guest?"

"Yes, sir. As far as I can see."

He heard the fear in her voice and fed on it. "More brandy," he shouted, gesturing toward the empty decanter. As again he heard a reassuring flurry of footsteps, he bent low over the table, trying to hear the distant conversation. Outside the window, he saw the boy driver just unloading the trunks from the top of the carriage, a handsome lad.

Without warning he felt his breath failing him. At the moment when he thought he could not endure any longer, he heard a voice, the one voice in the world capable of comforting him, and felt a hand on his shoulder. "Worse tonight, eh? Here's succor."

He looked up and saw a fresh decanter of brandy on the table, took note of the white, well-tended hand wrapped around cut glass, then looked slowly up into Bobby's face, with his bland, wide-set blue eyes, fair unruly hair, like an angel.

"Oh, God, Bobby," he moaned, shaking his head. "There are times when I don't think that I can survive."

"Of course you can," came the reply.

Then Humphrey felt the hand move with tenderness to his neck. "Now, more than ever," came the voice again. "You will survive. I shall see to it."

Humphrey closed his eyes in a spasm of enjoyment, the first respite he'd had in over an hour. Yet there were dragons even in that moment, his fearful realization that the serving girls were watching. "Careful," he whispered to Bobby.

Under the gentle chastisement the young man withdrew his hand and slid into the seat opposite him. Humphrey shouted at the still-gaping, stupid-faced girls, "Be about your business. Go on with you. Look in on the new guest. See to his needs."

"Sluts!" Humphrey muttered after they had disappeared, and looked up to see Bobby grinning.

Alone, Humphrey took a moment to feed on the face opposite him, a remarkable face combining the beauty of a woman in the features of a man.

"Oh, Bobby," he whispered, and looked away from the fair face and the awareness of the acts they performed each night between the linens of Humphrey's bed.

"My, how gloomy we are this evening." Bobby smiled, and for a moment Humphrey resented the glibness in his tone. Generally Bobby was sympathetic to a fault, had been from the beginning, when Humphrey had shared with him the whole dismal tale of his various misfortunes. And Bobby had shared a tale or two of his own, the son of a rich northern banker from Newcastle, well-educated, whose father had followed him one night to a male brothel, a "distasteful scene," as Bobby had put it, resulting in his expulsion from the family.

It had been the young man's intention to make his way south to London, where in that rich and varied world all things were possible. But instead he'd stopped for a night's lodgings at the Mermaid, and he'd stayed the night, the week, the year, and seven years later, there he sat.

Humphrey shook his head, feeling his own demons withdrawing under the balm of Bobby's closeness. "What an incredible pair we are," he mused sadly.

"Oh, not so incredible, Humphrey." Bobby smiled, lifting a small piece of folded paper from the pocket of his crimson satin waistcoat. "Just blessed," he concluded.

"Blessed!" Humphrey scoffed, refilling his own glass and pouring one for Bobby. "Under no circumstances would I assign that designation to either of us," and he lifted his glass and drank deeply, his eyes over the glass rim fixed on his beloved's face. "And the new guest?"

Humphrey demanded, his attitude businesslike, though again he sipped deep of the brandy.

"Go easy," Bobby cautioned gently.

There was a nagging to the voice which Humphrey enjoyed. How good it was that someone cared. "Oh, Bobby, sometimes I see absolutely no point to this earthly existence."

"The bitch again, is it?" Bobby asked curtly, his fingers tapping lightly on the folded piece of paper. "What would you do, Humphrey," he asked with suspect lightness, "if you were to learn of her whereabouts?"

"What would I do?" he repeated. "An academic question, dear Bobby," he said. "The lady is quite gone from my life."

"But not from your mind."

He shook his head. "No," he said, staring with glazed eyes at the small white square of paper. "She will haunt me all my life," he concluded simply.

Abruptly Bobby laughed. "You asked about the new guest, Humphrey, and did not give me a chance to reply. Do you still want to hear about him?"

"The new guest," Bobby entoned. "From London, he is," he began, "a solicitor, or so he says, here on business."

"Solicitors are always involved in business," Humphrey said. "They never rest. It's what makes them so—"

"But fascinating business, this," Bobby interrupted.

Humphrey looked up. "What exactly is the nature of your fascination with the man?" he asked.

"Oh, he's not my fascination, Humphrey"—Bobby smiled—"and his name is Morley Johnson." Again he lifted the piece of paper. "But he might be an object of some fascination . . . to you. Mr. Johnson is here on business for his client. According to Mr. Johnson, his client desires a complete report on the present state of . . . Hadley Park. Mr. Johnson's client is curious about her childhood home. She wishes to know about its physical condition and the disposition of several favored childhood servants, and she also wishes to know . . ."

At some point Humphrey had ceased hearing words. "I . . . don't . . . understand," he faltered.

At that, Bobby laughed "Of course you understand,

Humphrey. My God, man, wake up! I've just provided you with a road map to the demon-bitch who has damn near sucked your blood dry. And there's more."

He lifted the paper and read, his words precise, incredible. "His client, or so Mr. Johnson says, is Lady Eden. Lady *Harriet* Eden." Slowly he shook his head. "Sweet Lord, how often I've heard that name, Harriet, before. And Eden. I've heard it as well. Have you heard of them, Humphrey?"

But Humphrey wasn't faring so well. There still was a blanket of disbelief covering everything. A devise—that's what it was—of Bobby's, to lift his spirits. "It's an . . . error," he stammered, "clearly an—"

"Good God," Bobby shouted. "Are you deaf? Shall I take you by the hand and escort you up to the man himself? There is no error. His client is Lady Harriet Eden. *Yes,* her maiden name *was* Powels. *Yes,* she is alive and well and residing at Eden Castle on the North Devon coast. *Yes,* she's married to Lord James Eden, fourteenth Baron and sixth Earl of Eden Point. *Yes,* the man had a brother, dead now, named Edward Eden."

The cries of yes became a refrain in Humphrey's ear. A feeling such as he had never known before rose up within him. He sat on the very edge of his chair, his mouth half-open. There still was an inclination not to believe.

Bobby leaned close, no longer shouting. "I'm only grateful that I could deliver this information to you, Humphrey, I who know better than anyone the depths of your agony. Now perhaps you can exorcise her once and for all, and be truly mine."

It wasn't that Humphrey didn't hear the expression of affection. It was simply that his mind was still spinning on other matters. How could such important news bring so many unanswered questions? *Lady Harriet Eden? Edward Eden?* What was that connection? And why had fate sent Mr. Morley Johnson on this night when Humphrey had been almost doubled over with memories of the past?

"By God!" he exclaimed at last, full-voiced, certain possibilities beginning to occur to him. But he needed more information, needed to interview the man himself.

On that note of resolve, he pushed away from the table, stumbling once in his eagerness, hearing Bobby call after him, but refusing to stop, moving steadily across the empty dining room, his eyes fixed on the doorway and the entrance hall, and beyond that the staircase and the second-floor guest chamber where, with luck, Mr. Morley Johnson could tell him precisely what he wanted to know, a glorious stroke of good fortune, the first time in his long and bitter life when fate had said to him, *"Now, Humphrey Hills! You call the tune!"*

Eden Castle, April 1852

ALTHOUGH HE WAS forced to operate within the boundaries of limited experience, John Murrey Eden knew, with a certainty that defied reason, that he would never again, under any circumstances, be as happy as he was now.

Though he was totally absorbed in his own happiness, he was not impervious to hers. Or for that matter, the happiness of the entire castle save for that one gloomy besotted chamber in the west wing where his uncle dwelt and from which that now constantly inebriated man never emerged.

But for the rest of them, it was a castle at last truly named, a rapturous place grown more rapturous with the coming of spring, all the casements thrown open, letting in the freshness of sea breeze and early-blooming lilacs, a gluttony of happiness filling all quarters.

On this mild April evening, he stood behind her where she sat before her dressing table, her hairbrush in his hand, and carefully guided the bristles through her luxuriant hair. It had become a ritual which brought both of them immense pleasure.

"It resembles the color of autumn," he murmured, stroking her hair, his hand cupped about her head.

She laughed and lifted her face. "Do you think Mary's will take on the red tint?"

He shook his head. "She's destined to be blond, like my side of the family, and it will become her."

John smiled, remembering how that very afternoon Mary had kept pace with him and Richard as they'd scrambled down the steep cliff to the ocean, then back up again. How he adored her, adored them all, having found at last the family he'd never had.

"Penny?"

He looked up to her reflection in the glass.

"For your thoughts," she added softly.

He laid the brush aside and sat in the near chair, his long legs outstretched, spying caked mud on his boots from their afternoon outing. "You know my thoughts," he murmured.

"I know," she said, "but I like to hear you speak them." When at first he did not reply, she prompted, "Are you happy, John?"

He laughed and pressed his head back against the cushions of the chair. "My father always said that it was wrong of a man to expect too much happiness. It spoiled him for day-to-day existence."

"Do you think he was right?"

"He was always right." He crossed his arms over his chest and again stared at her. During the daylight hours, he felt complete satisfaction in her closeness, her affection, the touch of her hand, the manner in which she spoke his name, the thousand little intimacies which seemed to satisfy and blunt the need for the greater one.

But on occasions, like now at night, when they were alone, he felt the hunger and wondered how long it would suffice merely to brush her hair and hear her speak his name lovingly.

"John?"

She was there again, leaning forward in her chair. "What is it?"

He shook his head. "Nothing."

"No," she disagreed, and left her chair and knelt before him. "You looked . . . desolate." She frowned.

"I'm sorry," he said, his hand cupped about her face. Then playfully he lifted her chin. "Will you marry me?" He grinned. "Will you come away with me and be my wife?"

At first she looked surprised. "Come away where?"

"India."

She laughed prettily. "Why India?"

"Why not? It's a world away from England, a new horizon, a place where we could—"

"And what about Richard and Mary?" She smiled, still playing the game.

"We would take them with us."

"And never return to Eden?"

"Oh, yes, we'll come home one day, as husband and wife."

Now she looked longingly at him, the sense of play diminishing.

Encouraged, he leaned closer and repeated himself. "Please come away with me and be my wife."

"But I *am* married, sir," she replied. "England frowns on a woman with two husbands."

"You have no husband," he countered. "I doubt seriously if you've ever had a husband."

Gently she broke loose and settled back on her heels, still at his feet. He noticed one hand drawing the dressing gown more tightly about her.

Without warning he slipped to his knees beside her on the floor, took her in his arms and kissed her, a bit crudely, but what matter? There were years separating them, to be sure, but he knew he would never love anyone else as he loved her.

At the end of the kiss, he caught a glimpse of her face and thought he saw despair there. Now he watched as she pulled herself to her feet and walked away, no words spoken.

Had he offended her? They'd kissed many times, even during the day with the children scampering ahead, and always at night she bade him farewell with a kiss.

"Harriet?"

But she merely hushed him with a raised hand and continued to walk away, to her bedstand now. When at last she looked back at him, there was an expression on her face that he'd never seen before, the kind of splintered peace that comes with hard-fought resolution.

Slowly she approached him, a small volume in her hand. "Do you know it?" she asked.

"The Book of Common Prayer. I have one of my own."

"Turn to page seventeen," she commanded.

Torn between her stance before him and her perplexing command, he did as he was told, and at last found it, page seventeen, the Ceremony of Marriage.

Again he looked up, then slowly rose, his eyes never leaving her face. "I . . . don't understand," he said.

Again she retreated, as though determined to keep a safe distance between them. "Have you ever made love to a woman before, John?" she asked.

Still grasping the prayer book, he looked down, embarrassed by the truth he knew he must speak. "No."

"Then what *do* you know of the union between a man and a woman?" she prodded.

In despair, he clutched the book. "Nothing," he snapped, anger joining his embarrassment, "but I did not realize it was a tutorial matter to be disussed along with the Dialogues of Plato."

"It isn't," she replied, her voice as level as his was rising. "Still, it must be understood—"

"What must be understood?" he demanded. "What must be understood beyond the fact that I love you, will always love you, will never love another as I love you . . ."

The impassioned repetition began to sound childish in his ear. In despair, he turned away and took his embarrassment to the window, where he saw the high April moon casting a warm light on the inner courtyard. He closed the book in his hand, seeing clearly her purpose now, a gentle dissuasion, trying to talk him out of his love.

"I'm sorry I brought it up," he said. "It was wrong of me."

"No," came the voice behind him, a conciliatory voice,

offering hope. "And I'm not sorry you brought it up. I think we've both known since"—she paused as though searching her mind for a date—"since the night of old Jane's death that neither of us would be capable forever of . . ."

Slowly he turned. "Of what?"

"Of denying ourselves."

He stepped down from the window, as perplexed as ever. Was she playing her old tricks, beckoning with one hand, slapping away with the other? "Then I don't understand," he confessed again.

"I know you don't," she agreed, "and you must." At last she stepped toward him, the light from the lamp illuminating her face clearly, a face which seemed suddenly drained of color, as though in spite of her appearance of calm, her turmoil was as great as his.

"You . . . claim you love me," she began.

"And I do."

"There are years separating us."

"Meaningless."

"There will be other women in your life."

"None."

"And you will truly marry one day."

"Never!"

"You may be shocked by the act."

"I want you."

Only the dressing table separated them. Still she spoke, as though determined to argue them both out of their need. "We would be committing a sin," she said bluntly.

"In whose eyes?"

"God's and man's."

"We're not responsible for their vision."

"Our lives would never again be the same."

"How would they be different?"

"The intimacy, once established, would have to be fed."

He found her hesitancy touching. "Our chambers are close. I'm here nightly . . ."

"To brush my hair."

"To want you. To look upon you and wonder how much longer I can . . ."

Suddenly she turned away. At first he was afraid he'd offended her. Then he heard her own whispered doubts. "I . . . wouldn't want to . . . disappoint you."

Still clasping the Book of Common Prayer, he came up behind her. "How could you disappoint me?" he said.

As she turned, he saw disbelief in her eyes. "Truly you've never known a woman before?" she asked again, as though amazed.

No longer embarrassed by his confession of truth, he shook his head. "I was offered a whore once, but my father interceded."

Suddenly she bent over, her hands covering her face.

"Harriet?" He leaned close in concern. But she moved quickly away, as though determined that he not touch her.

She clung to the dressing table as though waiting out the weakness; then, as though nothing at all had occurred, she sat primly down before the mirror and to his reflection said, "Read the Ceremony of Marriage while I dress—"

"Dress? Where are—"

"Please read," she whispered. "I want you to hear the words, and I want to hear them."

He looked at her and wondered wearily if all mating was so difficult and complex. If so, how did the world ever proceed?

Then he was no longer concerned with the world, for in the most graceful of gestures she pulled the ribbon at the top of her dressing gown, which released the pale pink silk about her neck, and in one fluid cascade the gown fell about her waist, revealing a portion of those mysteries about which he'd wondered so often.

"Read, John," she commanded softly, apparently impervious to his fascination. In the reflection of the mirror he caught his first unobstructed view of her breasts, perfectly molded, so full that the inside of her arm brushed against them as she reached for the pitcher of lavender water.

Unable to maintain his position, he'd just started up behind her when suddenly there came a soft knock at the door. He turned on it, fearful that at any moment the door might swing open, the tableau clear for all to see.

He moved quickly away and looked back at Harriet, fully expecting to see her in the frantic throes of drawing the robe up about her shoulders. But she sat perfectly still, naked to the waist, a damp linen in her hand, and called calmly out, "Who is it?"

"Peggy, my lady," came the timid voice on the other side of the door. "Shall I prepare you for bed?"

Without hesitation, she lied gloriously. "No, Peggy, I'm already abed. I need nothing. And come morning, wait until I ring for you."

"Very well, my lady. Pleasant dreams."

"You, too, Peggy."

During this brief exchange, John stood rigidly to one side, his eyes moving back and forth between the two female voices, confounded that neither of them shared his agitation.

But they didn't, and after listening a moment to Peggy's receding footsteps, he looked back toward the dressing table, to see a living painting, the voluptuous woman preparing herself, one hand now lifting the weight of auburn hair, the other guiding the linen dampened with lavender water across her neck, then down one shoulder, then gently down between her breasts, lifting them in a self-caressing gesture.

He was suffering terribly. Again he started forward.

"Read, John, I beg you," she whispered.

"Harriet, please—"

"Read," she said to his reflection. Then sadly she added, "At least we can commence with civility."

Laboriously he returned to the chair near the dressing table and opened the Book of Common Prayer with the intention of following her command to the letter, and for all his good intentions he saw the small black words swimming across the page.

"Begin," she urged. Again he tried to do as he'd been told, though at that moment he made the mistake of looking toward the dressing table and saw her standing, the robe totally abandoned now around her feet, her hips rounded, curving in on a soft dark triangle, a most unmalelike smoothness, a compelling absence . . .

The palms of his hands were moist, and he transferred

that moisture to the thin parchment pages, causing them to stick together. At last, in a voice that was scarcely audible, he read, " 'In the presence of God and His Holy Congregation, we are gathered here to join together this man and this woman in Holy . . .' "

He looked up, thinking he'd done quite well, and saw her listening, one hand clasping the dampened linen, arrested in its progress down the right leg. In the angle at which she stood, the line of her back and buttocks was one magnificent classic curve, like the curve of a newly risen moon, or a dawn sun just appearing.

"Please go on," she whispered, rousing herself out of her frozen reverie, and rousing him as well as through blurred eyes he saw the statue move, extend the white linen to her toes.

Making a massive effort, he lowered his eyes to the page. " 'Matrimony is an honorable estate, instituted by God, signifying unto us the mystical union that is betwixt God and His church.' "

At some point, his eyes became adept at devouring several lines at once, so that he could speak and look up all at the same time. The point of the ritual still eluded him, though it clearly was giving her enormous pleasure. He'd never seen her face so enraptured, though in truth his eyes were seldom on her face. At each angle in which she turned, new secrets were revealed; a tiny birthmark on her upper left thigh in the shape of a perfect circle, the smooth white skin on the inside of her upper arm, the small of her back, her breasts . . .

He lowered his head, sensing that from this night on the world would no longer be ordinary. How long she intended to continue his torture, he had no idea, but he suspected that his agony would end when the vows ended, and with that in mind, he read rapidly. " 'Will thou have this woman to thy wedded wife, to live together after God's Holy ordinance . . .' "

At times he thought he could not draw sufficient breath to continue, and a few minutes later he thought it a minor miracle when the end of the vows came into sight, and he heard his own voice, though it was scarcely recognizable,

" '. . . and keep thee only unto her so long as ye both shall live.' "

A short time later, he read the benediction. " 'God the Father, God the Son, God the Holy Ghost, bless, preserve and keep you and fill you with all spiritual benediction and grace, that ye may so live together in this life that in the world to come ye may have Life Everlasting. Amen.' "

Silence. He closed the book and closed his eyes as well. He leaned over and rested his head in his hands. At that moment a lovely fragrance, like roses, came closer, accompanied by a soft rustling and the almost indiscernible weight of a hand on his shoulder.

"Come," he heard her whisper.

He looked up to see her, a vision in white, a gown of such airy fabric it seemed to float about her.

Before he could respond, she was leading him toward the door.

"Where are we going?" he whispered.

But she said nothing and paused at the door, peered out as though to check for late-night servants, then again she grasped his hand and led him out into the dark corridor.

He followed after her in willing obedience. The apparition leading him through the darkness would have to stop sometime.

Then true knowledge would commence. Then he would discover for himself what every man must discover for himself, the secret at the heart of the world, how the designs fit together, why men penned verse and painted paintings and sculptured statues, all dedicated to the love of a woman.

Never in the history of the world had there been a more eager student. He tightened his grip on her hand.

She could lead him to the very pit of hell, and he would willingly follow.

She knew precisely what she was doing, had known from the beginning, when she'd rescued him from the odd-boy cellar and moved him into the luxurious chambers directly down the corridor from her own. She'd known that ultimately it would come to this, a late-night flight down the corridors of Eden, with him behind her, a willing lover, leading him stealthily as Edward once had led her toward the small door in the east wall, past the graveyard and gardens and finally out onto the freedom of the headlands, and on to the glen in the distant woods, the one spot at Eden she'd refused to visit since Edward had taken her there almost seventeen years ago.

She knew precisely what she was doing, and what sane woman would do otherwise? What reasoning woman would turn her back on such a gift from Providence, a chance to relive the one brief and truly passionate love of her life? No sane woman would do that, not even Harriet, though the battle had been long and arduous.

Through God's infinite mercy, Edward had reappeared, and it *was* Edward following behind her, a younger Edward to be sure, but that was perhaps the most glorious part of God's gift. This Edward needed *her*. Now it was her turn to perform tutorial duties, to lead and instruct as once she had been led and instructed.

So consuming were her thoughts that as they reached the lower floor, she almost took the wrong turn, to the right, which led into the Great Hall and the ever-constant eyes of the watchmen.

Taking the correct turn now, she was afraid to look back until at last she spied the east-wing door and pushed it open and felt the mild reviving April night air.

Then freedom. Then the first glorious ocean breeze, the headlands beautifully illuminated by the light of the full moon, his face before her, a smile on his lips as though now he had perceived her plan, as though he too suddenly felt the strictures of the castle fall away. As he gathered her to him, she responded by locking her arms about his neck, where, with mouths opened, their lips met, mutual identities lost and unimportant.

"Not here," she whispered at the end of the kiss. "Come, let's run. It isn't far."

How kind the night was and how rapidly they took the horizon line of dark woods, and a few moments later, pushing their way through the underbrush, it occurred to her that this would be different. The first time she and

Edward had come here had been in the high clear light of afternoon. Now they would be forced to rely upon their hands, the sensitivity contained within their fingertips, for the moon was obscured here by the thick canopy of foliage overhead.

She was aware of him standing beside her, an almost timid stance, still waiting for her lead. Then take it, she urged herself, and within the moment the white gown was loosed about her waist, her arms free.

"Come . . ." She smiled and led him to the center of the glen, her hands now removing his belt, moving down the buttons of his shirtwaist, a slow gentle disrobing where occasionally he seemed to help.

She sensed the apprehension within him and recalled her own and tried to remember how Edward had eased it. And finally, as he was removing his boots and trousers, she stretched out on the cool green moss, remembering before how she'd looked up into the very face of the sun through lacy green trees.

He stood beside her, as though awaiting her next communication. She reached up for his hand and drew him down beside her.

"Are you afraid?" she whispered.

"Yes."

"No need," she reassured him.

An inauspicious beginning. She would have to do more. Slowly her hand moved down, stroking, until at last a sound of deep breathing began to rise close to her ear.

Suddenly he gave a low constricted moan and rolled atop her with a force which startled her, his legs pushing hers apart, his hands pinning her wrists over her head. Beneath the weight of his body, she found she could not move, and with one urgent thrust he entered her.

Then it was over.

She closed her eyes and thought with a smile that rape had occurred, not lovemaking, and she indulged him a moment longer, gave him a chance to recover from sensations that must have been as unsatisfying for him as they were for her.

Then, "John," she murmured. "Release my arms, please. There's no need."

He drew back as though only now aware of what he'd done. "I'm . . . sorry," he gasped.

She waited, then slowly sat up beside him. "Are you well?" she inquired gently.

He nodded, though he sat in a despairing position, knees raised, head buried.

She knelt before him, still feeling the brief sensation of his weight on her body, but feeling little else. She'd never thought it possible, the speed with which he'd performed.

She brushed back his hair and felt his forehead damp. What a night of instruction she had before her. She lifted his hand and placed it over her breast.

The lessons commenced, the complex lessons of postponement and gratification, the subtle enjoyment of pressure and sudden lack of pressure, the art of deliberation, of savoring each sensation, of building slowly. He was a newly humbled student and she a patient tutor who on occasion surprised herself with her expertise, recalling that other time, that other Edward, who had with such gentleness taught her in one brief afternoon the miracles that could be wrought with the human body.

Finally, when the first streaks of dawn were altering the night sky, she looked up from an interval of rest and saw him approaching her, a different expression on his face now, a somber look of control. As she opened her arms to him, he surprised her by lifting her to him, where expertly he guided her legs around his waist, his touch firm and sure, and with ease their bodies fitted together, and with her eyes closed she felt his broad hands supporting her, pressing her closer, the warmth inside her now, the mystical center focused somewhere near the entrance to her womb, his lips gently pulling on her breast, his hair brushing against her throat, a skillful, expert invasion which caught her off guard, the crest commencing, a different memory, yet the same glorious sensation.

Still it came, a searing heat which culminated in an explosion that caused her to cry out and cling to him, her head limp against his chest, his mouth close to her ear, where all she heard was his whisper, repeating her name over and over again.

Blessedly their passion subsided, for neither could have

endured more. Now incredibly she felt shyness as he covered her with the crushed white gown.

"Are you cold?" he asked, lying beside her.

A foolish question, as she doubted if she would ever be cold again. She shook her head and gently caressed his face, pleased at his pleasure.

For a long while they lay silently and watched the dawn. At first she had worried that they should return to the castle under cover of darkness. But as the morning light spread and she saw clearly his face beside her, she put aside her fears and spread the white coverlet over him and nestled warmly into his arms.

In the rising light, she looked at him sideways and detected changes on his face. He looked older. Due to her guidance, he knew intimately his manhood and the rich power contained within. She raised up on her elbow, the better to see him, as alike to that other man as though they were twins. Her newfound happiness made her greedy, and she felt a compulsion to implore him never to leave her.

Apparently he saw her distress and intuitively pulled her down on his chest and locked his arms about her. "I will never leave you," he vowed, as though he'd read her mind. "Never," he repeated.

She closed her eyes in the sheltering warmth and wondered how she could ever reassemble the fragments of that pathetic woman known as Lady Harriet. How could she again become Richard's and Mary's mother, and mistress to the servants? And the most difficult question of all, how could she survive the coming daylight hours without him, knowing the thousand meaningless rituals she had to struggle through before nightfall and once again they might be together.

As though he shared her silent bewilderment, and as though in fortification against the coming abstinence, he entered her again, gently, slowly, almost sadly. Now above her head she saw the brightness of sun, a leafy greenness, that other scene recreated perfectly.

As he kissed her, she closed her eyes and at the moment of greatest happiness felt a sudden sadness, felt time slipping by, one drop at a time.

In defense against the sadness, she closed her eyes and made herself blind, and wrapped her arms tightly about his neck and buried her face in his flesh, and with great effort shut out all thoughts, all sounds save for the distant shrill early-morning screams of circling sea scavengers.

❦

The Mermaid,
Late April 1852

ALTHOUGH DISINCLINED TO believe completely the incredible story, still Morley Johnson sat opposite the two sodomites, eager to hear more.

Would God be so capricious as to lead him on a fruitless search clear across the face of England, only to provide him with the prize on his last stop before heading home?

"Mr. Johnson, are you with us?"

He looked up from his bafflement to see Humphrey Hills staring earnestly at him. "I'm sorry, Mr. Hills," Morley muttered, shaking his head. "I'm simply dumbfounded, that's all." He sipped brandy and peered over the rim of the snifter at the two opposite him. "Are you . . . certain of your facts?" he asked again, enjoying his superiority. Rural inkeepers may traffic in gossip and speculation, but London solicitors required facts.

"Now," he began, "you say you have the privilege of Lady Eden's acquaintance?"

Hills shook his head. "Of Lady Eden, no," he replied. "I know no Lady Eden."

Morley sat up. A retraction so soon?

"I know Lady Harriet Powels," the little man went on. "As I've said before, I've been the proprietor of the Mermaid for many years. The Powelses have been my nearest neighbors." He smiled. "I know their history as intimately as though it were my own, and all their scandals as well, of which there are many."

Morley listened closely. "Then Lady Harriet is your friend?" he questioned further.

At that, the two men across the table laughed. "Friend? No," Hills replied at the end of the laugh. "Acquaintance, yes."

"Would she remember you?"

"Oh, I'm sure she would"—the man nodded eagerly—"though we were closer when we were children, the social barriers not so great." He seemed to falter here. "I'm sure you . . . understand."

Morley let his eyes wander over to the other gentleman, a Mr. Bobby Berents, who seemed to be silently encouraging his friend. A pretty man, if men could be called pretty.

"Mr. Berents," Morley asked, trying to establish the involvement of all present, "did you know Lady Harriet as well?"

"Oh my, no," Mr. Berents responded. "She was among the missing, thank God, when I arrived in Humphrey's life." He lifted a white linen handkerchief to his lips as though to hide a smile. "I doubt seriously if poor Humphrey could have coped with both of us, Mr. Johnson."

For the moment, no one spoke, Morley momentarily distracted by the interplay taking place opposite him at the table. Then he forced his attention back to the matter at hand. "Very well, Mr. Hills," he commenced in a businesslike tone. "Tell me again about the secret pregnancy."

Hills shrugged. "What's to tell that I haven't already told you?" he muttered. Then, as though he knew that his cooperation would serve him best, he went on. "Some time ago it was, sixteen years or so. The rumor the family put out was that she was ill, a highly contagious fever." He looked up at Morley and grinned. "Highly contagious, my ass. It was the swelling sort of sickness, it was, the kind that goes completely away at the end of nine months, unique to females, if you get my drift."

Morley did, as did Bobby, who snickered again into his handkerchief. Morley went on, warming to the interrogation. "And if the family was prudent enough to plant a rumor, how did you hear otherwise?"

Hills smiled. "Great God, Mr. Johnson, and you a London man! Don't sit there telling me that it's not come to your attention that certain lips open quickly for a thick purse?"

Yes, Morley knew that, though he resented the man's condescension. "Go on, Mr. Hills," he said. "Whose tongue did you buy?"

Hills looked up and took in the ceiling with a quick glance. "An old foreigner, she was," he began, "Swedish, I believe, or German. Hired by Lord Powels, she was, to see her ladyship through the embarrassment."

Still determined to discredit the man's tale, Morley asked, "If she was confined with her ladyship, how did you make her acquaintance?"

"Oh, there was no confinement in the beginning." Hills grinned. "She was brought over and established in Hadley Park simply as a lady's maid. It takes a while for the swelling to show, or the fever to commence," he added sarcastically.

"Then you met her before the confinement?"

Hills nodded. "I did. She took to coming down here for a pint, and though it grieves me to say it now, we got on well enough, and before long she'd told me all, how her ladyship had let someone between her legs, and how shortly she wouldn't be seeing me anymore, as it was her job to accompany her ladyship to the fourth-floor storage attic . . ."

Morley shook his head and again sipped his brandy. "Do go on, Mr. Hills," he said.

Now the man seemed uncertain, as though he'd come to a difficult part of his story. "Well, Mr. Johnson," he began, "when I got wind of what was going on and got a good strong whiff of the nature of the foreign bitch, I said to myself, Humphrey, what chance is that babe going to have? You see, she'd told me by then that part of her bargain with Lord Powels was that she take the babe out of England and never return. Well, I knew her character well enough by then to know that that babe would never survive his first day on this earth, that she'd probably drown him in the first stream, or else sell him to the gypsies."

"So you bargained for the child yourself?" Morley asked, finding this part of the tale the most incredible of all.

Hills nodded broadly. "I did indeed, sir. What Christian gentleman would have done otherwise?"

Bobby Berents turned away as though hiding a smile.

"And what were your intentions toward the child?" Morley asked.

"Honorable, sir, completely honorable. As you can see, I'm an unmarried man. God has not seen fit to send me a mate. Yet I long for a son, someone to raise as my own, someone to care for me in my twilight years."

Morley listened closely. "So the babe was delivered to you?"

Hills nodded. "The very night of his birth, for a pretty price, I might add."

"And what happened?"

Hills looked up at him now as though experiencing an insufferable weight. "Fate intervened, or the Devil." His eyes narrowed. "There were guests in the inn that night, a peculiar pair, one clearly a gentleman, Mr. Edward Eden by name . . ."

Morley sat up.

". . . and his old coach driver, the name I looked up for you this morning."

John Murrey. At Morley's insistence, Mr. Hills had spent the morning going through old registers, and at last had found the day, the date and the name. *John Murrey.* The name of the young man now in residence at Eden. Could it be mere coincidence?

Morley leaned closer over the table, fascinated by the puzzle. "Go on," he urged again.

"Not much more to tell, sir," Hills mourned. "I had a son for one night. I'd just tucked him into his little crib when this deranged gentleman, this Edward Eden, and his equally deranged manservant broke into my chambers, knocked me senseless and kidnapped the babe."

Suddenly he covered his face with his hands, as though

overcome. "When I came to, I was bloodied and dazed, the crib was empty and the gentleman gone."

Morley looked away. He drew a deep breath and tried to understand all of it. Why would Edward Eden kidnap a babe? He had hundreds of babes in his notorious Ragged Schools in London, all the available street rabble. Why would he journey to the Midlands to kidnap another? Yet the dates corresponded and could not be denied. A fortnight later, he had returned to London, the babe in arms, and had identified him to all, including the whore Elizabeth, as his son.

Well, Morley doubted that. When could he have come in intimate contact with Lady Harriet? And there was the most miraculous revelation of all. If indeed, as Hills claimed, she had given birth that night, and if indeed that same babe had been delivered to Humphrey Hills by the foreign woman, and if indeed that same babe had been kidnapped by Edward Eden, taken to London, raised as his son, then the only conclusion was that . . .

Suddenly he stood, feeling an acute need for movement in order to digest the revelation. If there had been a secret pregnancy and an abandoned babe, how would her ladyship react to the news that her secret had at last been found out, that the young man in residence at Eden Castle was her own son?

Morley closed his eyes, excitement and apprehension blending. Yet it had been her command, her need to know that had launched him on this prolonged search. Was he now to turn his back on the very truth he'd been sent to find? And perhaps his news could be the cause of great jubilation and celebration, the prodigal returned, the young orphan welcomed into the loving arms of his mother.

With his eyes still closed, he smiled. What a glorious scene, and how grateful she would be, his position as the Eden solicitor sealed for all time. Oh, great heavens, what a stroke of fortune had led him here to this rural retreat!

Gratefully, he looked back to the two sodomites and returned hurriedly to the table, his mind alive with plans and projections. "You must return with me immediately to Eden Castle," he proposed now to Humphrey Hills.

He started to speak on, but halted, amazed by the look of disbelief on the pudgy face opposite him.

"To . . . Eden?" the man stammered, and gripped the table.

Morley nodded. "She must hear it from you, from your own lips. I fear she would never believe me. You said you knew her once. Then she'll trust you."

The two across the table exchanged a rapid glance. Berents recovered first. "Of course you must go, Humphrey," he pronounced coolly to his friend. "It is quite simply the opportunity you have waited for all your life."

As for Humphrey, he seemed beyond speech. "To . . . Eden?" he repeated, to no one in particular.

Then a broad smile covered his face as he proudly announced, "I shall willingly accompany you to Eden Castle, Mr. Johnson."

Eden Castle,
May 2, 1852

IT WAS LIKE an illness, a suffering yet pleasurable illness, the love he felt for her. For days he'd tried to understand it, but apparently understanding had little to do with it.

Merely the sound of her voice, the echo of her footsteps, was enough to weaken him.

Now seated opposite her in the Banqueting Hall, in the torture of a public room, he rested his fork on the side of his plate and fed himself on the only true nourishment in his world. *Her.*

On either side of her, Mary and Richard were chattering simultaneously, and she was trying to hear them both, her face alive, yet evoking a tranquil charm.

"Herr Snyder said it was Sophocles," he heard Richard announce with conviction, some playful academic debate arising between them. Luncheons frequently were extensions of the morning classroom, Harriet encouraging both her children to academic excellence.

As John half-listened, he hoped that she would not involve him. How much more enjoyable it was simply to sit and absorb her beauty. He closed his eyes and saw her still as though she were permanently etched on his consciousness, her bottle-green silk dress with black buttons and braid trimming with white undersleeves and lace collar, her hair done up this morning.

Suddenly he opened his eyes to confirm his memory and saw the reality exactly as he had seen it with closed eyes, though much more powerful, those eyes gazing straight at him. "Are you tired, John?" she inquired softly, interrupting her debate with Richard.

He did well to shake his head. "Not at all tired." He smiled, amused by the daytime formality which had sprung up between them.

"Your eyes were closed," she said. "Does Sophocles bore you so?"

"Nothing that interests you, my lady, could ever bore me."

Delighted, he watched a blush creep up the sides of her cheeks. With suspect speed she launched forth once again into her conversation with Richard.

By way of distraction, John reached for his fork and commenced dragging it across the white linen, the sharp prongs leaving white tracks. Best not even to look at her. His head began to grow unclear. He felt a curious need to clasp something until the roar in his head ceased.

"Come, Mary," he said to the little girl, who was squirming restlessly in her chair.

A delighted grin broke on her face, as, pleased, she slipped from her chair and scrambled up into his lap and gave in completely to his tight embrace, her boredom with her mother and brother relieved in her curiosity about the fork and the lines it made on the table.

Now, as though Harriet sensed the restlessness at the end of the table, she brought the discussion with Richard to a halt. "Let's pursue the matter later, dearest. I fear we are boring those two. Look at them."

"Not at all." John smiled. "Mary and I are quite capable of amusing ourselves, aren't we?"

The child nodded and commenced stabbing at the cloth with the fork, making deep perforations.

Harriet leaned forward, concerned. "Take the fork away from her, John, before she hurts herself. It could be dangerous."

Gently he removed the utensil, and as the child protested, he suggested, "A walk. It's a May sun and high. What do you say?"

"We've not had our sweet yet," Richard protested. "Clara said it was fresh gingerbread."

"Fresh gingerbread!" John exclaimed. "Well, we mustn't miss that." As he commenced tickling Mary, Harriet laughed and lifted the bell beside her plate and rang it once.

As three stewards filed in through the small door on the right, he released Mary with a pat and told her to return to her chair. As the child obeyed, he looked back at Richard, the boy's face still lined with angles of concentration.

"It needs a rest, the brain does now and then." John smiled, leaning forward and tapping Richard's forehead. In an affectionate gesture, he ruffled the boy's dark hair.

Predictably, Richard protested, a ten-year-old whine of "Don't—"

"Why not?" John grinned, deliberately baiting him, as his father had so often baited him in an effort to lighten a mood.

As he ruffled the black hair again, Richard rose to meet the challenge and took up a position behind John's chair, giving him the same treatment.

As John's long fair hair fell in disarray over his forehead, he lifted his head in a mock battle cry and reached behind and pulled the boy forward, the tussle on.

But at some point, John was aware of the hilarity melting away. The servants, he noticed, had withdrawn to a safe distance. Through the muss of his hair he saw Harriet turn in her chair and glance toward the large arched doorway which led into the Great Hall.

He followed her gaze, and saw Mr. Rexroat, his face

clearly censoring the fun. "A carriage, my lady, has been seen by one of the watchmen about a quarter of a mile distant, heading this way." He seemed to stand a bit more erect. "Is it possible, my lady, that you are expecting guests?"

"I am expecting no guests," Harriet replied, "and want none to be admitted."

For a moment there was silence. Then John was aware of Rexroat's retreating footsteps. Richard began to stir, ready and willing to resume the playful battle.

In fact, everyone in the room seemed to be themselves again, except Harriet, who continued to stare toward the now empty archway. "I used to loathe the isolation of Eden," she murmured. "Now I resent a carriage passing a quarter of a mile distant."

"Were you expecting anyone?" John asked.

"Of course not," she protested. She lowered her voice. "The last thing I want now," she whispered, "is company."

"Well, then," he exclaimed, "I suggest that we indulge in Aggie's hot gingerbread, then a long walk across the headlands. Mortemouth today, I propose," he said, knowing that the steep cliff walk down to the little fishing village was always a treat for the children. "We've not been to Mortemouth since winter broke."

Predictably his suggestion was greeted with hearty approval from the children. Even Harriet seemed to relax a bit after the threat of guests.

John smiled at the sense of life resumed, feeling almost paternal, indulging himself in a familiar fantasy, that *he* was lord of Eden Castle, Harriet his wife, Richard and Mary the result of their passion, their offspring. What a fantasy that was. . . .

Then, as Richard and Mary commenced chattering happily about the proposed expedition of the afternoon, he again watched her. She had a characteristic gesture which he adored, a habit of smoothing her hand over her throat, then allowing that hand in its downward motion to slide quickly over her breast. She did it twice now, lightning-fast in its execution.

But as he leaned backward in his chair, the better to

catalog her beauty, he saw Mr. Rexroat again, appearing in the archway, his normally pallid face flushed as though he'd run a distance, a silver tray in his hand. My God, would the man give them no peace?

"The carriage is at the gate, my lady," he called out. "Two gentlemen, it is. One sends his card and begs an audience with you on a matter of great importance."

John watched her face carefully. He saw her brow furrow, as though her initial reaction was one of bewilderment.

"Who is it?" he asked.

She looked up, puzzled. "It says Morley Johnson, Solicitor."

Since she seemed disinclined to speak, and since Rexroat was waiting, John took the lead. "Then perhaps you'd better see him." He smiled. "Surely he wouldn't have come all this way without important news." His smile broadened as he tried to lighten the tension coming from her end of the table. "Perhaps he's found a mother for me"—he grinned—"a frail gray-haired lady whom we can move into the castle to take old Jane's place."

But apparently she could not be stirred by any degree of levity and continued to hold the white card, as though simultaneously repelled and fascinated by it.

Now she placed the card on the table beside her fork and looked again at Rexroat. "Two gentlemen, you say?"

"Yes, my lady, though the second was not identified."

When again she seemed to slip deeper into a kind of lethargy, John again took the lead, and grabbing Mary's hand, called for Richard to follow. "Come"—he smiled—"we all will go and greet this mysterious carriage."

As he passed behind Harriet's chair, he noticed that still she had not moved.

"Come, my lady," he said tenderly to the top of her head. "He is your solicitor, returned from your errand. We really should do him the courtesy of briefly receiving him."

In spite of Mary's shrieks that he "come on," he waited behind Harriet's chair, still baffled by her new mood, saw her head incline forward as though uttering a brief prayer.

Then, in the next minute, apparently restored, she

stood and straightened her shoulders as though she were walking toward an abyss instead of to the top of her own Great Hall stairs.

John fell in behind with Richard. "Who is Mr. Johnson?" Richard whispered as they passed beneath the arched door and started across the Great Hall.

John looked down on the boy, exploiting the sense of mystery. "We shall find out shortly," he whispered, and looked ahead to the bright splash of early-afternoon sun beyond the Great Hall door and earnestly hoped that the matter, whatever its nature, did not take too much of her time and attention. Mortemouth would be lovely at this time of the year.

Ahead, he saw Harriet step out of the shadows of the Great Hall into the blaze of sun, one hand still clasping Mary's, her other hand shading her eyes, her head turned stiffly toward the gatehouse and the carriage waiting patiently, held at bay beyond the twin grilles.

As John and Richard drew up behind her, Mr. Rexroat stepped around the congestion in the doorway and lifted a white-gloved hand in signal to the gate.

Within the moment John heard the cranking of the grilles, then saw the carriage moving slowly through. As the young driver guided the horses into a broad turn before the Great Hall steps, John glanced at Harriet. The tension was still there on her face. "I don't know why he couldn't have sent a courier with the report," she whispered.

"He's probably merely striving to please you," John comforted, still baffled by her curious apprehension.

With a rattle, the carriage came to a halt at the foot of the stairs. Within the moment two stewards stepped forward, one placing a low stool into position beneath the high carriage step, the other opening the door.

A man stepped out and seemed to draw himself up. "My lady," he murmured, bowing stiffly, "my deepest apologies for arriving unannounced. I considered sending a courier ahead, but I have important news and I wanted to deliver it to your ears alone."

"Important . . . news?" Harriet repeated, as though

willing to receive it here, on the steps, with dozens of ears listening.

But Mr. Johnson had other plans. "With your kind permission, my lady. I've brought an old acquaintance of yours. Would you be so generous as to allow me to present him to you?"

Mr Johnson was in the process of stepping back toward the carriage when suddenly he stopped and looked at the small congregation on the steps with a searching expression. Apparently someone was missing. "His . . . lordship?" Mr. Johnson queried.

"My husband is ill," Harriet said, obviously feeling no stress about lying before the servants who had gathered about the carriage.

"I'm most grieved to hear it," Mr. Johnson exclaimed, his manner as elaborate and artificial as his dress. At last he seemed to shake off the bewilderment of the missing Lord Eden and lifted a gloved hand to the steward standing near the carriage door.

Although the door was open, it seemed an interminable length of time before anyone appeared, all eyes focused on the small dark cavity beyond which, from John's angle, he could see a man's leg.

At last there was movement, a hunched male form, his brushed beaver hat clutched beneath his arm, his shiny bald head glistening like a small eye in the heat of the day, the man himself at last standing upright at the foot of the stairs, a most strange-looking man, painfully self-conscious at the center of attention, his neckerchief and waistcoat a flaming pink satin which seemed to accent his limited stature, his narrow-set dark eyes darting in all directions at once, to the heights of the battlements, to the small knot of servants standing to one side, to John himself and finally at last coming to rest on Harriet.

While there seemed to be recognition aplenty on the little man's face, Harriet seemed to be at a disadvantage. Again she brushed her hand over her eyes as though the glare of sun were hurting them. After a prolonged moment of nonrecognition, she shook her head apologetically. "I'm . . . afraid that I don't . . ."

Mr. Johnson took the lead. "May I present, my lady,

your childhood companion, an ardent admirer, by his own confession, and as proprietor of the Mermaid, your nearest neighbor, Mr. Humphrey Hills."

Mary suddenly broke free from her mother's hand and darted back into the shade of the Great Hall. John started to follow after her, but as he turned, he caught a glimpse of Harriet's face. He saw her close her eyes again. Then, "Mr. . . . Hills?" she stammered.

"Aye." The man grinned.

"From . . . Shropshire?"

"Aye, the same," the man confirmed, bobbing his head.

He had thought she might take the man's hand, but she didn't, and it was left to Mr. Johnson to bring them together. "In what glowing terms, my lady," he gushed, "has Mr. Hills spoken of your childhood friendship. It was the only melody he sang all the way from Shropshire, a moving refrain about a little girl in a blue velvet riding habit and a young boy who watched her with—"

"I remember him," Harriet said abruptly. After an awkward pause, John heard her speak again, her voice and manner as faltering as he'd ever heard them. "Mr. Hills, I . . . welcome you to Eden. I'm . . . not certain that . . . I understand . . ."

At last John could watch the embarrassing scene no longer and took the distance to her side. "I'm sure the gentlemen are thirsty, Harriet. Why don't we—"

"Of course," she murmured. "How thoughtless of me. Won't you both follow . . ."

As the awkward procession started up the stairs, John was in the lead, his hand on Harriet's arm. In their last moment of privacy, he leaned close, still alarmed by the expression on her face. "Are you well?" he inquired.

"I don't understand . . ."

"Who does?" He smiled. "Clearly they have a report of some sort."

"But why Humphrey Hills?"

"Did you know him?"

If she'd heard, she gave no indication of it, and instead looked around at the confused gathering and commenced dispatching people. "Richard, go back to the table and wait with Mary. Our walk will be delayed. And

Mr. Rexroat, a bottle of sherry please, if you will, in the small library. And Peggy, find Clara and have her stay with the children in the Banqueting Hall."

As everyone scattered, John held his position and looked back at the men just entering the Great Hall. On their upturned faces were identical expressions of awe and impression.

Then the two were upon them. When Harriet still seemed disinclined to speak, John again took the lead. "This way, gentlemen," and gestured toward the open door that led into the small library.

But Mr. Johnson stopped a few feet away, some objection forming on his flushed face. "With your kind permission, sir," he began, "I think it . . . advisable if we make our report to Lady Eden—in private. I do hope you understand . . ."

No, John didn't, nor did Harriet, whose face now clouded at the suggestion. John watched her carefully, thinking she might issue a protest for him.

But she didn't. She merely bowed her head and rested one hand lightly over her eyes as though suddenly fatigued. She looked so alone, as though she were being driven into the room by some terrible force.

"Please, sir," Mr. Johnson added, "indulge us for . . . say, half an hour, and there may be cause for general rejoicing at Eden tonight."

A curious comment. John now saw Mr. Hills grinning and nodding, his beaver hat still clutched under one arm, the other involved in constant adjustment to his person. John wondered briefly why he loathed the man so.

As the two men passed him by, following after her, they both bowed low, as though thanking him for his cooperation, and long before he was ready for it, the door was closed and he found himself alone.

He stood motionless, staring at the floor at his feet, the questions coming faster than he could consider them. Suddenly in anger he looked up toward the closed door, fully prepared to intrude despite their requests for privacy. But at the last minute, prudence intervened.

He could wait. If she desired his presence, she would

have said so, and now he smiled, amazed at the confidence he felt in their relationship.

His thoughts led him into an isolated corner of the Great Hall. He had thought once that he'd return to the Banqueting Hall and the company of the children.

But he changed his mind and settled instead for quiet pacing. A half hour wasn't so long, though about fifteen minutes later he stopped pacing.

Listen! He turned his ear in the direction of the small library, confident that he'd heard an outcry. He held still, his eyes focused on the blinding rectangle of light beyond the Great Hall door.

Apparently there had been no outcry, only Mary's sharp laughter coming from the opposite direction in the Banqueting Hall.

He listened a moment longer, then commenced his steady pacing again, trying to soothe his feelings of apprehension with thoughts of her.

Now and then he glanced toward the brilliant May sun at the door of the Great Hall. But it hurt his eyes and he concentrated instead on the slow steady clack of his boots on the parquet floor, and on the silence coming from behind the closed door of the small library.

A half hour wasn't so long, and he lowered his head and saw her in his imagination, a stray wisp of auburn hair wandering from the rest, a pale cheek, the depths of those eyes. . . .

When he first heard the library door opening, he thought how accurate Morley Johnson had been, for about a half hour *had* passed.

He moved to the center of the Great Hall, ready to greet her, to receive from her lips the nature of the private report. But from that distance, he saw her only in outline, the glare of sun coming in through the library windows behind her obscuring her features, though not obscuring her stance, a peculiar one, head down, both hands grasping the door frame, as though she were on the verge of collapse.

He tried to peer around her to catch sight of Johnson

and Hills. But they apparently were lingering in the recesses of the library.

Still she stood as though afraid to let go of the support of the door frame. Something was wrong. She appeared physically weakened.

"Harriet?"

Though he'd spoken her name, he knew that she had not heard. The distance between them was still too great. He moved forward, placed himself in her direct path.

"Harriet . . ."

Though he called again, louder this time, still she gave no indication of having heard him, and continued to walk in that blind fashion.

At last he hurried toward her, fearful that without his support she would collapse.

Apparently in spite of her blind walk, she'd heard him drawing near, and now she stopped, a frozen stance, both hands lifting as though to hold him at bay, a fierce gesture, warning him, without words, not to come any nearer.

Then slowly she was moving again, her step seeming to gather strength, as though relieved to be beyond him.

He watched her torturous progress across the Great Hall, heading apparently toward the Banqueting Hall, his bewilderment and anger rising. What had he to do with it? Whatever the nature of the report delivered by the two jackals, how did it concern him? And why had she taken it out on him as though he were a conspirator against her instead of a loving ally?

He glanced back toward the library door, hoping to catch a glimpse of the messengers who had delivered such a dark message. But he saw nothing and wondered if they too had been undone by their own words.

Again he looked toward the Banqueting Hall, seeking her out, that slim bent figure feeling her way along like a blind woman.

He would give her a moment, confident that sooner or later she would summon him to her and share with him this new weight of agony. Still he heard distant chatter coming from the far end of the Banqueting Hall, the children and maids apparently unaware of the corpselike woman who had just joined them.

From where he stood, he could see her moving toward the table. How rigidly she sat upon her chair.

He closed his eyes a moment to rest them from the unhappy vision, and vowed to go to her, regardless of her rejection of him. She appeared ill. One forgave an invalid for not knowing what she was saying.

Then he saw her make a curious move, a glint of silver grasped in her fists, her head lifting at last in a rapid reflexive movement, then both her fists thrusting upward into her eyes, a single sharp outcry escaping her lips, her head thrown back, someone screaming as again she drove her fists into her eyes, her whole body seeming to recoil. She did it yet a third time, something dark running down the sides of her face, though not a sound was to be heard coming from the Banqueting Hall now, all screams silenced in an apprehension of terror.

At last John was running, shouting her name as though he hoped to bring a halt to the bizarre violence with the mere force of his voice.

The screams had commenced again. Still John was running. Why could the distance not be bridged? Over the screams and the play of sun and shadow in the Banqueting Hall, he prayer, "God, help . . ." and at last approached her and dropped to his knees beside her and put his arm beneath her head and turned her toward him.

At first his mind refused to record anything. Then he felt as though an ax had been lowered against the back of his neck. The powerful impact seemed to push him forward as he bent low over her.

Dear God, would the screams and weeping never cease? He needed neither screams nor weeping. There were screams enough inside his head, and an insistent vision which forced him to look down on her face, scarcely recognizable as a human face now, resembling more a butchered animal left half-dead in a slaughter pen, the specific wounds obscured by the flow of blood, the instruments of her mutilation still clutched in her fists, two silver forks, fragments of tissue and blood coating the sharp prongs.

Something inside his head was screaming at him, informing him that the boy who had run, too late, to her aid, was as mufflated as she, that whoever it was now holding her, his sleeve soaked with her blood would arise a very different man. In spite of the voice, he managed to lift his head and cry, "Fetch the surgeon!"

Looking up, he saw Richard and Mary less than five feet away, their young faces drawn in terror.

"Get them out of there," he shouted to the sobbing Clara, who stood nearby. Though the storm was still raging within him, he heard steps and knew without looking up that his command was being obeyed. He reached out for a linen napkin and tried to stanch the two wells of blood that once had been her eyes. But within seconds the linen was red.

In the next instant he heard a familiar strong voice and saw the voluminous black skirts of Aggie Fletcher. When the old woman caught her first glimpse of the self-inflicted damage, she seemed to withdraw a step. "Sweet Jesus . . ."

"Help her," John begged.

Within the instant the woman took over, stooped down and lifted Harriet effortlessly into her arms, shouting at the top of her voice for various items. "Fresh water, linens, and camphor," and at last echoing John's initial command, "and bring the surgeon."

Still on his knees, John watched as Aggie carried her across the Banqueting Hall, a parade of weeping servants following behind, both children blessedly gone, removed to some position of safety, John left alone in his foolish kneeling position, the abandoned forks lying innocently in red pools.

Suddenly he reached out and lifted both utensils and hurled them the length of the table. Then he heard something else, footsteps in the distance, the two jackals who had delivered some message that had plunged her into total darkness, and plunged him as well.

He stared at them, both keeping to the safety of the small library door, as though too cowardly to step forward.

He rose from his kneeling position, the boy within him safely buried, the man in control as he retraced his steps, though twice a fit of trembling took him, and still he continued in a measured tread, wanting first explication, and then revenge.

Though the young man was still a distance away, Morley Johnson sensed his mood and tried to speak calmly to him. "I say," he called out, "did she faint?"

Then the young man was close enough for Morley to see him clearly, a fearful apparition, his face blood-smudged and deranged, his garments from his shirtwaist to the front of his trousers soaked with blood.

"I say, sir, would you be so kind as to . . ."

But there was nothing of kindness in the force with which the young man grasped Morley's shoulders and shoved him violently back into the library, where he collided with Humphrey Hills, who had pushed close to the door behind him.

"Sir, I beg you," Morley gasped, "inform us as to the nature of—"

"No! You inform me!"

Clearly the young man was not in his right mind, an observation which compounded Morley's apprehension and sent him backward into a retreat similar to that of Humphrey Hills.

So! This was him, the offspring of Lady Harriet. Then Morley's observations came to a halt as he saw the young man steadily approaching. "What did you tell her?" he demanded.

"I told her the . . . truth," Morley began. "She had sent me on an errand of considerable importance, and in my travels I discovered the truth and I thought it would please her."

If only Morley could lift his eyes from that blood-soaked apparition. "Please," he began gently. "Would you be so kind as to speak first? Your . . . appearance demands an explanation. If her ladyship is in any way injured . . ."

At that, the young man seemed to falter. Morley felt relief. "Please, sir," he began again, feeling that perhaps the man was coming to his senses. "Here, let me pour you a sherry. A good deep swallow will clear the head and put everything to rights again."

He was just offering the young man a glass, confident that they could sit and talk calmly, like gentlemen. Thus he was in no way prepared for the young man's sudden movement, his hand reaching out like a piston and knocking the glass aside, where it crashed to the floor, that same hand now moving toward Morley himself, where it grasped his neck and pushed him backward against the window seat, the man whispering fiercely, "What did you tell her? What did you tell her?"

Physically Morley was no match for him. All he could do was talk, as fast and as hard as he'd ever talked in his life. "I brought her a message, sir, I did, nothing more, a message and a messenger which I thought would bring her great happiness. I still don't understand, but Mr. Hills there, he's the one to tell it. I beg you, sir, speak to him. I'm merely the go-between, nothing more."

Flattened on the window seat, the hand still gripping his throat, Morley had taken the only course open to him, and had passed the responsibility on to someone else, to the little man lurking in the recesses of the room.

"You!" John called out.

Hills stepped forward, drew back a near chair from the table and sat. "I am the messenger," he began, a sense of pride filling his voice. "The one Mr. Johnson spoke of."

"What was your message?" the young man demanded again.

Morley listened halfheartedly to the now familiar tale, detecting a slight change in the performance taking place at the center of the room. When Hills had told the tale to Lady Harriet, he'd been much more delicate, never mentioning the word "bastard" once. There was in his attitude now a witless attempt to make the tale as grim as possible, a foolish tactic, Morley thought, for the young man was not to be trifled with. The outrage still was present. He was simply holding it at bay.

"So when the old Swedish midwife confirmed my suspicions," Hills went on, "I made her an offer for the babe, provided of course it was delivered safe and sound with ten fingers and toes, if you know what I mean."

Humphrey stopped talking for the first time and leaned back in his chair, clearly assessing the infant grown to manhood. Then he reached the climax of his tale, the very information that had sent Lady Harriet out of the room locked in that fearful silence. "But fate conspired against me that night," he went on. "Cruel fate that arranged for a Mr. Edward Eden to be a guest in my inn, and his old manservant by the name of John Murrey."

From where Morley sat, he thought he saw the young man step back as though to avoid the information.

"And those two undid me, beat me, left me for dead and kidnapped the bastard babe who was rightfully mine."

There was no sound in the library save for the newly risen breeze off the channel. From where Morley sat, the young man's reaction was almost identical to that of Lady Harriet, his head inclining forward, his hands reaching quickly out for the support of the table. And the expression on Hill's face was the same as before, one of enormous self-satisfaction, as though a score had been settled, a debt paid.

At last the young man stirred. "I . . . don't believe you."

Challenged, Humphrey Hills rose to meet it. He stood from his chair and pointed at the young man. "If I may be so personal," he began, "may I ask if you bear a small scar on your chest?"

Morley saw the young man push away from the table.

"Only a small scar it would be." Humphrey smiled. "In the shape of the letter B, if I remember correctly." His manner changed. "It was, I believe, a birth injury of some sort," he stammered uncomfortably.

All at once the young man turned away.

Hills concluded, "If you still bear the scar, then I must inform you that you are indeed Lady Harriet's bastard."

So engrossed was Morley in Hills's strutting manner that he did not at first notice the young man, his eyes lifting to Hills, his hands reaching out and finally the violent lunge forward, his whole frame seeming to shiver as he effortlessly grasped Hills's throat, in the process pushing him back and down, a single shriek leaving Hills's lips, his own defense as useless as Morley's had been against the superior strength of the boy.

The two of them stood upright for a moment, then crashed backward, Hills's head striking the round mahogany table with a fearful blow, the pupils of his eyes rolling upward, the boy atop him now, both on the floor, while Morley tried to encircle the thrashing turmoil of arms and legs, shouting, "Don't, I beg you, Mr. Eden. Release him!"

But still the young man pinned the now motionless Hills, his hands planted about his throat, channeling such awesome strength down into his fingers that his shoulders shook.

In rising desperation, Morley pushed roughly though ineffectively against the young man. "Let him go. You must let him go. You are doing murder."

But apparently that was precisely the young man's intention. Morley watched for as long as he could, and was just starting toward the door to issue a cry for help when at last he saw those hands lift from that throat, saw the boy on his knees straddling Humphrey Hills, saw Hills himself, his tongue slung grotesquely to one side of his mouth, a blue tint to his skin, his eyes white ovals, and a small spreading stain of red seeping out beneath his head.

From the door, Morley took in the scene, his pulse racing, fearful that the young man's murderous instincts had not been satiated and now he would turn on him.

But he didn't. In fact, it was quite the opposite. The boy lifted his hands and looked imploringly at Morley, as though at last the commanding voice which had ordered him to murder had ceased, leaving him alone with the sprawled lifeless body beneath him.

Still Morley kept to the door, not faring so well himself. That Humphrey Hills was dead, there was no doubt. That John Murrey Eden had committed murder, there was even less doubt.

He gaped at the appalling scene. Unwittingly he had set grim forces in motion by coming here. He still could not even imagine why the two, Lady Eden and the boy, had reacted as violently as they had.

Well, there was no time to mutter to himself. There was a need for positive action. But what kind? Under ordinary circumstances he knew precisely what to do. Murder had been done, and Morley Johnson had been an eyewitness. Under normal circumstances he would take the young man into immediate custody and deliver him before nightfall to the authorities in Exeter.

Under normal circumstances this is precisely what he would do, what English law dictated that he do. *But!* How often he had heard Sir Claudius Potter say that the Edens were a law unto themselves, and now that Morley Johnson was filling the role of Eden solicitor, it might behoove him to acquaint himself with Eden law as thoroughly as he was acquainted with English law.

He felt his mind move into action, providing him with a welcome distraction from the bleak scene at his feet, the young man at last finding the energy to remove himself from his close proximity to the dead Humphrey Hills, although that energy failed him as soon as he reached the first chair and he now sat slumped sideways.

Morley watched him, then stealthily slid the bolt on the library door, making certain that no one entered the death chamber until he'd had time to think through to a course of action which would be beneficial to all.

Beneficial to all! There were the key words. If Morley's perceptions were accurate, Lady Eden surely would not appreciate seeing her newly discovered and handsome son hauled unceremoniously off to prison. And no Eden, he recalled Sir Claudius Potter saying, enjoyed the public spotlight, particularly since the days of Lord Thomas Eden and his obsession for the fisherman's daughter.

And what could be more public, more humiliating than a murder trial, the case perhaps even moved to London due to the importance of the principals involved.

Good heavens! As the hideous projections whirled out of Morley's mind, he glanced at the boy. His life and future in England would be ruined. He would have to emigrate after prison, an act which undoubtedly would cause his mother great grief.

No! There would be no custody, nor any hurried trip to Exeter, no "prisoner" to deliver to the authorities.

Then what? Then concealment, although there were risks there as well. He could do it, pass the corpse off as the victim of a domestic accident, and in the process force the final bond of dependency and trust with the Eden family. They would in *his* debt, including the young man who might conceivably rise to a position of considerable power within the family.

"Mr. Eden, I beg you listen," he began urgently. "You must leave here immediately. Pack only what you can safely carry on horseback, wait in the stables for cover of night, then ride directly to London."

He paused for a response from the young man. When none seemed forthcoming, he shook him soundly by the shoulders, fearing him no longer. "Can you sit a horse? Answer me!"

At last the young man looked up. "Yes . . ."

"Then good. You can't stay here. I want no trace of you when the constable arrives. Do you understand what I'm saying to you? Look at me! Do you understand?"

Slowly the young man nodded, though his eyes fell on the sprawled body of Humphrey Hills at his feet. "Is . . . he dead?" he asked.

Morley nodded broadly. "Oh, I assure you he is dead, Mr. Eden."

In spite of the need for haste, Morley felt a strong wisp of moral outrage. "I begged you, sir, repeatedly to cease. I even tried physically to dislodge you. But to no avail. And now that the deed is done, we have the entire family to consider. And as you have only recently been proven a member of this noble family, I offer you my advice and assistance. If you will depart here tonight under cover of darkness, I believe I can conceal the true nature of the crime." He paused for emphasis, wanting to make certain that the boy understood precisely what he was doing on his behalf. "It will not be easy," Morley went on, hovering close, "and you must understand that I am jeopardizing my own career, my own future as well."

He broke off speaking, pleased to see the new expression on the young man's face, one of gratitude. Still, when he seemed incapable of movement, Morley grasped him by the shoulders, urging him to, "Hurry, I beg you. Pack only what you need, and wait in the stables until nightfall. Then, make for London."

"And . . . there?" the boy stammered, as though at last beginning to understand.

Momentarily stymied, Morley gaped down on him. Would everything be left for him to figure out? "Surely you have friends," he scolded. Then an idea occurred. "The woman Elizabeth," he whispered. "The little house in Bermondsey would be perfect. Go there."

At last the young man moved under his own volition, though it was merely a step away from Morley's side, where apparently the sight of Humphrey Hills stopped him again. "I . . . did not . . . intend to . . ."

Enough, Morley thought. Time was passing, the corpse at their feet growing colder. In London now, scientific advances were such that a medical inspector frequently could determine the approximate hour of death. Morley prayed that such advances had not yet made their way to the rural western edge of the country, for it was his plan to saturate Mr. Hills with brandy and have him drunkenly fall against the table about four hours from now, whereupon Morley would sound the alarm, send a courier for the nearest authority, wait "grief-stricken" for the death certificate and then bury the man as quickly as possible in the first public cemetery. Of course, in addition to all his other responsibilities, he would have to pen an aggrieved and diplomatic note to Mr. Bobby Berents at the Mermaid in Shropshire, and pray to God that the man did not force an inquiry.

Again he turned his attention toward the distraught young man. "You must hurry," he implored. "I will not sound the alarm until you are safely removed from here."

Morley waited until the young man had disappeared up the staircase. Then, confident that everything was going precisely as he had planned it, he slammed the library door, slid the bolt and sat awkwardly on the window seat, trying to keep his eyes off the lifeless body.

Sweet God! Who could have predicted this? As his agitation mounted, only one thought brought him comfort, the realization that though his present plight was hazardous, if he could make his way safely through this storm, he might just conceivably face a lifetime free from any other storms. Or if they came, he need have no fear of them, for the Eden wealth was an enormous, all-protective umbrella, and with his actions here today he had, for all time, earned himself a privileged position under that rich shelter.

The trick of life, according to his mentor, Sir Claudius Potter, was to take black disaster and convert it into golden opportunity.

For the first time in several hours Morley smiled, pleased at how skillfully he had mastered that lesson.

He knew what he had done.

He knew better than anyone what he had done, had been aware of the very moment when life had departed from the despicable little man's body, and even now he recalled how regretful he had been that there had not been additional life to extinguish.

As John rounded the landing on his way to the third-floor corridor, he stopped and leaned over the banister, thinking with extraordinary calmness that he was a muderer.

As he neared the third-floor landing, he heard a mix of voices coming from the far end of the corridor outside her chamber door. It was as though every servant in Eden Castle had selected that spot in which to wail.

Keeping to the safety of the shadows, John longed to join them, considered even pushing his way through them and demanding entrance to her chambers. But he didn't. It was a reluctance as complex as the day. Instead he felt his way down the corridor to his chamber door, pushed it open and slipped inside.

He moved his hands over the wooden door as though longing for a way to seal it. Had the man named Hills spoken the truth? Was Harriet the beautiful lady who, according to his father, had died giving birth to him?

"Damn him!" he whispered to the door, seeing his father's face before him, a lying face now. "Damn him!" he cried, and lifted both fists and drove them into wood.

Behind him he heard a voice. "If it does any good, I'll come and help . . ."

He whirled on the voice, thinking he was alone. Then he saw him standing in the far corner of the room, the long, lean figure of Dana, the old footman who had first befriended him.

"I did not send for you," John snapped, turning away before the man read his face too deeply.

"No, but I'm here anyway," Dana replied.

"Then leave," John commanded. "I have no need of you."

Slowly Dana emerged from the shadows. "I suspect you will never have greater need of me."

His anger still rising, John shouted, "Get out."

When still the man refused to obey, John lunged at him, more than willing to duplicate the crime he'd just committed downstairs.

But Dana offered no resistance. In fact, as John sprang forward, the man appeared to open his arms as though to receive his assailant, and at last the one-sided grappling match changed in nature, and as John felt Dana's arms move around him, he suddenly grasped the man and pressed against him in an awkward embrace.

All at once John felt a need so acute that his legs refused to support him, and Dana was still there, going to the floor with him, holding him tight until at last John had no choice but to let the man cradle him as though he were a child.

How long he lay thus in Dana's protective shelter, he had no idea. When he opened his eyes the sun was falling in crisscross patterns on the floor. Then certain imperatives filled his mind, and still aware of the hand resting lightly on his forehead, he spoke. "I must leave here, Dana," he murmured, and felt the force of the words for the first time as he spoke them aloud. *Leave here.* Leave *her.*

Dana agreed. "It would be best."

"Have you . . . seen her?" John asked.

"I have. Briefly. I brought the surgeon up."

"Is she . . . ?"

The man seemed to hesitate. "She will survive."

John at last dragged himself upward into a sitting position. He leaned back against the side of the bed as Dana was doing, both of them seated upon the floor. A thought occurred to him. He wondered how much Dana knew, how much any of the servants knew.

He returned the man's gaze, seeing neither condemnation nor accusation. Finally the need to share the weight became too great and he asked quietly, "How much do you know?"

A red tinge seemed to creep up the sides of Dana's face. He lowered his head. "I know little, sir, and prefer to keep it that way.'"

John understood, though still within him there was some terrible need to confess. But better judgment intervened. There were only two who must share this burden of guilt, who would live with it every day of their lives.

He left the bed and went to the wardrobe, where on the floor in the corner he found the satchel with which he had arrived. He emptied it of the old garments, too small for him now, and refilled it with a single change of clothes.

"Where will you go?" Dana asked.

"Back to London, where I came from."

He thought he saw an objection forming on the man's face. "You belong here," Dana muttered.

"I'll return one day," John promised.

An awkward moment followed, the two of them surveying each other. As though to break the mood, Dana commenced to fish through his pockets, his manner gruff. "I doubt seriously if you have a shilling on you."

Before John could protest, Dana was thrusting a pound note upon him, shoving it at last into his top pocket.

"I'll repay you one day," John promised.

"Don't want repayment," the man grumbled. He glanced up at John. "A word now and then, though, a letter . . ."

How curious, John mused, that sadness that always invested love. Now he found that he could say nothing, and merely dropped the satchel to the floor and reached out for his friend and clasped him to him.

"Well, now"—John smiled, hearing the man's sniffling and realizing for both their sakes, he must depart immediately—"one last favor, Dana," he asked. "I need a horse, a good sturdy one to carry me to London. I trust your judgment. Would you prepare one for me and have him waiting outside the door in the east wall?"

Dana nodded, as though grateful for the chance to flee the room. Then he was gone, letting in the sounds of mourning coming from the end of the corridor, shutting them out again as he closed the door behind him.

John stood motionless in the center of the room, a need still strong within him. If only he might see her for one last time. He did not want to cause her additional pain, and still remembered the manner in which she had lifted her hands to his approach in the Great Hall.

Slowly he reached for his satchel, amazed that the love which he felt for her was still intact. If only she might have lived with the message, the knowledge that he was . . .

He hurried to the door and stopped for a final look at his elegant chambers, and felt again a slow rising hate for his father. His judgment of the man had always been that he was foolish and weak. Now he must add deception and dishonor to that list of epithets. How would it have hurt him to tell John the truth, that the beautiful lady who had given him life was not dead, but living at Eden?

But he hadn't, and now the events of this day were his father's burdens as well as John's, *his* fault, *his* guilt.

Weakened by his hate, he stepped rapidly out into the corridor, his eyes moving immediately toward the confusion outside her chambers. From that distance he observed that the crowd had diminished, only Harriet's most loyal and trusted maids remaining.

He held his position, still debating with himself whether or not to invade their grief, when suddenly the door to her chambers opened and he saw Aggie Fletcher step out. She appeared exhausted, her face even from that distance reflecting the horror of the room she'd recently departed.

Once Aggie had been an ally. Surely she would grant him a moment's access to the chamber, permit him to look upon her one last time.

On this note of hope he started forward, but after three steps he stopped. She'd been in the process of wiping her brow with the hem of her apron when she saw him. At first a look of sad pleasure had crossed her face.

But it was the expression immediately following that caused him to halt his progress, a peculiar expression, as though defying him to come closer, the angles of her stern face cast downward in condemnation, as though *she knew*.

Before such a wall of suspicion, he had no defense. Then he was running, determined to put as much distance as possible between himself and the nightmare that was now Eden Castle, not consciously knowing where he was going, where he might safely pass the last few remaining hours of daylight before his departure from Eden.

But his steps took him there, through the blur of the castle, out through the narrow gate in the east wall, across the headlands, his breath catching in his throat as he plunged into woods, then at last seeing it up ahead, their temple of love.

Breathless, he dropped his jacket and satchel and fell to ground, his face buried in cool grasses, both hands outreaching as though to gather only the good memories to him.

But after a time of fruitless effort, when he had gathered nothing but shame and remorse and new grief, he tried to ease his agony with thoughts of London and Elizabeth, good Elizabeth. Might he tell her? Would God be so merciless as to deny him the relief of one confession?

No! How shocked she would be, Elizabeth more than anyone, delicate Elizabeth who in her great love for his father had denied herself all companionship, all intimacy. How could he plead a case of love and need to her?

His punishment was clear. There would be no willing shoulders strong enough to share his burden. How unique his suffering, to lose a mother and lover in the same moment.

Eden Castle,
June 21, 1852

SHE KNEW LITTLE in her newfound darkness and preferred it that way. Three weeks after she'd denied herself the world, she sat in her chamber, in a straight-backed chair, in her dressing gown, her eyes still bandaged, awaiting the knock on the door, and realized with pleasure that she'd lost even the diffident pride in her own suffering, which was a human being's last resource in misfortune.

Frequently throughout her ordeal, she had thought on Christ, had wondered if He, crucified on the cross, had been aware of Himself as spectacle. In the beginning, she had been, had carefully recorded the sound of each footstep moving across her bedchamber floor, knew intimately the sound of the surgeon who had dressed her wounds, removing all the damaged tissue, muttering over and over again, as though she were deaf as well as blind, "Christ, Jesus Christ . . ."

Abruptly she sat straighter in the chair. Her initial impulse had been for death, suicide by the quickest, surest means possible. But since she'd first come to Eden, years ago, she'd thought so often on death that it had been almost as though she were contemplating a reunion with an old friend. Far too easy. Not at all negotiable when placed beside that mountainous debt she had to pay.

Sharply she bent her head over. She'd discovered days ago that she could control the pain by adjusting the angle of her head. With her head erect, the nerve ends seemed more alive. Bowed, the pain subsided.

The chamber was quiet about her, the emptiness heavy. Good. It must become more so, and as the pain diminished, she thought calmly on the next step of her penance.

There was this to be said for her plight. No one seemed to have the will to cross her. That she'd requested audiences this afternoon with first the surgeon, then the master carpenter seemed not at all unusual to anyone. And all her other requests had been granted as well.

Though bewildered, only yesterday Peggy and Aggie Fletcher had directed the stewards in the removal of all furnishings save her bed and this chair. How fearfully they had moved about her, rolling the carpets, removing the fine old Brussels tapestries, all the expensive luxuries that once had pleased her and supported her in her false role as Lady Eden.

Slowly she stood, her hands outreaching, her sense of balance still off. Yet in spite of everything, how comforting it was, that safe blackness. Her bare feet felt the absence of sun, and the sensation informed her that she was moving into the shadows of the chamber, the stone floors cool beneath her feet.

A few steps later, she felt the weakness increasing. Softly she fell to her knees, the sudden jarring motion causing new fires to erupt beneath the bandages. Supporting herself on one arm, she welcomed the pain and waited it out, her head filled with a thousand voices, some ancient, some recent.

Your horse is dead, Harriet. We had to put him down.
You're speaking foolishness. One cannot chart passion.
Slowly she reached one hand up, her fingers touching her butchered hair.
You must cut it. Beneath the bandages, lice will breed.
Suddenly she lifted her head to the door, thinking she'd heard footsteps. The door still bothered her, her vulnerability to curiosity seekers who came to stare at her. At first she'd thought that she must endure that as well, but later she'd changed her mind. She had detected a quality in certain voices, Peggy's for one, and Aggie's and Clara Jenkins', a texture of love, a willingness to forgive her anything, a warmth that she knew she could very easily come to rely upon, and worse, to need.

While still confined to her bed, she'd formulated the last step in her plan, the step which would be executed today. Then true penance would begin.

Now she drew herself up onto her hands and knees and crawled the rest of the way to her bed, one hand reaching ahead, until at last she was kneeling beside the bed, her mind moving easily into prayer.

Only in prayer could she confess to the specific nature of her sin. Only in prayer could she think on what she had done, asking God to share her burden, which still was a mix of remorse and longing.

I will not perish under the will of God unless I myself will it.

How thoroughly over the last few days she'd been cursed with total consciousness. How she'd listened for John's step, hearing many others, but never his. She'd thought that he might try to see her, and had prayed that he wouldn't, and ultimately she'd taken her grief to prayer, where on her knees she had found relief.

Again she tried to adjust herself to prayer, to make her mind silent and submissive.

"My Father in heaven, hear . . ."

Listen!

She lifted her head, a wobbling, unhinged movement. She heard something, a step, movement near the door.

"Who is it?" she whispered, hearing the pleading in her voice. "Please," she begged, and again as small fires ignited in the ruined tissue about her eyes, she collapsed against the side of the bed, her arms wrapped about her as the footsteps drew nearer.

Then someone turned away, as though shocked. It was while he was still moving away that she at last heard a voice, scarcely recognizable. "Your . . . husband. I trust I'm not . . . intruding."

In spite of her new apprehension, she was conscious of a silent thankfulness. It was not John. They both had been spared. "James?" she asked, scanning the room with sightless eyes. When at first he did not reply, she considered raising herself to a position of greater dignity, perhaps to the edge of the bed, or better, to the chair.

But she changed her mind. That short journey to the chair from where she crouched was a distance of indescribable hazards, and the greatest hazard of all was herself as spectacle, the awkward jerking motions of her head, her butchered hair.

Without warning a new fear entered her mind. Had she been so busy concentrating on his heavy step that she'd failed to discern other lighter ones? Rapidly she started forward, clutching at the side of the bed. "The . . . children?" she whispered.

"They're not here," she heard him say from the window.

Weakened with relief, she slipped back to the floor and tried to deal with the man standing by the window. What was his purpose in coming here?

She was on the verge of asking when suddenly he stepped forward until, by her best estimate, he was standing directly over her. "I did not bring the children, but they have been asking for you. What am I to tell them?"

"Tell them I am dead."

"They know better."

"Tell them they mustn't come."

"I would not permit them entrance to this chamber," he replied, no pity in his voice, only a heavy condemnation. How soothing was condemnation.

"Then the matter is closed."

From the area near the foot of the bed she heard him again, softer this time. "I pity you," he murmured.

"I do not ask for your pity."

"Still I offer it, as any husband would to any wife—"

"I am not your wife."

"No. And you never have been."

On her knees, she clasped her hands before her. She needed prayer.

But as the soothing sound of "Our Father" was forming on her lips, he commenced pacing again, directly behind her, so close she could feel the displacement of air caused by his movement. His voice had grown harsh again, mocking.

"I wish you could see me, madam," he said. "Quite a transformation, I'm sure you would agree. I've shaved and bathed and am standing upright. Not a drop of brandy has passed my lips today. How curious that we derive our strengths from each other's weakness."

She listened, head down.

"You see, I felt compelled," he went on, "to come and see for myself if the tales circulating through this castle from servant to servant were true, or simply figments of their imagination."

Poor James, she thought, how consistent he was in his inability to understand her. What her soul desired more than anything in the world was to hear someone speak her sin aloud. What a balm that would be, what a foundation on which to build a lifetime of penance.

Knowing that he would not speak it as long as she appeared docile before him, she gathered what strength she had left and struggled upward.

Predictably a hand tightened on her arm. "No, Harriet, we will have this one last conversation. Then you'll be dead to me."

A prisoner now, she waited.

"Answer yes or no," he persisted, his voice close. "Did you bear my brother's child?" he whispered, as though fearful that other ears might be listening.

She nodded. What blessed relief.

"And was that infant the boy who has lived in this castle for the past year?"

Again she nodded.

The hand on her arm tightened. "And did you take that boy to your bed as lover?"

"Yes."

She had only a dim foreboding that he was going to strike her, and when the blow came, a sharp slap with his left hand, she fell backward at his feet.

On the floor, half-senseless with pain, she was vaguely aware of him standing over her. She knew that he was angry and stupid enough to kill her, and waited for the death blow.

But instead, at that moment she heard a confusion at the door, Peggy's voice raised in a horrified scream at the tableau before her.

Then she heard another voice, the old surgeon's who'd attended her for the last three weeks. "I say," she heard him sputter. "What is the meaning—"

But he did not finish, for at that moment she heard

heavy boots rushing toward her, heard James's protest, heard Peggy's weeping. "He escaped the guards, my lady. I had no idea that he'd come here."

Then the confusion of sounds became too great in her ear, matching her disappointment that the ill-timed intrusion had altered James's course of action. She was aware of him being escorted out, the guards, once remiss in their duties, now performing with greater determination. She was tempted to call after them, to instruct them to give him all the brandy he wanted, for now he sorely needed it.

Then she felt the sensation of many hands lifting her, the broad familiar hand of the surgeon cradling her head, and in the next instant she felt the security of the bed beneath her and heard again Peggy's tearful voice. "Is she hurt? I really had no idea that he . . . Why would he want to harm her further?"

On the opposite side of the bed was the surgeon, Dr. Addley, a man she had never looked upon, but one she knew intimately, his huffing manner bespeaking a large portly man, his rough, smelly fingers bespeaking a third-rate surgeon.

As his hands hovered about her bandaged head, she tried to draw a deep breath, the better to digest what had just happened, the better to face what was yet ahead.

To that end, she mustered enough energy to push away the fluttering hands, to silence Peggy's voice. "I'm well," she said, turning her head from one side to the other, the habit of sight still strong within her.

"You must let me see for myself, my lady," Dr. Addley contradicted sternly. "If there are repetitions of this domestic warfare, I must warn you that your injuries will never heal."

"I *am* healed, Dr. Addley," she said, "as much as I will ever be."

"I beg your pardon, my lady, but—"

"And I summoned you here today to remove the bandages."

"Oh, I'm afraid I can't do that."

"You can and will," she went on, allowing the classic petulance of the invalid to invade her manner. Now she gave in to self-pity, always effective where Peggy was concerned. "I have few pleasures left, doctor," she said softly. "One to which I look forward with anticipation is the ability to sit in the sun and feel its warmth on my face. Will you now deny me that simple pleasure?"

She heard Peggy sniffling, heard as well the reluctant silence of the surgeon. "I had . . . thought to remove them next week," he commenced hesitantly.

"Remove them now."

"There is the risk of infection."

"The wounds are healed. I have felt with my fingers beneath the bandages."

At last she felt the surgeon's hand gently lift her head, his fingers carefully unwinding the layered bandages, her head growing lighter with each turn until the last fell away.

She heard a gasp, Peggy's, and realized for the first time that the mask of bandages had protected others as well as herself. One hand moved tentatively up to the rough scar tissue, to the useless folds of dead skin about her eyes, the ridges of torn flesh moving out in all directions.

Slowly Harriet lifted her hand toward the surgeon. "I . . . thank you, sir"—she smiled—"for your diligent attendance."

"I wish, my lady, that I might have done more."

"No need." She smiled. "I have given Mrs. Swan instructions as to the size of your purse. I think you will be amply rewarded for your many trips up the cliff walk during these last few weeks."

"The purse means nothing to me, my lady, if only I could restore—"

"Peggy! See the surgeon out," she commanded, "and send the master carpenter to me immediately."

"Yes, my lady," came the tearful voice.

Harriet waited until they were gone, then commenced a slow inspection of her face with her hands. There was one small band of smooth flesh that covered her forehead, then the damage commenced, the rough script clear, extending to the cavities that once had been her eyes, on down over her cheeks where the last few perforations of the forks had cut into her skin.

Suddenly a cry surfaced, a soft wail which broke into sobs as continuously she cast her head about, thinking that with the bandages removed, she might see light, but seeing nothing.

In the last spasm of grief, she divined without fear that in the bleak stretches of her past life, what she had interpreted as loneliness had been nothing compared to what was ahead of her, that from this time on she was a force enclosed within herself. Each day, each hour, each moment would be an obstacle course through which she must successfully make her way in order to face another.

And when God felt that she had served her penance, and not a moment before, He would mercifully stop her heart from beating and draw the breath from her lungs, and the thought of that blessed state swept over her now like a cool chaste caress.

God, what a madhouse, Morley Johnson thought upon opening his eyes after a sleepless night, hearing constant hammering, as he'd heard it all night long, coming from the upper regions of the castle.

He shifted upon the stiff couch in one of the lower-floor guest chambers, still musty-smelling, though he'd inhabited it for three weeks.

Again he turned uncomfortably over, appalled at how his stay at Eden had stretched on. Twice he'd tried to depart, only to be restrained by pleading servants who sensed the rudderless ship that now was Eden Castle.

His first attempted departure had been almost three weeks ago to the day, after he had successfully resolved the embarrassment of the corpse in the small library. Now he rolled onto his back and stared upward at the elaborate plasterwork ceiling, rather pleased with his expertise in that awkward affair.

How effortlessly he'd appeased the local constable, a jackass, really, fisherman turned petty bureaucrat. Without question the man had signed the death certificate and had gratefully accepted Morley's twenty-pound note, a token of "appreciation from the Eden family."

Thus a murder had been concealed, a victim buried, a murderer gone free. Abruptly Morley closed his eyes. What a farce, the law! And what in God's name was that incessant hammering all about?

He sat up and clamped his hands over his ears, his head pounding in time with the hammer blows. No, he must leave here as soon as possible.

Sitting on the edge of the bed, Morley recalled the second time he'd tried to leave. For days he'd asked to see Lord Eden, to plant the seed in his mind concerning rising taxes, a simple business discussion between a solicitor and his client. And since Lord Eden had not yet put in an appearance in a public room, Morley had bribed a serving maid into escorting him to his lordship's private chambers, where he'd found a most curious sight, two burly watchmen standing guard on the door. When Morley had demanded that they announce him to Lord Eden, how they had laughed, though one had unlatched the door and had drawn it open a crack, and Morley had seen the ruin for himself and smelled it as well, an almost overpowering odor of brandy, as though the chamber were a brewery, and sprawled facedown upon the table he'd seen the collapsed figure of Lord James Eden, the side of his face resting in spilled brandy, his arms hanging limp, legs sprawled, garbed only in a soiled shirtwaist, no sign of trousers or stockings or boots, senselessly drunk, and from the ample assortment of bottles on the sideboard, likely to stay that way.

Morley felt a flush on his cheeks, thinking now what he'd thought then. How tragic, but how convenient. Obviously his lordship was in no condition to go over figures, or leases, or deeds of ownership. Was it possible that Morley Johnson now possessed a power that poor old Sir Claudius Potter had dreamt of all his life—complete control of the Eden estates?

The thought of that possibility brought him to the reason why he had remained this long at Eden Castle. He needed an interview with her ladyship, for he knew all too well that the true power at Eden had never resided in his lordship's weak hands. Oh, to be sure, his signature was required from time to time.

But the true decision-making chambers were on the third floor, her ladyship's apartments, and the various maids and the old house warden, Mrs. Swan, had put him off long enough, claiming "Her ladyship suffers terrible from female miseries," and "Her ladyship's done harm to herself," and "Her ladyship's nerves is a bit skitterish."

Damn, but his own nerves were a bit skitterish, he thought angrily, hearing that constant hammering.

Then it stopped. He lifted his head, recording the silence. He padded barefoot to the door and opened it a crack. An army of servants, or so it seemed, were running past his door, a look of shock on their faces as they hurried toward the central staircase.

Dear Lord, what now? As soon as the undisciplined parade had passed his door, he closed it and hurled himself into activity. Using stale water left from the night before, he bathed himself and dressed quickly in his traveling clothes. A few moments later he made a final adjustment on his jacket, then stepped out into the corridor. He started up the stairs, hearing the chatter of voices growing louder as he ascended, the turmoil seeming to emanate from the third floor.

As he rounded the landing and glanced toward the end of the passage, he saw chaos, every servant at Eden, or so it seemed, clustered outside her ladyship's apartments, all gathered about a strange focal point, a muscular workman, with sleeves rolled up, a scattering of saws and fragments of metal littering the floor, clearly the scene where the incessant hammering had originated.

Confronting this workman was the mountainous old cook, Mrs. Fletcher. From where Morley stood, it appeared as though these two were on the verge of fistcuffs.

After listening for a moment and finding that he was unable to make sense out of it, he at last stepped forward and raised his voice, ready to take charge.

"Enough!" he shouted. With relief he saw their plain dull faces fall into an attitude of respect, the old cook turning away first, juggling a serving tray bearing someone's uneaten breakfast in one hand, while the burly workman stepped away, rubbing his hamlike arm with one blackened hand.

As he caught sight of Morley, he swept off his flat shapeless hat and bobbed his head. "Guv," he muttered.

Morley waited for the residual chatter to cease. Then he stepped forward. "If it wouldn't be too rude of me," he began, "would someone be so kind as to inform me what this is all about?"

Within the moment the voices rose again, old Aggie Fletcher leading off. "Ask the simpleton behind you. He's the one. Ask what he's been up to this night, witless oaf."

"Me duty," the workman cried out. "Just me duty," he repeated. "I does what I'm told, was brought up that way, a faithful servant."

"A jackass," Aggie cried, topping him. "Look for yourself, sir." With a stabbing gesture she pointed toward the door which led into her ladyship's chambers, a new door, for just then Morley spied the old one resting against the corridor wall.

So? Her ladyship had requested a new door and a workman had obliged. Bewildered, Morley shook his head. "I fail to see—"

"Oh, you bet you do, sir," Aggie broke in, her broad arms again flailing in all directions, the items on the breakfast tray slipping dangerously about. "All you see, sir, is a closed door. But what I have here is her ladyship's breakfast. Now, would you be so kind as to tell me how I am to serve it?"

"Why don't you try knocking?" he snapped.

But she merely smiled. "Oh, I've done that, sir, till me knuckles is raw, bleeding practically. Would you care to try?"

In the awkward silence, Morley turned his attention to the workman. "What's your name?" he began, the ritual of the law courts strong within him.

"Boaz, guv," the man muttered.

"Now, Boaz," Morley went on, "tell me about this," and he gestured toward the new door.

The man shrugged. "What's to tell, guv? I was summoned to this here spot yesterday afternoon by her ladyship. She said that she required a new door, one that would make her feel safe, you know, one she could control, no one entering lest she says so."

With the sense of having answered all questions, Boaz moved back. "If you'll excuse me, guv," he muttered, "I been up the night, I have. Her ladyship said I was due a day of rest. Now, if you don't—"

"You can rest in a moment," Morley said, eyeing the awesome door with new respect. There was something different about it. No knob on the outside, nor hinges, a smooth heavy barrier neatly sealing the entrance to the chamber.

Well, sooner or later he'd have to find out for himself. He stepped forward and lifted his fist and rapped once, a civil sound befitting the station of the gentlewoman on the opposite side.

No response.

He knocked again. "My lady?"

Still no response.

He lifted his fist and knocked loudly three times. "My lady, with your forgiveness. It's Morley Johnson. I beg an audience with you, on a matter of importance."

But there was nothing, not even a hint that there was life behind the door. He turned to face the staring servants and shouted, "Then fetch a battering ram and a crew of your strongest—"

But the carpenter Boaz was merely shaking his head. "Oh, guv," the large man mourned, "ain't a battering ram devised by man capable of knocking that door down. Solid metal it is at the center, with thick English oak on either side, four solid metal hinges I forged myself last night on the inside, and a sliding bolt the length and breadth of a man's arm penetrating solid stone."

As the description trailed off, Morley was aware of increased weeping, the servants seeming to know what had happened, her ladyship sealed behind the impenetrable door.

"Get on with your duties," Morley commanded. "I'm sure you have enough to keep you more than busy."

At last Morley turned to face the two combatants who still glared at each other. "Go along with you, Boaz," he concluded. "You've earned your rest."

When he too had disappeared around the corner,

Morley leaned wearily against the wall, returning the old woman's stare. "What about the windows?" he asked.

"Accessible," the old woman conceded, "if you're a sea gull. If you're a man, you have three stories of sheer wall with no foothold between you and the gravel of the inner courtyard."

He thought he detected a sly pleasure in the old bitch's face. Coldly he suggested, "Why don't you run along with the others. Clearly there's nothing for you to do here."

Then she was gone, leaving him alone in the corridor, his boots scraping on wood shavings, his eyes focused intently on the new door.

But the longer he stood in the quiet corridor, the more aware he became of a will stronger than his own, and finally he pushed away from the wall in resignation, feeling a peculiar mix of disquiet and relief, and simultaneously thinking that he must hurry now, leave this place of madness and move back into the real world.

As his thoughts gained momentum, so did his steps, and he took the third-floor landing running, thinking ahead to the brief journey to Exeter, his conference with the estate agent, and ultimately to London, a humbly requested hearing with a sympathetic magistrate who would understand the plight of a hardworking solicitor with his hands tied, and who after having been informed of the shambles that was now Eden Castle, would grant him full power of attorney.

And with that awesome weapon in his hand . . . The thought almost hurt. Midway down the steps, he stopped and grasped the banister as though for support, and stared blankly ahead into space, a radiant smile on his face, as though he were glimpsing the shores of heaven.

On the Road to London,
June 1852

ACCORDING TO THE last road sign, he was a mile and a
half southwest of Salisbury, near a place called Harrington Hall.

What matter to him? His feet were blistered, the back
of his neck was baked red by the June sun, and it made
no difference whether he tried to think on where he had
been or where he was going. There was no hope in either
direction.

Since he had been in no rush to reach London—what
was there in London for him besides good Elizabeth and
her honest poverty?—John had sold the horse in Barnstaple
and with the extra pounds in his pocket had started
off on foot.

The climate was that of a warm June, the countryside
ripe and kind, and he desperately needed an interval
alone.

He knew he couldn't wander directionless forever. And
he wouldn't allow himself to become a burden to Elizabeth. Perhaps after a brief stay in London it would
be best if he fulfilled that childhood dream of escaping
to India. There were ships embarking weekly from the
London docks. He was young and able, could read and
write. It would be a simple matter to sign on with one of
the crews.

India! The name alone was capable of evoking dreams
of riches, adventure, a landscape free of memories. Perhaps in that hot, dusty clime, Eden and all it stood for
would relinquish its hold on him. According to the recent
books he'd read, a man, any man, could make or find his
fortune in India. For a moment he recalled certain exotic
place names: Bombay, Delhi, Agra, Meerut . . .

He closed his eyes and saw himself in fantasy, his skin darkened, a turban on his head, moving easily among dark-skinned men. He would think on it seriously. It could provide him with an escape route, and he desperately needed one.

Abruptly he halted his pace, feeling a sudden compulsion to leave the road. He wandered into the inviting shade of an apple orchard, and using his satchel as a back rest, he sprawled beneath a tree and closed his eyes, his sense of his father, of betrayal, still strong within him. Why had he deceived him? How would it have hurt to have told John the truth? But what was the truth? And the battle was on again. How many times he had explored all aspects of it, his confusion mounting.

Suddenly he leaned over, his forehead pressed against his knee. How he missed Harriet, would always miss her.

"Hello."

The voice was near. Sharply he looked up, his head swiveling in all directions. But his eyes, blurred with grief and sun, could find nothing. Had he imagined it? On his knees, he looked again down the long row of apple trees and saw nothing save the skittering of sun and shadow.

Then he heard a laugh. "Up here."

On his feet, ready to spring as though under attack, he lifted his head and saw only a thick leafy foliage.

"To your left," the voice instructed. "See the crook in the trunk?"

Then at last he saw her, or more accurately saw a single soft kid slipper, then the hem of a green dress, a mottled pattern resembling the profusion of leaves. No wonder he'd failed to see her. Perched on an uppermost branch, she blended perfectly with the tree.

Still unable to see any more than slippers and the hem of a gown, he shaded his eyes and moved rapidly around the tree. "You have a clear advantage," he called up, spying now a slim waist and a cascade of hair the color of the sun.

He heard the laugh again and the voice, just barely concealing its merriment. "That doesn't very often happen to me. I like it, though," she said.

"But it does make conversation difficult." He smiled,

still encircling the tree, seeing more each turn, a white hand grasping a limb, the angle of a jaw where the sun struck it.

His neck began to ache from its rigid angle. He felt ridiculous conversing with the tree. "Won't you come down?" he asked.

"Why should I?" the voice inquired, a tutored voice, calm, genteel. "You might be a highwayman or a murderer. You're unhappy, I can tell that much."

For a moment he gaped up at the talking branches. "To the first charge, I plead innocent. To the second and third, guilty."

He looked up to see what reaction, if any, would be forthcoming. He heard a soft "I thought so."

"The man deserved to die," John added, confessing to the tree.

"Many men do," the voice replied, then added curiously, "you'll probably kill again before you die yourself."

He lowered his head. "I . . . hope not."

"Where do you come from?" the voice asked.

John started to reply, then changed his mind. "From . . . that way," he said, and vaguely pointed back down the road.

"I know that much," the voice scolded lightly. "I've been watching you for ever so long, since you first appeared over the last down. I'm the one who made you leave the road." There was a pause. "I have magic powers, you know."

Again John gaped upward, recalling his strange compulsion to abandon the road. "Are you a witch?" he asked, smiling, keeping his eye trained on that one small slipper.

Abruptly she laughed. "I've been called one before."

"By whom?"

"By people who have reason to fear me."

"Do I have reason to fear you?"

The laugh died. Her voice changed, seemed to soften until it was little more than a part of the gentle breeze blowing through the tops of the trees. "I would hope not."

Weary of encircling the tree and craning his neck upward, yet enjoying the distraction from his grief, John at last settled against the trunk of a near tree. "I would never harm a witch," he said, entering effortlessly into the pleasant madness.

"I know that," the voice replied. "Still, there are impulses within you. I've known about them for ever so long."

As the voice trailed off with the wind, John sat erect, cross-legged upon the ground. "Known about them?" he questioned. "You've never seen me before."

Again the breeze seemed to break into a peal of laughter. "My goodness," she exclaimed, "I saw you only this morning, in my chambers. I asked Wolf if you were the one, and he said yes, and I argued with him. But he won out. He always does."

Beginning to feel uneasy, John asked tentatively, "Who is . . . Wolf?"

"My cat. He'll be so pleased when I tell him how right he was."

"I'm . . . glad," he murmured, thinking that perhaps he should leave. The wind seemed to have turned suddenly chill.

Although he had yet to move, she said, "You don't have to go yet. You'll spend the night in Salisbury, at the Red Lion, and it's an easy walk from here."

He looked up, beginning to feel annoyance at the invisible presence. "I've not been sleeping in public houses," he said. "I'm afraid I have a limited purse."

"Oh, it won't always be so, I promise you that," she soothed. "I have it on good authority that one day you will be one of the richest men in England."

He laughed openly at the preposterous suggestion. "On whose authority? Wolf's?"

"Who else?"

Still the wind was increasing, the clouds overhead growing thick. Well, he'd rested enough. It had been at best an interesting diversion, a fanciful, other-world quality about it. But unfortunately he was still of this world. As he rose to his feet, he glanced upward again. "I thank you for talking with me," he said, bowing to the tree. "If I should ever pass this way again . . ."

"Oh, you'll pass this way many times," the voice said,

"so often that you will cut a new road between London and North Devon. And if I'm not here, look for me in that large house which sits just over the north down. Harrington Hall, it's called. And my name is Lila."

Again his eyes began to blur from searching the upper branches. Once he thought he saw the gleam of an eye looking down on him. "Lila," he repeated.

"And your name is . . ."

"John." Sharply he looked up. Had she said the name with him, or had he just imagined it? Then "John" she repeated, and he thought he detected sadness in her voice. "Please don't wait too long before you come again," she added. "Of course I'll be here, regardless when you come. But don't let too much time pass."

The rising wind lifted the hem of the green dress and blew it to one side, revealing a white lace petticoat. Apparitions did not wear lace petticoats. Though certain that he had fallen into a kind of madness, still he asked, "Won't you come down before I leave? You have climbed to a considerable height. You may be in need of assistance."

When at first she didn't answer, he dared to hope that she might be considering his request. But instead she said, "No, I need no assistance. I climbed up and I can climb down. Besides, it's not time yet."

"And when will that time come?"

"Oh, it depends on many things. We both have much to do. There's a chance that one or both of us will not survive." Her voice fell as though she were considering her own words. "But I think we will. Now, you must go. Look! The cat's told them where I am. Isn't that just like him? To send me out here, then tattle on me?"

At that moment he heard a horse neighing in the distance. He turned about and saw a lone rider on the far hill.

"Oh, dear," she mourned. "You must hurry. Take cover deeper in the orchard.

There was such an urgency to her voice, such a complete madness to the entire episode, that before he was consciously aware of what he was doing, he found himself retrieving his satchel and running deeper into the orchard, finding a safe shelter of trees about twenty yards away and taking refuge in the shadows.

From where he crouched he could see the horseman drawing nearer. He heard a voice, slightly cracked with age and thick with worry. "My lady?" the old man called out. "Are you here? I beg you . . ."

Carefully John watched, peering out from his hiding place. Suddenly he saw a figure gowned in green drop from the tree, her hands outreaching to break her fall, a small, slim figure it was, almost childlike. As she picked herself up, he saw the rider turn in that direction and gallop eagerly forward, reining his horse in directly before the girl.

"My lady," the old man scolded. "I hope you know what you've done? You've upset the entire household. Your father and mother are—"

"I'm sorry, Max," John heard her say, approaching the horse. He had yet to see anything but her back and the long strands of fair hair, mussed by the wind. "I don't know why everyone gets so upset," she murmured. "I always tell my cat where I'm going. All you must do is ask him."

John saw the old man's face fall, as though a mantle of sorrow had just been dropped over his shoulders. "I know, my lady," he said, as though humoring her. "But you see, I have trouble understanding what the cat says."

"I don't see why. He speaks perfectly respectable English."

Then John observed the old man's eyes moving heavenward. "If her ladyship is ready to return, permit me to . . ."

As he bent over and extended his hand in assistance, she placed her slipper in his stirrup and swung up in the saddle with him, her face still obscured, but her voice clear. "Oh, Max," she said, speaking with childlike excitement. "I just met the beautiful boy. He was standing right here."

"Of course, my lady. Are you secure?" There was a hint of disbelief in the old man's voice, as though he were accustomed to hearing incredible stories.

"If you had come earlier, you could have met him too,

Max. But I had to send him away because it's not time yet. He'll come back and you can meet him then."

"It will be my pleasure, my lady."

"Of course, he's a murderer, but in time we all will forget that." .

"If you say so, my lady."

"Of course I say so." John heard a sudden sharpness to her voice, as though she were aware that she was being humored. How terrible, he thought, to know that nothing you said would ever be taken seriously.

Then, "Take me home, Max," she commanded. "I must speak with Wolf."

"Of course, my lady."

As the horse started slowly forward, John dared to leave his hiding place, longing to call after her. At that precise moment she turned toward him, a smile on her face, a most beautiful face, clear wide-set blue eyes, conveying a message without words, as though thanking him for talking with her, for taking her seriously.

He had only a glimpse, then she was gone. Still John watched, thinking surely she'd turn and look at him once more. But she didn't. Not until the horse reached the crest of the down and disappeared on the other side did he venture all the way out of hiding, and even then he approached the tree where she had perched with caution. Carefully he looked up and would not have been surprised to see that same soft slipper, the hem of that green patterned gown.

But he saw nothing except the tree limbs dipping under the stress of the rising wind and saw beyond to the churning clouds. Rain by nightfall was his grim prediction.

London was still miles ahead, and suddenly he discovered that he'd lost his appetite for the open road. The adventure of sleeping in barns and hitching rides in the backs of hay wagons no longer appealed. Perhaps it would be more prudent to stop at the Red Lion tonight in Salisbury, and come morning he'd spend his remaining money on a coach ticket to London.

He turned sharply and glanced toward the crest of the down where the horse and riders had disappeared.

You will spend the night in Salisbury at the Red Lion.

Then he felt the first cold pelting of rain upon his head and broke into a run, the rain increasing with each step.

My name is Lila, and you'll find me at Harrington Hall.

It was impossible for him to think any longer. The cold rain was coming at him from all directions, and the nonsensical present had been replaced by memories of the past.

Harriet.

Normally at this hour they were taking tea in her chambers. In spite of the rain, he could detect her fragrance, the way her hand brushed across his forehead.

Suddenly as he ran, tears came, the first release he'd experienced since he'd left Eden. In spite of his grief, at odd moments a quiet voice sounded in his ear, along with the rain.

You'll be one of the richest men in England one day.

Had he dreamed it? Or was he too mad, his mind unhinged by past events? Still he ran, the rain increasing, his thoughts growing as blurred as his vision.

By the time he reached Salisbury, the storm had increased to dangerous proportions, and only a fool would have refused shelter.

Now seated on the edge of the bed in his chamber in the Red Lion, wrapped in a blanket and shivering, John watched as the young maid fussed with the reluctant fire in the grate. She was talking all the time of something or other, talking lightly, as only women can talk.

Beneath the influence of her voice, a small fire, no larger than the one in the grate, began to warm John, and something inside his heart thawed in consequence.

By nature unsuited for self-pity, he pushed the mysterious past out of his head and concentrated on the flickering red light coming from the fire and the way it played over her earnest pretty face.

He did not know her name. It was not her name that interested him. "It's going well," he suggested, referring to the fire.

"Smoking a bit too much," she worried, fanning the air with her hand. "The wood is damp."

"Everything is damp." He smiled. He lowered the blanket from his head. "Do you live in Salisbury?" he asked, observing a small roll of soft flesh beneath her chin.

She nodded, her hands still outreaching with the poker, prodding the logs to burn. "Not far from here. With me mum."

"Where's your father?"

"Ask God," she replied without hesitation, "for I'm sure I don't know."

There was no anger or regret in her voice, simply a statement of fact.

"Have you always lived here?" John asked, enjoying the sound of rain on the roof, the pleasant lassitude that was beginning to extend to all parts of his body.

"Aye, always," the girl replied. "Least, as long as I can remember."

Then to the heart of the matter. "Would you know," John began, "of an establishment in these parts called Harrington Hall?"

She looked up at him with a roguish grin. "Coo, I'd have to be blind and dumb not to have heard of Harrington Hall, sir. They're our gentry, they are, though all of 'em's as balmy as a March day."

John allowed the blanket to fall down about his shoulders. The fire was beginning to blaze well. The warmth felt good on his bare shoulders. "Tell me about them," he invited, "unless of course you have duties elsewhere."

She glanced slyly up at him, her dark brown eyes catching sight of his bared torso. "The inn's full, sir," she said, "ever-body abed, 'cept you. I won't be needed, or missed, for a while."

He smiled. Obviously something she had seen had caught her fancy. "Then tell me about them," he urged, slipping to the floor before the fire, the blanket lowered to his waist.

His closeness seemed to distract her. Carefully he charted the course of her eyes over his chest. "Ooh, what happened here, sir?" she gasped sympathetically, her fingers reaching out to the small scar in the shape of a B.

"A fall," he said, and tried to turn her attention away. "Tell me of the Harringtons," he proposed in a playful mood, "then I'll tell you about the scar."

She shrugged. "A good family they was, in the beginning. Quite noble, till her ladyship strayed over to Ireland and brought back his lordship."

"They're Irish?"

"His lordship is. Black Irish is what we call him. But her ladyship is good solid English." She leaned close, as though to share an intimate secret. "It was the witchcraft that done it, the Catholic witchcraft. Oh, he worked it on her right enough and come back with her from Ireland."

She leaned closer. "They say he keeps the Virgin Mary's finger with him at all times."

"The . . . what?"

She nodded broadly. "Her finger. He carries it with him in a little gold and jeweled case and it gives him magic powers. Devil powers, some say."

John listened to the madness and mourned the loss of her good sense.

" 'Course, like I say, they're harmless enough," she went on, "though some think different. And generally they're kind as well. Once, twice, on some special festival day, Catholic day," she added, clearly condemning, "they open the gates at Harrington Hall and invite all us plain folk to come in." Somberly she shook her head. "I went once with me mum when I was little. A spooky place, it is, with Mary statues all over, and candles burning." She stared glumly into the fire. "We ain't been since that once. Me mum says they're after our souls, that's what."

John watched her closely and wondered to what degree her bizarre tale was truth or fiction. "Are there . . . children?" he asked.

"One," the girl replied, drawing her knees up, enjoying her position of authority. "Last Easter they found her before the altar of the cathedral, meowing like a cat. On all fours, she was, crawling around through the arrangements of lilies, and meowing like a cat."

"How old is she?"

"Oh, a child is all, really, thirteen, maybe fourteen by now."

"Would you know her name?"

"Who doesn't? Lila, they named her. And there ain't been no more since."

Lila. You'll pass this way again. Next time, look for me at Harrington Hall.

"Lila, yes, that's what they call her," the girl went on. "And she's forever gettin' loose. There's an old man who is supposed to keep his eyes on her, but sometimes she's too quick. Once they found her all the way over to Stonehenge."

It was several moments before he realized she'd ceased speaking. Then he saw her face, a frightened expression. "Gawd, I hope I ain't said too much. You . . . wouldn't be friends of them, now, would you?"

The earnest nature of her inquiry made him laugh. "No, I assure you, I'm not a friend of theirs. I was just passing through and heard the name and was curious."

Relieved, she clasped her knees and carefully tucked her long black skirts about her legs. "Well, if you wish, sir, I could go on all night about the Harringtons, but . . ."

No, he had no desire for her to go on all night. Now his close proximity to the fire made the blanket altogether unnecessary. In fact, if anything, it was overwarm. Slowly he unwrapped the blanket and pushed it to one side.

At first he thought he saw shock in her face, a tentative movement backward, which he halted by reaching for her hand. Would it be the same, he wondered, or was that mysterious ecstasy only possible with . . . ?

Harriet. He merely thought her name and suffered a small death and withdrew his hand from the girl's arm.

No longer retreating, she knelt before him, one hand fumbling with the buttons on her high collar. "I ain't a . . . virgin, sir," she whispered. "Don't pretend to be one . . ."

He looked at her, his memories still punishing him.

"Generally," she went on, "it's old men we get here, trying to outrun their wives, or merchants whose bellies protrude beyond the reach of their . . ."

Her hands were still moving down the buttons, the

black fabric falling away, revealing freckled shoulders. "Most always," she went on, not looking at him, "I tell 'em they must put a bob on that table there."

"I have no intention of leaving a bob on any table," he said quietly.

The dress undone, she pushed it off her shoulders, revealing small breasts. "I have no intention of asking you." She smiled. "A girl does it for herself now and then, if you get what I mean."

Then because she was near and apparently willing, and he was in need of finding out if it was a matter of one woman, or if any woman would do, he guided her gently backward on the floor before the fire and tried to approach her slowly as Harriet had taught him. But his need was great, and hers apparently greater. As her legs wrapped about his waist, he closed his eyes and felt the release, but little else.

"I'm . . . sorry," he whispered close to her ear.

Apparently no apology was necessary. As he raised himself above her, she grinned. "What for sir? We've the whole night, we do," and she wrapped her arms about his neck and again drew him downward.

Amazed that he'd brought her pleasure without half-trying, he tried again, hearing that distant soft voice of instruction in his ear.

A few minutes later, "Oh, lord, sir," the girl beneath him cried out.

Smiling into the darkness of her hair, he sent the instructor's voice away and the loneliness with it, until the sound of the rain blended with their thrashing, and nothing mattered but the fire and the warmth and the receptive female body beneath him.

London,
Late June 1852

WITH THE PROLIFERATION of railways, the coach companies, sensing the end, had clearly allowed their conveyances to go to seed. John had considered the comfort of one of the new shiny trains, but had lacked the fare.

Now, after the most torturous journey he'd ever made in his life, he alighted from the Salisbury-to-London stage and limped toward the White Bear Terminus in Piccadilly.

As he moved through the crush of foot traffic, he wondered bleakly if he even had enough coin in his pocket to cover the modest cost of a pint of ale. His throat was parched, the late-June sun high and hot at midafternoon. Clearly he did not have enough for the comfort of a conveyance, so he'd have to walk all the way to Bermondsey, and God only knew what hideous poverty he'd find when he got there, Elizabeth still trying to operate his father's Common Kitchen, undoubtedly half-starved herself.

His annoyance mounting, he stepped to one side out of the crush of foot traffic and into a quiet harbor near an old costermonger hawking onions. He plunged one hand down into his pockets, his fingers finding a single half-penny. In the heat of the pavement, with the smell of pickled onions filling his nostrils, he closed his eyes and felt momentarily defeated. What a strange journey it had been.

He keeps the Virgin Mary's finger with him at all times . . . Lila's her name . . . they found her meowing before the altar of the . . .

He shook his head, dismissing the curious interlude, preferring to recall instead the willing little serving maid who had stayed with him all night.

Standing on the crowded pavement, he was aware that only in her embrace had the past released its hold on him. Then he must remember the antidote and pray that the world was filled with willing and able females.

Of course the relief hadn't lasted. No sooner had he climbed aboard that dismal coach than the feelings of grief had returned, the realization that with each turn of those coach wheels he was being carried farther and farther away from Eden, that golden dream which had obsessed him for most of his life, now denied to him, perhaps for all time.

By dusk he'd reached the Thames, and all his thoughts were moving in one direction, toward Bermondsey, toward that small timber-frame house that his father had purchased years ago with the remainder of the moneys from the sale of the house on Oxford Street. And to Elizabeth, perhaps the only true mother he would ever know.

As the river rushed beneath him, fresh sorrow rose within him, and he thought again of Elizabeth. Hadn't she always comforted him as a child, loved him out of his sadness, spoken coolly to him of God and grace and duty?

Hungry for that saintly presence, he pushed away from the side of the bridge and the currents of water—like his thoughts, moving too fast for coherent understanding—and he ran all the way, not stopping once for breath until he rounded the corner and saw the house, as humble and as simple and as good as Elizabeth herself, his refuge, his last hope.

Curious, how heavy her thoughts had been all day of Edward. She'd kept four appointments—Lord Kimbrough, Lord Bolton, Sir Embry, and Reverend Hawkins —good lovers, all, any one of whom in the past had been able to coax her out of her loneliness.

But today they had been simply ordeals to get through, though they'd been most generous with her, Lord Bolton arriving first, this morning at ten, bearing three dozen red roses in a silver urn. Then Lord Kimbrough, with his constant pleas that she accept without further hesitation the handsome rooms on Park Lane, overlooking Hyde Park.

To the new flat, she'd said no. There still was too much of Edward in these rooms. To the pearl necklace, she'd said yes, and had lovingly tucked it away in her rosewood jewel box, a gift from another client.

Now, weary at dusk, she eased down into the elegant brass hipbath, a gift from Mr. Jeffries, and allowed the perfumed fragrance of steaming lavender water to envelop her. To one side, her eye fell on the hand-painted Japanese screen, another gift, and from there she indulged herself in an inspection of her bedchamber.

A splendid bedchamber it was now, not at all in keeping with the plain exterior of the house. And in all honesty she could not say that her new luxuries had been "hard-earned." This life suited her very well, allowed her to fight off the loneliness which still affected her, evil moments when, on thinking of the past, her heart seemed to sit like a stone in her breast. Only in her awareness that others suffered as much, if not more, had she been able to find relief.

And profitable. There was that to be said for her new life and profession. Again from where she sat, relaxing in the tub, she lovingly cataloged the mahogany table and sideboard, the new armchair and sofa covered with pale rose damask, and the variety of little tables and cabinets.

By craning her neck, she could see into the front parlor, the long velvet drapes at the windows, patterned carpet of intricate frond and lily design, and there, her new prize, the lovely upright piano, a gift only last week from Henry Cardew. And next to the piano, her own bureau for writing and her needlework table, and the elegant wallpaper, heavily patterned in damask and floral design.

Her eyes satiated, she leaned back in the hipbath as she beheld the center of her profession, the massive four-poster bed, constructed of mahogany and rosewood, with side curtains of velvet which had been delivered to her last month with a simple card, no signature, and a loving message, "For your blessed comfort."

To this day she had no idea who her beneficiary was.

She'd delicately questioned all of her gentlemen, and all had displayed a convincing ignorance.

At the end of her inspection, as she was preparing to sink deeper into the soothing water, her eye fell on the small trunk in the far corner of the room, Edward's trunk, looking ordinary and out of place amidst the new elegance. Within the instant, her mood of self-satisfaction faded.

Would there never be an end to it, to the almost penal servitude which his memory demanded of her? How many times she had considered removing the trunk. It did not belong here, certainly not in this room.

Abruptly her thoughts relapsed into silence, and she stared into the still water. How was it possible that she could cure unhappiness for others, yet be so unhappy herself?

But there was no answer, and as she reached for the sponge, she clung to only one awareness, that in a very real way she *was* loved, treasured in certain cases, her presence sought out by gentlemen of the highest caliber. And she served them in her own way, and God and the world and Edward must understand that, and she owed no one explanation or apology, and her greatest rewards were not the new luxuries which now surrounded her, but rather the blessed look of relief on a furrowed brow, the slow unclasping of a fist, and the grateful tears which on occasion had streamed from the most manly face.

Her defense over, she bathed herself carefully, keenly aware of the needs of her next visitor, his note just visible on the silver tray which rested on the sideboard. Delivered by special courier, written in bold, familiar hand, it said simply, "In from Hawarden. Catherine ill again. Must see you at five this evening. Please. W.G."

Now, if she hurried, she might have time before Willie's arrival to read the latest London *Times*. He appreciated her being well-informed, clearly enjoying using her as a sounding board.

Then hurry she did, concluded her bath and stepped out onto the soft carpet, drying carefully, then dragging the Japanese screen forward until it obscured all items of her bath.

From her wardrobe she withdrew the dressing gown which she'd made months ago from Willie's gift of Florentine lace. She wore it for no one else. Though she'd attached a full silk petticoat to the waist, she'd left the top unlined, and if anyone chose to look, he might see her flesh beneath the patterned lace.

The clock on the mantel said four-forty-five. Fifteen minutes in which to gather herself together and perhaps scan the newspapers so that she might speak intelligently with Willie. And fifteen minutes in which to send the ghost of Edward away.

To that end she went about the comfortable parlor making small adjustments to the clutter of knickknacks. From the sideboard, intent on keeping busy, she spied her two large potted palms, pushed away from the window and the direct rays of high summer sun. Now at dusk the light was soft and diffuse, and she went forward hurriedly to push them back in front of the window.

As she tugged the first palm into place, she stopped to adjust the folds of velvet drapes. From this angle through the window she saw a figure standing across the lane. She pulled back in annoyance. Jack Willmot's guard dog was still in place. What a presumptuous and foolish expense!

For several moments she stared bleakly at the hulking figure. Then she noticed another man, approaching slowly from the left. Two? Had the guard now been increased to . . . ?

Suddenly her hand tightened on the velvet drape. She blinked, the shape of the man growing clearer, the stance, the carriage of the body, the color of the hair as the dying sun struck it, all painfully familiar.

Edward.

Abruptly she dropped the drape, both hands pressed against her mouth as though to prevent an outcry. Was she losing her mind? Was the grief that refused to heal turning her into a madwoman?

She stood motionless. It was only that she had been thinking on him, that was all, only his presence which still permeated the small house in spite of its new furnishings. With strict discipline she ordered herself to breathe calmly. Willie was due any moment. He appreciated as much as anything her calmness and peace of mind.

Then, as though to test her new calm, she again drew back the drape. Quickly she searched the street in all directions, blessedly finding nothing but the first bully boy, a heavyset man in a loose-fitting jacket who lounged against the streetlamp.

As for the other, he was gone, if indeed he'd ever been there at all. As she lowered the drape, she thought sternly that she must watch herself in the future. Edward was dead, and all that remained of him was that one small trunk resting in the corner of her bedchamber.

A knock sounded at the door. The sudden noise startled her, her nerves still on edge. Willie was never punctual. And where was his carriage?

The knock sounded again. She looked almost fearfully toward the door. Willie never knocked more than once. Then who?

The knock came a third time, a sharp impatient rap accompanied now by a voice. "Elizabeth?"

As the voice, rife with familiarity, bore down upon her, she saw the door open, saw first the resurrected head of blond hair, the features identical, dark blue eyes, tender smile, then the whole of him appearing before her in the blaze of evening sun spilling in through the open door, the specter complete, the winding sheet gone, the grave apparently a kinder place than anyone imagined.

"Edward . . . " she gasped, and as the apparition refused to fade, she felt the room and all the objects in it begin to whirl about her, and her mind, in defense against that which it would never understand, simply shut down. Reaching out in an effort to both banish him and draw him closer, she fell to the floor and welcomed the rationality of the unconscious world. . . .

The faint did not last long, and a few moments later she awakened to find herself on the sofa. He was still there, bent over her in concern, though not the "he" she had imagined, but the nearest duplicate she would ever find this side of heaven.

"John?" she whispered, unable to believe that the

young man who knelt before her was the same boy she'd left standing in the rain on the steps of Eden Castle only a year ago.

But his relieved grin confirmed his identity and his soft apology anchored it. "It's me." He smiled. "I'm sorry if I took you by surprise. Perhaps I should have—"

"No," she said, feeling unbearable happiness at seeing him again. Belatedly she opened her arms to him as she'd done a thousand times when he'd been a child, and as he leaned forward into her embrace, she closed her eyes and clasped him to her, feeling the shoulders and torso of a man.

"Oh, John," she whispered. "How I've missed you. How often I've longed for word . . ."

Still he clung to her as though reluctant to let go, as though all he needed at this moment was her closeness. At the same time, she sat up on the sofa, still feeling light-headed. As she made an attempt to straighten the white lace dressing gown, she looked down, feeling a moment of chagrin. Hurriedly she glanced over her shoulder at the rosewood clock. Five-fifteen. Willie due at . . .

"Come John," she said, moving toward the sideboard. "I think we both need a drop of sherry."

As she filled the glasses, she was aware of him staring at her. "Come," she urged again, lifting a glass, aware of his close scrutiny of the room.

A few moments later he stood before her and took the glass from her, his eyes still relentlessly inspecting her.

"You've . . . changed," he said simply.

"As have you." She laughed. "My goodness, I've never seen such a striking resemblance. If your father were here . . ."

Abruptly he turned away and walked toward a near armchair. From the angle of his head, she knew he was still inspecting the room, trying to draw a conclusion between the humble sparse furnishings he remembered and these new opulent ones.

Behind her the ticking of the clock seemed to grow louder, as though trying to warn her of the impending collision. "John," she said cheerily, ignoring the clock's warning, "you must tell me everything. How is Eden? Are

you here for a short visit? I started so many times to
write to you, but I . . ."

In twin movements, as he sat in the armchair, she sat
on the sofa opposite him. Strange, but it had never occurred to her that this moment might take place. She had
been so certain that she would never see him again, confident that everything he would ever need was at Eden.
Again she looked up to see him staring at her.

"Well?" she asked gently, longing to shift the focus of
attention back to him. "Tell me everything. It's easy to
see the Devon air agrees with you."

Still no response.

"John? Is everything . . . ?"

He waved his hand before him as though to dismiss her
questions. "Everything is well," he lied, and she knew he
had lied, but let it pass for the time being.

"I felt the need to return to London," he said. "I missed
you, and was worried"—and again his eyes made a wide
arc of the room, still inspecting—"though I see that my
anxiety was . . . unfounded."

She looked down at her glass, wishing she'd known in
advance of his arrival. At least she could have put away a
few items. Then in the next moment she brought herself
sharply up. Why should she have to put anything away?

She said simply, "I'm doing well, John. I'm sorry if I
caused you anxiety. I should have written."

"And I, too," he murmured.

Outside on the street, she thought she heard a carriage.
As it rattled past she looked down at her glass, surprised
to see the amber liquid trembling.

"Were you expecting someone?" he asked.

She nodded.

"Then I must leave," he said, standing.

"No, please," she begged, seeing for the first time the
state of his garments. Most soiled they were, as though
he'd not changed in days. She suggested, "Why don't you
go up to your old room, wash up, and perhaps have a
nap. Later, we'll have a quiet supper together. I'd like
that very much."

It was her guess that he had not slept soundly for days.
Now with relief she saw that her proposal held some ap-

peal for him as well. Wearily he shook his head. "I . . . have no place else to go, I'm afraid."

"You need no place else," she said, coming up before him and taking his hand. "This is your home. Wherever I am, that will always be your home. Do you understand?"

Never had she seen such a sorrowing expression in one so young. When she couldn't bear the look any longer, she again opened her arms to him, and as he came, she whispered, "I've missed you so much."

Suddenly there was a knock at the door, a single rap, the clear signal of . . . "No, wait," she said as John reached for his satchel. True, she hadn't heard the carriage, but on occasion she'd known Willie to alight a distance away. "Wait," she said again to John. "I would like for you to meet this gentleman."

Satchel in hand, he paused midway across the room. As she moved past him to the door, she was again painfully aware of his eyes upon her, bewildered eyes. In defense against such a look, she flung open the door in warm greeting to the tall smiling man on the opposite side.

"Willie, I . . ." Abruptly she stopped. The man was not Willie Gladstone. "Jack . . . ?" she murmured, thinking perhaps that the dim light on the stoop had altered her vision. But it hadn't.

The man grinned. "Jack Willmot, at your service," he said, and bowed low in a courteous gesture.

She stared doggedly at his face, all aspects of recognition clear now, from the red hair to the massive shoulders to the weathered and newly tanned complexion. "Jack," she murmured again, thinking what a night of homecoming this was proving to be.

When she seemed incapable of inviting him in, he invited himself. "It's a long road from Canada"—he smiled—"and I made every step of it thinking of you. I know I'm unannounced, but might I . . ."

"Of course," she said. "I'm sorry, I . . ."

As Willmot moved past her, he apparently spied John standing at the center of the room, and for a moment the large man suffered the same shock that Elizabeth had suffered earlier.

"Is . . . it . . . ?" he gasped, and obviously could not continue.

With peculiar strength John stepped forward, hand extended, "John Murrey Eden, sir."

It was several moments before Willmot could speak. "My God," he muttered at last, extending his hand. "Gave me a start, you did. I don't suppose a day has passed since I last saw you that I haven't thought of your father."

From where she stood just inside the closed door, Elizabeth observed that the confession seemed to annoy John.

"It's a common mistake," she heard him say. "There have been times when I wished I might alter my physical appearance. It's like living in another man's skin."

"Oh, don't think that, lad," Willmot cut in. "Your father was a great man, perhaps the greatest I've ever known, and I've known some great ones."

As Willmot's voice drifted off into ancient grief, an awkward silence filled the room. Elizabeth had looked forward to Willie Gladstone. Instead fate had produced the two most preeminent ghosts from her past. Though her instinct was to retreat, she tried to stir a semblance of life back into the frozen room.

"I thought you were in Canada, Jack." She smiled, taking his arm. "At least the last I heard—"

"I was." He grinned, still eyeing John as though in disbelief. "A dreadful country, that is. But we laid the groundwork. Now it's up to the navvies to finish the track."

That was it, she thought, get him talking about distant lands, and try to remove that grim look from John's face and pray that Willie was detained a bit longer. "Come, both of you," she urged. "What a grand reunion this is, and what a surprise. Let's talk until nothing has been left out."

But John protested. "You're expecting a guest . . ."

"But he's not arrived yet," she said lightly, aware of Willmot's eyes upon her, as though in the confusion of greetings he'd failed to see her clearly, and certainly had failed to see her provocative gown. From there, she saw him launch forth into the same surprised inspection of her front parlor that John had just made. There was one small difference. Jack Willmot knew the reason for her new affluence. John, as yet, did not.

"Come, Jack." She smiled, eager to limit the boy's knowledge for as long as possible. "Tell us all. You have before you a captive audience, two simple islanders who have never stepped foot off their island. So tell us of your adventures in Canada. We'll not interrupt once, will we, John?"

Relieved, she saw John sit slowly opposite them, his expression still uncertain.

At the center of attention, Willmot appeared not to know what to do. "I . . . don't know what you want to hear, Elizabeth," he confessed, still trying to digest the new opulence of the room.

"Anything, Jack," she said, a bit desperately. "Everything!"

He paused, his eyes moving over the heavy velvet drapes at the window. "Well, I can tell you one thing," he commenced. "I've not sat in a room of such . . . comfort since I left London."

"What were you doing in Canada, Mr. Willmot?" John asked, and Elizabeth gave him a grateful look.

Willmot smiled. "Well, that depends on who you talk to, John. Building a railway, according to Mr. Brassey. Extending the empire, according to the directors of the Hudson Bay Company. Spreading Christian principles, according to the missionaries, and stealing their bloody land, according to the Indians." He laughed and shook his head. "Take your pick. I spent six months in that wilderness and I'm sorry to say I'm inclined to agree with the savages."

"Were they savages?" John asked, leaning forward in his chair.

Willmot nodded. "Some were, some weren't, like us English."

"Did you ever see any of them?"

"See them!" Willmot laughed. "I worked alongside them and lived with them." He lowered his head. "On occasion I preferred their company to that of the Hudson Bay agents."

Elizabeth listened carefully, her attention torn between what Willmot was saying and the increasingly rapt expression on John's face. Perhaps at last events would go well, though there still was the clock ticking behind her. Almost six o'clock, Willie later than usual.

"And who is Mr. Brassey?" she heard John ask, his satchel abandoned at his feet.

"A king." Willmot smiled instantly. "At least, one of the new kings. We breed 'em now without bloodlines, lad. There's scarce a railway or dock in all of England and the better part of the world that Thomas Brassey hasn't had a hand in." He paused, relishing the effect his words were having on John. "You're growing up in great times." He smiled, his attitude paternal. "The classes are crumbling. Any man of talent and vision and determination can rise through the ranks."

Suddenly he lifted his hand and started marking off an impressive roll call. "In cotton you have Strutt and Peel and Owen, not a blueblood among them, but giants all. In machinery you have Nasmyth and Maudsley, and among the ironworkers, consider Crawshay or Wilkerson . . ."

As he ran through his illustrious roll call, Elizabeth again glanced at John. Never had she seen an expression of such intense concentration.

"And all these men are rich?" she heard him ask.

"Rich!" Willmot parroted, laughing. "Any one of them could put Midas to shame. And one of the richest of all is Mr. Brassey."

"What do you do for him?" John asked.

Again Jack laughed. "Anything he asks me to do."

"Including building a railway in a country that doesn't want one?"

Momentarily taken aback, Willmot lowered his head. "I'm not a . . . king," he said, "only a lackey."

"Why?" John persisted. "You said yourself that any man can rise as high as—"

"Any man with brains—"

"You have brains. My father said so."

The report seemed to undo the large man. "Your father,

John," he began, "saw good in every man, frequently where none existed."

"Still, why are you the lackey and Brassey the king?"

Again Willmot faltered. Elizabeth hid a smile. She had forgotten, and poor Willmot had never known the boy's relentless curiosity.

She looked up to see Willmot slowly shaking his head. "I'm satisfied with who I am, John," he said. "I live a simple life, a good life, following orders, enjoying a few . . . friendships." As he said this, he reached out for her hand. She started to withdraw it, but changed her mind. He'd said friendship. Most willingly she would be his friend. It had been his earlier talk of marriage that had put her off.

Unfortunately at the very moment that she had thought things were going well, she *did* hear a carriage, unmistakable this time. They apparently heard it as well, for Willmot released her hand. As for John, he seemed unconcerned by it, his interest engaged by Willmot's earlier statements.

As he leaned forward, asking, "Tell me more, Mr. Willmot, about everything, about Mr. Brassey and Canada and the red savages," she did not wait for the rap on the door, and went to open it, wondering what course she should follow now. Send Willie away? She couldn't do that. Send them away? She couldn't do that either.

As the confusion grew within her, she swung open the door and saw the worn though handsome features of Willie Gladstone.

Suspended awkwardly in his left hand was a beautiful gilded cage, about eighteen inches tall, and perched gracefully on the little gold swing at the center was a delicate, perfectly wrought china bluebird.

"Willie, how beautiful." She smiled.

"My dearest," he murmured, "I'm sorry I'm late. I had to track this down in a craftsman's shop beyond Kings Cross Station. An aide saw it and told me about it. I thought . . ." He broke off and looked at her with clear affection. "I thought it might . . . suit you."

The silence coming from the room behind her was heavy, the silence of two men listening. "It's beautiful,

Willie." She smiled, feeling an urgent need to acquaint him as soon as possible with the other two waiting in quiet concealment behind the open door.

"Please come in," she said. "I confess I was worried about you."

She had intended to say more, but as he passed her by, he kissed her on the cheek, a gesture which, coming from Willie, meant nothing, but in her awareness of the other two waiting, caused a hot blush to cover her face.

"Look," he said, still blissfully ignorant that they were not alone. He lifted the little golden cage into the air, wound a small button beneath it, and lowered it for her inspection. Awed, she saw the tiny bird twist its head up and down in a delicate musical birdsong.

"Willie, I've never seen anything so beautiful."

"Nor have I," he said, his eyes on her breasts, one hand lifting as though to explore the softness partially concealed beneath white lace.

"Willie," she said quickly, over the birdsong, "while I was waiting for you, I had two unexpected though delightful surprises."

He stepped back, perceiving her message. She saw a look of apprehension in his eyes, the look of all men who were blessed and cursed with a double life.

"No need, Willie," she soothed. "Good friends, these two, and I'd like very much for you to meet them."

She guided him out from behind the door, her arm tucked through his, the musical bird cage suspended between them, the little china bird at last winding down its song.

She saw Jack Willmot stand immediately, as though he'd recognized Willie. John followed more slowly, the expression on his face one of distraction, as though he were still trying to work out to his satisfaction the difference between lackeys and kings.

"Mr. Gladstone," she pronounced a bit formally, suffering a twinge of awe herself. *Mr. Gladstone!* The Chancellor of the Exchequer, the man who only last week according to the *Times* was closeted in private conference with Queen Victoria, the man who was keeping both the Whigs and the Tories waiting in suspended animation to see to which party he would give his allegiance and considerable voice.

"Mr. Gladstone, permit me to present Mr. Jack Willmot, a good friend, only recently returned from Canada, and in the employ of Mr. Thomas Brassey."

He thrust the music box into her hands as though belatedly aware of how foolish he must look holding it. "Mr. Willmot," he said graciously. "And how is Mr. Brassey progressing in the Canadian wilds? While the empire is grateful for his adventurous spirit, it would be bereft if harm should befall him."

Jack heard him out, smiling. "When I left Mr. Brassey, he was well, sir. I believe he's due back in London any day."

As the brief exchange came to a natural end, Elizabeth guided Gladstone's attention toward John. "Willie," she said, "allow me to present Mr. John Murrey Eden, the son of Mr. Edward Eden, whom I believe you knew."

Gladstone extended his hand to John, his voice falling as though in regret. "My boy . . ." He smiled. "No, I never had the privilege of knowing your father personally. I believe my wife had the pleasure of meeting him once, in the company of Lord Shaftesbury. And of course all of London is grateful to him, specifically the thousands of once homeless children who have benefited immeasurably by his Ragged Schools."

Elizabeth expected to see a look of pleasure on John's face at the generous tribute. But instead she saw annoyance, John only briefly taking Gladstone's extended hand, then stepping back. Now he maintained his silence, which spread like a contagion to the others standing awkwardly about.

"Come," Elizabeth urged. "Everyone sit down, please. I doubt if there's a salon in all of London with company as distinguished as . . ."

But Willie seemed loath to sit and pulled away from her hand. "I mustn't stay, Elizabeth," he said. "I . . . sense that I've interrupted a reunion, and I wouldn't dream of—"

Then Willmot was protesting. "No, Mr. Gladstone," he said, skirting the sofa on the opposite end as though in a race for the door. "I was just leaving. Clearly you had an . . . appointment, and . . ."

As his voice drifted off into an embarrassed confusion, Willmot glanced around the room as though he'd forgotten something. "Ah, John," he said, lifting his hand toward the boy. "Come, I suggest we find a good public house. I know of one not far. If it's Canada you're interested in, I have several evenings of stories to tell you."

Then his efforts became clear, and Elizabeth realized that he was trying very hard to clear her house so that she could keep her appointment. While grateful, she suffered a sense of shame, and following fast on the heels of shame was anger, that she was allowing these two to affect her in this manner. Suddenly weary, she turned away. Let them work it out for themselves. At that moment it mattered little to her who remained, who departed.

Taking momentary refuge in the arrangement of the music box on the sideboard, she heard two of them speaking simultaneously, Willie offering again to leave, Jack Willmot trying again to summon John out of his innocence. "Come, lad," Willmot practically shouted. "We'll return . . . later. I have stories to tell you unfit for a woman's ears."

"But I had thought to wash up first and—"

"Come, you can wash up at the pub."

"I'm very tired . . ."

"Then you need a pint. Leave your satchel, and *come*—"

Finally she heard John's reluctant boots moving slowly behind her. She dared not look at him. She would have to try to explain later.

She heard Willmot bidding Gladstone a respectful good evening. In an incredibly short time she heard the door open, a scuffle of boots on the stoop, then the door was closed.

Well, she'd hoped to handle it all with a bit more grace, and she suffered a moment of apprehension, thinking on what Jack Willmot might tell John. And why was Willie standing so solemnly behind her?

As though to avoid the answers to all those questions,

she lifted the gilded music box, turned the button four times, placed it on the sideboard and watched the pitiful efforts of the little china bluebird as it tried to drown out the silence in the room.

Every time Jack Willmot had thought of her since he'd been away, he'd always imagined her in the degrading position of sin. Yet now, why was he so shocked to arrive unannounced and find her anticipating the arrival of a client, even so distinguished a man as "The People's Willie?"

Still embarrassed, he glanced back at John and saw the confusion on his face.

"I should stay, Mr. Willmot," the young man pronounced earnestly, and as he reached back for the door-knob, Willmot warned sternly, "No!"

Was he really so innocent? Had he no conception of what would shortly take place behind those velvet curtains?

"Come," Willmot urged, placing his arm about John's shoulders. "I promise we'll return—later. And I *would* like to lift a pint with you. Is that asking too much, for old times' sake?"

Under the duress of kindness, the young man softened. "Of course not, Mr. Willmot. It's just that—"

"And don't call me that. My name is Jack."

As they walked up the lane in the gathering dusk, he saw the young man glance back twice toward the small house and the handsome carriage standing at the edge of the pavement.

"Well, a bit of luck, this, wouldn't you say?" Willmot smiled. "I've thought on you often," he went on. "Quite frankly, I never thought to lay eyes on—"

"I wasn't aware that you knew Elizabeth," John interrupted.

"Of course I knew her," he said. "If you recall, I was the one who—"

Again John interrupted. "I mean, after my father's death. I assumed that she returned to London, and that you—"

Disliking the sensation of being questioned, Willmot

broke in. "No, I was still here, and she was in desperate need." He paused, expecting John to interrupt again. "She was quite alone, you see," he pointed out gently. "Loneliness isn't so hard for a man to bear. There are a hundred ways in which we can lose ourselves. But for a woman, particularly for one like Elizabeth, she—"

"What do you mean?" Abruptly John stopped walking.

For a moment Willmot thought he gleaned the purpose of the entire conversation. Clearly the young man had his suspicions, but now he needed to have them confirmed. No, thank you, Jack Willmot thought grimly, returning that earnest young gaze, then retreating from it. "She missed your father enormously," he said. "Still does."

Slowly they commenced walking again, Willmot setting the pace. "Well," he said, "you must talk to me. You know more about me than I know about you. Have you been at Eden for the entire year? And what brings you back to London? A visit? Family business?"

It seemed a sensible subject. But in the next minute, when the young man ignored the questions and posed a different one of his own—"Tell me more of Canada and Mr. Brassey"—Willmot stole a glance at that profile, seeing again the father in the son plus a new characteristic, a certain hardness, a stubbornness, certainly a will to have his own way in all matters, even conversational ones.

"Well, Canada . . ." Willmot smiled, missing the father's gentleness. "What's to say? It's vast, beautiful in places, harsh in others. Quite insect-ridden in the warmer months." Thinking that perhaps the young man would enjoy a tale of the grotesque as all young men did, he added, "In the North Woods, the mosquitoes are said to inhabit in an incidence of five million to the acre. For the tribes in the area, it is a convenient form of execution. A naked man, bound, is sucked dry of all his blood in three and one-half hours."

Ah, at last, a look of interest on that young face. "Good God," John whispered, clearly absorbed in the image of such a death. "Did you see it done, for yourself, I mean?"

Willmot laughed and shook his head. "I was there to build a railroad."

"Then how did you hear it?"

"From trappers, mountain men who lived among the Indians."

"Mountain men," the young man repeated. Then in the next breath he blurted, "I'm sick of England."

That was all he said, and since they were approaching the Seven Men, raucous laughter greeting them, accompanied by the shrill whine of a fiddle executing a jig, Willmot held all his questions and pushed open the doors and saw a solid crush of people.

Leading the way, Willmot pushed through the crowds, making it to the safe ground of the opposite side, where thin partitions divided low wooden tables. At last he found an empty one and slid along the bench on one side, motioning for John to sit opposite him.

Willmot thought it strange that the boy had never been here before. It was the nearest pub to the house in Bermondsey. Surely his father had come here often to quench his thirst.

Then he looked up to see the young barmaid who'd just appeared before them, a pretty lass with coal-black hair and matching eyes that seemed fascinated by John's blond good looks.

"What'll it be, gintlemen?" She grinned.

"A pint of ale and a sausage roll, if they're fresh." Willmot said.

"The same for me," John added.

The girl seemed to linger a moment longer in clear fascination of John, then reluctantly she turned to respond to a call from across the room.

As the voices in the crowded pub continued to reverberate behind him, only silence filled their table. Willmot leaned back on the bench. Something was wrong, and while he had no idea what, he was determined to find out. While he had no real responsibility to the boy, he still felt a debt. If only he'd exercised a bit more caution that last night on the Great Exhibition site, perhaps the boy's father would be sitting here with him now, instead of Willmot.

Feeling paternal, Willmot tried to project his voice over the din coming from the area of the dart boards. "Tell me of yourself." He smiled. "Did Eden suit you? Quite a change for a lad between this London and that paradise. Were you warmly received? Not a particularly happy homecoming, I wouldn't imagine, though still . . ."

He broke off, feeling that he was rambling, that little of what he was saying was reaching the ears opposite him. Or if his words were being received, they were being ignored.

In the midst of this small defeat, he glanced sideways into the room. Near the serving bar he spied the young barmaid. She seemed in close huddle with the barkeep, her hand pointing in their direction, the heavyset man's head swirling about and at last bringing them into focus.

Willmot continued to stare at them, baffled by their interest. He looked back to see if John had noticed that they were being stared at. Apparently the boy hadn't. He continued to sit stiffly, his hands gripping the edge of the bench.

Suddenly, when Willmot least expected it, the boy looked up. "Tell me more about Mr. Brassey, if you will. Everything—"

"Mr. Brassey?" Willmot stammered.

"Yes," John said, "the man you were speaking of earlier, the contractor, I believe you said."

Willmot nodded, not wanting to appear simpleminded. It was just that for the last few minutes Brassey had been very far from his mind. "Mr. Brassey," he repeated, failing to see how that topic could hold much interest for the lad, yet willing to oblige if he could. Stealing a moment to gather his thoughts, he glanced again out over the crowded room. The group at the bar had grown, five or six now, all in a close huddle, all pointing and looking in their direction. What in the . . . ?

"What do you do for him?" John asked.

"I'm a foreman," Willmot said. "A professional foreman, the same as when I first met you and your father."

"Were you working for Mr. Brassey then?" John asked.

Willmot laughed. "No, the Crystal Palace wasn't Mr. Brassey's cup of tea, and I'm afraid he still fails to see the practicality of it. No, you'll find Mr. Brassey where there's a job that nobody else wants to do, and where there's money to be made."

If the young man's interest was intense before, now it bordered on obsession. He leaned over the table. "Is he very rich?" he asked.

Again Willmot laughed. "Beyond what either of us will ever know or can imagine. I've heard it rumored— though mind you, it's just a rumor—that his net worth is approaching five million pounds."

"Five . . ." John gasped.

Willmot nodded, pleased by the boy's attention. "He's the best," he went on, "a true gentleman in a field known for its quacks." He leaned closer. "And most remarkable of all"—he grinned—"is that he told me once that he had arrived in London in 1820 with three shillings in his pocket."

For some reason, the large room seemed to have grown quieter. It was possible now to talk at a normal pitch. Was the dart competition over so soon? Generally they were only warming up in the early evening hours. Well, whatever the cause for the new quiet, Willmot was grateful for it. It meant that they could talk, that perhaps he could establish some bond of trust with the boy. Now generously he offered, "I'd be happy to introduce you to Mr. Brassey when he returns to London. I think you'd like him. He has many qualities not unlike those of your father, quite a . . ."

All at once that blond head bowed.

"John . . . ?"

As Willmot started to lean forward with a concerned inquiry, he was aware again of the increasing silence coming from the room behind him, as though all activity had ceased and the scattered attentions of some sixty-five or seventy people were now otherwise engaged.

What in the hell was going on? Mildly annoyed, Willmot shifted around on the bench as though to confront the silent starers. He tried to read the expressions on their faces, and from where he sat it seemed as though they were staring, not at him, but at John.

Then, without warning the heavyset, heavy-jowled barkeep was moving toward them through the closely arranged tables, his soiled apron tied tightly over his protruding stomach, his long black hair catching glints of light as he passed beneath the oil lamps. He was headed their way, and in the last moment of privacy, Willmot whispered, "If we've caused offense, let me do the talking."

While he was still a few feet away, the barkeep ducked his head and commenced wiping his hands on his apron. In an attempt to blunt the man's approach, Willmot swiveled to meet him. "What's the cause of all this?" he called out in good humor. "My friend and I are just passing a quiet hour. If we've caused offense . . ."

The barkeep halted in his approach, his massive head wagging back and forth. "Oh, it's not offense you caused, sir, jus' the opposite." Now he gave John a close inspection.

" 'Tis him," he gasped, "or . . . his ghost."

Behind him hovered the little serving maid, clearly the one who had sounded the alarm. "See, I told you so, didn't I now? I said look over there if you want to see a face from the grave."

At that several chairs scraped as others tried to get a closer look. Across from him, Willmot saw the boy, his eyes down, as though the weight of embarrassment was too much to be borne.

Still mystified, Willmot was on the verge of questioning the barkeep further when behind him at a table not too far removed he heard a gruff voice shout, "Couldn't be him, though, not the Prince of Eden. We seen him off last spring."

Then Willmot knew. Why hadn't it occurred to him? He had made the same mistake himself a few hours earlier. Coming upon that strong fair face so unexpectedly would test the nerves of a stone. And these folks here in the Seven Men were bound to suffer a painful recognition as they had suffered a painful loss. The passing of the Prince of Eden surely had been like a light extinguished in their lives. Before his death, they had been able to count upon at least one refuge of warmth, one man who had treated them with human dignity.

With a sense of reverence Willmot looked out over the gaping faces, proud to have known such a man. As several more pushed closer, he thought how pleased John must be, receiving this silent tribute to his father. Because words of some sort seemed called for and because clearly John would not be capable of delivering them, Willmot stood and cleared his throat.

"You've made one small mistake, my friends, but an understandable one. This is not Edward Eden, though pray God that he was here. This . . . duplicate as you called him is just that, his son, John Murrey Eden, a lad as fine and as upright as his father, and I think I can speak for him when I say—"

Suddenly from the young man there came a strong protest. *"No!"* Willmot only had enough time to look down before the young man rose with such force that the bench clattered backward.

"John . . . ?" But as Willmot's hand moved forward, the boy shot past him, knocking noisily against the partitions, and with his head still bowed, he ran through the crowded room, his hands outreaching as though to clear all obstacles.

For a moment Willmot continued to stand, only vaguely aware of the whispering going on around him. Then he too was moving, running the same obstacle course that John had run, trying to dodge the clutter of tables and the press of people who clearly had a tribute to make and no one to whom to make it.

Once out on the pavement, he noticed that night had fallen, the shadows obscuring the street in all directions. "John?" he called, foolishly thinking the boy might be waiting nearby and would answer.

Then a grim thought occurred to him. Of course, where else would he go but home, to the house three blocks away, to that obscenely luxurious front parlor where Elizabeth was at this moment entertaining her most distinguished client.

No, he thought, and broke into a run. Not until he'd turned the corner did he spy him, about fifty yards ahead and still running. "John, wait . . ." Willmot shouted, knowing he could hear now, but knowing as well that he would not stop or turn back until it was too late.

While he was still a distance away, Willmot saw the elegant carriage still waiting before the house. Was there no warning he could give? To anyone? "John, please wait . . ." he called a final time, and saw the boy take the front steps and push wildly at the door.

Breathing heavily from his sprint, Willmot started to take the three small steps in one, then suddenly changed his mind. Though the door was open, he heard not a sound coming from the room. While he felt a responsibility, perhaps it was not his place to intrude. As he retreated back to the pavement, he wondered if he was acting with prudence or cowardice.

His anxiety increasing, he continued to strain his ears, trying to hear something. To his left he spied a spill of light coming through the incompletely drawn drapes. Disliking what he was about to do, yet doing it anyway, he stepped to one side and with instantaneous regret saw clearly through the crack a most bizarre tableau, like mannequins in a store window, the man Gladstone seated upon the sofa, the specifics of his features as frozen as the entire room, Elizabeth lying lengthwise, her head in his lap, the obscene white lace dressing gown down about her waist, his hand cupped about one breast.

But worst of all was John, literally a statue, as though upon his rapid entrance he'd collided painfully with an invisible barrier beyond which he could not move.

Still Willmot watched, thinking that someone, anyone, must move and speak soon. It could not persist, the shocked embarrassment coming from the two on the sofa, and the nightmare on the face of the young man. Clearly he'd had no notion of what was going on. None at all.

Then she moved first, though such a slow movement it was, her head lifting from the lap, one hand reaching downward for her garment.

In need of respite from the scene, Willmot closed his eyes. It might have been worse, though he doubted it. If the boy had discovered them in the middle of the act itself, it couldn't have been more obscene.

He noticed that Elizabeth was on her feet, the dressing

gown partially restored, her face desolate. "John . . . ?"
she begged softly, and was not given the opportunity to
finish.

Drawing on some mysterious source of strength, the
statue moved. Apparently he'd spied his abandoned
satchel on the floor near the sideboard. Still moving as
though in a trance, he retrieved the satchel and cast a final
look at the woman drawing nearer. Some new expression
cut through the masklike features, first hurt, then anger,
then the plainest of all, accusation. Judgment passed, he
stepped backward, and from where Willmot stood, he
thought he saw the young man's lips move, a single word,
but he could't hear, and could only faintly see Elizabeth's
reaction. No longer advancing, she stood still, the extended hand slowly withdrawing, her head lifting as though
she were having difficulty breathing.

Willmot had seen enough. Should he simply slip away
and pretend it had never happened? Or should he remain
and attempt to gather all the fragments of Edward Eden's
son together and take them to some safe place?

While he was still in the process of making his decision,
the young man appeared on the darkened stoop. Willmot
looked up. "John, I tried . . ." But as Willmot attempted
to explain, John started walking slowly down the street,
satchel in hand.

Torn between the disintegration on the pavement and
what surely must be matching disintegration taking place
inside the house, Willmot foundered. He looked up at the
closed door, half-expecting to see Elizabeth. Why hadn't
she called the boy back? Why hadn't she at least made
an effort to explain?

"John, wait," he called out, thinking perhaps that they
would walk for a while, with Willmot doing the talking,
trying to assist him in understanding. Then, in Willmot's
opinion, it would be best if the boy returned to Eden.
It was where he belonged. Certainly he did not belong
here.

Having thus plotted the direction of the immediate
future, he drew up alongside John, who had yet to look
back and acknowledge his presence in any way. No

matter. Willmot did not require acknowledgment, merely a listening ear.

"John, let me—"

But again that one hand lifted in a sharp gesture, as though he needed no help, or if he did, he would ask for it later.

Seeing the gesture and the blond bowed head, Willmot held his tongue and contented himself with merely walking alongside the boy. Perhaps later words would be negotiable.

But they weren't. For the better part of the night, Willmot followed behind him as he walked the streets of London, his head still down.

About midnight Willmot found that they were approaching Oxford Street. The traffic had thinned with the late hour, though an occasional carriage rattled past and several costermongers working late tried to hawk the tail-end of the day's wares.

But nothing, no encounter, no voice, no sound was enough to cause that head to lift in either interest or curiosity. And though an occasional bobby strolling in the late-night hours eyed them with mild suspicion, no one seemed inclined to halt or question them.

So they were free to roam the streets, with John setting both the pace and the direction, a topsy-turvy route as far as Willmot could determine. The only time that John halted his step altogether was at a point midway down Oxford Street, when in a crush of commercial shops and linen establishments he stopped and looked about, as though lost, and finally fastened his attention on one shop front, clearly new—constructed within the last five years was Willmot's guess.

Standing behind the young man, Willmot followed the direction of his gaze, baffled why this particular shop held such interest for him. He was on the verge of breaking the silence and making inquiry when John volunteered the information himself.

"This was my father's house," he said, his voice so low that Willmot moved a step closer.

"This?" Willmot puzzled. "It looks . . . newly built."

"The house was destroyed to make way for the shop."

It wasn't condemnation in his voice, merely bewilderment, as though he'd hoped to return and find the house exactly as he'd remembered it.

At some point in the early-morning hours, a faint rain began to fall. Willmot turned up his collar and buttoned his jacket to the top and watched to see if John would do likewise. He didn't. If he was aware at all of the falling rain, he gave no indication of it.

Looking up into the fine mist, Willmot got his bearings and realized that they weren't too far from his own flat behind St. Paul's in Warwick Lane. It seemed the sensible thing to do, to suggest that they make for those rooms, and if John chose to pass what was left of the night staring into emptiness, then at least he could do so in dry comfort.

With this suggestion in mind, Willmot drew closer and stood over him for a moment, still finding his silence incredibly difficult to penetrate. He'd not thought it possible for the human body to endure such a siege of silence.

Then without warning the young man spoke. "How much did you say Mr. Brassey is worth?" he asked, as though nothing had transpired since their earlier conversation at the Seven Men.

So surprised was he by the sound of the voice and the curious question that it took Willmot a moment to adjust to both. "According . . . to rumor," he stammered, "approaching five million."

"And how much did you say he arrived with in London?" the young man asked further.

Again Willmot struggled to answer. "According to his own accounts, less than . . . three shillings—"

He was aware of movement next to him, the young man fishing through his pockets for something and apparently finding it, holding it out before him, palm open.

Willmot looked closer at something shiny in that open palm. A coin of some sort. He leaned closer. A halfpenny.

The young man stepped forward as though on a burst of energy, swinging his satchel. He looked at Willmot and smiled. "I thank you for your company," he said. "And now, if you could direct me to a near boardinghouse, I'd be most appreciative."

"A boardinghouse?"

"I need a place to stay, Mr. Willmot. Obviously I cannot return to the house in Bermondsey, nor can I go back to Eden."

Willmot looked at the boy. "I know of . . . no boarding house," he faltered. "There's no need anyway. My flat is not far, and there's plenty of room."

The boy looked at him. "I am grateful, and I assure you it will only be temporary." He stepped closer. "You offered once, Mr. Willmot, to introduce me to Brassey. Does that offer still hold?"

"Of . . . course," Willmot stammered again, "as soon as he returns from—"

"Good! Well, then, come. You lead the way for a while and I'll follow." In spite of his words, he strode to the intersection, leading the way, his shoulders back as though drinking in the perfume of an early-summer morning.

Again Willmot shook his head and hurried to catch up. As they started across Southampton Row, the young man drew farther ahead, his stride long and purposeful now. Willmot had never seen such a rapid transformation.

"To the left," Willmot called out as John veered to the right. No longer was he interested in keeping up with him. His own weariness after the long night was beginning to take a toll. Then, too, of greater interest to him was that miraculous resemblance, the way he carried his shoulders, the angle of the stride, the swing of the arms, the daylight on his hair.

But there *was* a difference, deeper and more profound than mere physical resemblance. And it was his awareness of that difference and his inability to identify it that disturbed Willmot and caused him then to hurry to catch up, as though the young man were an incomprehensible force that must be watched.

Eden Castle, North Devon, January 1853

THOUGH ELEVEN, GOING on twelve, and considered by all to be still a child, nonetheless Richard was capable of overhearing the whispered conversations of those around him, and assessing the dimensions of that bleak existence which now passed for life at Eden Castle. The trouble was that he understood all aspects of the tragedy. Except one.

On this cold January morning, bent over his desk in the small library, near the warmth of a flickering fire, he leaned over the fine print of Homer's *Odyssey* and pretended to be reading. But all the while his mind never traveled further than the third-floor corridor above him, that grim place where daily there could be heard voices calling out to his mother. A macabre ritual had been established. The awesome door opened only briefly, late at night, and for one person, Peggy, who was granted quick access for the purpose of serving a simple tray. Then she was banished, and tearfully she had informed all that if anyone tried to enter when she did, her ladyship had vowed to bolt the door forever.

Still everyone tried to talk to her through the closed door. Such a variety of entreaties: Peggy's soft concerned one, Mrs. Swan's pragmatic one, Aggie Fletcher's harsh angry one. And once, some months ago, they'd even enlisted him.

"Talk to her, Richard," Clara Jenkins had instructed. "Tell her that you need her, that Mary needs her, that everyone . . ."

He had obeyed in all respects, had stood outside the ominous door, her daily tray of food and the fresh chamber pot resting near his feet, aware of the others hovering in the shadows a distance away. He had commenced talking, at first of superficial things: Mary's stomachache, his progress in Latin and French, the new colt. And all the time he'd talked, he'd kept his eye on the door, a continuous prayer running through his mind, *"Please, God, let her open it."*

But she hadn't.

Suddenly Richard shivered. The small fire was dying, the storm outside the window increasing. His thoughts labored painfully to lift everything that had happened to the light of an ultimate meaning, and while he understood a great deal, there still was one missing link in the chain of understanding.

John.

Why had he left them when they needed him most? Why had he been there one day and gone the next?

John. How he missed him.

"Very well. Enough!" The voice was Herr Snyder's, sharp and drained of patience. "Clearly you have succumbed to self-indulgence, as has everyone else. Oh, I've been watching you. A page hasn't been turned in the last fifteen minutes."

Richard did not look up. Neither did he offer any sort of denial. How could he? Herr Snyder had spoken the truth.

Apparently having received no denial or apology or explanation, Herr Snyder washed his hands of the entire matter. "Then I'll leave you to your own devices," he pronounced, marching toward the door.

From where he sat at his desk near the fire, Richard followed his progress until he disappeared up the stairs, clearly on his way to his second-floor apartment to write more letters of inquiry, searching for new employment.

Upon the instant of his departure, Richard felt a curious splintering of emotions, partly relief to be out from under the weight of those sharp eyes, and partly regret, an awareness that perhaps he needed the anchor of Herr Snyder's iron discipline to keep him from drifting like the other lost vessels in the castle.

Alone in the small library, his sense of relief won out. He would miss Herr Synder, but he could manage without him. Of late he'd felt a strange impulse to cease exploring other men's minds, and for a while at least, explore his own. Now he would have freedom in which he could pursue to his heart's content the massive old fifteenth-century Bible which was chained to the pulpit in the chapel.

He loved the Parables best, the Prodigal Son, the Coat of Many Colors, Daniel and the Lions. All these tales transfigured the world and expanded his temporal boundaries.

Thinking on his place of refuge, he closed the volume of Homer. In a surge of excitement he stood. Then he was moving across the Great Hall to the steps.

He increased his pace and was well on his way to the safety and warmth of the chapel when at the top of the third-floor landing he heard a voice, a familiar one, though the words were unfamiliar.

In spite of the instinct which warned him not to stop, he stopped and pulled his jacket up about his neck. Suffering from that unfortunate faculty of comprehending everything and feeling its nature in an instant, he turned toward the distant voice. It was Peggy. Forbidden to speak a word to his mother at night she was holding her conversation with the door early today. Drawn forward by grim curiosity, Richard glanced down the corridor and saw her seated upright upon the floor, a piece of newsprint in her hands, laboriously reading.

"It's the Russian influence at Const-ant-i-nople, my lady, that might cause the war. What with Napol-e-on inclining toward military ventures for prest-ige, and the Czar interfering as always in everything, England will soon be drawn into the conflict . . ."

Richard closed his eyes, feeling ill. Apparently Peggy was determined to involve his mother in the foolish affairs of the world, whether she wanted to be involved or not.

"I hope all that war talk makes sense to you, my lady," she said, looking up at the door, "because I assure you it makes no sense to me."

From where Richard stood near the end of the corridor, he saw Peggy draw her cloak more tightly about her and turn the page of newsprint. "Let's find a happier item, my lady, shall we? Ah, here, the Queen and her Albert are at Osborne for a brief holiday. And here's a darling sketch of the little princess, my lady, quite a plump cherub, she is. How I wish that you could see it."

Suddenly she broke off, her head lifting regretfully to the door. "I'm . . . so sorry, my lady," she said, her voice breaking.

The poor woman leaned forward, her hands pressed against the cold unresponding barrier, openly crying. "I can't bear the thought of you imprisoned like this, my lady," she sobbed. "Whatever you done, or didn't do, it's a loving God that looks down upon you. He wouldn't want you to do this for His sake."

Abruptly Richard stepped back. He didn't want to hear any more. There was nothing he could do about anything. If Peggy chose to talk with a locked door, that was her business.

As for himself, it hurt too much, even to watch from a distance, and sharply he turned and started running through the corridors. Out of the turmoil of a thousand contours gradually emerged the features of his mother as they had appeared to him before she'd done the damage.

Oh, dear Christ, how he missed her and wanted her, and he ran toward the chapel in sore need of refuge, sobbing like a child.

London, March 29, 1854

THOUGH USUALLY PUNCTUAL, this morning John slipped behind his desk in the outer office of Peto, Betts, and Brassey one hour late and mildly hung over.

At the far end of the high-ceilinged room he saw the other clerks huddled about Andrew's desk in close examination of something.

Well, there was a break. Perhaps no one had noticed his late arrival. Weary at eight-thirty in the morning and breathless from his high-speed sprint up three flights of stairs, he opened his portfolio to a scattering of papers, the report which Brassey had assigned him to make over a month ago: *Laissez-Faire and the Development of British Industry*.

He would never survive this day. Still he scattered the papers about, determined at least to give the appearance of working. At the end of the long room, Andrew's voice rose above the others in a single exclamation. "What sport it would be . . ."

Slowly John looked up. He squinted down the length of the dimly lit room. Quickly he glanced behind toward Mr. Brassey's closed door. The cat was either busy or away. Again he tried to overhear the specifics of the conversation coming from the opposite end of the room. But he could hear nothing clearly, and the sight of those "fellow prisoners" simply served to deepen his depression, and with newly sinking spirits he glanced about at the cold gray office which once, or so he'd hoped, would be the door to his future.

Door to anonymity, more likely, he brooded. He should have followed his instincts months ago and departed for India. Even now the only respite he had from this mind-dulling work was an occasional excursion to the docks, where he'd watch the giant sailing ships arrive, the Indian porters grinning down at him as though trying to lure him on board.

But no. He'd decided that Willmot's contact with Thomas Brassey would be more promising. Promising! For fourteen months he had been "one of ten" clerks, filing letters, copying graphs, running witless errands that a child might do as well. Oh, the pay was adequate, no more. It enabled him to pay Jack Willmot a few shillings a week for sharing his flat, though each time John paid him, Willmot insisted it wasn't necessary. And it enabled him as well to slip five shillings a week into old Mrs. Pendar's apron pocket, a generous payment for her housekeeping duties and for the hot meals she delivered to their second-floor flat. As for the rest of his salary, it was sufficient to cover his nightly drinking.

Slowly he pushed back in his chair, his head tilted upward. He must watch himself this morning. He knew the price he always paid for dissipation. Normally in the mind-numbing activities of the day, and the feverish activity of the night, he could successfully hold memory at bay. But in certain transitional periods, like now . . .

Eden.

One word, capable of undoing him, and he leaned forward across the desk, cradling his head in his hands.

Her.

There was another word, one *her* out of a world of hers. Was she still alive?

Beneath his hands, he stared, eyes blurred, at the column of figures which Mr. Brassey had given him the night before. They were to be tabulated, copied in triplicate, the papers on Mr. Brassey's desk first thing this morning.

"John! There you are!"

The voice was eager and warm and belonged to Andrew Rhoades. Grateful for the reprieve, John looked up, aware that he'd been discovered. The lot of them, headed by Andrew, were now moving toward him, their faces, to the man, alive with some new enthusiasm.

And to the man, John had ignored them for over fourteen months for the ciphers that they were, all except Andrew, and there was a special bond, or more accurately, a two-edged knife which cut both ways, simultaneously attracting John, then repelling him, for at their introduction and upon hearing the name of Eden, Andrew had gaped, claiming surely it wasn't possible that John Murrey Eden was the relation of Edward Eden, the man in whose Ragged Schools Andrew had grown up and received his early education.

But of course it had been possible and true, and the foundation for the bond between the two young men had been laid. When John's loneliness threatened to unhinge him, he could always count on Andrew's company for a good night's debauchery.

Now they were upon him, Andrew still in the lead, waving a large cardboard poster of some sort.

"How long have you been sitting here with your head between your shoulders?" Andrew grinned. "When all the time I hold the key to your future."

John looked up at the poster. "It doesn't resemble a key." He smiled, trying to send the ghosts away and rise to the optimism of the moment.

"Oh, but it is," Andrew responded with mock sternness. "While you were dallying this morning, the rest of us have decided to give a fortnight's notice and join up."

This was greeted with a rustle of approval from the men behind him, though John still hadn't the faintest idea what they were talking about and said as much. "Join up what?"

"My lord, man," Andrew exclaimed, "haven't you heard? Every news-hawker in London has been screaming it."

"Screaming what?"

"War!" Andrew grinned. "That's all. Just war."

As the others laughed at his sarcasm, John sat up, interested. "With whom?" he asked, puzzled that he'd missed so important an announcement.

"Russia," one man said with assurance from the back of the group.

"No," another disagreed. "Turkey. The *Times* said it clear as day."

"You're both wrong," exclaimed a third. "The way I heard it, it's Moldavia."

Suddenly Andrew raised a hand into the air. "If the dunces will cease talking, I will inform the man—"

"Please do," John murmured, amused by the prospect of war without a clear-cut adversary.

With a sense of melodrama Andrew took the floor, his sandy-colored hair and flushed complexion the only color in the drab room. "It's the Czar all right." He nodded, confirming the first man's guess of Russia. "He wants Constantinople, and all the rest of Europe, according to what I hear." He peered closely at John, as though amazed by his lack of knowledge. "You've . . . heard nothing?" he repeated.

Rather proud of his ignorance in such a foolish matter, John shook his head. "Nothing."

"My God, it's filled the newsprint for the last six weeks."

"Then it's true, is it?" John asked, respecting his friend's somber demeanor. "Truly war?"

"Truly war." Andrew nodded. "Last night France and Britain agreed on armed intervention in support of Turkey."

"Against . . . Russia?" John faltered, unable to make sense out of the confused allegiances.

Andrew nodded.

"And where will this . . . war be staged?" he asked, still unable to take any of it too seriously.

"The Crimea, most likely, midpoint between Russia and Turkey."

"Sounds cold," John said.

"Most likely it will be," Andrew agreed. "But look," and at last he forced the poster down onto John's desk. "Look at the pay listed. Great God, it's more than Brassey pays in a—"

John studied the poster, designed for purposes of recruitment. Fifteen shillings for a cavalry recruit and four pounds for an infantryman, with monthly pay at seven and six pounds respectively. Clearly the government needed soldiers and needed them in a hurry.

"What do you think?" Andrew asked.

John hesitated a moment. "I thought you wanted to study law."

"I do," Andrew exclaimed, "but how can I study anything on what Brassey pays?" He again pointed to the poster. "With that salary, I can save. I can serve my country and return with a sizable purse, enough to pursue a career. Look again!"

John eyed the poster and the listed sums. "It's a lot of money, but not enough to get blown to bits." His negative comment had a dire effect on the enthusiasm of the potential soldiers.

Someone suggested coldly, "Not a very patriotic bloke, are you?"

"For such a senseless conflict, no."

"How do you know it's senseless? The Czar has already walked over two countries—"

"The Czar can walk where he pleases," John replied.

"What if he walks to England?" someone protested hotly. "What will you do then?"

John grinned. "If he walks to England, I'd like a ring-side seat for his channel crossing."

As muttering broke out around him, he saw Andrew looking down on him, the disappointment clear on his face. "I . . . thought you'd be excited."

"I am, for you, if that's what you want."

"You're as sick of this place as I am," Andrew protested, leaning over the desk. "I know. You've told me so."

"I am," John agreed, "but not so sick that I'm willing to play target for a bunch of cossacks."

Suddenly Andrew stood erect, the determination clear on his face. "Well, I've tallied my last column of figures, transcribed my last letter, and filed my last graph. In two weeks I'll be a soldier in Her Majesty's Service."

At the conclusion of this brief speech, the others broke into a cheer. Clearly Andrew had spoken for the lot of them.

"Then I wish you well." John smiled, extending his hand to his friend.

As Andrew took it, the others began to drift back to their desks, resigned to at least a few more days of tedium before they entered the great adventure of war.

"Are you sure you won't come with us?" Andrew asked. "We'd make a grand team. The Czar would know he'd tangled with someone when we finished with him."

"I'm sorry," John murmured. "I have no desire to involve myself in the Czar's affairs."

"He'll involve us all before it's over."

"Not me, he won't." John smiled. "Now if you'll excuse me, Andrew, since I'm not moving on to more gainful employment in Her Majesty's Service, I'd better turn to my work here. I assume that Brassey is lurking about someplace . . . "

"In his office," Andrew muttered. "He's been closeted there with several gentlemen since early this morning."

John glanced toward the door which led to the inner

sanctum, the simple chambers where decisions were made which affected the lives of thousands: where to build a railway, whose farmlands to disrupt, what tariff to charge that would inevitably add new weight to Midas' wealth. With longing John continued to stare at the closed door, wishing that he were seated in there instead of out here.

When he looked back, with an invitation to Andrew to join him for dinner—burned bridges must be mended —he discovered that Andrew had returned to his desk, a few of the clerks still in close conference with him, all of them excited over their new futures.

Alone, from his end of the room John watched them, momentarily regretting his decision not to join them. Why was it that every decision he'd ever made in his life always left him in a state of aloneness? As he saw several of them look up in his direction, he lowered his head over the scattered papers and again gave the impression of industry.

His eyes fell on the words *Laissez-Faire and the Development* . . . , the study which Brassey had ordered on government regulations since 1793. With interest he read the report, written in his own hand over the last few weeks, a new awareness beginning to move over him. He *had* learned something in this grim office.

Suddenly a new idea occurred to him, the most dazzling of the morning. One of ten? No longer. Not with nine going off to fight Her Majesty's war. For a while at least, until Brassey could replenish his work force, John would be one of one.

Buoyed by hope that things might be different, he carefully placed the report on the desk and drew forth clean pages. It must be recopied, must appear the epitome of accuracy and neatness to Brassey, who would look upon it and certainly view its author in a different light.

Through the entire day he worked, and when at last he looked up, he saw night outside the high window and the office empty, the other clerks, including Andrew, long since gone off to drink to the future and the glories of war. Over his shoulder he glanced toward Brassey's door, the light still visible through the crack. Good! By John's estimate they were here alone. Difficult for one man to ignore the other when both were alone.

With care he copied the final paragraph of the lengthy report. Again he glanced over his shoulder at the door, as though it had spoken to him. On his desk the solitary lamp flickered low, casting his own shadow in massive proportions on the high wall. For a moment he watched, fascinated by the magnification, a pleasant respite from the tedium of the day's work. So engrossed was he in himself grown larger than life that at first he failed to notice the door open, or the man standing on the threshold, his spectacles in his hand, coat off.

"Shadow play?" the voice inquired.

John stood immediately. Behind him on the desk, he felt of the carefully stacked edges of his report.

Brassey took a step farther out of the door, squinting at John from across the room. "And you are . . . ?"

"Eden, sir," John replied, mildly hurt that after all this time in the great man's employ, he still was a nonentity.

"Ah, yes." Brassey nodded. "You are Willmot's young friend, of course."

Willmot's young friend! Damn! What a way to be remembered. Just as he was on the verge of stepping forward with his report, Brassey inquired further, "Where is Willmot? I haven't seen him about lately. I could have used his expertise today."

"He's in Brighton, sir. An aunt is ailing."

"Of course." Brassey nodded. "Now I remember." For a moment he appeared to look vaguely about the floor.

John had never seen the man so addled-appearing.

"Well," Brassey said, and turned away as though he were about to take refuge in his office.

Quickly John stepped forward, determined that when they met again, the man would remember him. "Mr. Brassey . . ." he called out.

Slowly Brassey looked back, still holding his spectacles in his hand. But before John had a chance to speak, Brassey apparently had a question of his own. "Why are you still here, Eden?" he asked. "I thought I'd lost all my clerks today to Her Majesty's Service."

"Not me, sir."

"Why not you?"

"War holds little appeal."

As though stirred to interest in spite of his fatigue, Brassey appeared to look more closely at John. "Then am I to understand that you'll be remaining in my employ?"

"If you'll have me, sir."

Brassey laughed. "If I'll have you. You may find yourself doing the work of ten men, at least for a while."

"I'll do my best, sir."

Again Brassey looked at him, as though seeing him in a new light. "I thought all young men were attracted to war."

"Not I."

"Why?"

John smiled, pleased by their easy give-and-take. "I have no quarrel with the Czar, sir."

"But apparently your country does."

"And there will be plenty of soldiers to fight for her," he added, motioning to the nine empty desks.

"But not you?"

"No, sir. With the departure of the others, you are merely left shorthanded. If I had gone as well, you'd be left empty-handed."

For a moment they looked at each other across the empty desks. John tried to read the expression on Brassey's face, but could not. However, his next question was a sharp one. "You're not a coward, are you, Eden?"

Taken aback, John could not immediately reply. "I've never been tested, sir," he admitted, "but I hope not."

"Well," Brassey said finally on a deep expulsion of air, "I appreciate your . . . loyalty, and wish that I could assure you of a safe harbor here. But I can't. Even if you stay with me, I fear that sooner or later, all of us will get a close-hand look at the Czar."

"I . . . don't understand, sir."

"Study your maps, Eden," Brassey called back, turning into his office. "From where our troops will be forced to land to where the fighting will take place, you'll see miles of virgin territory. Men and materials will have to be moved across it at the greatest possible speed."

John was following after the trailing voice now. "I still don't understand, sir. Surely the army can take care of—"

With his hand on the doorknob, Brassey turned back. "The army does well to wipe its nose on a rainy day. No! Before it's over, they'll need us practical men. So be warned. Stay with me and you'll end up in the frozen mud of the Crimea anyway."

Baffled, the report still in his hand, John tried to halt the retreating man.

"Later, Eden," Brassey said sharply. "Go home for now. As I said, I appreciate your . . . loyalty."

As the door was closing, John again called out, "The report, sir, it's finished."

But the door was closed, and in the new silence John heard a bolt slide, clear indication that the man wanted no further interruptions.

For a moment he stared at the closed door, anger increasing that he'd been dismissed as though he were nothing more than a common clerk. When the truth dawned on him, that indeed he *was* a common clerk, and now perhaps, at least in Brassey's eyes, a cowardly one, he lifted the multi-paged report and in anger hurled it across the room.

As the pages floated in disarray over the empty desks, he glanced again at the closed and bolted door, and ran from the room, taking the three flights downward in broad strides, until at last he was standing on the pavement in the traffic of midevening, even then considering returning to the bolted door and demanding the time that he felt was due him.

But after several deep breaths of cold March air he changed his mind. Such a confrontation would accomplish nothing. What precisely had the man been talking about? *Even if you stay with me, sooner or later you'll find yourself in the frozen mud of the Crimea.* How was it possible that civilians could be summoned to a theater of war?

With his hands shoved into his pockets, his coat collar turned up, he commenced walking against the traffic, his mind still turning on the frustrating encounter. Well, this much was clear. The time had come to leave. His future was as ill-defined now as it had been fourteen months ago. He was sorry for Jack Willmot's sake that the "promising position" with Brassey had failed. But there was the truth of it.

Then leave! Go back to the flat on Warwick Lane, pack, leave Willmot a note and go to the docks. India was still beckoning, still pushing against his conscience as though it were an unrealized dream. He had no idea what he would find there, but it could be no worse than what he had here, which was exactly nothing.

Was he a coward?

No! But why must he prove it to Brassey? *Damn Brassey!* Then leave. A ship may be waiting now. India! Blazing sun, dusty plains, treasures to be plucked from off the ground.

In his excitement, he stepped blindly out into the traffic and heard the neighing of horses reined sharply in, and looked up in time to see a carriage veer to the right, a collision avoided at the last minute, the enormous carriage rumbling past so close he could feel the displacement of air.

"Watch out!" someone shouted.

"Idiot!" another cried.

Quickly he stepped back to the pavement, the driver of the carriage still struggling for control. He looked up, brought to his senses by the near-calamity. Inside the carriage window he saw one small gloved hand draw back the velvet curtains. Then he saw the side of a cheek, a bonnet tied snugly about a small chin, long fair hair arranged over a fur cape, the eyes, the cheek, the chin familiar, all familiar . . .

My name is Lila Harrington. Don't let too much time pass before you come again.

"Wait!" he called after the carriage.

The face was still there, craning forward as though in an attempt to see him more clearly.

"Wait!" he cried again, leaving the pavement in pursuit of the smiling face.

But as the carriage resumed speed, she merely waved at him, her face little more than a flesh-colored disk now, surrounded by the darkness of fur and shadows. Then she was gone.

For a moment he stood on the pavement, shivering from cold as well as from recognition. Had it been her, the same one who'd spoken to him from the apple tree? But it couldn't have been.

Yet, if it hadn't been her, why the smile and the wave? For a few minutes he felt a compulsion to follow after the carriage, to pull the door open and see for himself.

But he didn't. It hadn't been her. That pretty piece of madness who had spoken to him from the branches of the apple tree was safely confined in Salisbury. And concerning India. Good sense intervened there as well. He couldn't just walk away from his responsibilities, thus confirming Brassey's suspicion of him as a coward. And he owed Jack Willmot more than a hastily scribbled note. If it hadn't been for Willmot's kindness . . .

No, India would again have to be postponed. But one day, he was certain, circumstances would conspire in his favor, all omens right, and he would at last gain access to that massive frontier of empire, and pit his ingenuity against its vastness and take away with him what he needed.

For now, he felt bereft, confused, weary.

Ahead of him he saw a prostitute, very young and appealing. There might be sport. Surely he could afford her. But just when he thought he had found his diversion for the night, his spirits sank mysteriously lower, memory always a potent enemy.

Elizabeth. How stealthily and without warning that name entered his mind. In the past, it had been capable of lightening his steps as well as his mind. But now, how barren it made him feel. With his hands shoved into his pockets, he turned his back on the prostitute and his head sank lower between his shoulders, as though matching his thoughts.

Elizabeth. How many men had she entertained? he wondered. And when had she started? The day after she'd taken him to Eden? Had she healed her grief in this fashion, welcoming men to her bed while still deep in mourning for . . . ?

The thought was so awesome that it seemed literally to spin him about. Then he was running, without destination, simply eager to pass the night, to try by any means at his disposal to obliterate the loneliness which again was settling about him.

London,
June 1854

NOT UNTIL ELIZABETH held the document in her hand did she fully realize its import and value. Yet there it was, in fine scroll, proclaiming to all men that she was the legal householder of the elegant property at number seven St. George Street.

In spite of the bustle of moving men about her, she glanced up at Lord Kimbrough, who had just placed the deed in her hands. "I . . . don't know what to say, Frederick," she murmured.

"Say nothing." Lord Kimbrough smiled. "It's yours, legally and forever."

She closed her eyes to the complexity of the deed description, strangely saddened by the accomplishment of what she had worked so hard to achieve. Part of it was simply her reluctance to leave this house in Bermondsey, in spite of the fine new house awaiting her only a block removed from Westminster Hall.

Apparently Lord Kimbrough sensed her sadness and thoughtfully invited, "Come. It's not necessary that you remain here." He cast a critical eye over the small front parlor. "The workmen have clear instructions. And you have yet to inspect your carriage. Come," he added gently, "a turn around the park and I shall, with immense pleasure, deliver you personally to number seven."

The carriage! In the excitement of the deed, she'd almost forgotten about the elegant new carriage which had preceded Lord Kimbrough's larger one and which was at this moment waiting beside the pavement, two beautiful brown horses in harness, her own driver, a rotund Father Christmas of a man perched smartly in the high seat.

In spite of the enticement, she begged off. "Not now, Frederick, please." She smiled. "You go ahead. Let me finish here and we will have a late supper together tonight at number seven. Our first."

Apparently her reciprocal gift was adequate to the occasion. With a grateful smile Lord Kimbrough kissed her lightly on the cheek, adjusted his top hat under his left arm and without further protest bowed to her. "It will be pleasant to have so short a journey this evening," he whispered. "A five-minute walk from Westminster and I'll be at your door."

She returned his smile, fully aware of what the move meant to him and to the others as well. No longer would they have to run the hazardous course from Westminster to Bermondsey, through the ever-worsening London traffic, along with the fear that a private investigator or a suspicious wife was trailing behind them. Now, at the closing bell, they could merely slip discreetly out of Westminister, cut a circuitous path across the green and within moments be granted the safe refuge of her new dwelling.

As though to speed him on his way, Elizabeth grasped his arm and again thanked him. "I *am* grateful, Frederick. It will be a new life."

"In exchange for the one you have given me," he replied gallantly.

Now he walked rapidly down the steps, sidestepping a workman with a crate of china hoisted upon his shoulders. "Not one crack," he called out good-naturedly to the man. "Not so much as a chip. The lady requires beauty and she shall have it, I swear it."

Blushing at the public proclamation of his affection, Elizabeth waved to him and remained on the stoop until his carriage had maneuvered a path through the congestion on the pavement.

Now the confusion in the room behind her caught her

attention, and she turned back, the deed still in her hand. "Be careful with that," she warned one of the men who was just in the process of removing a large gilt mirror. She should assist them. It was the reason why she had remained behind. Yet she discovered curiously that she had no desire to witness the dismantling of the front parlor. It was like a dismemberment, and feeling an increasing need for a moment of seclusion, she took refuge in her bedroom, already stripped of all furnishings save one. Edward's trunk.

Closing the door behind her, she leaned against it, eyeing the trunk. It was her intention, had always been her intention, to leave it behind. It had no place in the house on St. George Street, certainly no place in her new life.

Suddenly she bent over, the pain of memory too great. She'd called to John too late. But he hadn't come back. And though she had sent countless messages to Willmot's lodgings in Warwick Lane, none had been answered. Where he was now, and what doing, she had no idea.

She raised her eyes to Edward's trunk. If only he were still alive, how different her life might be.

But at the very moment that she was sinking into a sense of her own degradation, with a conscious act of will she lifted her head and wiped away her tears. What in the name of God was she doing? Edward Eden was dead, John as good as dead.

All she had to do was rise from this bare floor and walk out of the front door and into her own carriage and a brand new life.

Then do it! As she stood, her eye fell again on Edward's trunk. Why should she take it with her? It was filled with nothing of importance.

From the front parlor she heard someone calling. "Miss?"

Quickly she wiped at her face to clear the last residue of tears, then opened the door. A workman stood on the other side, hat in hand, his face glistening with perspiration. "We're done here, miss." He smiled. "Just wanted to know if there was anything else . . ."

She hesitated. Then, "No," she said, "everything else I intend to leave."

She watched him go, rounding up his two mates in the process. Still she stood, gazing at the spill of sunlight streaming in through the open front door. On the pavement she heard the large wagon rumble forward. At last the street was empty and quiet, as was the room around her.

Leave! It was all over for her here. Let someone else inhabit this place of sorrow. Quickly she reached for her valise, avoiding Edward's trunk. Not taking the time to affix her bonnet, she grabbed it with one hand, the luggage with the other, and ran through the empty parlor and out onto the pavement, where she saw her new carriage, the driver holding the door open for her.

"Miss . . ." He smiled.

She'd wanted to chat with him for a moment, but chatting could come later. It was most important that they leave immediately.

"St. George Street, is it, miss?" he called back as he climbed atop his seat.

"Yes," she replied, amazed at the impatience in her voice.

As the carriage started forward, she closed her eyes and gripped the armrest, trying to keep her mind busy. First she must see to the dispersing of the furnishings. Then she must unpack her valise. Lord Kimbrough had said a maid would be waiting, someone to shop for her and do her errands. Then the pantry must be stocked, ample quantities of everyone's favorite: port for Lord Kimbrough, champagne for Lord Hopkins, sherry for Willie . . .

Oh, she really should write it all down. Suddenly her shoulders trembled. "Wait . . ." she whispered. Realizing that no one had heard her, she pulled down the window and cried, "Wait! Turn back, please."

She saw the driver angle the carriage about and with an air of confused resignation drive back down the street.

They had traversed only two blocks, and a moment later she looked out of the window at the house she'd just left.

"May I be of assistance, miss?" the old driver called

down. "If you forgot something, I'd be more than happy to—"

"In the back room," she said, her voice without inflection, her eyes straight ahead. "There's a small trunk. Fetch it for me, if you will."

A few moments later he returned, Edward's trunk hoisted on his shoulder. "Shall I put it up, miss, with your other—"

"No," she said. "There's room back here. Place it on the seat opposite me."

As she felt the carriage moving again, she at last settled back in the seat, staring at the trunk. Curious. Already she felt a new peace, as though a portion of her soul had been restored to her.

"Edward," she whispered, the image of the man sitting opposite her. "Do *you* understand?"

The only answer she received was a clearing of the turmoil in her mind. But whatever hopes she once had had of fleeing to a new life, unencumbered, now disappeared. She might very well be fleeing toward new lodgings, but the truth of the matter was that part of her was still held a prisoner in that plain trunk. As for John, that was a sorrow that she'd have to learn to live with.

"Westminster ahead, miss!" the old driver called out. "Not far now."

Not far indeed, she mourned, and felt a peculiar need to cry.

❧

London,
December 1854

THOUGH FEELING PRIVILEGED to have been included, nonetheless John stood at the back of the crowded office and listened skeptically to all that was being said.

Brassey was poised before an enormous map of the Crimea, wielding his pointer like a general wields his baton, having earlier pointed out the Black Sea, Turkey on one side, Russia on the other, and the British harbor at Balaklava.

Clustered in chairs around the desk were four army officers—they had been introduced, but their names had escaped John—and standing behind the chairs were Brassey's trusted "lieutenants," twenty-five of his professional foremen, Jack Willmot among them.

For hours—since midafternoon, and it was now early evening—the military men had sung a grim chorus, graphically describing horror after horror: the climate apparently as effective as the enemy itself, rain, snow and frost making movement a nightmare, clearly stating that the British Army was no longer in a state to bear the burden.

As the voices droned on, John leaned wearily against the wall. He didn't need to listen. During the past year he'd received countless letters from Andrew Rhoades telling him everything. He'd told him as well about the oceans of blood and the constant screams of pain, long letters which suggested more a need to talk than anything, his dreams of a law career apparently forgotten in the carnage.

John had replied as sympathetically as possible, wishing Andrew well and bidding him to take care, and trying to bring him up-to-date on the tedium that was Peto, Betts, and Brassey, and the hysteria that was London.

From where John stood, he saw Willmot glance over his shoulder as though to confirm John's presence. John returned the look with a nod, grateful for the man's concern. What fast friends they had become, despite the years which separated them. Though John had been promoted to head clerk months ago and his weekly salary now was such that he could have had a flat of his own, Willmot had insisted that he stay in his comfortable chambers in Warwick Lane. As Jack Willmot had pointed out, John could put the saved rent into his bank account, which was only nine hundred and ninety-nine thousand, nine hundred and fifty pounds short of his first million.

Suddenly the room went silent, and John's attention was dragged forward to the cluster of men about the desk.

To his surprise, he saw that Brassey had abandoned his position by the map and had taken a seat behind his desk, focusing on one of the officers, who apparently had been successful in shocking the entire room. Now John noticed all heads slanted toward the officer.

Brassey seemed to straighten in his chair. "Withdraw?" he said, doing little to mask the disgust in his voice.

"It's been suggested, yes, sir," the officer confirmed, holding his shako on his lap, one finger moving nervously back and forth across its visor. "At the British Council of War just last month. You see, sir, after each battle, we seem to come to an abrupt halt. Little or nothing can be sustained in the face of—"

"But withdraw!" Brassey exclaimed.

Finally one officer took the floor with renewed aggression, as though he were unaccustomed to the censure of civilians. "I beg your pardon, sir," he pronounced firmly. "It's quite a simple matter to play armchair general from the safety of a London office." His voice fell. "It's quite another to be there and see what happens, and suffer the cold and the—"

"But withdraw!" Brassey exclaimed a third time. The mood in the room was grim and growing more so. John's attention was fully engaged, his mind running to Andrew, good, decent Andrew, who wanted only to pursue a quiet study of the law. Had he been in those cold trenches that resembled dikes? Had he come face to face with a Russian peasant or a Russian sword?

At last Brassey stood, his awesome height towering over the seated men. John wished he'd given the colonel a chance to explain. But Brassey had other options on his mind. Retrieving the pointer from the desk, he approached the map. "What would it take, Colonel, to turn the British forces about and set them on the road to victory?"

The colonel smiled. "Short of a miracle, sir?"

"Including a miracle," Brassey said. "Your superiors and Lord Aberdeen notwithstanding, withdrawal is an obscenity which we will not consider."

"I was sent to London, sir," the officer began, "in search of a miracle. But I have been here a week and I've been told a half dozen times that my . . . miracle is not possible, this side of divine intervention."

"Name it," Brassey demanded, "or better still, let me name it for you."

He stepped up to the map. "Here," he commenced, pointing to the British harbor at Balaklava, "is where the men and materials are landed."

He looked back over his shoulder. Obligingly the colonel nodded.

"And here," Brassey went on, pointing to the black dot of Sebastopol, "is where the bulk of the fighting takes place."

Again the colonel nodded.

"And between here," and the pointer stabbed at Balaklava, "and here," quickly it slid up to the black dot of Sebastopol, "there is one single country road which is impassable from October to March.

"A railway," he pronounced. "The British Army does not require a miracle." He smiled. "They simply need a railway."

A hush fell over the room, all minds turning on the preposterous suggestion. The colonel stirred first. "I've been told, sir, that they are one and the same, a miracle and a railway, that is—"

"Nonsense," Brassey scoffed. "You should have come to me first, Colonel, and not gone to the weak sisters who serve as my competitors." Abruptly he turned back to the map.

"Of course, it wouldn't be easy," Brassey admitted. "But then, the Grand Trunk wasn't easy, was it, men, or the Paris—Le Havre."

The direct question elicited a few mutters, as obviously the insane proposition was beginning to take hold in other minds.

Generously the colonel stepped forward with a suggestion. "It wouldn't be necessary to stretch the line the entire distance, sir, between Balaklava and Sebastopol. A trunk line extending to . . . here," and he came around the desk and pointed to a destination. "That would be sufficient. You see, the most difficult terrain is the incline itself, a distance of approximately seven miles. Beyond that, horses and wagons are most effective."

Seven miles, a mere seven miles, John thought, uphill, in the dead of winter, caught in the crossfire between British and Russian troops. Was Brassey mad? Were they all mad?

As though in answer to his unspoken question, Brassey turned about with renewed energy and confronted his men. "We can do it, can't we?" He smiled. "We can perform this miracle that will save both British lives as well as British honor."

For a moment there was no response, as though that villain, good sense, had tempered their replies. Then some idiot standing not too far removed from John shouted, "With you leading us, we can, Mr. Brassey," and the floodgates opened, the cry of faith taken up by others, everyone shouting his confidence, the colonels and Brassey shaking hands, the entire room a furor of insanity.

John still couldn't quite believe what he'd seen or heard. Obviously Brassey had permitted himself to be swept up in a hysteria of patriotism. Well, it was none of John's concern. It simply meant that life would be very quiet for the next few months at the firm of Peto, Betts, and Brassey, and the flat in Warwick Lane would be quiet as well.

As two men filed past him, John assumed that it was safe for him to leave. He'd wait for Willmot in the outer office, although he doubted seriously if the man would be fit company tonight. He took a last look at the map, the colonel's horrors still fresh in his ear. Good God, had they all lost their minds?

Having seen and heard enough, he turned toward the door when suddenly . . .

"Eden!"

He looked back at Brassey, the officers standing to one side of the desk, Willmot and another man to the other.

"Sir?" John inquired, a bit embarrassed by the attention.

"Come forward," Brassey commanded. "You've kept a safe distance all afternoon. Now, step forward."

John glanced at Willmot. Then he did as he had been told. Before the desk he stopped.

"Where were you going?" Brassey inquired almost pleasantly.

"I thought the meeting was concluded, sir," he said. "The hour is late and I—"

"No, quite the contrary." Brassey smiled. "The hour is early. We all have round-the-clock days ahead of us. Might as well accustom ourselves to them now."

You have round-the-clock days, John thought.

"Well, then, Eden," Brassey began, settling back in his chair as though ready for some diversion, "you've held your tongue all afternoon and well into the evening. Don't ask me to believe that there is nothing going on in that keen mind."

"No, sir," he began. "My mind is anything but empty."

Brassey nodded, as though he'd won a point. "I thought as much. Then what, might I ask, is your opinion of what you have heard here?"

"My opinion, sir, of what I've just heard?" he began, repeating the question for the benefit of all. "My opinion is this. If I were, at this moment, to shut out the world and channel all my concentration for the next twenty-four hours in one direction only, I could not possibly conceive of a scheme more deserving of the designation lunatic than the one I've heard here today."

It had been his intention to go right on. His mind had already compiled a dozen salient points with which to buttress his initial statement. But for the moment the reaction of the others held him in some fascination. The four army officers were no longer smiling. In fact, one by one those faces turned in his direction. To the left of the desk was poor Jack Willmot. In the act of searching through the files, he now froze.

Ultimately there was Brassey, no longer interested in his notepad, but settling back in his chair, looking directly up at John.

When out of all these shocked expressions, no words seemed forthcoming, John drew a breath and went on. After all, he had been invited to speak.

"I've listened carefully, sir," he began, "to everything,

and while the tales were shocking to be sure, I heard nothing that I had not heard before. From Andrew. You remember Andrew Rhoades, sir. He was a clerk in your office before the 'Glorious Conflict.' All he wanted here was to save enough to study law. But the Czar changed all that."

"I've received several lengthy letters from Andrew, sir, each filled with tales as horrible as the ones we have heard today. No, more horrible in a way. We were informed of the pain and suffering here today, but we were told nothing of the bewilderment . . ."

Out of the corner of his eye, he saw one of the officers stiffen.

". . . which plagues the ordinary soldier. You see, sir, according to Andrew, they haven't the faintest idea what they are doing there. Oh, to be sure, it seemed like sport in the beginning, but after one has seen certain sights of war, the element of sport recedes, and men, unfortunately, need a reason for pain and suffering."

"Need a reason?" one of the officers exploded. "What better reason than Russia's imperial lust? The Czar was clearly the aggressor, both in Moldavia and—"

John smiled. "The Czar was the aggressor in his own garden, as it were. By that definition, sir, we English are aggressors in Ireland. Yet I see no ally rushing to Ireland's aid."

"It's . . . not the same," the officer sputtered.

"How is it different?"

When the officer either couldn't or wouldn't reply, Brassey urged, "Go on, Eden."

"Well, sir"—John smiled—"my point is this. If the average soldier hasn't the foggiest idea what he is fighting for, it doesn't require too much thought to figure out why the British troops are being defeated. And according to Andrew, whose opinion and judgment I respect, the true enemy is not Russia or the climate, but rather the British military establishment itself, who, ill-prepared and ill-advised, appears to be waging the war as though they were on holiday to Brighton."

"I beg your pardon," another officer angrily interrupted. "You've gone too far."

John too a step back from the angry barrage, his attention focused on Brassey alone. "You asked for my opinion, sir," he gently reminded everyone in the room. "As I've said before, to subject your civilian navvies, none of whom will be armed to the stresses of the winter, to the meaninglessness of the conflict, to the apathy of the British troops, to the Russian crossfire, to the insanity of power politics, for the purposes of constructing seven miles of railway which could be obsolete on the day it is completed, to build a supply link from fleet to army, to ship out materials and men, to engineer the line and then run it, all at cost, expecting no profit, is, with your forgiveness, sir, the height of lunacy."

There! Rather succinctly he'd combined all his points into one barrage. Now all he had to do was wait for the smoke to clear. And from the sputtering coming from the officers on his right, that might be some time.

To his left, he observed poor Jack Willmot, who looked stricken.

Brassey was stirring, two fingers rubbing back and forth across his lips. When he spoke, his question was brief, almost simpleminded. "You . . . see no point in the venture, then?"

"None at all, sir,"

Abruptly Brassey sat up, rubbing his forehead, his face totally obscured. "And you see no . . . profit in the venture, Eden?"

"No monetary profit, sir. In fact, I predict a loss. You will have to provide everything, tents, tools, vessels—I doubt if you can count on the British Army for anything."

John watched, fascinated, as the man slowly lowered his hands from his face. Somehow he looked martyred, as though in front of witnesses his dream had been destroyed.

As John stepped back to execute a quick exit, Brassey did a peculiar thing, not at all in keeping with the mood of the room. He grinned.

While John was still trying to interpret the grin, he saw Brassey clap his hands together as though with undisguised glee. "Then it's settled, Eden," he announced.

"I . . . beg your pardon, sir?"

"I said it's settled," Brassey roared, the grin exploding into an outright laugh. He lifted both hands and smoothed back his long white hair. "I never thought I'd hear myself say this, but what I need for this venture more than anything is one good hard-minded pragmatist, someone to keep me in line and remind me of my limitations as well as those of my men."

John listened, half-turned away. "I'm afraid I . . . don't understand, sir."

"Don't understand?" Brassey bellowed. "Don't understand!" he repeated. "You who have just given us a succinct appraisal of the British Army, the French Army, and the Russian Army, including a concise definition of goals and capabilities of each?"

"You asked for my opinion, sir, and—"

"And you certainly gave it," Brassey said. "And an interesting opinion it was, quite illuminating, I'm certain, to everyone in this room, most particularly to me, who now has the pleasure of informing you that you will go to the Crimea with me as my first assistant."

John's hand, lifting toward the door, froze.

As Brassey laughed heartily, all the others joined in, the officers grateful that nothing John had said had altered the man's initial insanity. Even Willmot was laughing, a look of pure rapture on his face, as though John had been singled out for a spectacular honor.

While John was struggling to understand this curious turn of events, Brassey came out from behind the desk, hand extended. "Well, what do you say, Eden?" he demanded. "Shall, together, the two of us take on the Czar as well as the inept British Army and show them both what Englishmen are capable of accomplishing?"

John still couldn't believe what he was hearing. "I . . . can't—" he began, and was not given a chance to finish.

"Of course you can." Brassey grinned. "Didn't I say I needed you? First assistant? Do you have any notion what that means?"

For a moment John considered laughing. It would have been sport to mimic the man. Instead he stepped away. "I say no thank you, Mr. Brassey," he called over his shoulder.

"First assistant, Mr. Eden!" Brassey repeated. "You haven't answered my question. Do you know what that means?"

"As I said—"

"It means prestige."

"If you will excuse me, sir—"

"It means advancement, and for one as ambitious as you—"

"I'm not ambitious, sir," John replied, his hand on the door.

Again Brassey laughed. "Not ambitious!" he repeated. "I look at you, Eden, and I see myself a quarter of a century ago."

John had heard enough, and for the second time tried to take his leave.

For the second time Brassey halted him by the mere force in his voice. "Then, profit, Eden."

John held his position by the door.

"Profit!" Brassey repeated. "The chance to learn the art of contracting from the inside. Simple lessons, Eden, which I have perfected and which have transformed me from a very poor man into a very rich one."

With his face averted so that no one might see and interpret it as weakness, John closed his eyes. At last the man had said something that interested him. But abruptly he turned, his defenses back in place, and only slightly weaker than before. "I have a blueprint for my life, Mr. Brassey, as all sober men do, and it does not include a diversion in the Crimea."

He succeeded in opening the door this time, though a curious clucking noise prevented him from passing through it.

"What a shame," he heard Brassey say, "to have an early opinion confirmed. How . . . disappointing."

John turned back, something ugly in the half-formed accusation. "What is it you're saying?"

Brassey shrugged. "Nothing, only I thought it strange last year when you allowed all your friends to enlist without you."

It had been mere innuendo, but the outline was very

clear. "I had no more appetite for war then, Mr. Brassey, than I do now."

"Appetite?" Brassey parroted. "Or inclination?"

The men clustered about the desk had grown silent. "What is it that you're trying to say, Mr. Brassey?"

Again the man shrugged. "Nothing, nothing at all. It's just that in my day . . ."

John had had enough, of everything, of thinly veiled accusations, of allurements, of resistance. There was always the possibility that Brassey had made the offer of first assistant, secure in the knowledge that John would never accept. But of greater importance was the awful weight which seemed to have settled over the room, a weight which was centered in the eyes of the men watching him, specifically in Jack Willmot's eyes, looking at John as though seeing him for the first time, a clear look of disappointment.

In an effort to alter that expression, John announced, "Then I accept your offer, Mr. Brassey, most particularly your promise of profit." Even as he was speaking, the full meaning of what he was saying had yet to settle over him. All he knew was that somehow he must remove the taint of that unspoken accusation, the brand of coward. "I'll join your venture," he went on, anger rising, "and serve you as best as I know how, and expect to be served."

In his growing anger, he was aware of Brassey, a look of satisfaction on his face. The awareness of such a look only fed his outrage. "I still think it's insanity," John went on. "No, worse than insanity," he added. "Perhaps approaching criminal."

Brassey appeared to draw himself up, and in spite of the tension, still he extended a hand to John, his closing advice succinct. "Say your good-byes, then, Eden. Tell the girls they will have to do without your charms for a while. Pack your warmest clothes and meet me on the docks of Portsmouth in a fortnight."

John listened, loathing both the man and the words. There was a new weight in the room now, the weight of defeat. For all of John's rhetoric, Brassey had ultimately defeated him, and he knew it, and Brassey knew it.

Ignoring Brassey's outstretched hand, he grasped the

door, feeling relief in escaping from the watching eyes, though still suffering defeat so acutely that he slammed the door behind him with such violence that he felt the vibrations run across the floor, an explosion which he felt certain would be recorded by the man standing victorious on the other side.

It brought him only small satisfaction, but for the moment it was all he had.

Not until Jack Willmot felt the cramp in his hand did he realize how tightly he'd been gripping the desk. The violence with which John had slammed the door brought him to his senses, and quickly he turned loose of the edge of the desk and massaged his wrist where the muscles were painfully contracting.

What had happened here? Why had Brassey placed John in such a position, then literally run him to ground? And John! Why had he spoken thus, his words sounding dangerously close to treason, particularly with army officers present. And first assistant! Was the young man totally dense and self-absorbed? Had he no conception of what that advancement would mean to him?

As the muscle spasm in his hand relaxed, the tension seemed to move up to his shoulders. Before he could deal with it, he saw Brassey slowly turning away from where he'd faced the closed door for several moments without moving.

"See to him," Brassey instructed Willmot. "In his present state, he will probably drink himself senseless and stumble into the Thames, thus depriving us and the world of his . . . wisdom."

Mockingly spoken, the sentiment provoked laughter from the officers. But from where Willmot stood, he saw no smile on Brassey's face.

"See to him," Brassey commanded again.

Hurriedly Willmot moved to obey, though on his way to the door he stopped, feeling the need to say something. "I'm certain the lad did not mean anything he said, sir," he began.

"Nonsense," Brassey contradicted. "He meant every word of it, and more." Abruptly he drew a noisy breath.

"And the damnable thing about it is that he may be right."

From where Willmot stood, he could see the reaction from the officers.

"Go ahead, Willmot," Brassey said almost brusquely. "He's still your charge, at least for a while. Just have him standing upright and sober on the Portsmouth docks in two weeks. Is that clear?"

Willmot did well to nod, for in truth nothing was clear. He closed the door behind him and looked out across the large room in time to see a shoulder, with a coat loosely swung over it, just leaving the room.

"John, wait," he shouted, and knowing that he wouldn't, Willmot grabbed his own coat and raced after the departing figure, and at last caught up with him on the pavement, where, to Jack's surprise, he saw that night had fallen and a light snow had commenced.

As he drew his coat about him, he observed John standing on the edge of the pavement, angry puffs of fog escaping his mouth, mute evidence of his lingering rage.

Expertly Willmot took in all aspects of the brooding figure. With an experience based on the two years they had shared the same flat, he knew that the best approach to John was a circuitous one. He watched him a moment longer, newly aware of the depths of affection he felt for him. In a very real sense, this was the son that Willmot had never had.

"Come," Willmot urged, taking John's arm. "I propose dinner, a feast if you will, one of Childe's beefsteaks as large as a hindquarter and still smoking from the fire."

"I'm . . . not hungry, Jack . . ." John faltered, head down. "You go ahead. I'll walk a bit."

"John, wait," Willmot called out, and caught up with him only a few steps away. "Please," he urged. "Come with me to Childe's. It will serve no purpose to—"

John smiled. "No cause for alarm. I'm simply following Brassey's advice. Remember? Say your good-byes, he said. Didn't he say that?"

Willmot listened, appalled at how angry the boy still was. He noticed something else, that self-imposed isolation into which he always locked himself when troubled.

A cold wind suddenly gusted in their faces. John turned away. When he looked back, all the walls were intact. "I don't think you'd find it to your liking, where I'm going," he said. "I won't even find it to my own liking," he added, "but I'm going anyway."

"Where would that be?" Willmot inquired.

"I'm going to Bermondsey. I have no one to say my good-byes to, except you, and you apparently will accompany me. So that leaves Elizabeth."

Willmot looked up. This was an unexpected turn. *Elizabeth.* That name had not been spoken between them for months. To be sure, for a while after John's painful discovery of what she had become, Willmot had tried to help him to understand. But each conversation had always concluded in anger, and ultimately they had made an agreement that her name was never again to be mentioned.

Now John had broken the agreement, and if Bermondsey was indeed his destination, Willmot had sad news for him. But first he had to make certain that he had understood correctly. "Bermondsey?" he repeated.

"Of course," John said. "I can't leave things between us as they are now, can I? Someone must know where I'm going and care."

Peculiar. Willmot had never heard that before, that hint of self-pity, or was it something else? "Are you so . . . apprehensive, John?" he asked, amazed. "Do you really see potential . . . danger in—"

"Indeed I do," John said, "and I'm amazed at your loyalty to the man."

"Brassey would never engage in any undertaking that might prove potentially harmful to his—"

"Brassey is totally unconcerned with the welfare of anyone but Thomas Brassey."

"That's not true."

"Oh, isn't it? Who will profit if the scheme is successful? Who will the press lionize if that damnable railway *is* built? Will it be you, or the other foremen, or the navvies who will freeze and be shot at and suffer illness?"

Willmot retreated a step and drew up his collar. "I . . . doubt if we will ever see fighting."

"See it? Did you hear nothing of what was said this afternoon?"

Willmot watched, helpless, as John paced back and forth. Again he tried to reassure him. "Nothing will happen." He smiled. "I give you my word. We will go and do the job for him, as I've done countless jobs all over the world. We'll collect our pay and return to London by spring, richer men, you richer than most."

He stepped closer, still failing to see why the evening wasn't cause for celebration instead of angry exchanges. "My God, John," he said. "Aren't you aware of what happened in that office? Out of all those men, many of whom, like myself, have been with him for years, *you* were singled out for an opinion, and for advancement. First assistant!" he marveled. "I can think of fifty men who would fall on their knees for such advancement."

"Then seek them out and tell them the job is theirs," John responded coldly.

"I can't do that. Brassey chose you to honor—"

"Or destroy."

If those last words had not been so soberly spoken, they would have been laughingly melodramatic. As it was, Willmot smiled. "Now, why should he want to destroy you, John?"

Newly impressed by the depths of the boy's mood, Willmot had one last question. "If you feel this . . . strongly, John, why did you agree to go? You're a free agent. It's your right to say no."

For a moment he did not speak. Then all he said was, "I had no choice. In effect he called me a coward. Now I must go and find out if he's right."

From the look on John's face, it was clear that nothing Willmot said could dissuade him from his fears. Apparently he would have to play out the whole ridiculous melodrama, up to and including a "soldier's good-bye."

As John started away, Willmot called after him. "If you insist, let me save you a trip. You won't find Elizabeth in Bermondsey."

John looked back. "I . . . don't understand."

"She's moved."

"Where?"

"If you like, I'll take you there."

Slowly John returned. "How do you know?"

Embarrassed, Willmot shrugged again. "Habit." He smiled. "Since your father's death, I've felt . . . responsible."

Still John stood, his eyes fixed upon Willmot. "Do you love her?"

Willmot had not been expecting so direct a question.

"You do, don't you?"

"I did once." Willmot nodded.

"Is she still . . . ?"

"Oh, indeed, very much so. A peer it was, or so I heard, that purchased her new lodgings for her."

John stared downward at the pavement. "Show me where she is, Willmot."

Resignedly Willmot drew a deep breath. What was the point? She was lost to both of them. With a sense of futility he increased his pace, determinedly leading the way. The sooner they arrived, the sooner they could depart.

About twenty minutes later, the hulking facade of the Admiralty came into view. And beyond that, the Horse Guards, and beyond that the Government Offices. Without breaking speed, he turned into St. George Street, a respectable street inhabited by successful surgeons, a few members of Parliament, and at number seven, Elizabeth.

Not until he'd crossed the narrow street and taken refuge in the shadows near a black iron fence did he look back at John and see the puzzle in that face as he took in the quiet lane and its unspoken wealth and respectability.

"She's . . . here?" he asked, bewildered. "Where?"

Willmot lifted a hand numb with cold and pointed to the house across the way. "Number seven," he said. "She owns it. Some generous gentleman put it in her name."

He might have said more, but slowly John stepped out of the shadows, his attention held by the house. The massive front door was a colorful explosion of stained glass. The lamps were lit in the entry hall. To the right were the heavy drapes of the drawing room. Willmot had never seen inside. The drapes were always closed. But to the left he saw something he'd never seen before, the drapes opened on that room, a dining room, the long table covered with white linen and a glittering array of crystal, while overhead a gold chandelier supporting at least a hundred lit candles shed a bright light on the gentleman at one end, a middle-aged man with graying hair formally dressed in black, and at the opposite end of the table, the woman, scarcely recognizable, her fair hair done up and intertwined with pearls, her gown rose satin, both the lady and gentleman chatting amiably while a maid moved silently about the table.

Willmot watched longingly. How beautiful she looked, how much the "lady" in her new setting. Could one pretend such a look of happiness, and where was the sordid degradation he thought of whenever he thought on her?

The gentleman was saying something now. Then he was on his feet, his hand extending to her. She reached for it and stepped gracefully into his embrace, her head tilted backward to accommodate the force of his passion.

Willmot watched the kiss a moment longer, then turned his attention back to the rigid figure standing on the pavement. "Come, John," he whispered sternly. "We've no right to be here."

But the boy merely shook his head, all of his attention still focused on the window across the street, the kiss ending, the gentleman lifting her into his arms and carrying her out of the room.

Willmot bowed his head, his heart going out to the boy. How could he explain that which he himself did not understand?

For over an hour they stood thus. In the agony of waiting, Willmot had long since ceased to feel the cold. A comforting numbness had set in, which he kept hoping would extend to his brain, or at least to the feeling part of him so that his heart would no longer ache for the young man who had yet to lift his eyes from that darkened second-floor chamber.

When Willmot did not think he could endure a moment longer, he saw John straighten his shoulders. He seemed to take a final look at that second-floor chamber; then for the first time he turned toward Willmot, his face clearly visible in the spill of light from the near streetlamp, revealing tears which he tried to wipe away with his hands.

Willmot stared at him. What could he say? Nothing, and in silence the two of them turned their backs on number seven and walked steadily through the cold night, the streets devoid of all traffic.

During that long walk back to Warwick Lane, neither of them spoke, except once, when unexpectedly John reached out and placed his arm around Willmot's shoulders and drew him close and said softly, "What would I do without you, my friend? What in the name of God would I do without you?"

"No need," Willmot whispered huskily, embarrassed by the expression of affection, suffering acutely from the cold now, the chilling wind stinging his face, leaving a rim of salt moisture about his eyes.

❧

Eden Castle,
December 24, 1854

CLARA JENKINS COULD hardly make herself heard over the weeping servants, yet someone had to take charge. "It will serve no purpose," she scolded, "no purpose at all." Then she turned away, weeping.

The word had only just come down. Having received no answer to their morning call, the two guards had entered the chamber and had found his lordship dead, lying in a pool of vomit.

Clara pressed her apron tightly against her lips, striving for control. What were they to do now? Surely there was ritual involved. But what? The word should go out, shouldn't it, that Lord James Eden, fourteenth Baron and sixth Earl of Eden Point, was dead. Though she'd only been a girl at the time, Clara remembered vividly the pomp connected with the death of Lord Thomas Eden.

Sweet Jesus, she groaned, the thoughts distracting her from her grief. How could they be expected to perform all those rituals? And who would even pen the obituary? With Herr Snyder gone, only two of them, herself and Mrs. Swan, could even write.

As the wailing about her increased, she glanced up the stairs, hoping to catch sight of Aggie Fletcher, who bravely had offered to go up and confirm the death. Feeling sick, Clara reached out for the banister.

Craning her neck upward, she peered through the railings and saw the white soiled gown of Miss Jennifer.

Angrily Clara started up the stairs. Someone had to be concerned for the dignity of this disintegrating family.

"Here, now," she scolded gently, taking one thin arm and trying to turn her about. "Look at you, wandering about these cold corridors without your cloak. Come, Clara will walk with you back to your chambers. I'm sure your maid has laid a lovely fire for . . ."

Abruptly her thoughts stopped. There was no maid. The woman assigned to Miss Jennifer had been let go only last month, along with forty-three others. All that remained of what once had been the largest staff of domestics in the West Country were those weeping creatures below, scarcely more than ten in number.

At that moment, coming from the third floor, she heard a determined step, someone marching rigidly through the chaos. A second later, Aggie appeared on the upper landing.

"He's dead, right enough," Aggie announced, full-voiced. "Been dead the better part of the night is my guess," she added. "Stiffening already. We best move quick or we'll never get him in a box."

As the wailing increased, Clara saw a tinge of red rising on the old cook's face. "Well, we bloody well can't keep it a secret," she snapped. "Now, can we? As for them weak sisters down there, I'll take care of them right enough."

Brushing past Clara and Jennifer where they stood mid-step, she sent her voice ahead in a barrage of abuse, shouting orders, yelling at one to fetch her boiling water, commanding another to fetch the coffinmakers from Morte-

mouth, and yet another to see to the beef joint she'd
left boiling on the cook stove in the kitchen court.

Shielding Miss Jennifer, Clara watched as Aggie sent
the weeping servants running, dispatching everyone save
old Dana, the footman, who since Mr. Rexroat's departure
several months ago now served as senior adviser to the
crumbling household.

Oh, lord, Clara couldn't even think on all the tragedies,
and there was no time anyway, for she looked down to
see Aggie and Dana climbing the steps.

Then Aggie caught sight of Miss Jennifer. "What's
she doing here?" she demanded.

Clara explained. "I found her wandering about. Quite
chilled, she is. I had thought to . . ."

Aggie stepped forward, her eyes fixed on Jennifer.
"Run along, child," she commanded. "Go to your chambers and keep warm."

Suddenly Jennifer wrenched free from Clara's grasp
and cowered against the banister, her eyes distended
with fear. "I want Daniel," she whispered, tears beginning.

Clara scolded Aggie. "Look what you've done now."
She started toward the hysterical woman. "Miss Jennifer,
you must . . ." The weeping only increased. She was on
the verge of trying again when she heard a voice coming
from the top of the landing.

"Please leave her alone. All of you."

The voice was young, quiet, slightly cracking, midway
between boyhood and manhood. Clara looked up to see
Richard, his face drawn. "All of you," he repeated gently.
"Please move away from her. She'll be fine if you give
her her freedom."

As he started down the steps, Mary in hand, Clara
wondered mournfully where her two lovely "children"
had gone. Though Richard was twelve and Mary almost
seven, still they were no longer children. Of all the various tragedies which had descended upon the Eden family,
here Clara thought, were the two most pitiful victims.

Below her on the steps, she saw Aggie and Dana retreat, as though contained in this frail and brooding twelve-
year-old boy was the only true voice of authority at Eden.
Suffering a shock of recognition, Clara realized that the

assessment was true. It was not merely Richard kneeling beside his aunt Jennifer. He was now the fifteenth Baron and seventh Earl of Eden Point. Clara wondered if those shoulders could support such a weight.

She watched as Richard knelt beside Jennifer, his voice soothing, telling her precisely what she wanted to hear, that all was well, that he'd seen Daniel himself only a few hours earlier.

As the quiet monologue persisted, Clara reached inside her sleeve for her handkerchief. As embarrassing tears clouded her eyes, she found it impossible to believe that those three, the boy, the child and the madwoman, were all that was left of what once had been one of England's noblest families.

Fortunately she was not given a chance to pursue that bleak thought, for Richard having soothed and joined Mary and Jennifer, now stepped toward the center of the staircase.

He ran a hand through his long black hair and seemed to straighten his shoulders. "My father," he began. "Is he . . . dead?"

Dana stepped forward. "Yes, my lord. With your permission, my lord," Dana went on, "I recall the ritual of your grandfather's passing, and while I'm afraid that circumstances prohibit us from duplicating all tradition, there are certain steps which could be taken."

Richard nodded. "I'd be most grateful, Dana, for all your assistance."

The old man drew a step closer. "Well, my lord, I know where the mourning banners are stored. Folded them myself, I did, after your grandfather's passing. There's three good guardsmen left. With their help, I think we can get the banners flying."

"Then do so, Dana."

"And further, my lord," Dana went on, "someone must pen the obituary. I recall last time, it went out to dozens of newspapers, all the London ones, of course."

Richard appeared to glance about him. With reluctance he said, "I'll do it."

"I'll help, my lord," Clara offered. "Tonight, the two of us will—"

"I'll do it, Clara."

Before she had time to fully understand why her offer of assistance had been turned down, Dana went on. "And Mr. Morley Johnson should be notified as well," he said, his voice cold, reflecting his feelings for the London solicitor, who kept sending them smaller and smaller monthly allotments.

But if Richard had any opinions on the subject, he kept them to himself, and again simply stated, "I'll write to him. Anything else?"

Dana paused, indecision on his face. "I was . . . wondering, my lord," he began, "if Mr. John Murrey Eden shouldn't be notified as well."

Clara saw the taut expression on Richard's face. She knew better than anyone how much Richard missed his cousin, how bewildered he still was by his mysterious departure from Eden so long ago. "If I knew where to write, Dana, I would have written long ago," he said simply.

The old man nodded. From where Clara stood, it wasn't difficult to follow the progress of his thoughts. How much Eden Castle needed that firm, confident hand of John Murrey Eden. Yet, in a curious way, it seemed to her that the present disintegration had commenced with his arrival, on that rainy May evening.

"Anything else?" he asked of Dana, glancing over his shoulder to where Jennifer and Mary were patiently waiting.

The old man lowered his head. "Well, of course, there's the preparation of the . . . body, but Aggie and I will see to that."

"I'd be most grateful."

"Any particular location in the graveyard, my lord?"

"No, no, of course not."

Clara heard a slight edge to the boy's voice, as though the new burdens were beginning to take a toll.

"A simple service, then?"

"Yes, simple."

"Tomorrow?"

"Yes, tomorrow."

"If the gravediggers can break ground . . . "

Clara saw the boy's head lift. "Yes," he whispered.

"Well, then," Clara said, interrupting the male counsel for the first time, "I think that everything has been covered." Belatedly she looked back to where Richard stood, afraid that she might have spoken out of turn. "Is there anything else, my lord?"

He gave her a strange look. "Please come with me to the nursery and stay with Jennifer and Mary." He closed his eyes as though a thought even more unbearable than all they had discussed had just entered his mind. "Someone . . . must tell my mother."

The three of them, Clara, Aggie and Dana, protested simultaneously. "No, my lord," Aggie begged. "It isn't necessary."

But he merely topped their protest. "She must be told," he said, then, with wavering conviction added, "It . . . might make a difference."

A difference, Clara thought angrily. If the clear abandonment of her children had not made a difference to that selfish woman, why would the death of a husband whom she had never loved affect her?

Lost in the depths of her own censure of Lady Eden, Clara was not at first aware of the meeting breaking up. Proceeding up the stairs ahead of her, she saw Richard, one hand grasping Jennifer, the other, Mary, leading both his frail charges toward the warmth of the nursery fire.

"Wait, my lord," Clara called out.

But he led the way to the nursery door without speaking, and gently guided Jennifer to a chair near the fire, while Mary sat cross-legged on the floor at her feet. Clara watched as he kissed them both and whispered, "I'll only be a moment. Warm yourselves, and upon my return I'll read to you."

Richard watched a moment longer, as though to make certain that they were placid, then without a word to Clara he started toward the door, apparently determined to carry out his grim errand.

Well, lordship or no, Clara had wiped his nose and rocked him to sleep, and on the basis of that investment, she caught up with him at the door, eager to speak her mind.

"Richard, wait." She stepped closer. "Why put yourself

through more pain? She won't hear, you know that, and if she hears, she won't respond."

He appeared to be listening. "We must continue to try," he said.

Before such a plea, she had no choice. Wearily she shook her head and stepped back to the nursery door, as though to demonstrate that she would do anything he asked of her. "Of course, my lord," she murmured.

She was just turning back into the door when she heard his voice again. "One thing more, Clara," he said. "Please don't call me that."

She looked back, puzzled. "Call you . . . what?"

"My lord."

"But . . . that's what you are."

"No, I'm not. I dislike it intensely. Please don't call me that again."

Before she had a chance to reply, he turned and started off down the corridor, a small figure growing smaller in the gloom.

Suddenly Clara shivered, partly from cold, partly from premonition. If the fifteenth Baron and seventh Earl of Eden Point refused to accept his new mantle, then there was no future at all for Eden Castle.

Shivering again from the bleak vision, she stepped inside the nursery, closed the door firmly behind her, and saw the two at the fire, gazing back at her, their faces identical, eyes wide and staring, as though they too had suffered the same vision.

London, January 1855

"THIS WAY," MORLEY Johnson called out to the workmen following behind him. "This way, I say, and be careful!"

He looked down the arcade in the encroaching dusk at the two workmen, relics really, far too old to have been entrusted with Morley's new treasures. Yet what was a man to do? With the Crimean conflict draining off all the able labor, Morley had paid a pretty penny for these two ancients.

As they drew nearer, huffing under the weight of Morley's new mahogany desk, he cautioned again, "Do be careful. One scratch and I'll dock your wages. In there. Right through those doors."

As the two passed him by, Morley sent his eyes heavenward, then looked about him, still unable to believe where he was and how far he'd come.

The Temple! By God, he still couldn't believe it. Morley Johnson, solicitor, with chambers in the Temple.

He shivered from the cold and glanced in either direction, regretful that he had chosen nighttime to move from that smelly office on High Holborn Street. The Inns were practically deserted, and it would have been pleasant to have executed the move in daylight when the courts were bustling so that students and barristers alike could have taken note, could have whispered among themselves, "Isn't that Morley Johnson?"

Quickly he removed his top hat and gloves and placed them on one of the desks and approached the door to his inner chambers. For a moment he stood in the doorway, saddened by the realization that the chamber did not quite live up to his expectations. Empty, it had appeared so large.

Still, he must not be too critical. He was here, wasn't he? Where he'd always wanted to be, one of the few barristers and solicitors who was not a Sir or a Lord, here by virtue of a handsome bribe. So who was to say that next year, or the year after, when his new and effective tool of general power of attorney had cut deeper inroads into the Eden wealth, that he might not occupy those most impressive chambers which once had belonged to Sir Claudius Potter?

Outside he heard the grunting approach of the two old workmen again, and looked up to see them carrying a crate of his lawbooks between them. "That's it, guv," one said, grinning. "The wagon be empty."

Morley reached inside his waistcoat pocket and withdrew two one-pound notes. "Go along with you now," he said, frowning.

As the two old men shuffled out of the chamber, Morley moved closer to the fire and warmed his backside. He smiled. Never had events gone so well for him. Of course, he had taken certain steps. With the death of Lord James Eden, he'd effortlessly talked an old magistrate into awarding him general power of attorney. And early last year he'd had to replace the estate agent in Exeter with a more cooperative gentleman of his own choosing.

And now, what *was* the last count of North Devon land safely deeded to Morley Johnson? Over two thousand acres, pushing three, if he remembered correctly.

On a burst of energy, he left the fireplace and commenced to arrange his law volumes on the shelves. That done, he inspected the small alcove on the far wall, a discreet chamber, only large enough for a comfortable couch. With Minnie and the children gone to visit her parents in Sussex, he quite possibly could pass a few nights here as well, as Sir Claudius used to do, in the company of a female.

The thought caught his attention. Still gaping into the darkness of the alcove, another thought occurred to him, a fascinating one which he'd entertained off and on for the last year: the possibility of constructing a country estate on a hundred acres or so near Taunton, where Minnie and the children could be safely confined, leaving him free for his various London pursuits, business and otherwise.

It was not unheard-of, far from it. Quite the fashion it was for great men to lead two lives, a respectable domestic one in the country and a professional one in London.

Yes, why not? Not right away, of course. He'd have to wait for the war to conclude, those vague hostilities going on in the Crimea that seemingly had disrupted all of London life, stripping the streets of all young men.

But it would end soon, the Czar on his knees before the superior British forces. Then, in the flush of victory, with the streets thronging with unemployed labor, then would be the time to build.

Quickly he took a final look about the chambers. By

God, equally as grand as Sir Claudius', they were. Then he went into the outer office, retrieved his hat, whirled his cape about his shoulders, and marched forth into the night in search of some discerning group who would recognize quality when they saw it and welcome him into their fellowship.

He walked erect, in spite of the January wind, confident that he would not have to look very far.

Harrington Hall, Salisbury, January 1855

LADY LILA HARRINGTON, age sixteen, her nose and fingers nipped from her winter walk in the apple orchard, had just seated herself before the fire in her sitting room and was on the verge of serving her cat, a great gray-and-white-striped Maltese named Wolf, a cup of tea, when a remarkable thing happened. Wolf, who generally adored a good cup of tea, jumped down from his chair and ran to the locked door, confronting that barrier as though he meant to attack it.

Lila watched and was on the verge of calling him back when suddenly she understood. Someone was coming, someone unexpected. In a surge of annoyance, she returned the china teapot to its cozy and leaned forward to warm her nipped fingers, closely watching Wolf, who continued to watch the door, the hair on his back bristling.

Who in the world could it be? Hadn't they already played all their games for the afternoon? Hadn't old Max let her "escape" shortly after luncheon, and hadn't she scampered dutifully across the frozen meadow and sat atop her tree until she'd thought she'd freeze to it and become a part of it?

Suspiciously she eyed her cat. He *was* getting old, approaching two hundred years, according to her best estimate. She'd read in her great-grandmother's diaries of a massive gray-and-white-striped feline named Wolf who had inhabited the Hall when it had first been built. Then one spring morning several years ago, she'd found him and had spirited him up to her chambers, and he'd been with her ever since, though old Max had tried to do away with him once and still bore on his left arm the ten-inch scar left by Wolf's claws when he'd objected to being put in a sack weighted with stones.

She smiled lovingly at the big cat, still stalking the door. "Come, Wolf," she scolded. "I think you're just imagining things. There's no one—"

Then she heard it too, footsteps moving along the corridor outside her door. Wolf was beside himself, alternately scratching at the door and meowing in his most powerful voice.

"All right," she soothed. "I believe you. Come. Over here," she commanded, motioning toward his chair. "Let's see who it is and get on with our tea."

Reluctantly the cat obeyed. She waited until he'd hopped up on his chair, his eyes bloodred, reflecting the fire, his ears still alert.

"A good watchman, you are, Wolf," she whispered, stroking the coarse striped fur. "I apologize for—"

She heard a soft knock at the door—not Max's knock, she knew that much. She held still in her chair, baffled by this remarkable occurrence. Then she heard the key in the lock, another game she willingly played, permitting them to lock her in after five o'clock. What harm, if it made everyone feel safe.

She sat erect, never taking her eyes off the doorknob, which was slowly turning. To her left, Wolf hissed. Slowly she lifted a restraining hand. Though the occasion was without precedent, there was no need to overreact.

She was on the verge of leaving her chair when suddenly she saw the door push open.

"Papa," she whispered, struggling to overcome her initial shock. And equally as remarkable as Papa's presence was "Mama," she added, on her feet now, trying to recall the last time her parents had visited her private chambers. But with growing amazement, it occurred to her that there was no "last time." This was the first.

Belatedly remembering her manners, she started toward them, more than ready to deliver kisses to both, when she noticed their withdrawal, her father moving forward into a protective stance before her mother.

"Papa, how pleasant," she said, withdrawing to her tea table, hoping that Wolf behaved himself today. She looked toward the door, where they continued to stand, and thought how beautiful they were, her father tall and slim and dark, a fine counterpart to her mother's pale English beauty. With all her heart, Lila wished now that these two were not afraid of her. She'd never do anything to hurt them. Surely they knew that.

Still aware of the tension in the room, she decided to let them take the lead. At last her father started forward, a white envelope in his hand, his polished boots carrying him to mid-room, where abruptly he stopped. "I hope we're not disturbing, Lila," he said.

"Of course not, Papa," she reassured him. "We were just having tea. Won't you—"

Her mother stepped forward, a portrait in red velvet with high rolled collar and long tapered sleeves. Lila wished she looked more like her mother. Oh, the hair was the same, to be sure, but instead of those eyes as blue as English lakes, she'd inherited her father's dark ones, which looked totally out of place in her pale face, which freckled in the summer sun.

Now her mother drew even with her father, one hand nervously adjusting the collar of her gown. "No, no tea, Lila, thank you." She smiled stiffly. "We've come to you on a . . . matter of some concern."

A matter of some concern! Lila had heard that phrase before, last year when the stables had burned down and three horses had died, the time Cook had terrible pains in her stomach and had started foaming at the mouth, the time the hysterical villagers had found Lila crawling about in the cathedral calling her cat, oh, just countless times she'd heard that phrase, a matter of some concern, as though she and Wolf were responsible for everything that happened.

Out of consideration for their obvious discomfort, Lila stood. "What matter of concern, Mama?" she asked calmly. "I went no place today and did nothing except play the games with Max. Ask him if you don't believe—"

"Oh, it's not a matter of belief or disbelief," her father said, advancing one step, then again holding his position.

"No," her mother agreed. "You've been a very good girl of late, and we're both grateful."

Annoyed, Lila walked rapidly to the window seat. Behind her she heard a sharp cry and looked over her shoulder in time to see her mother recoil as Wolf jumped down from his chair and trotted after Lila to the window seat. As he curled up in her lap, she noticed that his eyes were no longer bloodred.

"He won't hurt you, Mama," she said, softly caressing his enormous head.

"Lila, your attention for a moment," Papa said. As he stepped toward the window seat, Lila saw him examining the white envelope in his hand.

"What is it, Papa?"

"This," he replied, extending the envelope. "This . . . letter was delivered to you today. It's caused your mother considerable torment, and myself as well."

Lila looked up. A letter! Why hadn't Wolf told her what a remarkable day this would be? "A letter?" She grinned. Had *this* ever happened before? No! Never! Not once in her entire sixteen years had anyone ever knocked on her door and announced, "A letter for you, Miss Lila."

"A letter." She laughed, truly impressed by the miracles of the world. But as she reached out for it, her father withdrew a step, holding the letter just beyond her reach.

"What we must know first, Lila," he cautioned sternly, "is how did this happen?"

Oh, Wolf, was the man an idiot? As though in response, Wolf meowed and jumped down from the window seat and commenced rubbing against her gown.

"I don't know how it happened, Papa," she said. "Is there a name attached to it?"

Her father nodded. "Indeed there is, a man's name. John Murrey Eden."

John Murrey Eden. Then she laughed, remembering it

as clearly as though it had happened only yesterday, that high blue summer day when she'd scaled her apple tree for a world view and had seen the young man while he was still a distance away on the road, walking head down, as though a gigantic foot were pressed against the back of his neck. As he'd drawn even with her, she'd summoned him without words to the shade of the apple orchard.

Oh, yes, John Murrey Eden. She remembered him well. And she'd seen him once more, on the London street corner, but that had been no surprise, for she'd willed that as well.

"Yes, Papa," she said, again reaching out for the letter. "I know him."

But again he withheld it. "Where?" he questioned. "How?"

"In the orchard," she replied. "He was walking on the road to Salisbury and we talked briefly."

Her mother peered nervously around her father's shoulder. "And you told him your name?"

"Of course I told him my name," Lila exclaimed. "How can two people talk if they don't know what to call each other?"

"And you did . . . nothing to him?" her mother asked further, the fear in her voice clear.

Lila shook her head and retreated back to the window seat, tired of reaching for the letter. "No, I did nothing to him, Mama," she said wearily. "Someone else had done quite enough."

Still worried, her father asked, "But why did he write to you?"

"I suppose he had something to say."

"No, he says nothing of import," her father replied. Then, by way of explanation he added, "Of course I opened it. For your own protection."

How often she had heard that as well. *For your own protection.* Every restraint they placed upon her was for her own protection, old Max's constant watch—no female servant would come near her, not since her first and last lady's maid had given birth to a two-headed infant. Keeping her under lock and key, that was for her own protection, and hiding her away from all society, that too was for her own protection.

Suddenly someone within her rose up in anger. "Give me the letter, Papa," she demanded. "You had no right to open it, none at all."

Within the moment the letter was dropped on the floor, as though the envelope had turned hot in his hands. By the time she'd retrieved it and returned to the window seat, she looked up to see her parents retreating to the door.

Her father spoke first, an expression of regret on his face. "We *are* concerned for you, Lila. You know better than anyone the threats and accusations which have been leveled at you." He glanced back at her mother. "It would break both our hearts if you were taken from us," he said. "You must understand that whatever we do, we do for your own good."

Moved by the declaration and by the look of concern on both their faces, someone within Lila commenced to cry. She possessed no powers, was incapable of causing any calamity to happen. And Wolf was as innocent. That they talked between themselves was merely a matter of convenience. And loneliness.

"I'm . . . sorry, Papa," she whispered, trying to hold the tears back. She looked down at the letter in her lap and read the remarkable salutation.

My dear Lady Lila Harrington, and within the moment she felt such a surge of excitement that the tears went away and quickly she read the rest of the brief message, Mr. Eden kindly refreshing her memory of the hot summer day and the talking apple tree, their chance encounter—*chance*, she smiled at that—on the London street corner. And the concluding paragraph, written in a winter mood again, that he was going off to a place called the Crimea to build a railway, and if she could find it in her heart to write to him, he'd answer back, and would she kindly remember him to her cat and ask him to exert any influence he could over fate.

In the quiet interim of reading, she was aware of her parents still standing at the door. Wolf had settled down into a deep and placid sleep beside her, apparently finding nothing in the letter to object to. And why should he? He had been mentioned as well. Oh, Wolf, she marveled silently, and stared out of the window toward the gray clouds.

"I don't think it would be wise to reply," her father suggested from the door.

"Why not?" Lila asked. "I am invited to reply, the address included here at the bottom of the page."

While her parents held a whispered conference, she found herself already imagining the first line. "My dear John Murrey Eden . . . "

"We must be allowed to read your reply," her father stated cautiously.

"Of course." Lila smiled. "I want you to read it. My spelling is appalling, as you know, and I want it to be proper." From where she sat, she could see the worry on her mother's face. If only she could say something that would reassure her.

But suddenly a series of images appeared before her, hideous images she'd never seen before, of men screaming, their limbs torn off, a smoky hillside, rocky, with great pools of blood turning the snow pink, more screams and more explosions, and pain more acute than any she'd ever imagined in her life.

Someone within her was crying aloud, and she could not hold the tears back, and as she felt a stabbing pain in her right shoulder, she stood, her head tilted back, a moan escaping her lips. She was cold, so cold, and as she stumbled to the fire, she was only vaguely aware of her parents' frightened faces, her mother weeping as her father quickly ushered her out of the room.

As Lila knelt on the floor before the fire, she heard the door close, heard the key turning in the lock, as though it were someone's desire to contain both the pain and the cold. Not that she blamed them. She too would have liked to take refuge in the safety of the corridor outside the locked door.

But she couldn't. This was her domain, and she had work to do. She waited for the pain and cold to pass; then slowly she sat erect before the fire, the crumpled letter still in her hand. With Wolf purring at her side, she lifted the sheet of writing paper and held it in both hands, and within the moment she saw his image on the paper, with the flickering fire behind it.

She was warm now. Smiling at his image, she crawled on hands and knees to her bureau, fetched her writing pad and inkwell and her best point and returned to the fire, where she knew, in time, her response would be made clear in the flames.

She was interrupted only once by Wolf, who insisted upon having his cup of tea, diluted with heavy cream.

As Wolf lapped contentedly nearby, Lila kept a constant vigil on the flames, the message becoming clearer, until at last she dipped the point into the ink, shook the excess off into the fire, where for a moment the ink droppings resembled a new cosmos evolving out of the flames. Then very carefully, in her best penmanship, she commenced writing,

My dear John Murrey Eden . . .

Balaklava Harbor, the Crimea, February 1855

JOHN SAW IT first through the small porthole beside his hammock, a scene so dismal that he turned over and tried to recapture the comforting warmth of his dream, which was fast fading. In the dream, he had seen himself seated before a fire in a strange chamber, while nearby . . .

"My God, are you still abed? We're here!"

The voice belonged to Jack Willmot. It was very near, filled with excitement, and shattered the fragile fragment which John had brought back with him from sleep.

No matter. Dreams were nothing of very great import. John had been plagued with them every night of this miserable voyage. In a way, it was a relief to have arrived. It would be good to feel solid earth beneath his feet again.

"Well?" Willmot grinned from the narrow door. "Up and dress. You must see the sight from the upper deck."

Turning in the hammock, John smiled at the phenomenon known as Jack Willmot. When precisely had it happened, this bond between the two of them?

At last John raised up on one elbow and looked his fill through the porthole at the dismal scene. As well as he could tell, the ship was in a holding position at the mouth of the small harbor, and upon closer examination, it was John's considered opinion that they might be held at bay for the rest of the day. As far as he could see, ships of all sizes and descriptions were lined up on both sides of the harbor, every available mooring occupied and even more ships trying to angle their way toward a touch of land.

"My God," John muttered. "What a mess."

"The captain says we'll probably have to hold here until afternoon." Willmot nodded.

"Afternoon of what day?" John asked, impressed as always by the efficient planning of the British War Council.

"Oh, it'll right itself soon enough." Willmot grinned. "According to the captain, it's Brassey's vessels that are causing the trouble."

John turned on the idiocy of that statement. "Then may I suggest that we all simply turn about and head for home," he said. "Let the soldiers build their own bloody railway."

But as soon as he had said it, he regretted it, seeing on Willmot's face the tension which he had exhibited every day of this voyage. In the beginning, when Willmot had offered to bring John his meals here, John had interpreted the gesture as merely a considerate one. Then at some point it had occurred to him that Willmot was trying very hard to keep him segregated from the soldiers, for fear there would be trouble.

Slowly now John looked up to the Highlands, to that terrain he knew so well after countless hours of map study. Access to the Highlands, across which ran the route to Sebastopol, the theater of all the major fighting now, was by one difficult narrow road. There John sat up, looking closer. How curious it was to see the reality after studying the map. It was steeper than he had imagined.

Had he requisitioned enough explosives? According to his estimates, they'd be doing little but blasting for the first few weeks, a great way to call attention to what was going on. The explosives would summon every Russian regiment within thirty miles. Spies, under cover of darkness, could easily report back the cause and nature of the blasting. And unless "Ivan" was more stupid than John thought, he doubted seriously if the Russians would merely turn their backs while British navvies built rail links which could improve the troop and material movement and affect the outcome of the war.

He continued to look out of the porthole, all his earlier apprehensions rising up as one. Before they'd left London, he'd registered a strong opinion with Brassey that he at least provide a portion of the navvies with arms. Oh, there would be no trouble on the first link. They were close enough to Balaklava and the protection of the British forces stationed at the base.

But beyond that rocky slope there were miles of empty, cold and frozen terrain. What a simple matter it would be for Russian units to advance on the unarmed navvies and . . .

"God," he muttered.

Apparently Willmot heard his whisper. "There's no danger, John," he said, retreating from the hammock and beginning to strip off a few layers of garments. "All our allies are scattered beyond that ridge. The French, the Turks, the Sardinians, the Algerians . . ."

John looked away from the argument, having heard it so many times before. As the ship took a slow roll to the left, he threw back the heavy cover and met the Crimean cold for the first time, dressed only in a nightshirt. "Christ," he gasped as his bare feet touched floor.

Willmot laughed, as though grateful that John had abandoned his fears. "Then get some clothes on, lad," he ordered. "You'll empty your trunk if you're wise. Put on two of everything. I'll go fetch you hot coffee. That'll warm you right enough."

Then he was gone, slamming the narrow door behind him before John had a chance to object. It had been his intention this morning to dress and go to mess himself.

He disliked having Willmot "wait" on him. Nothing to do but hurry and catch up with him.

Still shivering, he withdrew his trunk from beneath the hammock and donned two of everything. Inside the cocoon of thick garments, he found he could not move as easily. But no matter. The only movement he planned to execute today was to walk off this miserable ship as soon as possible, find Brassey and commence this insane job. At last ready, he started out into the narrow passageway.

A young seaman was just hurrying by, his face red from cold. As he stood back to give John passage, he grinned. "Not headin' toward the mess, sir, I hope."

John nodded. "I thought I might. Why?"

"Oh, the soldier boys is havin' themselves a time, they are. Passin' bottles around like they was in the Leicester Square pub. Listen! Can't you hear them?"

Then John heard the drunken discord coming from the end of the passage, slurred choruses of "Annie Laurie" mixed with "Auld Lang Syne," both punctuated by raucous laughter.

"Our fightin' finest," the seaman muttered. "All Ivan will have to do is give 'em a bottle of vodka and they'll follow after all the way to Moscow."

John looked toward the drunken discord coming from the end of the passage, hoping to catch sight of Willmot. He couldn't believe that he had joined the early-morning revelry.

Still Willmot was no place in sight, and the seaman was right. It would serve no purpose to walk into that drunken crew. They were hard enough to endure when they were sober.

He started off in the opposite direction, heading toward the upper deck. A few moments later he scaled the narrow ladder and pushed open the door and received, like a slap in the face, the coldest blast of winter wind he'd ever felt. His eyes tearing from the cold, he made his way to the railing and stared out at the bleak scene.

It was approaching four o'clock in the afternoon when the *Tyrone* was finally cleared for passage into Balaklava harbor. Even then it was touch and go, her bow literally scraping the hull of an outgoing vessel as the two captains tried to manipulate their ships through a passage scarcely large enough to accommodate one.

At three different times John had been forced to take refuge down in the comparative warmth of his compartment. On the second time down, he'd encountered a very drunken Jack Willmot collapsed across his hammock, all apology and regret.

Now the man was standing beside him, erect at least, if only mildly bleary-eyed, while all about them soldiers leaned over the railings, vomiting up their early-morning celebration.

"Damn," Willmot cursed. "I should have known better."

John smiled, enjoying this turn of events. How many times Willmot had put him to bed with a stern lecture on the effects of inebriation. Now, however, John was in no mood to return the sermon. He accepted Willmot's explanation of how he'd been "drawn in" to the festivities. What harm? In a way, John wished that he had joined them. Perhaps this grim harbor would be more palatable drunk than sober.

Beyond the crowded dock he saw the ragged edge of Balaklava, plain rough dwellings, mostly of cinder block, with a curious-looking church steeple here and there.

"How in the name of God are we going to find Brassey in this mess?" he asked.

Slowly Willmot lifted his head to the chaotic scene, though clearly it was agony to do so. "He said he'd send transport," he muttered. "Keep your eyes open."

John was doing just that, but saw no one who even vaguely resembled any of Brassey's men. All at once the ship scraped against the dock in a grinding sound and came to a halt, while at either end John saw seamen throwing out enormous coils of rope to waiting dockmen, where, struggling, they looped it over the moorings, and for the first time since he'd left Portsmouth, John felt the world grow blessedly still.

He was in the process of leaving the railing, and vacating this place, when suddenly over the shouts of the men he thought he heard his name being called.

Again he held his position and looked out over the sea of pushing men. But he saw no one he recognized, and convinced that he'd merely imagined it, he was turning away when he heard it again.

"John! John Murrey Eden!"

Squinting into the gray afternoon, he swept the crowded dock and at last found him, a man standing at the far edge of the mob, waving a red scarf in the air, shouting, "John, over here."

John gaped at the man, not recognizing him, thinking finally that it probably was one of Brassey's men sent to fetch them. But as the man pushed a few yards nearer, John took a closer look, some element of recognition dawning.

Good God! John leaned closer over the railing, the voice clear now, reminding him of Brassey's outer office back in London, a bleak period in John's life that might have been unendurable had it not been for the fellowship and warmth of . . .

"Andrew! Andrew Rhoades!"

By way of reply, the man removed his heavy cap, as though belatedly aware of the need to make himself plainly visible.

But the gesture, instead of reassuring John, caused him to look closer, half-convinced that he'd made a mistake. The voice was the same, but the face and features were entirely different, older, even some gray visible in the once dark hair. And the eyes, once alert, were now lost in shadows, the cheeks gaunt, the skin almost chalk-white, a rough, unkempt beard obscuring both the chin and the line of the jaw.

It *was* Andrew Rhoades, or what was left of him. In a surge of old friendship and new concern, John gave a final wave and pushed through the soldiers in search of Willmot.

He found him slumped against the partition which led to the officers' mess. "Come, Jack," he urged, reaching a hand down in assistance. "Andrew Rhoades has come to fetch us. Can you stand?"

Willmot looked slowly up through glazed eyes. "Our luggage," he muttered.

"I'll send someone for it later, or fetch it myself," John said hurriedly. "Come, let's get out of this place."

As they stumbled down the gangplank, John looked ahead to see Andrew beating a similar path in an attempt to meet them. Up close, the devastation on his friend's face was even worse. How was it possible, John brooded angrily, for a man to leave London, age eighteen, and three years later resemble a man of fifty?

But there was no time for answers. Andrew was upon him, the cold wind ruffling his graying hair, moisture about the corners of his eyes which John suspected had nothing to do with the cold.

It was several moments before the embrace ended. Andrew stepped away first, wiping at his eyes. "I'm sorry." He smiled. "I couldn't believe it when Mr. Brassey said you were following . . ."

Then he spied Willmot, and as the two shook hands warmly, John was brought forcibly back to the reality that was his purpose for standing on this wretched dock. "Ah, Brassey," he said grimly. "And where is the great man?"

"He arrived about a week ago," Andrew replied. "You wouldn't believe it, but there is already a tent city set up in the large valley on the edge of town. His engineers have started blasting, and he was most anxious for your arrival. He said that . . ."

Then obviously he saw Willmot's deteriorating condition and suggested, "Let's get out of here. Brassey sent a carriage. It's not far, if it hasn't been stolen."

With that he commenced to clear a path through the crush of men. Again John lent Willmot a supportive arm and followed after.

Beyond the push of the crowd, John found that they were on a commercial street, a narrow muddy artery from which were being hawked a variety of wares, skewers of lamb cooking over open fires, loaves of flat dark bread, sheep and goats and chickens running through the crowds.

At last, at the top of an incline, John saw a remarkable sight, a small but stolid English carriage, looking out of place in the stinking alley, a large man in civilian clothes in the driver's seat, his whip raised at the ready.

"Any trouble?" Andrew called out as they approached the carriage.

The large man grinned, a good plain English face to match the carriage. "Not to speak of, sir, though a few of the bloody bastards has got new stripes on their hides."

Still trailing a yard or two behind, John saw Willmot slip in the muddy terrain, and ran to his side just as he was starting down, Andrew joining him, the two of them helping him into the carriage.

"Is he ill?" Andrew asked, concerned.

John smiled. "Not seriously. Just a little shipboard celebration."

Willmot confirmed this diagnosis with a low groan.

As Andrew and John assisted him into the carriage, he fell forward, holding his head, occupying the entire seat.

Andrew assessed the problem of limited space and suggested, "Let the driver take him to the tents and he can come back for us."

But John had another idea. "How far is it?"

"A little over a mile."

John called up to the driver. "Take him on. We'll walk and be along later."

"But you must be exhausted," Andrew protested. "And Mr. Brassey said—"

"Brassey can wait." John smiled, relishing the words. "It's been far too long since I've seen you. A few hours' delay won't make that much difference. Come, lead the way to a local spot and let's at least lift one glass together."

At first John saw a strong look of objection on Andrew's face. Then apparently he warmed to the suggestion and lifted a hand to the driver.

With a rattle the carriage started forward. "See him safely delivered," John called out, and the last view he had was of Willmot curled comfortably into the cushions.

As they started at an easy gait down the narrow street, Andrew restored his sealskin cap and John followed suit, drawing on his gloves, as the bitter cold seemed to increase with nightfall. Andrew walked for a few minutes in silence. Then, as though trying to lift himself out of his mood, he said expansively, "Well, I'm afraid I can't offer you either a Childe's or White's," mentioning their two favorite London restaurants. "Actually, the food at the tents is by far the—"

"Oh, come now," John chided, "surely somewhere in this exotic landscape we can at least—"

Andrew nodded, and as they entered the commercial street again, lined now every twenty or so feet with flaring torches, John again saw the ruin in his friend's face, felt his shivering inside the warmth of his heavy coat.

"Have you been ill?" John asked, knowing the answer, but wanting specifics.

"A minor wound in the leg," Andrew said, "from a Russian saber, and a not so minor case of dysentery that has sent me to the hospital in Scutari twice."

"Are you well now?" John asked.

Andrew laughed. "I've been granted a reprieve, at least a temporary one. My commanding officer has assigned me to Mr. Brassey until the railway is completed. Military liaison, I believe they call me."

"Splendid," John said with enthusiasm. "Then we'll have many such evenings, won't we?"

Again Andrew gave him a curious look. "I doubt it. We're in desperate need of the railway, John. Without it, we face certain defeat."

He'd become so earnest. As though just thinking on Brassey had reminded him of certain duties, he sternly added, "I think we had better proceed immediately to the tents. Mr. Brassey gave me strict instructions to bring you—"

"Damn Brassey!" John exploded. "Damn Brassey," he shouted again. Caught between the ruined features of his friend and the projection of the impossible task ahead, he strode past Andrew, ignoring his startled expression, and led the way through the crowded streets of Balaklava as though he knew precisely where he was going.

But of course he didn't. A few steps later, Andrew caught up with him, turned him in the proper direction with a soft apology. "I'm sorry, John. It's just that I'm sick of this place. We must end it soon. So many have died."

Abruptly he broke off. Again John saw the confusion

that he'd discerned so often in Andrew's letters, a simple question, obviously still unresolved. What were they doing here? What were any of them doing here?

Lacking an answer, John pulled his collar up about his face in an attempt to block out the stinging cold and walked silently beside Andrew, at least giving the appearance of passive acceptance.

❧ London, St. George Street, March 1855

"'THEY HAVE WHAT?" Elizabeth gasped.

She sat up on the velvet settee in her drawing room, certain that the early-morning hour had affected her hearing. Still half-asleep, her hair undone, she clutched her dressing gown and stared disbelieving at Willie Gladstone opposite her. In spite of her shock, it suddenly occurred to her that she'd never seen him at this hour of the day. She'd seen him last night, to be certain, a pleasant evening spent in the manner of old friends, during which she'd expressed concern that Edward Eden's son and Jack Willmot had apparently disappeared from the face of the earth. Time and again she sent her card around to Jack Willmot's address in Warwick Lane, begging for a reconciliation. But she'd received no reply.

Thoughtfully Willie had promised to look into the matter himself. Now here he was, at nine-thirty in the morning, seated before her in her drawing room, delivering this most alarming message.

"I'm afraid it's true," he soothed. "I sent an assistant to Mr. Brassey's office first thing this morning. A clerk there confirmed what I suspected. Both Mr. Willmot and Mr. Eden sailed for the war zone the first of January."

For the second time Elizabeth heard the words, and still she couldn't believe them. "The war . . . zone?"

He nodded, then stood and commenced pacing before

the fire. "Hysteria," he pronounced angrily. "All of England has gone slightly mad."

His words, instead of soothing, caused great agitation. "Then . . . there's real danger?" she asked.

Abruptly he stopped pacing. "For them," he mused thoughtfully, "perhaps not. After all, they have gone as civilians."

Civilians! Elizabeth didn't understand and said as much, and listened carefully as Willie explained the nature of Brassey's expedition.

All the time Willie talked, Elizabeth heard the words, though at one point her mind wandered to an image of John as a little boy, his abhorrence of violence, how even the sound of a voice raised in anger was capable of unsettling him. Now she simply couldn't imagine him in a "war zone."

"There's really no cause for worry, my dearest," Willie murmured, sitting opposite her again in an attempt to ease her fears. "I know Thomas Brassey well, a man renowned for his kindness and thoughtfulness to his men."

She looked up from her memories, wanting desperately to believe him, though now there was another worry. Had John gone off to war in an attempt to escape the pain that she obviously had caused him?

The possibility could not be digested, and she moved away from it, her steps carrying her to the window.

Willie came up behind her, his hands on her shoulders. "But there's good news as well," he said. "According to my assistant, Brassey's clerk said that the project was going so well that the entire expedition expected to return to London by April."

She turned to face him, grateful. That *was* good news. By April. Only a month or so away. Then God grant that he return safely, and that he would answer her card and come to see her. Surely in an atmosphere of calm and reason she might help him to see and understand who she was, and that in no way did it have any effect on her deep love for him, and the deeper love she still held in special reserve for his father.

Edward. At the mere thought of his name and the realization that she had failed his son, her eyes filled with tears, and she saw Willie open his arms to her, and without hesitation she stepped into the embrace. "I'm sorry," she whispered.

"No need," he replied.

Still drying her eyes, she said, "It's just that I feel a . . . responsibility to the boy."

"And a deep love," Willie added.

"He's the only son I'll ever know."

As though he sensed that what she needed most was brusque reassurance, he gave it to her. "And he shall be returned safely to you. I promise it on my name." He guided her back to the fire, his mood altering, his arm still about her waist. "If I could be granted one wish today, it would be to stay here with you."

She heard the wistfulness in his voice and discovered that it matched her own. At least with company she could keep her mind busy and away from war zones. "Then why don't you?" she asked.

"Don't tempt me," he said, moving away. "I'll see you tonight. Now I'm afraid I must go and deal with Little Johnny Russell."

In spite of her disappointment, she recognized both the name and the problem, having heard Willie talk about it at length the night before. A member of the cabinet, Lord John Russell was claiming that the government had no defense against the charges of mismanaging the war and therefore should resign. Willie apparently was in complete agreement with everything except the last, claiming that if the government resigned, Russell would head the new cabinet, and that, for some reason, would be disastrous.

Whatever the outcome, Elizabeth knew that he was fully preoccupied and she had no right to keep him away fom Westminster.

"I thank you, Willie," she said, reaching for the bell cord. "At least I know now where John is, and with your word on his safe return, I'm sure the days will pass quickly."

She kissed him farewell and walked with him to the door.

Back in her bedchamber, she moved close to the fire

and tried to perceive of John in something called a war zone. He was just a boy. Didn't Willmot realize that, and she was certain now that it had all been Willmot's idea.

But standing before the fire, she was forced to abridge her condemnation of Jack Willmot. Obviously he'd stood by John, perhaps when he'd needed him most, certainly when she'd disappointed him so bitterly.

Remembering that horrible night, she clasped her arms about her, feeling a chill that the fire could not dissipate. Shivering, she turned away and crawled between cold linens.

From the limited perspective of her pillow, she surveyed her grand surroundings, fully aware of what she'd done to climb to this luxurious setting. Could she ever make John understand? She must try, for now it occurred to her that if *he* didn't understand, she might be compelled to doubt herself.

Out of a morning of grim thoughts, this was the worst, and she turned on her side. Without warning, her eyes fell on the small trunk almost hidden in the corner behind the mahogany wardrobe.

As tears came, she closed her eyes and gave in to her loneliness and regret, and as her grief mounted she buried her face in the pillow and forced herself, in spite of the pain, to take a hard inventory of her deceits, her failings, her emptiness.

❧

Balaklava Highlands, March 1855

SHIVERING, JACK WILLMOT lay on his cot beneath three fur rugs in the small tent and decided that compared to the Crimea, Canada had seemed like a tropical clime.

Never had he been so cold, and it was little comfort that everyone felt it as acutely as he did, including John, who had refused even to get undressed for this rest period and who now huddled under his blankets, fully clothed, rereading his last letter from Harrington Hall in Wiltshire.

Since sleep was out of the question, Willmot turned on his side and studied the young man, full bearded now, looking not so young. There were new lines on his face from squinting at the snow, and new hollows beneath his eyes from too many sleepless nights.

What a vast inner change had taken place in the boy as well, Willmot thought. What pride Willmot always felt when he saw John, on horseback, leading Brassey along the line, pointing out this inefficiency and that need.

Leading Brassey! The incredible words echoed in his head. Yet they were true. Time and again Willmot had seen Brassey seek out John, ask his opinion, listening carefully to his response. Of course there had been violent battles between the two men. In fact, one was raging now, unresolved. But for all the fireworks which erupted from the collision of their strong personalities, Willmot had to admit that never had a Brassey project progressed as efficiently as this one.

With pride Willmot looked at John across the way. How many times Brassey had told Willmot that he'd never encountered so quick a mind in any man. Of course —and this was a cause of bafflement to Willmot—he'd never heard Brassey make these tributes within earshot of John. Quite the contrary; when the two of them were together, they shouted at each other like bitter enemies, though again Brassey had told Willmot that upon their return to London he was planning to give John a contracting job of his own, only a small project in the Scottish Highlands, but nonetheless an opportunity that could lead to a future, if only the two did not kill each other first.

Without warning, Willmot thought of Edward Eden, and how proud he would be of his son. If only the man had not died so early.

He was summoned out of his old grief by a rustling of pages, and looked across the tent to see John lying on his back, the letter clasped atop his chest, his eyes staring upward, as though relishing the words he'd just read.

Peculiar, how much those simple, almost childlike letters meant to him. And from a young girl he'd never formally met. Oh, to be sure, John had told him about Lila Harrington, as much as there was to tell. On occasion he'd even shared her letters, allowing Willmot to read for himself the delicate penmanship on the pale blue writing paper, accounts concerning the antics of her cat, the condition of a winter orchard, the shades of pink in a March sunset, and always, at the end, warning John to take care.

Most peculiar, Willmot thought again as he pulled the fur rug higher to cover his frozen ears. Yet, perhaps not so. He knew for a fact that John had never recovered from the loss of Elizabeth, and before that, the loss of Eden. In the harsh cold male world of the Crimean winter, Lady Lila Harrington probably appeared before him like a saint, a soft voice and pretty head filled with nothing of greater importance than the care and feeding of her cat.

In spite of his efforts to keep warm, Willmot shivered. At the faint sound, John looked up.

"I thought you were asleep," he said, refolding the letter.

"Who can sleep?"

"Still you need your rest," John scolded, "if you plan to keep pace . . ."

Pleased by the realization that John cared for him, Willmot sat up, drawing the fur rug about his shoulders. "I can work you under the bed any day, my friend." He smiled. "As for the navvies, I'm the one who prods them. Remember?"

John looked across at him. "I don't know what I would do without you," he said, slipping the letter inside his coat. "God," he muttered, drawing his blanket up. "Will we ever get out of this frozen hell?"

He sounded so tired. Quietly Willmot reminded him, "By your own estimate, about three weeks should see us on the ship home."

"Not by my estimate," he corrected. "Those words were Brassey's, not mine. The estimate his as well, and based on his ego, as always."

There! The outline of John's latest and most violent

disagreement with Brassey. When work had first started back in Balaklava in January, at John's urgent recommendation, Brassey had pulled one hundred and seventy navvies off the line, armed them, briefly trained them with the help of the army, and had sent them out to act as scouts. Thus, with this slight protection the other fifteen hundred navvies had proceeded with the blasting and the laying of track. The work had gone well, with round-the-clock shifts, the men driving themselves as never before.

But now, with the end in sight, Brassey wanted to pull the armed scouts back in. He'd called a counsel only the day before in the large mess tent, with five foremen present, including Willmot, though the true battle, as always, was between John and Brassey. And what a battle it had been, the worst to date, both men shouting at each other from opposite ends of the table.

Brassey's contention was simple. The Russians had not felt compelled to attack in three months. Why should they marshal a force now when the railway was ninety percent completed?

John's argument had been valid as well. Why not now? The army did not have the personnel to defend the newly built railway. What a simple matter it would be for the Russians to dispatch a unit to the rear, come upon the navvies by surprise, decimate their numbers, then, working backward, systematically plant explosives and destroy three months of hard labor.

In a surge of pity Willmot watched John as he stared at the canvas floor covering. Whatever diversion he'd found in the young girl's letter was now gone, obliterated by his conviction that Brassey's judgment was flawed.

Willmot started to speak, then changed his mind. In a way, he had to admit that he agreed with Brassey. The likelihood of a Russian attack seemed remote. There had been countless times in the past when they might have done so. But according to the scouts, they'd seen nothing in the frozen wilderness but bedraggled and retreating British soldiers. Then too, the job was so near completion. Those one hundred and seventy navvies back at work on the line could make a vast difference.

If only he could convince John of this.

Suddenly the flap of their tent was pushed open. From where Willmot sat on the edge of the cot, he saw the tall figure of Thomas Brassey, the tip of his nose and cheeks ruddy with cold, the rest of him so encased in cloaks and wrappings that he looked twice his normal size, filling the narrow tent opening and obliterating the still-gray afternoon sky beyond.

John did not turn, as though he'd identified the man from the expression on Willmot's face. Without acknowledging Brassey in any way, he moved to his cot, retrieved his blanket and stretched out as though the most sensible course of action for all men now was sleep.

Annoyed by John's rudeness, Willmot stood. "Mr. Brassey . . ." He nodded courteously, trying to compensate for the disrespect coming from the cot.

But Brassey had not come to see Willmot. From the moment he'd entered the tent, his eyes had never left John's face, and now, in spite of the rudeness, Willmot thought he detected a look of humor in Brassey's eyes. "I've come to effect a truce," he announced broadly, looking down on John. "There's enough warfare going on around us. I prefer not to engage in hostilities with my . . . valuable assistant."

My God! This was as close to an apology as Brassey would come. And considering that Willmot wasn't absolutely certain that Brassey owed John an apology, he looked down on the young man with increasing irritation.

But John showed no sign of making a response.

Brassey stared down on him a moment longer, then took one step toward the cot, his manner changing, becoming more businesslike, "I come with news," he said bluntly. "Czar Nicholas died on the second of March. Alexander has succeeded, and his first official act was to recall General Menshikov."

The incredible message had been delivered in rapid-fire succession. Brassey smiled. "The Russian Army is in complete disarray, and my courier tells me that a tentative peace conference was opened in Vienna on the fifteenth of this month."

Willmot grinned. Then it was almost over. Home to an

endless hot bath, good English tea and one of Childe's massive beefsteaks. "Did you hear, John?" he exclaimed, puzzled by the continuing lack of reaction coming from the cot opposite him.

Apparently Brassey was suffering from the same bewilderment. "Well, Eden, did you hear?" he shouted. "Please make a comment, suitable or otherwise."

At last the head on the pillow shifted. "Our work here is completed, then?" he asked.

Willmot was on the verge of answering when he saw Brassey's head moving back and forth. "Not . . . quite," he said, stripping off his fur hood. "The government wants us to finish what we've started."

As though John sensed the man's hesitancy, he sat up, swinging his boots over the edge of the cot, his manner as cold as Willmot had ever seen it. "Why go to the trouble of completing a line that will never be used?"

"I said . . . a tentative peace conference," Brassey repeated. "There's still the matter of Sebastopol."

John looked up. "The matter being that the Allies have it and the Russians want it?"

Brassey nodded. "Undoubtedly it will be settled at the peace table."

"And if it isn't?"

Brassey hesitated, his pleasure at his own announcement rapidly receding. "It will be," he snapped. "In the meantime—"

"In the meantime," John interrupted, "little or nothing has changed. We continue to survey the terrain, blast when necessary, lay the tracks and drive the spikes."

Brassey nodded, losing patience. "Of course, of course," he muttered. "But under different conditions."

"How different?" John asked.

"My God, are you totally dense?" Brassey exploded. "Didn't you hear what I said? The Russian Army is in complete disarray. They pose no threat now. To anyone."

John smiled as though he were dealing with a child. "Did your courier tell you that, Mr. Brassey, your half-frozen British courier who is beginning to wonder if he'll ever get his feet warm or see the hop fields at harvest time?"

Brassey glared down at him, the exchange becoming as angry as the one the day before. "I must confess, Eden," Brassey went on, making an effort to rein in his anger, "I am as baffled as ever by you. In a way, your assistance on this project has been invaluable, and in another way you have made it one of the most complex and difficult undertakings of my career."

"Then I offer my apologies and tender my resignation," John replied. "Give me a horse to get back to Balaklava, and I will not further impede your progress in any way."

Apparently the deliberate manner in which he had spoken only served to enrage Brassey further. He stepped closer to the cot. "What precisely is it that you want, Eden?" he shouted. "I've followed your suggestions from the beginning, frequently against my better judgment, when my natural inclination was to toss you out."

John rose, though not with any sense of outrage. "Then why didn't you, Mr. Brassey?"

For a few moments a taut silence filled the tent as the two men faced each other. At last Brassey stepped away from the encounter, one gloved hand pushing back the unruly white hair. "I've one more piece of news, gentlemen," he announced coldly from the tent opening. "I have this morning given orders for the scouts to return to their jobs on the line. With their numbers, ten days will see us to completion, and we all can leave here."

Suddenly John stirred, his earlier air of relaxation replaced by shocked anger. "You've . . . done what?" he demanded, following after the man.

Brassey turned, a faint smile on his face. "I believe you heard me well enough, Eden. In essence, what I've done is regain command of my own men, my own expedition."

"Your men?" John shouted, his outrage filling the small tent. "To what extent are they your men? Does that give you the right to jeopardize their lives? At least give them arms if you call in the scouts."

"They are navvies, not soldiers," Brassey snapped. "Most of them illiterate at that. They wouldn't know one end of a rifle from the other." He turned toward the tent opening and jerked the flap back. "And the scouts *are* in," he added, "have been since midmorning, doing what they have been trained to do, which is to build a railway."

For the first time he looked sharply at Willmot as though in the simple act of sharing a tent with John Murrey Eden he shared his madness as well. "And what are you doing in here?" he shouted. "Number Three Section needs a foreman. I believe that's what you were hired for."

Taken aback by this tone of voice from the man he revered, Willmot struggled with an explanation. "It was my relief, sir . . . " he began. "I was on the line until dawn—"

"I've been on the line since yesterday morning," Brassey boasted, "without respite."

He paused as if to see if any further rebuttal would be forthcoming from any quarter. Willmot looked across at John, saw his eyes leveled, some private assessment going on inside his mind. Blessedly he kept silent, as though aware of Brassey's state of mind.

As for Brassey, the silence now seemed to anger him as much as words. "Nothing further to say?" he demanded sarcastically of John. "I can't believe it. That tongue motionless? For the first time?"

As his voice rose in sarcasm, Willmot was forced to look away. It was as though the man were disintegrating before their eyes. Of course, Brassey had admitted to no sleep in over thirty-six hours. Then why didn't he have the good sense to take himself away until . . .

Then he did. He looked back into the tent for a final time, all of his attention focused on John again. "Forgive the . . . harshness of this exchange, Eden," he muttered. "I would be less than honest if I said anything but that your services to me have been . . . invaluable." Then he was gone.

"He's mad," John said quietly, staring at the tent opening flapping in the wind.

"Just fatigued," Willmot corrected, turning back to his cot. The encounter had worn him out and left him as baffled as always. What peculiar forces were at work between these two men?

He sat wearily on the edge of the cot and urged John to, "Come. No point in pursuing it further. It's not so bad," he added. "Home by the first week in April. Surely you have no objection to that."

John looked at him, an expression of incredulity on his face. He seemed on the verge of saying something, then apparently changed his mind. Without a word he retrieved his heavy gloves from the end of the cot and left the tent, and left Willmot to puzzle over both his expression and his sudden exit.

Willmot shrugged. No point in asking what the sense of it all was. In an unnatural situation, men behaved in an unnatural manner.

That was all.

March 21, 1855

FROM THE TOP of the high plateau, John could just see the first light of dawn. Below, the bonfires which followed the line resembled a hundred small suns, while the real one on the black horizon paled in comparison.

He'd lost track of the numbers of times he'd been up and down the line, his attention divided between the navvies on one side and the blackness on the other. Now almost frozen and in need of a fresh horse, he was starting down toward one of the fires.

Night was by far the worst, and for the last three, since that afternoon when Brassey had revealed himself to be wholly mad, John had appointed himself a search party of one and had spent each night riding the escarpments which bordered the narrow canyon where Section Three was being laid. If there was need for a cry of alarm, his most surely would be weak and inefficient. But it would be better than nothing and it might give the unsuspecting navvies an extra minute to find a mount and perhaps a weapon.

With less than four hundred yards to go, he drew up on a level stretch of ground for one last look. Below in a red-black scene that looked like something out of Hades, he saw the navvies working, the resounding echo of their hammers and picks shattering the still night. There were little more than two hundred in all working on Section Three, the tip of the spear known as "Brassey's Miracle." The others were working at various places back down the line, crews following the branch lines in all directions.

But this particular terrain, at least in John's opinion, was the most dangerous. On either side, this formidable escarpment dissolved into flat plains pierced at a few points by old roads which were largely impassable, though once they had been the main routes to the front before Brassey and his men had arrived.

Again John looked down on the feverish activity. Lower down he saw the small tent city, the gray smoke of early-morning fires beginning to rise and mingle with the fog of night. In a way it was a peaceful scene.

Perhaps he had been wrong all along. Who was he to second-guess the Russian intent? Surveying the dawn in a wide arc, John lifted his head and thought unexpectedly of Eden, a world remote from this one, warmed by the channel breezes in spring, the headlands a soft carpet of wildflowers, little Mary weaving him a crown of clover while Richard read aloud to all of them the latest offerings from Mr. Wordsworth. And Harriet, close beside him, her beautiful hair undone and falling over her shoulders, one slender hand finding John's in the protection of thick clover, their fingertips just touching, nothing visible even to the most watchful eye.

He bent his head lower. It was easier to think on the dead and wounded of the Crimea than to dwell on the dead and wounded of Eden.

It was while his head was still down, his thoughts fully occupied, that he heard a peculiar disturbance, little more than a distant rumbling, as though the supply wagons had arrived earlier than usual from Section Two.

Harriet. Was she dead or alive?

What was that noise? Hadn't he told them repeatedly not to bring up the supply wagons until the shifts had changed? Let the crew going off do the unloading rather than sap the strength of the fresh crew. How many times did he have to tell the foremen before—?

Suddenly he looked up, the new sound clearly audible over the picks and hammers of the crew below. Horses? Surely not.

The noise was increasing, hundreds of horses, or so it seemed. From where he sat astride his horse, halfway up the incline, John looked down to see if anybody else had heard it. Apparently not. The exhausted navvies appeared to be moving at half-speed, many of them looking toward the tents as though hoping to catch a glimpse of their relief shifts.

The increasing sound now seemed to filter dully through his head. Perhaps it was merely an echo of distant troop movement. The rocky ridges and valleys of the Highlands were like that, filled with downdrafts and echo chambers. But as the sound increased, he sat erect and looked in all directions.

What in the . . . ?

As his alarm increased along with the noise, John was on the verge of reining his horse about and climbing back to the top of the escarpment. But no sooner had he brought his horse about than his eye fell on the escarpment across the valley. In the half-light of dawn there appeared to be dust rising on that distant ridge, either that or mysteriously swelling ground fog. He rubbed his eyes in an attempt to clear the fatigue and looked again. Now the silhouetted outline of the rocky escarpment appeared to be changing shape, the rock juttings growing, then diminishing, the entire horizon line alive with mysterious movement.

Urging his horse up the rocky incline, he tried to look backward and keep a steady vigil on the ridge across the way. The black horizon line now possessed a life of its own, as within the instant it seemed to elongate into a solid black layer that had not been there before.

God . . .

Suddenly he leaned forward in his saddle. The sun had at last spotlighted certain specifics. The new layer atop the ridge was a solid line of men on horseback, and the rectangle of black to their rear appeared to be . . . artillery.

Yet a moment later he held still, his mind grasping frantically at the possibility that they were British troops, or French. But what would British troops be doing poised on top of the escarpment looking down on their own, with a fortification of artillery behind them! And why would . . . ?

The sun singled out a color, not the cherry-red tunics of British squadrons, but the somber gray overcoats of Russians.

It was the last coherent thought he had, for at that moment a battle cry arose from the throats of hundreds of men across the valley, and John saw wave after wave of Russian infantry start down the incline, swords flashing in the new dawn.

In spite of the rising sun, John watched the incredible sight enveloped in a sense of darkness. From where he sat in his position of safety on the opposite ridge, he saw the sleepy-eyed navvies look up at the thundering descent as though at a mirage, no one making the smallest effort to prepare himself for the descending waves of Russians. From the tent settlement he noticed other men, still holding their coffee mugs near the small fires, their suspenders down about their waists, many drawing curiously forward as though to get a better look at this most peculiar spectacle.

At that moment he saw a fiery explosion at the top of the escarpment, heard the dull report of the Russian artillery in place now, and a moment later the shell exploded near the front of the tracks, a dusty flaming cosmos spewing out fragments of men, the single volley seeming at last to raise the alarm as now the terrified navvies commenced running in all directions.

The first line was upon them, the Russian horses stampeding through the disarray, the riflemen pulling back as though realizing belatedly that there were no effective arms here, and swords were quite adequate to the job.

John felt the breath choking in his throat as he looked from one scene of terror to another, the encounter scarcely worthy of the name "battle." "Massacre" would be more appropriate, as wave after wave of fully armed Russian soldiers swept down and through the unarmed navvies, a few men trying to fight back with picks and hammers, the earth around the newly laid track glistening red in the rising sun.

In spite of the shouts and cries, a heavy curtain of silence dropped over John. The sounds of battle grew muffled, the tension within him stronger. At last he felt the heels of his boots digging into the horse, saw in that last moment of lucidity a wounded navvy fall backward into a bonfire, heard his shrill cries as his body twisted grotesquely, consumed by the flames.

Then John was moving, the gray overcoats coming closer, their sense of victory transfiguring their countenances, laughing with relish as they pursued the navvies.

In a flurry of hooves, John crashed into the Russian center, into the mass of men jostling and screaming. To one side he noticed a fallen Russian soldier, slipped from his horse, his boot still caught in his stirrup, being dragged by his frightened mount. With deliberation John angled his own mount into position, then urged the horse forward to top speed, directly over the man's head until at last it cracked, the upper part of the skull seeming to shift as blood poured out of the eye cavities and mouth.

Without hesitation John reached down and relieved him of his sword in time to raise it into the face of the second soldier, who obviously had witnessed the act. Without taking aim, John raised the sword to the man's throat and plunged it forward, a curious smile on the soldier's face as he fell backward, John feeling for the first time the pulling sensation of the blade as it cut through human flesh.

On horseback he was able to see better than the navvies who were run to ground while in the very act of trying to escape, though now as a gray overcoat started toward him John urged his horse to a short retreat, then turned about and saw out of the corner of his eye blood dripping from his sword, then again plunged blindly forward at the Russian soldier, striking with a single thrust in the heart. At some point he was no longer conscious of who he was or what he was doing. His only goal was to stay erect on his horse while inflicting as much damage as possible to those who swirled about him.

The fighting began to break up into a series of isolated encounters, and still John looked in all directions at the Russian soldiers, who continued to emerge out of the fog, and at the fallen navvies strewn about the ground, a few trying to drag themselves away from the battle, only to be trampled underfoot by the horses.

The churned-up ground was slippery with mud and blood, causing more Russian soldiers to slip from their mounts, thus providing the navvies who were still on their feet with ready weapons. Thus armed, he saw them fling themselves at their stolid and determined foes, Russian soldiers now joining the wounded on the slippery ground.

To one side he saw a familiar figure engaged in hand-to-hand combat with a Russian soldier over the possession of a sword, but at that instant a cloud of smoke separated them and John urged his horse in that direction, sword raised, shouting, *"Willmot . . ."*

Through the smoke, he brought his horse up short in time to see the soldier in possession of the sword, raising it high in the air and plunging it into the man's stomach, the beloved face turning before he fell, meeting John's eyes.

The Russian looked up at John's approach, as with one cry he ran the man through. As he jumped down from his mount, he pulled his sword free, the soldier stiffening for a moment, then going limp.

"Jack," he shouted, turning back to the man who lay facedown in the mud. As he struggled to lift him, he was aware of his horse running off, but was aware of little else, save the man in his arms, the blood spreading over his coat, his eyes closed against the pain.

"Get . . . to your horse," Willmot whispered. "Get to . . ."

John held him close and looked about, trying to find a safe harbor. But he saw nothing but screaming men and fleeing horses, and he held Willmot closer in a convulsive grip, something cold splattering against his face now, one large black horse coming nearer, its rider ele-

gantly garbed in a spotless gray overcoat, spiked helmet
on his head, something glittering overhead, drawing yet
nearer until at last John saw the glittering something
poised over him, their eyes meeting in that single instant.
Then a sharp force of indescribable weight cut into his
right shoulder, dislodging Jack Willmot from his arms,
the soldier on horseback looking down on him as waves
of pain swept him into a safe warm darkness. . . .

He was enjoying a peaceful walk along the headlands
of Eden with Jack Willmot, on his way to visit his father's
grave, when without warning the darkness lifted.

At first he saw nothing but shadows. He was cold,
though there was an isolated caldron burning in his right
shoulder. His head was resting on something damp and
faintly moving, and as the shadows receded into mosaics
of light and color, he realized that he'd returned too soon.

He knew where he was. Little had changed except
his own helplessness. The noises about him, those too
were different, the air no longer rent by stampeding horses
and exploding rifles. Now all he heard were moans and
cries for help, and one voice very close panting,
"Jesus . . ."

Recognizing the voice, he made the mistake of trying
to lift himself with his right arm. As the caldron in his
shoulder exploded, the agony seemed to lift him, then
drop him again, where through glazed eyes he saw
Jack Willmot, in profile, his head pressed backward into
the blood-soaked ground, his hands clutching at his
stomach, his teeth chattering.

"Jack," he whispered, trying to move closer in an attempt to warm the man with his own body. In the process he glanced down at his right arm, saw the arm and
hand coated with blood. If only he could go back to sleep
again. If only sleep would claim him, or death, anything
that was black and feelingless.

But neither sleep nor death would have anything to
do with him, and he was forced to drag himself to a half-
sitting position, Willmot's head in his lap now.

Struggling to hold his head erect, he heard what he
thought were French accents moving among the wounded,

and looked up to see a contingent of the French Foreign
Legion, their overcoats flapping open in the wind as they
tried to do what they could for the wounded.

"Jack," he whispered, bending over Willmot's head.
"We're going home," he promised, holding him close.

Willmot opened his eyes, "Are you . . . hurt badly?"

John shook his head. "Nor are you," he said sternly.
"We'll lift a pint again."

Willmot looked up. Then new pain invaded him. His
hands clutched at his stomach. He twisted his head toward John's chest.

"Jack," John pleaded, not knowing precisely what he
was asking except that somehow they both be made whole
again. But he did not finish his request, and instead
continued to focus on those about him who were beyond
help.

John lowered his head. The stain of blood was spreading, covering his right side. Would he die here, he wondered, would both of them die? *Die?*

Then he heard horses' hooves, a curiously energetic
sound over and above the moans of men. In his lap, Willmot stirred, breathing in hoarse gasps. Momentarily John's
attention was torn between the suffering in his lap and
the sounds of horses drawing nearer.

Still not looking up, he heard a familiar shouting,
"Donnez premiers secours à ces hommes!"

Slowly John raised his head, his eyes falling first on an
enormous white stallion, brought all the way from England
for the pomp and ceremony of one man. The animal's eyes
showed white, his massive head lifting against the tight
rein, one hoof stamping at the earth only inches from
John's foot. Astride the horse, seated erect in his saddle,
hatless, his white hair blowing in the cold wind, giving
him a demented look, he saw Thomas Brassey.

"Prêtez la main ici!" Brassey shouted again, and at
that several French soldiers ran up bearing two litters.
They seemed to hesitate as they approached Willmot
where he lay on his back, his hands clutching at his
stomach.

"Dépêchez-vous! Hurry!" Brassey ordered.

With Willmot's weight removed from his lap, John

began to feel weaker, as though it had been his friend's body that had kept him strong and anchored. His eyes blurred.

Then he was aware of another litter close by, two French soldiers approaching him, one on his legs, pulling his boots forward, the other lifting his arms. As his body weight pulled against his wound, he cried out and momentarily lost consciousness, and revived on the litter, the pain so intense that tears filled his eyes.

Still he managed to clear his head long enough to look up. And there was Brassey, still seated astride his fine horse, safely removed from the blood-soaked mud, his boots in the stirrups polished, his coat thick and dry. The only feature about him which marked the occasion as unusual was his hatless state, that, and his face as he stared down on John. A portion of the customary arrogance seemed to have left it. His mouth was open, and his lips appeared to be trembling.

John lifted his eyes, forced them into direct contact with Brassey's. Before the Frenchmen lifted his litter, in that one brief instant when he was certain that Brassey's attention was his and his alone, he whispered, "Damn you! God damn your soul to hell!"

His head dropped back onto the litter and he closed his eyes.

❧

Balaklava Harbor, Aboard HMS <u>Perseverance</u>, April 1855

CAPTAIN J. M. Broadwood was standing near the top of the gangplank looking out over the grim scene, firm in in his mind that after two years of transferring the sick and wounded from Balaklava to Scutari across the Black Sea, this was the worst.

"Gawd," he muttered to his first mate, who was standing nearby. "Soldiers are bad enough, them that knew what they were letting themselves in for. But civilians . . ."

The first mate, a good man named Margate, stirred from his position near the railing where together they had kept a vigil for over two hours as ambulance wagon followed ambulance wagon to the docks from the Highlands. "Just another blot, it is, Captain," Margate muttered. "Name me one thing that's went right with this bloody war, just one."

Captain Broadwood heard the despairing tone and recognized it. It matched his own as well as the rest of his crew who had been pressed by the government into this grisly duty. They were all seamen, and damn good ones, at home on the high seas, their hold normally filled with tea from China or cotton from America. He'd heard no grumbling from his men on runs from Hong Kong or Savannah Harbor. No, the grumbling had started when they'd had to swab the deck three, sometimes four times a day in an effort to cleanse the blood, when with every sailing they could look forward to the grim ritual of burials at sea.

Margate had seen enough. He walked away a few steps and looked respectfully back. "With your permission, Captain," he said, "I'll press the crew into duty to help with the loading. I think it best if we get under way as soon as possible."

Captain Broadwood had no intention of disagreeing with him. Men were not designed to be heaped in such a miserable mass as that on the docks. He moved back to the top of the gangplank, assuming a captain's stance, his eye falling on a strange conveyance just entering the crowded dock area, a black carriage which looked out of place among the gray of the ambulance wagons. Compounding this strange conveyance was the fact that it appeared to be dragging a small enclosed sled behind it.

Grateful for a diversion, Captain Broadwood watched as the carriage penetrated as far as possible onto the dock, then was brought to a halt by the press of wounded lying on litters. A moment later the door opened and he saw a British soldier climb out.

Broadwood saw the driver of the carriage hop down from his perch and run to the covered sled at the rear of the carriage. He threw open the narrow door and looked inquiringly in. Then Broadwood's attention was drawn back to the carriage as he saw the soldier reach a hand in and guide a young man forward, clearly wounded and weakened, his right arm and shoulder swathed in bandages.

Captain Broadwood frowned at the scene. As diversion it left a great deal to be desired. It was simply the arrival of more sick and wounded. Now he saw the young man, dressed in ill-fitting civilian clothes, pull away from the support of the soldier and move rapidly toward the rear of the sled, where two litter bearers were withdrawing a man lying prone, covered with a blanket and strapped onto a litter.

It was apparent to Captain Broadwood that the wounded young man was refusing to leave the side of the man on the litter. The soldier appeared to be begging him to do so, but in spite of his obvious weakened condition, the man stood as though a guard, his good left hand grasping his friend's.

Finally the argument was settled by the superior will of one man over the other, and Broadwood saw the soldier step back in an attitude of resignation and start slowly through the wounded.

A moment later the soldier stood before him. "Corporal Andrew Rhoades," the man said, "temporarily released from the Sixty-third to escort the civilian wounded to Scutari."

Broadwood smiled. *"All* of them, Corporal?" he asked gently. "Quite a job that would be."

"Two in particular, sir," the soldier admitted. "Mr. Brassey's assistant and one of his foremen." The young corporal reached inside his pocket and withdrew a crushed sheet of paper.

Broadwood knew what it was without looking, an official order. "Were you there?" he asked, referring to the recent massacre.

"No," Corporal Rhoades replied, a reluctance in his voice which seemed to say that he wished he *had* been there.

The captain put a hand on his shoulder. "Bring your two friends aboard, Corporal. We'll be under way as soon as possible."

At that moment Margate's voice boomed across the deck. "Stores secured, Captain. Way's cleared for the litters."

It had not been Captain Broadwood's intention to watch the grisly procession. He'd seen quite enough from the deck of his ship. But as litter after litter passed him by, he found himself searching each face, passing judgment on who, in his opinion, would survive the voyage and who wouldn't. The fortunate ones were half-delirious, the truly fortunate unconscious.

As he was about to turn away, having looked his fill, he saw the young corporal starting up the gangplank, his friend leaning heavily upon him, a greatcoat swung loosely over his bandaged shoulder, his eyes lifting now and then to check on the litter which preceded them, that man's face as bloodless as any Broadwood had seen during his watch, a noticeable thickness about his middle, bespeaking bandages.

Broadwood watched until they had disappeared through the narrow passage which led to the deck below. Then he looked back in the other direction and saw the wounded still coming, and unable to look any longer, he fled down the deck in the opposite direction.

In the meantime there was a bottle of brandy in his cabin which offered relief, and he ran toward it, feeling as battered and bleeding as those British navvies now filling the lower deck of HMS *Perseverance*.

They left Balaklava late in the afternoon with their shipload of sick and wounded—some for Scutari, some for the hospitals on the coast, a few officers for Malta. It had been reasonably good weather when they had left the harbor, but at this season of the year, the Euxine was seldom quiet for many hours together, and before they had got halfway across, a storm was raging furiously, the black waves upheaving as if they would at every moment engulf the ship with her cargo of life and half-life.

Captain Broadwood stood on the quarterdeck speaking with the first mate, Margate, when the young corporal with the badge of the Sixty-third approached them, making with one hand a military salute while with the other he held on to save himself from being washed overboard. "Captain, will you be in smooth water soon?" he shouted. He lowered his head, an expression in his eyes which reflected the scene of human misery he'd just left below deck.

What was Captain Broadwood to do but tell the truth. "Lad," he shouted, "the ship scarce makes any headway in this sea. There will be no smooth water for the next twenty-four hours anyway."

The corporal nodded slowly, as though in resignation. As he turned away, the captain called after him, "Wait," feeling the need to offer some solace to such a despairing face. "Isn't all taut and dry below? And the doctor's with your mate, isn't he? All the ship's comforts are at his service. Does he want anything?"

The corporal turned back. "He won't live much longer, Captain. He never could stand the sea, or so he says, even when he was the man he used to be. He wants . . . fresh air, that's all."

In the face of such an earnest entreaty, Captain Broadwood weakened. "Go ahead," he said gruffly, "bring him up, though I can't imagine what healing powers you'll find in that sea."

As he gestured roughly toward the swells beyond the deck, he saw the corporal hurry off; then he stepped inside the captain's bridge. Which friend? he wondered. The corporal had boarded with two.

"Bear a hand," he shouted to several of his crew. A few minutes later, they had arranged a makeshift bed beneath one of the quarterdeck boats. And a few moments after that, the grim procession emerged from the lower deck, a doctor in the lead carrying one end of the litter, the corporal supporting the opposite end, and hovering close was the young man with the clipped right wing, his good hand tightly grasping the limp hand of his friend.

Captain Broadwood indicated the makeshift bed, then stood away. It had been his intention to take refuge in his own cabin. But something caught his interest, some measure of devotion with which the young man knelt beside his friend. The captain noticed then that everyone else was standing away, the doctor as though to say that he'd done all that medical science could do, and even the corporal, clearly not wanting to intrude on so intimate a moment. He did linger long enough to place his own coat about the kneeling man's shoulders, then stepped back and left them alone, the young man on his knees beside the litter, the older man lying motionless, as though death had already descended and had somehow failed to announce its presence.

But a few minutes later, with the wind shrieking about him, and the salt sea foam splashing on his face, he revived for a time. His eyes opened and moved directly to the young man's face. He whispered something, though Captain Broadwood couldn't hear over the wail of the wind. But whatever it was, the young man smiled, a stiff muscle spasm which did little to alleviate the desperate look of grief on his face.

As the man revived even more, Captain Broadwood moved a step closer, drawn forward by a combination of pleasure that perhaps the harsh air was proving medicinal, and his curiosity to know the nature of the bond between the two men. Clearly they were separated by age, and something else, class perhaps. There was a roughness to the man on the litter, something about the texture of the complexion which suggested that he was a man who had worked outdoors most of his life, quite opposite from the young man bending over him, whose features, while strong, bore a refinement.

They were not of the same fabric, these two. Yet how to account for the clear love which existed between them? In that moment the wind seemed to subside, as though nature herself saw the need for a moment's calm, and for the first time Captain Broadwood heard the young man's voice clearly. "Jack, we'll go to Eden Point when we get home. You'll be welcome there, I know. You'll see for yourself how beautiful it is, a perfect place to heal."

But the man on the litter merely looked up into the gray churning heavens. "John," he whispered, "promise me . . . that you will . . . see Elizabeth," he begged, "and forgive her. She . . . loves you so much."

Suddenly he pressed his head back against the litter, one hand grasping his stomach. The corporal started forward and was restrained by the doctor, who with a shake of his head sealed the man's fate. Nothing could be done.

The young man was kneeling over him again, speaking his name. "Jack, listen to me, please . . ." Captain Broadwood heard the break in his voice, saw that left hand trembling as it moved over the man's chest, caressing, always caressing, then back to his forehead, lovingly stroking the graying hair.

As for the man on the litter, his lips and face were as pale as wax, his eyes sunken in their blackened sockets, his features damp from the salt spray.

Again he seemed to revive, though energy was fast going. Grasping the young man's hand, he drew him close. "Take care of yourself, John," he said. "Years from now . . . remember me." He drew the young man close and kissed him. With his eyes closed, he said softly, "I . . . had not planned on . . . loving you. But I do."

The young man grasped the hand so feebly outstretched, and bent over him, tears streaming, mingling with the spray of sea which flew around that strange bed of death. "Jack . . ." he cried, half-raising the dead man to him.

One by one all turned away from that intimate embrace, unable to look any longer. Above the swells and wind, the sobs of the young man could be heard, unearthly weeping, as though he'd repressed tears for too long, and now with the legitimacy of a dead man in his arms, he could weep for everyone.

Barrack Hospital, Scutari, Mid-April 1855

WITH A SENSE of amazement Andrew sat upon his camp stool beside John's bed, a vigil which he'd maintained for the last four days, and focused on the miraculous changes which had taken place in the British hospital since he'd last seen it over a year ago.

It was a forced diversion. Anything to keep his eyes off that pale face on the pillow, growing paler in spite of the fact that according to the nurses his shoulder wound was healing.

Then why the pallor? Why were the eyes sinking deeper into shadows, and why had he refused all food and drink for four days since he'd been here? And why no response to anything Andrew said, no response to anyone for that matter.

Andrew looked closely at his friend, trying to put the horrible shipboard death of Jack Willmot out of his mind. Never had he heard a man mourn as John had mourned that day.

Overcome with his own feeling of helplessness, Andrew left the camp stool and walked a few steps to the window, seeking momentary solace in the bright warm day, again trying to absorb and digest the incredible changes which had taken place in the hospital. How changed it was, and in a rush of gratitude he thought of the Englishwoman who had almost single-handedly wrought these miraculous changes.

At some point, despite British mismanagement, hope had dawned at Scutari. Everyplace he looked, Andrew saw new order, the sick and wounded in the wards using towels and soap, knives and forks, combs and toothbrushes. The walls had been whitewashed, the beds separated a decent distance, the sheets were clean and white, and here and there the indelible signature of a true Englishwoman was visible in the lovely bouquets of wildflowers, bringing light and color and fragrance to men who sorely needed it.

Andrew had never seen her, that Englishwoman named Nightingale, but he'd heard about her, chatting softly with other men in the ward, soldiers who wanted news from the front. Andrew had told them what he could, and in exchange had posed questions of his own, sharing tales of the old Scutari, where men prayed for death rather than recovery, and more often than not had their prayers answered.

"It's her," one had told him, his eyes seared by an exploding shell. "The lady," he whispered, "she makes the difference. Afore she come, they was cussin' and swearin' but now it's holy as a church."

Over and over again during the last four days Andrew had listened to such testimony, sensing a passionate idolatry spreading among the men. One confessed to having kissed her shadow.

Now slumped on the camp stool, Andrew brought his brief inspection to a close. Whatever her magic, Andrew's only regret was that she'd arrived too late for the thousands who had already died. Slowly he turned back to John's bed, as though his brief recess was over and now again it was time to concentrate on his friend.

"John?" he whispered. "Please look at me. You must eat. The nurse says . . ."

Feeling the need to touch him, Andrew reached for his left hand, which lay limp on the bed. But there was no response.

For a moment longer he lingered in close scrutiny of the face he knew by heart, charting the many changes, so vast that at times Andrew wondered if a mask hadn't been slipped over the old features. The long fair hair was still there, though no longer brushed, now encircling his face in a snarled and oily mat. The mouth and chin were all but obscured by the full unkempt beard which had grown in darker than his hair and showed small streaks of gray. His complexion, turned rough by his constant exposure to the Crimean winter was that of a man in his middle years. And his loss of flesh was apparent in the thinness of his neck, which stood out in sharp contrast to the heavy bandages encasing his right shoulder.

But for all that grim inventory, nothing was worse than his eyes, and before that devastating emptiness Andrew retreated. There was an additional worry plaguing him. He couldn't stay here forever at Scutari. But how could he leave John in such a condition? Confident that Mr. Brassey would not want him to leave until all was well, he'd stayed four days, thinking every day his friend would stir and request water, a biscuit, something.

In a rush of despair Andrew was about to try again when suddenly he heard a disturbance at the far end of the ward. He looked up to see a dozen or so litter-bearers bringing new wounded through the double doors.

Andrew glanced out of the window. He'd seen no hospital ship, no new arrivals on the landing stage from Balaklava. As the ill moved past him, he saw that a few were dressed in military garb, though mottled and strange-appearing, and others were clad in plain civilian clothes, quite ragtag they were, and most peculiar of all were their faces, bronzed and sun-baked, not the rough chapness caused by the Crimean cold, but the dark brown burnt look of constant exposure to extreme heat.

As litter after litter filed past him, he noticed something else as well, the telltale symptoms of dysentery, the legs drawn up in an attempt to accommodate the searing pain in their guts, the spreading stains of brown beneath their hips, their lips parched and open.

Suddenly two orderlies shouted at him, "Move back, soldier. This one here is in need of that empty bed next to your friend."

Andrew grabbed the camp stool and moved to the window, staring in sympathy as the large man turned and twisted on the litter, his hands clutching at something about his throat, begging them to leave him be.

As the nurses approached, his screams increased, and from where Andrew stood he noticed that not once did the man's hands leave his throat. They appeared to be clasping a leather pouch of some sort.

"Here, now," one of the nurses soothed. "All we want to do is make you comfortable. You'll let us do that, won't you?"

As one of the nurses reached again for his neck, the man struggled with all his might to flee the bed, and would have, had it not been for the quick action of the three orderlies who stepped forward and restrained him.

"Very well, no need," one of the nurses said, seeing the cause of his fear. "You may keep your toy, whatever it is. I promise, we won't touch your pouch, but do let us bathe you. We only want to . . ."

About twenty minutes later the man had been bathed and dressed and now lay upon the bed, his eyes still keeping watch on all those around him. At last the orderlies stepped away, and the man, sensing his increasing weakness, stuffed the leather pouch into his mouth, as though to say, "Try to remove it now."

As the nurses gathered up his soiled garments, Andrew moved to assist them. As he handed over a pile of soiled linen, he asked quietly, "Where are they from? I saw no ship dock at—"

The nurse shook her head. "Their ship docked at Malta, an unscheduled stop due to an outbreak of dysentery. The hospital there was filled, and we inherited the overflow. From India they are."

"Are they soldiers?" Andrew asked.

"A few," she replied. "He isn't, however," she said, looking down on her new charge. "Just an Englishman, soldier of fortune, you might say, gone off to see the world." She looked down on the man's feverish face. "Seen a bit too much of it would be my guess," she added sympathetically.

Someone called for her assistance from the end of the ward. Before she left, she glanced down on John. "And what are we going to do with your friend, Corporal?" she asked sadly. "He must eat soon." Her hand brushed across John's forehead in a loving caress. "Wouldn't it be lovely to hear him screaming like his bedmate there? I never worry quite so much when they are screaming," she concluded.

The voice from the end of the ward called to her again,

and with an air of resignation she started away. As she passed the foot of John's bed, she looked back at Andrew. "Does he have a favorite food?" she asked brightly. "Our stores are somewhat limited, but Miss Nightingale believes in fighting pain with pleasure. If there is a certain treat that he might respond to . . ."

Her voice drifted off as she waited for Andrew to respond. But try as he did, he could think of nothing. Faced with his silence and the voice coming from the end of the ward, the nurse gently shrugged. "Well, I'll tend to his tray myself this evening. Perhaps between the two of us we can coax him into swallowing a few bites."

He started to thank her, when again she turned back. "What's his name again, Corporal?" she asked, an air of apology in her voice.

"Eden," he said. "John Murrey Eden."

She nodded, then she was gone.

Slowly Andrew drew a deep breath, lifted the camp stool and placed it again at John's side. As he sat wearily, he looked over at the newcomer from India in the next bed. He appeared to be sleeping. But that curious leather pouch was still in his mouth, the line of his jaw suggesting that his teeth were exerting pressure, that no one had better dare try to remove it, or in spite of his weakened state, he'd come fighting out of his semisleep.

India, Andrew mused. What had he been doing there? For a moment he felt a surge of resentment. The man appeared able-bodied. Hadn't it occurred to him that England needed him in the Crimea, not India, where the empire was secure?

As his weary mind built a connection between the wounded silent John Murrey Eden and the man on the other side, Andrew rearranged the camp stool and turned his back on the soldier of fortune and concentrated anew on the ravaged face of his friend. He leaned forward with a resolute beginning. "John, remember Childe's, remember how we used to . . ."

But after those few words, he was defeated by the still face and the fixed staring eyes, the parched lips which were moving now, as they frequently did, in delirium, whispering only one recognizable name, though Andrew had no idea who it was or how to respond to it, a name spoken so softly that on occasion it sounded like little more than a gentle expulsion of air, the same name he'd heard John utter over and over again during the last four days and nights, a simple name which seemed to soothe him just to speak it.

"Harriet . . ."

It was a slow-falling dusk, typical of the Crimea, when the sun seemed to hang forever on the black horizon line. On the small table near John's bed rested the tray of untouched food, a tribute to female ingenuity, a deep bowl of rich red beef stew and to one side a sherry trifle, a delicacy which Andrew had never seen in the Crimea. In addition there was a pot of tea, now grown cold, and a wedge of soft white bread.

After a half hour of gentle pleading with John, the nurse had urged Andrew to eat it himself, and at first he'd been tempted. But instead he'd taken a cheese roll from the trolley as it had come through the ward, always hopeful that perhaps sometime during the night, John might stir and request sustenance.

With the coming of night, the ward was growing quiet. Bedtime medicines had been administered, the moans of pain subsiding. Andrew stood up and tried to stretch the tightness out of his legs and shoulders. He eyed the stone floor beside John's bed. For the last four nights he'd napped there, brief intervals of sleep.

How much longer could he wait here? Was John purposely starving himself? Was it an act of premeditation, or had his grief literally unhinged his mind?

Hurriedly Andrew moved to the window as though to move away from such thought. If only Jack Willmot were here. Willmot had been the only one who could handle him.

Though not by nature deeply religious, it occurred to him to pray, though to what God he would speak and how he would address Him, he had no idea. How to begin? *Our Father in Heaven . . .*

It sounded stiff and childish, and in a rush of self-consciousness he lifted his head and turned away from the window. As he turned, his eye fell on the double doors at the end of the ward, on the figure of a woman standing there, looking back at him.

She appeared thin and angular. Her hair from that distance was indistinguishable, though it appeared dark, parted in the middle and drawn tightly back, a cap of white lace covering all but the rim of her face.

As she drew nearer, Andrew noticed other specifics; in her arm she clasped a heavy black notebook, and her face, coming closer, was not as old as he had first thought, scarcely a middle-aged woman.

Less than twenty feet away, she stopped. Would she stand there all evening merely gaping at him? If she had business with him, let her come forward. Growing exhausted by the curious encounter, Andrew at last rose to face her. Perhaps she was a relative and had come to visit someone, as soon as she could find him in the long rows of silent beds.

To this end, he asked courteously, "May I assist you? If you're looking for a specific patient, I'd be happy to summon a nurse."

Was he mistaken, or was that a smile on those small features?

"I need no assistance, Corporal," she said, "at least none that you can give me."

Though plainly spoken, the rebuke was not offensive.

"You don't know me, do you, Corporal?" She smiled, stepping to the foot of John's bed, her eyes falling upon that still face. Suddenly the smile faded, as though something in those ravaged features had caught her attention.

"It *is* him," she whispered. "When the nurse told me his name, I thought it might be, but . . ."

Andrew stepped forward. "You . . . know him?" he inquired.

Without looking up, she replied, "I knew his father, Edward Eden. And him as well," she added, "when he was just a babe. I spent my eighteenth year as a volunteer in the Ragged Schools of London." She shook her head, obviously falling victim to nostalgia. "How much I learned from his father, Edward Eden. Oh, not scientific knowledge to be sure. Mr. Eden was sadly lacking in that department." She laughed softly, her eyes holding fast on John's face. "But what a master the man was in the art of caring. No matter how small or dirty or diseased the child, Mr. Eden's arms were always broad enough to hold it, his heart always open and receptive to the faintest cry."

Her voice seemed to drift off, and Andrew felt himself leaning forward as though fearful of losing a word. When she seemed disinclined to say anything further, Andrew said, "I'm afraid you have the advantage. My name is Andrew Rhoades. And you are . . ."

She looked up with an expression of apology. "I'm sorry," she murmured, and extended one thin white hand in an almost masculine gesture. "Miss Nightingale," she said.

It was a few seconds before Andrew recovered, and by then she'd already withdrawn her hand, placed the notebook on the foot of the bed, dragged the camp stool close and sat upon it, her head and shoulders erect, her hands folded primly in her lap, demanding of Andrew in an efficient voice, "Tell me about him. What's causing this?"

After the amazing announcement, Andrew did well to stammer, "He . . . was in the massacre, in the employ of Mr. Thomas Brassey, the . . . rail link at Section . . ."

The sound of his own voice flustered him even more, and grateful for a reprieve, he watched her bend over the bed, draw back the blanket and commence an examination of John's shoulder wound, unwrapping the bandages, asking only of Andrew that he, "Bring the candle closer."

He did as he was told and found his attention torn between the red and angry-looking shoulder wound and the woman herself, this frail female who, single-handedly, had taken on all the stupidity and inefficiency of the British Army.

"Healing well enough," she pronounced. "I've seen men up and about with more."

The wound rebound, she lingered over John's face, one hand stroking his brow. "The resemblance is quite unique, isn't it?" she commented quietly.

At last Andrew felt himself recovered enough to speak.

"It is," he agreed. "I too knew his father. I grew up in the Ragged School near Jacob's Island."

She looked at Andrew as though with new respect. "I'm afraid, Corporal," she began, "that the nature of my duties here has taken a heavy toll of my respect for the . . . maleness of the world." She looked back down on John, the brusqueness softening. "However, I can say without hesitation that Edward Eden was one of the rarest individuals it has ever been my privilege to know."

In the face of such a tribute, Andrew thought it safe to remain silent. Then again she seemed to shake her head and in a clear tone asked, "Now, tell me everything."

As succinctly as possible, he recounted all the grim events of the last few days. Not once did she interrupt, and at the conclusion of the brief account, she continued to sit primly upon the stool, as silent as the man in the bed.

At last she lifted her head, as though an approach had been decided upon, and in a clear voice which exuded self-confidence, as though it had never occurred to her that she would not receive an answer, she said, "John? Can you hear me?"

Andrew stood still, his eyes moving back and forth between her face and the unresponding one on the pillow.

"Of course you can," she went on, undeterred by the silence. "I'm sorry I wasn't here to welcome you four days ago. But I'm certain that you'll forgive me. Men with mere arm wounds do not, of course, warrant the same attention as men with no arms. But now I'm here, with a few minutes to spare, and I'd like nothing better than to pass them with you."

In a mix of amazement and despair, Andrew watched. How many times during the last four days he'd tried the same approach.

But whereas, in the past, Andrew had retreated after a few such words, Miss Nightingale persisted, nothing in her manner to suggest that she was, in essence, conversing with herself.

"Now," she went on, "what I want to know is where do you intend to go from here? You see, in a few days you'll be able to get about quite handily on your own power.

Will you be returning to the war zone or going back to England? The war zone," she went on, answering her own question, "is in my opinion quite unrealistic, don't you agree? I must confess I can't for the life of me understand what we are doing there at all. Can you? Of course not. Clearly you were 'talked into' something. Am I correct? Of course I'm correct."

Andrew listened closely, amazed by his impression that John was actually responding. But of course he wasn't. Her voice simply gave that impression. And how clever, her denunciation of the war, how close she was moving to John's heart.

"But the fact remains," she went on, "for whatever foolish reason, here you are, at the end of one road, and now you must select another, mustn't you? Of course, that shouldn't be too difficult, a young man like yourself. The most pronounced difficulty will arise in the variety of roads open to you."

She laughed softly and seemed to relax a bit, one hand smoothing the lace collar at her throat. "I'll now confess to you, John"—she smiled—"all my life, in secret, I've wanted to be a man. But merciful heavens, the agony of choosing which worlds to conquer. To have every horizon open to you, and to know that you can accomplish *everything.*" She shuddered. "What hell that must be. For the female of the species, the decisions are so simple. Still, there have been many times when I would willingly change all that deadly simplicity for just one day of your glorious hell."

Andrew had the feeling that she was no longer speaking for John's benefit. Some essential aspect of her personality had without warning surfaced, and the self-revelation had to be dealt with before she could go on.

But deal with it she did, and once again restored, she talked on.

"I knew your father, John," she began, one hand grasping the limp one on the bed, "knew you as well when you were the length of a man's arm. Merciful heavens, what a weight we all put upon you in those days, long before you were ready to carry it. And the weight is still there, the weight that the gods place on all gifted individuals, the willingness to be tested to the very limit of one's endurance and capacity."

She abandoned the limp hand as though it had offended her in some way. "What a baffling inconvenience," she pronounced in a mocking tone. "How skillful we all are at raising false issues. The death of a good friend, the horror of a stupid war, the old phalanx of weakness bristling with its accustomed spears. So easy to say I'm beaten. Much more difficult having to admit that you've simply thrown away the game. And with all the winning cards in your hand! And so noble a game! John Murrey Eden threw the game away!"

There was mockery in her voice, as harsh as any man's. Andrew moved a step forward, amazed to see John's eyes upon her.

Then, in a curious reversal of both mood and manner, she announced bluntly, "I will not speak to you of God. The subject is beyond me. I have been accused of viewing the Deity as little more than a sanitary engineer. A man's god is something personal." Her manner and voice altered as though for a confession. "Not that I haven't dwelt on the puzzle long"—she smiled—"though I'm afraid that the fruits of my efforts are thin and lacking."

She seemed to warm to the "thin-and-lacking" subject, leaning close to share an intimacy. "The most fascinating approach that I can devise for the matter is a simple question. What beings should we conceive that God would create? Now, He cannot create perfect beings, since essentially perfection is One. If He did so, He would only be adding to Himself."

She paused as though aware of her audience of two, for at some point Andrew had lost interest in John's reaction and was listening to her words as though they were being spoken for him alone.

"Thus the conclusion is obvious," she went on. "God *must* create imperfect creatures." Again she smiled down on John. "All that will be asked of us at the end is whether or not we have been unprofitable servants. He gives us a lamp by which we shall stand, and frequently the lamp shows us only our own shipwreck. No wonder at times our feelings are mixed to the point of a confused silence," she said softly. "And yet, at other times, I fancy there are possibilities of human character much greater than have ever before been realized."

In spite of the abstract nature of her words, Andrew had the feeling that at the heart of the matter was a soul made of steel. He found it difficult to believe that such a woman had ever truly agonized over the mystery of God. If anything, the Almighty had better be careful lest He too fall into her clutches and she reorganize heaven as she had reorganized Scutari.

In the semidarkness of the ward, Andrew saw her eyes still focused downward on John, and he listened closely for the parting words, expecting some moving summary to everything she had said earlier. Instead, to his surprise, she said simply, in a manner so positive, and practical, "I'll give you a week, John. Then I want you up and about. You see, I need your bed, for others less fortunate."

Without hesitation she walked rapidly away, never once turning back, as though the possibility that she would not be obeyed was simply beyond her.

Andrew held his position beside the table and watched her the length of the ward, was still watching even after the double doors had closed, her presence lingering in spite of the physical vacuum, like the hallucination of the eye when it continues to see a flame after the candle has burned out.

It was some minutes before he shook off the mood and drew near to John's bedside. He looked down. Nothing. The eyes had returned to their customary spot on the ceiling. For all her noble efforts, Miss Nightingale had accomplished nothing.

Suffering a strange weakness brought on by the encounter, Andrew sat on the camp stool, his eye in the process falling on the man in the next bed, his cheeks still bulging with the leather pouch, though from all signs, he was fast asleep.

It wasn't until Andrew turned back toward John's bed that he saw the first faint movement, that left hand suddenly stiffening with new energy, the arm following suit, and arm and hand together lifting the torso, the body angling to the right as it fought for a center of balance, John himself at last seated upright on the edge of the bed.

The face lifted with a stubborn concentrated expression, and as the eyes, buried in hollows, met Andrew's, two words left those parched lips.

"My . . . friend," John whispered, lifting his hand.

The next evening, with Andrew packed and ready to leave, John sat propped up by pillows and tried to manipulate the spoon in his left hand. He finished the bowl of stew and pushed the tray away, a little annoyed by the grinning Andrew and greatly annoyed by the delirious mutterings of the man in the bed next to him.

"It's like Bedlam," he muttered, feeling irascible, in the manner of an invalid.

"It's paradise"—Andrew smiled—"compared to what it used to be."

"Then spare me paradise," John grumbled, and slipped down beneath the blanket, amazed by his presence in this place. Still struggling through a degree of confusion, he looked up at Andrew, neat and polished in his scarlet tunic and white shoulder straps. "When are you leaving?" he asked, as quietly as the ravings in the next bed would permit. He knew the answer anyway.

"With the evening tide," Andrew said.

John was on the verge of expressing his gratitude when suddenly the sun-baked lunatic in the next bed let out an unearthly scream which brought nurses scurrying from all quarters of the ward. Even Andrew hurried to offer his assistance. For the first time John felt a wave of sympathy for him. Perhaps the poor man had simply fallen into the pit out of which John had recently climbed.

As the man's howls increased, John sent his attention in the opposite direction. Slowly he lifted his hand to his right shoulder. The only remaining sensation was a burning, a negotiable discomfort, but still something new, considering that for four days he'd felt nothing. During that strange time, apparently every nerve ending in his body had been occupied elsewhere, trying to assist him with that mysterious and difficult passage which at one point had deposited him at Eden, a scene of crystal clarity, withered leaves blowing about the inner courtyard.

Again the man screamed. God, what were they doing to him? Unable to bear the sounds of misery any longer, John threw back the blanket and stood, a bit wobbly on unsteady legs, and cut through the barrier of nurses and orderlies with a single command.

"Leave him be!" he shouted.

One by one, the nurses looked up in surprise, Andrew with them, their expressions registering amazement that so firm a command could come from such an unlikely source.

Without warning, he felt weak. He took a step backward until he felt the bed behind him, and sat, trying to maintain the impression of strength.

One of the nurses offered an explanation. "He must be bathed, Mr. Eden," she said kindly. "That's all we were trying to do."

John felt the recently consumed stew turn in his stomach. "Clearly he does not want a bath," he muttered.

Apparently Andrew saw the approaching weakness and moved back to John's side, throwing out a suggestion to the waiting nurses. "Perhaps he's right," he said. "Later. He might be more cooperative later."

From where John sat on the edge of the bed, he could see the objecting patient in the next bed. The hospital robe had been stripped down to his waist. Apparently someone had tried to remove a small leather pouch which hung about his neck. The man now clutched at it, his eyes white and darting, his cheeks ablaze with fever.

John watched him for as long as he could; then, using the last of his energy, he walked to the bed next to him and with his good hand drew the blanket over the man's chest, muttering angrily, "Damn nurses . . ."

The man looked gratefully up out of his fear. "Thanks . . . mate," he whispered, both hands clutching at the leather pouch.

John lingered, moved by the helplessness of so strapping a man. Under better circumstances, no one would lift a hand to him without his permission. While he was still standing there, John saw the man's eyes close, as though convinced that now it was safe to sleep.

"Where did he come from?" John asked, stepping back to his own bed.

"India," Andrew said, "or so one of the nurses claims."

John looked up, newly interested. "India? How did he get here?"

"Aboard a troop ship heading for England. Dysentery caused them to put in at Malta. Some were sent here."

As a new wave of weakness swept over John, he leaned back against his pillow and closed his eyes, wishing that the whitewashed walls would stop whirling about him.

As Andrew drew up the blanket about him, John asked a question. "Have . . . you been here all the time?"

Andrew nodded, smiling.

"Without sleep . . . or respite?"

Again Andrew nodded.

John watched his friend's face closely. There really was no need to pose either question. The answer was clear in the lines of fatigue about Andrew's eyes.

Suddenly John caught the hand that was arranging the blanket and held it fast. Something had to be said. "There was no need, you know."

"There was every need."

"I would have survived."

"I wanted to see for myself."

A tension had fallen over both, a unique defense against rising emotions. John released his hand. "You really insist upon returning?"

"I have no choice," he repeated.

"That's nonsense and you know it," John snapped. "The rate of desertions each day is high, and climbing higher."

"And I will not add my name to the list," Andrew said with conviction. Apparently he saw the look of annoyance in John's face and moved to dispel it. "Oh, don't get me wrong, my friend." He smiled. "I should have listened to you back in London, on the day we signed up. But then I thought you were wrong."

"And now?"

Andrew lowered his head. "It was a stupid venture to start with. And you?" he asked. "What will you do? Is it back to London or Eden for you?"

Such a simple question! Still gaping, as though the answer were written on Andrew's face, John realized for the first time the full measure of his recent estrangement from life. The immediate future had come to a halt on that escarpment above Section Three. And with Jack Willmot's death, it had vanished altogether.

John shook his head. Was it necessary that he address that black vacuum of the future so soon?

While Andrew detected his mood, he obviously did not know its cause. "Shall we plan to meet in London, then? Within the year? Together we should be able to plot some sort of negotiable future, don't you think?"

John nodded, shocked by his ability to deceive. Meet in London! He had neither appetite nor desire for London. What was there in London except the empty flat on Warwick Lane, filled with Jack Willmot's memories? What was there for him in that obscene house in St. George Street? And he would never again step foot in Brassey's office. The generous wage and assistantship that was to have been his future had been shattered on the bloody field of massacre at Section Three. As for Eden? On that thought his mind disintegrated into the fragmented images of a madman.

"Then London, is it?" Andrew asked.

John nodded. He would write to Andrew later and abridge the lie, after he had settled upon a destination.

He looked up to see Andrew moving back to the foot of the bed. "Must you leave so soon?" John asked. "There's time yet."

But Andrew shook his head, a helplessness in his expression which suggested that the parting was no easier for him than it was for John. "I need to report to the docks early," he murmured. "I heard this morning that the ship will be full to capacity. A new regiment was brought in from India. Reinforcements." He grinned. "Don't worry. In no time we'll have Ivan on the run back to Moscow."

John's suffering was acute at the imminent loss of this

last good friend. He thought that it would be best if he said only what Andrew wanted to hear. "Then go and fight your war." He smiled. "Go along with you."

Andrew lifted the valise at his feet. He started to lift his hand to his forehead as though in salute. But something altered in his face. He dropped the valise and started forward, and John was there to receive him, his good arm returning the embrace, the mottled patterns of late-evening sun dancing in liquid movements across the bed.

Then he was gone. For a moment John held still, his eyes fastened on the vacuum at the end of the ward. Finally he fell back into the pillow, appalled at the tears in his eyes. How long would it go on, this unfortunate propensity of his to lose people he loved?

Lacking the energy and will which might have led to an answer, he turned on his side in an attempt to conceal his tears from the passing nurses. He swallowed hard and was in the process of wiping his face with the back of his hand when suddenly he felt eyes upon him and glanced across at the bed opposite. The man lay in his exact same position, on his side, one hand crooked beneath the dark matted hair, the other still grasping the leather pouch about his neck, his pale watery eyes open and fastened upon John.

Neither spoke, as though both were shocked by the intimacy of the confrontation. Finally, in a voice so low that it was scarcely audible, the large man smiled. "Rough, ain't it, losing a good mate?"

John said nothing. For the first time he noticed a front tooth missing in the broad flat mouth, and took in the rest of the face and was on the verge of turning in the opposite direction when the man spoke again.

"Didn't mean to pry," he said. "No offense?"

Still uncertain whether he should respond to the strange man, John returned his stare, fascinated and curious about the way in which the man maintained an iron grip on that soiled leather pouch. When the man seemed disinclined to speak again, John closed his eyes, assuming the episode was over.

Then again John heard his voice, weakened now, but

audible. "I meant what I said," he whispered, "about losin' a friend. I . . . lost mine, just three days ago. At Malta. Went to India together, we did. Saw good times and bad, fortune and misfortune . . ."

His voice seemed to be fading. John raised himself up on his elbow, the better to hear. India interested him as always and here was a firsthand witness. The man's eyes were open, though fixed and staring at the ceiling. "But we was headin' home, with our just rewards, and he . . . died." The voice broke. John saw tears running out of the corners of his eyes. "Oh, lord," the man murmured, "how can the world and ever'thing in it look so right one morning and so wrong the next?"

John listened sympathetically. "Sleep now," he urged quietly. "I'll stand watch, if you wish. No one will come near you. I swear it."

There was a moment of doubt. Once John saw him make an effort to throw off his fatigue. But he couldn't do it, and as his head tossed back and forth on the pillow, John urged, "Please. Whatever the nature of your treasure, I promise it will be safe."

The man looked up at him. "That's what me mate was told as well," he whispered, "and he ended up with a knife between his ribs."

"I have no knife," John reassured him, startled by the account of murder.

"Them didn't either," the man said, his speech beginning to slur as sleep crept closer. "But they found one quick enough when they learned what me friend was carrying."

In one last effort he tried to lift the small pouch. But even that was too much to ask of him now.

Still watching, John was certain a few minutes later that he was fast asleep. But as he was on the verge of drawing a breath of accomplishment, the man opened one eye. "Forgive me, lad," he whispered, "but what's your name? Something about you tells me you couldn't knife a man you'd exchanged names with."

"Eden," he said, "John Murrey Eden."

The man seemed impressed. "Suits you, it does," he murmured. "With luck, you'll grow into it one day. Beats hell out of mine." His eyes were closed now. John was beginning to wonder if the mouth would ever follow suit.

"You might as well hear it right off . . ." He faltered. "Alex. Alex Aldwell, and I don't recollect who gave it to me, but . . . I'll catch up with them one day, and when . . . I do . . ."

The threat was never completed. At last the massive head rolled to one side, mouth open, though silent.

John held still a moment. There had been false alarms before. But no. At last the large man was safely submerged in sleep. As John expected, the last area of the man's body to relax was that left hand, the fingers uncurling from about the leather pouch.

Again he looked closely at the sleeping man. His precise age, John could not even guess. Fifty perhaps, the same as Jack Willmot.

A bad move, that. Best to stay safely lost in the mystery of Mr. Alex Aldwell. The longing for Jack Willmot behind him, John took up a vigil on the edge of the bed, determined to serve the man by keeping his word.

From the end of the ward he heard the approach of the dinner trolley. He'd eat again tonight. Practically speaking, a man didn't stand a chance of putting his world together again on an empty belly.

He heard the trolley making its slow progress down the hospital ward. But his attention was now focused in another direction, on one small object, that leather pouch which hung, unattended, about the man's neck. What was it? And what a simple matter it would be to . . .

No. When he became rich, he might indulge in a harmless deception. But he was a poor man now, and when a poor man gave his word, it was all he had to give.

A week later, John sat in the large solarium at the end of the central ward, looking out over the blue waters of the Bosporus at Constantinople, a blaze of early May sun on his face, trying to coax Alex Aldwell into telling him about India.

John leaned back against the wicker chair, a little amazed at how well he felt, both physically and emotionally. His constant companion for the last seven days had been Alex Aldwell, a not-so-peculiar bond springing up between the two, considering that both had lost good friends during the last fortnight.

Of course, as far as John was concerned, there was no point of resemblance between his new companion and Jack Willmot. There were the physical attributes, for one. Though strong, Jack had been normal size, while Alex Aldwell standing was an even more awesome sight than Alex Aldwell lying prone on the bed. A good foot beyond John's six feet, he literally towered over all, and added to that was the girth of a chest which resembled an apple barrel, and arms and flanks the size of quartered cattle, and in every sense of the word he was an awesome sight. Once past the more weakening stages of his dysentery, he had shown no anxiety at all over that damnable leather pouch which still hung on the V of white flesh about his neck. And no wonder. Any man would be a fool to try to remove it against Alex's wishes.

"Tell me of India, Alex," John began on a fresh breath. "Everything," he added, smiling. "How did you get there? Why did you leave?"

The big man looked sideways at him, his expression one of suspicion. "Why?" Alex demanded bluntly.

"Why not?" John countered.

Alex averted his face, his mammoth hands locked together between his legs, the pouch bobbling gently about his neck. "What's to tell?" he muttered to the floor. "Suffice it to say that it's . . . Eden, that's what it is."

John looked sharply up, amazed that that one small word could render him speechless. Surely it had been mere coincidence. Not once had he spoken of his past to Alex Aldwell.

A broad grin broke on Alex's face. "At least as close to paradise as any man has a right to expect, a gorgeous land, really," he added, warming to his subject.

John was on the verge of prodding the man to speak further when he saw there was no need. Alex leaned back into the settee now, his legs sprawled before him, his eyes fixed on the ceiling, a new calm on his face. "Would you believe me if I told you I was never cold there, not once? Lord, I grew up with ice in me blood, and it took that Indian sun to thaw it proper."

"How did you get there?"

"How else?" Alex muttered. "John Company." He looked over at John and apparently saw the question on his face. "East India Company," he explained. "Twenty-five years ago, it was the new horizon. If you had no future in England, join the company and go to India. There was future enough for all."

Sternly he shook his head. " 'Course, all that changed right enough. I signed on simply as a guard for the company. Then one day, about ten years ago, I looked up and it had the smell of the military about it, more sepoys than whites in the ranks, and officered by English 'gintlemen.' "

He said this last with a pronounced sneer. "Bloody aristocrats," he cursed. "The plain blokes does the work, and they move in to take the credit."

John agreed with a nod, recalling the stupidity of the British officers in the Crimea, who frequently were more concerned with getting their boots polished than finding a warm dry place for their men to sleep.

He was about to make this contribution when he saw that Alex needed no help. The man was talking effortlessly now, of exotic scenes, vast official palaces, and dark-skinned veiled beauties, of the fierce Indian sun and the liquid seduction of the Ganges. "So I roamed for a while, I did." He grinned at John. "Me and Rod, that is, who had no more stomach for the military than I did. We'd saved a good purse between us, thanks to John Company, and one day we took off on our own." The grin broadened. "Went native, we did, lived good and bad from Bombay to Delhi." For a moment he sank into a kind of trance, the calm of his voice spreading to the expression on his face. "Lord, but I loved it," he whispered. "A world where the sun reaches its zenith before noon, the sweltering heat of the plains, the shuttered houses with only the slow wafting of a punkah to move the air, the shimmering afternoons, the courtyards emptied of all white men, and only a few natives visible, dozing in the shade like bundles of old rags."

The spell was complete, skillfully woven. Surprised by

the man's eloquence, John found that he was almost afraid to breathe.

" 'Course, don't get me wrong," Alex warned. "It's a harsh land with lots that takes gettin' used to. They do things different, they do, but I figured it was still their country in spite of John Company, and they had a right." He leaned closer. "Like suttee. Ever heard of it? No, of course you ain't. Well, what that is in two words is widow-burning."

John listened closely, amazed by the new light in the man's face and the grim tale he was telling. " 'Course, our missionaries has stamped it out in most places now. In His Name, they calls it. But Rod and me seen one once in a village near Meerut. Some Moghul had died and we saw the natives building this bier. All night long they worked on it, and at dawn they carried out the dead man and laid him atop it, then went back for his widow."

The light of excitement on his face dimmed. "She didn't seem to take to the idea at first, and they had to drag her through the dust, not ten yards from where we was standing. But they managed to get her up there with her dead husband, and suddenly she wasn't objecting no more. Just sittin' there on top of that bier with her face raised. And she was still sittin' there when the flames took her."

He broke off speaking, his left hand kneading the back of the settee. "Lord, but it's awful, the smell of burning flesh."

John felt himself accompanying Alex back into that exotic world, and finding it, if not preferable to, at least different from any he had ever known before.

"Where did you go from there?" he asked eagerly.

"After Meerut?" Alex grinned. "Well, it was our intention, Rod's and mine, to find our fortune, you see. Plenty of others had found theirs before us, so naturally we figured why not us?"

There was a spirit of joking about him now, as though he were secretly laughing at his own foolishness. "Instead, for a period, all we found was plenty of soft brown spread legs." He laughed aloud, a look of affection on his face. "Never seen such willing females. And gifted, too, they are. Like brown macaroni, wrapping themselves about a man."

Overcome by the memories of his sexual exploits, he couldn't for the moment go on. "Lord, forgive me," he apologized. "You shouldn't have started me talking. You really shouldn't have."

"No, please," John said urgently, leaning forward. "Go on. I want to hear more. Everything, please, I beg you."

Alex looked at him closely as though trying to determine his sincerity. At last he commenced speaking again, lounging back against the cushions, a faint look of superiority on his face, as though his various experiences were a source of pride to him. "After Meerut," he mused to the ceiling. "Hard to say. Outside of the cities, time in India don't mean much. I know we traveled its length at least twice, exhausting that purse of ours in the meantime, as well as exhausting ourselves." He closed his eyes as though again feeling the fatigue. "I remember Rod saying one day that if we really wanted to find our fortunes, we'd better go where fortunes existed, 'cause we sure as hell weren't going to find them in any of those poor villages."

While he lapsed into a momentary silence, John looked about. For the first time he was aware that the solarium was empty. Good! This world seemed to be dying just as the other one was coming vividly to life. He listened attentively now as Alex filled the quiet air with strange names, recounting his progress up the Ganges, through Benares to Fatehpur, on up to Cawnpore, which boasted a sizable British settlement, then across the dusty plains to Agra and Aligarth, and at last . . .

"Delhi!"

With a sense of awe the simple place name seemed to fill the empty room. Even Alex sat up straighter as he spoke it, then leaned close with an important intimacy. "Whoever commands that walled city will command the respect of all of India," he said with conviction.

"Who commands it now?" John asked.

Alex shrugged. "The British, of course, who else? For the time being, that is. Men from all parts of Asia meet in Delhi," he went on, keeping his voice low, as though someone were listening in the empty room, "and someday or other much mischief will be hatched within those walls."

The warning was cryptic and briefly spoken. In the very next breath, he was speaking again, rubbing his hands together. "Lord, after the dust and poverty of the villages, Delhi was our mecca, for three hundred years the capital of the Moghuls, the rulers of the Muslim Empire in India, and though old and reduced by the British to virtual bondage, the last Moghul king still lives there."

He sat erect, his legs apart, his massive hands planted on his knees. "I knew him, don't you see?" he boasted. "Yes, I did. Rod, too."

He laughed as though in a way he found it hard to believe his own words. "We were—how shall I put it?— thrown together, you might say. Mutually joined, don't you know, by our loathing of the British military."

John leaned slowly back, not wanting to distract the man with sudden movement, sensing that the already fascinating tale was on the verge of even greater excitement.

"The main road into Delhi," Alex went on in the manner of a storyteller, "crosses the River Jumna—at one point almost a mile wide—by a bridge of lighters lashed together and covered with logs. Now, this road and bridge is under the domination of the Red Fort, the King's personal palace and in sight of his private quarters."

He'd begun to use his hands, massive gestures depicting the size of the river, the curious log-covered bridge. "Now, here we come to a difference of opinion." He smiled. "There are two forces that think they control that bridge. One—and need I say it?—the bloody British Army, and two, poor old Bahadur Shah Zafar, the last descendant of the Moghul conquerors."

He shook his head sadly. "Poor old man, he's long since ceased to hope that he might throw off British domination. Eighty-two if he's a day, he is, kind of womanlike in size, brought up in the vicious atmosphere of his own court, and now with the British boot on the back of his neck, a tiny, ailing man, none too clean, let me tell you, wandering of eye, and toothless."

He paused, some new expression on his face, a look of affection for the old man he'd just described. "Well, he sits up there in his private quarters, he does, day in, day out, and watches his bridge, and somehow in his mind is the idea that anyone the British hate is automatically his friend."

He chuckled and leaned back, his hands laced behind his head. "Well, as you can imagine, Rod and me that day weren't greeted with no brass band. Oh no, Johnny Company had sent out our names and faces on posters as deserters."

As his outrage increased, he stood suddenly and commenced pacing, as though to walk off the excess energy. When after several minutes of angry pacing he still showed no signs of going on with his tale, John asked, "What happened then?"

"What happened?" came the thunderous echo from the window. "I'll tell you what happened. We was met on the Delhi side of that bridge by six armed guards, with rifles raised, pretty little soldiers they was, warning us that another step would be our last."

Although he'd been standing erect, now he crouched down as though recreating the scene in pantomime. "Well, I knew Rod wasn't of a mind to obey them little boys, and Rod knew I wasn't, and the last hope of our salvation lay in gettin' past them and into the foot traffic of Delhi itself."

He bent farther over, his arms raised in an attitude of combat, a completely absurd position for the hospital at Scutari, but at that moment John was not aware of the reality of his surroundings. He, along with Alex, stood on that hot, dusty bridge, with the gates of Delhi only a few yards beyond and six soldiers blocking their path.

Suddenly an unearthly war cry issued from Alex's lips and his raised arms lifted in a rapid-fire movement, until all John saw was the gray blur of his hospital robe. "We took 'em, we did," he shouted triumphantly, "Rod flattening three of them on the right, and me the other three on the left, and while they was lying stunned, old Rod and me, we were two blurs racing through them gates, knocking peddlers aside, catching a chicken or two in our face, but running like hell."

Still breathless from his recent theatrical, Alex smoothed back his long hair, sank into the chair near the window and nodded broadly for a moment or two while he tried to catch his breath.

"Well," he commenced, "that's when the fun really started. No more than through the gates we were, skirting the walls, keeping close in the shadows, when suddenly a door opens out of the wall and there's these two Indians motioning us to come in. All turbaned up, they was, in white coats and wrapped leggings, and I'm here to say we didn't ask 'em twice what they meant, and before we knew what had happened we was inside that courtyard and facing the old Muhammad himself who told us we was safe, and if the British hated us so, he was bound to love us."

His expression froze. "Muhammad Bahadur Shah Zafar," he said, as though treating the air to the sound of the name. "He took good care of us, he did, set us up in a private quarter next to his retinue."

For the first time he looked at John, as though at last aware of an audience. "A world within a world, that's what the place was, lad. Old Rod and me, we prided ourselves on having seen it all. But . . ." Here he shook his head. "We hadn't seen nothing till then. Dusty blood-red, the earth was there, where filth lay side by side with rich carpets, and ivory and silver chairs covered by dirty rags."

He stopped speaking and looked across at John with a mischievous grin. "That's where I wore me cock out, lad, I'm sure of it. Seems like everyplace me and Rod looked, there was a set of brown eyes looking back at us, promising us paradise."

Predictably the memory of sexual pleasure was more powerful than combat. John waited patiently.

He didn't have the heart to interrupt such pleasant suffering.

When Alex started speaking again, it was on the same subject. "Cock, it was," he announced bluntly, "that endeared us to the Muhammad forever. *His* cock." He grinned further. "Can you imagine the old geyser, at eighty-two, still lusting?" He shook his head. "But he did, and you see, he had a special appetite. Oh yes, and a difficult one for his retinue to fulfill."

He walked back to the settee, John following every movement with rapt attention.

"Englishwomen." Alex grinned down. "The old bastard liked Englishwomen. And one day he approached Rod and me with a bargain. Ten pounds a head for every piece of white flesh we brought him."

John stared upward. "What did you do?" he asked.

Alex shrugged. "We obliged, of course, though we weren't too happy with the price. Ten pounds out of that treasure house was like one grain of sand from Brighton beach."

"Could you find them? Englishwomen, I mean, who were willing—"

Alex laughed and settled back into the settee beside John. "Find 'em!" he parroted. "We had a selection as grand as the lanes of St. James Park. In fact, old Rod laughed once and wondered what the English gents were doing with all their whores on Indian soil. And they weren't all whores either," he added slyly. "Oh, no, not at all. There was fresh young maids who'd come over with officers' families, and a few grand ladies themselves, bored, with their soldier husbands gone off hunting, wanting to see if it was any different with an Indian."

He grew reflective. "Oh, we was good whores' bullies, we was, slipping out under cover of night to avoid meeting up with our soldier friends, and bringing back fresh white meat for old Muhammad. You see, they trusted us, the bitches did. White men would take care of them and see they got safely home. And we did. We had all that understood with the old man. No branding, no white slavery, no drugs, just a set of white legs he could play with all night, just so long as them same legs could walk her home come dawn."

He winked at John. "And of course, like the enterprising businessmen we was, we kept upping the price a little and claiming a diminishing market, and the old man's supply of pounds became exhausted and one night he came to us in his grand robes and said the words we was waiting to hear."

All at once he stopped speaking, casting only a sideways glance at John. Within the instant everything about him had changed, his manner, his volubility, his own interest and enjoyment in his tale.

John gave him all the time he needed, concentrating anew on the small leather pouch which swung gently against the broad barrel chest. A moment later, his voice, muffled behind the barrier of his hands, Alex commenced speaking again. "I've done some god-awful things, lad," he confessed. "When I buried Rod, I . . . kept wanting to jump in the grave with him."

John listened, amazed at the sense of childlike shame which was emanating from the man. He had to get him back to his story somehow. "Tell me what happened, Alex," he prodded gently.

Drawing a massive breath, Alex looked up with a peculiar expression of indifference on his face. "What happened?" he repeated. "Betrayal, that's what happened. The old man begged us to wait one night, claimed he'd pay us right enough, if we'd just continue to bring him white flesh."

Again he shook his head. "Rod was the one who suggested we follow him. And we did. He moved like a ghost across that courtyard, and disappeared into a mound of dirt, and we were moving right behind, down a narrow passageway, following his small torch like it was the evening star itself. My God," Alex whispered, "we must have burrowed under half a mountain, like a mineshaft it was, pitch black except for that beacon light carried by the old man."

Suddenly he stood again, strode rapidly around the settee, forcing John to crane his neck for fear of missing a word.

"Then, there it was," Alex said, a strange calm in his voice, "just as Rod had predicted, a low wooden door which wouldn't keep a healthy flea out, leading into an underground chamber. Oh, mind you, it was pitch dark at first, till old Muhammad lit the wall torches. Then . . . a scene out of Ali Baba, it was," he gasped, "trunks, caches, chests filled with jewels, like the spilling of a rain-bow, and ivory and silver and gold mixed in, for as far as the eye could see in every direction, the light of the torches catching the brilliance and damn near blinding the both of us. Gold chains, I seen, lad," he whispered, bending close, "the size of a man's arm, and ropes of emeralds, and silver chairs, the treasure of the Moghul Empire, all sittin' unattended in that mole's hole, just waitin' . . ."

He raised up. "I was the one who did it," he confessed bluntly, "gave the old man a light tap was all, enough to knock him senseless. And we wasn't greedy, no sir, we wasn't," he protested. "Rod took what he wanted, and I took what I wanted, and left enough for the whole bloody world."

John saw the man's strong right hand move up to the pouch about his neck, a reflexive gesture, as though he'd been threatened in some way. "I got scores to settle, I have," he said, his voice suddenly hard. "Alex Aldwell ain't going to be a joke anymore."

He said something else, but John didn't hear. Slowly rising from the settee, he found that he was unable to take his eyes off that fist that covered the leather pouch. "Come on, Alex," he begged. "Give us a look. What harm?"

But the man merely tightened his grip on the pouch and stepped back, a look of defiance in his eyes.

"Come on, Alex," John wheedled. "It was a grand tale, but how am I to know you didn't make it up?"

Fortunately the man rose to the challenge. He stepped back to the settee, looked carefully about the large room and at the same time lifted the pouch to his teeth and commenced to chew loose the tight leather cord.

Amused by the melodrama, yet curious to see the contents of the pouch, John followed after him, saw the massive hands shift, the leather pouch upended, the object, whatever it was, now cradled in the palm of Alex Aldwell's right hand.

For a moment the man's own broad shoulder blocked John's view. Then Alex shifted to one side and John saw clearly, yet not clearly. My God, what was it? An ice crystal the size of an apricot? A pool of fire cupped in the broad palm?

Aldwell sensed his awe and grinned approvingly. "A right pretty bauble, wouldn't you say?"

John stepped closer, incapable of saying anything. He'd never seen such a gem, never even dreamed that one like this existed, a diamond of inestimable value.

While he was still gazing upon it in disbelief, it was gone, slipped stealthily back into the leather pouch, the pouch itself shoved protectively inside Aldwell's robe.

"And that's it," Alex pronounced in a strong voice, moving away from John as though intent on putting distance between them. "Come on, lad, let's eat now. I've worked up quite an appetite, I have."

But food was not paramount in John's mind. "Wait," he called out, wanting to hear more. "Was it . . . really that simple?" he asked, following after the retreating man.

"Simpler." Alex grinned. "You see, everyone inside the palace walls trusted us. We just crawled up out of that mole's hole and left through the gate, and walked out of Delhi and kept walking to Bombay. There we bought ourselves passage on a troop ship leaving for Portsmouth." Here his voice fell. "And we almost made it, we did, 'cept for the sickness that sent us sailing here instead of home."

Still John pursued him. "And there's more?" he asked, frantically trying to bring the man back. "In the treasure house, I mean?"

"Lord! More?" Alex threw back his head, laughing. "This here dangling from me neck is modest compared to what we left. You see, we had to be mobile, we did, but Rod said he'd given his right arm for a good packhorse."

Again as he started toward the door, John called after him. "And what next?"

With the length of the room between them, he saw Alex grin. "Back to England, what else? I've sealed me fate in India, I have. Can't go back there, now, can I?" The grin widened. "But with this"—and he clutched at the pouch about his neck—"I can fix meself up right proper anyplace. Wouldn't you say?"

Then he'd at last exhausted himself. "Dammit, come along, lad. Me ribs are playing a tune on each other."

But John had no appetite. The mood and meaning of the story hung heavy on the air. He wanted to ponder it and think again on the contents of that soiled leather pouch. "You go on, Alex," he called out. "I'll be along later." He turned back to the settee and had sat in thoughtful silence for almost five minutes when suddenly he had the sensation of eyes upon him and looked up, and to his surprise saw Alex Aldwell still standing in the door watching him.

Startled, he was in the process of standing again when he saw the man smile at him and lift his hand in salute. Then he was gone.

What was that all about? Had the man wanted to say something else? No matter. John would rejoin him shortly in the ward. Whatever it was would keep until then. For now he meant what he had said. He needed a brief interim alone to deal with the memory of that amazing gem and his keen awareness of how it could serve a man.

He stared out across the waters of the Bosporus. No matter how hard he tried to discount the story, no matter how numerous the loopholes and how incredible the specifics, one unalterable fact remained: the diamond itself.

How theatrical, he thought, sinking into a near chair. He sat crumpled over and watched night fall, the room behind him growing dim. Yet paradoxically, as the light diminished, his vision grew clearer, his sense of purpose and direction sharper. It was what he had wanted, what he had always wanted, access to that rich land.

My God, Alex Aldwell was an oaf, a lovable oaf. Yet look what he carried about his neck. If he could do it, why not John? In that moment was contained the shock and forewarnings of enormous possibilities, and most gratifying of all, the sense of a future, and ultimately he saw a dazzling scene, a triumphant processional to Eden, an entourage of elegant carriages thundering across the moors, the gates thrown wide, a hundred voices shouting welcome, and in the lead, moving toward the steps where Harriet was waiting to greet him, John himself,

clothed in rich fabric of fashionable cut, his carriages
laden with gifts for Richard, for Mary, and tucked in his
pocket in folds of blue velvet, a diamond resembling Alex
Aldwell's.

He bent lower, overcome by the vision.

For two hours he sat thus, his mind working first in one
direction, then in another, weighing all aspects, trying to
temper the scheme with reason and prudence. In broad
outline, the plan seemed foolproof. What he desperately
needed was more specific information.

Then what was he sitting here for? Perhaps fortified
with dinner and a pot of tea, Alex would be willing to
talk the night away. All John wanted was harmless information; the cost of passage from Constantinople to
Bombay, the length of the overland route from Bombay
to Delhi, the supplies he might need, small questions
requiring only small answers, no reason why either of
them should even mention the now shared knowledge
of the fortune which hung about Alex's neck.

Then he was moving across the now darkened room.
As his thoughts increased, he broke into a run, and a few
minutes later he spied the broad double doors of the ward
up ahead, and he was already calling out the man's name,
"Alex!" scarcely aware of the men on either side who
raised feeble heads at his rapid passage, aware of nothing
but the curious congregation of nurses in the area around
his bed.

They appeared to be talking together in an excited
manner, at least a dozen, their full dark skirts obscuring
both his bed and Alex's. Behind them in the broad aisle,
he noticed the abandoned dinner trolley.

Whatever the nature of their distress, it did not concern
him. All he wanted was the attention of one man, and
accordingly, while he was still about thirty feet away, he
called again "Alex!"

As one, the huddled nurses turned, varying degrees of
surprise and worry on their faces. One, a tall stern-faced
woman, confronted him. "He's with you, isn't he?" she
asked, glancing beyond him as though he were being
followed.

As she leaned to one side, he looked toward Alex's

bed, thinking that perhaps the man had taken a turn for the worse. But he saw nothing except a stripped bed, a neat pile of used linen on the foot and a pillow which had been neatly rolled and placed at the head.

John took a step forward. "Where is he?"

The old nurse cut in. "We were hoping you might tell us." She cleared the nurses with a wave of her hand and pointed downward as though the bed itself were the culprit. "Look," she ordered.

"I . . . don't understand," he faltered.

"Neither do we," the nurse snapped. "But as you can clearly see, Mr. Aldwell is gone."

A nurse nearby murmured, "Even his things. Look. His valise is gone as well."

As the female voices buzzed around him, John continued to stare down on the empty bed. The old nurse moved closer. "If you can shed any light on the matter, Mr. Eden, we'd be most appreciative. We frown on patients simply packing their belongings and walking away."

Then all at once he began to understand. Of course. He should have known. The moment Alex had loosened that leather pouch about his neck, he must have known that he would have to flee. The contents of that pouch prohibited trust in any man. Besides, he had the tragic lesson of his friend to live with, the man called Rod who'd trusted someone and who now lay in a grave in Malta.

As understanding continued to illuminate his disappointment, John massaged his right shoulder in a thoughtless way, the bulk of his concentration aimed on his earlier scheme. Was it still negotiable? Did he really need Alex's experience in such simple matters? Routes to India were open to all. Still, he would miss the man.

Behind him he heard a soft step and looked over his shoulder to see the old nurse drawing near. "I'm sorry, Mr. Eden, that you've lost a new friend. This might lift your spirits, however."

She reached beneath her apron and withdrew several envelopes. "Mail." She smiled, then added, "A bit worse for wear, I'm afraid." She tossed the letters onto the bed. "They arrived from Balaklava this morning and were hand delivered by a gent along with that large envelope there."

He stared down at the scattered envelopes and from that distance recognized on several the delicate penmanship of Lila Harrington.

"Thank you." He smiled, then turned to the window and the night beyond. Somehow, after the excitement of the afternoon, he wasn't ready to step into the cloistered existence of the young girl on the Wiltshire downs. Again he picked up the thread of that earlier inspiration. Why not? Why not India? Admittedly it was a gamble, but it was better than England, an ancient dream waiting to be fulfilled.

Then it was settled, at that precise moment and in that tortured manner. And it remained settled for all of about three minutes until his head, moderately cleared of all drama and romance, started moving in another direction, along the bleak path of pragmatism.

He was penniless, his trunks were gone, his purse with his first month's wages from Brassey gone, everything destroyed in the massacre at Section Three.

He leaned forward until his forehead was resting against the stone windowsill. How briefly the gleam of hope had lighted his thoughts. How black now was the reality of his situation. What was he to do? Stay in this damnable hospital, shuffling about with the other invalids? Suddenly he brought his fist down against the stone sill, with an accompanying curse of violence. *"Damn Thomas Brassey!"*

It was several minutes before he was even aware of the hand on his shoulder, a soft voice urging, "Mr. Eden, come. I think you've been up and about long enough."

He looked over his shoulder and saw a young nurse balancing a dinner tray in one hand while she tried to turn him about with the other.

"Come . . ." She smiled. "A bit of food and a good night's sleep will put you in fine fettle again."

Still watching, he saw the carefully balanced tray begin to slip to one side. Quickly she righted it and placed it on the bed, brushing the letters to one side. As the various envelopes slipped to the floor, she caught the last one in time, a large brown packet whose weight had held it steady.

"I'm sorry," she murmured. "Here, you take this one and I'll retrieve the others for you."

He took the brown envelope and stared down at it, his name printed in a neat familiar penmanship on the front, and in the upper-left-hand corner in broad block letters an equally familiar name: THOMAS BRASSEY, CONTRACTOR.

He continued to stare down on it as he moved slowly back to the window, reaching for the candle as he passed by the table, arranging both candle and letter on the sill, and with his good hand he ran his fingers beneath the seal, lifting the flap, seeing the thickness of several pieces of stationery at first, then seeing more, the thick curled edges of . . . banknotes.

Quickly he stripped off the stationery, in the process releasing the contents, amazing contents, one, two, three, four, five, six fifty-pound notes, three hundred pounds altogether now scattered across the sill, and as though to make certain that his eyes had not deceived him, he thrust the candle forward and counted again.

His hand was trembling as he shook open the pieces of stationery, searching for a clue. But he found them mysteriously blank, not a sentence, not a word penned in explanation.

He stared at the pages, seeing no written word, but sensing volumes of unwritten ones. Those blank pages fairly reeked of confusion, of guilt.

Three hundred pounds! His full salary for four months plus a bonus of one hundred pounds. A fortune, at least a limited one, funds enough to purchase a most comfortable passage to India, with enough left over to see him well into the Muhammad's treasure room.

"Mr. Eden, here's the rest of your mail. Now, come along and eat your dinner." The thin voice came from behind, the little nurse again, unaware of the miracle that earlier she'd placed in his hands.

Suddenly he felt beside himself, and grinning, he reached forward with his good arm and encircled her waist, lifting her off her feet, whirling, her startled screams filling his ear.

"Mr. Eden, please . . ." she gasped.

At the end of the whirl, he released her. A most becoming blush covered her face as she stepped a safe distance away. "Mail is . . . generally medicinal," she stammered. "I'm afraid I've dropped the rest of it again." She pointed to the envelopes which had scattered during his mad whirl. Still backing away, she gained the center aisle. "I do believe I'll let you retrieve them this time." She smiled.

He grinned back at her, then returned to the bed and the dinner before him, the other letters still ignored. All he could think of was Alex Aldwell and his tales of the afternoon. For a period of time, both the living and the dead would have to be put behind him.

All that mattered was that he'd found his future, and more important, had found the means to take advantage of it.

It was all he had ever asked of life. Why up until now had it been denied him?

Three weeks later he stood on the poop deck of the elegant French sailing frigate *Belle Poule*, listening to the grumblings of the equally elegant Captain Romain Desfosses. For four days the beautiful sailing vessel had sat in the becalmed waters of Constantinople harbor, encircled and threatened by a flotilla of squat steam tugs.

"Horrible, aren't they?" the dapper little captain pronounced stiffly, glowering out at the tugs. "What could be more dreadful than the belching black smoke from those monsters?"

John nodded, concealing a smile, trying to appear sympathetic, yet enjoying literally everything. The delay of four days was nothing to him. He was comfortable enough in his spacious accomodations below deck. And he was certainly more than comfortable in his new fashionable wardrobe, courtesy of the sole English tailor who resided in Constantinople, who had provided him with a gentleman's wardrobe at half of what it would have cost him in London.

And he was greatly enjoying the semideserted French ship, which had been commissioned by the British War Council to make way for Malta, where it would pick up one hundred and seventy British dependents and take them on the prolonged journey to India. And he was even enjoying the constant company of the little French captain, who for four days, over magnificent port served in French crystal, had talked almost constantly on every subject imaginable.

And all the time that the captain talked, the uncooperative wind remained becalmed, and the steam tugs continued to circle, threatening. The harbor master had served notice. If the *Belle Poule* had not vacated the crowded harbor by the end of the week, he would be forced to attach a towline and let the steam tugs drag her out in a humiliating spectacle. Of course, John was pulling for the wind and for Captain Desfosses.

He leaned on the railing next to the captain and tried to look suitably sympathetic. He was on the verge of expressing that sympathy when suddenly from the top of the crow's nest he heard a cry. While he was in the process of looking up, he felt it on his face, a scarcely discernible sensation, little more than a caress. Quickly he looked at the captain, who had felt the same thing and who now stood frozen on the deck as though fearful of making a move.

Again from overhead John heard a faint cry from the crow's nest. Behind him on the broad deck he saw the seamen begin to stir, a few raising a tentative hand to the air as though testing.

As the tension about him increased, John had the feeling that he was standing in the center of a slowly whirling vortex. The ship began to rock, ever so gently, and looking out at the harbor, he saw a small white froth, some force ruffling the surface, the same force causing the planks beneath his feet to creak.

"Captain," John whispered hopefully.

"Shhh!" Still the taut waiting persisted, trained eyes and ears alert.

Then all at once it came, the cry from the crow's nest which thundered down on all, "WIND HO!" and the deck was alive with hundreds of seamen scampering up the main mast, loosening the upper sails without the help of even an elementary platform, clinging to the cobweb rigging like small blue spiders, defying gravity, releasing sail after sail, shouting joyously at each other as the wind caught in the billowing cloth and pulled the ship forward.

So scattered was his attention that John turned in all directions and caught only a glimpse of Captain Desfosses grinning broadly. "Weigh anchor!" the man shouted the length of the deck, and as a heavy metal clanging joined the wind sounds, John felt himself caught up in the excitement.

Overhead the stately sails were now filled to capacity, the magnificent vessel gliding through the green waters. The captain had disappeared, his short legs carrying him in a run to the bridge, where with what must surely be unbearable pride he would navigate his great ship through the harbor and point it toward the Mediterranean.

John grasped the railing and lifted his face to the wind. Below, he saw the steam tugs retreating, several dipping their flags in salute to the sailing ship. Hundreds of dinghies had appeared as if by magic, their oars also raised in salute.

Slowly he leaned forward, never dreaming that such a depth of emotion was possible for a mere wind and a stately sailing ship. Of course there was more to it than that, and he knew it. As the breaking waves and hiss of waters slapped against the side of the *Belle Poule*, he glanced over his shoulder back toward the green waters of the Bosporus and the Black Sea beyond. Very softly he told Jack Willmot good-bye, and immediately turned his attention to the passing silhouette of Constantinople.

To his left, over the sprit sail he saw the gray hulk of Scutari and the Barrack Hospital, and he said good-bye to that as well. As the *Belle Poule* cut swiftly through the waters, he turned his vision toward the Mediterranean and the prolonged journey ahead, first Gibraltar, around the coast of Africa to Free Town, then Luanda, Walvis Bay, the rigors of the passage around the Cape of Good Hope, up the other side to Port Elizabeth, past Malagasy and across the Indian Ocean to Bombay.

He stared downward at the breaking waves. Had there ever in the history of man been a more circuitous route? Considering his only true and ultimate destination, he had to answer himself no.

In spite of the cold cleansing stream of wind and spray, he smelled heather and lavender, and saw across the churning waters of Constantinople harbor a clear silhouette of Eden at sundown, when she was at her loveliest, in black outline against a fiery dusk.

Whatever was ahead of him, of this he was certain. That vision of Eden would be with him, would always sustain him and give him purpose.

London, June 1855

ELIZABETH HAD LOST track of the number of times she had written to John and addressed the letters to British Military Headquarters in Balaklava. What she'd not lost track of was the fact that she'd received no answer. In the vacuum caused by his silence, she found herself turning more and more to the comfort of Edward's old trunk, poring over the meager contents as though in search of a voice to end the silence.

Her house was quiet this night, Lord Kimbrough on holiday with his family in Brighton. And to the best of her knowledge, Willie Gladstone was on a hiking holiday in North Wales. She only received these two now in her bedchamber, and while each knew about the other, there appeared to be no resentment. For the rest of the time, her salon was filled with gossiping, chattering gentlemen who, weary of the affairs of state, looked to her to provide them with a relaxed safe setting where they might sip a glass of sherry, exchange a raucous joke.

Now, no one demanded more of her but Lord Kimbrough and Willie Gladstone, and she preferred it that way. She felt a bond of affection for both men, and there were other concerns filling her life now, namely her one consuming passion, which was to locate John, to make amends to him in whatever way was necessary, and to resume a life with him, giving him the support and loyalty she'd given to him as a child. With Willie Gladstone's help, surely they would locate him soon and bring him home safe and sound to her.

For several moments she knelt before the trunk, her hands flattened on top. "Pray God keep him safe," she whispered, and vowed to work overtime during these summer days at the large warehouse near Newport Market, where volunteer women met daily to prepare parcels for the front.

Thus resolved, she turned her attention back to Edward's trunk and with childish delight dragged it out from its hiding place behind the wardrobe and into a position where the lamplight was bright. In a state approaching reverence, she had just lifted the lid when suddenly she heard a sound in the entrance hall below.

Newly alert, she listened, her hand suspended in midair. She'd given Doris the night off and had extinguished the lamps in all her reception rooms. Then she'd locked the front door and had taken refuge in her bedchamber. She was expecting no one.

She heard it again, a discernible step on the stairs, and as her pulse increased, she drew herself slowly up from her seated position. It occurred to her to call out for the identity of the interloper. But at that moment she heard an enormous crash, a splintering of glass and a deep hoarse "Dammit!"

The voice was familiar if the curse was not, and feeling a surge of relief, she was on the verge of calling out his name when suddenly her door burst open and there stood the man himself, his gray cloak hanging limp off one shoulder as his hand massaged his knee.

"Willie!" she gasped, stifling a smile. "You're not hurt, are you? What in the world . . ." In addition to the rather comic appearance of one of England's most prestigious cabinet members rubbing a bruised knee was her own somewhat bewildered state. "I wasn't expecting you," she murmured.

With a smile she urged him, "Come, sit by the lamp and let me examine your wound. You gave me quite a start, you did."

He followed after her, his hand smoothing back his long graying hair. "Why did I startle you?" he asked. "There are only two keys loose, aren't there? Mine and Freddie's? Surely you knew it would be one or the other of us."

Belatedly she remembered. "Of course. You're right. I'm afraid I wasn't thinking clearly."

"Are you sorry," he asked, "that it's me and not Freddie?"

Taken aback by the question, she drew her dressing gown about her and considered restoring Edward's belongings to the trunk. "I'm always delighted to receive you, Willie," she murmured tactfully, "and I miss you sorely when you're gone."

He sat wearily in the comfortable wing chair, his long legs spread before him, seeing for the first time Edward's belongings scattered about the floor. "If I knew that you spent every night of my absence with a ghost, I'd have no cause to worry."

"You have none now." She smiled and knelt before him, blocking his vision of Edward's trunk. As she settled comfortably between his legs, she lifted one hand to the injured knee and commenced a gentle massage, while he responded by stroking her hair.

"You loved him very much, didn't you?" he asked, a sadness in his voice which she couldn't quite understand.

"He was a remarkable man," she said, and hoped he'd let it go at that.

But he didn't. "How often do you go through his things like this?" he persisted.

"As often as I feel it necessary."

"Does it bring him closer to you?"

"He inhabits me now. He can come no closer," she said. In a way she regretted the direction of the conversation. Edward occupied a portion of her heart which she allowed no other man to enter. "What has brought you to London?" she asked.

"You," he said.

There it was again, that sadness, as though he were facing a dreaded ordeal. "What is it, Willie?" she asked, settling back between his legs.

"I have . . . news, a most difficult message."

Again she heard it, that ominous tone, as though he were trying to warn her of something. Alarmed, she pulled free of his arms. "What message?" she asked.

He shook his head. "I considered sending a letter," he muttered, not looking at her. "But I found the courage to come myself."

A thought was forming in her head which she rejected. "Willie, what is it? Have you received word concerning . . ."

Still she could not speak the name. Then she had no need, for he inclined his head forward, confirming her fears.

"I received the dispatch while I was in Wales," he began, his normally rich voice a monotone. "I'm afraid it's several days old. There was an attack on civilian navvies by a large Russian contingent at a place called Section Three below Sebastopol." His voice broke. "Over two hundred fatalities, and scores wounded, the rail link destroyed by explosives."

As his voice rose, she realized that at some point she'd ceased hearing individual words.

His name is John Murrey Eden and he's my son, she heard Edward say, as clearly as though he were standing beside her.

She looked up into Willie's face. "John . . ."

He nodded. "He was in charge of the crew, along with his friend Jack Willmot. We've not received a complete fatality list, but . . ."

Silence closed about her. She glanced up toward the window, where the moon shone through the mist. Briefly she breathed her fill of stillness. Then someone was calling her name, but she had no idea who. All sense of the room, the house, even her own name vanished. She was cut adrift.

"Elizabeth, please," someone begged close behind her. But the terrible silence continued to encompass her, giving her the impression that she had destroyed something. Again Edward's voice came to her from a distance.

If something happens to me, take care of my son for me. Promise?

Then the voice disappeared, taking all light and warmth and hope with it, leaving her with the sensation of arms about her, trying to support her grief.

❧

Aboard the Belle Poule, First Night Out of Malta

FROM HIS TABLE for two near the bulkhead beneath the oil portrait of Louis-Napoleon, John looked apprehensively out over the crowded dining room, his eyes fixed on the far arch through which at any moment would appear the albatross with which he'd been burdened for the duration of this lengthy voyage.

Now look at him, palms sweating, out of sorts, awaiting a man he'd never met, a "cultivated English gentleman," Captain Desfosses had said, "the only other single civilian gentleman besides yourself, Mr. Eden, and with the dining room filled to capacity with officers and their families, would you be so kind as to allow this gentleman to share your table?"

But that was not the worst of it. The worst had come as the sly dapper little French captain had been departing from John's stateroom.

"Fraser Jennings is the gentleman's name," Desfosses had announced. Not until he had been halfway out of the door had he turned back, grinning. *"Reverend* Fraser Jennings, it is, Mr. Eden. *Merci!"*

John had called him back, or tried to, but by the time the awful realization had fully swept over him, that he would be taking every meal for the next six months with *Reverend* Fraser Jennings, it had been too late. The cheeky little French captain was no place in sight.

Reverend Fraser Jennings!

Damn! It wasn't fair, not fair at all, and he was on the verge of leaving his chair and letting his absence speak for itself, when, at that moment, a most unusual sight appeared in the archway. Now, *there* was a suitable dinner companion. Why couldn't Desfosses have guided that specimen to John's table, an Indian gentleman clearly, tall, most distinguished-looking in his slim white coat and wrapped leggings, an elegant white turban encasing his head.

So dramatic was his appearance that John noticed others looking up, a hush falling over the once chattering room. Strange, but John did not remember seeing an Indian embark at Malta. Now he leaned up in his chair as the gentleman continued to stand in the arch, as though aware of himself as spectacle.

A moment later John saw Captain Desfosses appear at the gentleman's side. Of course, what else? The scheming captain had kept this prize for himself. His annoyance mounting, John was in the process of looking away when suddenly he saw Desfosses take the Indian gentleman by the arm and point him toward . . .

John sat up. They were heading his way, the Indian carrying himself with great dignity through the crowded tables, both men drawing nearer, until at last they stood directly before John where he sat at the table.

"Ah, Mr. Eden," Desfosses beamed, "allow me to present your dinner companion, the Reverend Fraser Jennings, and, Reverend Jennings, may I present Mr. John Murrey Eden. I'm certain you two gentlemen will . . ."

But John was certain of nothing. As the man inclined his head in a formal Indian greeting, John slowly rose from his chair, his attention drawn to the "Indian's" eyes, as blue as Wedgwood plates, and to the fringe of sandy blond-gray hair which was visible beneath the white turban.

"Reverend . . . Jennings?" he stammered.

"Mr. Eden," the "Indian" responded stiffly. "I thank you for the generosity of sharing your table and I trust that my companionship will not be too tedious for you."

Still John gaped and was only vaguely aware of

Desfosses slipping away, as though he'd done his duty. Then he saw the "Indian" withdrawing the chair opposite him, sitting erect and launching immediately into the fruit salad, leaving John in a rather predominant standing position with the weight of approximately seventy sets of eyes upon him.

"Please do sit down, Mr. Eden," the man murmured. "We've provided theater for the others long enough."

At last John came to his senses and sat rapidly, aware of the sound of cutlery scraping against an empty bowl. In less than a minute the fruit salad opposite him had been devoured, and now he saw Reverend Jennings lift an imperious hand to the nearby steward, informing him without words to bring the next course.

Never had John seen such an appetite. In less than twenty minutes, without a word spoken between them, the man had consumed the complete menu, two stewards hovering over them now, one to accommodate Reverend Jennings, one to serve John, who was just commencing his oxtail soup.

Well, thus occupied, the man would require no conversation, although now curiously John found himself suffering from an acute desire to learn all about this blue-eyed Indian.

But to his disappointment, he saw the man conclude his cherry tart with a flourish, wave aside the offer of coffee, press his napkin primly to his lips and start to rise from the table.

"I thank you again, Mr. Eden," he said stiffly, "and because we must share this table, I see no reason for us to intrude into each other's privacy. I shall not be a burden to—"

Quickly John cut in. "I assure you, Reverend Jennings, you are not a burden. In fact, I was wondering if you would care to join me later in an after-dinner drink."

"I do not consume spirits, Mr. Eden," the man said, looking down his long slender nose, "and for the first three months of this voyage, I will not partake of any of the public rooms."

"For the . . . first three . . ." John tried to repeat, his bewilderment increasing.

"I am in a state of mourning, Mr. Eden, having recently buried my wife of forty-seven years."

Sobered by the grim announcement, John murmured, "I'm sorry . . ."

"Don't be, Mr. Eden. May was a good woman, a faithful partner, but she loathed India. There was a sense of shared relief as I lowered her into her English grave. Now, if you will excuse me . . ."

And with that he was gone, moving with dignity back through the tables, leaving John with his mouth open.

It was several moments before he shook the strange mood completely. At the same time, he made a quick reassessment. Whatever Reverend Fraser Jennings was or wasn't, he would not be a bore. In fact, John found himself eagerly looking forward to breakfast.

But the place opposite him was empty the next morning, and remained empty throughout luncheon, and it wasn't until nine o'clock that evening that John caught his next glimpse of Reverend Fraser Jennings, clad again in Indian garb, blue this time, matching his eyes.

"Ah"—John smiled as he approached the table—"I missed you this morning and at luncheon. I trust you are—"

"I partake of only one meal a day, Mr. Eden," the man said. "God frowns on dietary excess," and following this rather pompous announcement, he launched forth into one of the most impressive displays of gluttony that John had ever seen, consuming everything in sight as rapidly as possible. Throughout the silent meal, John found himself fascinated at the speed and skill with which the man could transport food to his mouth.

As the platters were emptied, John leaned forward, determined to engage the curious man in at least limited conversation. To this end he pushed aside his own dinner and subtly inquired, "May I ask your destination, Reverend Jennings?"

The man looked up as though startled both by the question and by John's presence. "You must make up your mind, Mr. Eden," he said sternly.

Taken aback, John faltered. "I . . . don't . . ."

"Do you want conversation or not? When I approached

this table last night, I felt a negative presence, a resentment that I—"

"What nonsense." John laughed nervously.

"It isn't nonsense, Mr. Eden. Mother India has taught me much. Generally I can discern a man's thoughts with great accuracy."

Embarrassed, John took momentary refuge in his napkin. "Perhaps in the beginning I was skeptical," he confessed.

"But you're not now?"

Damn! Why was it necessary to hold a discourse on the art of social conversation?

"You anger very easily, Mr. Eden. Did you know that? It could be a fatal flaw and should be checked."

Truly annoyed now, John was in the process of continuing his dinner, when without warning the man across from him laughed.

"Of course, I don't deny that this tedious voyage would be more pleasant with companionship," he said, a degree of warmth in his voice which John had never heard before. "But the desire must be mutual. In the process of talking, we will reveal parts of ourselves to each other, give ourselves away, as it were. Is that a gift you are prepared to receive, Mr. Eden?"

Dumbfounded, John did well to nod.

"Well, then"—Jennings smiled—"in answer to your question, my destination is India. Where else? I have a mission school in Delhi, established it thirty-five years ago. I've turned many a native eye toward redemption, Mr. Eden."

As the words tumbled out, John briefly regretted his insistence on conversation. Abruptly he caught himself. If the man *could* read thoughts . . .

"Born in Alfriston on the southern coast of England," Jennings went on, "and received my call from God while a boy of thirteen beneath the very tree where John Wesley preached his first sermon."

Still the words came, his voice growing lighter, a brightness in his eye which did not seem wholly appropriate for a grieving husband who had just buried his wife of forty-seven years.

"Educated at Oxford. I speak French, German, Arabic, Italian, Persian and Urdu. I prefer the rationalist philosophers such as Locke and Hobbes, and I play an aggressive and warlike game of chess. Do you play chess, Mr. Eden?"

Taken off guard by the direct question, John nodded. "On occasion I—"

Reverend Jennings beamed. "Then we have found our true salvation. Come, my boy. I never travel without mankind's two major supports, the Holy Bible and a chess set. Come, we'll have coffee in my stateroom, and I warn you, watch your queen. I'm barbaric where queens are concerned."

Before John could protest or decline, Jennings was standing behind his chair, taking him by the arm and literally propelling him through the dining room.

Great God, what had he done? Condemned himself to six months of chess, that's what he had done, condemned himself further to the companionship of a man who in a good clinical sense could be considered totally balmy.

"Come along, Mr. Eden." Jennings grinned again. "What an adventure we have before us! The only accurate way for one man to get to know another is over a chessboard. There true colors are revealed, philosophies made clear, souls purged. What a stroke of good fortune for both of us. Wouldn't you say?"

Then John heard it again, that slightly nasal Oxford purr. "Too late for doubts, Mr. Eden. At least for the duration of this voyage, we are bound together. At your insistence, if you will recall. . . ."

Six months later, John stood on the deck of the *Belle Poule* watching the crowded dock at Bombay, certain in his mind that he never wanted to see another chessboard as long as he lived.

In spite of his present irritation, he was forced to admit that the tedious and at times hazardous voyage had passed fairly rapidly. Not that he had learned a great deal more about Reverend Jennings. The man played chess the same way he ate, with an astonishing single-mindedness which did not permit too many verbal exchanges.

Still John was relieved that their companionship was coming to an end. He glanced over his shoulder now, waiting for the man to appear so that they might say their good-byes.

Below, John looked out over the dock at the fascinating scene with rising excitement. *India!* How often he had dreamt of this moment. The Great Adventure, the new horizon which had beckoned to him since he was a boy. Looking down, he saw hundreds of dark-skinned people, women with their faces concealed behind veiled saris, a solid crush of ox carts, cows roaming at will.

"Quite a pageant, isn't it? Can you imagine the challenge of diffusing among those inhabitants the light and influence of the Truth?"

John recognized the voice without looking, having heard it shout "Checkmate" countless times. "Reverend Jennings"—he smiled, extending his hand—"I wanted to say good-bye and thank you for an . . . interesting voyage."

"A pleasure, my boy," the old man replied, as though touched by sentiment. "Your chess tactics are rudimentary but sound. Stick with it and you could be a master one day."

John bobbed his head in thanks and reached behind for his valise. As he started toward the gangplank, a thought occurred to him. "One last favor, Reverend Jennings. Would you be so good as to direct me to the nearest railway station. As I said, Delhi is my destination and I—"

But he was not given a chance to finish, his voice obscured by the sudden laughter coming from Reverend Jennings. "Railway station?" the man gasped at the end of the mindless hilarity. Now he drew closer, still wiping at his eyes. "My poor boy," he mourned, "to the best of my knowledge, the nearest railway station is Euston in the north part of London. There *is* a narrow-gauge which departs from Calcutta when the times and the spirit permit, but . . ."

Shocked by the news, John lowered his valise to his

feet and stared with sinking spirits out over the bustling dock.

It was several moments later before he was aware of Reverend Jennings standing beside him, his arm about his shoulder in a paternal gesture. "God's hand again." The old man smiled benignly. "He brought us together six months ago, and now He is insisting that we stay together. As long as we are both going to Delhi, we might as well extend our companionship and travel as one."

Everything within John resisted the invitation. But how many options did he have? There was not a doubt in his mind that Fraser Jennings knew India, perhaps better than any other white man on the ship. And looking out again over that crowded dock, John was at last forced to admit that perhaps a trained and knowledgeable hand could be of assistance to him.

"I don't want to . . . intrude," he faltered.

"What intrusion!" Jennings responded expansively. "Come. Leave your luggage. We'll have it brought north at a later date. I have an extra pack. Fill it with what is essential to your comfort and soul. And don't be alarmed. Mother India will provide us with everything we need. She always has and always will."

Before John could speak, the tall lean man strode away to where the luggage was being disbursed. John saw him say something to the Indian porter, and a few moments later he heard Jennings calling to him from the top of the gangplank.

"Come, Eden," he shouted. "The greatest adventure of your young life awaits you." Without waiting to see if John was following after him, he started in great strides down the gangplank, his head lifted, shoulders back, as though he were marching toward Paradise.

In that instant John heard the foreign tongues on the dock raised in excited cries and shouts. He looked about once again at the elegant and safe decks of the *Belle Poule*, and he caught the spirit of the adventure and ran after Reverend Fraser Jennings, shouting, "Wait!"

Harrington Hall, Salisbury, Wiltshire, February 1856

ALTHOUGH SHE WAS capable of enduring much, it was as though the season were testing her.

From where she sat at her window seat, with Wolf curled comfortably beside her, Lila Harrington looked out over the frozen dusk. She had not enjoyed fresh air for days. According to Max, it was too cold for safety's sake. Thus denied the endless variety of her world, she'd been forced deeper into her imagination. But even that rich resource had faltered when confronted with events around her.

Her mother was seriously ill, the physician in constant attendance, her father plunged into deep grief. Lila had been forbidden to enter the sickroom.

There had been a tragic carriage accident on the road near her apple orchard. The injured, a woman and three small children, had been brought to Harrington Hall before being transported to Salisbury. All last night she had heard their cries.

And the worst, the open letter in her lap, usually the source of incredible happiness, now thrusting her deeper into a mood as frozen as the day.

Again she lifted the soiled, mussed paper, foolishly thinking that perhaps the message had altered since she'd first read it at noon. From John it was, dated May 1855, so long ago, and written in haste from Constantinople. When Max had delivered the envelope to her and she'd seen the familiar handwriting, she'd thought that it was an announcement of his homecoming. Instead she had read:

My dearest Lila,

Great news! At last circumstances have conspired in my favor, all omens are right and I'm off to India. Although I could write volumes, I must keep my message short, as time is pressing upon me. Suffice it to say that a dream is coming true for me, and I will try to the best of my ability, and when time permits, to share with you all the sights and sounds and sensations of my destination. I know it shall be a marvelous adventure, and although I don't know when I shall return, I will think of you always with fondness and devotion. Please give my best regards to Wolf and your parents. Find India on your world globe and think of me in my new happiness.

> Your humble servant,
> John Murrey Eden

She closed her eyes and let the letter fall limp in her lap. "Oh, Wolf," she whispered, "will we ever see him again?"

The big cat pushed lightly against her and lifted his chin so that she might stroke his whiskers.

"Why India, Wolf?" she demanded, her confusion rising. But there was no answer.

Again she closed her eyes and kissed the warm soft fur of the purring cat and hugged him close, although he disliked such a show of affection.

"Keep him safe for me, Wolf," she murmured, "and bring him back one day. Please . . ."

Then, in an attempt to dispel the tears in her eyes and banish her loneliness, she went to the fire and knelt before it and studied the flames until she found his face.

Kwandwa, Central India, February 1856

DAMN, JOHN CURSED as he trudged behind Reverend Fraser Jennings.

Damn, he cursed again, wishing that Jennings would hear him and halt his pace. For a brief respite, John was even willing to endure one of those blasted sermons. But either Jennings didn't hear or was locked into his own peculiar meditation, a mystical trance which seemed to make him immune to such human suffering as hunger, thirst, heat and fatigue.

For seven weeks, since December, they had been walking north to Delhi, a mere seven hundred miles distant from Bombay.

On occasion, Reverend Jennings, speaking a peculiar mix of Arabic, Persian and Urdu, had managed to get them a place in the back of a passing ox cart. Of the two modes of transportation, John was forced to admit that walking was preferable.

But fatigue and blistered feet were only part of his misery. The rest had to do with his shrunken belly and the perverse temperature which alternately left him with chills and fever, and his growing apprehension concerning Reverend Fraser Jennings himself.

As though Jennings was aware that he'd entered John's thoughts, he looked back, a smile on his tanned face. "God has provided us with a very comfortable place to make camp up ahead. I've stopped there many times, in that lovely grove of lime trees." He saw the fatigue on John's face and stepped toward him in concern. "Can you make it, my young friend? Here, lean on my arm."

John shook his head. He would collapse on this dusty road before he took the arm of a sixty-five-year-old man.

"You're unusually quiet this evening, John," Jennings said, walking easily up the incline. "Of course, I think I know the reason," he went on in his customary fashion, posing questions and answering them all at the same time. "It's this land, isn't it?" he asked, rhapsodically gesturing ahead to the Vindhya mountains.

The mountain range had been in view for three days. At some time they'd left the flat plains behind them, the terrain rising all the time, the countryside on occasion appearing as verdant and green as England.

"Ah, yes, this land," Jennings went on. "In this place, one is left with a mysterious crystallization. Even to the wayfarer such as yourself. "Do you feel it, John?" he whispered.

"I'm damn hungry, Jennings. That's the only communication going on within my spirit now."

As always, instead of being put off, Jennings laughed heartily, and patted John on the back, praising him for his honesty. "An honest spirit is close to God." He nodded admiringly. "Come. Not far now to rest and sustenance." Again he set a fast pace, leaving John with a rearview study of his grasshopperlike frame, his lankiness accentuated by his Indian garb.

John brushed aside a buzzing insect, winced slightly as his foot came in painful contact with a sharp pebble, and tried to take his mind off his various miseries. It had been days since he'd bathed, his trousers were torn from repeated contact with bramble, and his once white shirt-waist was now stained yellow from his own sweat. He'd not worn a coat since shipboard, and the gray one rolled in his knapsack served as his pillow each night.

But—and here was the mystery—as John seemed to be disintegrating, Jennings appeared to be embracing life with all the enthusiasm and zeal of a man half his age. Every day of the wearisome trek he'd managed to find the energy to lecture John upon the nature of Indian life, waxing eloquent on the immense structure of Indian society, which was based upon complications of caste, religion and land ownership.

During these long monologues, nothing had been required of John but the appearance of a listening ear, and that he'd given because he'd had no choice. But most of the time his attention had wandered in one of three directions, either back to Eden, which now seemed so remote as to belong to another planet, or to Lila Harrington, or ahead, to the mystical Delhi, where, with luck, he'd rapidly find his fortune and flee this place of vast uncharted distances and timelessness.

Suddenly he heard Jennings shout, "There! Just ahead, John. See it? Our place of refuge for the night!"

In spite of his fatigue, John increased his pace, caught up with his companion, and for the last few yards even led the way until at last he was seated beneath a tree on a cool carpet of moss, his head tilted upward, eyes closed.

He heard movement about him but did not have to open his eyes to know what was happening. The sounds were unmistakably those of Jennings "pitching camp," a euphemism which meant that the man had removed his knapsack, had spread out a cloth and on it had placed their "supper," another euphemism, which meant two pieces of dried fruit and a flat round cake of flour which tasted like wood and was called chupattis.

The next voice he heard was Jennings' inviting him to "Come and wash before partaking of God's bounty." Now he trudged wearily after the man to the edge of a small brook, where, bending down, the two of them washed the dust from their faces and hands.

Somewhat restored by the cooling water, John sat back on the bank and unlaced his boot, searching for the pebble that had caused him grief for the better part of the day.

A few moments later, stripped and fully submerged in the shallow water, he looked up into the night sky and saw a familiar configuration of stars, the same he'd seen many nights walking the headlands of Eden.

Was there anywhere in this world a place called Eden?

Before he had a chance to search for an answer, he saw a small beacon fire at the top of the incline, saw the familiar lank figure holding a worn Bible, intoning, "The Lord is my Shepherd, I shall not want . . ."

But John *did* want, would have given anything that it was in his power to give to be away from this place and from that man who clearly coveted after the ways of those he saved.

Jennings had roused John early this day, telling him they must walk twelve miles beyond their prescribed course the day before. Jennings had promised a group of Thuggees, religious zealots, that he'd visit their temple in Bindhachal in exchange for safe crossing of their territory. This had enabled their journey to proceed on a direct line to Delhi rather than having to skirt the huge territory held by the potentially dangerous warriors.

All morning long, Reverend Jennings told him that it was just a theatrical show, and that he was not to take anything he saw at Bindhachal too seriously. Still, apprehension accompanied John on the day's long walk.

About midafternoon they came down from the foothills of the Vindhya mountains and John found himself once again on a dust-swirled plain. The traffic on the road seemed to be increasing. Now and then a caravan of camels passed them by, the heavily veiled riders scarcely looking down from their rocking perches. And there was an almost continuous line of ox carts interspersed with steadily increasing pedestrian traffic.

But worse than anything was the proliferation of beggars. Most of them were maimed, a few eyeless, one with half his face eaten away by disease. They ranged in age from very young children to old men and women, most of them sitting in numb despair by the roadside.

On the other side of this town, Saugor, John looked up to an impressive sight, a second settlement, light-hued sandstone structures, one building the largest that John had seen for several weeks, a multistoried affair of mixed architecture graced with two copper-domed mosques, as though medieval Muslim art had joined tentative forces with staid, mid-nineteenth-century English architecture.

The building was surrounded by several smaller ones and the entire compound sat in the middle of a vast parade ground. Treeless, the settlement rose with the suddenness of a mirage, and crowning all, on an arrow-straight standard planted atop the largest structure, was the Union Jack, fluttering now and then under the pressure of a tentative breeze.

John needed no identification, but Jennings gave him one anyway. "British Cantonment for Central India," the man muttered, revealing his feelings as he generally did in all matters.

As they topped a rise of land, they stopped for an unbroken view. A large regiment was on parade. From this distance they looked like toy soldiers.

"Good little boys, aren't they?" Jennings grumbled.

Puzzled, John asked, "Would you have them go home?"

"They never should have come," Jennings said, "and one day they *will* go home. The sepoys will see to that."

"Will you go with them?" John smiled, playing a half-hearted devil's advocate.

Jennings looked at him. "God sent me here, not to corrupt or exploit, but to spread His Word. When my work is over, He will tell me."

Against such quiet conviction, John, as always, had no effective rebuttal.

Beyond the parade ground, in the shadow of the cantonment, John saw an appealing spectacle, a cluster of whitewashed bungalows, each house bordered by flowers and hedge. On the lawns fronting these inviting bungalows, he saw colorful arrangements of ladies in billowing gowns, seated beneath the trees, waited on by white-jacketed natives, the silver of a tea service glistening in the afternoon sun.

As they drew closer, John heard the sound of a woman's laugh and the delighted squeal of well-fed children as they romped over the green, two fat terriers joining in the fun. It might have been a scene in Hyde Park. Of one thing John was certain. The lovely white-and-green spectacle bore no relationship to anything else he'd observed during their long trek.

Finally he trudged after Jennings, though a few yards down the road he stopped and looked back, suddenly aware of how low and weak the wall was surrounding the ladies, not strong enough to keep out anything of substance, let alone the dramatic differences between two worlds.

As Jennings had predicted, they approached Bindhachal at dusk, a fiery sunset outlining the temple itself. They had not stopped for food or rest all day save for the slowed pace at Saugor, and now John found himself gazing upon this remarkable sight through eyes dimmed by hunger and fatigue.

Never had he seen anything like it, a broad dusty road leading past a line of low cottages, the road itself clogged with people, all eyes turned toward the shrine, a dazzling arrangement of gold spires, set in gradations, the uppermost pointing heavenward. Ornately carved columns, six on each side, supported the roof and gave access to the inner chamber of the temple. Hundreds of supplicants crowded on the steps and across the pavilion, apparently having come from all over India to propitiate the goddess.

Jennings whispered, "This is it, the holy place of the Thugs."

Although impressed, John had seen enough. Caught in the push of supplicants, he had just managed to catch the sounds coming from within the dark recesses of the temple, shrill cries like bleating sheep or weeping women. Since there was no aspect of mind or dimension of imagination in his entire existence to prepare himself for the sights and sounds, he felt only a powerful compulsion to vacate the place and leave the incense and cries to those who worshiped here.

As he was about to turn away, he felt an iron grip on his arm and looked back into the amused eyes of Fraser Jennings. "No cause for alarm." The man smiled. "Come, we must humble ourselves before the goddess Kali." With a sense of melodrama, he leaned closer. "We are being watched," he whispered. "Make no mistake of that."

While John was listening, his attention was drawn away by the sight of something at his feet on the temple steps, a stream of red spilling down the stairs, bare feet walking through it, leaving red footprints.

"It's blood, all right," Jennings whispered, "but harmless, I assure you. The British permit them to slaughter animals."

"Jennings," John began, "I think I'll wait—"

"No, you won't," Jennings said sternly. "I promised them your supplication, too, and they will see you bowed."

Hurrying to catch up, he drew even with Jennings as they passed beneath the arch. His eyes at first had difficulty adjusting to the torchlit interior, but a moment later he saw all too clearly and too much.

The inner chamber was vast, the floor covered with black mosaic tile, about forty priests arranged in a circle near the end, some engaged in self-flagellation, the screams of their pain blending with the shrieks of goats and lambs whose throats were being cut before the monstrous goddess, the entire room one screaming, bloodsoaked arena, presided over by an immense ebony statue, Kali the Terrible, the blood goddess, consort of Shiva, naked, with her sword, noose and bludgeon, and stuck all about with human skulls.

John took three steps inside the arch, then stopped. The priests appeared to be in a trance of ecstasy, though now he noticed that one or two looked up from their bloody rituals, their dark eyes focused on Jennings, then himself. With no words spoken, the message spread, and one by one, the men, their robes bloodied, stepped away from the goddess.

Where only moments before the chaos had been deafening, now all that could be heard was heavy breathing, and on occasion the pitiful bleating of a lamb whose life had been briefly extended by the appearance of two Englishmen.

John heard Jennings whisper, "Come near. Kali awaits us."

In spite of the new tension in the chamber, John followed after, keeping a wary eye as they passed down the line of priests, a few holding at the ready yellow silk nooses tied around a silver rupee with which the stranglers had been killing the animals prior to cutting their throats.

Ahead, he saw Jennings standing before the goddess as

though transfixed. Watching closely, John saw the man lift his arms to his chest and incline his head. Three times he performed this ritual of supplication.

All about him the priests seemed to push closer, those nooses still clutched in their hands, their dark faces revealing nothing at Jennings' worshipful stance. It did seem a weak gift in contrast to the bloodied floor. The place demanded more than three short bobs of the head.

Suddenly—and where the instinct came from, he couldn't say—John experienced an urge, not merely to witness, but to participate. For all the horror surrounding him, there was an honesty to the place, a sense that here, if nowhere else, a man could give vent to his baser desires and impulses.

For a moment longer he tried to defeat the impulse. But it was strong, and demanding to be acted upon, to provide a fitting finale for this "theatrical."

With a lightning-quick movement his hand shot forward and grabbed the yellow noose from a near priest, and still moving at top speed, he came up behind Jennings, thrust the noose over his head, duplicating the sensations which he'd just witnessed—the knee thrust forward against the back, the noose drawn tightly about the man's throat, the coin angled into place near the windpipe, then a sudden thrust of energy which toppled the victim backward and left him gasping, his face upside down in John's vision, his hands clawing at the stricture about his neck.

But of greater interest to John than Jennings' fear-stricken face was a peculiar sound he'd heard at the instant of attack, a collective intake of breath, as though the priests themselves had been shocked by the reenactment of their own religion.

His attention was drawn back to the sputtering upside-down face of Jennings. "What in . . ." the man gasped, his fingers still clawing at the noose about his neck.

John grinned. "Just a theatrical, Jennings. No cause for alarm."

The parroted words seemed to bring the man little comfort, and he continued to thrash about. For a moment John pulled the noose tighter, feeling adrift somehow, as though his body in some miraculous way had been taken possession of by the ghosts of the ancient Thugs. Not until he noticed Jennings' face turn a shade of blue did he ease his grip on the noose. At the same time he looked up into the priests' faces and was granted a reward almost as great as that collective gasp. In those dark visages which once had caused him such fear, he saw fear.

It started with the priest from whom he'd grabbed the yellow noose, only a flicker of a smile. Slowly it spread, splitting one dark face after another, joined here and there by a giggle, that sound amplified into full laughter as the circle of priests pushed closer, their hands outreaching as though desiring to touch the one who so effortlessly mastered their sacred religion.

John grinned back, feeling a kinship. Suddenly the priest on his right lifted his head and shouted a sharp command to the rear. A few moments later, John found himself standing at the center of their circle while three adorned him in a black turban, then draped a long black robe over him, bringing up the tail between his legs and securing it to a leather girdle.

He permitted the adornment, relished it, catching sight now and then of Jennings, who apparently had had all his pompous authority squeezed out by his brief tenure under the noose.

Well, John would make his apologies later. For now he was enjoying himself. At some point an earthenware bowl of wet mud appeared, and with his eyes and mouth tightly closed, he permitted them to rub it over his face and neck.

Then the adornment was over. Lacking a mirror, John had no conception of the total picture. But he could look down at the curled sandals on his feet, the robe drawn tightly between his legs, the leather girdle securing the upper half of the robe, draped over one shoulder. The mud was drying on his face and neck. He returned the gaze of his admirers, feeling less an Englishman and more an Indian than he'd ever dreamt possible.

The priest who had issued the command for the transformation stepped forward, his dark face sobered. In his hand he held the long yellow noose, the silver rupee knotted at the middle.

"Rumal," he pronounced, and extended the noose to John.

John looked to Jennings, who was now on his feet. The old man smiled. "He wants you to take it."

Then the priest was speaking at a rapid pace, apparently unmindful of the fact that John was not understanding a word. Abruptly John lifted his hand and summoned Jennings to step forward. The man came, obviously bearing John no ill will and grateful to be included in the ceremony.

With his translator beside him, John nodded to the priest, indicating that he could continue, and he did, the staccato sounds blending with the soft Oxford hum as Jennings translated. "He says that although you have not been initiated stage by stage into the art of Thuggee, you have nonetheless proven yourself worthy to wear the rumal. And further, he says let any man once taste of the Goor and he will be a Thug, though he know all the trades and have all the wealth in the world."

The voices fell silent, and as the sense of ceremony increased, John saw the priest withdraw a coarse-looking yellow lump from the folds of his robe and extend it forward.

Ever helpful, Jennings whispered, "You're to eat it."

Hesitating for the first time, John looked at the lump in the man's hand.

"Take it," Jennings whispered. "It's a rare honor."

Finally John lifted the lump to his mouth. The taste was sweet, the texture like sand. But as all were watching, he had no choice but to bite down and swallow the mixture.

With a lift of his hand, the priest signaled for attention. Again the twin voices took over. "He says," Jennings whispered, "that you are a brother, that you have demonstrated the instinct of the wild beast, and that from now on you shall ride a horse like a true Thug and wear your rumal and show a front."

Ride a horse! John could think of nothing he'd like better, but he had no horse. Jennings was there, still translating, "And finally he says that the sanctity of this temple is always open to you, that no matter what, you are now a true son of Kali and she will protect you from all adversity."

Apparently the presentation was over, and John was aware of the priests on either side moving him toward the arch which led to the door of the temple.

Outside, he noticed that the dusk had turned to night, though in the area surrounding the temple there were dozens of lit torches, casting a red glow over the scene.

Jennings saw it first, for John heard a gasp and only then did he look toward the bottom of the steps, where he saw a massive black stallion, saddled, a priest holding the reins.

"It's a gift," Jennings whispered as the priest placed the reins in John's hand, "befitting a brother Thug."

John stroked the flank of the magnificent animal. "You must thank them for me."

As Jennings' voice filled the hushed silence, John placed his foot in the stirrup and swung up into the saddle, consciously striking a pose.

They saw him astride the handsome animal and heartily approved. Lifting his hand in salute, John urged the horse forward, suddenly desirous of leaving the place while his luck still held and while he was still vaguely aware of who and what he was.

With Jennings trotting behind, John led the way down the road at a slow pace, a peculiar sound following after him, more than just the rhythm of Jennings' sandals slapping against the dirt. This new sound was a high-pitched lament, wailing voices raised in wordless cries.

In spite of his instinct to look back, John kept his eyes straight ahead. What he felt was inconceivable and irrational, a sense of melancholy at his separation from a group of barbarians who earlier had terrified him.

It wasn't until they were two or three miles removed from the shrine that John reined in the horse and led him to one side of the deserted road and waited for Jennings to catch up. The mud on his face and neck had now dried, causing a pinching sensation. The girdle had been pulled too tight and his hair beneath the turban begged to be scratched. But he waited out all these discomforts and watched the trotting figure approaching in the night.

As Jennings drew near, John prepared himself for the apology that he knew he must deliver. But he was never given that chance. Instead, the man burst upon him with a breathless enthusiasm that had nothing to do with his recent exertion. "My God, what a master stroke!" Jennings grinned. "You're an Indian, that's what you are," the man went on. "By God, but you almost fooled me, you did. I thought you were English through and through, to the quick, to the marrow, to the heart." He laughed outright, lavishing John with affectionate attention.

At the first break, John ventured a tentative apology. "You're . . . not angry?"

"Angry! It was a master stroke, that's what it was. I'm only regretful that I didn't think of it myself."

"Your . . . throat?"

"Is fine, fine. What an experience! I've never seen the Goor ritual before. I daresay no white man has." He stepped back. "Do you realize what an honor has been bestowed upon you?"

Impressed by the man's enthusiasm, John still was suffering from the rapid transition of Thug back to Englishman. "Surely you don't approve of their cutthroat ways?" he asked.

For the first time since they had paused by the side of the road, Jennings appeared to be speechless. He contemplated John and his question with an intense gaze. Clearly the battle was a painful one, his Christian god in open warfare with his Indian gods.

There was a sense of incompleteness to the exchange, and John was on the verge of pursuing it further when suddenly Jennings suggested that they pitch camp here for the night, get a good rest before starting on the road to Delhi in the morning.

But in the quiet of the evening, John thought he could still hear the priests' keening. "No, let's go farther down the road." Tossing the reins of the horse to Jennings, he suggested, "You ride."

He didn't wait to see Jennings mount, and led the way back to the deserted road, where a half-moon struck the dust and caused it to resemble snow. He was aware of the horse walking behind him, Jennings giving him the lead for the first time in weeks.

"Walk like an Indian," Jennings shouted. "You have been blessed beyond the conception of most men. You are now Kali's son. Walk like it!"

But John did nothing to alter either his stance or his pace. His head down, he wondered if Fraser Jennings had any notion of how close he'd been to death this day, how it had consumed all the rational discipline at John's command to resist the mysterious forces loosed at Bindhachal.

Delhi,
March 1856

THREE WEEKS LATER, having followed the left artery of the Ganges through Cawnpore and Agra and Aligarh, leading the black stallion between them, they came out onto a high plateau and looked down upon an incredible sight.

There was Delhi; and high above the Jumna River, presiding over the bazaars and teeming alleyways of the walled city, stood the fortress palace of the Moghul emperors.

For once Jennings was silent, apparently sensing John's awe and sharing in it. "No matter how many times I leave and return," he murmured, "the sight of that city always brings tears to my eyes."

John glanced at him, impressed to see moisture on his face. During the last few weeks, since Bindhachal, he'd grown fond of the old missionary, and now that the time had come when they would shortly part company, John found himself dreading it. Still, his "business" in Delhi had nothing to do with Jennings, and the sooner the separation came, the better.

There were a few hours left. John had promised to take

a look at Jennings' mission school and to have dinner with him. Though the man frequently had been a bore and a puzzle on their long journey, John felt indulgent of him, the kind of indulgence which always marks imminent separation.

"Have you seen inside?" John asked, motioning toward the fortress palace, knowing that such a simple question would keep the man talking for half an hour.

"Oh my, yes." Jennings smiled, wiping away the tears of homecoming. "I've been a guest there many times. I've played chess with Bahadar Shah Zafar, though he's a godless man. He's little more than a pensioner, you know, lives altogether at the mercy of the British."

John saw the scowl on the man's face as he turned to the right. "There it is, there is the contagion," and he pointed toward a large cantonment on the outskirts of Delhi. "There are our British brethren," he muttered.

Nothing more was said all the way down to the banks of the river, though now John noticed an increase in traffic, hundreds, or so it seemed, passing back and forth across the curious boat bridge.

Presiding over all this multitudinous activity was a scattering of British soldiers, looking stylish and well-fed in their red tunics and white shakos, like large clear targets in a sea of brown and gray and black.

But of consuming interest to John was the palace itself, looming larger, protected by high red sandstone walls, perhaps two miles around.

Again Jennings' pace increased. John trotted behind, his head swiveling in all directions. It wasn't until they were approaching the main gate which led into the Red Fortress that Jennings slowed his pace. He drew to one side out of the crowded street and waited for John to catch up, then pointed up to the beautifully carved central arch.

"Do you know what it says?" Jennings asked. Without waiting for the answer, he squinted upward toward the massive arch and read, *"If there be a paradise on earth, it is here, it is here, it is here."*

A dust cloud swirled up. Grit stung John's eyes. It would be paradise if those red sandstone walls were as generous with him as they had been with Alex Aldwell. "Is this the only gate?" John called out above the noise of street traffic.

"Oh, no," Jennings shouted. "There are four gates, but they are kept locked now."

The "now" was significant, and John wanted to explore it, but again Jennings was pushing through the narrow streets, as though to signal there would be no more stops, not with the anticipation of "home" drawing him like a magnet.

John tried carefully to note the twists and turns. The next time he passed this way, he would be alone, though it occurred to him that finding his way back to the Red Fortress would require no intelligence. The walls and onion domes of the palace loomed over every other structure in Delhi.

As he walked, he ran through in his mind the plan which he'd half-concocted during this interminable trek. He would see Jennings to his mission school. Then he would take his leave this very night. If an oaf like Aldwell could gain access to the palace, he was certain that he could as well. He still had over a hundred pounds left, sewn inside the leg of his trousers. If he needed to offer bribes, the money was there.

Once inside the gates, he remembered specifically Alex Aldwell's direction to the underground treasure house. If all went well, he would retrieve his horse and be across the river by first light. Again, fate and God willing, he could reduce the torturous ten-week walk to a swift three atop the horse. Back in Bombay, he would take his remaining moneys and purchase a ticket on the first sailing ship leaving for Portsmouth.

So engrossed was he in these thoughts that at first he was unaware of Jennings calling to him. "John, this way! Hurry, they have spotted us."

Running to catch up, he saw Jennings waiting for him beside a low whitewashed stone wall. The gate was open and he saw a small courtyard, a proliferation of chickens running loose, and beyond the dust and chickens, he saw a small compound of bungalows, one large one with a broad portico, while stretching out to the left were three smaller cottages.

As John drew near, he saw the emotion in Jennings' face and heard it in his voice as he muttered, "Home!" That was all he said, for at that moment the double doors of the large bungalow flew open and about thirty dark-skinned children ran down the steps, their eyes bright with affection, their arms outstretched. In the next minute Jennings was inundated, laughing and crying all at the same time, his broad arms trying to lift as many children as he could, his hands constantly stretching forward to pat a head or stroke a cheek.

John stepped back out of the turmoil. As the reunion showed no signs of breaking up, John settled wearily on the low stone wall. Gazing over the tops of the children's heads, he saw a new gathering on the steps of the bungalow, several adults, natives in native dress, save one, a dark-eyed, dark-skinned young woman who seemed to be focusing on Jennings with the same degree of adoration displayed by the children.

She was coming slowly down the steps now, her long black skirt and white shirtwaist reminding John of Harriet on days when she'd visit the kitchen court.

From where John sat she appeared young and very pretty, her dark hair pulled back and fashioned in a knot, a shyness apparent though blending compatibly with her bearing. A little boy accompanied her, five, perhaps six, in native dress, tightly wrapped leggings, white slim jacket.

Intrigued, John continued to watch as step by hesitant step the young woman and the boy approached the circle of children. As far as John could tell, she'd never taken her eyes off Jennings, though he was certain that Jennings had not seen her as yet.

All at once he did. That bending white head suddenly froze in its greetings. Simultaneously John saw the young woman duck her head and draw the boy even closer, as though embarrassed by the intensity of Jennings' gaze.

The peculiar encounter held for several minutes. Then Jennings lifted a hand toward the three Indian women standing on the steps, and within the moment the women were herding the children back into the bungalow.

In an incredibly short time the courtyard was empty save for Jennings and the young woman and the boy.

Would he never greet her? John wondered, feeling an intimacy in the moment, but refusing, out of curiosity, to turn away. At last the old man was moving toward her, one hand outstretched as tentatively he touched her face.

There was a bond between them, of that John was certain. But what sort of bond, he had no idea. He saw a sadness in the young woman's face now, a remarkable face, rich smooth olive complexion, dark eyes, perfectly sculptured nose and cheekbones.

Then the strange nongreeting was over and John saw Jennings scoop up the young boy, who, unlike the other children, seemed ill-at-ease in his arms and within the moment struggled for his freedom and hopped down to the woman, burying his face in her full black skirt.

So engrossing was the encounter that again John was caught unawares as Jennings called to him. "I'm sorry," he apologized.

John smiled, still unable to take his eyes off the young woman, whose beauty increased close at hand.

As though eager to put his blunder to rights, Jennings said to the young woman, "This is John Murrey Eden, Dhari. We passed several enjoyable months together at sea, over endless chess games, and we've been companions on the road." He looked back at John, as though to confirm his identity. "While not quite brothers, we are, I hope, good friends. Please greet him warmly and make him feel welcome."

He was in no way prepared for her response, one slim hand outstretched in greeting, and a musical, cultivated English voice saying gently, "Mr. Eden. I'm grateful for your fellowship with Reverend Jennings, and I'm certain that you were a source of spiritual strength in his grief."

John gaped. Grief? What grief? He'd witnessed many moods in Jennings, but grief had not been among them. Then he remembered the dead wife, May.

Jennings said almost brusquely, "Well, come. As you can see, Dhari, we're both in sore need of a hot tub. Tonight at dinner we will fill your pretty head with tales beyond your imagination. Won't we, John?"

John did well to nod, and picked up his knapsack and trailed behind as Jennings gave the young woman a spate of instructions having to do with dinner and the children, a brief discussion of menu, and finally, "Take Mr. Eden to May's room, would you, please? See to his needs. I can see to my own."

From where John stood, he thought he saw an objection on her face, but at that moment the little boy, ignored for long enough, made his presence known by a sharp tug on her skirt. Smiling, she caressed the child's head. "This is my son, Mr. Eden. His name is Aslam. He's six and is trying very hard to master your beautiful language."

His mind still splintered by the confusing circumstances, John nodded to the little boy. "Aslam." He smiled and extended his hand to the child. Mother and son! Where and who was the father?

"Go with Dhari, John," Jennings insisted, climbing the steps to the bungalow, for the first time displaying a weariness of both step and mind. John watched until the man had disappeared from sight. What had happened to his incredible endurance? There hadn't been a day on the road when he hadn't outwalked and outtalked John.

"If you're ready, Mr. Eden, I'll take you to Mrs. Jennings' room."

He hurried after her, his eyes struggling to adjust to the shadowy interior after the brightness of sun. As they passed the kitchen, he looked in and saw several of the native staff filling two large copper tubs with steaming water.

"This way, Mr. Eden. Here it is."

And there it was, the dead wife's room, small, though comfortably arranged, with an inviting feather bed covered neatly with a flowered coverlet, one bureau with a well-worn Bible resting atop, one wardrobe, one straight-backed chair beside a small table with a wicker sewing basket, and two large color reproductions, one of Christ at Gethsemane, and the other a likeness of Queen Victoria at her plump stern worst.

While John was briefly inspecting the room, he saw the young woman place his knapsack on the bare floor, then lovingly smooth the coverlet, her eyes filled with mourning.

"If it's any comfort, Dhari," John said, "I won't be here

long. If there's any other room in which I can simply wash and—"

"Oh, no," she said hurriedly. "Reverend Jennings wants you here, and here you shall stay."

He watched as she continued to move about the room. "Did . . . you know her well? Mrs. Jennings, I mean."

She looked up, her slight frame seemingly inadequate to support her grief. "She saved my life," she said, and could not finish and turned away to the small window which gave a view of the rear courtyard and rows of long clotheslines adorned with what appeared to be hundreds of small white shirts.

John focused on the drying clothes, not certain what kind of comfort he should offer the young woman.

She turned back to him with a smile. "I'm sorry. I've tried for months to prepare myself. She was so ill when they left here. I knew then that I would never see her again." She shook her head, one hand smoothing back a strand of ebony hair. "I *am* grateful to you for accompanying Reverend Jennings. Rosa said he would not come back if Mrs. Jennings died. Thank you for returning him to us."

Again he had the uneasy feeling that they were talking about two different men. In spite of his fatigue, he longed to change the subject, to make inquiry about where she came from, and how she had mastered English so beautifully, and what precisely was her role in this mission school. But he felt the questions would be inappropriate, and at that moment two Indians appeared in the doorway carrying an enormous copper tub of steaming water between them, and following behind was a woman bearing a stack of linens.

Dhari was transformed into a blur of efficiency, instructing them in native tongue where to place the tub, taking the linens from the woman and turning at last to John with a startling order. "Take off your clothes. Rosa will wash them and have them pressed in time for dinner."

He hesitated, thinking of the pound notes sewn inside his trousers. "These are beyond restoration." He smiled, indicating the clothes on his back. He handed her the knapsack and a weak explanation. "There's a soiled change in there which could do with some attention, though."

She took the knapsack and handed it to Rosa. Alone, she again ordered, "Take off your clothes," and at the same time drew open the top drawer of the dresser and took out a long-handled scrub brush and a dish of soap.

John counseled himself to be calm. "I've taken up quite enough of your time, Dhari. I'm certain you have other—"

"Don't you want me to scrub your back?" she asked, surprised. "Reverend Jennings would be angry with me if—"

"No," John said as gently as possible, part of his mind censoring the old buzzard for placing such temptation in his path.

"Then there's nothing more I can do to make you comfortable?" she asked from the door.

"You've done enough." He smiled. "A bath, a rest, and I promise to be better company at dinner."

Again she gave him the gift of that remarkable smile. "And I, too," she said. "We'll make it a fete and put all death and grief behind us." The smile faded. "Mrs. Jennings would have wanted it that way."

Then she was gone. Never had he seen such exotic beauty. What were the rules here, he wondered, and should he take them seriously? And why was Mrs. Jennings' bedroom on one side of the bungalow and Reverend Jennings' on the other? And how often had the old man allowed Dhari to scrub *his* back?

Struggling against his fatigue, he stripped off his foul-smelling clothes, grabbed the brush and soap where she'd left them on the table and sank slowly into the water, his eyes closed in enjoyment.

With his knees raised, he leaned back against the copper tub.

Dhari. A pretty name. Damn the rules! Was it too late to call her back? Even now she might have been wielding the scrub brush.

He was halfway out of the tub, water dripping, when

suddenly his eyes lifted to the opposite wall, to the suffering face of Christ.

But it wasn't that. He could deal with that face. It was the other, the one next to it, the stern flat eyes and fleshy jowls of Queen Victoria that sent him sinking backward into the tub.

Oh, God, he was too tired anyway.

The dining room was small, with Spartan furnishings, reminding him of farm cottages at Eden. But that was the only point of recognition. For the rest of it, he felt bewildered and groggy from his heavy nap.

As the woman named Rosa served his plate with a rich red pungent mixture of chicken and vegetables, he looked about the table and thought how helpful it would be if everyone could just manage a degree of consistency.

For instance, there was Dhari seated opposite him at table, her Western dress gone, adorned beautifully in a pale blue silk sari, one shoulder bared, the fabric so fine as to reveal her breasts in perfect outline. Her hair was loosed in a black shimmering cascade which extended below her waist.

Then there was Reverend Jennings, conversely clad in a somber, tightly cut black frock coat, highly polished black boots, and resting beside him on the table, within easy reach, a well-worn dog-eared Bible. In addition to these obvious changes, there was something else as well, a subtle inner change, the light of childlike enthusiasm gone from his eyes. Now he looked old, his graying hair brushed rigidly back, something alarming in the zeal with which he stared ahead as though aware of besetting temptation on either side.

After all plates had been served, John heard Jennings command, "We will bow our heads in prayer."

And they did, Dhari's falling forward as though it had been snapped downward by a cord, and Jennings following suit. As the man intoned, "But when I looked for good, evil came, and when I waited for light, darkness came . . ." John lifted his head just enough to make an attempt to understand where he was.

Four servants, two male, two female, he noticed, were

standing near the door with bowed heads. All in native dress, they seemed to be responding to the dismal voice reciting the dismal tale. Job, most likely.

"And we thank thee, O Lord," Jennings prayed, "for our safe return to our children, who need us, and for the companionship of John Murrey Eden. Be with this child of Yours during his stay in Delhi and assist him in finding what he is searching for, peace for his heart, and strength for his soul."

John felt a blush along the edge of his face.

There was a flurry of prayers for everyone; then he heard a muttered "Amen" and the ordeal was over. Rosa broke the silence by placing a basket of brown bread on the table. For the first time, Jennings smiled, reached for the bread and commenced eating.

Dhari followed suit, then John did likewise, and true to the nature of the room, they did nothing but eat for about twenty minutes. The clink of flatware against the china plates increased to deafening proportions, and finally John felt compelled to say, "It's very good," referring to the food on his plate.

But if anyone agreed with him, they kept it to themselves, and it was only as Rosa was filling Jennings' plate a second time that he looked up and ventured a word. "Did you sleep well, Eden?" he inquired, a stiffness to his voice.

"Very well, thank you. The bed is quite comfortable."

And that was that, at least for the second go-around, and during the silence, waves of melancholy beat upon John's brain along with the rising conviction that he was seated in the heart of a mystery. He wanted to ask questions of everyone, particularly Dhari, but that fine countenance had not looked up once during the entire meal.

At last, as Rosa was serving tea, Jennings asked, "Well what now, Eden?"

While John had hungered for conversation, he was not prepared for so blunt a question. "I'll strike out on my own. I can't impose upon your hospitality—"

"Nonsense," Jennings interrupted. "There are only two safe places for an Englishman in Delhi now. One is the

British Cantonment outside the walls, and the second is this mission school."

Dhari leaned forward. "He's right, Mr. Eden. Delhi is filled now with suspicious old men and plotting young ones."

"And what are they plotting?" he asked, feeding on the beauty opposite him.

But Dhari refused to say anything else. He saw her glance toward Jennings as though afraid she'd already said too much. The man reached out and covered her hand with his.

The quiet moment held, almost to the point of embarrassment, John entertaining a brief though unthinkable theory having to do with an old man, a young girl, and a dead wife.

Finally Jennings withdrew his hand, though he continued to focus on the girl as he spoke. "Dhari serves as our eyes and ears here." he said. "She has total access to the fortress palace and to her grandfather's ear as well."

In response to this remarkable information, John sat up. "Grandfather?" he repeated.

Jennings nodded. "You are in the presence of the granddaughter of Bahadur Shah Zafar," he intoned, a mocking smile on his face that seemed to war with the nature of his words. "And Aslam, the little boy you met earlier is his great-grandson." His eyes fixed on Dhari's bowed head. "The royal princess," he pronounced, "who owes her life and that of her son to Christ. Isn't that correct, Dhari?"

John watched intently. Was it his imagination, or was something cruel taking place at the table. "I . . . don't understand," he said.

"Tell him, Dhari," Jennings urged, "tell him all."

But either the young woman couldn't or wouldn't. She sat now with her hands clasped in her lap, head bowed. John noticed a trembling about her shoulders.

"Then I'll tell him." Jennings smiled, apparently unmindful of her discomfort. He adjusted himself in his chair, facing John now. "Suttee," he pronounced simply. "Have you ever heard of it, Eden?"

Yes, he had, from Alex Aldwell, back in Scutari, but

with his attention torn between Dhari and Jennings, John did not answer.

"Widow-burning," Jennings went on. "Another aspect of Indian religion which we have almost destroyed."

John's eyes were still on Dhari. He saw her glance over her shoulder as though contemplating leaving the room. But Jennings reached for her hand, a restraining gesture.

"Dhari was living within the palace at that time," Jennings said, "though she'd been coming to the mission school since she was a girl. My wife was very fond of her, called her the daughter she'd never had. Then shortly after Aslam's birth, about six years ago, Dhari's husband, one of the royal princes, died."

The discomfort across the table was increasing. Twice she tried to pull free from Jennings' grip, but he simply moved his hand up about her wrist and held it fast.

"We didn't see Dhari for several days," Jennings went on. "May was worried sick, and one afternoon one of the native servants told her that suttee was planned."

The man's face clouded. "I told May to stay out of it, that there was nothing we could do, that gods, all gods, must be obeyed. But she wouldn't listen. And that night she took a small pistol that I kept locked in my wardrobe and went to the palace, gained entrance at the point of a gun and spirited Dhari and the infant out."

One candle stood between John and the bowed young woman across the table, and at that moment the fire seemed to leap up under the duress of a breeze, encompassing the bowed head in flame. Briefly he closed his eyes and began to understand Dhari's devotion to the dead May.

But as always, what he didn't understand was Jennings. "And you took no part in it?" John questioned.

Broadly Jennings shook his head. "My relationship with Bahadur Shah Zafar was based on mutual trust. Wouldn't I have been wronged if he had said: No more communion at your mission school, no more baptisms." His voice was rising. "Then what right have I to interfere with his gods? None, none at all, and I tried to tell May that, but she wouldn't listen. And the very next day, the palace gates were closed to me forever. The royal wrath was not aimed at Dhari or at Mrs. Jennings, but at me. A man is expected to control his wife, and if not, then he is held accountable for her actions."

He leaned back in his chair as though puzzling an ancient dilemma. "Since that day, I have not once looked upon the Peacock Throne, or shared the splendor of the royal chambers, or enjoyed the serenity of the courtyard. We were so close, Bahadur and myself . . ."

His voice trailed off into a wistful tone. Dhari apparently saw the weakness and decided to take advantage of it, and once again tried to leave. But again, and with greater violence, he pulled her back down into her seat.

John eased up to the edge of his chair. He was a guest, but if it went on much longer, he would be forced to act.

Then all at once, of his own volition, Jennings released her arm. "I'm . . . sorry," he muttered to no one in particular.

Across the table, John noticed Dhari still in her seat, as though in spite of her instinct to run, she knew she must stay.

"So Dhari and Aslam came to live with us," Jennings concluded. "And of course, nothing really changed for her. She now enjoys both worlds, again has total access to the palace. The priests have convinced her grandfather that she is leading a charmed life. Saved by the white goddess, they say. And May is enjoying the peace of her grave. I'm the only one left to suffer."

John heard the martyred quality in his voice and looked down at his napkin and vowed silently to leave this place as soon as possible.

Suddenly Jennings stood, the self-pity gone from his face, replaced by weary efficiency. "It's late," he said, "and I'm certain you are as tired as I am. I must go over the books yet and see if chaos has descended in my absence."

On his way to the door he called back over his shoulder. "Sleep well, John. Tomorrow at breakfast we shall plot your future. I can always use an intelligent young man here. I weary of female company."

John started to protest everything, but decided this was not the time. Besides, Dhari was still at table, and he looked forward to time alone with her. Then he heard the flat monotone at the door. "You come with me, Dhari," Jennings ordered. "I need you to assist me with the books."

She was gone, following after Jennings down the long corridor which led to the rear of the bungalow, leaving John alone with the residue of old food odors and a sensation of unease.

Rosa came in to clear the table. John nodded to her and left by the opposite door. Midway across the entrance hall, he stopped. Beyond the front door he saw the quiet night. Perhaps now was as good a time as any. There was nothing waiting for him in Mrs. Jennings' room. And he had no desire to "plot his future" with Jennings come morning. And he certainly had no desire to pass the night in this house.

He stood a moment longer, then he walked to the front door, and stepped out into the quiet night. A stroll, perhaps that was all he needed, a convenient stroll along the walls of the palace.

For about twenty minutes he stood thus, contemplating the possibilities of the night. He looked about on either side. The cottages where the children slept were quiet. It occurred to him then that if by some miracle his "stroll" proved successful, if out of one chance in a hundred he could gain admittance to the palace grounds and to the treasure house, then he must be prepared to make a quick exit from Delhi. With that in mind he made a brief detour around the side of the compound in search of the stable where his horse had been lodged. He found it beyond the rear courtyard, found as well a sleeping native boy who never so much as opened his eyes at John's approach.

He checked on the horse, made sure he had feed and water, and was just heading around the other side of the compound, passing close to the rear rooms, when suddenly he heard a familiar voice, Jennings quoting Scripture again, and something else, a low female voice trying to keep pace under duress.

The window was directly before him, the shade incompletely drawn. Quietly he approached, some stray voice telling him not to, but approaching anyway. He peered through the slit between shade and windowsill and wished instantly that he'd obeyed the voice inside his head.

The scene was one of copulation, the specifics blessedly obscured by the spread dressing gown on Jennings' back, his bare feet pushing against the foot of the bed while beneath him lay his partner, her ankles loosely secured to the bedposts, her face covered by the crush of his body, only a soft voice escaping over the panting groans of the man who was raping and quoting Scripture at the same time.

John stood a moment longer, magnetized by the ugly scene. Then he turned away. His eyes in passing fell on an abandoned light blue sari.

Cautiously he stepped backward; then he was running, his legs devouring the distance to the front gate and the road beyond.

Not until he reached the north gate of the fortress palace did he slow his pace. Breathless, he leaned against the wall and looked back the way he had come and tried to put the image out of his mind. It was his avowed intention then to seek immediately what he had come for, and to leave this wretched place of mixed gods. He did not belong here. But as long as he was here, he would make an effort to find what he'd come for, then leave before dawn, before he had to face Fraser Jennings again and perhaps carry out the instinct which he'd ignored in the temple of Bindhachal.

Thus resolved, he looked about at the deserted streets which earlier that day had been filled with people. Twice he encircled the Red Fortress, taking careful note of the torchlight beyond the wall.

As well as he could determine, there were four main gates giving access to the palace and courtyards. Three were heavily though sleepily guarded by dozing men in black turbans.

According to Alex Aldwell, the treasure house was removed from the palace. John recalled the man saying that he had followed the old Emperor to a deserted mound. Then it must be in the opposite direction, away from the palace itself, toward the one area where he had seen no protruding structure over the wall.

The feel of the night was strange. There were sounds, but they seemed to come from no specific source. No matter how hard he tried to discipline his mind, he still saw the image of rape. Running, he felt his way along the wall, coming at last to the grillwork gate, the grounds beyond empty, a garden of some sort, only the faint rustling of trees as a breeze brushed through them.

Without giving himself a chance to debate the widom of his actions, he pulled himself up the grillwork, finding ready footholds, and in a remarkably short time dropped undetected on the other side.

He felt a surge of excitement. How easy it had been thus far. He found himself in a garden which seemed to turn on a spiral around several mounds of earth.

A long avenue of trees confronted him then, leading to the largest mound, the branches indistinguishable against the night sky. He could not see the end of it. It seemed to him that he had been walking along this avenue for too long, and still no end in sight. The mound seemed to be moving farther away. Somehow in the dark he'd lost sight of the other mounds.

A few minutes later the large mound of earth again came into sight, and he ran across an open space, experiencing a state devoid of good sense, intent only on his goal.

He approached the mounded earth slowly, seeing to his amazement a small unguarded door. Though he found it incredible to believe that the bastion was not under guard, still he drew nearer.

He had just touched the metal bolt when he heard, or thought he heard, a single step behind him. Confident that his ears were playing tricks on him, he turned rather slowly to confront the ghost sound, when something of incredible strength struck a blow across the back of his head.

In a curious way, he had long expected it. He felt his knees give way, his body whirl around in a half-turn.

Then a second, more powerful blow struck him across his forehead, and all became quiet. There was a white light inside his head and a distant mocking voice which chanted, "Fool!" before the ringing of bells deafened him and plunged him into darkness.

Upon the instant of awakening, he turned away from the temptation of reason. He opened his eyes to find his face resting on damp dirt. It was dark, but not so dark that he couldn't see the three dirt walls about him and the bars in front of him, the entire cubicle measuring no more than four by four.

He tried movement and instantly regretted it as pain cut across his forehead and down between his eyes. Reflexively his hand moved up, felt a dried substance on his face, coating the bridge of his nose, and his fingers touched the wound itself, a gaping hole which felt as though his forehead had been split open.

Groaning, he gave up movement for a while and lay back against the dirt, his eyes staring sideways through the bars toward a steep dirt path which appeared to lead upward toward the spill of light at the top of the path. He was buried in earth somewhere.

Stirred to new activity by the helplessness of his position, he again struggled to a sitting position, noticing for the first time that his shirt was gone, as well as his boots, as well as one leg of his trousers, slashed at the very place where he'd sewn his English pounds.

In the dark, he dragged himself toward one of the dirt walls and rested against it. His worst enemy was his sense of his own stupidity. What in the name of God had possessed him? As self-abnegation burned into his consciousness, he rested his head against the wall and closed his eyes. Now and then a fresh trickle of blood slid down the bridge of his nose. He thought grimly though not too seriously that if someone didn't come soon, there was a remote possibility that he would bleed to death.

But two days later, after having tested the bars and found them unmovable, after having tried valiantly to cover his urine and defecation with loose damp dirt, and after having watched the patch of light at the top of the tunnel fade and reappear at twenty-four-hour intervals, he clung to the bars in his weakened condition and found the courage to think the unthinkable.

No one was coming, no one had any intention of coming. He had been placed in this hole for the purpose of starving to death. Who would hear his screams? In all the countless hours he'd spent in this pit, he'd heard nothing at all from above. Who would miss him and come looking for him? Hadn't he stupidly announced that night at Jennings' that he was striking out on his own?

No! Slowly he dragged himself to the bars, lifted his head and shouted with what energy he had left, "Help . . . someone!" continued shouting these two words in sequence until his throat burned and the echo of his voice fell back upon him, unheeded.

Through one entire interval of light he shouted, and when darkness fell, his lips were still moving, though no sound came out.

His last conscious thought was of Harriet. How was it possible in so short a life for a man to take so many wrong steps? Still the temptation gripped him to rise up just once more and tear the net of stupidity and circumstance in which he was entangled.

But there was no energy for such an action. He charted one more interval of light and dark at the top of the tunnel. Or was it two, or twelve?

He lost count.

❦

London, February 1856

ANDREW RHOADES SAT behind his desk in the outer office of Sir Arthur Chesterton, pushed his lawbooks to one side and studied the brown envelope which only moments before had been delivered to him.

From British Military Command Headquarters in Balaklava, it read. Momentarily the snow falling outside his window in the Temple faded, as did the street sounds of carriages on cobblestone. Both these sounds were replaced by the memories of bursting shell and screaming men.

He shook his head in an attempt to shake off the memories and consciously reminded himself that he was safe in London, facing no greater threat than the gentle disappointment of Sir Arthur over his failure to complete the briefs before him.

Andrew's entry back into civilian life had been easy enough. Armed with the Crimean Medal of War, he'd found doors opening to him that before had been tightly closed. After the senselessness of war, he'd discovered that his earlier dream of a career in law had been even more powerful than before. He'd made application, had passed the initial tests and had been called to the bar. With Sir Arthur as a considerate sponsor, he'd taken joyously to his lawbooks and now found himself working overtime in an effort to pass the final examinations and launch a small law practice of his own.

Thus the war and all its accompanying horrors had been put far behind him. Seldom did he look back except at times like now, when it was thrust into his hands in the form of an envelope from British Command Headquarters in Balaklava.

Curious, he turned the envelope over and felt the shifting of smaller envelopes inside. He rubbed his eyes for a moment and reminded himself again that he must consider the practicality of spectacles. The densely packed print of lawbooks was beginning to take a toll, and with his eyes still closed, he thought incongruously of John Murrey Eden.

There too was a piece of unfinished business, prompted no doubt by the presence of the strange envelope in his lap. Since his return to London over a year ago, Andrew had followed every lead in an attempt to track down his friend. He'd gone by Jack Willmot's flat, thinking perhaps John might have returned there. But the landlady had said she had not seen him, and if Andrew did, to tell him to come and fetch Jack Willmot's belongings, which she'd stored in her attic.

Andrew had even made a trip by Thomas Brassey's office, only to be greeted by an array of new faces, one dour man informing him that Mr. Brassey was out of the country, and no, he'd never heard of the gentleman named John Murrey Eden.

The snow beyond the window had turned to sleet and rattled against the glass. He finished rubbing his eyes and opened them to a million spiraling suns out of which evolved one clear image of his missing friend. If only he knew where else to look!

With the aid of a letter opener he slashed the heavy seal on the back of the packet and upended it over his desk. To his amazement, about thirty smaller letters fell out, some well-worn, mute evidence of their lengthy travels, and all bearing the remarkable name of John Murrey Eden.

Bewildered, Andrew shuffled through them, his hand falling on a single sheet of paper, folded once, the unmistakable stamp of the military on it.

Quickly he opened it, carried it to the window, and in the gray light of the snowy afternoon read:

Dear Corporal Rhoades,

As you well know, the day for which we have fought and prayed is upon us. With the Peace Conference in Paris going well, it has fallen our task to disperse all undelivered post addressed to our gallant men in the Crimea. We are sending along for your inspection and assistance a correspondence addressed to one Mr. John Murrey Eden. We admit that it would be a simple matter to return the various letters to the senders. But we are loath to return unopened mail from the war zone, as the senders are inclined to think the worst. Unable to locate a fatality sheet on John Murrey Eden, we must assume that he is in transit. A gentleman from Mr. Brassey's expedition has informed us that you and Mr. Eden were close friends. We located your address through army files, and if you know where Mr. Eden is, or where to reach him, we would be most appreciative if you would deliver this correspondence to him.

> Major Christopher Denning
> Army Post-Master General
> Balaklava

Andrew stared at the letter, slowly returned to his stool and sat heavily. Obviously he wasn't the only one who couldn't locate John Murrey Eden. He looked at the scattered letters.

Slowly he lifted one, observed the delicate penmanship and light blue paper, turned it over and read on the back: "Lila Harrington, Harrington Hall, Salisbury."

Bewilderment increasing, Andrew searched his mind for any reference that John had ever made to one Lila Harrington. But he found nothing.

One by one, he commenced stacking the letters, all addressed in that same hand, all signed by one Lila Harrington. Could there have been two John Murrey Edens?

As he brooded, he continued to stack the letters, an ardent and intense correspondence, all from Lila Harrington. Then all at once he lifted a letter that broke the pattern, the handwriting different, and on the back a new name: Elizabeth Eden, 7 St. George St., London.

To the best of his recollection, John had never spoken this name either. Quickly he sorted through the rest of the correspondence. Out of twenty-four letters, sixteen were from Lila Harrington, eight from Elizabeth Eden.

Andrew thought he had known John fairly well, knew certainly his proclivity for London whores. But he had the feeling that neither of these women fit that description. For one thing, the writing paper in both instances was too fine. Generally whores did not have a stationer's account. Neither did whores live in places called Harrington Hall or St. George Street. But if John had been involved with gentlewomen, wouldn't he have told Andrew?

Obviously not. Well, there was at least one bonus to the mystery. He now had two more addresses, locations where perhaps at this very moment John Murrey Eden was sitting cozy and warm before a fire, enjoying the companionship of one lady or the other.

Hurriedly he slipped the letters from Salisbury back into the large envelope. Those would have to wait. He had neither the time nor the money for a trip to Salisbury. But the one at St. George Street held promise. He knew the location well, an easy walk which he'd make as soon as he completed the briefs for Sir Arthur. If he found John Murrey Eden alive and well and in the arms of a lovely lady, he'd feign anger before he embraced him. And if he didn't . . .

Abruptly he pushed the thought aside. How he hungered to see his friend. What a reunion it would be!

Then hurry! He returned all the letters to the packet, placed it to one side of his desk, like a treat which he would enjoy later, and drew the law volumes back and tried to concentrate on the difference between specific and general power of attorney.

It was approaching nine o'clock when Andrew stood on the snow-covered pavement of St. George Street looking up at number seven, seeing it dark with the exception of one lamp burning at the second-floor window.

Perhaps he should return at another time. But when? His studies kept him busy. He'd cut his work short this evening in order to make this trip. No, he must present himself and his inquiry now.

On this resolution, he left the pavement and climbed the stairs and knocked once on the elegant door, tried to peer in through the leaded glass panel and saw only darkness. He waited a moment, then knocked again, louder this time.

As he was about to turn away, the door opened a crack and a young maid peered out. "Who is it?" she demanded.

Andrew tried to put her at ease. "I beg your pardon," he apologized, "but I'm searching for one Elizabeth Eden. Would you have—"

"Gone to bed," the maid snapped.

As she started to close the door, he stepped forward. "I'm looking as well for John Murrey Eden. Would you know—"

From the faint spill of light from the lamp, he saw a

change on her face. "What would you be knowing of John Murrey Eden?" she asked suspiciously.

Grateful for the reprieve, he smiled. "I'm his friend. My name is Andrew Rhoades. We were in the Crimea together. I have some—"

"You were . . . with him in the . . . war?" she asked, as though this were remarkable news.

Andrew nodded. "The last time I saw him he was on his way home. I just wondered if . . ."

He heard the sliding of the bolt, and a second later saw the door open to him, the little maid stepping cautiously back as though still on guard. "Wait here," she ordered.

She closed the door behind her and circled him wide. "I don't know if she'll see you or not," she warned. "She's been . . . ill, but . . ." Again she hesitated. "You may be good medicine."

As she hurried up the darkened stairs, Andrew felt a slight apprehension. Perhaps he should have sent a card around first.

Too late now, and he shivered in the cold entrance hall. Clearly the reception rooms of this house had not been in use for some time. He peered through the doorway into what appeared to be the drawing room, though he saw the furnishings shrouded in white cloth. A gloomy place, he thought, and somehow a strong instinct told him he would not find John here.

Perhaps he should leave before . . . Then he heard female voices coming from the top of the stairs, one insisting, "Show him in, Doris, please. Don't keep him waiting."

He saw the maid hurrying down the stairs. "She'll see you, she will." She grinned. "It's the first time I've seen her out of that chair in . . . Please, this way, Mr. Rhoades, if you will."

As he hurried up the stairs after her, he thought it unusual for a reception room to be on the second floor, and a moment later he realized with a start that he was being received in the lady's bedchamber. From where he stood in the door, his eye fell first on the mussed bed, then on the lady herself, who stood at mid-chamber, gazing expectantly at him, a frail slim woman, somberly clad in a dark dressing robe, her fair hair loosed about her face and down her neck, mussed, as though she'd not taken the time to groom herself.

But it was her face that held him, a lovely face with delicate features which bore the ravages of illness. The young maid performed the introductions. "Mr. Andrew Rhoades, miss," she said. "And this here is Miss Elizabeth Eden," she concluded, then added thoughtfully, "May I fetch you something, Mr. Rhoades? Coffee? Brandy?"

To both he said no, still concentrating on the woman, who was staring upon him as though he were a ghost risen from the grave. At last, when the taut silence was approaching embarrassment, she seemed to draw herself up. "Forgive me, Mr. Rhoades," she murmured. "I've not received company for so long. Doris, please take his wraps, and two toddies would be lovely."

As Andrew handed the maid his cloak, he noticed the woman walking slowly to the fire and noticed for the first time a curious sight to one side of the fire, a trunk, well-worn, simple compared to the lavish furnishings in the room, and on top of the trunk, two white candles, the whole spectacle resembling a shrine.

She looked back at him and motioned for him to take the chair opposite her before the fire.

"I'm sorry if I disturbed you," he began, feeling mild discomfort at sitting in a lady's bedchamber.

"You did not disturb me," she replied. "I seldom leave these chambers now, and I seldom sleep. You could have called at dawn and I would have been awake, seated where I'm sitting now."

Andrew struggled to make a connection between this woman and John Murrey Eden. But there was no connection to be made, and as his discomfort increased, he decided to state his business immediately and take his leave.

To that end he withdrew the large packet of letters. "I received this in the morning post," he began, "from the army postmaster in Balaklava. It contains letters addressed to John Murrey Eden."

He thought he saw her stiffen. "Go on, Mr. Rhoades."

"There's not much else to say." He smiled. "I noticed

that a few of the letters were from you, and I came here tonight hoping to find John and deliver them myself."

He saw new suffering on her face, watched, shocked, as she bent over, both hands covering her grief.

Alarmed, he stood. "Please," he begged, and looked helplessly toward the door, longing for a glimpse of the maid. "It was not my intention to . . ." He broke off and stepped closer. "If he isn't here, perhaps you could tell me where—"

"I was . . . hoping," she faltered, "that you could tell me the same." She withdrew a handkerchief. "My apologies, Mr. Rhoades," she murmured. "I was hoping that you were bringing me a message. Now I'm afraid I must give you one." She dabbed at her eyes and seemed to concentrate on the lace-trimmed edge of her handkerchief. "Did you know John well?" she asked.

Relieved that the worst of her mysterious grief was under control, Andrew returned to his chair, still holding the packet of letters on his lap. "Well enough." He smiled. "We first met as clerks in the office of Mr. Thomas Brassey."

"John is dead, Mr. Rhoades," she said bluntly, as though feeling the need to deliver herself of the message all at once so that someone else might share her grief with her.

For a moment Andrew felt incredible heat on his face as he tried to confront both the woman and her insane message. "Dead?" he repeated.

She nodded. "I received the message some time ago, from a dear friend who is in a position to know."

"Who?" Andrew began, still not believing the words. "Where—"

Her voice was a monotone as she worked with intense concentration on the task of smoothing the white lace handkerchief across her lap. "He was with Brassey," she began, not looking at him, "at a place called Section Three. They were building the last link of a railway, the Russians attacked, and—"

"No!"

The force of his rebuttal caught her attention.

"No," Andrew repeated. "No offense, please," he said, "but the source of your information is wrong."

A look of confusion crossed her face. She appeared to be on the verge of speaking, but he didn't give her a chance. "You see, I was there"—he smiled—"only hours after the attack. There were scores of dead, but John was not among them. Oh, he was wounded, to be sure, but I personally escorted both of them, John and Jack Willmot, to the base hospital at Balaklava."

She was looking at him as though he were speaking a foreign language.

"It's true," he insisted with conviction. Suddenly he stopped, recalling the tragedy on board ship, wondering if she knew Jack Willmot, if he meant anything to her. "John's friend . . ." he continued. "Mr. Willmot's injuries were . . . serious. He. . . . died aboard the hospital ship and was buried at sea."

She had known him, of that Andrew was certain. There was shock on her face. Feeling the need to break the brittle silence, Andrew went on. "But John, I assure you, was alive and well. The wound, while painful, was superficial, a deep cut across his shoulder, caused by a Russian saber. But I sat with him at Scutari, saw him on the road to recovery, and left him to return to the war zone only after I had extracted his promise that he was returning to London."

He was about to say more, but he ceased talking as she stood. If Andrew hadn't stepped forward and caught her in his arms, she would have fallen.

As she wept against his shoulder, he held her, embarrassed to be holding her, yet enjoying the sensation.

The embrace lasted for several moments and might have lasted longer if the maid hadn't reappeared in the door bearing a small tray with two steaming mugs, her watchful eyes monitoring the tableau by the fire. "Is everything . . . all right, miss?" she inquired.

At that Elizabeth left his arms, laughing through her tears. "Oh, indeed it is, Doris." She smiled. "This gentleman has just brought me the most miraculous message. He claims to have seen John alive after the attack, says he was wounded, but well recovered from his wounds and on his way home."

With no sense of putting a damper on the good news, but because she was a practical woman, the maid asked flatly, "Then where is he now?"

Andrew saw Elizabeth glance his way as though he were the font of all information. "I don't know," he admitted, "but I know he's not in his grave. I'd swear to it."

Elizabeth took the mugs from the tray and offered one to Andrew. "You have given me hope, Mr. Rhoades," she whispered, "and for that I will be eternally grateful."

He took the mug and drank too quickly and burned his tongue, all the time never taking his eyes off her.

"Thank you, Doris." She smiled, dismissing the girl, settling once again in the chair and inviting him to do likewise. When they were alone again, she leaned back, a smile on her face. "You wouldn't believe me, Mr. Rhoades, if I told you . . . what I have been through. Days, months of remorse, grief. You see, his father entrusted him to me, John's father, I mean."

Andrew settled back in his chair, sensing a story. It didn't matter, so long as he could watch her.

And it was a story, Elizabeth talking compulsively as though she'd been alone for too long, as though single-handedly Andrew had broken her acquiescence toward everything, even toward death.

At dawn, after the most absorbing night he'd ever passed, Andrew sat relaxed in his chair before the dying fire, aware that he knew more about John Murrey Eden than he'd ever known before, and very aware that he knew all about the lovely Elizabeth as well.

Apparently Elizabeth saw the look on his face and rose from her chair, and with an almost embarrassing intimacy stood before him. "I . . . don't know how to say it," she began. "It's such a comfort to be able to talk with someone."

He'd never known a woman quite like her, exhibiting all the traits of a gentlewoman, yet so at ease with him in her bedchamber. "And I enjoyed it." He smiled.

"Will you come again, Mr. Rhoades?" she asked.

"I'm . . . very busy," he confessed, "with my law

studies . . ." He saw her disappointment. "Of course, I'll come," he said, "whenever I'm welcome."

"Tonight." She smiled, extending a hand to him. "For dinner. Around eight."

She took his arm as he walked to the door. "We still have a problem, Andrew," she mused softly.

"The missing John." He nodded. At the door an idea occurred to him, and he voiced it, hoping it would reassure her further. "I'll speak with Sir Arthur," he promised. "He's a prominent solicitor, and a most compassionate man. Perhaps there is a way to trace—"

"I'd be most appreciative," she interrupted. She stared at him a moment longer. "How fortunate John is to have such a devoted friend," she said, and without warning, and with no sense of shame, she stood on tiptoe and lightly kissed him.

"Until tonight." She smiled. "And thank you, Andrew, for my resurrection. You saw him alive. How I'll cling to that."

Wordlessly he started down the stairs. He found his cloak on a chair in the entrance hall, took it up and looked back to see her waiting at the top of the steps.

"Good night," she called down.

"Good morning." He smiled up, then let himself out of the door and stood for a moment on the steps, charting the passage of a milk wagon through the cold dawn as though it were the most fascinating sight in the world.

Delhi,
March 1856

THE FIRST FACE he saw was Queen Victoria smiling down on him. Was it heaven or hell? he wondered.

He closed his eyes and felt something heavy pressing against his forehead. The pain was still there in his head, sharper than ever, and though he tried to cling to consciousness, he slipped back into the dark pool which he shared with a mass of blackened skeletons.

The second time he opened his eyes, he was aware of someone lifting his head, trying to force a warm liquid between his lips. A soft voice urged, "Swallow, Mr. Eden, please. You need your strength."

He needed more than that, though in the instant before he lost consciousness again his vision cleared and he saw a set of worried black eyes and a smooth brow.

Then he knew precisely where he was and where he'd been, and lacked only the bridge connecting the two.

"Water . . ." he whispered, his mouth feeling as though it were filled with sand.

Never had such a simple request been so gratefully received. Dhari's smile broadened, and again she called over her shoulder, "Rosa, hurry, he's truly awake."

While he was still pondering the mystery, he saw her drop to her knees beside the bed.

"Dear Heavenly Father," she prayed in flawless English, "thank You for sparing this life and for giving us courage to seek him out. We thank You, too, for placing Your hands in ours as we nursed him and we pray always that we will be worthy of your continued mercy and forgiveness. In His Name we pray. Amen."

He closed his eyes, moved by the prayer, by the one who prayed, by his awareness that if it had not been for her, he would be dead. "Dhari—"

"Don't," she urged, standing beside him, one hand pressing gently against his lips. "Say nothing."

He looked up and tried to put that earlier vision out of his head, seeing her submitting to rape.

"Jennings—"

"He's been praying for your recovery for the last month." She smiled. "He's with the children. I'll have Rosa give him the news."

Her face was so forgiving that he thought for a moment he'd imagined the rape. Then something else caught on his slowly awakening mind. *"For the last month . . ."* He tried to repeat the words and failed, and grew angry at his recalcitrant lips. In frustration he tried to turn his head on the pillow, but he was blocked even there.

As he groaned at his own helplessness, Dhari leaned close. "You must lie still, Mr. Eden. I'll tell you everything, I promise."

There was such urgency in her voice, and besides, he had no choice. Rosa appeared, carrying a cup of cold water.

He drank the cool water until it was running down into his beard and Dhari took the cup away, murmuring, "That's enough for now."

She closed the door and stood leaning against it, filling the room with the warmth of her smile. "It's so good to see you awake," she murmured. "How many times we lost all hope. Reverend Jennings said not to worry when you didn't come for breakfast the next morning. But about noon, Aslam, my little boy, sought you out." She smiled self-consciously. "I would never have given him permission to disturb you. But I'm so glad that he did. He wanted to show you how well he could read Shakespeare, and when he didn't find you in Mrs. Jennings' room, he came and told me."

She hesitated, one hand smoothing the edge of her pale yellow sari. "Still Reverend Jennings said not to worry, that you were merely a young man in search of adventure, and like a tomcat, you'd return when you'd had your fill."

He closed his eyes, and apparently she interpreted it as fatigue. "Why don't you rest now?" she suggested. "We can—"

"No, please," he managed, his curiosity growing to anxiety. "Tell me."

She nodded as though to spare him the effort of speech. "Four days later," she went on, "I was visiting my grandfather and I overheard one of his wives whispering to my cousin about a white man in the dungeon cell." She shook her head. "At first I paid no attention. They gossip constantly. But as I was leaving the palace courtyard, I noticed that one of the guards was wearing your boots. Oh, I remembered them. I polished them myself that first afternoon. I considered approaching him, then changed my mind." Again she lowered her head. "None of the lower caste care for me much, I'm afraid. They take their rituals very seriously, and most of them feel I should be dead."

A few moments later she recovered. "I waited until the next day and asked two of my cousins to take me to the dungeon. At first, they refused, saying it was none of my concern. But I bribed them, and they took me to you and helped me carry you home."

It was several moments before she spoke again and came slowly around the bed until she was standing beside him.

"You were more dead than alive," she said. "I sent for the physician from the British Cantonment, though Reverend Jennings said it was a waste of time. He said you'd suffered a concussion, a very serious one, that you were half-starved and that probably you'd never wake up."

Gently she lifted his hand. "Oh, how I prayed," she whispered. "Rosa and I bathed you every day, kept you clean and comfortable, saw to it that you swallowed broth, and now . . ."

As she clasped his hand to her breast, he wondered if he would ever live long enough to repay her.

At that moment the door was pushed open and he saw Fraser Jennings, his white hair ruffled from the wind, his face stern, though softening. "So! You're awake."

Dhari turned immediately. "Yes," she whispered joyfully. "I've given one prayer of thanksgiving. Shall we kneel together and offer another?"

As Jennings' Christian voice rose into the theatrics of prayer, John closed his eyes and wondered about the heavy weights on either side of his head. He wondered why his vision was blurred, and why he was feeling only the need to escape from this room filled with Christ, Queen Victoria and Jennings.

Just when he thought he could not endure, another voice cut in, brash, arrogant, masculine. "Oh, lord, Fraser, not trying to reach God again, are you?"

John opened his eyes and looked toward the door to the most incredible man he'd ever seen, a man who literally filled the door with his ball-like frame, as wide as he was tall, with a smaller ball for a head, which sat directly on his shoulders. Capping the bald head was a hair covering

of white tufts which looked as though they had been in-
dividually attached. He was wearing a dark brown coat
which strained mightily to contain the girth of his arms
and chest, and moving down the front of his brown waistcoat, John noticed a line of ovals where buttons tried to
meet buttonholes and failed, revealing the white of under-
clothes beneath.

"So! You're at it again, Fraser." He laughed. "When
will you get it through that thick Methodist skull of yours
that there is no one in heaven? It is all part of the massive
joke the Jews played on us centuries ago. There's nothing
in Rome or Canterbury either, except piles of poorly
arranged masonry and two senile old men like us."

John blinked, thinking that his vision was deceiving
him again. No man could be that obese and still move. A
moment later, he saw Jennings get to his feet with Dhari's
help and confront the enormous man with admirable
Christian kindness.

"Oh, God hears us, Reggie, make no mistake about
that. Blame not the world that your eyes are blind, your
ears deaf—"

"Hell," the big man snorted. He gave a little laugh of
derision and for the first time looked toward John and the
bed. "Good lord," he gasped. He pushed through the
door with some effort and gazed in red-faced amazement
down upon John. "Are . . . you awake?" he whispered.

"Only a short time," Dhari said, coming up on the
other side of the bed. She looked so pleased at his return
to the living. The other two looked simply amazed.

"Well, good lord," the fat man marveled, his fleshy
hands outreaching.

Suffering no desire to be touched by the man, John
tried to pull away.

"It's all right, Mr. Eden." Dhari smiled. "This is Dr.
Taylor from the British Cantonment. He's cared for you
from the beginning."

"Get these damn things away," the man shouted, and
John opened his eyes in time to see two Indian servants
rush into the room, each lifting what appeared to be
sandbags from either side of his head.

"There, that's better," Taylor muttered. "Well, I'm

pleased to inform you, Mr. Eden, that you are alive, though according to all the rules of medical science, you should not be." He leaned closer, displaying yellowing teeth. "Have you ever cracked a good English walnut, Mr. Eden, and observed the manner in which there is always one central split with small ruptures running out on either side? Well, that was your skull a month ago, sorry to say."

John listened, holding his head very still now.

"I've never seen anything like it," the doctor marveled. Suddenly there was a new look of alarm on his face. "You're not addled, are you?" he asked sharply. "Or simple-minded?"

He pulled himself out of the chair, a laborious process which left him panting, and pulled back one of John's eyelids. "What's your name?" he demanded.

"John Murrey Eden."

"How many fingers?"

John looked up at the fat hand. "Three."

"Where are you?"

"Delhi."

"Who is on the throne of England?"

"Victoria."

"Who is the consort?"

"Albert."

"How many royal children?"

John hesitated. The old doctor grinned down on him. "Oh, never mind. I couldn't answer that one myself. The royal womb is fertile, even if the royal brain is not."

He beamed at John, then leaned close, as though for a confidence. "I don't suppose you'd care to tell me what you were doing inside the palace walls, would you?"

John decided to feign that obstinate egoism peculiar to sick persons. He said nothing.

The doctor smiled. "No, I didn't think you would. I would advise against further adventure, however. Another blow like that and someone will be able to pick the sweetmeats of your brain."

As the old man leaned forward, John was aware for the first time that his head was heavily bandaged. He felt the pull this way and that as the man unwrapped the dressing, was aware of Dhari watching, her lovely dark eyes filled with concern.

As the last bandage fell away, he saw the expression on her face and needed no mirror. The doctor confirmed the worst. "You're going to carry quite a scar on your forehead, Mr. Eden, for the rest of your life. You can tell all it's a battle wound. Choose your own battle. It makes no difference."

As he commenced rewrapping the bandage, he asked considerately, "Are you feeling any discomfort? I have innumerable elixirs in my bag in the carriage, designed to numb the senses."

John muttered, "No," then, because it was beginning to bother him, added, "I . . . can't see very clearly."

The man exploded with a hearty laugh. "No damn surprise. Your eyes probably rattled about like marbles during the assault. I think they'll clear, though. Don't overwork them, and draw that damn blind."

As he pointed toward the small window on the far wall, Dhari lowered the blind.

In spite of his initial aversion to the man, John was beginning to soften toward him. "Thank you," he began weakly, and was immediately relieved of the need to say anything else.

"Don't thank me," the doctor snapped. "You'll pay before you're done by coming to Sunday dinner as soon as you're able. My wife adores young men, particularly prime specimens such as yourself. I try to deliver as many as I can to her. For myself, as you can see, a conventional marital bed no longer suffices."

John looked about at the other faces around the bed, wondering if any were embarrassed or offended by the man's bluntness. Apparently not.

"So, Sunday lunch, it is." The man grinned. "Just as soon as you're able. I'll send my carriage for you and introduce you to a bevy of English beauties who will feed on your masculine charms and wear you out in the process. So, get your cock ready, and I've seen it, and a gorgeous cock it is, and soon you'll learn why the average Englishman has no desire to return to England."

John felt the heat of new embarrassment on his face,

and wondered why no one else displayed the slightest discomfort at the man's crude ways.

Now to Dhari Taylor commanded, "Feed him anything he wants and as much as he wants. The man will need all the strength at his disposal."

John saw the man's watery blue eyes focus on Dhari, moving from her face in an appreciative line to her breasts.

"If you're in a thanksgiving mood, Mr. Eden," he said to John, though not looking at him, "give thanks to that nigger there."

Shocked by the designation, John looked toward Dhari, surprised to find her serenely smiling back at the doctor.

The man was caressing his belly below his waist in a vulgar, sensuous gesture. "They have a magic touch, the niggers do." He smiled, still devouring Dhari's breasts with his eyes. "And that one hovered over you long after Fraser and I both said give up. Isn't that right, Fraser?"

Jennings nodded. "Correct." He smiled, apparently not offended by anything that had been said the last few minutes. "Dhari has an incredible faith," he went on. "She has sustained me on more than one occasion."

Then the examination was over. From the door the doctor looked back toward the bed. "Welcome to the living, Mr. Eden," he said, his voice suddenly sobered. "Fraser tells me you're a gentleman recently come from the Crimea. Do come to Sunday dinner, and I'll fight off the ladies and keep you all to myself. You've no idea how weary I get of women and niggers and soldiers."

John heard loneliness in the man's voice. "Dr. Taylor?" he called out with effort. "Are you . . . with the military?"

The man looked surprised. "Of course. What did you think? A forty-year veteran I am." A light dawned on his face. "Oh, of course. No, no uniform." He smiled, holding up the tail of his coat. "I outgrew the largest years ago. Besides, none of us are too spit-and-polish in this godforsaken outpost," he added. "And why should we be? We have niggers to do our work for us. Very little is required of an Englishman here, Mr. Eden, except that he devise a way to retain his sanity."

With that, he led the way through the door, Jennings

following after him. A few moments later, Rosa appeared with a tray.

Dhari returned to the bed, a bowl in her hand, a spoon lifted toward John's lips. He swallowed several spoonfuls of the rich broth, felt them resting uneasily in his stomach and said, "No more, please."

"You must," she insisted. "Dr. Taylor said you—"

He looked up at her, bewildered by her serene acceptance of everything. "Why did he call you . . . nigger?"

She sat on the edge of the bed. "I am," she said. "At least that's what the British call us. Any flesh darker than theirs is nigger."

"Why don't you object?"

"Why should I? What would it gain me?"

"Does he come here often, Dr. Taylor, I mean?"

"Oh, yes, they're good friends. Dr. Taylor sees to the children once a month. Sometimes Reverend Jennings can pay him. Most of the time he cannot. But he comes anyway. He's a good Christian."

Since there was still an air of bluntness lingering in the small room, John heard himself speaking bluntly. "The first night I was here," he began, "I went to the stable to check on my horse—"

"Oh, he's well. The stableboy is taking good care of—"

"And I happened to pass near the rear of the compound. I saw into Jennings' bedroom . . ."

He looked up, afraid he'd said too much. Instead he found her smiling as placidly as ever, a quizzical look on her face as though she was not quite certain of his point.

"I . . . saw you," he went on, "with Jennings. You were . . . bound . . ."

"Loosely, yes," she admitted. "I could have freed myself at any moment." She shook her head as though experiencing a bewilderment of her own. "It brings him pleasure," she murmured, "and it doesn't hurt me."

Apparently she saw the confusion in his face, and with her fingertips commenced stroking his brow. "Is it so wrong to give pleasure?" she asked. "I've been taught since I was a little girl that my only purpose is to bring pleasure."

"Do you . . . love him?"

"Of course," she said without hesitation. "I love all men who possess kind hearts and generous spirits. If it weren't for Reverend Jennings, countless Indian children would be dead now, including myself." Shyly she looked up at him, the beauty of her face so near. "I have been blessed," she began softly, "with the gift of giving pleasure. Why should I withhold it, or deny it, or limit it?"

He had no answer, was capable of giving none. Her hands were moving across his chest, pushing the coverlet down. "How many times," she said, "I've bathed you, and wondered about . . . that." She pointed to the small scar just above his right nipple, an ancient wound which once had fascinated another, a half world away. Thinking on Harriet and his awareness for the first time of his nakedness caused a strange sensation.

"I . . . don't know," he murmured, concerning the scar.

"Of course you do." She laughed. "Children are not born scarred. Someone did that to you, although I can't imagine why."

Her hands continued to stroke his chest as she moved closer, her long black hair falling forward, partially obscuring her face.

It occurred to him that perhaps she should cease. Just then she leaned down and kissed him, a sweet harmless intimacy that stirred him and set him thinking on that distant bedchamber where another had so effortlessly taken control of him.

"Dhari . . ."

He must stop it. There would be no hope for control past a certain point. Still she prostrated herself over him, edging down the side of the bed, her hand covering him.

Upon the instant of intimate contact, he felt a curious lassitude in his arms and legs, as though all the energy and heat in his body had been drawn to one point. He shut his eyes, feeling no need for vision. The sensations were clear.

He felt the skin of his upper legs tighten, felt her lips on him. She was whispering something, but he couldn't hear.

No sooner had she closed her lips about him than the tension crested, and he pressed backward against the pillow, a tremor of vast proportions, reminiscent of Eden and Harriet. Long after the actual moment passed, he felt his eyes fill with tears, thinking on how innocently she had performed, without shame, as though in sequence she had given him food and water and herself, a natural healing progression.

For a moment he fought a silent battle with his pride, remembering what she had said about loving all men.

"How do you know," he began, still not fully recovered, "that I have a kind heart and a generous spirit?"

She laughed, the most beautiful creature he'd ever seen. "I think you do," she said simply.

If it had been left to him, he would have been more than content simply to lie beside her for the rest of the evening. He had not dreamed that such effortless satisfaction was possible.

Then she was scrambling off the bed, causing him to look up in alarm. "Don't go," he begged, "please . . ."

"I have duties," she said. "Reverend Jennings needs my help with evening prayers. Sometimes we have quite a large gathering in the evening. The children bring their parents." Again she bestowed on him that warm smile. "What fun it is to see the child instruct the adult in the ways of Christ."

He held her hand a moment longer. Perhaps if he could get her talking again. "Do . . . you really believe in Christ, Dhari?" he asked softly.

She seemed surprised at the question. "Of course I do," she replied, "and so do you, though you won't admit it. You're like Dr. Taylor, perhaps one of God's most blessed children, yet full of denial."

She drew away from his hand and walked to the door. She looked back. "May I ask a favor of you?" she inquired.

"Of course."

"May I bring Aslam in to see you for a moment? He's quite worried about you, has come daily to see you during your long sleep." She looked self-conscious. "He's fascinated by you, by your . . . youth. All he sees here are old men."

"It would be my pleasure." He smiled, drawing the coverlet up.

A moment later the little boy appeared, his dark eyes wide, dressed as John had seen him that first day. "This is Aslam, Mr. Eden," Dhari murmured.

"Aslam," John repeated, and lifted his hand to the boy. Grinning, the child took it, his dark smooth face a miniature of his mother's. "I was afraid you would never wake up," the boy said soberly. "Everyone said you wouldn't."

"Well, we proved everyone wrong, didn't we?" John said. He saw that the boy was clutching a slim red book in his hands. "What are you reading, Aslam?" he inquired.

"Mr. Shakespeare," the boy said.

John looked up with interest. "And what is your favorite," he asked.

"This," and proudly the boy thrust the volume forward. *"Hamlet,"* he added. "I like the ghost on the battlement."

Apparently Dhari saw John's increasing fatigue and placed a restraining hand on her eager son. "Not now, Aslam," she counseled. "Come, we're both late for prayers, and Mr. Eden needs to rest."

At first the boy objected, more than willing to initiate a new thread into the conversation. "May I ride on your horse one day, Mr. Eden? I'm helping the stableboy to look after him."

John nodded. "Take good care of him for me, Aslam, and as soon as I'm able, we'll ride him hard."

At last the maternal voice won out, though the boy moved close to John's pillow before he was again turned away. "I'm glad you're here," he said with sweet simplicity.

In the distance, John heard the strains of a pump organ wheezing out a melancholy hymn. Dhari heard it too. "Come, Aslam, we're late."

Without a word she ushered her son out of the door and closed it behind her.

John closed his eyes. What series of blunders had led him to this helpless predicament? Even if he were well and able, would he want to leave here? And where would he go? Back to England? Penniless as always. . . .

He turned his head too suddenly and for his efforts suffered a pain across his forehead. Soon enough he would have to rise and make a decision and choose a new direction.

But for now the distant hymn of the children kindled thoughts of his own childhood, of the Ragged School on Oxford Street, the presence of many children, his father . . .

For several minutes he enjoyed memories he'd long since forgotten, and realized now that he'd missed them.

Four weeks later, John sat on the cool veranda of Dr. Taylor's bungalow within the British Cantonment, drinking tea and looking out at the parade ground where the Thirty-eighth Native Infantry was performing regimental drills. Dr. Taylor had promised him that it would be quite a spectacle, with a grand finale, and well worth waiting for.

It was an awesome sight, the row upon row of men, British-appearing from the distance, with their scarlet tunics and white shakos, though not British, as his present company had repeatedly told him all afternoon.

He looked about at the others on the veranda with him. Dr. Taylor was there, of course, filling a wicker chair like an overfed Buddha.

To his right was his wife, Violet, a harmless creature, as fragile as her husband was massive. After Taylor's initial words several weeks ago concerning his wife, John had come on guard. But she had been gracious to him during the meal and after. Now she presided over her tea table, looking like the displaced Englishwoman that she was.

More threatening were the two ladies on his left, Mrs. George Smyth, Marjorie, as she'd informed him upon introduction, and Mrs. James Metcalfe, Hazel. Their husbands, both officers in the Thirty-eighth, were absent, in Nepal on a tiger hunt for the fortnight.

Gazing out over the shimmering heat waves, John wondered why he had come. He'd known beforehand that it would be dreary, a small suffocating world struggling to keep up the appearances of England. But Reverend Jennings had insisted, pointing out that the doctor had saved John's life and at least John owed him the decency of "breaking bread with him." Even Dhari had joined the conspiracy, producing a decent Western suit of clothes for him from God knew where. Only little Aslam had protested, claiming that if John was well enough to go riding off in the back of a carriage, he was well enough to honor his promise of long standing to take him horse-back riding.

John closed his eyes to rest them from the glare of sun and the meticulous formation of marching men, thinking on the little boy with real affection. How many pleasant hours they had passed, Aslam perched cross-legged on the foot of his bed.

Even more appealing than Aslam's company was Dhari's. Dangerous thoughts there. With his eyes still closed, he saw her so clearly, the most innocent, loving creature he'd ever known. The image that raced through his mind could not be borne in silence, and he must have made a sound, for at that moment Violet Taylor was hovering over him. "Mr. Eden, are you well?"

He looked up, embarrassed, to see all eyes upon him. His embarrassment increased as he saw the two ladies on his left on their feet as well, their hands pressed against his forehead where a single bandage still covered his head wound.

"He feels feverish," one exclaimed. "I'm afraid you let him get up far too soon, Reggie."

John tried to protest. "I'm . . . fine."

"Of course he's fine," Taylor grumbled. "If all of you would stand back and give him air . . ."

Reprimanded, the ladies retreated. Violet summoned a servant and ordered him to fan John.

"No, please," he begged, shaking his head at the approaching boy. "It isn't necessary."

Apparently the flurry of activity had roused Dr. Taylor out of his somnambulant state. To a nearby servant he bellowed, "Gin for two," and a few moments later, as the young dark boy served two appealing glasses of gin and lime, John sipped and felt the abrasive spirit cut through his earlier discomfort. As the ladies gossiped softly, he saw Taylor angling his chair closer, the lethargy of the afternoon apparently dissipated by the cool drink and the separation of the women.

"Well, Eden, what do you think of our coloreds?" He motioned toward the dark-skinned soldiers.

"Impressive," John said politely.

Taylor nodded. "Damn right it is," he muttered. "Look at them. Who'd believe that two thousand niggers could be trained to those maneuvers."

Beyond the man's fleshy shoulder, John saw a "nigger" fanning, listening closely.

"They're children, you know," Taylor went on. "But if you keep a tight rein on them, they'll do all your dirty work and smile while they're doing it."

John sipped his drink.

"Of course, we've had our troubles with them in the past. Every now and then you have to hang one or two just to remind them who the master is. Actually they make better servants than soldiers." He drained his glass, burped pleasurably and immediately called for another. As the young Indian boy stepped forward, John caught a glimpse of his eyes, brooding beneath his tightly wrapped turban. Had he understood anything that had been said?

As Dr. Taylor prattled on about the difficulties of Empire, John felt his mind wandering back to the mission school and took the first step in what he hoped would be a quick exit. "I really should be getting back to Delhi," he began.

"Nonsense," the man scoffed. "Old Jennings sleeps of a Sunday afternoon. And the nigger goes around to visit her grandfather in the palace." He looked up to John. "You have no immediate plans, I hope, to do an encore of your earlier escapade? You might not be so lucky the second time."

Without replying, John circled behind the man and looked longingly toward the broad central gate which led to the road beyond.

"Oh, come now, Eden," Taylor prodded. "What *were* you doing inside the Red Fort in the first place? It wasn't very intelligent, you know. That's their world. This one is ours. You can expect a measure of mercy from white Christians. Expect nothing from the savages."

The degree of hate in his voice was so heavy that John looked back, curious to see where the jocular fat man had gone. "Why do you stay, sir?" he asked.

"Where would I go?" The man grinned. "In exchange for setting limbs, delivering a babe or two, putting a cracked skull back together, I'm free to satisfy all my appetites." He shook his head vehemently. "I couldn't stand England after this. No, the truth of it is I love it here. Oh, I admit it would be better without the niggers. But you take one, you have to take the other. Right?"

With the next breath Taylor was waving him back into his seat with a mild scolding. "Now, sit down and be the proper English gentleman I told the ladies you were."

John held his position by the veranda railing, thinking how pleasant it would be to bury his fist in that grinning face.

Apparently Taylor saw his expression and lightly apologized. "Oh, come now, Eden, sit down again. I meant no offense. And believe me, the best is yet to come. Shortly we will treat you to a mild display of British authority. You might learn a thing or two from it."

Reluctantly John did as he was told, a bit curious about the "grand finale" which now had drawn others out of their bungalows into the fierce heat. The green surrounding the British bungalows was filling rapidly, pale English ladies with white parasols held aloft, a large contingent of scampering children, a sense of pampered boredom heavy on the air.

John looked away. Then he heard a rustle of excitement from the crowd gathered on the green and noticed simultaneously that the muffled thunder of thousands of marching feet had ceased.

"Ah," Taylor exclaimed. "Enough talk. Pay close attention now, Eden, and you'll see the British imperial hand at its best."

All across the parade ground the regimental drill had come to a halt. The two thousand native soldiers stood erect, their discipline dazzling. The dust blew in eddies about their feet, the air stilled, no sound at all except for the residue of laughing children being summoned and hushed by their mothers.

Slowly, out of the extreme right side of John's vision, he was aware of movement, a small contingent of men emerging from one of the distant buildings, a curious procession, six native soldiers, formally garbed in military uniforms, surrounded by a larger guard of twelve men.

Curious, John asked, "What is it?"

"Punishment," Taylor said. "Oh, not of a very serious sort," he added. "Don't worry. Nothing to offend."

John observed a thin red line of soldiers encircling the waiting native troops, a rapid cordon resembling a tightened knot, their rifles at the ready. Something about the scene struck him as bizarre, armed soldiers encircling armed soldiers.

Ever helpful, Taylor leaned closer with a succinct explanation. "The niggers' guns are not loaded." He grinned. "Ours are."

John received this information as simply one more piece of the puzzle, other events beginning to take place near the center of the parade ground as now six British soldiers marched forward in close formation until they were facing the six sepoys. The rest of the guard stood back, supporting what appeared to be heavy chains between them.

To one side stood the commanding officer, who lifted his hand in signal, and one by one the six British soldiers stepped forward and pulled the shakos from the sepoys' heads and hurled them into the dust. Next, in precise gestures they tore the gold buttons from the front of the scarlet tunics, then the white cross belts, the ritual stripping proceeding at a rapid pace, the prisoners themselves removing their boots and trousers, standing ultimately naked on the hot parade ground, save for the narrow strip of white loincloth between their legs.

John looked away from the humiliating scene.

"What did they do?" he asked Dr. Taylor.

"Spread rumors, they did," the man replied. "Those six bastards circulated word that we had polluted their sugar and mixed ground bullocks' bones with the flour and that disguised in their food was cow's flesh."

"Any of it true?"

"Of course not. Well, I don't know. Christ, I'm not responsible for their feeding, thank god."

Again John looked out toward the parade ground, wishing more than ever that he'd taken an early leave. For several moments the six men stood erect in their seminaked state, not stirring. Then the remaining guard moved forward, dragging the heavy chains between them and, bending down, commenced one by one to fetter the men's ankles.

All at once, the first man who was being placed in chains lifted his head and cried out a single word.

"Asking for forgiveness." Taylor smiled.

"What is their sentence?" John asked, wondering how women and children could gaze upon such a sight.

"Ten years' hard labor on the roads," came the pat reply. "Oh, they don't like it. I can tell you that. Look! Look at them."

As the second man was placed in irons, he looked over his shoulder and shouted something to the waiting sepoys.

Taylor giggled. "That one's asking for help. Can you believe it?"

John was prepared to believe anything, his mind still occupied with the harsh sentence. Ten years' hard labor, for spreading rumors about sugar!

The fettering was a slow and clumsy process, and nerves were taut as one by one the prisoners shuffled off, some of them crying for mercy, some for help. Moved by their grief, John was in the process of looking for a more compatible horizon when suddenly he saw movement from the last of the prisoners, the only one who had yet to be fettered. Darting forward, the man in his terror raced across the parade ground, his brown legs blending with the dust, only his white loincloth sharply visible.

The unexpected escape stirred the troops, as with one accord they shifted forward. The encircling red cordon moved closer, and at the same moment, John observed a single guard raise his rifle with deliberation and sight carefully down his barrel as though he were gauging his range on a rabbit.

A single sharp report rang out over the stilled parade ground. The fleeing man's back exploded into a mass of red and he fell forward, one hand clawing for a moment, then growing still.

Nearby a small girl in her mother's arms started crying. Shocked, John stood up and turned away, facing the house now and the small congregation of servants, tears running down the women's faces, the young servant boy's face reflecting the shock that John felt.

"Oh, come now, Eden, you've seen worse," Taylor chided behind him. "There's this to be said about niggers. There's an endless supply of them, and the man *did* bolt."

But John could not take his eyes off the native faces. Ultimately they turned away first, leaving him gaping at the empty doorway. The sound of muffled marching and the shouts of the commanding officer filled his ear as the troops withdrew from the parade ground.

As always, Taylor was there, a puffing mountain of flesh and words. "Are you truly offended, Eden?" he inquired. "Surely I don't have to point out to you what would happen if such strict disciplinary measures were not taken. They outnumber us eight to one."

"No," John lied. "I'm not offended. If you'll excuse me, I must be getting back."

He saw Dr. Taylor signal the ladies that their guest was leaving. Then the large man followed him to the top of the stairs as though eager for a last private exchange. "How long will you be staying in Delhi, Mr. Eden?" he asked.

"Not long," John replied, looking out over the now deserted parade ground, where the dead man still lay, unattended.

"Does that mean"—Taylor smiled—"that you've found what you came for, or you've given up?"

"I came for nothing, Dr. Taylor," John said, "except adventure, which I've found. I'll be leaving within the month."

At that Taylor gave him a knowing grin. "I think not," he said, and lifted a finger to summon his carriage forward. "Life is too easy here, Mr. Eden. A man would

have to be a saint to deliberately remove himself from it."
His grin broadened. "And you are no saint."

Before John could offer a rebuttal, the ladies were upon
him. Graciously he thanked Mrs. Taylor for her hospitality.

Before he stepped into the carriage, he turned for a final
wave, the smile dropping from his face as he caught a
last glimpse of the dead man, still sprawled face down in
the dust.

He paid uninterested attention to the short drive to the
gate, then settled back against the cushions, trying not to
dwell on what he had seen.

Life is too easy here, Eden. A man would have to be a
saint to deliberately remove himself from it.

As the carriage picked up speed on the road leading
back into Delhi, John vowed to himself to prove the man
wrong. By the end of the month, he'd be on his horse
heading for Bombay, where he'd be more than willing to
work for passage home. He'd thought he had witnessed
the height of British stupidity in the Crimea. But that futile
exercise paled in comparison to this one.

Of course he would miss Dhari and Aslam. But they
belonged here, and he in another world. He'd give himself one month to fully regain his strength. Then he'd return to London, where he'd look up Andrew Rhoades,
perhaps even seek an audience with that dim though
lovely memory named Lila Harrington, would somehow
try to put a life together for himself, without Eden, without Harriet.

Perhaps it wouldn't be a glowing, joy-sated world. But
he'd try to make it at least endurable.

Delhi,
April 1857

WHAT PRECISELY HAD detained him for the last thirteen months, he had no idea. First, there had been the rainy season, a time when, according to Jennings, "no man in his right mind left the protection of his shelter." Then there had been Jennings himself, who had begun to exhibit all the characteristics of a graceful loser, stepping aside in the face of John's growing adoration of Dhari, even suggesting that they resume their shipboard battle of chess, Jennings playing aggressively as always, and John letting him win, wise enough to know that every man has to win at something.

Then there was the mission school itself, its routine seeming to absorb John, to fill him with an unprecedented sense of being needed. He performed an odd variety of jobs, from stacking wood to assisting Jennings with the children's lessons. Since that afternoon in the British Cantonment, it brought him incredible satisfaction to see a dark-skinned, black-eyed child smiling in pleasure.

Then there was Aslam, who had become the most persistent shadow that John had ever known. The boy dogged his steps, finding in John perhaps the father that he'd lost. The two of them enjoyed long horseback rides along the Jumna River, John thoroughly enjoying the little boy's adoration, marveling at his quick intelligence, and secretly marveling at the realization that this small brown bundle of curiosity and energy was the great-grandson of the last Emperor of the Moghul Empire.

And of course there was Dhari, who quite simply made the world beautiful for anyone fortunate enough to fall within her spell. Never had John felt so filled with well-being and gentleness. With melancholy he always watched her leave, like primordial man must have felt watching the sun go down, as though something too great to under-stand had withdrawn its warmth.

Though John had not once returned to the British Cantonment since that first disastrous afternoon, Dr. Taylor had established the habit of coming to the mission every Sunday, to "escape the bloody women," as he put it.

On this Sunday in mid-April, John sat on the steps of the mission porch, listening to the two old men behind him. He was waiting for Dhari and Aslam so they could commence their usual Sunday excursion out into the countryside. But something had detained Dhari, and Aslam was playing marbles contentedly in the courtyard, and as always the lethargic peace of the hot afternoon and the quiet Delhi streets wove a powerful spell. John lounged against the railing, only half-listening.

"Terrified of it, they are." Dr. Taylor laughed. "Won't come near it. Have you heard of it, Eden? The new rifle?"

John shook his head. The man prattled on so that it was difficult to follow him even when one was paying close attention.

"The new Enfield rifle," Taylor scolded, as though aware that he did not have the undivided attention of his limited audience.

"Well, what about it?" Jennings snorted, shifting in his chair in an effort to stay awake and hospitable.

"What about it!" Taylor parroted. "It's just set all the sepoys on their ears, that's what. You see, the gun takes greased cartridges, which must be bitten open to release their powder. Half the grease is animal tallow"—he leaned up in his chair—"made partly from pigs, it is, abominable to Muslims, and partly from cows, sacred to Hindus."

He laughed. "We have them coming and going with this one."

Reverend Jennings looked at his friend, not sharing his amusement. "Then why doesn't the army select another material?"

"They have," Taylor thundered. "But the dumb niggers won't believe us. Oh, they're convinced that we intend to defile all sepoys and break their castes."

From where John sat on the steps he could see that the

two men's expressions did not match. Jennings sat up in obvious alarm, while Taylor leaned back chuckling.

"Then they must be told the truth," Jennings insisted.

"Oh, God, they've been told the truth in every language imaginable. They're stupid, Fraser. They simply lack our intelligence."

Here was the beginning of the ancient debate which obviously had raged between the two old friends for years; the one trying to subjugate their souls, the other exploiting their services. "Still, it could be dangerous," Jennings muttered.

Taylor laughed. "Oh, nonsense. The troublemakers are few and far between, I promise." The large man stood now and stretched. "Just last month," he concluded on a yawn, "we had to shoot one at Barrackpore. Took a shot at his commanding officer, he did. Fortunately he missed. Then he turned the gun on himself and missed again. Would you believe it? At least he survived to be executed in public."

The yawn over, John saw him glance at his pocket watch. "Oh, God, Violet will be furious." As he started toward the steps, John moved to one side to give him easy passage and for his trouble received a scolding. "It's your fault, young man," Taylor grumbled genially. "You know that, don't you? I'm having a hell of a time explaining your prolonged absence to the ladies. Their inquiries are continuous. You should hear the number of ways I cover for you. Of course I'll never tell them the truth, that you've found paradise between a pair of brown legs."

From the bottom of the steps Taylor grinned up at both of them. "I'd take to locking my doors at night, Fraser, if I were you. Most of them hate your Bible as much as they hate our new rifle. And all you have for protection here is a brood of children, a native staff and a wandering Englishman."

He shook his head as though concerned. Then he burst into laughter. "A jest, Fraser, that's all," he shouted, waddling on to his waiting carriage.

John watched until the carriage was out of sight. Without looking at Jennings, he asked, "Was he serious?"

When after several moments the man had not replied,

he looked back to see him relaxed in his chair, his eyes closed. "Reggie is never terribly serious about anything," Jennings muttered.

John was on the verge of pursuing it further. But as he saw Jennings' head nod to one side, he kept his questions to himself and looked again out over the quiet courtyard. Everything was so peaceful. Here and there a wandering chicken pecked at the dirt, searching for something edible, and on the street beyond the mission, nothing stirred but dust eddies and an occasional passing beggar.

Where was Dhari? If she didn't come soon, he felt as though he would fall into a sleep as instantaneous and as deep as Jennings'. He closed his eyes to rest them from the glaring sun, Taylor's words still fresh in his ear.

We had to shoot one at Barrackpore the other day.

He saw again in memory the dead man sprawled in the dust of the parade ground with his glistening red back.

They hate your Bible as much as they hate our rifle.

"Dhari?" He opened his eyes and called inside the bungalow.

But there was no answer, only the soft click of boys playing marbles, and the screech of a kitehawk as it wheeled high in the burnished sky.

May 10, 1857

SOMETHING WAS WRONG.

John noticed that at services that morning about half the children were absent. Jennings had waited until almost eleven before starting the lessons. He'd sent John out to ring the bell again, and as he'd passed through the normally bustling kitchen, he'd found it empty, the native staff gone.

Shortly before eleven a few children had appeared,

mostly offspring of Europeans living in Delhi who sent their children for Christian training to Jennings' mission.

Dhari had appeared briefly at the beginning of the service, but at one point John had looked up to find her gone, only Aslam sitting on the rough pew, looking frightened.

At the end of the service, the white children had run out to the waiting carriages, and with undue speed the various conveyances had drawn away.

Now John watched carefully as Jennings discovered his compound deserted, and was amazed to see nothing of anxiety on the man's face. "Feed the animals, John," he ordered kindly before starting back toward the bungalow. "Then come to the kitchen. We'll have to fend for ourselves today."

Bewildered, John watched the tall figure disappear into the coolness of the house. With Aslam's assistance he fed his horse, Black, and the other animals, longing to speak, but not wanting to say anything that would alarm the boy.

Finally he couldn't resist and asked, "Do you know where Dhari is, Aslam?"

The boy was scattering feed to the chickens. "She told me to wait with you." His small hand froze in midair as he looked apprehensively up at John. "Is that all right?"

John detected the boy's worry and moved to dispel it. "Of course it is." He smiled. "Do you know where she went?"

Aslam shrugged. "She said she would be back."

"Has this happened before, Aslam?" he asked, gesturing about the deserted compound. "I mean, has everyone run off like this before?"

"No," Aslam replied, meeting John's eyes.

"Well, come," he said abruptly. "We've fed the animals, now let's feed ourselves."

They were just securing the latch on the stable door when John heard voices coming from the kitchen annex.

"Dhari . .

Then the two of them were running across the dirt courtyard and into the cool shade of the kitchen, where

Dhari was speaking with unprecedented urgency. "You must, Reverend Jennings, please."

As they entered the kitchen, she drew Aslam to her and looked at John with clearly entreating eyes. "Make him see," she pleaded. "You must leave here, both of you, and take Aslam with you."

Again Jennings interrupted. "I will not leave, Dhari," he said firmly. "I have no cause to leave."

"You will soon."

"This is my home," he repeated, "my mission. If in the past I were to have deserted it every time I heard a rumor, I would have spent more time away than here. Can't you see, the children need me."

"And can't you see there are no children. They've gone home, Reverend Jennings." Her voice softened. "Their parents know what's coming."

As Jennings turned away, John stepped forward. "What is it, Dhari?" he asked quietly, trying to offset the tension.

"Mutiny," she said simply, and gathered Aslam closer, as though for protection against the word. "I've just come from the palace," she went on. "My cousins are trying to talk my grandfather into taking command."

"A futile attempt, that," Jennings muttered. "I've tried to talk him into it myself on occasion."

"This is different, Reverend Jennings," she said, a new pleading in her voice. She shook her head as though trying to clear the confusion. "I've never heard so many rumors," she murmured, "so much activity. The palace is alive with—"

"What did you hear?" John asked.

"Everything. That the native regiment at Meerut is already in mutiny, that they will ride here during the night and join forces with—"

"Not a chance," Jennings declared. He was moving toward the door. "The rumors will be dead by morning, as will be the scheme. For now, might John and I prevail upon you for a bite of lunch? Rosa and her staff apparently elected to have themselves a holiday. Well, that's all right. We'll manage, won't we?"

"Reverend Jennings, wait." Dhari tried to call after him. But he was gone.

In despair she leaned against the table. John felt as though he were suspended between Jennings' reassurance and Dhari's distress. "Do you think there is real danger?" he asked.

"Yes," she said with conviction. "Oh, John, talk to him," she begged. "Maybe he'll listen to you. I can find a wagon for us now. We can pack a few belongings and be well away from here by dawn. Please, I beg you . . ."

He was moved by her fear, half-convinced of the validity of her words. Suddenly he had an idea. "You wait here," he ordered. "I'll be back in half an hour."

"Where are you going?"

"Fix Jennings his lunch," he called back, "and yours as well. And don't leave the compound."

He ran out of the back door, heading toward the stable, aware that she was calling after him. Hurriedly he saddled Black, aware of Dhari and Aslam at the back door watching him as he rode past. "Stay inside," he shouted, then urged the horse to a trot around the compound, guiding him carefully through the gate and onto the deserted road.

About thirty minutes later he saw the British Cantonment in the distance, placidly resting under the noon sun. The parade ground was empty, but he remembered that regimental drills did not commence until late afternoon.

He slowed at the gate, expecting to be interrogated. But the sentry boxes were empty. Obviously everyone was either napping or at Sunday dinner.

His destination was military headquarters, the large building on the right, and here he encountered a young corporal, his rifle abandoned to one side. He looked sleepily up as John approached.

"Cricket match don't start till three, mate." He grinned.

"I've not come for cricket," John said, reining Black in. "I'd like to see your commanding officer, please."

The corporal chuckled. "No chance of that. Colonel Wilson, he's gone, he is."

"Could you tell me where?"

The man shrugged. "Who knows? His wife has a sister in Agra. I think I heard he'd gone visitin'."

"Your second in command, then," John asked. "Who would that be?"

"That would be Colonel Hewitt."

"And where is he?"

"At dinner I suppose."

"Would you take me to him?"

The corporal grinned. "Ain't allowed to leave me post, sir. But he's right in there," he added, motioning through the door behind him. "Help yourself. I'll watch your pony for you."

John was tempted to turn back. Then he remembered Dhari's fears and climbed down from his mount, determined to find out what he could from whoever was in authority here.

He tied the reins to a near post, thanked the corporal and walked into the shade of the building. At the far end of the central corridor he heard men laughing, heard the clink of silverware. As he approached the double doors, he saw a sergeant in full dress who bluntly demanded, "Stop and state your business."

John obliged, stating his name and saying he'd come to see Colonel Hewitt on a matter of importance.

"Nothing more important than the colonel's dinner," the sergeant declared flatly.

John suggested that he call him out and let the colonel be the judge of that.

From beyond the door he heard several men laughing, one shouting, "More wine!"

"You see?" The sergeant grinned. "They're getting themselves ready for the cricket match this afternoon. A bloke needs lots of liquid to survive cricket in this hellhole."

John was on the verge of pushing the sergeant aside when suddenly an officer appeared beyond the door. "Didn't you hear me, Sergeant? More wine. Are you deaf?"

John took note of the scarlet tunic, unbuttoned at the neck, the slight list to the man's walk and the insignia of colonel on the sleeve.

"Colonel Hewitt?" he called through the door.

The man squinted into the corridor and seemed to pull himself erect. "Yes? I'm Colonel Hewitt. And you?"

Again John identified himself and stepped closer. "I'm staying at the mission school in Delhi," he began. "We received a rumor of an uprising at Meerut. I was wondering if you had heard—"

"Meerut?" the colonel repeated, glancing back at his fellow officers. Suddenly he looked accusingly at John. "Who sent you?" he demanded.

"No one sent me," John said, beginning to lose patience. "I was just wondering if you had heard—"

"Meerut?" the officer repeated mindlessly. The other officers were shaking their heads as though sharing his bewilderment. At last the colonel looked back at him. "No, all is quiet in Meerut. We had trouble last month at Barrackpore, but nothing to amount to anything."

John stared at him a moment longer; then, "Thank you," he said, eager to leave the place. As he started down the corridor, the colonel called after him, "You'd better stay for the cricket match. British soldiers against sepoys. It's always a good game."

But John merely waved a hand behind him and by the time he reached the front door and the blazing sun beyond, he looked back to see the colonel gone, the distant sound of men laughing striking the silence of the afternoon.

As he reappeared on the steps, the corporal looked up at him. "That was quick. Take it you found him."

John nodded and swung up on his horse. As he started back down the road, he saw a few children playing croquet around the bungalows. The tedium of a Sunday afternoon was commencing.

Once through the gates, he looked back at the cantonment, which seemed to be sleeping in an immense dream. Even the Union Jack atop headquarters hung limp on its standard, this little pocket of England fast asleep in its foreign clime.

When he reached the mission, he turned the horse over to Aslam and found Dhari and Jennings in the kitchen. Briefly he told them where he'd been and what had happened.

Jennings grinned. "There, you see. And you should have stayed," he scolded lightly. "That's always a first-rate cricket match. I saw it several years ago. Of course, the British always win, but the natives give us a run for our money."

John glanced toward Dhari, who seemed to be looking at him as though he'd betrayed her. "Dhari . . ." he began.

But she left the room, left him standing before the table, his sentence half-formed.

"Pay her no mind," Jennings counseled. "She's a woman and tends to moods. They all do. Come, now, have a bite of lunch, and let's take advantage of the quiet afternoon for a game of chess."

John said nothing and looked with regret at the open door through which Dhari had disappeared. Would it have made her happier if he had brought her news of murder and rioting sepoys?

Maybe Jennings was partially right. A game of chess, then he'd seek her out and make his apologies for the absence of hard facts to support her fears.

The truth was that the only excitement taking place in all of Delhi this afternoon was the cricket match at the British Cantonment between Englishmen and Indians.

Delhi,
May 11, 1857

IT WAS THE silence that awakened him, the same heavy silence they had endured all Sunday afternoon and evening.

He opened his eyes and saw a morning sun. The courtyard was usually alive with children at this hour, their voices shattering his early-morning sleep.

He sat up, still hearing nothing. From the window he saw nothing but deserted streets, and beyond that the brown plain.

Quickly he dressed, repeatedly thinking he'd heard something. But nothing moved except the morning wind.

As he hurried out into the hall, he glanced toward the central corridor, where normally the children were being lined up by staff members, all speaking that peculiar mix of Urdu and Hindi and English, hoping to say something that someone understood.

Now? Nothing but the shadows of the sun on polished hardwood floor.

Suddenly he started toward the front door at an increased pace, needing to see for himself that the children were at their desks.

Hurrying toward the classroom, he looked back over his shoulder, thinking he'd seen fleeting movement beyond the wall. Then he was running, taking the three steps in one stride, pushing open the classroom doors.

The rows of desks were empty, the windows closed. He heard his own deep breathing and was on the verge of retracing his steps when, peering closer toward the front of the large room, he saw a figure on his knees, clearly at prayer before the simple altar.

"Jennings?"

But there was no response. He started to call again, then changed his mind. At least he'd found someone. Now, Dhari? And Aslam? Where were they?

Midway between classroom and bungalow he lifted his head and heard a curious popping sound in the distance. It came in a sporadic flurry, then ceased, then commenced again. Gun reports?

Suddenly, on the road beyond the mission compound he saw three men running. They passed through the shadows and were gone before he had a clear look at them.

He gained the steps, his head turning in all directions. Blindly he reached out for the door, his hand stopping in midair as from the right he heard the muffled sound of horses, coming fast. He stepped back into the shadows of the porch, feeling the need to conceal himself. A few moments later about half a dozen horses galloped by, their riders, excited Indians, waving swords and torches.

He stared after the curious charge, holding his position until they had disappeared. He'd just stepped inside the door when he heard a distant explosion.

Then it came again, another explosion, louder than the first, causing the floor beneath his feet to vibrate. He braced for a third explosion, peering skyward, searching for the smoke which would identify the location and cause of such explosions.

He stood a moment longer, then turned back into the house, shouting, "Dhari," as he ran down the entrance hall and burst through the kitchen door. He saw her seated calmly at the broad kitchen table, Aslam beside her, two bowls before them.

"Did you hear?" he shouted.

She looked up, her face composed in its customary serenity. "I heard," she said. She pointed toward the corner of the kitchen, toward a shattered pile of china fragments. "It broke Mrs. Jennings' china platter."

John only glanced toward the broken china. "What was it?" he asked, hurrying toward the back window and looking in the direction of the British Cantonment, where he found his answer in the distant boiling clouds of black smoke. "The . . . arsenal," he murmured in disbelief.

"I'd say yes," Dhari commented quietly.

John watched the smoke as it rose higher into the sky, and finally looked back at Dhari.

"Perhaps we should leave," he said.

She smiled. "I'm afraid it's too late for that. You wouldn't get to the city walls."

"We could try."

"You would fail. It's best now to stay here."

Suddenly her serenity began to annoy him. "Then what do you suggest we do?" he shouted. "What's going on out there? I've seen men riding . . ."

She nodded. "They're from Meerut. I spoke early this morning with one of my cousins. According to him, there's no one left alive in Meerut."

"I don't believe that."

"It's true," she said. "The sepoys have ridden all night. This morning they will be joined by an armed force within the palace."

As her voice droned on, it was momentarily drowned out by thunderous hooves coming from the road in front of the mission. Aslam left his chair, his curiosity drawing him to the window with John. "What is it?" the boy asked.

John shook his head. "You wait here. I'll—"

"I wouldn't, John," Dhari suggested strongly from the table. "I think it's best to stay out of sight."

Still annoyed by her passive acceptance of a world going mad, John snapped, "I'd better get Jennings. He's in—"

"I know. He's been at prayer all night. He'll be along soon enough. I have his breakfast ready."

"Breakfast!" John repeated. "We must leave here, Dhari. Can't you see—"

"I saw it yesterday," she replied, her voice suddenly cold. "We could have been far away by now." She bowed her head. "Now we must wait and hope that . . ."

At that moment, Jennings appeared in the doorway, his cheeks ablaze with color. "Did you hear?" he demanded excitedly. "Did you hear the explosions?" He hurried to the window and peered out. "Look at that." He grinned. "It's happening. My God, it's happening at last."

He commenced pacing about the kitchen. "I never thought it would, you know, not in my lifetime. Oh, I knew they would rise up one day, but I never dreamed—"

"What are you talking about?" John demanded, trying to cut through the man's bizarre joy.

"Rebellion!" Jennings shouted. "Hindu and Muslim, high caste and sepoy, forgetting their difference in a common hatred for the British." Suddenly he clapped his hands together as though in joyful thanksgiving. "Oh, God, how long I've prayed for it, for the resurrection of the Indian spirit, the courage to reclaim what we've taken from them."

John could only stare, suffering the rising conviction that he was listening to a madman.

"Come," he commanded Aslam, gathering the boy to him, hoping by the force of his voice to stir the other two to good sense. "We must leave. We'll go the back way. I'll saddle Black and—"

Over the urgency of his command he heard Dhari's voice. "Reverend Jennings, your porridge is waiting."

With his arm still about Aslam's shoulder, John watched as Jennings sat at table and bowed his head in prayer. "Who among all these does not know that the hand of the Lord has done this?" he prayed, his face lifted with a smile. "In His hand is the life of everything and the breath of all mankind."

"Jennings!" John commanded. "Dhari!" But both heads were bowed in a murmuring recitation of the Lord's Prayer, while beyond the window the noise increased, the sounds of a world disintegrating, women's screams now blending with the shouts of men.

John lifted Aslam into his arms, feeling himself somehow allied with the only intelligence in the room, and carrying the little boy, he hurried out of the kitchen toward the front parlor, whose window gave a perfect view of the courtyard and street beyond.

As he passed by the front door, he shut it and threw the bolt and glanced through the lace curtains in time to see two white women running down the street, their skirts billowing, hair undone, their arms flailing uselessly at the four men on horseback who pursued them. One stumbled and fell, disappearing behind the low wall, and within the moment the men were upon her, bending over in their saddles, driving their long swords downward again and again, lifting them into the air after each thrust. The second woman stopped and looked back, and was instantly hacked down by a long curved cavalry tulwar.

John shut his eyes, still grasping Aslam to him, and tried desperately to conceive of a mode of escape. Not on foot. Dhari was right. They would never get to the city walls. But there still was a chance on horseback, leaving by the rear.

As he turned to execute his plan, he saw Jennings and Dhari coming toward him down the long hall, one face placid, the other wreathed in a smile.

Aware of the carnage taking place beyond the wall, John warned, "Get back, both of you."

Still they came, Jennings sending his voice ahead in reassurance. "There's no need to be afraid, John." He smiled. "They have no quarrel with us. We've done nothing to offend them."

Dhari passed him by and went into the front parlor and took up a vigil by the window there, throwing her voice back into the hall with a soft warning. "You'd better get away from the door, both of you. If they see you . . ."

Then they did. Still peering through the curtains at the door, John saw a large contingent of armed men riding up from the direction of the palace, at least thirty horsemen and as many on foot, their faces indistinguishable from the distance. Then effortlessly the first line of horsemen leaped the wall and led their mounts around the dusty courtyard.

Quickly John withdrew, taking Aslam with him, joining Dhari at the window in the parlor. "We could still leave," he said urgently.

But she shook her head, an expression of sadness in her face as she peered through the curtains at the clouds of dust rising about the stamping hooves, the courtyard filled with laughing, shouting men, their figures black against the flames of the burning huts across the road.

Several carried torches, and as they started toward the steps of the bungalow, John heard the bolt at the front door slide, saw that Dhari had heard it as well, and for the first time saw fear in her eyes.

"No," she whispered, and pushed past him, calling out, "No, Reverend Jennings, don't . . ."

They reached the entry hall at the same time and saw Jennings smiling at them, his hand on the bolt. "Don't worry," he said. "I know these men. They are your grandfather's guards. I've taught many of their children to read and write. I'll talk to them."

"No, please," Dhari begged. "Don't go out."

But the bolt was sliding again, the door opening, and again Jennings looked back at them with a radiant smile. "And I heard a voice from heaven saying, write this." He quoted, " 'Blessed are the dead who die in the Lord henceforth. Blessed indeed, said the Spirit, that they may rest from their labors, for their deeds follow them.' "

He passed through the door, accompanied by one final cry from Dhari.

From outside, John heard a sudden cessation of voices as the sepoys caught sight of Jennings. John moved to the window and stood behind Dhari, one hand grasping Aslam's wrist, ignoring the little boy's pleas to "Let me see!"

At the moment there was nothing to see but the stillness of the confrontation itself, the men with torches moving slowly back before the black-clad figure.

Then he saw Jennings lift both arms into the air, speaking full-voiced in native tongue, moving down the steps, several of the horsemen parting to make way for him.

"What's he saying?" John whispered.

"He's . . . praising them," Dhari murmured, "for their courage, for reclaiming what is rightfully theirs."

The waiting stretched on, Jennings filling the quiet with his resolute voice, smiling now and then up at a dark face, patting a horse's head, reaching out to touch a hand.

John felt the tension, his eyes watering at the intensity of his gaze. Overhead, the sun, rising to midmorning, beat down, catching and reflecting the glitter of a sword.

Suddenly the once-stilled men erupted into a frenzy of movement, shattering the stillness as all pushed forward toward the core, the place where Jennings stood. Dhari screamed as time and time again the men lunged forward with their swords, plunging them downward.

John watched as though in a trance, as if such a catastrophe were not possible, mindlessly clinging to the hope that somehow Jennings was not at the center of that bloody attack.

But that frail hope was shattered by one sharp cry from Dhari, who had never taken her eyes off the scene and who pressed back against John, both her hands covering her mouth. Her eyes clearly reflected the atrocity which John saw now, Jennings' decapitated head lifted aloft on a sword, the severed tendons and muscles dripping blood, that beneficent smile still on his face, as with a great roar the men shouted their approval and passed the sword among themselves, causing the head to tremble as though it were still alive.

John twisted away, dragging Aslam with him.

Again he heard Dhari's voice behind him, as though, past the initial shock, she'd scarcely been affected by the tragedy.

"Listen closely," she said. "Wait here with Aslam. I'll lead them away. As soon as we're gone, take Aslam, get the horse and ride out the back."

"No."

But she rushed over his protest. "Aslam," she whispered to the boy, "take him the secret way."

The little boy nodded solemnly.

Again John tried to protest. "I'm not leaving without you."

"I'll meet you beyond the toll house at the lower end of the bridge," she rushed on. "There's a grove of trees there. Wait, and I'll come as soon as I can."

Still not convinced of the validity of the plan, John begged, "Come with us now. We could still—"

But she was shaking her head. "No, please, do as I say. They won't harm me, I promise. It's your only chance."

As once again the cries arose from the courtyard, John pulled her to him. Wordlessly she kissed him, drew Aslam to her for an embrace, then she was gone. At the door she stopped for a final instruction. "Stay out of sight until I lead them away," she whispered, "then run."

John nodded and once again lifted Aslam into his arms. He carried the boy to the window and abruptly lowered him to the floor as he saw Jennings' decapitated head still being passed among the men.

When the men caught sight of Dhari, they fell silent. To John's amazement, she moved directly toward them, her hands waving excitedly toward the road, clearly relaying the false message that the other white man had fled. Several of the horsemen started out at a gallop toward the wall, only to be stopped by a shout from the others, who now encircled Dhari cautiously, looking down upon her with suspicious eyes.

Aslam started to speak. John clamped his hand over the boy's mouth as again a stillness descended on the courtyard. Apparently the men were divided, half wanting to take off immediately in pursuit, the other half doubting her words.

One of the men slid from his mount, grasped the sword bearing Jennings' head and thrust it before her face.

John saw her draw back. Then he saw her recover, step forward and spit into the dead face.

All at once a roar of approval went up from the watching men. The sepoy who had dismounted climbed back onto his horse, and grinning, reached down and swung Dhari up into the saddle with him.

With a triumphant yell, still holding the sword aloft, he led the way back into the road, the others following after him, and in a miraculously short time the courtyard was empty save for the settling clouds of dust and the mutilated body of Fraser Jennings.

John pushed away from the window and leaned against the wall, clasping Aslam to him. A smell of smoke was now filling the room, the crackling of flames growing louder. He looked out at the front porch and saw it on fire, lit apparently by a torch which had been tossed backward.

The small hand suddenly twisted in his, the child leading. "Come, John," the boy whispered, "I know the way."

Then they were running back through the bungalow. They ran across the rear courtyard toward the stable, where, even before he'd opened the door, he heard Black neighing in fear as the smoke reached his nostrils.

"No time to saddle," John shouted as Aslam started toward the tack room. Quickly he threw the harness on, drew back the reins, lifted Aslam up onto the broad black back and pulled himself up behind.

With only a few words, Aslam directed him through the rear gate and down the narrow alleyway, past low bungalows, bypassing the central bazaars altogether. He heard shouts and screams in the distance, and the continuous muffled reports of rifles. But not until they entered the lower street did they encounter anything, and then he tried to draw the boy closer to him and shield his eyes from the scene, the ground littered with corpses, dogs already foraging on the dead flesh.

His thoughts moved to Dhari, and he felt a prayer forming in his head. He wrapped his arms more tightly about Aslam and wondered how the boy would survive with images like these burned into his consciousness.

Ahead he saw the Kashmir Gate, and beyond that the toll house. He drew Black to one side, thinking that the rampaging sepoys would surely place a guard at the gate.

But to his surprise, he saw the gate empty save for the sprawled bodies of British soldiers where apparently they had pursued the marauders as far as the gate before being hacked down.

West of the gate he looked up toward the settlement of Daryaganj, a small suburb occupied by minor European families and Eurasian officials. Coming from that direction he now heard cries and shouts, saw the sky overhead black with smoke, and realized that the rebels were going through the city, a section at a time, thus accounting for their absence here.

Then hurry! Tightening his grasp on Aslam, he urged Black forward, and felt the horse respond with a sudden burst of speed. He would have passed the grove of trees altogether had it not been for Aslam's cry, "There! We're to wait there."

Sharply John pulled back on the reins and guided Black into the shelter, moving immediately toward a vantage point where he could see through the foliage in all directions.

"Can we get down?" Aslam asked.

John hesitated. Unarmed, his only defense for himself and the boy was this fast horse and a moment's head start. He looked over his shoulder toward the gate, trying to remember if Dhari had set a time. One hour? Two? But he couldn't remember and had no intention of leaving without her, and in order to pacify Aslam, assisted him down to the dirt and urged him to "Stay close."

John remained on the horse. With the exception of the fires and smoke, he saw nothing moving, though he continued to hear the reports of distant guns, which told him the rebellion was far from over, their escape not yet completed.

It was late that afternoon when John heard approaching horses. He looked through the trees toward the Kashmir Gate, and with one hand drew Aslam close. Still keeping his eyes on the approaching horsemen, he moved slowly to where he'd secured Black to a tree. He swung Aslam up and was in the process of following suit when suddenly he noticed something different about the riders. They were riding their horses at a slowed, almost ritualistic pace. These men were drawing near with due deliberation.

No matter, thought John. Again he grasped the horse and was in the process of swinging up when he noticed something else. The lead rider was not alone. Someone was sitting with him in the saddle.

Still grasping the reins, he whispered to Aslam, "Keep still," fairly confident that the man could not see into the thickness of the grove, and curious about the passenger whose head and face seemed to be obscured by a black hood and whose hands he now saw were bound in front.

At what point recognition became clear, he didn't know. Perhaps it was the hem of the sari he'd seen earlier that morning in the kitchen annex. Or perhaps it was Aslam's whisper, "Mama . . ." the child's voice breaking for the first time into a tone which resembled adult fear.

Still the riders drew nearer, until they were less than fifty yards from the grove of trees. The others halted, and that one lone rider proceeded forward at a slowed pace, the specifics of his passenger clearer. It *was* Dhari, of that he was certain, but why was her face hooded, her hands bound, and why . . . ?

Then all at once the rider pushed her off the horse; she landed on her feet and seemed to stand erect for a moment, then suddenly collapsed, falling to her knees, then the rest of the way to earth, her bound hands clasping something which spilled in her fall, scattering small glittering lights of reds and greens across the brown earth.

The rider watched her for a moment, then reined his horse about and galloped back to the others.

"Mama," Aslam whimpered.

As John saw him struggling down from the horse, he warned sternly, "Wait! Do you hear me? Don't leave Black."

Reluctantly the boy agreed, his eyes still focused on his mother. "Go get her," he whispered, "please."

John moved cautiously to the edge of the trees, his attention divided between the lifeless figure of Dhari and the band of horsemen a short distance away. Why didn't they leave? They must know he was here. Were they using her as a decoy to draw him out?

All at once he heard her groan, a sound of pain mixed with fear. She turned weakly over onto her back in the dust, scattering more of the small glittering objects; then she was quiet.

Still keeping to the meager protection of the trees, John looked again toward the waiting horsemen. Suddenly he darted forward in full view, approaching Dhari at top speed, intent only on lifting her into his arms, then retreating.

But as he drew near her collapsed body, he saw the spilled objects in the dust, gems, countless in numbers, a dazzling array of diamonds, emeralds, rubies, the empty pouch still clasped between her bound hands. He fell on his knees and lifted her, while with his other hand he reached for as many as he could gather, was still struggling to collect them when he heard the sharp reports of rifles, the bullets hitting nearby, raising small explosions of dust.

The riders in the distance commenced shouting now and firing another round. John gathered her to him and left all the stones save for the few scooped up in his hand, and ran with her back toward the trees, feeling her head inside the black hood bob lifelessly against his chest.

"Move back!" he shouted to Aslam, and saw the boy slide toward the horse's rear, his hands outreaching to assist John up, dragging Dhari after him.

"Hold on tight," he shouted to Aslam, and cradling Dhari in his arms, he dug his heels into Black, and with a cry urged him forward, exploding out of the thicket of trees at top speed, seeing the horsemen still grouped nearby, but not looking back to see if they were in pursuit, certain that they were.

Not until he was approaching the rise of land where he and Jennings had stopped for a rest on that day so long ago did he cease pounding the horse's sides. As Black slowed to a canter, he looked back for the first time and saw the riders in the distance, still on the other side of the bridge, filing slowly back through the Kashmir Gate. Clearly they had let them escape. For what reason, he had no idea.

From that vantage point he viewed the entire city, saw it in flames, every structure burning, the only portion of the horizon intact and not on fire the Red Fort and the palace within.

"Is Mama . . .?

"I don't know," John said. "We can't stop here." He urged Black forward, trying to keep his eyes on the road and at the same time on the hooded head.

They rode without speaking for over an hour. Shortly before dusk, John left the road and took off across the open fields, heading for a distant fringe of trees.

With the flame-streaked sunset behind them, he guided Black into the dense trees and heard water nearby. He brought the horse to a halt and slid down, carrying Dhari with him. He was aware of Aslam following closely behind as he placed her on the grass.

"Take Black to the stream," he ordered Aslam.

At first the boy glared defiantly down on him, as though he knew he was being sent away.

"Please," John whispered, relieved to see the boy obey.

Slowly he approached the hooded face, and with one hand cradling her head, withdrew the hood and stared down. Her eyes were closed, her mouth distorted by a blood-soaked cloth which had been stuffed between her lips. Quickly he removed it, felt it so filled with blood that it dripped freely as he tossed it into the grass. Yet what was the source of bleeding? He saw no cuts on her face, her lovely features intact except for the smeared blood about her mouth, her lips parted from the thickness of the gag, revealing . . .

No, God!

Had he cried aloud? He closed his eyes, then opened them, then leaned closer, his fingers gently separating her lips, growing red with her blood.

She had no tongue. They had cut out her . . .

"John?"

He looked up through blurred eyes to see Aslam standing nearby, and could not find any words to keep him from coming closer.

"Is she . . . dead?" the little boy asked fearfully.

It was that simple question which stirred John out of his grief and into action. No, she was not dead, and gently he lowered her to the grass and commenced tugging at the rope about her wrists, trying to keep his eyes away from the atrocity of her mouth. He pulled his shirtwaist free from his trousers, ripped the tail and handed the material to Aslam with an order, "Soak it with water. Hurry!"

As the boy dashed off into the shadows, he raised her head and slipped beneath her, cradling her in his lap, his hands mindlessly smoothing the blood-soaked sari as though feeling the need to put something in order.

Why hadn't they just killed her, killed him as well? But no. Obviously they had discovered that she had lied to them, and apparently lacking the will to kill the granddaughter of the Emperor, they'd merely rendered her silent so that she would never lie again to anyone.

These suppositions only heightened his grief, and as he lifted his head to shout for Aslam, the boy appeared, holding the dripping cloth in front of him, his eyes wide with fear.

"She isn't dead, Aslam," John soothed, taking the cloth, "and she won't die, I promise you." He commenced gently to cleanse her face, guiding the cloth about her lips.

Opposite him, Aslam squatted, watching closely, holding her hand. A few moments later, John felt her stir in his arms, her head twisting, and at last, her eyes opened, first to him, then to Aslam, then grew wider in terror, apparently at the memory of her torture.

A strangling sound escaped her lips, the voice box intact but the instrument of speech gone. She tried again, louder this time, the grief and frustration clear upon her face, her eyes searching John's, one hand grasping his shoulder as though begging him to help.

"Don't, Dhari," he whispered.

It came a third time, a moan which rose to a wail, her hands moving to her mouth as though to deny what she knew was true. Suddenly she seemed to suffer a spasm; her head fell backward, a low gurgling sound rose in her throat and almost violently John pushed her onto her side as the vomit of blood erupted in a crimson stream, Aslam on his knees staring in fear, John bent over her as though wanting to take the racking convulsions into his own body, enclosing her tightly, unmindful of the warm red liquid spilling out over his arm.

Not until the sky was streaked with the light of dawn did he feel it was safe to close his eyes and not keep a watch on the field and the road beyond.

At several intervals during that long night he'd heard horses on the road, and drunken cries, and had seen torchlight, all confirming what he feared, that the mutiny was spreading, that it would be impossible to travel in safety on the road.

Worse than that, all night long he'd observed the red glow which had filled the night sky in the direction of Delhi. All hope of a quick military put-down was lost, as was the hope of returning and seeking medical aid for Dhari. There was only one safe direction now, and that was south, either to Bombay or Calcutta, a torturous journey he knew well from experience, made doubly impossible now by the fact that he was traveling with a child, a seriously ill woman, no food, no blankets, no money.

All at once the bleak inventory blended with his fatigue and his sense of horror at the various atrocities he'd witnessed firsthand, and he stumbled on a protruding root and went down on his knees. As he fell, he heard a curious clinking sound inside his pocket and with a strange listlessness reached inside with one blood-caked hand and withdrew three gems: one a ruby about the size of his thumb, another slightly larger, and one emerald of equal proportion. He stared at them, at first unable to identify them.

Slowly he sat upon the ground, remembering all. Why had she gone back inside the palace? For these? Suddenly he enclosed the stones in an angry fist and looked up toward the crude pallet of banyon boughs less than ten feet away, an equally crude coverlet of reeds and brushes covering the two small figures, both of them sleeping soundly despite their makeshift bed.

He'd have to awaken them soon. They must put distance between themselves and the burning city, the possibility that the sepoys would change their minds and come after them, for he was certain now that they had been allowed to escape. On whose orders, he had no idea. Perhaps her grandfather's, or a sympathetic cousin's. Or perhaps they had been permitted to escape because the rebel sepoys had known that they would never make it to safety, that a prolonged dying on the road would be more agonizing than a decisive thrust of a sword.

The sun was climbing. It was time to move. They must find food before too long. He was aware of the gems still clutched in his fist. Curious, these had been his purpose for coming here. Now they were of no value to him whatsoever, and willingly he would have given them all over for transportation away from this place of danger.

He heard a soft moan and looked toward the pallet. Dhari was stirring, one hand lifting as though to fight off unseen assailants. He hurried to her side and knelt down, held her hands between his own until the terror of her nightmare passed, until she found the courage to face the terror of the day.

Close beside her, Aslam was still sleeping. Carefully John drew back the covering of boughs and lifted her in his arms, noting an increase in the bruises and swelling about her face.

Gently he carried her to the banks of the stream, went down on his knees with her in the mud, lifted the dried cloth which had fallen onto her breasts, soaked it with water and applied it to her bruised lips.

Once she'd had her fill of water, he moistened the cloth again and tried to cleanse her face, aware of her eyes upon him. He found himself praying for both their sakes that she did not try to speak again. The sound he'd heard her make the night before still echoed in his ear. Silence was better.

"We must travel today, Dhari," he began. "Are you strong enough?"

She nodded.

"We'll go slowly," he promised. "Has the bleeding stopped?"

With her head pressed against the trunk of the tree, she opened her mouth as though for his inspection. The small cavity was dark, but he saw the severed ends of the tongue, the jagged tissue white now, the bleeding stopped.

Gently he leaned forward and kissed her. He reached down for her hand and placed the three gems in her palm. "I'm afraid the rest spilled," he said.

She looked down as though in surprise, and returned them to him, her lips moving in that same low monotone. She tried to form words and failed, and as her frustration mounted, he drew her close, her sobs filling his ear.

"Don't, Dhari, please," he begged, knowing what she had wanted to say.

The gems were his. She'd gone back. *For him.*

"I'll never leave you," he whispered. "You'll be with me always. Do you understand?"

He held her face between his hands, needing her reassurance that she understood. Slowly her sobbing subsided, and with one hand she reached out to him, caressed his forehead as though he were the one in need of comfort.

At first her recovery and their progress had been nothing short of miraculous. But ten days later, as they were approaching the outskirts of Mirzapur, she fell forward across the horse in a faint, and John, walking ahead, was summoned by Aslam's cries. Running back, he caught her before she dropped to earth, lifted her down into his arms, felt her brow on fire and saw a black foam issuing from her lips.

Quickly he made camp, and as always sent Aslam on ahead into the village. He'd learned long ago that his white face would gain them nothing. But apparently no one could resist the beautiful little boy. Daily Aslam had done the scouting, had wandered into the village of the moment and had always returned with something, chuppatis, fruit and on occasion a roasted chicken. John had never quizzed the boy too closely on whether the food had been given or stolen.

Now at midafternoon, with Aslam still gone, he cradled her in his arms, fearing the worst. She'd not regained consciousness once. As he held her, he rocked gently back and forth, suffering that peculiar awareness that he'd lost a portion of his senses, that the events of the last two weeks had taken a toll from which neither of them would ever fully recover, hiding from black and white alike, for to the Indians *she* was traveling with the enemy, and to the whites *he* was traveling with the enemy.

At last, though untutored and unskilled, he lifted his head and prayed to whatever god happened to be in the vicinity, tried to remember how Reverend Jennings had done it, what words he had spoken. But he could remember nothing that made sense, and settled at last for simply admitting to the green boughs overhead that he had done all he could do, and if there was any truth to divine intervention, he needed it now, for Dhari's sake.

He closed his eyes and waited, sensing, in spite of his amateur's prayer, that no one had heard. It was while his eyes were still closed that he heard horses, looked up and saw a half dozen fierce-looking riders drawing near, their black robes blowing backward, their bearded faces obscured. And in the lead, as though that most horrible nightmare were being performed in repetition, he saw Aslam, his eyes wide with fear, held a prisoner by the lead rider.

Hurriedly he placed Dhari on the grass and stumbled upward, and had taken only three steps forward when the horsemen surrounded him, their faces smeared with white dust, the leader grinning down.

Frantically John turned in all directions, bitterly thanking God for his answered prayer. As he heard an outcry from Aslam, he looked back to see the rider holding a knife at the boy's throat.

Then, because he could endure no longer, because he'd seen more spilled blood and mutilated bodies than a man could see and still survive, he lunged toward the knife-

wielding rider, was just outreaching to pull him down and
wrest the knife from him when he felt a noose go around
his neck.

He struggled uselessly, then fell backward, seeing the
sun explode into a thousand fragments overhead. As the
earth rose up to meet him, he thought quite lucidly that
this was for the best. At least he could die with Dhari.

Compared to what he'd recently seen of living, death
seemed a worthy alternative.

He awakened to two companions: one, Kali the Terrible, Kali the blood goddess, consort of Shiva the De-
stroyer, naked, stuck all about with human skulls.

And two, a fat, well-fed, massive black-and-white-
striped cat who licked his face with a rough tongue and
brought him back to consciousness. If this was death, he'd
been here before.

Slowly he raised up from the pallet and saw a third
companion seated near his feet.

"Aslam . . ."

As the temple spun about him, he lay back, aware of
the boy hovering over him.

Not far away he heard the high chatter of men's voices
raised in dispute. He looked in that direction, recognized
the rider who'd held the knife to Aslam's throat. And another, an older priest with graying beard who seemed to
be speaking with authority. He'd seen that face before as
well.

They were in the Thuggee Temple at Bindhachal. The
old priest was the one who had adorned him, given him
the gift of the rumal and the horse.

The men saw him looking at them. Steadily they returned his gaze and came forward until they were standing over him. He was aware of Aslam's hand in his and
thought with grief on Dhari.

Laboriously the old priest squatted beside him, his
leathery face a network of wrinkles. He said something
and waited for an answer. Helpless, John looked to
Aslam.

The boy smiled. "He wants to know if you've made up
your mind yet? Are you a white man or an Indian?"

John failed to see the humor in the question. "Tell him I'm neither," he muttered. "Tell him at the moment I'm simply a lost man."

As the boy repeated the message in his high clear voice, John raised himself to a sitting position.

After the translation, the old priest laughed, and spoke again, his face growing suddenly sober.

Again John was dependent upon Aslam, who relayed the message. "He wants to know where we have come from."

"Tell him."

John watched the exchange, trying to read the moods on their various faces. The talk was concluding now. The group of black-robed men standing behind the priest still glared down on both John and Aslam, as though they had been deprived of something.

Sensing an impasse, John reached into his pocket and withdrew one of the gems. He handed it to Aslam and said, "Tell them that in exchange for food and shelter, we will give them this."

Aslam looked at the ruby, then extended it toward the priest. Suddenly the men standing behind leaned forward.

The old priest shouted them back, and with the cunning of a bargainer grinned slyly at Aslam.

The boy translated. "He wants to know if you have more."

John tried to stare the old man down, but realized ultimately they could take whatever they wanted, including their lives. Reluctantly he dipped into his pocket and produced the remaining two gems. Reverently the priest studied the stones. A broad grin cut across his face as he handed the emerald to one of the waiting men, kept the larger ruby for himself, and apparently suffering from some sense of fair play, returned the smaller ruby to John.

The men drifted off, appeased, admiring their new wealth. Slowly the old priest stood. John started up after him, struggling to ask the most difficult question. "Dhari . . ." he whispered to Aslam. "Ask him about . . ."

Drawing Aslam close as though for protection against what they might find, they followed the priest around the goddess Kali, down a corridor to a cell near the rear of the temple. The old priest pushed open the door, then stepped back, allowing them access to the room, to the low bed and the figure of a woman lying prone, another priest bending over her, applying what appeared to be a coating of moist red mud to the inside of her mouth.

John moved to the foot of the bed and stared down on a glorious sight, Dhari alive, her eyes open, one hand lifting toward him.

He knelt beside her while the priest applied the curious compound, which, up close, smelled of herbs.

Suddenly he felt shy. Were thanks due? And to what god? Surely not to Kali, whose heritage was strangulation and death?

Then who? Lacking an answer, he merely drew Aslam beside him and let their closeness and the fact of their survival suffice for prayer.

Three weeks later, he stood on the crowded docks of Howrah outside Calcutta, with Dhari and Aslam waiting in the cart behind him, and tried to do business with Captain Lewis, whose sailing ship the *Bluebeard* would be the last to leave India for the next six weeks.

"Full!" the old English captain pronounced. "Full, as you can see," he grumbled, motioning behind him to the stream of people filing up the gangplank.

John saw all too well, had been watching for most of the morning the procession of women and children with meager belongings, all victims of the mutiny, whose carnage had spread, or so John had heard, as far as Cawnpore, where not one man, woman or child had been left alive.

"Please," John begged, trying to keep his voice down, not wanting to alarm Dhari and Aslam. "We'll take any accommodations."

The ruddy-faced man laughed. "Any accommodations," he parroted sarcastically. He pointed toward Dhari and Aslam waiting in the cart. "With garbage like that, even if I had room, I'd have to put you in the hold. No decent Englishwoman would want to breathe the air with the likes of them."

John lifted his head and tried to look beyond the mean-faced old man to the ship itself. "The hold will do fine," he said. "Name your price."

But the captain merely glared at John's persistence. Then something crossed his face, the look of the predator. "Two thousand pounds," he pronounced flatly. "For the three of you, that is, for yourself and the garbage."

John turned away. He'd hoped to make the transaction using the ox cart and two horses which the old priest at Bindhachal had given them.

"Two thousand pounds," the man repeated, grinning.

John looked over his shoulder toward the cart. Dhari gazed back at him, her beautiful face fully restored now, not one sign of her ordeal visible even to the most careful eye. But he knew all to well the full extent of her agony, the persistent difficulty in swallowing, the painful recuperation, and the even more painful acceptance that she was condemned to a life of silence. How often he'd found her kneeling in prayer in that small cell behind the pagan goddess Kali. Gradually her spiritual strength had returned, along with her physical strength, and both John and Aslam were becoming quite skillful in reading her eyes. Not since that first night had she made any sound at all. And John suspected that she never would again.

Yet, curiously, without speech she had grown more beautiful, her serene spirit more articulate than ever.

"Two thousand pounds," the captain repeated. "Take it or leave it," and immediately he turned away as though certain that he'd closed the door.

But John caught his arm and turned him back and reached into his pocket for the remaining ruby. He held it up for the man's inspection and saw the light of new interest spread on the corrupt face.

"Ah . . ." He grinned. "You're taking more than garbage with you out of Mother India, I see."

As he reached eagerly for the gem, John withdrew it. "Three beds," he demanded, "and three meals a day and transportation from Portsmouth to London when we reach England."

"My Gawd," the man muttered, "do you want me to piss for you as well?"

"Take it or leave it," John said, still holding the gem just beyond the man's reach.

"Oh, I'll take it right enough." The captain grinned. "And do your bidding." He shrugged. "What's it to me what you take back with you?" He smiled and leaned close. "I understand the woman right enough," he whispered. "She'll bring you a pretty penny on the London market. But the boy, what in God's name do you plan to do with him?"

John felt his right arm stiffen, felt that if he did not escape the man's presence soon, the *Bluebeard* would not have a captain. Yet, paradoxically, at the moment he felt the need to strike out, he felt equally old and tired, felt as though his shoulders were sagging, that if he were to walk away now, he would not be able to walk erect.

"Then it's settled," he said, and thrust the gem into the waiting palm and hurried back to the cart. Without a word he motioned for Dhari and Aslam to get out. He nuzzled Black's nose and looked around the crowded dock. No one there was in need of a cart and three horses. They were all fleeing this place with the same urgency as was John. At the edge of the dock he spied an old Indian, footsore, his hand outstretched, begging.

John brought the horses about and guided the cart to where the old man stood. He placed the reins in the man's hand, ignoring the surprised look in the face. Hurriedly he hugged Black one last time and ran back to where Dhari and Aslam were waiting, aware that they both had been closely watching.

"Must we leave him?" Aslam begged.

"We must," John said, wishing his voice had not sounded so sharp.

With his arm around Dhari's shoulder, Aslam's hand in his, he led them toward the gangplank, where he was suddenly aware of white women drawing back, clutching their children to them.

Well, at least they would be left alone, John thought grimly, and proceeded with head erect to the top of the gangplank, where Captain Lewis was waiting.

Their accommodations were only slightly larger than a closet, with three hammocks and one washstand. But it was dry and private, and that evening as the *Bluebeard* set sail with the tide, they were on deck, John feeling the sea breeze, daring to relax for the first time in several long weeks.

Home! The simple word resounded like a temple bell inside his head. London. Elizabeth. He hungered to see her, and warned himself that she must be allowed her life as he was his. He'd seen enough anger and hurt and pain and death. It was time to build bridges, design a future.

Home! As the wind filled the sails, he felt his excitement increasing and drew Dhari and Aslam close beside him. He'd come to India for treasure, and unwittingly he'd found it.

"Wait until you see London, Aslam," he promised excitedly.

But as he looked down on the little boy, he saw tears in his eyes, and turning to Dhari, he saw the same expression, both of them looking out over the water at the dim outline of land slipping farther into the distance.

He was going home. They were leaving theirs, and he tried to think of consoling words. But remembering the night he'd left Eden, he realized there was nothing he could say to ease their pain.

"Come," he urged kindly, sheltering them against the cool wind and diminishing land, intent upon turning their eyes away from what was behind to what was ahead, hoping with incomprehensible need that it would be better, for all of them.

London,
December 24, 1857

FROM HIS POSITION near the wassail bowl, Andrew looked out over the crowded drawing room, amazed that there were so many lonely people in London. Elizabeth had warned him in advance. Only the lonely attended her Christmas Eve party.

Again he looked about at the faces, amazed at the

prominence of the gathering, many gentlemen from Parliament, and there, a renowned Fleet Street publisher, and several well-known illustrators, and Lord Kimbrough. Mr. Gladstone had been here earlier and had promised he'd try to return, "if Catherine nods off early."

Moving around all like a dancing flame was Elizabeth, a vision in red velvet, her fair hair piled high atop her head, speaking to one and all with the greatest intimacy, as though without their singular presences her party would have been a failure. That the gentlemen responded to such flattery was understandable. But the ladies were equally as receptive, kissing her warmly, their eyes lingering in admiration of the diamond necklace that adorned her throat. A Christmas gift from Lord Kimbrough, or so Andrew had heard.

In the far corner, about the pianoforte, a rousing version of "Good King Wenceslas" broke out, the wassail glasses lifting high, keeping time with the music. In the fire well the Yule log popped merrily, enhanced by several guests throwing pine cones on the blaze.

Perhaps the most popular spot in the entire drawing room, however, was the table to his right beyond the wassail bowl, a heavenly arrangement of tiny cakes and candied fruit and golden buns and a long silver platter arranged with sliced roast beef and goose, and game loaf.

The climax of the evening was yet to come, the promise of Lord Kimbrough that before the evening was over, a "Christmas tree" would be delivered which they must all decorate in honor of Christ's Mass, a new and curious tradition which had been started at Windsor by Albert, part of his German heritage which still surfaced with shock waves on the placid English world.

All in all it was a glorious scene, the Christmas spirit alive and flourishing in spite of the tragic events which had befallen England this year. Earlier in the evening, as the guests were first arriving, before the warming intoxication of the wassail bowl had taken effect, Andrew had participated in hushed dialogues concerning the tragic mutinies in India, the London *Times* still filled with horrifying accounts, though the rebels had long since been hunted down and brought to justice.

Oh, yes, the talk was on every tongue, the journalists fanning the fires with explicit accounts of raped white women, dismembered children, the well at Cawnpore. And after all the anger and horror and revulsion, two strong emotions remained: a seething resentment of all dark-skinned people, and two, a rather poignant bewilderment that one of Britain's most promising colonies had dared to revolt against English benevolence.

"Sweet heaven, Andrew, I wish you could see your face."

He looked up from his wassail cup, in which he'd been seeing a cavalcade of tragic events, and into Elizabeth's face.

"I'm sorry." He smiled. "I was only thinking—"

"Not a very wise thing to do," she chided, "particularly at a party. Come, you've been lurking in this corner long enough."

But as she took his arm, he drew her back, longing for a moment alone with her. "You're so lovely," he whispered.

She looked up into his face. "I have much to be thankful for this Christmas," she said. "You, primarily."

He accepted the compliment with a smile, yet knowing that the true basis for their relationship was John Murrey Eden. In the past they had talked endlessly of him, as though as long as they spoke his name, they somehow kept him alive.

Now he pulled her closer, and in spite of the crowded drawing room, kissed her. She caressed the side of his face as though aware of his need. "Later," she promised. "We will watch Christmas dawn together."

It was a generous promise, considering the number of other gentlemen here who would like to share the same experience. But he believed her and released her hand and watched lovingly as she moved back into the heart of her party.

Everyone needed Elizabeth's harmony. Andrew wondered how many of those guests laughing with her now knew or even suspected how unharmonious her own inner life was, still in mourning for the dead Edward Eden, suffering nightmares over whether or not she would ever see John again, feeling that she'd failed him, and in turn had failed Edward.

As the voices rose about him, he refilled his wassail cup, recalling the false leads he'd followed in his search for John. All paths stopped at the hospital in Scutari. From there the man had disappeared, and though Andrew had never let on to Elizabeth, after a fruitless two-year search he feared the worst.

At that moment a thunderous shout from the door signaled the arrival of the Christmas tree, and as all rushed in that direction, Andrew looked up to see a massive evergreen being angled through the double doors. With excited cries from all, four workmen carried it across the room and into position by the window, lopsided at first. The entire gathering shouted instructions, and at last the tree was upright, though looking a bit bizarre.

"Most peculiar," he heard someone comment. "They do this at Windsor, you say?"

"It's free of squirrels, I trust," another murmured.

Before the festive mood could be wholly dampened by the natural suspicion that follows innovation, Lord Kimbrough took the floor with his customary exuberance, bidding the little maid Doris to follow after, bearing a tray filled with delicate sweet cakes to which loops of gold cord had been attached.

"I assure you," he bellowed out over the crowd, "it *is* done at Windsor, and in every other fashionable house throughout London, or will be shortly. We must be the pacesetters. Come, lend a hand. It lacks only decoration." By way of demonstration, he lifted a small cake and fastened it to a bough, where it swung as prettily as a miniature bird's nest.

Within the moment everyone saw how it was to be done and all pushed forward, attaching the cakes and small white candles and nosegays of holly and mistletoe.

Beginning to weary of his observer's position, Andrew noticed Elizabeth standing near the edge of her guests, a glowing smile on her face, as though nothing delighted her more than the delight of others. Thinking to share the moment with her, Andrew drained his cup and was just starting around the table when simultaneously he heard the front bell ringing and heard Lord Kimbrough signal Elizabeth's attention.

"Needs more decoration at the top, right?" Kimbrough called from atop his chair.

As Elizabeth turned her attention to the question, Andrew held his position, seeing Doris hurrying to answer the door. Damn! It probably was Gladstone, early returned after "Catherine had nodded off." Andrew didn't stand a chance vying for Elizabeth's attention with Kimbrough and Gladstone both on the scene.

Now across his legs he felt the blast of cold air from the open door. Someone was keeping it open for an undue amount of time. He noticed the candles on the wassail table leap higher in the chill draft. Elizabeth was still focusing on the tree, waving one hand toward the bare upper branches.

As Andrew glanced back through the arch, he saw Doris, a most peculiar expression on her face, backing away from something that was still out of sight by the door.

His attention momentarily torn between the drama taking place at the unseen door and the smaller drama of the partially decorated tree, Andrew saw several of the ladies clasp their bare arms as the chill spread throughout the entire room.

He saw Doris hurrying toward her mistress. But Elizabeth could not be deterred from the task at hand, and while she was aware of Doris, she simply placed a restraining hand on her arm and warned Lord Kimbrough to make sure the candles were secured, lest the small flames ignite the tree.

Partly in curiosity and partly because the chill was becoming damned uncomfortable, Andrew was in the process of going and closing the door himself. But at that moment a figure appeared in the archway. Andrew held his position, understanding Doris' dilemma. Obviously a passing beggar had seen the festivities through the window and had barged in, hoping for alms or a sweet cake.

Quite disheveled he was, Andrew noticed, lean, with full unkempt beard flecked with gray, his long hair snow-dampened and plastered about his face, his trousers mottled, ill-fitting, his ragged coat beyond description. In his hands he held a worn crushed hat which he kneaded continuously while he looked with hollow eyes out over the . . .

Christ!

Soundlessly Andrew whispered the word, squinting toward the specter in the archway.

He took one step forward, when about ten feet ahead he saw Elizabeth at last turn to the urgent whisperings of her maid. No message was relayed. None was needed. The man stood at the exact center of the arch, as though framed for all to see, the cold winter wind racing around him, his eyes, buried in dark circles, moving slowly over the drawing room, coming at last to Elizabeth, where they stopped.

His lips seemed to part as though he'd spoken a word, though none was audible, as the bulk of the party's noisy attention was still focused on the Christmas tree.

But Andrew was aware of nothing but the man and Elizabeth, two mismatched statues staring at each other with an intensity which stretched between them like a solid cord.

Endlessly they stood, generating an invisible energy which slowly attracted the attention of the chattering crowd, who in groups of twos and threes, commenced turning, voices caught in mid-sentence falling until in all corners of that festive room there was silence.

As for himself, Andrew was certain now, though he still could not believe his eyes. Compounding the miracle of the man's appearance was his wretched condition, looking more dead than alive, one hand clearly trembling even from that distance.

John. It *was* John, or what was left of him.

Then Elizabeth moved, only a step at first, as though fearful the apparition might disappear. After two steps, Andrew heard her whisper his name, as though some instinct had warned her not to go forward until the confirmation was complete, as though she were accustomed to dealing with ghosts.

"John . . . ?"

At the sound of his name, he too moved, only a step, but it was enough. Then Elizabeth was running toward him, sobs tearing at her voice with every breath, and as his arms opened to her, Andrew saw a new light on his ruined features, as he literally reached out and pulled her to him, enclosing her in his arms, only his face visible, his lips moving soundlessly, repeating her name over and over, while she sobbed openly and clung to him.

Andrew stepped back into the shadows, smiling and crying all at the same time. Wiping at his eyes, he ached to go forward and join in the reunion. But he dared not. It was too intimate, and he was aware now of the guests as they whispered together, each seeking an explanation from the other. He saw tears on John's face, one broad hand cupped about Elizabeth's head, still holding her close.

Andrew dug inside his waistcoat pocket for a handkerchief, blew his nose and wiped at his eyes. By the time he looked up, he saw that they were simply gazing at each other, her hand caressing his forehead, her fingers, lingering in examination of a pronounced scar which ran the length of his brow and disappeared into the mussed hair.

From the area near the Christmas tree Andrew saw Lord Kimbrough moving through the crowd until he stood only a few feet away from Elizabeth, as though to remind her that she had guests.

But there was no need, for at that moment she turned and looked past Lord Kimbrough directly toward Andrew, her face still glistening with tears, one hand extended as though beckoning him to come forward.

And he did, without hesitation, observing that John had not yet seen him, had instead turned back toward the doorway as though something of great concern lay in that direction.

It was Elizabeth who summoned his attention by gently taking his arm, whispering something, and stepping back. Then the full weight of those eyes were upon Andrew, accompanied by a puzzled expression, one hand self-consciously smoothing the worn coat, then moving shakily forward. "Andrew?"

Andrew could only grin, silently cursing his damnable emotions. Then, remembering what they had been through together in the past, he found a mere handshake unsatisfactory, and feeling John's arm go around him, he gave in to the embrace.

As he clasped the thin shoulders close, he looked beyond the arch and saw two shadowy figures. He started to take a closer look, but sensed the embrace coming to an end and stepped back, wanting to ask him where he had been and what various crucibles could account for the lines and scars and fatigue on his face.

But he said nothing, and neither did John, and it was Elizabeth who stepped between them. In a scarcely discernible voice, as though words were still beyond her, she addressed the gaping guests. "This is my son," she said simply.

As murmurs arose from the company, Lord Kimbrough suggested considerately, "Perhaps we should leave, Elizabeth. Clearly you have a much more important party to attend . . ."

"No," she said, "I won't hear of it. Now it's truly Christmas," she added, taking John's arm. "Stay. All of you, please, and share this miracle with us. You see, we thought he was . . . dead."

Her voice broke again, and John put his arm around her and drew her close.

Lord Kimbrough stepped forward and extended his hand. "John Murrey Eden, isn't it?" he inquired softly. "I feel as though I know you. Elizabeth has spoken endlessly of you."

Again silence. Lord Kimbrough rallied first. "Elizabeth," he pronounced, as though to shake the mood, "he looks as though he could go a few rounds of your banqueting table. Shall I escort him to the bounty or will you?"

"I'm sorry," Elizabeth murmured, still in a state of shock. "Come," she said, taking John's arm, "you must be—"

But suddenly he pulled away, his eyes moving back toward the arch. "I'm . . . not alone."

"Someone's with you? Well, bring them in. My goodness, to keep them waiting in that cold . . ."

Even as she spoke, John disappeared around the corner. Standing close behind Elizabeth, Andrew saw her shoulders trembling.

Concentrating on Elizabeth, he was not aware that anyone had reappeared in the archway. What he heard first was a collective gasp from the guests, then the entire room falling into a new silence, a sense of shock compounding the mystery.

Andrew looked toward the arch to a most astonishing sight, John, his arm about the shoulder of a dark-skinned young woman, his other hand clutching a dark-skinned young boy, both the woman and boy staring about the room with frightened eyes, their appearance as pitiful as John's, the woman in a long soiled black skirt, its filthy hem dragging the floor, bits of straw stuck here and there. her small frame lost in a man's coat, a tattered shawl covering her shoulders and matted black hair. And the little boy clung to John's hand, his timidity getting the best of him as he buried his face in John's coat.

The tableau held, as though John were giving everyone a chance to look their fill. Someplace near the edge of the guests, a woman gasped, "They're . . . Indians."

Immediately following, someone told her to hush. John looked down, a tightness covering his forehead. Without looking up, he said, "We've traveled a great distance. We're . . . very hungry."

He might have said more, but Elizabeth came forward until she stood before the young woman. Smiling, she reached for her arm. "Come." Without another word, she led her toward the banqueting table. Andrew stepped forward and took John's arm. "I haven't eaten yet." He smiled. "I'll join you."

As John looked up, he seemed to lose his balance. Andrew moved to his side, his arm about his shoulder. "Are you all right?" he whispered, hoping to mask his friend's weakness from the curious onlookers.

John nodded. As he took the little boy's hand, he said to Andrew, "I'd not expected to find both faces I love under one roof."

Andrew smiled. "We wanted to make things easy for you."

Suddenly John looked at him with an intense stare. "You are the first, my friend," he murmured, "in a long time."

Before Andrew could reply, he saw John look ahead to the table, where Elizabeth was filling a platter for the young woman, who continued to stand self-consciously to one side.

Before the bounteous spread, John looked down at the roast beef, the golden chickens, the elegantly arranged platters of fruits and cakes. "If starvation didn't kill us"— he smiled—"this very well might."

From across the table, Elizabeth looked up at the sound of his voice, her recent emotional upheaval still clear upon her face. "I can't believe it," she said. "Is it really you?"

Andrew saw a tinge of embarrassment on John's face. He nodded briefly before he shifted the attention. "This," he commenced, trying to turn the little boy at his side, "is Aslam."

To Andrew's amazement, he heard the child respond in shy though flawless English. "It is my pleasure," the boy said, making an effort to be grown-up.

Taking the boy with him, John moved toward the young woman and completed the introductions, his arm about her waist, a discernible love in his voice as he said, "And this is Dhari."

The young woman did not respond and appeared even more painfully shy than the boy. Upon introduction, she bowed her head, and Andrew noticed John drawing her closer, as though offering support.

They formed a strange tableau, and while the specifics of the ordeal that had rendered them thus were still unknown, Andrew found himself looking with dread to the account which would inevitably come. He'd seen those expressions before, after the Battle of Inkerman, on the heights of Sebastopol, in the faces of men fresh from battle who had taken part in atrocities that had taxed their abilities to endure.

Unfortunately, Andrew realized that they all were

causing greater pain by staring. Then, by God, enough! Clearly the other party had ceased, the stunned guests incapable of speech or movement. Then life must originate here, for none of them could survive in this awkward state for very long.

Accordingly, Andrew stepped forward, a volume to his voice that surprised even him. "Come, Aslam." He grinned at the little boy. "Point out what suits your fancy, and we'll fill a dozen platters if need be."

Again the child seemed to hesitate, but at last he let go of John's hand, drawn forward by his own hunger and the dazzling array of food.

And Elizabeth was moving again, asking kindly of Dhari if she preferred this or that, and filling the platter anyway, in spite of the fact that she'd received no answer.

As the plates were being filled, Andrew noticed John sit slowly in a near chair, his eyes closing as though feeling a burden lifted from his shoulders. Watching him, it occurred to Andrew that he'd never seen such consummate fatigue. Only once did he lift his head, and at the sight of the heaped platters he whispered, "Not too much, please, I beg you. Our fare of late has been . . . simple and limited."

Lord Kimbrough drew near to the end of the table. Although he made an attempt to keep his voice down, Andrew heard, "I really believe, Elizabeth, that the rest of us will take our leave now. It's a private party and that's as it should be. We are—"

She started to protest, but he didn't give her a chance. "We're going to the Benthalls'." He smiled. "They tell me their Christmas tree needs my expert advice."

As Andrew glanced over his shoulder, he noticed that many of the guests had already departed, and others were in the hall.

From where he stood, Andrew thought he saw a look of sadness on Elizabeth's face. "There's no need, Freddie," she whispered.

"No, my dearest," he replied. "There's every need." He raised his voice into an encompassing warmth which included John. "Your prodigal has returned. The rest of

us will come around and greet him later, when he's
. . . restored. For now, I think that all of you need
privacy. It's a great occasion. I want to do nothing to
spoil it for you."

The sentiments were thoughtful, the delivery more so.
For a moment Andrew felt a pinch of envy as he saw the
obvious love which existed between Elizabeth and the old
man. She placed the platter on the table, called back to
Andrew, "I'll see my guests out," and she took Lord
Kimbrough's arm and walked with him to the door.

John was watching, Andrew observed. "Come," Andrew called out to him. "I'm afraid you must prepare
your own platter. Hurry, though. We'll wait for you by the
fire." Lifting both platters into the air, he smiled at the
young woman to follow after him, and as the last guests
were filing through the archway, he settled Aslam on the
floor near the blazing Yule log, and the woman in a near
chair, and urged them gently, "Eat now," and stood back,
marveling at their dark beauty which shone through despite their worn garments.

A few moments later John caught up with them, and
ignoring the chairs, sat on the floor near Aslam, warning
the child to eat slowly and not too much.

Andrew heard the outer door close for the last time,
saw Elizabeth and Doris in close huddle in the hall, the
girl shaking her head as though giving a negative
response.

"Your luggage, John." Elizabeth smiled, reentering the
room. "Where is it? I'll send someone to fetch it."

For the first time John looked up from his plate. "We
. . . have no luggage," he said.

Andrew offered to prepare a plate for Elizabeth, who
was still struggling to digest the mystery of travelers without luggage. "No, thank you," she said. "I'm far too excited to eat." Smiling, she slipped into a chair opposite the
young woman. "Dhari," she said softly, as though testing
the name on her lips. "Doris is preparing a hot bath for
you, for all of you, and afterward, we'll find fresh
clothes."

The young woman nodded, but still said nothing. Apparently she understood, but was not as well-schooled as the boy. A short time later, one by one, they pushed back their plates, all only partially eaten.

"Enough," John groaned pleasurably, reaching out and drawing the boy closer. "You see, Aslam, I told you that we all would be warm and dry and well-fed again."

The boy nestled close under John's arm. From where Andrew stood, he could see the questioning look on Elizabeth's face. But still it was not the right time to ask questions. There were more urgent needs to attend to. John, holding the sleepy boy close, spoke of one of them. "Elizabeth, would you be so kind as to give us shelter for the night? Come morning, I'll look for—"

"For the night!" she repeated, shocked. "For this night and all the others. This is your home. You'll look for nothing come morning but rest and peace and a return to good health."

Apparently the avowal moved John. "I'm without . . . funds," he said.

"I'm not," countered Elizabeth. She left her chair and went down on her knees before him. "Please," she begged softly. "Never let us become separated again." Her voice broke. "I don't think I could endure losing you a second time."

He drew her close, and though the tears were silent, Andrew was aware that both were crying.

Suddenly he felt like an intruder. "Elizabeth," he began, "I'd best be going as well."

"No, don't please," she begged. "Someone had better stay and give us direction. At the moment, I feel quite incapable . . ."

John too urged, "Please stay, Andrew."

A moment later, Doris appeared in the door, her sleeves rolled up. "Hot water's ready," she said, "and I've another kettle boiling for the gentleman and the little boy."

As John pulled himself wearily to his feet, Elizabeth took the boy's hand and extended the other to the young woman. "Come." She smiled. "This is woman's work." To Andrew and John she added, "You two sit and talk."

But John would hear none of it. "No, I'll go with them. They may be frightened in strange—"

"It isn't necessary, John," Elizabeth countered. "They've nothing to be frightened of here." She reached for Dhari's hand, impervious to the fact that the woman had pulled back. Ignoring her hesitancy, Elizabeth walked with her to the door, chattering lightly. "A hot bath and you'll feel right enough." She smiled. "And fresh garments. We'll raid my wardrobe. Green! Oh yes, green would be a lovely color for you. What *is* your favorite color? Do you have one? Or yellow?"

At the bottom of the steps, the young woman looked at her, an expression of sadness on her face. She reached out for the boy and started up the stairs after Doris, her head bowed, as though she'd averted her face just in time to conceal her grief.

From where Andrew stood, he saw the hurt in Elizabeth's face. She was accustomed to people responding to her warmth, not ignoring it. Still puzzled, she looked back at John. But he pushed past her without a word, a peculiarly hard expression on his face.

He was midpoint on the stairs, the other two having already disappeared down the second-floor corridor, when Elizabeth stepped forward. "John? Have I offended her?" she asked.

He did not reply.

"I only meant to . . ." She faltered. Then all at once an idea blossomed. "She doesn't speak English, does she, John? Of course, that's it, isn't it?"

Slowly he turned. "She speaks perfect English, Elizabeth, flawless English, in the most musical tones."

The strange reply brought comfort to no one. "Then what did I say?" she begged. "Why won't she speak to—"

"Because she can't." These three words were merely whispered, but they seemed to drain John of his last reserve of energy. "We're alive tonight because of her. She aided our escape by betraying her own people." For the first time, his voice broke. "Before they returned her to me, they . . . cut out her tongue."

Andrew saw Elizabeth's back stiffen; one hand reached

out for the newel post. By the time they both had recovered, John was proceeding up the stairs. He said nothing further. In the skeletal outline of that one announcement, Andrew's suspicions were confirmed. John had been caught up in a nightmare, and had been dropped back into the civilized world vastly changed, permanently scarred.

Cut out her tongue. The inconceivable words continued to assault him. When he looked up, he saw Elizabeth moving up the steps. As she reached midpoint, he felt a greater urgency to leave, to give everyone under this roof a chance to adjust to each other. To that end he called up, "Elizabeth, I'll take my leave now. You need time to—"

Abruptly she turned, her face drained of color. "No, please. I'll see to their needs. Then I'll come back down." Again she repeated with almost desperate urgency, "Please, Andrew, please stay."

"I'll wait by the fire." He smiled up at her.

Alone, he turned back into the drawing room, still cluttered with the remains of the once festive party. He headed wearily toward the fire, glancing at the chair where the young woman had recently sat.

They cut out her tongue.

Slowly he closed his eyes, still trying to digest the image of pain. But it was not possible.

About a half hour later, Elizabeth returned. From the archway she made a soft incredulous announcement. "He . . . bathed them himself. He sent Doris to the other room, and . . . bathed them . . . himself. He said that they would require only one bed. Only one bed," she repeated, "for three."

He reached out for her. "Obviously they've gone through much . . . have formed a dependency . . ."

She looked up at him as though wishing he'd talk on, as though needing to hear explication.

Instead he drew her into his arms and held her close, tried to provide a negotiable shelter for her bewilderment. "We'll know everything in time," he soothed.

They settled on the large sofa near the fire and stared

into the flames. Neither spoke on what was behind or what was ahead. The spirit of Christmas lay in disarray about them, shattered by a single announcement. The pulse of history had been slowed by the mutilation of a young dark-skinned woman.

Whether or not it would ever commence to pump again at a healthy rate, Andrew had no idea.

※

London,
Christmas Night

THE FOLLOWING EVENING, still at table after three hours, it was Elizabeth who felt the need to break the silence. Seated opposite her, John had just concluded the most terrifying story she'd ever heard, ending with a hoarse account of their arrival six days ago at Portsmouth, their ride to London in the back of a hay wagon, and their appearance the night before at the Christmas Eve party.

At times during the prolonged monologue she'd felt physically ill, had tried not to look at either Dhari or Aslam as John had recounted the specifics of their ordeal. Now, seeing the young woman with bowed head seated on her right, she reached for her hand. "You're safe now, Dhari," she said with conviction. "Do you believe me?" To her incredible joy, the woman smiled.

Beyond Dhari sat Aslam. Not once during the long account had he stirred, his childish restlessness subdued by his interest in his own ordeal.

Next to Elizabeth sat Andrew, the expression on his face reflecting what she felt as a look of relief flooded his features, grateful that the monotone voice had at last talked itself out.

Over the burned-down candles and scattered glasses, she looked at John, saw him shaking his head, staring, unseeing, at the white cloth. "So many died," he murmured.

"On both sides," Andrew said. "It's been put down now, of course, you know. The mutiny, I mean."

John nodded. "I heard only sketchy reports from a dockman at Portsmouth. Tell me more."

As Andrew commenced speaking, Elizabeth dared to relax, though she glanced about her dining room, feeling a need to confirm the reality of this world as opposed to that dark one of which John had just spoken. She looked at Dhari. How different the young woman looked tonight, gowned in dark green taffeta, her black hair, which she'd allowed Elizabeth to brush and style, drawn becomingly back in a French knot. They'd passed the afternoon together, Elizabeth becoming skilled in carrying on a conversation which required no direct answers, Dhari responding without words to the love and attention being heaped upon her. In time they would become fast friends, of that Elizabeth was certain. Clearly John adored her, and on that basis alone, Dhari would always have a home under Elizabeth's roof.

As Andrew and John continued talking, Elizabeth noticed Aslam at last giving in to boyish restlessness. He slipped from his chair and walked around it, his hands slipping in and out of the carved wooden slats, looking quite handsome in his new sailor suit.

And finally Elizabeth looked toward John. Thoughtfully Andrew had brought around a suit of his own when he'd come for dinner, and though ill-fitting, at least John looked warm and clean, his beard brushed, though his hands still trembled and his eyes tended to stare too long on certain inconsequential objects.

In spite of everything, Elizabeth felt suffused with a sense of well-being. He was home, they were reunited, and Edward's spirit seemed very close, no longer confined to the meager belongings in that trunk in her bedchamber.

She bowed her head and gave a prayer of thanks, then looked up in time to hear Andrew announce quietly, "Force was ever the fuel of empires, John. You know that. England's wars have always been nicely balanced between the philanthropic and the belligerent. And whether we contend with a civilized or barbarous enemy, the nature of empire will always lead us to a perpetual battlefield."

Suddenly the male voices at the end of the table fell silent. Elizabeth looked up to see John staring sadly toward Dhari. "For all your rhetoric, Andrew, the price is too high."

"It's not my rhetoric," Andrew said. "It fills the Temple. One can't walk the Common without hearing it. The subject of empire is quite the most fashionable one in London nowadays."

Elizabeth saw John look up, a new light on his face, as though something had dragged his attention away from the horrors of the past. "The Temple?" he repeated. "The law courts, you mean? What business do you have in the Temple?"

With the spotlight thrust upon him, she saw Andrew blush. "Although at times I'm loath to admit it, I'm a solicitor now," he said.

The news had a pleasing though surprising effect on John. He laughed, a glorious sound after the mood which earlier had permeated the room. "A lawyer?" he repeated. "Quite a step up from Brassey's clerical room." He leaned forward, grasping his friend's arm in affection. "Well, tell me all. How did it happen? And are you a good lawyer? Do you have your own practice?"

Andrew lifted a restraining hand. "I have a practice, yes, a small one." He ducked his head in becoming modesty. "I'm told I'm good, yes, though I've never been tested."

John gazed upon him with an expression of admiration. "How well you have done for yourself, Andrew," he murmured, "and how far I lag behind."

Andrew countered graciously. "I could never have survived what you've been through, John, what all of you have been through," he added, his eyes encompassing Dhari and Aslam.

Briefly the mood seemed to threaten them again, and hurriedly John moved to dispel it. "One additional question." He smiled. "Which I shall toss delicately out for whoever cares to answer." He paused. "How was I so fortunate to find the two people I love under one roof?"

Elizabeth felt a blush on her cheeks and glanced toward Andrew, trying to determine whether he would take the question, or she.

Finally he took it, reaching for the decanter of port, leaving his chair and filling the glasses around as he spoke. "I received a packet of unopened letters addressed to you from the army postmaster in Balaklava. Apparently the army was the first to lose track of you. The postmaster thought I might have a lean on you, which of course I didn't."

He moved beyond Aslam until he was standing near John. "There were two packets of letters," he went on, "one bore Elizabeth's signature and address." He looked toward Elizabeth. "I delivered them, hoping for news of you, and in a way, I've been here ever since."

"Nothing could please me more," John murmured, and lifted the glass in toast to Andrew and Elizabeth. "And the other packet?" he inquired.

Andrew shook his head. "From someone in Wiltshire. I believe Elizabeth still has them upstairs. What was her name, Elizabeth?"

Elizabeth sat up, ready to reply, but there was no need.

"Lila Harrington." John smiled.

"Yes, that's it," Andrew confirmed. "Quite a lot from her, really. Who is she, John? Some prize you've kept from me?"

Responding to the good-natured bait, John smiled cryptically. "You will meet her one day." Then he was standing before the table, looking down on Elizabeth. "May I see them? The letters, I mean."

She stirred herself into action, a bit confused as to whether she should drag them all up to her bedchamber or bring the letters down.

John saw her confusion. He turned to Andrew, his good spirits rising. "Have you had the humiliating experience yet of confronting Aslam over a chessboard?"

Andrew shook his head.

"Then now is as good a time as any. It must come to all men, the realization that they can be effortlessly defeated by a seven-year-old boy."

Aslam popped up from beneath the table, his handsome

face wreathed in a smile. "Would you care for a game, Mr. Rhoades?" he inquired politely.

"I'd like nothing better," Andrew said.

John gave him a grateful pat, then moved to behind Dhari's chair and held it for her as she stood. "I'm counting on you," he whispered, loud enough for all to hear, "to keep your son honest."

Elizabeth saw him lean forward and kiss her on the cheek, Dhari responding with admirable warmth. They made a striking couple, Elizabeth mused, John so tall and fair, Dhari dark and delicate. But who was Lila Harrington?

There was no time for answers as Aslam ran eagerly from the room heading for the drawing-room fire and the chess challenge, Andrew calling back good-naturedly, "Care to place a wager on the winner?"

John laughed. "Only a fool would accept that offer. His chess master was Fraser Jennings, who quoted the Bible like a saint and played chess like Genghis Khan. Watch him," John concluded. "He's brighter than both of us put together."

Elizabeth saw Andrew wave a casual hand backward, then saw that same hand rest protectively about Dhari's shoulder, as though he too were trying to eradicate the horrors of the past in a loving and warm present.

Obviously John saw the gesture as well and was moved by it. "My father once told me that a man was wealthy if he had one good friend."

Elizabeth closed her eyes, aware of him standing behind her chair. Edward's spirit *was* very close. To the best of her memory, she had never heard John quote his father before. On any subject.

"Come." She smiled, relishing the moment alone with him, their first since his return. "Your letters are in your father's trunk."

But as she moved to pass him, he caught her and drew her close. "Elizabeth, I'm so sorry . . ."

Caught in his embrace and wanting never to leave it, she asked, "Why? What have you to be sorry for? I'm the one—"

"Jack Willmot is dead," he said.

"I know," she murmured, holding his face between her hands. "Andrew told me everything." In his eyes she saw the reflected horror of the last few years. "Oh my dearest," she whispered, and clung to him, seeing him not as a grown man but as the handsome little boy who'd clasped her hand tightly for fear of falling down the steps in the old house on Oxford Street. How many times she'd served as the buffer between that vulnerable innocence and all dangers, real and imagined. If only she could have spared him at least a portion of these present crucibles.

But she couldn't, and concentrated now on what *was* within her capability, which was to give him vast amounts of love and understanding. With their arms linked, they left the dining room, moving slowly up the stairs, hearing in the drawing room Aslam's delighted shriek as he took an early lead.

"Poor Andrew," John muttered.

"He'll survive," Elizabeth countered. "He's a remarkable man."

John nodded in agreement, and they climbed the rest of the stairs in silence.

John knew precisely when she had left the room; he had started to call her back, then had changed his mind. Clearly it had meant a great deal to her, his confrontation with his father's trunk. How effortlessly she had read rapture on his face, when in truth, all he'd felt was depression at the sight of this fragment from his boyhood.

Staring at it, he saw that it reeked with that poverty in which he'd passed most of his life, and poverty of the worst kind, foisted on him by the man who had owned this trunk, that foolish man who had fathered him in secret, lied to him about the identity of his mother, thrust him early on into a zoo of wretched, half-starved children, and as though the list of offenses already was not long enough, he'd then committed the most stupid blunder of all, had given his fortune away, *his* fortune, the Eden wealth, that ancient inheritance which would have made such a difference in John's life.

Abruptly he pushed away from the trunk, wanting

to have nothing to do with it. He leaned back against the chair and lifted his head.

Eden.

There was that, too, the painful realization that it still was beyond his reach. Yet how hungry he was to see it. He started upward as he effortlessly recalled the happiest days of his life, with the reassuring comfort of Eden Castle surrounding him, glorying in that first love, the only love that mattered, Harriet's love, mother or wife, it made no difference.

In a surge of longing he leaned forward and threw open the lid of the trunk, determined to fetch his letters from Lila Harrington and return to the drawing room.

He turned them slowly over in his hand. Of course he must write to her and thank her for such unwarranted devotion. Yes, he would write to her soon and request the privilege of calling on her. What harm?

He smiled and felt partially restored by the mere memory of Lila Harrington. He was on the verge of closing the trunk when his fingers brushed across the worn fabric of an old shirtwaist. Without warning, his father was upon him.

"I'll take you to Eden one day, John, I promise."

Damn the man! Angrily John lifted the shirtwaist and saw beneath it another.

Damn him! Still he plunged deeper into the trunk, his hands clawing at the objects, one hairbrush, a pair of shoes, a nightshirt, and near the bottom, a muss of papers and letters, all bearing his father's handwriting.

He closed his eyes, feeling as though he'd fallen into an abyss, or more accurately, had never really crawled out.

As he commenced refilling the trunk, he saw a large brown packet resting on the bottom, almost obscured by the yellowed letters and clippings. With a sense of having examined everything else—and why not this?—John pushed the papers aside and lifted the packet. Constructed of coarse brown cardboard, it had appeared at first to be merely the bottom of the trunk itself.

As he lifted it, he examined it for handwriting and found none. Clearing a spot among the old garments, he placed it on the floor. Reaching in, he felt of two separate thicknesses, and withdrew the first, a large envelope with Elizabeth's name on the front in his father's handwriting. Turning it over, finding no wax seal, he withdrew a short letter in his father's hand and a neatly tied stack of banknotes. He looked closer. My God, each note was in the denomination of five hundred pounds, and there were—quickly he counted—twelve of them. *Six thousand pounds!*

He stared incredulously down. But there they were, neatly folded and resting inside the letter, which he opened and lifted toward the light of the fire.

It was his father's handwriting, instructing Elizabeth that if anything happened to him, she was to take John to Eden Castle, and with the sum enclosed see to her own needs if she chose to return to London.

That was all, a hastily scribbled message, posing more questions than it answered. *If something happened to him.*

As John stared, mystified, at the letter, he glanced to the top of the page, to the date: April 10, 1848. Then it dawned. The Chartist Demonstration, that gloomy morning when, led by Feargus O'Connor, twenty-five thousand men had met on Kennington Common with petitions for the male franchise. While John remembered the incident only dimly, his father had told him about it countless times, how nervous the city had been, how the army had been called out, how hysterical editorials had predicted that the Thames would be red with blood by nightfall. Of course, nothing had happened.

With a sense of wonder, John stared down at the notes in his hand. Obviously the letter had been penned early that morning when his father had not known what to expect. Upon his safe return that night, he'd apparently forgotten about the letter with the small fortune in it and had shoved it into the back of his desk.

A curious thought entered his head. Did Elizabeth know about it? It was her money, then and now. If only she had found it earlier, how different her life might have been, and his as well.

He must tell her immediately. Returning the notes to

the envelope, he felt the second weight in the packet, and reached in and withdrew a thick bundle of neatly aligned parchments, each bearing an official seal on the folded side.

Eager to share his discovery with Elizabeth, he decided not to examine them now, but changed his mind and drew off the cord and saw the folded parchments scatter about his lap, one falling partially open in the process, revealing the dark blue embossed edge of a legal document.

He flattened it before him and saw what appeared to be a deed, signed by his father, witnessed by a Sir Claudius Potter, and made out in the name of . . .

John Murrey Eden.

Unconvinced that his eyes had not deceived him, he lifted the parchment to the light of the fire and saw it clearly, his name on a deed of ownership, near Blackfriars, Plat 34, north-northwest, section two, adjacent property 341.

It was gibberish. What did it mean? He stared down on it, and noticed the other papers spilling on the floor.

He lifted a second and pulled it open, saw another deed, his father's signature again, the flourish of Sir Claudius Potter, and again under the title of landowner,

John Murrey Eden.

This one was near Adelphi, Plat 14, south-southwest, section . . .

For a moment the silence of the bedchamber seemed alive, so great that he heard his own breathing, his eyes fixed on his name. He looked at three deeds, then in a frenzy he opened each parchment, confirming his suspicions, deed after deed opened and examined until he found himself covered with them, his mind exploding with questions, talking aloud now, reading from the various parchments, then at last counting, "Two, four, six, eight, nine, eleven, fourteen, fifteen, sixteen, seventeen."

Seventeen!

Seventeen pieces of London property in his name, the locations of his father's Ragged Schools, purchased for the good of all children, yet made out in the name of one child who, at some later date, in need of direction, would find them and . . .

Without any forewarning he was crying, for himself, for his father, for the distance between them which extended beyond the grave, for the fact that even now, with this bounty in his lap, he still did not comprehend him, and that the loss was his, as was the loneliness.

Carefully he reached out to the parchments, as though he were afraid of breaking something. Then he was moving, wiping away the tears, gathering the parchments, thinking that he needed a trained eye to view them, someone who could tell him, yes, they are valid, and yes, they are yours, thinking of Andrew, then speaking the name softly as he continued to gather the deeds. He retrieved Elizabeth's letter and money at the same time, stuffing it all into the brown folder which had lain undiscovered for years at the bottom of the trunk.

He was on his feet now, rushing to the door, clasping the folder to him, calling aga n, "Andrew," taking the steps downward three at a time, shouting at the top of his voice, *"Andrew!"*

One week later, after having inspected each site with John, Andrew aligned the deeds on Elizabeth's dining-room table, weighting the curling edges with salt cellars, and stood back.

Every afternoon and well into the evening for the last seven days, the two of them had searched out each piece of property, generally finding only empty lots where obviously the old structure had been cleared but the disreputable property had been ignored. The deeds were legitimate, weighted with back taxes, but legal all the same. Andrew had confirmed that. Of course, he had doubts as to their real value, but as yet he hadn't the heart to tell John.

It hadn't been too difficult to discern that Edward Eden's estate investments had formed an interesting pattern. Because of the nature of his Ragged Schools, he had been forced on every occasion to buy into the most undesirable parts of London where there were no near neighbors who might have been offended by the sight of half-starved and malformed children.

"Well?" John prompted, leaning over the back of a near chair.

Still Andrew hedged, not wanting to give him false hope. "Let me show you something," he suggested, reaching for the map of London which he'd brought from his office. He placed it atop the spread deeds, aware of Elizabeth hovering close, sharing in the excitement, still astounded that she'd not discovered the deeds earlier, for John's sake.

Dhari was there as well, engrossed in the needlepoint which Elizabeth had given her. And Aslam was there, ignoring his French primer and drawn to the excitement at the table.

"Look," Andrew urged, pointing with his free hand. "Over the years, London has naturally divided itself into distinct segments. Here the fashionable West End, with the royal palaces of Whitehall, Westminster and St. James, and opposite you have the commercial and mercantile East End, with the ports and heavy industry. I'm not implying that there is a clear dividing line, but as you can see, money follows money, and the landed gentry and the aristocracy tend to buy land on the western outskirts, rather than to the east of the city or the isolated districts south of the river."

Andrew looked up, surprised to see everyone listening except John, who was now straddling the chair backward, apparently more fascinated with Aslam's jet-black hair than he was with anything Andrew was saying.

Smarting from the lack of attention, Andrew released the map and let it roll itself up. At the sound of the flapping parchment, John looked up, apologetic. "I'm sorry, Andrew." He smiled. "What were you saying?"

"It isn't important," Andrew replied, and now found it relatively simple to say what had to be said. "You asked for my estimate of the total worth of all seventeen deeds," he began, not finding it any easier at all. "Of the two finds you made upstairs in your father's trunk, John," he began gently, "I'm afraid that Elizabeth's is the more valuable. You would do well just to match her by selling all seventeen properties."

Though he was looking at John, he heard Elizabeth's disappointment first. "Oh no," she murmured. As for John, he was still straddling the chair, a distant expression on his face, as though if he'd heard anything that Andrew had said, it hadn't made the slightest difference.

Suddenly he looked up as though amazed to find others in the room with him. "We're not going to sell, Andrew," he announced. "We're not going to sell so much as a parcel of it."

"Then you won't make a penny. You might as well place the deeds back in your father's trunk for all the good—"

"We're not selling, Andrew," John repeated.

How often Andrew had seen that look before, and now braced himself for his next question. "Then . . . what do you intend to do?" he asked cautiously.

"Develop!" John replied without hesitation.

Standing opposite him, Andrew returned his stare, struggling to keep from smiling. "Develop . . . what?" he managed.

"Whatever the various areas need," John replied, at last raising up with a broad gesture that encompassed all the deeds. "Or," he added slyly, "what I tell them they need."

Andrew continued to gape at him, aware of the tension building in the room. There were so many arguments whirling through his mind that he did well to say, "You're . . . joking, of course."

"I've never been more serious in my life."

"John," Andrew commenced delicately, "forgive me, but you know nothing of general contracting."

"I can learn."

"It's a highly speculative business. Men work a lifetime and—"

"I intend to work a lifetime."

"Have you any conception of the hazards involved?"

Instead of being angered by Andrew's rapid-fire questions, John seemed to delight in them, as though unwittingly Andrew was filling his proper role. "I know some of the hazards." John smiled. "I did learn a few things from Brassey. And together we can learn the rest."

"We?" Andrew inquired.

"Of course, we." John grinned. "I'll need your help. I'll need everyone's help."

Slowly Andrew returned to the table, unable to believe what he was hearing. "John," Andrew began kindly, not looking at anyone, lest he falter. "Private speculation is the worst sort of gamble, an organized and highly risky business. Believe me, no one profits."

"Someone must."

"Oh, yes, the large contractors with a million pounds of government contracts in their portfolio, like Brassey."

"Any others?"

"An individual has about one chance in five hundred of succeeding. The subcontractors make it impossible."

"Then what if . . ." John started to speak, his fingers tapping the edge of the table in a short staccato rhythm. "Then what if one went around the subcontractors? What if a man erected his own workshop, purchased horses, carts and materials and engaged his own crews of carpenters, smiths, glaziers, bricklayers and other workers? Do you see what I'm getting at, Andrew? A large-scale building firm, employing men from all the old separate trades on a continuous-wage basis?"

Great God! Andrew closed his eyes to rest them from the excited face hovering near. "It's never been done," he said flatly.

"Never?" John repeated, suspicious.

Caught in his own excess, it was Andrew now who felt the need for a chair. He walked wearily to the sideboard and sat in a straight-backed chair against the wall. "There have been one or two successful master builders," he confessed. "Cubitt, and perhaps Burton."

He looked up, ready to qualify his last words, only to see a new light in John's face.

"Master builder," John repeated. "I like that. Master builder."

"Oh, my God, John," Andrew groaned. "Do you have any conception of what you would need to maintain an establishment as expensive as your own workshop?"

Without waiting for the reply, which he felt certain would be less than satisfactory, he rushed on, leaving his chair in the process as though drawn forward by his own urgency. "You would need an uninterrupted sequence of work, and an equally uninterrupted flow of capital."

Suddenly it dawned on him. Capital! What was he arguing for? He was confronting a man who by his own admission was without funds. "Capital," Andrew repeated, as though at last he'd put an end to the madness. "Where is your capital, John? You can't plunge one shovel into one square of earth without capital."

He was looking at John, expecting a response from that quarter, and thus was in no way prepared for Elizabeth's voice coming to him from across the table. "He has capital." She smiled. "Six thousand pounds from his father, and I have more if he needs it, investments up to and including this property."

Even then Andrew did not look at her, did not take his eyes off John, whose expression had softened. "I can't let you—" he began, and that's all he had a chance to say.

"Nonsense," Elizabeth cut in. "I have friends who have taken my limited assets and converted me into a fairly rich woman. I have no need of the money. It's rightfully yours."

The two gazed at each other, some form of silent communication taking place.

John looked back at Andrew, that damnable grin still on his face. "Well, then," he beamed. "What next? We have our capital."

"Enough to commission an architect, hire a surveyor and perhaps fifty workmen? You need more," Andrew said bluntly, throwing diplomacy to the wind.

It was Elizabeth's turn again. "As I said, I have more," she repeated, "and many friends who are constantly looking for a place to invest a few pounds. A word from me and they—"

"A corporation!" John exclaimed, as though the simple idea had just dawned on him. "We'll sell stock."

"You still need a larger, more dependable flow of capital."

"We'll borrow."

"Banks are skeptical."

"Insurance companies."

Momentarily stymied, Andrew was forced to concede, "Perhaps . . ."

"Perhaps?" John laughed. "I'm not totally ignorant, Andrew. I'm perfectly capable of figuring five-percent interest on, say, a twenty-thousand-pound loan."

Andrew nodded, a recent statistic from the London *Times* surfacing through the doubt in his head. "The London Assurance lent one hundred and thirteen thousand pounds to speculative builders last year alone."

"Well, then?"

"You need collateral."

Again the answer came from Elizabeth. "He has it. This house," she announced. "I own it free and clear. It's quite valuable, according to Lord Kimbrough."

For the first time John said, "No."

"Why not?"

As the battlefield shifted to John and Elizabeth, Andrew stepped back from the table, amazed that the discussion had pressed this far. Yet for the first time, and with a feeling of amazement, Andrew was forced to admit that it might, with large portions of cunning and daring and luck, work.

As the argument continued behind him, Andrew paced as far as the arch which led into the drawing room, feeling a need for distance, for a clear perspective of the mad scheme.

He ran through in his mind all the pitfalls and hazards, and with complete astonishment found himself thinking again: *It might work.*

As his thoughts increased, growing more positive in nature, so did his excitement. By God, it might work. Of course, John would need a good solicitor, someone trained in the matter of drawing up agreements, leases, mortgages, bonds and all the other instruments of property which would become necessary throughout such complicated and intricate transactions.

Suddenly he was aware of a cessation of voices behind him. He looked back, amazed to find expressions of victory on both their faces. Collateral was no longer a problem.

"Well?" John said, as though they had wasted enough time on inconsequential matters. "Any more arguments, Andrew?"

Not quite able to believe what had happened, Andrew shook his head. "About a hundred," he said bleakly.

"Any with weight behind them?"

"If posed to a sane man, yes. To you, no."

John laughed, though the expression faded as rapidly as it had appeared. "As I said before, Andrew, I need help, most specifically yours. Do I have it?"

In spite of the urgency on John's face, Andrew withheld his answer. He knew John Murrey Eden too well to commit himself lightly. He knew further that a firm commitment meant one of two things: they would either rise together to incredible heights, or fall to equally incredible depths. And he knew that he would have to abandon his own fledgling law practice.

"Well?" John prompted, his face reflecting the tension of the moment. Everyone else in the room was looking toward Andrew as well, not a sign of doubt on any of those faces. The man they adored had formed a plan. How could it possibly go wrong?

Stalling for an additional moment, Andrew turned away and tallied up a credit sheet which hopefully would match the debit ledger. There was this to be said. Those early years of apprenticeship under Thomas Brassey would now serve John well. Of all the clerks in the office, John had been the brightest, the quickest to grasp the endless rows of statistics and figures concerning cost overruns, capital investments, stock percentages.

His steps took him as far as the drawing room, and he looked back, amazed that John was being so patient with him. In the continuing silence, Andrew glanced over the spread deeds scattered about the dining-room table. The primary assets for a master builder were land and materials. John possessed the first. In addition he certainly possessed the fool's daring necessary to any speculative venture. Of greatest importance, he possessed, perhaps to a damaging degree, the need to succeed. All he lacked were the sources for the enormous sums of capital needed to keep his enterprise going. But with Elizabeth's help, Andrew could foresee a way around even that.

Then what stood in the way of giving an answer? Nothing. After murmuring a prayer in the direction of the ceiling, he stepped toward John, extended his hand and smiled. "I'm with you."

At first, John seemed too stunned to respond. Slowly he received Andrew's outstretched hand and drew him close into a warm embrace and heard him whisper, "Thank you."

Then the quiet moment was over and he turned energetically to the table, calling, "Come, Andrew, let me tell you my plan."

As Andrew drew near the table, he saw John shuffling through the deeds, searching for one. "There!" he exclaimed finally, flattening one deed atop the others. "We'll start there."

Andrew leaned close. It was the Paddington property, near the new railway station. As John unfurled the map of London, Andrew peered closer, feeling another objection forming. "Not a very good place for houses, John. The traffic and noise—"

"I don't intend to put houses there." He beamed. "Look at the area, Andrew. Can't you see the need?"

Andrew looked again. Opposite him he was aware of Elizabeth drawing close, attracted to the puzzle. She too bent over the flattened map, one hand playing distractedly with the strand of pearls about her neck. All at once she looked up. "A hotel," she exclaimed. "There's not a decent hotel of any size in the area."

"Precisely." John smiled. "A hotel, Andrew. Can't you see?"

He could now, and nodded, though still he warned, "It's an ambitious undertaking for the first—"

"Then all the more reason to do it," John said. "Let's call attention to ourselves right off, shall we? And no simple medium-priced place, this, Andrew," he went on. "You said it yourself. Money follows money. I intend it to be the grandest hotel in all of London, first class, for the bloody aristocrats and landed gentry and anyone else who can afford the tariff."

He grew expansive, encircling the table, stopping once to kiss Dhari's hand, though not missing a beat in what he was saying. "The finest materials, Andrew, the finest artisans, the most modern kitchen, and of course we will hire the chef from Europe."

"You will need an architect," Andrew said.

"I have design ideas of my own," he protested, coming around the table.

"You are not a draftsman," Andrew reminded him.

"Then we'll hire one," John conceded, "but he will take direction from me." He continued filling the air with his glorious description of the new structure, standing beside Elizabeth, one arm about her shoulder, his voice lifting as he announced, "And we shall call it, 'the Elizabeth.' "

"No," she protested.

"Yes," and apparently suffering an irrepressible surge of joy, he lifted her into the air.

Amidst her faint protest, he lowered her to her feet and confronted Andrew with a direct question. "Where shall we work?"

"You'll need an office."

"You'll work here," Elizabeth said, straightening herself. "In the drawing room. It's never used."

"It would save money at first," John agreed.

Andrew nodded. "Then the drawing room it is, though I warn you, it will be quite disruptive."

"Dhari and I will stay out of the way, won't we?" Elizabeth smiled, retreating to where the young woman sat. "Unless, of course, we're needed."

Dhari looked as though she wanted to speak. Elizabeth hugged her.

If John saw the little drama, he gave no indication of it. Instead he continued to hover over the scattered deeds and map of London, his mind clearly moving ahead to other projects. Without looking up, he said, "Why are you standing about, Andrew? There's work to be done. How long will it take you to draw up instruments of corporation?"

Andrew faltered. "About a week," he murmured. "And the deeds must be brought up-to-date as well, the taxes paid." He smiled. "I wonder how many times in the last few years other builders have searched for the owner of those lost deeds?"

John seemed to relax. "Well, we're found now, aren't we?"

"We are indeed," Andrew agreed, then added, "I have a few cases I must finish first, before I can—"

"Finish them quickly," John urged.

"I will. In the meantime, I'll compile dossiers on all the practicing architects for you."

"And bring me everything you can find on the financial structure of Cubitt, and who was the other?"

"Burton." Andrew smiled, seeing the intention behind John's request. He would be an apt student, but he needed a body of knowledge, and how better to learn than from the mistakes and accomplishments of those two great master builders?

Then Andrew saw a look of fatigue on John's face, as though the expenditure of energy during the last hour had drained him. He leaned against the table and cast a final glance over the scattered deeds. "It *will* work," he murmured. "We'll make it work."

As the echo of the whispered vow hung heavy over the quiet room, Andrew realized that he had no further objection. There wasn't a force in the world equal to that avowal.

He saw John glance toward Aslam, as though reminded of his presence, though in truth the little boy had never left his place at the end of the table, had listened to every word that had been said.

Gently John reached out and ruffled his hair. "You'll help me, won't you, Aslam?" he asked, and in characteristic fashion answered his own question. "Of course you will. I'll make you a partner one day, so that fifty years from now, the richest man in all of London will have dark skin."

Suddenly he threw back his head, laughing. "Oh, God, how marvelous that would be."

Aslam watched intently, his patrician features breaking

into a smile, as though he was well aware of the joke he shared with John.

John reached for the little boy and invited, "Come, one quick game of chess before bed."

Andrew watched along with Dhari and Elizabeth as the two headed into the drawing room. But a few steps this side of the door, John stopped, as though a pressing thought had just entered his head. He did not look back, his voice low, as though on this point, he wanted no rebuttal. "The corporation, Andrew," he began. "I want it in my name."

"Of course," Andrew agreed. He'd never entertained any other possibility.

"In my name," John repeated. "But I want the 'Eden' dropped."

Out of the corner of his eye, Andrew saw Elizabeth start forward. As though John had sensed the objection, he repeated himself, in a voice without margin. "I want the 'Eden' dropped."

Andrew saw Elizabeth retreat, no match for the will of the man standing in the doorway. To Andrew it seemed a petty request. After all, it had been Edward Eden's foresight in signing over the Ragged School properties to John that was making this entire venture possible. "Are you certain?" he began.

"I'm certain," came the strong reply. "I want the 'Eden' dropped. My father was well known in the city. I don't want my competitors to get us confused. Edward Eden was the philanthropist. I am not."

He waited to see if there would be objection coming from anyone. Then on a fresh burst of energy he led Aslam into the drawing room, proclaiming, "Be on your guard tonight. I'm feeling victorious."

With that, the two disappeared around the corner, heading for the gaming table.

Andrew looked back toward Elizabeth. The disappointment on her face was astonishing. But at last she was calm, looking back at him with a bewildered expression, as though she were suffering from the sensation of riding on the tail of a comet, wondering whether it would rise to the rarefied air of the heavens, or plunge to earth.

London, Late January
1858

IN SPITE OF the mountainous problems pressing upon him, John glanced about the drawing room, which now bore no resemblance to a drawing room, and thought, quite simply, that he'd never felt more alive, thought too how much he missed Jack Willmot. With the hiring of the workmen ahead of him, he needed one good professional foreman. In short, he needed Jack Willmot.

From his cluttered desk near the window, he looked out at the wintry day, amazed at the line of men stretching around the corner. The firm had run four simple adverts for men from separate trades who wanted employment on a continuous-wage basis. He'd expected perhaps fifty to appear for the interviews. He glanced again out of the window, seeing at least double that number, a continuous line of burly unemployed men, slapping their arms and stamping their feet against the cold.

Although he hated to do so, he called to the young clerk at the desk near the end of the room. "Hold them a moment longer. I expect Mr. Rhoades at any moment. I want him to be here."

The young man nodded, a bright eager fellow named Archie whom Andrew had recruited from somewhere.

John cupped his hands about his forehead and stole a look upward at what once had been Elizabeth's drawing room. Early on, that first week, all the furniture had been moved out. Now a solid row of filing cabinets lined the far wall, the room stripped of all furniture save for his desk, and over there, Andrew's, and the clerk's desk at the end of the room.

The same day that the carpet had gone into storage, John had had several large display boards delivered, which now stood about the room bearing large maps of

central London, and pinned to the largest, the magnificent
drawings done by the architect Mr. Lewis Chiswell of
"The New Elizabeth" which shortly would rise out of the
congestion around Paddington Station.

Lowering his hands and leaning back in his chair, John
gazed in admiration at the elegant structure. A "domes-
ticated and practical Blenheim," Chiswell had called it,
incorporating all the theatricality of that great estate with
the exigencies and needs of a modern hotel. "Think of all
the ordinary people who would like to pass a night at
Blenheim," he'd joked with John.

Now, for an exorbitant tariff, they could. John gazed
upon the drawing, an intricate composition of Baroque
movement, arched windows, the segmental colonnade of
the main front and the interplay of convex and concave
forms. In a way, it was an intensely emotional design,
eliciting either instantaneous adoration or revulsion.

Fortunately the board of directors at the Metropolitan
Equitable Investment Association had fallen into the
former classification, had been so smitten with the idea of
royal lodgings for affluent commoners that they had readily lent him fifty thousand pounds of the Association's
money plus another twenty-five thousand pounds from
private investors.

Thus armed, he had been able to listen to Chiswell's
suggestion of Italian marble for the large reception rooms.
Although he'd spent hours studying the drawings, he
looked at them as though seeing them for the first time.
They *were* impressive. It would be a landmark.

Suddenly he heard the front door burst open, and saw
Andrew in the archway, his arms bulging with portfolios,
a scowl on his face. "My God, John, we mustn't keep
those men standing out there any longer. Why didn't you
start?"

"I was waiting for you," John called back, in high
spirits, ignoring the scowl. "Did you find him?" he asked
urgently. "The man named Hazlitt?"

"I found his boardinghouse," Andrew muttered, moving to the warmth of the fire. "According to his landlady,
he is in France. Seems there's a Frenchwoman—"

"Damn!" John exploded, leaving his chair and striding

toward the window, where he saw the line of men still growing. He had been counting on Hazlitt, though he'd never met the man. In his search for a professional foreman, the name Hazlitt had come up again and again. Employed for years by Thomas Cubitt, and largely responsible for the efficiency of his crews, John had heard that the man had taken only occasional jobs since Cubitt's death in 1855. John had hoped to hire him, knowing better than anyone the need for a strong voice of authority to keep the workmen in line and extract their best labors.

"Surely he's not the only foreman in London," Andrew soothed.

"Then find me another," John muttered.

"I thought that tomorrow I might call on Thomas Brassey. His files are extensive and—"

"No!" Abruptly John turned from the window, amazed that Andrew would make such a suggestion. "I want nothing from Thomas Brassey," he went on. "If it weren't for Thomas Brassey, Jack Willmot would be here instead of lying at the bottom of the Black Sea."

"I'm sorry," Andrew murmured. "We'll find someone. Perhaps one of the men outside."

John appreciated his understanding, but doubted seriously if there was a mentality in that frozen hungry line of men capable of performing the duties of a foreman.

"Let's get it over with," he said, dreading it, the inevitable process of selecting some, rejecting others, all in need. To the young clerk at the end of the room he called out, "Let them in, two at a time. Take their names and experience. And don't forget. I want only skilled workmen. If they're just looking for a week's wages, send them packing."

The young man nodded. As he disappeared into the entrance hall, Andrew drew close to the desk. "Chiswell finished the last of the drawings today, including the elevational designs." He pointed toward the portfolios on his desk. "They're marvelous. As soon as this is over, I'll show them to you. The detail in the individual chambers is elegant. London will never have seen anything like it."

Sitting behind his desk, John smiled. The praise was good, especially coming from Andrew, who'd seemed hesitant at the beginning. With every passing day, Andrew's enthusiasm had increased, and now it was he who kept John bolstered when the problems mounted. And how they had mounted, and with what skill Andrew had solved most of them, from negotiating to retain the freehold to buying up additional properties, thus giving them the space they needed on which to erect the Elizabeth. He was a skilled solicitor and a good friend, and the awareness of both softened John's newly awakened loss of Jack Willmot.

As the front door opened again and the cold draft of air raced across the floor, preceding the two disreputable-looking men who appeared, hats in hand, John and Andrew were both seated behind their desks, ready to commence the hiring.

John waited while the clerk took down their names and experience, recalling how often he'd done this for Thomas Brassey. It served one best to put aside all humanitarian tendencies and let only the conservative instincts hold sway. They were a clever lot, the poor and unemployed, capable of spinning heartbreaking fiction. Every one had an ill wife, crippled children and a hungry white-haired old mother. Unfortunately, as John knew all too well, most of the fictions were true.

For over an hour John and Andrew sat at their desks, enduring the stream of unemployed workmen. Their hiring goal for this first job had been three hundred men. By four o'clock in the afternoon they had less than half that number, always holding out for the most skilled, the most experienced, the healthiest. At some point, Archie had taken pity on the shivering men, and had tactfully suggested to John that they let as many into the warmth of the house as the entrance hall would hold, the others outside moving in to take their places as space permitted.

John had agreed, though now he was well aware of the crowded foyer, literally packed with frozen, hungry men.

Shortly after four, he glanced out of the window, amazed to see the line still growing, men with white slips of paper in their hands looking for the proper number where the hiring was going on. It was obvious that they would never see them all today, and it was equally obvious that someone would have to step outside and tell them so.

A hard task that would be. Most of the men he'd seen today were hungry to the point of desperation. From where John sat by the window, he'd already seen examples of shoving, men quarreling over their places in line, afraid that the quota would be filled before they had had a chance to apply.

All at once he heard a loud voice coming from the entrance hall, then the low rumbling of men arguing together.

"Damn," John muttered beneath his breath.

"What is it?" Andrew inquired.

At that moment John saw one of the men reach out, his massive hand shoving the man in front of him, and with one violent movement he jerked him out of sight beyond the archway. Suddenly a yell shattered the silence, the sound stirring the other men out of their lethargy, and as the entrance hall erupted into cries and shouts, John left his chair running.

Foolishly he tried to shout over the din, but to no avail. He was aware of Andrew behind him, apparently stunned by the sudden violence which had erupted in the entrance hall.

"We must stop them," Andrew gasped, and he too tried to push into the circle of men, and for his trouble was shoved roughly back.

John encircled the brawling men, calling to Andrew to see if Elizabeth had a weapon in the house. At first Andrew seemed not to hear, and as John was on the verge of shouting again, he saw the front door burst open, saw in silhouette a giant of a man filling the door, and thought with increasing anxiety that the din had reached the pavement and the remaining men would come streaming in.

For a moment the mountainous man stood there, his features obliterated by the glare of daylight behind him. Then he was pushing the men aside as though they lacked weight and substance, his massive arms effortlessly clearing a path until at last he stood over the three men fighting. He reached down and lifted the main offender to his feet by the scruff of his collar. Without warning he drew back his arm and pistonlike delivered a blow to the man's jaw that sent him sprawling, knocking over several others in the process.

John watched the remaining two men start forward. The large man turned with deliberation, grabbed their shoulders and with one resounding thud knocked their skulls together and tossed them toward the slowly retreating group of men.

The mood in the confined area was still ugly, and John was on the verge of stepping forward and dismissing the lot of them when the big man spoke, talking to the sullen workmen as though they were misbehaving schoolboys. "Now, what you done here, mates, wasn't exactly proper, was it? We all come here looking for a chance to work, and you act like you was in a dockside pub."

With growing amazement, John saw the men nod, self-conscious as schoolboys. John had yet to see his face, though at that moment, the large man said, "Now, someone here is due an apology, and I think that the sooner we . . ."

With that, he turned toward the archway, his massive features catching on the light from the drawing-room windows, his shock of red hair as luxuriant and thick as the rest of him. The face was vaguely familiar, the features growing more so, incredible features, or their exact duplicate, which John had last seen in the hospital ward at Scutari.

"Alex?" John whispered. "Alex Aldwell?"

A grin broke on the man's face. "Eden, is it?" he inquired in turn. " 'Course it is, the young man from the hospital, with a thousand questions."

With a laugh, John extended his hand and bridged the distance between them and felt his arm being pumped vigorously up and down.

"I . . . don't believe it," John managed, freeing his hand, recalling the number of times he'd cursed this man during that hot trek across India, recalling at the same time the enormous diamond which Aldwell had kept concealed in the leather pouch about his neck. The memory only heightened the mystery of what Aldwell was doing here, clearly a workman, in workman's clothes.

"What happened, Alex? The last time I saw you, you were a wealthy man."

At first Aldwell seemed at a loss to know what he was talking about. Then a smile lightened his look of confusion. "Oh, that," he said. "Well, I tell you, Eden. I got separated from it three days out of Constantinople. Bloody Turks did it to me. Come up from behind and left a knot on my head the size of the stone itself."

He shook his head. "I was ready to commit murder at first, but I guess some men were meant to be rich, and some weren't, and I'm head of the second group."

John listened sympathetically, detecting a change in the man, less belligerent, less arrogant, his garments speaking of hard times.

Aldwell stepped closer, suffering a question of his own. "Are you applying here as well, Eden?"

John laughed. "No, I'm taking applications."

Puzzled, Aldwell reached inside his coat and withdrew a soiled bit of paper. He read, "John Murrey Firm."

"That's me," John nodded.

"Where's the 'Eden'?"

"Dropped it."

The man looked closely at him. Slowly he stepped back, apparently aware of the new distance between them. "Sorry for the ruckus here," he murmured. "I'll get 'em back in line for you if you wish."

But John had no intention of exploiting his position as employer. They had far too much to talk about. The hiring was over for the day. He stepped after Aldwell, one hand on his arm. "No, wait here. There'll be no more interviews today. Stay close, though," he added. "I doubt if they'll take too kindly to it."

"Oh, I'll tell 'em for you," Aldwell volunteered. "They're a good lot, really. You want them back there same time tomorrow?"

Grateful and impressed with the man's efficient manner, John watched as Aldwell herded the men out of the door and onto the stoop where the others were waiting. In a booming voice he shouted, "That's all today, mates. Don't leave downhearted, though. Tomorrow is yet ahead, and the gent says to come back then."

Keeping an ear on the activity outside, John looked over at Andrew and saw the look of bewilderment on his face. "I met him in the hospital at Scutari. I never expected to see him again."

"He handles men well."

"Indeed he does."

"I'll leave you two alone," Andrew went on. "I'm certain that Elizabeth and Dhari heard the noise and are concerned."

Alex Aldwell reappeared in the door and closed it behind him. "Done." He grinned. "Though ever' last one of them will be back tomorrow."

John thanked him and motioned for him to come close. "Alex, I would like you to meet my friend and solicitor, Andrew Rhoades."

As Andrew extended his hand, John saw him wince at the strength in the man's grasp. With the intention of sparing him before his arm was pumped off, he suggested kindly, "Alex, go on in by the fire. There's tea there. You look frozen. I'll be with you in a moment," John called after him, "and this time, I have a tale or two to match your own." He dismissed the clerk, sent him home for the night and called up to Andrew, who was just starting up the stairs. "Wait a moment."

As Andrew looked back down, John asked, keeping his voice low, "What do you think?" bobbing his head toward the drawing room, where Alex was waiting.

"He's your friend. You know him better than I do." Andrew looked down on John again, smiling. "I don't know what we would have done today without his assistance." He shook his head as though reliving the brutal moments, then slowly he proceeded up the stairs.

John stood alone in the entrance hall, looking out over the smudged prints left by muddy boots. Still he missed Jack Willmot, and while he didn't understand the tragedies of the past, he thoroughly understood the needs of the future, and now he lifted his head and felt his spirits follow, and entered the drawing room with the rising optimism of a man who had just found himself one hell of a foreman.

London,
August 1859

ANDREW SAT ON the brocade sofa in the sitting room adjoining the bedchamber in John's new town house in Belgravia. His attention was torn between not mussing his new dress blacks and the clock atop the marble mantelpiece, which was devouring the minutes at a rapid pace.

"John, you must hurry," he called out. "I told Elizabeth and Dhari we would be there before nine o'clock."

No answer. There had been no answer for the last half hour, not since John had angrily dismissed his manservant, shouting that he was capable of dressing himself.

Nerves!

Andrew was certain it was nerves. He felt the pressures himself, the opening of the Elizabeth tonight, the thousand and one details which had inundated both of them.

He started to call again, then changed his mind. If *he* felt the pressure, what must John be feeling? In an attempt to get his mind off the ordeal of waiting, he reached for the latest edition of the *Illustrated London Chronicle* resting on the low marble table before him. For a moment he bounced it nervously against his knee, not really in the mood to read.

He looked about, taking a pleasing inventory of the richly decorated sitting room, which in reality paled in comparison with the rest of the Belgravia mansion. The move had come six months ago, instigated by no one in particular, but simply a need for more space for John's growing firm, plus the fact, as John had pointed out, the Belgravia house itself would be a good investment. Also Andrew was certain that living in the mansion that had been built by Thomas Cubitt held great appeal for John, the young master builder displacing the old one, in more ways than one.

For the first time since he'd arrived that evening, Andrew leaned back against the sofa, amused at the quixotic nature of his good friend and business associate, who for the most part thumbed his nose at decorum, and yet who had insisted that for appearance' sake, Dhari and Aslam remain under Elizabeth's roof, though he'd furnished private apartments for each in his new Belgravia house. Now three, sometimes four times a week, Dhari would arrive in her private carriage and pass the night with John, only to be whisked away before dawn back to Elizabeth's house on St. George Street. And John had succeeded in fooling no one, as all the tattlers in London were gossiping about the dark-skinned and curiously silent mistress of its new young master builder.

Aslam was a more frequent visitor, his carriage arriving at nine sharp every morning, when John would escort him up to his apartments, which included a classroom where four tutors were waiting.

On occasion, Elizabeth called in for tea, or dinner, making sound business suggestions, acting as liaison between John and her many and influential friends in Parliament.

Andrew had been relieved when John had established his own household and had given Elizabeth back her drawing room as well as her privacy. In a way, Andrew had suffered most when they had all been confined in the house on St. George Street. Now he was able on almost any evening to avail himself of Elizabeth's company, though frequently he had to wait patiently for Lord Kimbrough to leave.

He smiled, aware of his role as "waiter." No matter. The truth was he was happier, more prosperous than he'd ever dreamed possible. The success of the firm had been nothing short of miraculous. Under John's leadership, they'd scarcely broken ground for the new hotel when he'd launched half a dozen other projects: the new modern dock in St. Katherine's, the large Methodist church in Bloomsbury, and the most profitable of all, the government contract for new barracks near Hyde Park, with the promise of more government involvement to come.

In order to accommodate all this feverish activity, John had set up offices on the street floor of his house in Belgravia, and there was scarcely a night when the lamps did not burn late.

Now all of London, particularly financial London, was keenly aware that a new, young wizard had arrived among them, and through the art of competitive tendering was in the process of driving all his near competitors out of business.

The primary result of all this confusion could be stated in one simple fact. John Murrey Eden was well on his way to becoming one of the richest men in London. A "scrambler," the London *Times* called him, who was not above undercutting the Archbishop if it meant profit to his stockholders and fiercely loyal crew of five hundred workers.

Thinking on the man now, Andrew opened his eyes and called again, "John? Do you need assistance? Time is passing and we really must . . ." He glanced at the clock. Eight-thirty. They should be in the carriage now. The traffic would be fierce.

"John?" he called again, and still receiving no answer, slapped the folded newspaper against his knee and considered charging into the bedchamber himself. But he changed his mind. The world wouldn't come to an end if they were a few minutes late. On more than one occasion both he and Elizabeth had expressed concern over the pace that John had set for himself.

Every morning for the past year and a half, John's day had commenced at six-thirty and frequently had not come to a halt until well after midnight. There had been no holidays, no respites, and if he wasn't in committee meetings or closeted with an architect, then he could be found on the building site of the moment, chatting with his men, frequently accompanying them in the raucous company of Alex Aldwell to a local pub, where they would lift a pint together.

Elizabeth had called him obsessed and feared for his health. But in Andrew's opinion he was simply a man who at last had found an outlet worthy of his incredible energies.

Eight-forty! In an attempt to quiet his rampaging nerves, he opened the folded newspaper on his lap and read the headline:

THE NEW ELIZABETH AND ITS YOUNG GENIUS.

He blinked and withdrew his spectacles from his pocket. Though the London papers had been filled with accounts of the new hotel for weeks, he'd not seen this one.

He adjusted his specs and lifted the paper toward the lamp and read aloud, full-voiced, in an attempt to penetrate the silence coming from the bedchamber.

" 'The New Elizabeth and Its Young Genius.' Have you read this, John? How's that for a headline?"

Still no response. "Let me read it to you," Andrew called out. "Perhaps it will spur you on to greater speed."

An occasion of note will take place in this city on August 9, 1859, the formal opening of the most elegant hotel to grace London in over two decades.

The New Elizabeth, adjoining Paddington Station, is a marvel of old-world grandeur and modern technology, a grandiose, declamatory structure more like a mountainous work of sculpture than architecture.

Seldom has London seen a public house on the scale of this one. Reminiscent of one of England's Great Houses, it will provide luxury and comfort for the weary who have the purse to match the tariff.

For the opening ball on this coming Saturday evening, the gallery will be filled with twenty thousand crimson roses, and while the invited guests feast on the eighteen-course banquet provided by the artist-chef Laguerre, a full stringed orchestra will perform a concert of Strauss waltzes to aid their digestion and heighten the glories of their surroundings.

Andrew stopped reading with a wry smile. How effortless it all sounded. Who would know the hours, days, months of laborious planning which had taken place prior to this evening? No one but himself and John and the staff of sixty who had been hired specifically to arrange the opening ball.

Andrew looked up, thinking that the effusive journalism might draw John out or at least elicit a response. Unfortunately it did neither, and Andrew read the closing paragraphs, determined to enter the bedchamber at the conclusion of the reading.

But of greater interest to informed London than the hotel itself, which is certain to become a landmark, is the driving creative force behind it, a young man about whom little is known except that he appeared two years ago on the London financial scene, and through methods orthodox and unorthodox is well on his way to becoming the premier master builder in all of London.

Who is he and where he came from, no one knows. But where do any of them come from, those amazing industrial czars? From every rank of society they have come, and royalty has smiled on them, politicians have cleared their way, and the city has put its money at their disposal. The roll call is impressive: Stephenson, Naysmyth, Brunel, Tangye, Bessemer, Murrey.

Consider the Empire Builders, the men who invent, design, organize, contract. When historians look back on our remarkable empire, they will note that during the reign of one of our greatest queens, we also enjoyed an age when kings were common.

Andrew blinked at the newsprint, rather impressed by the unique tribute. He removed his spectacles and wiped at his eyes, and it was while he was thus incapacitated that he heard a familiar deep voice.

"You read very well, Andrew, even when you're reading nonsense."

Thank God! At last. Quickly he looked up, expecting to see a fully dressed John standing before him. Instead he saw the man still in his dressing robe, loosely knotted about the waist, revealing bare legs and feet, his hair mussed as though he'd recently been lying on his bed, a maddening smile on his face.

Andrew started to his feet. "What in the—"

"We must be on guard against believing such rubbish," John went on. "The journalist who wrote that should be drowned in his own ink."

"Damn the journalist!" Andrew exploded. "Why aren't you dressed? It's nine o'clock. The guests, Elizabeth, Dhari all waiting . . ."

But if the man was aware of Andrew's anger, he gave no indication of it. Instead he strolled to the sideboard, lifted the decanter of port, poured a glass, sipped and announced calmly, "I'm not going."

For a moment Andrew had to struggle with the incredible announcement. "Not . . . going?" he repeated, his anger rising along with his nerves. "What do you mean, you're not going? Everyone's expecting you. My God, man, have you lost your senses?"

To this impassioned plea John simply repeated himself. "I'm not going. You run along, Andrew. You can handle it all very well. In fact, you'll be far better at it than I would be."

Andrew shook his head, still not able to believe what he was hearing. "You're . . . joking, of course, John."

"I'm not joking at all."

"But you have responsibilities, obligations . . ."

Without warning, John exploded in a burst of anger, slamming the glass down upon the tray, shattering it in the process. "Don't speak to me of obligation and responsibility. I've put in eighteen-hour days for the last two years meeting both. My enterprises are now feeding and clothing hundreds of people and will continue to do so in the future. I build buildings, Andrew," he concluded, his anger receding. "Does that mean that I have to socialize with their inhabitants?"

Before this outburst, Andrew retreated. "No," he conceded softly. "But the ball was your idea."

"And I'm certain it will be a success." Almost in surprise he looked down at the shattered crystal on the tray, his manner apologetic. "The hotel is no longer mine, Andrew, indeed it holds no interest for me. I built it, but now it belongs to others, like yourself, and all those ladies and gentlemen who will partake of Laguerre's sumptuous feast."

A brief smile crossed his face as he quoted from the flowery newspaper account. Though they were no longer shouting at each other in anger, still Andrew was almost beside himself at this sudden change of plans. My God, the Lord Mayor would be there, a guest list which represented every titled family in England.

He watched as John sank into a near chair, lifted his bare feet to the ottoman and smoothed back his long mussed hair. "I'm tired, Andrew," he confessed softly. "Do this favor for me, will you?"

Did he have a choice? Of course he didn't. "What will you do?" Andrew asked, still not resigned to the ordeal yet ahead of him.

At the direct question, John smiled. "I don't inquire into all aspects of your life, do I?" He shrugged. "I feel the need for fresh air. I may take a brief journey . . ."

"Where?"

"No more questions," John begged, lifting both hands in a restraining gesture. "Look at the clock, Andrew," he added. "You'll be late as it is. You'd better hurry. Make my apologies to Elizabeth and Dhari, and lift a glass of that French champagne for me. We certainly paid enough for it."

All at once he leaned his head back against the cushions and closed his eyes, his customary signal for the end of a conversation.

At last resigned, Andrew backed away. He did look tired. But they all were tired. And what journey was he talking about? And how could he ever explain such a notable absence to such an illustrious company?

At the door he lifted his cape and top hat and looked back at the sprawled figure of one of the new "kings." Unfortunately, at that moment he looked most unregal. Although Andrew still had a hundred questions, time did not permit him to pose any of them. Someone must keep the machine running, and in a terse voice he called back, "I'll report to you later," and received in reply a sleepy, "You do that."

Still angry, Andrew slammed the door and hurried down the stairs, taking the marble entrance hall in a dead run, and emerging at last on the darkened pavement to see his carriage, and parked in front of it, John's large one, the four horses stamping at the cobbles. Lounging against the door he saw Alex Aldwell.

"Alex," he called out, mystified at the presence of the large man, who was lightly snapping the whip against the side of his leg.

"Good evening to you, Mr. Rhoades." Alex grinned. "You look right smart tonight, you do. A big occasion, ain't it?"

Andrew ignored the remark and drew close. "Where's Jason?" he asked, looking about for John's customary driver, a West Indian whom John had hired about eight months ago.

Alex shrugged. "Asleep would be my guess."

"What are you doing here?"

"Mr. Eden told me to have the carriage waiting at ten o'clock, and here I am."

Andrew stepped closer, loathing his role as spy, but knowing from past experience that when Aldwell drove, John was up to no good. "Did he say where he was going?"

"Didn't say and I didn't ask," the man replied, displaying his blind loyalty to the man who'd lifted him out of the ranks of workmen and made him foreman, an awesome task which Andrew was forced to admit that Aldwell performed brilliantly.

Momentarily stymied, aware of passing time, Andrew stepped wearily toward his own carriage, calling back, "Look after him, Alex."

"I always do, Mr. Rhoades. I owe him this grand life, as we all do in a way. Ain't that right?"

Andrew did not offer a rebuttal. He gave his driver instructions and pulled himself up into his carriage.

What was John up to now? Where was he going? And what possible excuse could Andrew give to the waiting dignitaries? As the carriage pulled out and around, Andrew looked back at the mansion, dark except for the lights on the top floor, where at the moment of his greatest triumph the new "king" sat brooding in solitary confinement.

Would Andrew ever completely understand him? Probably not, and on that note of despair he called out for his driver to, "Hurry! Please hurry!"

At ten o'clock, clothed in a dark cloak and carrying one small portmanteau, John walked across the pavement toward his carriage.

He tossed the portmanteau to Aldwell, and watched as the man secured it atop. As he was crawling back down, John spoke his destination for the first time.

"Do you feel up to a drive tonight, Alex?" he asked.

"Name it and I'll take you there, John."

"Wiltshire. Salisbury."

Alex grinned. "Are we going to prayer?"

"Perhaps, among other things."

"It'll be a night's drive."

"Make an easy one of it. Stop when you wish. I'm in no hurry."

"Then it will be pleasant enough," Alex added, holding the door open. "It's the rushing about that gets to a man."

As John pulled himself up into the carriage, he smiled back. "In a while, I'll come and ride up there with you. We can pass the night telling tales of India."

The man nodded enthusiastically. "I'd like that!"

As the carriage started forward, John admitted to himself that he would enjoy it as well. How many pleasant hours he and Aldwell had passed, reliving their experiences in that dark mysterious world. Of course, John suspected that each tale grew a little taller with the telling, but out of the hundreds of people who moved through his world now, Aldwell was the only man who knew and understood that terrifying chapter from his life.

The carriage was picking up speed now, heading toward the western edge of the city, and for the first time in several hours John dared to relax, though he still carried with him the angry bewilderment of Andrew Rhoades.

Perhaps he should have attempted an explanation. But how could he have explained what he himself did not understand, his need for a brief interval away from the committees and charts and stockholders' meetings and arrogant architects? Days ago he'd made his plans to flee the city on this night. The very thought of the festivities chilled his blood, the fawning and obsequiousness, the rather tasteless opulence which he himself had created.

He shuddered, relieved that the ordeal had been avoided. Of course, he would have to mend his bridges and tender countless apologies, but for one brief interval he wanted to stand in a world that had nothing to do with the past or the future, to lounge beneath an apple tree in the warm August sun and perhaps hear a sweet voice inquire from the upper branches, "Where are you going? You look weary."

And he felt weary. At least he'd spoken one truth to Andrew. But as the speed of the carriage increased, he was aware that this sojourn might well be a mad goosechase. Well, nothing new there. He'd been called mad often enough, and he'd had only limited contact with Lila Harrington since his return to London two years ago, through her letters, which continued to move him by their innocence and her deep concern for him.

With what obvious devotion she continued to fill page after page, spirited epistles informing him of the "great" events in her life: the nest of newly hatched robins in the tree outside her window, Wolf's refusal to let the field mice alone in spite of his well-fed belly, the miraculous night she'd seen three shooting stars over the horizon . . .

He smiled, remembering these dear letters which he kept hidden in a special drawer in his bureau. One, two, three letters might have been forgotten. But seventy-nine! Now he at least owed her the courtesy of a personal thanks for her continued devotion.

Glancing out of his window, he discovered that they were on the outskirts of the city. He lowered the window and let the breeze blow over him, cleansing his mind of the turmoil of the last two years.

Abruptly he laughed. After so many days of meticulous planning, weighing somber architectural masses and figuring to the last decimal point percentages and cost overruns, the sheer whimsy of his present escapade began to have a medicinal effect on him. He leaned up and rapped

on the front window, signaling Alex to bring the horses
to a stop.

As the man did so, John crawled out of the isolation of
his carriage and hoisted himself atop the high seat, took
the reins from Alex's hand, slapped them gently across
the horses, urged them to top speed and shouted over the
whistling wind, "Did I ever tell you about the Thuggee
temple at Bindhachal?"

"No, I don't believe you did," Alex shouted back in a
good-natured lie.

John glanced over and saw his friend grinning in anticipation of the tale he'd heard at least a hundred times before. And catching the spirit of the occasion and the romantic excitement of the night, both men commenced
laughing, their hilarity joining with the wind as the carriage sped down the narrow dark turnpike.

The following afternoon, after a comfortable morning's
sleep at the Red Lion Inn in Salisbury, John directed Alex
to leave the turnpike and take the dusty road heading
south toward Penselwood. About a half mile later, the
surrounding landscape grew familiar, the orchard on the
left now, the sandstone towers of Harrington Hall just
visible on the right beyond the rolling downs.

In anicipation, John sat up on the edge of his seat and
allowed Alex to pass the orchard by. Then he shouted,
"Bring the horses about."

Slowly John crawled down from the high perch and
thought of the difference between now and that hot morning so long ago when he'd trod this same path, leaving
Eden behind him, the burden of a murdered man on his
conscience, Harriet occupying his soul.

He clung to the side of the carriage, weakened by his
thoughts, as though no time at all had passed, as though
nothing had healed. He looked westward, as though if he
looked hard enough he might see Eden miles away. He
must return one day. He couldn't put it off forever. Too
much of his heart still resided there. But he couldn't go
back yet, not now. He must be stronger, more invulnera-
ble to what he might find.

He continued to stare toward the top of the hill, seeing through the shimmering heat waves the young boy with dusty boots and soiled garments, alone.

As sweat rolled down his forehead and into the corner of his eye, he rubbed the stinging sensation and realized that in spite of all his success, in spite of his five hundred workmen, his mansion in Belgravia, his various building projects, in spite of Andrew and Alex and Elizabeth and Dhari and Aslam, he was still, after all these years, alone.

In the stillness of the hot August day, the perception, so unexpected, worked a strange magic on him. Abruptly he looked in the opposite direction, down the hill toward the orchard.

"Wait here, Alex," he instructed. "I have no idea how long I'll be. You may want to wait inside the carriage. It will be cooler."

"I'm fine, John," came the quiet reply, "and take your time."

John walked away, moved by the loyalty of the man who obviously was not at all curious why John had directed him to this lonely, isolated spot.

Or if he had questions, he kept them to himself, and John proceeded alone down the hill, his eyes moving ahead to the orchard. A few moments later he left the road, as he'd done on that other hot morning, and headed toward what he thought was the same tree. In spite of feeling self-conscious, he found himself looking up into the high branches. But he saw nothing but the leafy green ripeness of August, the slight breeze blowing cool against his sweat-soaked shirt, his boots, he noticed, as scuffed and dusty as that other boy's.

He looked in all directions. Perhaps he had the wrong tree, and he walked deeper into the orchard, seeing nothing but the skittering play of sunlight and shadow. From this vantage point he looked over his shoulder and discovered that he could not even see his carriage, and briefly the limitations of time and space disappeared and he sat heavily in the shade upon the moist earth and rested his back against a tree trunk.

Perhaps the young lady was married now. He assumed

that for her it had been a fashionable diversion to pen
letters to the Crimea, and later to a scarcely known gentleman in London, her devotion the result of boredom as
much as anything.

Well, then, it had been as he'd suspected, a fruitless
interlude. Not a total loss, however. At least he'd confronted one ghost from the past, that young boy who'd
walked from Eden and taken refuge in the shade of these
trees. He'd come this far on this occasion. Perhaps on his
next flight from the pressures of London, he'd find the
courage to make it as far as Taunton. And the time after
that, Barnstaple, and the time after that, to Eden.

Thus resolved, John pulled himself up, dusted off his
trousers, and commenced walking back toward the road.
He was not particularly looking in the direction of the
towers of Harrington Hall, but as he stepped up onto the
road, out of the corner of his eye he saw something atop
the crest of the far down.

He looked away, then looked back. From that distance,
recognition was impossible, but it appeared to be a woman,
the wind blowing her skirts, one hand raised to her eyes
as though she too were squinting into the distance.

Although he had taken a few steps to the left, heading
back toward the carriage, he proceeded slowly to the far
side of the road. She was still standing, her eyes fastened
on him. Then all at once she was running toward him
across the down, the wind blowing her skirts and hair,
while at her feet, keeping pace, was an enormous gray
cat who leaped up out of the tall grasses, then disappeared,
only to leap up again, the two of them drawing nearer,
until recognition was complete.

Embarrassed though incredibly pleased, John felt the
heat of a blush on his face. It was her, looking even
younger and more childlike, as though the passage of
years had not fazed her. She was calling his name, a
beautiful sound which the wind caught and blew toward
him.

He couldn't believe it. "Lila?" he called out, laughing.

"Yes," she cried, still a distance away.

Thinking quite plausibly that this was a place of
either magic or miracles, he went to meet her.

She knew it!

It *was* him. She had known it since early morning, no, last night, really, when she'd seen his face in the moon, and Wolf had scratched endlessly at her window, wanting out. He never went out at night unless someone was coming.

And at dawn the feeling was so strong that she'd dressed early and gone to the orchard while her father was still at prayer. She'd waited all day, until, limp from the heat, and thirsty, she'd gone home for a brief respite.

Now, there he was, and laughing, she ran the rest of the way down the hill until she came to a halt about ten feet from where he stood, feeling out of breath, and suddenly painfully shy.

"John?" She smiled, trying to smooth her hair.

He nodded, looking very stodgy and grown-up in his hot city clothes.

"I . . . thought it was you," she said, amazed and moved by the changes which had taken place in him. His beard for one. She'd never imagined him bearded, and wondered if he would object if she touched it.

Apparently not, though he appeared to be holding very still, as though he were afraid to move.

"It's rough." She smiled and looked up to his forehead, her fingers moving over the long scar. "Will you tell me how this happened?" she asked. "But not now. That story doesn't belong to today." She laughed again, still unable to believe that he was standing before her. "Aren't you going to say anything at all?"

Finally he seemed to come to himself, as though he were awakening from a deep sleep. He glanced down at Wolf, who was rubbing against his leg and purring loudly. As though to Wolf, he spoke her name. "Lila. I wanted to come and thank you for your letters," he began hesitantly, still not looking at her. "I'm afraid I didn't receive them as you sent them. But they all were waiting for me when I got back to London and . . ."

For the first time he looked up, presenting her with the vast changes that had taken place on his face. "And I wanted you to know I was grateful."

She saw sweat rolling off his face and thought him the

most uncomfortable-looking man she'd ever seen. He stepped away, appearing shy. "And you?" he asked politely. "Have you been well?"

"My mother died."

He looked back at her. "I'm sorry. When?"

"Last June on a Saturday morning at six-twenty-five." She looked away, not wanting to recall the day. She shouldn't have told him. Something about his face suggested that he'd heard enough of death. "But I'm well and my father is well, though he says his beads and prays in secret."

She didn't want to discuss that either, or any aspect of the gloom which had descended on her house. "Come . . ." She smiled. "Let's go to the orchard. It's cool there."

As she led the way across the road, she looked up at the handsome carriage waiting at the top of the hill. "Is that yours?" she asked, scooping Wolf up into her arms.

John followed after her. "It is."

"Who is the driver?"

"A friend. Alex Aldwell."

She released Wolf with a warning to leave the field mice alone, and looked back up the road. "Max will adore him." She smiled. "Max adores anyone with flesh. He has so little of it."

Behind her she heard the sound of his laugh, and led the way into the shade, turning back with a suggestion. "Why don't you take off your coat? You'd be more comfortable."

When she looked back, she was pleased to see that he'd done just that. Slowly she knelt beneath a large tree and closed her eyes to the delicious earth odors which wafted in and out with the breeze. "Sit," she invited, and motioned to the tree trunk and watched as bashfully he did as she had requested.

Thus seated, with only a short distance between them, she warned herself not to prattle on, as her father had scolded her so often for doing. *Others want to speak as well, Lila.*

So she knelt before him and waited for all of his news before she told him hers. Just when she thought he'd never speak, he picked up a near twig and commenced making lines on the earth and said apologetically, "I should have written."

"You had no time."

"No, I mean from London, to tell you I was coming."

"I knew you were coming. I've been here all day waiting for you."

He looked up, as though surprised by her answer, though in the end a smile canceled the surprise and he said gently, "You haven't changed."

"You have. You look older."

"I *am* older, and . . ."

He seemed to lose his train of thought and looked vaguely about at the earth where he'd scratched a pattern of intersecting lines.

"Are you through?" she asked politely.

"Through with . . . what?"

"With your words. If you want to say more, I'll be quiet. If not, I'll talk."

"You talk, Lila. Tell me all about yourself."

She moved closer on her knees, delighted with the invitation. "Oh, I've nothing to say about me," she began, smoothing out the lines of intersected earth. "It's about something else, though. Quite a mystery it is. Would you like to see it? It isn't far, and perhaps you can explain it."

"What is it?"

"It's the stream," she began, amazed that someone was willing to share her mystery. "Over there," she went on, pointing beyond the orchard. "And it's rising, just a bit every day, but I've watched it for three weeks and dropped a measurement into it, and it *is* rising. Would you like to see? And on the way, I'll show you something else, a cocoon that for three weeks has been trying to become a butterfly." Suddenly she shuddered. "In a way, it's terrible. You can see it trapped inside. I've wondered if I shouldn't try to help." She looked at him, pleased by the interest on his face. "Do you know anything about butterflies?"

It was several moments after she had stopped talking before he said anything. But she'd charted the expression on his face, one of soft bewilderment. Oh, how lovely it was to have him back.

"Will you come with me, John?"

Slowly he reached one hand out and caressed the side of her face. "I'll come. Lead the way."

"Let's take off our shoes," she suggested. "It's very marshy and damp. And it feels so good, the wetness."

He laughed and immediately reached down to his boots.

"Let me do it," she begged, and without waiting for his answer, moved close and rested his boot in her lap and released the three large buckles, and with one effort jerked his foot free. She rolled down his stocking and pulled it free, and marveled at the white beauty of his foot, the skin so tender. When she looked up, she was dazzled by the radiance in his eyes, the tension she'd seen earlier almost gone.

Hurriedly she removed his other boot, then stood and kicked off her slippers, and seeing his sweat-dampened shirtwaist, made a second suggestion. "Why don't you take off your shirt as well?"

Without a word of protest, he followed her every suggestion, and stood before her at last, perfectly at home in his skin, bearing an incredible resemblance to the young boy she'd met here years ago.

"Well, then"—he smiled—"lead the way. I have an appetite for small perplexing mysteries."

She lifted her head and called for Wolf, told him they were going to the stream and if he wanted to come, he'd better hurry.

Then she led the way through the orchard, hearing his bare feet padding along behind her, hearing him laugh aloud as though shaken by some extravagant merriment.

From where he sat atop the high carriage seat, Alex saw the young woman and grinned, his suspicions confirmed.

So! It *was* a woman. But even from this distance he could tell that this one was different, no brassy London whore.

Alex knew he shouldn't be watching, and considered averting his eyes, but what else was there to watch on this deserted road? So he settled back against the seat and took it all in, the two of them standing at the bottom of the hill, John stroking the cat—that was a bad sign, when he had that pretty piece of fresh country goods standing before him.

Ah! There! At last. She had some sense if he didn't, and Alex watched, fascinated, as she led him across the road and into the shade of the orchard.

Squinting, Alex continued to watch. Jesus, they looked shy as children, her kneeling before him, him scratching at the dirt. Where was the old John who could disrobe a whore and mount her in twenty seconds flat? Alex knew. He'd timed him often enough. Yet now? Look at him there, ducking his head like some schoolboy.

Wait! There was an encouraging move, again coming from her. Doing something to his boots. Oh, yes, events were picking up, John shedding his shirt, the two of them standing . . .

Suddenly Alex leaned forward on the seat. What in the hell? Look at them, running through the orchard and through the meadow beyond, racing toward that dark fringe of trees.

Damn! They must have seen him watching, and now he'd be robbed of the best part. "Damn!" he cursed again, and crawled slowly down from his perch, sweltering, and into the cool interior of the carriage.

Well, no matter. At least he knew what they were doing here now, and knowing John, within the hour he'd have his fill of country air and country wenches, and unless old Alex missed his guess, they would be London-bound by nightfall.

Unfortunately, he missed his guess, and two weeks later, as he squatted on the flagstone terrace outside the kitchen entrance of Harrington Hall, scaling fish with a stick of an old man named Max, he sat flat down on his ass as though he'd just come to his senses, and wondered what in the hell they were still doing here.

Not that it was so bad. Quite the contrary. It was one

of the most enjoyable and prolonged holidays that Alex Aldwell had ever known, fishing every day in the Avon with old Max, enjoying a bountiful table in the servants' hall with the staff, though a weird collection of geese they were.

They'd spent the first two nights at the Red Lion in Salisbury, then the young lady had insisted that they stay at Harrington Hall, and Lord Harrington had agreed, though he wore a perpetually bewildered look and fingered pope beads all the time.

As the fish scales splattered about the flagstones at his feet, Alex was forced to admit that the most baffling of all was John Murrey Eden. Every evening that first week, he'd told Alex, "We'll leave tomorrow, noon at the latest." But tomorrow and noon would come and go and the young lady would appear with a picnic hamper and they would take off across the downs and return at nightfall with wreaths of clover in their hair.

Like children they were, the two of them, sometimes riding bareback over to Stonehenge, other times jumping out of the barn and onto the hay mounds, then John bidding her good night at the ungodly hour of ten o'clock and sitting with her father for the rest of the evening, then coming to bed himself about midnight, where he *stayed*, for Alex had heard him from the next room.

No, something was going on, or more accurately, nothing was going on, and wasn't likely to, and in the meantime, what must the folks back in London be thinking? Worried sick, that's what they'd be. Oh, yes, he could just imagine Mr. Rhoades. And Miss Elizabeth. It was a wonder she didn't have the soldiers out searching for them.

No, it would have to come to an end soon, and as Alex tossed the last fish over into the wicker basket, he ignored Max's invitation to share a pint, and walked determinedly around the side of the Hall, squinting over the wall into the garden, where he'd seen John and Lila Harrington walking earlier.

There they were, on their hands and knees, *planting*, John as mud-smudged as a farmer. *Children*. That single description kept coming to mind and seemed most accurate.

Kneeling beside John was the young lady, or more accurately, child, for Alex knew the female of the species very well, and that one, he would swear to it, was as virginal as the day she'd slipped from her mother's womb, and for all the progress John was making, she was likely to stay that way. He gazed a moment longer as they passed the trowel back and forth. Then Alex had seen enough and cleared his throat noisily.

At the rude noise of shifting phlegm, he saw John look up, an expression of concentration on his face as intense as when he did his cost charts. "Alex . . ." He smiled, as though just bringing him into focus. "Come, lend us a hand. We're making an investment in the earth, and according to Lila, the dividends next spring will be lovely, long fragrant trumpets of waxlike beauty."

Christ! Had the man taken leave of his senses? "I . . . was wondering," Alex began, "if I might have a word with you. Just a word, John, that's all, in private if you don't mind."

Gently John leaned close to Lila and delivered himself of a melodramatic stage whisper, loud enough for all to hear. "Look! Now, that's a London face. Can you see it? Look at the brow, the tightness about the eyes."

To Alex's embarrassment she said quietly, "It's a good face, John, the face of a man who loves you very much." She raised her voice to Alex. "Won't you come and help us, Mr. Aldwell?"

For a moment he almost succumbed to the sweetness of that face. But at last he saw John rising from his kneeling position. Brushing the dirt from his knees, he started up the flagstone steps which separated the terrace from the garden below. "Now, Alex, what's so important that it couldn't wait?"

"I was wondering," Alex began, "if perhaps I shouldn't send Mr. Rhoades a message of some sort."

It seemed a sensible suggestion, and he was in no way prepared for the surprised look on John's face. "Why?" he asked bluntly. "What sort of message?"

"Well, accounting for ourselves, you know, where we are and . . ."

John smiled. "We know where we are. What difference does it make to Andrew?"

"Don't you think he's worried, as are all the—"

"Why worried? I left him with enough work to keep him busy for several months. As for the crews, they certainly know what to do."

"We've been gone, John, for over two weeks."

"Yes?"

"Miss Elizabeth. Don't you think she's probably beside herself by now?"

Apparently Alex had said something that had penetrated. "I know, I know," John said, retreating a step, as though he did not like to be reminded of certain obligations. "You're right, Alex," he conceded, "and I promise we'll leave—perhaps tomorrow, no later than noon."

How many times Alex had heard those words before. "Just let me send a message, John, telling them all where we are and what—"

"No!" He stepped closer, with an expression which resembled anger. "Can't you see? Can't you understand?"

But Alex couldn't, though before John's anger he retreated. "Perhaps . . . tomorrow, then," he muttered, repeating the vague promise. He turned about and walked away from the mud-covered man, deciding just then to seek out old Max and lift as many pints as necessary to dull his thoughts of neglected duties, of the keenest mind in all of London gone suddenly balmy.

John watched him go and started to call him back, but ultimately said nothing. How could he possibly explain to that pragmatic man what he himself did not understand?

He turned back to the wall and looked out over the garden to the font of the mystery, the bowed head of Lila Harrington, who perhaps *had* worked a spell on him. She'd laughed about it often enough, and now he wanted nothing more than to remain in her presence, and now he wanted nothing more than to remain in her presence, to live forever in the atmosphere of boyhood and youth which she had created for him.

During these last two weeks he'd felt blood flowing in his veins for the first time in years. All the remembered tragedy through which he had walked had fallen away from him, and he was young again. Beyond a simple clasp of her hand, he had never touched her. It was as though he had willingly placed all his ardor and ambition before a temple of innocence.

He leaned heavily atop the brick wall, still watching her. How beautiful she was, how healing, freeing him from his deepest guilt. He'd never known anyone so confident of her right to be in the world.

And what a magnificent world she had shared with him these last two weeks. He'd seen things he'd never seen before: the way the sun striking underwater fern turned the stream chartreuse; the dilemma of the rising stream itself, which they had never solved; the awesome three-day vigil during which they had knelt in meadow grasses and kept a sharp watch on the butterfly struggling to free himself from his cocoon. John had never witnessed such drama, and as the creature had thrashed itself loose and soared to the tops of trees, John had felt tears in his eyes and had done nothing to brush them away.

Still he looked down on her. With absolute confidence he realized that he could survive and accomplish anything if only he had the assurance that this one small paradise would always be waiting for him.

But he didn't have that assurance. In fact, sitting with her father late at night, he'd heard tales that had chilled his blood, the hysteria of the villagers and even some of the staff who thought her a witch. He couldn't believe it, such mindless superstition in this modern age.

He'd learned more as well, not through direct confession from Lord Harrington. But there were worrisome signs which John had observed for himself, the reduced staff—merely six for a Hall this size, which meant that some had been let go; an obvious disintegration of the outbuildings, broken farm machinery, overgrown fields, crumbling stone walls.

Twice Lord Harrington had spoken of returning to Ireland and taking Lila with him. His only emotional link to England had been his wife, and now that she was dead, he was certain he would feel more at home on the old sod.

No, John wouldn't permit it. He needed the warmth and innocence and wonder of Lila Harrington to keep before him an unfaltering image of purity.

An idea occurred, incomprehensible at first, but flaring rapidly into the realm of rightness. Why not? All he needed of wifely love was that one sweet face. Even before he had fully grasped all the implications of what he was about to do, he left the wall and hurried around the path until he was standing directly over her, suffering anguish for fear that she would reject him, yet posing the question anyway. "Lila," he began, his voice low, "will you marry me?"

Her hand, reaching out for the trowel, halted in midair. Her head seemed to incline forward for a moment. She looked up at him almost shyly. "I've known for years that I'd marry you one day, John. Surely you knew it as well."

Before he could respond, she reached for his hand and drew him down beside her, and with great tenderness she pushed a soft mound of earth to one side, revealing an earthworm. "Look." She smiled, urging him to come closer. "There on his back. The colors of the rainbow. Do you see them?"

As she marveled at the mystery, he found himself as always captivated by the discoverer as well as the discovery. As he took careful note of the earthworm, he felt the world become quiet around him, as though eternity were smiling down on him, like a beneficent father who derives joy from the realization that one of his children has discovered the secret.

Later that evening, in the library, Lord Harrington threw open one of the windows, certain that his ears had deceived him. "You're asking . . . for what?" he said, looking at the young man.

Mr. Eden merely smiled, a rather indulgent expression, as though he were aware of the madness of his own words. "I'm asking for Lila's hand in marriage," he repeated, as though perfectly willing to give Lord Harrington all the time he needed.

Lord Harrington stared at him, then stealthily reached inside his pocket, enclosing his fingers about his comforting rosary.

Marry Lila! The incredible words echoed about the room, and he looked back at the young man who had posed them. "I'm afraid . . . I don't understand, Mr. Eden. Is this . . . a jest?"

"I assure you it is not, Lord Harrington."

"But . . . we scarcely know—"

"I know enough," he interrupted, displaying a forceful ego. It was not his knowledge with which Lord Harrington was concerned.

"You've only been here two weeks," Harrington went on.

"We have corresponded for the last four years," Eden countered. "Surely you were aware of that."

Lord Harrington nodded. Of course he had been aware of it, had within the last few months instigated a brief investigation of John Murrey Eden, had discovered through his solicitor's efforts that the young man was peripherally connected with the Edens of North Devon, and was now a successful master builder in London. Still, there was a vast difference between a romantic schoolgirl correspondence and marriage.

He looked back at the young man, beginning to fear the worst, that he was quite serious in his proposal. Then Lord Harrington would have to deal with it seriously, though he'd never felt less equipped to handle such a delicate matter in his life.

As he stared out of the window, over the dark peace of his Wiltshire estate, his fingers, out of sight in his pocket, worked steadily at his beads. If only his wife were here, and as fresh grief rose, he moved faster down the beads, as though to make up for lost time, connecting in his mind the recent disintegration in his life with his earlier rejection of his beloved Catholic faith. To be sure, God's punishment had been slow in coming, but it had been thorough once it had arrived. Now look at him. Childless, except for Lila, alone, his wife recently buried, his portfolio of stock melting away before his eyes, unable to pay for the services of a full staff, unable to make needed repairs. . . .

And now, here was another mystery with which he had to deal, and he looked directly at the prosperous young man who was asking to marry Lila, poor Lila, who in her entire life had never even managed to turn the head of a passing stableboy.

As though his confusion could not be contained, he muttered, "I . . . still do not understand, Mr. Eden."

"If you'll forgive me," the young man said, drawing near, "you're making it more difficult than necessary. It's a simple matter really. I've discovered during these past two weeks when you have received me with such hospitality that your daughter fills a very important vacuum in my life. I must return to London immediately and I don't want to return without knowing that she is safe, and mine."

Lord Harrington listened closely, trying to find something to which he could say no. But he was forced to admit that during the last two weeks he'd found the young man to be a gentleman and quite good company. He appeared to be well-educated and articulate, his wealth rapidly increasing, a prime catch for any number of titled young women. And again the overriding question. _Why Lila?_

"So in order to be assured of her safety," Eden was saying, "and to assure myself that her company will always be available to me, I feel that marriage is the only sensible solution."

Again Lord Harrington looked beyond Eden's shoulder to where Lila knelt before the fire. No response at all from that quarter. He wondered if she was even aware of this discussion, her future being plotted with such deliberation. He did love her, in spite of how difficult a child she had been, and he feared for her as well. At twenty-three she was well on her way to spinsterhood. Who would care for her if something happened to him? With the urgency of this last thought, he looked back at John. "She's . . . all I have now," he muttered.

But Eden merely stepped closer. "I'm aware of that,

Lord Harrington, and I have only one condition if you approve of the marriage, and that is that Lila be permitted to stay here with you."

Harrington looked up, amazed to hear Eden voicing his own fears. "She doesn't belong in London," John went on. "In spite of everything I could give her, I know she would be vastly unhappy. I'll come for her one day and take her to her proper home. In the meantime, I will send a generous monthly allotment for her care as well as yours, plus additional staff of my own choosing. With your permission, I want her protected at all times."

Lord Harrington continued to listen closely, amazed by Eden's businesslike approach. "The allotment will cover the cost of much-needed repairs," John went on, "and I think that with the exception of my occasional visits, you'll find your life little changed from before." He stepped back. "What I'm saying, Lord Harrington, is that the arrangement would be profitable to you as well as to Lila. I'm not asking her to leave your world. I'm asking for permission to enter hers."

Out of sight in his pocket, Lord Harrington continued to say his beads. Had God at last decided that he'd been punished enough? "The . . . banns, Mr. Eden, when would you want them—"

"No banns," Eden said.

Harrington looked up. "I . . . don't understand."

Eden smiled. "I find it difficult to believe, Lord Harrington, that anyone in England gives a damn what I do, or what Lila does."

"Still—"

"No banns, Lord Harrington, and I prefer that it not be a religious ceremony. The local magistrate from Salisbury will do nicely, a simple civil—"

"No!" Lord Harrington said, at last finding something to protect. "You cannot ignore the church."

"Whose church?" Eden asked. "Catholic or Anglican?"

Embarrassed, Lord Harrington turned away to the window. So! Apparently Eden knew his conflict as thoroughly as he knew everything else, and in a way he was now forcing him to confess his Catholicism. And that he couldn't do. He'd lose what little staff he had left, and bring the wrath of the high Anglican village down upon him and give them new cause to persecute Lila.

Again he agreed, and prayed for God's forgiveness, and with a nod confirmed that a private civil ceremony would be best, and asked the most fearful question of all. "When?"

Without hesitation came the reply. "Tomorrow."

"Tomorrow?" Lord Harrington repeated. It was out of the question, lacking even the most rudimentary outline of decorum and decency.

"Tomorrow, Lord Harrington," John repeated, "and shortly thereafter, I must return to London."

Feeling a pressing urgency to inform Eden of everything, Lord Harrington walked a step or two beyond the window and motioned for John to follow after him. "I feel you must know, Mr. Eden," he began, finding the words painful, "my daughter is considered by many to be . . . slow-witted."

Mr. Eden laughed openly. "We both know that's not true, don't we, Lord Harrington?"

Before such a confident reply, Harrington didn't even try to pose an argument. There were other, more important matters to be raised. He lowered his head in an attempt to hide his mortification at the mention of such a subject. "She . . . is still a . . . child, in all ways, Mr. Eden," he faltered. In the event that Eden had missed his point, he added, "She . . . knows . . . nothing."

"And I will place no demands on her," Eden said. "It is her innocence that I covet. How foolish of me to sully it." He pledged again, "I will place no demands on her—until I want children. Then she'll understand." His earnest face softened into a smile. "Can you imagine how richly blessed the child would be who found himself the beneficiary of that maternal love?" He shook his head, as though he were envying the unborn child.

For the first time, Lord Harrington felt almost pleased with this incredible conversation. Clearly the young man adored his daughter, had seen in her a richness that had eluded all other eyes, including his own on occasion.

Still there was one problem remaining, and as Lord Harrington left the window, heading toward the fireplace, he was aware of Eden following behind him. As he drew even with Lila, he waited for her to look up. But she didn't, her interest still focused on her cat.

"Lila . . ." Lord Harrington commenced, drawing a deep breath as though for a final ordeal, having vowed that at the first hint of her objection, the entire, unorthodox scheme would be abandoned. "I've been talking with Mr. Eden," he went on. "Have you heard what we've been saying?"

Without looking up, she whispered, "I've heard everything, Papa."

He waited to see if she would say more, and when she didn't, he urged, "Well? What is your wish?"

He was aware of Eden close behind him, both staring down with interest on the object of their discussion.

For several long moments he thought that she would not say anything at all. Then all at once she laughed and looked up. "I've never heard such a prolonged discussion on a matter that was settled years ago."

The laugh died, but the smile remained. "Of course I'll marry Mr. Eden," she murmured. "Tomorrow." She paused; then her eyes brightened as though an idea had just occurred. "In the orchard."

All at once she was scrambling to her feet, scooping up the cat in her arms. "Now, if you both will excuse me, Wolf and I have a hundred things to attend to."

With that she was gone, the room seeming to suffer from her absence, Eden standing as though in a trance, staring at the doorway through which she had departed.

Lord Harrington walked slowly back to his open window, his hand cupped about the entire rosary, still not certain what had transpired here tonight.

Perhaps one day he would understand it, but for now he closed his eyes and thanked God for what he hoped would be a blessing.

Sometimes it was so difficult to tell the blessings from the curses.

At twelve noon, on August 29, 1859, in the unique setting of an apple orchard, green with late-summer ripeness, John Murrey Eden, son of Edward Hartlow Eden, grandson of Lord Thomas Eden, wed Lady Lila Harrington, only daughter of Lord Liam Harrington of Tully Cross, Connemara, Ireland.

A bewildered and red-faced local magistrate with the ominous name of Josiah Blunder performed the brief civil ceremony, his bewilderment somewhat eased by the fifty-pound note in his pocket which had been given to him by the bridegroom to cover the inconvenience of the journey out from Salisbury.

The bride wore a becoming though simple gown of white silk and carried a small nosegay of lily-of-the-valley and watched solemnly as the bridegroom placed a simple gold band on her left hand. He'd purchased the ring only that morning from Mr. Tweeds, Salisbury's only jeweler.

The ceremony was witnessed by Lord Harrington, the bride's father, Mr. Alex Aldwell, the groom's friend and driver, and a handful of loyal servants, which included old Max, who wept throughout the brief interval.

The wedding certificate was signed and dated by both parties on the stump of a tree. Glasses of chilled champagne were lifted in brief toast to the newlyweds. Then, with her cat trotting behind her, the bride followed the groom to his carriage, lifted a sprig of lily-of-the-valley from her nosegay, placed it in his buttonhole and received his promise that he would be back, hopefully within a fortnight.

Then, with the somewhat stunned wedding guests looking on, the carriage rolled forward, picking up speed as it proceeded down the country lane, the bride waving until it was out of sight, then suddenly scooping up her large gray cat, lifting him high into the air over her head, and laughing with pure joy as she stared straight up into heaven.

London,
September 1, 1859

"YOU ARE WHAT?" gasped Elizabeth, staring at John, then glancing about the table to see if anyone else had heard the incredible announcement. Still exhausted from her worry of the last two weeks when John had simply dropped from sight, she was certain that her ears had deceived her.

She glanced to her left and saw the same shocked expression on Andrew's face, while opposite her Alex Aldwell grinned and launched forth into his fourth serving of steak-and-kidney pie. Beyond Alex, Dhari looked up.

"You . . , are what?" Elizabeth repeated, again looking at John, who lounged backward in his chair at the head of the table, clearly enjoying the shock waves caused by his announcement.

With deliberation he refilled his wineglass, sipped and again uttered the amazing words, which Elizabeth noticed had attracted the shocked attention of the servants near the sideboard.

"I am married." He smiled, measuring the words out as though astounded that he would have to repeat such a simple message.

Elizabeth *had* heard correctly, though still she couldn't believe it, and apparently neither could Andrew, who let his fork clatter noisily back onto his plate. "You're . . . joking, of course," he muttered.

"I'm not," John countered. "Ask Aldwell there. He saw me through the entire ceremony, a rock of a man, he was."

Elizabeth looked across the table at the now blushing rock of a man. Unfortunately he'd just inserted a forkful of kidney dripping gravy into his mouth, and his blush turned crimson as he was aware of everyone watching him.

John laughed heartily, taking mercy on him. "But please, if it's blame you're interested in placing, spare Alex. I sensed his opposition from the beginning. It was all my doing, though I don't know why such a felicitous announcement should warrant such shocked expressions." He paused, a look of delight on his face that Elizabeth had never seen before, not recently at any rate. "People do marry," he added almost shyly, "every day."

Andrew rallied first. "Forgive us, John," he muttered. "Would you indulge us in a few questions such as: Who is she? How did you meet? And where is she?" He looked comically about as though the mysterious bride might at that moment be hiding someplace in the room.

John laughed. Elizabeth had never seen him in such high spirits. Obviously whatever had happened had had a marvelously medicinal effect on him. She listened carefully as he addressed himself to the questions one at a time.

"First," he said expansively to the entire table, "her name is Lila Harrington, Lady Harrington, I might add. I came under her spell years ago when I was in dire need of a kind spirit."

"Then where is she?" Andrew demanded, apparently growing accustomed to the idea.

"Not here." John smiled. "She doesn't belong in London, though all of you will meet her soon enough. I promise you that."

Silence descended on the table, as though all questions had been answered, all mysteries solved.

John seemed to settle into a soft reverie, though Elizabeth noticed that he reached out one hand to Dhari, who received it without hesitation, as though nothing had been said during the last ten minutes which altered anything between them.

As for Elizabeth, she tried to deal with the shocking announcement, realizing that she still was weak with worry from his unexplained absence. How greatly he resembled his father in that respect as well, Edward tak-

ing off without a word, reappearing with a smile of innocence several days later.

John married! Softly she shook her head and looked
up, to see him watching her, as though awaiting her
approval above all others. And at last she gave it to him,
for who was she to withhold it?

"May I write to your new bride, John?" She smiled.
"From one who loves you as much as she?"

He seemed to regard her with silent gratitude. "She'd
like that very much, Elizabeth," he said. "And I as well."

Then, as though everything had been said, he clasped
Dhari's hand and with tenderness invited, "Come . . ."

The simple invitation carried a weight of meaning, and
everyone watched as he led her across the dining hall and
up the staircase, heading toward the privacy of his upper
chambers, where the bride in Wiltshire would be momentarily forgotten.

Elizabeth watched along with everyone else, as though
mesmerized by the sound of retreating footsteps, and
prayed that the new bride possessed vast quantities of
understanding.

"I still can't believe it," she heard Andrew mutter to
one side.

"Well, it's there to be believed, Mr. Rhoades," Alex
responded enthusiastically, "and I apologize again for
not sending word where we were."

As Andrew dismissed the apology, Elizabeth leaned
forward in her chair, hungry for specific information.
"What's she like, Alex?"

The big man seemed to think on the question. With
reflective tenderness he murmured, "Well, she's like a
child, she is, Miss Elizabeth, as innocent as the day she
was born. And John there becomes a child when he's with
her." He shook his head as though all aspects of the
curious episode were beyond him.

But suddenly Elizabeth understood, perhaps more than
she had a right to understand. John had recaptured his
own lost youth. And in order to assure himself that he did
not lose it again, he had married it.

Softly she laughed, and shook her head, feeling curiously alive and in need of love herself. Abruptly she stood, announcing that the hour was late, though it wasn't, and that she must return home.

Rather sedately, as though to mask her need, she walked the length of the dining hall and down the stairs to the foyer, where the old butler held her cape for her and bid her a courteous good night.

She paused on the threshold, listening, hoping that Andrew was following after her.

He was.

It was the March 16, 1861, edition of the London *Times* which noted in its financial section that there scarcely was a district of London now which did not boast a structure bearing the imprint of John Murrey Firm.

Has there been a more propitious meeting of man and age? John Murrey's genius has exploded at a time when the last vestiges of protectionism have been discarded, and industry, commerce, agriculture and shipping are all enjoying the benefits of their new freedom. Internally the penny postage, the electric telegraph and the completion of many railway projects are making their influence felt.

Now everybody is an investor, or anybody who has any spare cash. And what is the most popular stock among investors? The answer is simple. John Murrey Firm, which has taken common investment to a height never before conceived and who has made his stock available to his own crew of over a thousand workmen, a private guild whose membership boasts some of the finest craftsmen in all of England, and who now, possessing partial ownership in the parent firm, are more than willing to labor loyally and long for the man who has given them unprecedented prosperity, a man who at an incredibly young age is fast becoming one of the wealthiest men in England and who perfectly embodies the spirit and genius of our expanding empire.

On this night, the "perfect embodiment of the expanding empire" sat sunk with fatigue behind his desk, his head resting on his crossed arms, looking for all the world like an overtaxed schoolboy.

His day had commenced at six A.M. with a conference with three foremen over construction difficulties at the building site in Audley. From there he had moved through four meetings with boards of directors, one committee meeting which had been called by the Bank of England, and a prolonged conference with his new architect—one of six employed full-time by John Murrey Firm.

Now it was approaching eleven P.M. and he was aware of Andrew sprawled on the sofa a short distance away, devouring the financial page of the London *Times* as it was his habit to do, the two of them awaiting a late-night repast which John had ordered from the kitchen.

Never had he known such fatigue. Even his mind felt bruised, and as far as he could see there was no respite in sight. The meetings of each day only seemed to produce complications which led to more meetings, endless committees filling every hour of the day and spilling over into the night.

He lifted his head and his eye fell on that small stack of pale blue stationery, Lila still writing to him as she'd done years ago when he had been in the Crimea. Suffering an almost mournful feeling, he realized that he'd not seen her in over a month.

Slowly he lifted his head. "Andrew, do you think it would be possible for me to slip—"

But Andrew had spoken at the same time, tilting the newspaper nearer to the lamp. "John, did you see this?"

God! If it was another statistic or column of figures, he'd send the man packing. Before he'd had a chance to answer, Andrew spoke on, angling the paper closer to the lamp in an effort to accommodate his failing eyesight. "Listen," he commanded, "under the delinquent-tax notice, four columns down, Eden Castle, North Devon. In arrears two years. Debt one hundred and seventy thousand pounds. To be put on the block in six months."

John looked up. Andrew stared back, removing his spectacles. "How is that possible?" he asked, perplexed.

Still John stared forward. "What . . . did you just read?" he asked, thinking that his mind had wandered and he'd not heard correctly.

Andrew put on his specs, flattened the paper, and read, " 'Delinquent Tax Notice on Eden Castle. Debt one hundred and seventy thousand pounds. To be put on the block in six—' "

Still John wasn't certain that he'd heard correctly. Slowly he rose from his chair and moved around the desk. He lifted the paper from Andrew and carried it to the lamp, where he read for himself.

There it was, plain enough, though he continued to stare at the small print. Delinquent estate tax . . . . It wasn't possible.

He was aware of Andrew beside him, his voice reflecting John's bewilderment. "My God," Andrew exclaimed. "Who is the family solicitor? What idiot would let . . ."

Family solicitor. John closed his eyes and let the paper fall from his hands, seeing in his self-imposed darkness a precise image of Morley Johnson.

"Johnson," he muttered. "Johnson," he said, louder. "Morley Johnson," he said a third time, full-voiced.

All at once his fatigue disappeared, swallowed up by his apprehension. If the estate taxes were delinquent, what were the conditions of the castle itself, and worse, its inhabitants?

Suddenly he grabbed Andrew by the arm. "Come," he commanded. "There are files I want to see, questions I want to—"

"John, do you know the hour?"

"I know it well enough," he shouted back. "You have keys, I've seen them, and friends in the Temple. I must know what's happened, Andrew, as soon as possible."

"Can't it wait until morning?"

"No," John thundered. "Are you coming or not?" His voice fell. "I need your help."

At last Andrew started after him. "I do recall Sir Arthur mentioning a Morley Johnson. Perhaps he—"

That was enough. Then John was running, narrowly avoiding a collision with the maid, who was just entering the room bearing a tray laden with sandwiches. "Your meal, sir," she called after him.

But he was already on the staircase a flight below, and Andrew had to run to catch up.

It was approaching dusk the following evening before they managed to put all the pieces of the grim puzzle together. In chambers in the Temple borrowed from a sympathetic and helpful Sir Arthur, they slumped before a massive table cluttered with the results of their investigation.

Andrew spoke first, moved by John's quiet grief. "You have ample grounds to bring criminal charges against the man," he said bluntly. "I'm sure you realize that."

But Andrew wasn't certain if John realized anything. He sat before the table, his elbows propped up, his hands cradling his head. With his face thus obscured, it was impossible to read any expression, though from the slump of his shoulders and his prevailing silence, Andrew knew well the depth of his despair.

In the absence of a dialogue, Andrew commenced a monologue. "I don't know when I've seen a more blatant corruption of power of attorney," he began. "Is the man a fool? The youngest, most uninformed law student knows the ethics of principal and agent, and that both carry with them incredible responsibilities."

He talked on, warming to his subject. "The agent is bound to exercise proper skill and use the proper means for carrying out the functions which he undertakes. Thus when he is employed to buy, he must not be the seller; when he is employed to sell, he must not be the buyer."

He looked in amazement about the table at the proof that this simple law had been mercilessly trammeled. There they were, deed after deed, hundreds of them listing Morley Johnson as seller, Morley Johnson as buyer, not even bothering to reissue them under a false name, with the exception of the first eight or ten. So daring a criminal act, Andrew could not imagine, and he tried to stir John to speech with the simple announcement, "Well, no matter. We'll meet Mr. Johnson soon enough in a court of law. Then we'll let a magistrate decide the weight of his punishment."

He looked down on John's bowed head and saw his hands trembling. "John?" he inquired softly. "There's nothing more we can do here. Why don't you go home and rest? I'll take care of the next few steps. A courier will be on his way to Taunton by morning to serve Mr. Johnson with a list of charges. A court date will have to be set, but I—"

All at once John pushed away from the table and walked toward the windows. With his back to Andrew, he finally spoke, though his words were as incredible as the events of the long night and day. "There will be no court case, Andrew," he commenced quietly, "no criminal charges."

Andrew started forward. "I don't think you understand—"

John turned. In the light of dusk, Andrew thought he looked one hundred years old. "I'm afraid the lack of understanding is on your part, Andrew," he said, as though every word required a major effort, "and what I'm going to tell you undoubtedly will only compound your confusion, but you are entitled to know."

He turned back to the window as though he found it difficult to look at Andrew. "I murdered a man once," he began, "and Morley Johnson was the only witness to that murder." He looked down at his hands with a curious expression, as though they were appendages which did not belong to him.

As the astonishing confession filled the room, Andrew sat slowly in a near chair. "Who . . . ?" he began, and never finished, for John was speaking again.

"No one you would know," he said, "a piece of garbage named Humphrey Hills who had done terrible damage to someone . . . I loved very much. At any rate, I took it upon myself to relieve the world of his presence, and Johnson witnessed it, and covered for me."

At last he faced Andrew, a strange look of relief on his face. "I've never told anyone before." Curiously, he laughed. "No, Morley Johnson is not a fool, Andrew.

He's a very clever man who knew better than I what he was doing that day."

While Andrew had questions, he knew better than to ask any of them. "I'm . . . sorry," he murmured.

"Why?" John demanded with renewed energy. "Again, I am in your debt. Thank God for your obsessive habit of reading the London *Times*'s financial section. Otherwise we might have lost more than we've already lost. We might have lost Eden."

Suddenly he stopped pacing, as though the thought had descended upon him like a nightmare. The bleak mood lasted only a moment, then he returned to the table, dragged out his chair and sat again.

"I'm going to ask you to do some favors for me, Andrew," he commenced, his hands clasped before him.

"Anything," Andrew murmured, still stunned by the recent confession.

"First, I want you to go immediately and pay the delinquent tax. Then I want the deed to Eden Castle reissued in the name of Lord Richard Eden."

Andrew leaned forward with a question, though he never had a chance to pose it, for John rushed on.

"Then I want you to journey to Taunton, or wherever it was that Sir Arthur said Johnson was living now. And I want you to tell him that I am desirous of seeing him immediately. Tell him it will be to his advantage to come. He'll understand those words."

He hesitated, as though coming to the most difficult part of his request. "And then," he went on, "I want you to journey to Eden for me."

Andrew noticed that John's hands were trembling. "And I want you to report back to me on precisely what you find there." His voice fell. "Will you do that for me, Andrew?"

Andrew was moved by the silent suffering. "Of course," he agreed. "I'll do anything you ask."

Apparently the display of loyalty had a disastrous effect on John. As though to hide this new weakness, he stood angrily and glared down at the scattered proof of corruption. "Damn that man!" he exploded. He strode to the door and called back. "Be about it, Andrew. Immediately.

Leave tonight if possible. Stay as long as necessary. I'll look after things here. Keep me informed."

Then he was gone. Andrew heard the echo of his boots as he walked down the arcade, leaving only the memory of his amazing confession in the chamber.

Murdered a man! Under what circumstances? He'd failed to tell Andrew that, and for some reason Andrew had the feeling he would never know. And perhaps he didn't want to know. Again he thought with loving sympathy upon John Murrey Eden.

Just when he had worked so hard to arrange a dazzling future, his mysterious past surfaced in splintered disarray, and as always the primary victim in such a tug of war was the present.

Nine days later, in the morning post, John received the following letter postmarked Taunton, North Devon, in a familiar and meticulous handwriting:

> My dearest John,
> I arrived in the village of Taunton two days ago, and with my first inquiry concerning Mr. Morley Johnson, the local publican responded, "You mean the fool who lives in the Folly?" And that, my friend, set the pace for all further inquiry. The locals seem to feel real animosity to the Johnsons, though a few pointed out that they had brought business their way. But most viewed him with less than respect and many laughed openly as though he had become a humorous bit of local color.
> The following morning I set forth to find the man, and located him on a large estate at the center of which sat one of the most incredible structures it has ever been my misfortune to view. I would be fascinated to have Chiswell take a look at it and identify its style. I'm afraid that it would tax even his vast architectural knowledge.

Damn the house, John cursed impatiently. *Did you find the man?*

After having waded through hordes of children playing on the green, I found myself confronted with a disreputable-looking butler who informed me that Mr. Johnson was busy and not receiving this morning. I stated that I had journeyed from London and that it was a matter of importance, and as we were arguing, the man himself emerged from the solarium, announced that *he* was Mr. Morley Johnson and he was surprised to find such a crude display of manners on the part of a "Londoner."

Oh, my dear John, there is no way to describe the man except to state that he possesses not one redeeming grace. After much talking, I convinced him that it might be worth his while to hear me out, and I was promptly escorted into the solarium, where I met a bewigged woman whom he identified as his wife.

At this point I confess to a deception. I identified myself as the solicitor for the John Murrey Firm, withholding the name of Eden, and watched the interest on Johnson's face mount. Of course he had heard of you. "What Englishman that respects money has not?" was his reply. When I told him that you wanted to see him in your offices in Belgrave Square as soon as possible, he seemed puzzled. But it was the wife who coyly suggested that such a large and prosperous firm surely needed the services of more than one solicitor. I pleaded ignorance, of course, simply that I had been sent to fetch him. But that one veiled suggestion obviously set him to thinking, and finally he shook my hand warmly and invited me to stay for dinner, which I declined, and escorted me back to my carriage, assuring me that he would prepare immediately for the journey to London.

So in conclusion, I suspect that any day you will have him on your doorstep. Still, I am disappointed that we cannot bring criminal charges against him. Never have I seen a more worthy suit. But I'm respectful of your position and with all love and concern now warn you that it will not serve your purpose to do violence against him. My advice is that you relieve him of all further contact with your family, then sweep him from your doorstep for the trash that he is.

Trust everyone is well there. Give all my love. The weather here is wretched, a cold driving rain. I'm off to Eden now to do your bidding, and will return to London as soon as possible.

> Your devoted and loving servant,
> Andrew Rhoades

Slowly John folded the letter and slipped it into the envelope. He leaned back in his desk chair and took the letter with him as though he did not want to part with this frail link which connected him to Andrew's love and loyalty.

How blessed he was with Andrew's friendship. Yet how often had he told the man that? Never, to the best of his recollection. Now he admonished himself, vowed to be more verbal in his appreciation of those around him, of those who served him, and as though the admonishment itself was the solution to the problem, he leaned forward, slapped the letter on the desk, shouted to one of those faceless servants to come and light the lamps and looked forward with relish to the arrival of Mr. Morley Johnson.

It was as Andrew had predicted. The next afternoon, as John was discussing with Alex Aldwell the need to hire fifty additional men, John looked out of the window and saw a carriage stop before his house.

He'd never seen such a carriage short of a royal procession, gilt and purple with an indistinguishable coat of arms emblazoned on the side, while atop the high seat sat a coachman bedecked in a uniform trimmed with gold braid. He held a fine leather horsewhip in his hand.

Alex saw his interest outside the window and moved close to see for himself. "Gawd," he muttered, "is it the Queen we're doing business with now?"

John gave no reply and continued to watch the pretentious arrival, the footman hopping down, affixing a low stool before the carriage door. A few moments later, the man emerged, lavishing attention on his dandified garments, straightening his lavender satin waistcoat, stroking the small conceit of an Elizabethan beard which grew on his chin.

At first John didn't recognize him, would have passed him by in a crowd. Then recognition dawned and with it the memory of that day at Eden in the small library, the man Humphrey Hills speaking those most incredible words.

"Leave me," John whispered.

"About the additional men—"

"I said, leave me," John repeated.

"Will you be needing—"

"I need nothing now, but wait outside."

Then Alex was gone and John heard the butler open the door, and long before he was ready for it, though it was the moment he had wished for, the bastard appeared in the door, struck a pose, and pronounced, "Mr. Murrey, my name is Mr. Morley Johnson ·and I believe you sent for me."

John did not reply, curious to see if the man recognized him. Apparently not. The full beard and the passage of almost ten difficult years had created an effective mask. "Mr. Johnson," he said, not rising from his chair, not making any gesture for the man to come forward.

But he did anyway, as John knew he would, removing his top hat, revealing thin nondescript graying hair. He shook off his cape while casting a close eye over the opulent office. "Very grand, these houses," he pronounced, uninvited. "For myself, I would have been comfortable in one, but my wife insisted upon a country seat. I'm sure you know women, Mr. Murrey. Whatever it is the neighbors have, the wife wants one bigger and better."

He laughed knowingly and displayed his first awkwardness at not having been invited to take a seat. Clearly a man never to suffer from the lack of an invitation, he selected an overstuffed chair near the desk and sat.

John watched with an almost trancelike fascination. *There is no way to describe the man except to state that he possesses not one redeeming grace.* As that fragment from Andrew's letter crossed his mind, he was aware of the man gaping at him, as though at last John's prolonged silence was beginning to bother him.

"You . . . did send for me, Mr. Murrey?" Johnson began. "Correct me if I'm wrong."

John leaned back in his chair. "I did indeed, Mr. Johnson," he said, and found that he could scarcely look at the man.

Fortunately there was no need, for obviously Morley Johnson had worked out in his own mind the purpose of this interview and now took the floor as though it were his to take. "I must confess, Mr. Murrey," he began, "I was shocked when your man Rhoades told me that a firm as large as yours had the services of only one solicitor. I immediately thought how dangerous. One man, even an exceptional one, cannot possibly look after the vast entanglements of an enterprise such as yours."

"You've heard of us, then?" John prodded.

Morley Johnson laughed. "Heard of you!" he repeated. "Who in all of England has not? I may live in the country, Mr. Murrey, but I am not a rustic. London papers are delivered weekly to my foyer, and I read them from cover to cover, and for the last two years it has become quite impossible to pick up the London *Times* without seeing your name and your magnificent accomplishments written up in glowing detail."

John nodded, then moved to the heart of the matter, or at least the heart as Morley Johnson perceived it.

"Tell me, Mr. Johnson, about your . . . legal experience. I'll be blunt with you. I've heard of you. I've been told that a mere ten years ago you were a clerk in the offices of Sir Claudius Potter. And now . . ." He leaned back in his chair and with a nod of his head indicated the man's rich apparel.

For the first time, Morley Johnson seemed loath to speak. An expression of caution seemed to cover his face, and he looked suspiciously back at John. "You've been talking about me?" he asked, on guard. "With whom?"

Now it was John's turn to be expansive and generous. "My God, man, you too have a reputation. Damn clever is Morley Johnson, that's what I've heard. A legal wizard, an expert in the area of deeds and freeholds."

He paused, pleased to see the suspicion gone from the face opposite him. Johnson leaned close, his voice low. "I don't generally prattle on about such things, Mr. Murrey," he began. "I mean, a man's business transactions are an intimate area of his life. Wouldn't you agree?"

John looked back at the man across the desk. "You don't recognize me, do you, Mr. Johnson?" he asked quietly.

"Recognize you?" the man puzzled. "I'm not sure I—"

"We've met before," John went on. "Years ago, under tragic circumstances."

He could see the bewilderment washing across the man's face. The suspicion had returned as well, and now he seemed to be moving up to the edge of the seat. "I'm afraid you have the advantage, Mr. Murrey. I don't—"

"As you had the advantage over the Eden family?" John demanded, his voice rising.

Morley Johnson was on his feet. "I . . . don't believe I . . ."

"Please sit down," John said in a voice that left no room for debate.

Sensibly the man obeyed.

"Now, take a good look, Mr. Johnson," he invited, his voice cordial. "We *have* met before. Remember? Years ago, in the small library at Eden."

Morley's eyes were blinking so rapidly they resembled restless wingbeats. His lower jaw went limp as he continued to take in John's face with incredible intensity.

"Surely you remember." John smiled. "You were keeping good company then, fitting company, scoundrels together, the both of you."

"Eden," the man gasped, and stood rapidly up, the color draining from his face.

John moved around the desk until he was standing before him. Taller, younger, of sturdier frame, it required no great effort for John to push him back into the chair, thus blocking future escapes. For the first time during the distasteful encounter, John was beginning to enjoy himself. "I'm impressed, Mr. Johnson, with what you have done." He smiled. "And what did you intend to do when you put Eden on the block? Were you going to purchase the castle as well?"

He saw the man's apprehension vault, his tongue licking his lips as though his mouth had gone dry. "There . . . were delinquent taxes," he began, and never finished.

"Why delinquent, Mr. Johnson?" John demanded. "Surely the wealth of the Eden estates was sufficient to cover a tax debit?"

The man started forward. "I command you to let me pass, Mr. Eden," he pronounced in a quavering voice. "You . . . trapped me into coming here, and then tricked me into talking, but in spite of all that, you and I both know that you intend to do nothing about it."

John settled on the edge of the desk, his foot blocking Johnson's passage. "Oh?" He smiled. "How do we both know that I intend to do nothing about it?"

"Because there is a small unmarked grave in the middle of Exmoor," Johnson retorted with admirable courage. "And only you and I know the identity of the man buried there, and only you and I know who put him in that grave." A hint of a smile lit up his face, as though in spite of his predicament he knew he had the upper hand.

John gave him a few minutes out of courtesy to enjoy his false sense of victory, and even went so far as to concede his debt. "You're right, Mr. Johnson. Quite conceivably I would be in Newgate prison now if it weren't for you."

A look of relief flooded Morley Johnson's face. "Then we have nothing more to discuss," he said, again making an effort to rise.

And again John pushed him back. "One additional matter," he said. "You are to have nothing further to do with the Eden estates. Is that clear?"

Incredibly, the man laughed. "What estates, Mr. Eden? The only estate left is a rough five miles of rubble surrounding the castle itself. The rest has been profitably sold to the hands that worked the land so long. The tenant farmers are now the landlords," he added, "making their monthly allotments to me, Morley Johnson. You arrived a bit too late, Mr. Eden," he concluded sarcastically.

All at once he broke off, as though aware that he'd said enough. "If you will excuse me, I must—"

Again John pushed him back, and at the same time shouted, "Alex!"

Within the instant the big man was at the door.

Without taking his eyes off Morley Johnson, John said, "Alex, would you do a favor for me? There's a fancy carriage parked outside on the pavement with a fancy coachman sitting on the seat, with an elegant horsewhip in his hand. Since it all was undoubtedly purchased with Eden money, would you tell the driver that the owner of the horsewhip would like to inspect it for a few minutes? Tell him I'd be most grateful . . ."

He was aware of Alex's hesitation, as though in an effort to make sense out of the strange command. Apparently unable to do so, he disappeared from the door and left John to focus on Morley Johnson, his hands braced against the cushions of the chair. "If . . . this is a joke, Eden," he muttered.

"Oh, it's no joke, Mr. Johnson, I assure you. You see, we are perfect adversaries. I can't bring charges against you, and you can't bring charges against me. And since I intend never to look upon your face again, I want to remember it at a certain angle. Grant me that one indulgence, Mr. Johnson, I beg you."

At that moment Alex reappeared in the doorway, whip in hand. "John, I—"

"Close the door, Alex," John ordered, "and bolt it."

Aldwell did as he was told, though he continued to peer at the confrontation by the desk.

"Now," John said, standing before the ashen-faced Morley Johnson. "Will you remove your garments, or shall I have my friend here do it?"

As he gestured toward Alex, he saw Morley Johnson swivel his head about. The tension on his face broke into a nervous giggle. "Remove . . . my . . . garments?" he repeated. "I'll do no such thing, and neither will—"

It required only a scant nod of John's head to bring Alex forward. He handed the whip to John and with one fluid movement lifted Morley Johnson to his feet, and holding him steady with one hand, he commenced removing his coat and shirtwaist.

Predictably, the man protested, trying to fight off the massive hands. "Stop it! Stop it this minute. I swear, Eden, I'll bring charges—"

"You'll bring nothing." John smiled. "I have a dear friend—I believe you met him, Andrew Rhoades—who is longing to get you in a court of law. According to him, most magistrates come down very hard on corrupt solicitors."

He saw Alex was removing his undershirt, the man flailing uselessly against Aldwell's superior strength, flailing too against what he realized was the inevitable. "Oh, God, please, Mr. Eden, don't," he gasped, eyeing the whip in John's hand.

Alex was restraining him, holding both arms behind his back. "Are you sure you want to do what I think you are going to do?" he asked quietly over the almost continuous whimperings of Morley Johnson.

John had never been so certain of anything in his life, and he pulled the chair around until the back was facing him, then without a word indicated that he wanted Johnson stretched over it, Alex restraining his arms on the other side.

Seeing his fate, Morley Johnson made one last plea. "Oh, no, God, I beg you. I've been ill, and I'm not a strong man." Still Alex forced him into position.

John waited until Alex had the man's arms drawn tight. He ignored the questioning look on Aldwell's face, ignored as well the last high-pitched wail coming from Morley Johnson. Then he stepped back about three feet, lifted the whip high into the air and brought it down with a resounding snap across the white flesh.

He saw Johnson jerk like a puppet, Alex kneeling on the chair cushion, the better to restrain his arms. As John stepped back to lift the whip a second time, he saw a spreading circle of wetness at Morley Johnson's feet and smelled urine.

He lifted the whip again and brought it down, fascinated by the spastic movement of the man's body, seeing two long red ridges rising out of the plain of smooth flesh.

He commenced moving faster, the whip rising and falling in an easy rhythm, John thinking the name of everyone the man had wronged with each lash: two for Richard, who had befriended John upon his arrival at Eden, and who had lost the most, lost his entire future; and two for little Mary; and two for his aunt Jennifer; two for his father; two for all the Edens dead and buried, corrupt and honorable; and two for Harriet. . . .

Whether it was his thought of Harriet, or Alex's stern, "John, enough!" that stopped him, he couldn't say. All he saw then was the white back, no longer foundering, and the network of red lashes growing redder, a few seeping blood. Coming to his senses, he saw Alex's shocked face, and at last John turned away.

"Get him out of here," he muttered over his shoulder, leaning heavily upon the desk. "Put him in his fine carriage and tell the driver not to stop until he reaches home."

He heard a rustle of movement behind him, looked back and saw Morley Johnson slung over Alex's broad shoulder like a sack of potatoes. "And take those things with you," John added, pointing toward the heap of torn garments.

Finally he handed the whip over. "Tell the driver thank you," he said, and turned away.

He heard the door close, and with a sense of having paid all debts, he drew the drapes at the window and returned to his chair behind the desk and sat wearily in the semidarkness, the palm of his right hand aching from where he'd grasped the whip.

Well, where was it, he thought angrily, the satisfaction of revenge?

But it never came, even though he was sitting there at midnight. And still it hadn't come, even at dawn, with the first colors of morning sun penetrating the drawn drapes. All he felt was fatigue from the sleepless night, dread that he had yet to receive Andrew's report from Eden, and shame.

London,
April 3, 1861

THOUGH IT WAS approaching midnight and he was dusty from the road, Andrew did not take time to wash and change. Rather he directed his driver to proceed to the house in Belgrave Square, and as he brushed past the old butler and started up the four flights of stairs, he looked ahead and saw John, clad in his dressing robe, coming down the steps toward him.

Stopping at the third-floor landing for breath, Andrew grasped the banister and tried to think of a way to soften the terrible report. But he could think of nothing and John was upon him, embracing him warmly, hurrying him up the stairs and into his private chambers.

"It's good to see you." John smiled, closing the door. "I've missed you. May I get you something? Brandy? Coffee?"

Andrew shook his head to everything, hearing in John's voice a clear anxiety. Wearily he shook off his dusty cloak and apologized. "I should have waited until morning."

"No, no, I'm glad you came straight on. Come . . ." He took Andrew's arm and led him to the chairs before the fire. John sat first, drawing the cord of his dressing robe tightly about his waist. "Shall I build up the fire?" he asked.

Andrew shook his head, seeing a man who wanted to hear and yet who did not want to hear.

"And the weather?" John inquired.

"Miserable most of the time." Andrew smiled.

John shook his head in commiseration. "The West Country, I'm afraid, is not known for its fair climate at this time of year, though when the sun does shine, it's quite . . ."

Andrew nodded, wondering how long it would take for John to gather his courage and ask the one question that Andrew was fully prepared to answer.

Silence. Andrew bided his time. "And you?" he asked abruptly. "Have things gone well here?"

"Oh, yes." John smiled. "We broke ground last Tuesday, I believe it was. The school at Calthorpe, if you'll recall . . ."

Andrew nodded.

"And Alex talked me into enlarging the crews once again."

"My God, why?" Andrew exclaimed.

John shrugged. "Claims he was shorthanded, said we were working on so many sites simultaneously that he always finds himself shorthanded."

Andrew brooded a moment, looking down at the toes of his dusty boots. He was too tired for business matters. They would keep until morning. Of greater urgency was . . .

"You are the one with news, Andrew," John said softly. "Please tell me . . . everything."

So! It was to be now. Andrew closed his eyes to rest them and clear his head. "I don't know what the conditions at Eden were when you left, John," he began, "but I do know that now they are quite . . ."

He looked up to see John staring at him. "Did you . . . speak to anyone?" he asked, his voice hoarse.

"I spoke to everyone," Andrew replied. "There aren't many left, as I'm sure you know."

"No," John said, pleading. "I know nothing. It's been ten years. Tell me everything, Andrew. Leave nothing out."

Before such an expression, Andrew felt the need for movement, for distance. He stood and walked around the sofa. "I arrived on a Tuesday," he began. "I had to leave the carriage outside the gatehouse. One of the grilles had fallen, obscuring the passage, and as I learned later, there is no one in the castle able to repair it."

He glanced back at John, saw his expression unchanged, his face taut with listening. "As I was climbing over the fallen grille, I saw a young man approaching across the inner courtyard. He seemed alarmed at my presence, though ill-equipped to do anything about it. He was carrying as a weapon . . . a Bible."

"Richard?" came a whispered inquiry.

Andrew nodded. "An admirable young man, once I'd convinced him that I meant them no harm. He looked to be about eighteen, frail, with dark hair, and a pleasing manner." Andrew walked slowly about the room. "I became quite fond of him. We had good chats. And he spoke two names constantly. Yours, and God's."

Andrew looked back toward the fire. In spite of the fact that the length of the room was between them, he saw new despair on John's face. For the first time Andrew began to understand why *he* had been sent as the first emissary. Clearly for John there was a source of pain connected with Eden that was unendurable, even hearing about it secondhand.

Then Andrew recalled an incredible piece of news and hurried back to the sofa. "They didn't know, John. They didn't know about anything, about the delinquent taxes, why their allotments had ceased, had no idea that in six months the castle would have been sold out from under them."

Overcome by his own incredulity, he shook his head. "Of course, I presented him with the new deed, issued in his name, Lord Richard Eden, fifteenth Baron, seventh Earl of Eden Point. I told him that you were responsible. He was very moved. He asked endless questions about you, as did they all."

"All?" John repeated. "Who . . . else was there?"

Andrew spied the decanter of brandy, changed his mind, poured himself a small snifter and breathed heavily. "Mary," he said, in answer to John's question, "a shy thirteen-year-old girl who hid behind one of the columns in the kitchen and would not at first come out. I called her Lady Mary and she seemed surprised at the designation, as though no one had ever informed her that the title was her birthright. She looked more like a scullery maid, and her favorite companion, her only companion, is a white-haired senseless old lady named Jennifer. Your aunt, I believe Richard said, your father's sister."

He saw John nod, confirming the relationship, and heard his voice again in urgent inquiry. "And who else?" as though he were waiting to hear a specific name.

Andrew sipped at the brandy, thinking how much easier it would be if John would simply give him the name of the individual who held such interest for him. But he didn't, and Andrew struggled on.

"And I met the old cook, by the name of Agony Fletcher."

"Aggie . . ." John repeated softly.

Andrew nodded. "I suspect that she is largely responsible for holding things together even in so tenuous a fashion. And there was another woman named Clara Jenkins who received me warmly and again asked continuous questions about you."

He saw John nod, though saw no other movement in that hunched frozen statue.

"And there was an ancient man, I think his name was Dana, who said nothing and passed every day before the kitchen fire. Aggie told me he'd been a footman at Eden for over sixty years, and while he was good for nothing now, he had no place to go and none of them could bear to turn him out."

Andrew paused, seeing the bleak scene in his mind. "They all live together, John," he went on, "in the servants' hall. Richard told me that the rest of the castle had been closed off for years. He took me up to the Great Hall one morning and I could see why. Several windows were broken and sea gulls were nesting in the ceiling. It appeared as though at one time they had kept their livestock there. Bales of scattered hay were everyplace, as well as dried animal excrement . . . ."

Abruptly Andrew took a deep swallow of brandy and welcomed the burning sensation. "Richard informed me that everything of value within the castle had been sold over the years, for food, for fuel. He said he regretted it, but that they had had no choice."

He shook his head in an attempt to put the memories out of his mind. "I've never seen such wretched conditions," he muttered, "and I don't know how much longer they can persist. Richard told me that they tried to garden in spring and summer, and while I was there, two women from Mortemouth brought fish to the door, and freshly baked bread. According to Clara, they remembered the Eden family from better days, and not a week passed that some kind soul from the village didn't climb the cliff walk bearing a covered basket of some sort."

Abruptly he slammed the snifter down. "Charity, John. They couldn't have survived without the charity of the village. And you don't want to bring criminal charges?" he concluded in amazement.

He saw John's head still bowed, and at that moment heard in soft repetition that same question that he'd heard before. "Anyone . . . else, Andrew. Did you see . . ."

At last he looked up. Andrew had never seen such an expression on that normally strong face. "No," he said, shaking his head, "no one else, except those that I—"

"Are you certain?"

Mystified, Andrew nodded.

"A . . . lady," John whispered. "Her name is Harriet. She's . . . blind."

Again Andrew saw the incredible need on his face and wished that he could satisfy it. "No," he said. "I met no one by that name. And I was told that the rest of the castle was empty."

John's head fell forward until it was resting on his clasped hands. Andrew had never seen such desolation, and was on the verge of going to his side to comfort him in his mysterious grief when suddenly he stood and reached out for the mantelpiece.

"Then she must be . . . dead," he whispered.

For several minutes the room was silent except for the crackling of the fire. Then he saw John push away from the mantel, reach into the pocket of his dressing robe, withdraw a handkerchief and wipe it across his face.

He was still restoring the damage when he turned about, his expression outwardly submissive, though Andrew knew the man all too well, knew that something was beginning to churn behind that broad forehead.

Slowly he commenced pacing in front of the fire, then the area widened to include the sideboard. Andrew felt it as he'd felt it so many times before, energy being generated, plans being laid.

Fascinated by the metamorphosis taking place before him he sat up on the edge of the sofa.

Then finally: "I'm going home," John pronounced, his voice breathless, as though such an expenditure of energy had taken a toll within himself.

"I'm going home, Andrew," he repeated, hurrying back to the sofa, as though at last the scheme had to be shared with someone. "And you're coming with me." He grinned. "All of us are going, everyone, Elizabeth, Dhari, Aslam . . ."

Suddenly he laughed aloud, as though he'd moved so swiftly from grief to joy that he still hadn't found an emotional center of balance. "I want you to leave immediately, Andrew," he instructed, "and take a crew of workmen with you, as many as you need." He sat on the edge of the sofa, then immediately stood.

"I want you to stop first at Harrington Hall, and tell Lila to have her trunks ready. I'll come for her within a fortnight." From the fireplace he waved a hand backward. "And Lord Harrington, too. We mustn't leave him alone. He'll enjoy fishing off Mortemouth."

Andrew leaned back into the sofa, shaking his head. This amazing friend of his was up to his old tricks again, playing God, remaking the world, and reordering everyone's life in the process. And somehow he would make it all work. Andrew knew this from experience as well.

John was now hurling a barrage of instructions toward the sofa. "And after you stop at Harrington Hall I want you to proceed to Eden and start the construction of a barracks outside the gatehouse, nothing fancy, but comfortable. The workmen will have to have a place to stay. And fix that damn grille," he added. "It's on a system of pulleys, if I remember. The men will know what to do."

For the first time he paused as though his thoughts were coming too fast for his tongue and he'd momentarily lost the sequence of his new vision. Andrew asked quietly from the sofa, "To what end the barracks, John?"

"To what end?" John repeated, back on track. "The

complete modernization and renovation of Eden Castle."
He smiled. "That's to what end." He turned rapidly about
and grasped the mantel as though he needed support for
the weight and excitement of his vision. "Andrew, it will
be marvelous. Can't you see it? Those old stone walls
filled again with life. I want every chamber remodeled, I
want only the finest fabrics and furnishings. I want our
most skilled craftsmen on the job, woodcarvers, carpenters, designers."

Andrew nodded, "You want it restored."

"Restored? No, I want it better than ever. I want it to
be the most magnificent castle in the West Country, in all
of England, and I'll spare no expense or effort to accomplish that goal. Is that clear?"

It was, and Andrew began to feel the excitement himself. But there were one or two remaining questions he felt
he must raise. "And our work here?" he asked.

"What about it?" John demanded. "I pay handsome
salaries to eight professional foremen. If they don't know
what to do, then we'd better look about and hire those
who do."

"Aldwell?"

"Alex will go with us. I need him. He's the best of the
lot."

"And how long will we be gone?"

"As long as necessary." Then he was seated beside Andrew, color rising on his face as the dream grew. "A holiday, Andrew. Let's take a holiday. How long has it been
since we've had one? Things will progress well here. We
have a good organization with good men. I'll tell everyone
who needs to know where I can be reached. If something
goes wrong, one or the other of us can be back in London
in two days."

Andrew smiled at the soft pleading opposite him. He
looked almost boyish, this young "king," as though he
were pleading with his father to be taken to Eden.

Before such an expression, Andrew found he had no
resistance. "We'll need at least one hundred men," he
said, working out logistics in his mind.

John nodded. "Take fifty with you now to start on the

barracks. I'll bring fifty with me. But only the best, Andrew."

"And I'll have to replenish the staff at Eden. Poor Aggie can't—"

"Hire all of Mortemouth if you wish. The village has served my family for generations. They'll come willingly, I know."

"And we'll need buyers. Everything is gone, china, silver . . ."

Again John smiled. "Hire as many as you need. Give them unlimited letters of credit. My only instruction is that they buy only the finest."

For a moment both men stared at each other. John sat erect, as though he needed the answer to one more question. "Are you with me, Andrew?"

Without hesitation Andrew replied, "Haven't I always been?"

The brief declaration of love was warmly received. John grasped Andrew's hand, then strode toward his desk, taking a lamp with him, calling back, "Then we both have work to do. I want you to leave immediately, Andrew. Gather the men you need, and the equipment. Make a brief stop in Wiltshire, then proceed on to Eden." He sat behind his desk, drew the lamp close, the light casting a soft glow over his face. "Tell them I'm coming home," he said quietly.

He dismissed the mood and drew forward a scattering of ledger sheets, ready to get to work. A few minutes later he looked up, surprised to see Andrew still sitting on the sofa. "What are you waiting for? There's work to be done."

Andrew shook his head and pushed wearily to his feet. "Might I take time for a bath?" he asked in good-natured sarcasm.

A look of remorse crossed John's face. "Of course. I'm sorry. Take all the time you need. A full day, if you wish."

A day's rest after a tedious journey of over two weeks! "Thank you," Andrew said with mock gratitude. He gathered up his cloak and moved to the door, where he stopped and looked back at the man crouched over his papers. Andrew heard his voice in memory: *I'm going home*.

Perhaps there he would find the peace which had so consistently eluded him.

※

London,
May 1, 1861

AMIDST THE CONFUSION of carriages, John stood on the pavement outside his mansion in Belgrave Square and suffered a curious thought. It was ten years to the day that he and Elizabeth had taken his father's body home in that grim wagon with those thousands of pathetic mourners trailing behind.

The thought did not belong to the day. He called, "Aslam, come! You will ride with me."

As the little boy climbed down out of Dhari's carriage, he saw Elizabeth now climbing down from hers. She looked elegant in her pretty dark blue silk traveling suit, her face flushed with the excitement of the journey.

"No need for Dhari to ride alone," she called out cheerily, and John lifted his eyes heavenward, as a waiting steward assisted her up into Dhari's carriage. They should have been under way an hour ago, and would have been except for this constant shifting.

In the spirit of a harried father trying to organize a large family, he shouted, "Is everyone settled? Luggage secured?"

The various coachmen responded all along the line, and with a smile John took note of the lengthy entourage; his carriage in the lead, followed by Dhari and Elizabeth, followed by Elizabeth's empty carriage, followed by two large carriages filled with luggage, and two more filled with servants. Fortunately the hour was early and the traffic would not be too severe.

Now he hurried toward his carriage, where Aslam was waiting, his dark eyes reflecting the excitement of the adventure. As John swung the little boy up, he noticed the ever-constant book beneath his arm. "What did you choose for the road?" he inquired, climbing in after the child.

"Rousseau."

"Ah, good." John smiled. "A perfect choice. We'll have a discussion to pass the hours." He lowered the window and leaned out for last-minute instructions to his driver. "Take it slow through the city," he shouted. "We're to meet the men just beyond Bayswater. After we have joined with them, keep to the turnpike until Salisbury. I'll direct you from there."

As the carriage started forward, John looked back at the entourage. By God, they presented a spectacle, they did. With a growing sense of excitement that was almost insupportable, he leaned against the cushions and closed his eyes, allowing the fresh lilac-filled air to rush over him, his mind still turning on that other morning ten years ago.

How changed they all were! How hopeless the world had appeared that morning and how full of hope on this one. With the exception of that deep grief for Harriet which he knew would be with him always, he reached the conclusion that he'd never been happier, and suddenly he laughed and leaned forward and slapped Aslam's knee playfully and invited, "Tell me all you know about Rousseau."

It was approaching midmorning when they reached the outlying community of Bayswater. There Alex was awaiting him with fifteen wagons filled with equipment and men, all laughing and jostling as though they were going on a seaside holiday, which in a way they were. John had determined early on to make it a pleasant excursion for his workmen.

After greeting Alex warmly, they both stood beside his

carriage and watched as the fifteen wagons fell in at the rear of the entourage.

"Quite a tail we've got there." Alex grinned as he assisted John back into his carriage.

"Keep them close together," John shouted back in warning, and continued to lean out of the window until he saw Alex swing aboard the first wagon.

Then at last they were under way, an incredible train of over twenty conveyances rattling across the lush green English countryside, heading in a south-southwesterly direction toward Salisbury.

After two rest stops and two brief intervals for food, after having traveled all night and when the rosy streaks of dawn were just lengthening the sky, they pulled into the tree-shaded lane which led to Harrington Hall. Looking ahead, John saw a small and beloved figure standing on the terrace, her hand lifted in greeting.

Even before the carriage had come to a halt, John jumped out and ran to greet her, deriving continuous nourishment in her innocent beauty. How she would flourish at Eden, surrounded by nature's richness of both land and sea. And how good she would be for Mary, who might just once in her life find herself on the receiving end of sufficient love.

Then she was before him, her eyes lifted in an expression of adoration, and he embraced her lightly and whispered, "I've missed you."

"No more separations"—she smiled—"please," and in that gentle way told him that she had missed him as well.

A moment later, Lord Harrington emerged from the door, followed by a procession of stewards bearing trunks. He spied John and greeted him warmly. "Are you certain, John"—he smiled—"that I am included in this invitation?"

"Of course." John nodded. "There's work for all, and excellent fishing in both the ocean and channel." He clasped the man's hand. "No one is to be left behind, Lord Harrington," he said, suddenly solemn, "ever again."

"Then come," Lord Harrington said with dispatch.

"While our stewards secure the trunks, we'll partake of breakfast. The staff has prepared a light buffet on the terrace. Come, all of you."

As additional stewards commenced opening carriage doors down the line, John saw Elizabeth and Dhari step down and adjust their gowns, Elizabeth hurrying forward first, her face showing not the least sign of fatigue from the night's journey, smiling brightly as she approached Lila, eager to meet her for the first time, though John knew that the two had established a warm correspondence, Elizabeth frequently receiving news from Harrington Hall even before he did.

He stood back, fully aware that no formal introduction was necessary, Elizabeth approaching, her arms open, and Lila responding admirably, stepping into the embrace, as though they had known and loved each other all their lives.

"You're even more beautiful than I had imagined," Elizabeth murmured at the end of the embrace.

"And you as well." Lila smiled.

"Where's Wolf?" Elizabeth asked suddenly, looking about. "I must meet the cat. Come, Dhari, Aslam, remember the cat Lila wrote about so often? Now we can meet him in person."

With Lila leading the way, the three women started around toward the garden, their heads bent in close conversation, Aslam running around and between them, relieved to be out of the confinement of the carriage.

For a moment John stared after them and marveled at their individual and unique beauty, poignantly conscious of the role each played in his life, aware also that he desperately needed each to fill the vacuum, to take the place of that one miraculous woman.

He heard Lord Harrington calling to him from the terrace. "Come, John, before your hungry men devour it all."

Laughing, he walked directly into the crowd of familiar faces, calling them all by name, feeling a sense of fellowship with them, aware that they were mutually dependent upon each other.

He proceeded on, shaking hands, answering questions

about their destination, coming at last to the brick re-
taining wall which separated terrace from garden. There
he stopped and looked over the edge at the gray cat
luxuriating obscenely on his back, allowing the three
women and Aslam to rub his belly while he pawed
sleepily at the air.

John smiled at the tableau, worthy of an artist's canvas.
Yet with all the festive merriment going on about him, he
lifted his head and peered westward, as though in spite of
the felicitous nature of this brief stop his true destination
lay yet ahead.

Shortly before noon, their entourage swollen by the
addition of Lord Harrington's three carriages, Elizabeth,
Dhari, Lila, with Wolf in her arms and Lord Harrington
riding together, the procession started forward again.

John stayed alert until he saw that his driver was back
on the turnpike again. Looking opposite him, he saw
Aslam sound asleep, exhausted by the sleepless night and
the activity at Harrington Hall. Lovingly John studied
him. Such a beautiful child, and so bright. All he had to
do was outrace his past, which was what every man had
to do.

Then, thinking to join him in sleep, John too stretched
out in moderate comfort, wishing that he might close his
eyes and open them to see Eden Castle before him.

But he could not sleep and found his thoughts filled
with Eden, a curious mixture of the Eden he had left and
the sadder Eden that Andrew had described. Again that
awesome sense of grief descended on him, and with
Aslam asleep and nothing to divert him, he closed his
eyes and gave in to it.

Eden Castle,
May 3, 1861

RICHARD HAD BEEN on the battlements since dawn, searching the horizon in all directions. From this vantage point he could see everything, could see the new barracks outside the gates nearing completion, could see as well the feverish activity in the courtyard as the army of new servants scurried every which way, trying frantically to prepare for John's imminent arrival.

Coming from the courtard below, he heard a voice shouting up. "Do you see anything yet?"

Richard looked down on Andrew far beneath him. "Nothing," he shouted back.

"Keep your eyes open. He said a morning arrival."

Richard waved and lifted the spyglass to the distant horizon. Briefly he closed his eyes. Never had he felt God's hand so securely upon him, or God's blessing. How often he had prayed over these last difficult years, had vowed that if God saw them safely through their crucible, he would give his life to Him.

"Here I am," he whispered to the blowing wind, finding it a joyous promise to keep.

All at once, without the aid of the glass, he looked up and saw what appeared to be a sizable dust cloud on the horizon, coming from the direction of Taunton. He looked again with his naked eye, then quickly lifted the glass and saw it even more clearly.

Richard grasped the glass and tried to hold it steady against his eyes, but his hands shook. Still the dust eddied and swirled about the horizon, lifting in large brown clouds, something of tremendous force moving over Exmoor at a tremendous rate of speed.

Then all at once he saw it, the massive lead carriage

618

drawn by four black stallions. He lowered the glass and shouted over the edge of the battlements, "Andrew! He's coming!"

The cry seemed to echo about the inner courtyard. Other voices were shouting now, Andrew's predominant among them. "Lift the grilles!" he shouted to the men at the gate. "And tell all the stewards to stand by."

Richard gazed a moment longer at the feverish activity below, then looked back into the glass and saw the lead carriage followed by others, two, three, four, five, more carriages than Richard had ever imagined, and following those, more wagons of the sort that had arrived with Andrew over two weeks ago.

He smiled, thinking that all of London had come to Eden; and even more acutely aware than ever of an ordeal ending, he lowered the glass and lifted his head and with eyes open gave a short prayer of thanksgiving.

And at last he was running, hungry to see the face of the man he loved like a brother, taking the narrow steps three at a time, emerging at last into the third-floor corridor, hearing even there the first carriage rattling over the grates, its speed unbroken, as though the passenger could not endure the slowed pace of a more cautious approach.

Still running, Richard took the final staircase, half-stumbling, and entered the Great Hall to see the servants at work setting up the massive tables upon which Aggie was arranging a sumptuous repast.

"He's here," Richard shouted, and saw only peripherally the excited faces of Aggie and Mary, Jennifer and Clara. Dodging his way through the servants, he reached the Great Hall door just as the lead carriage was swerving wide for its final turn, the carriage door, Richard noticed, already opening, a tall man running alongside for a few moments, then turning loose and looking up in all directions at the facade of the castle.

At the top of the steps, Richard stopped, his eyes focused on the man, his heart filling with ten years of unspent love. He'd changed, looked taller somehow, fully bearded, his fair hair windblown about his face, but then, to Richard John had always been a giant.

Then all at once Richard saw him look up toward the top of the steps, look away, then look quickly back, as though his eyes had deceived him.

Although there was movement all about, Richard was aware of nothing but that strong face, the man himself coming slowly forward.

Promising to keep his emotions in check, Richard started down the steps, saw John still coming toward him, the warmth of a smile on his face. Though less than three feet separated them, still neither had spoken. Suddenly Richard found himself in John's embrace, the two of them clinging together against all those staring eyes, impervious to everything save the goodness of their reunion.

Let it last a moment longer, Richard prayed, at least until he could clear his eyes. Apparently John was having the same difficulty, and when they finally separated, each laughed at the indisposition of the other as both tried to wipe away the embarrassing moisture with the backs of their hands.

"I . . . can't believe it," Richard managed at last. "There were times when I was certain that you were dead."

John grinned. "There were times when your estimate was fairly accurate," he said, then added, "Now, come, let me look at you. What in the hell happened to that little boy who wanted to play marbles?"

Richard was on the verge of answering when suddenly he saw John gazing past him to the top of the stairs. Poor man, Richard thought happily, as again he saw his eyes fill, and glanced up to see Mary coming shyly down the stairs, her one good dark dress painfully mended, her light hair, though, still curly and lovely.

Then she too was in his arms and he was holding her gently, the two of them laughing together as though the passage of ten long years had never taken place.

Immediately following Mary, he saw Jennifer, then old Aggie and Clara and Dana clinging together against the vicissitudes of age and the moment. They inundated him, all clinging to him while he tried to embrace them, reaching continuously out and drawing them close. Again, under the emotional duress of the moment, Richard looked away.

For the first time since he had descended the Great Hall steps, he saw a most incredible spectacle, the inner courtyard filled with carriages, each spilling forth a footman and driver, the narrow doors opening to reveal several lovely women, one dark and quite beautiful, a dark-skinned little boy teasing a great gray cat, a tall, distinguished-looking gentleman with graying hair and a look of almost unbearable joy on his face.

This small group now seemed to huddle together, all smiling at the warm reunion taking place at the bottom of the stairs, and moving around them was a large collection of maids and stewards releasing trunks and hatboxes and dropping them from the tops of carriages like autumn leaves.

Filling the rest of the courtyard were the wagons, grinning strapping men leaping to ground, then turning to greet the other workmen who'd arrived two weeks earlier, who were now running in through the gates, their work on the new barracks temporarily abandoned in the excitement of greeting old friends.

In considerable amazement Richard looked around at the chaotic scene. After so many years of silence, when month in, month out, all he'd heard was the wind shrieking, the cries of sea gulls and his own persistent prayers, now the music of human voices raised in shouts and laughter seemed to him almost unbearably beautiful.

He might have been content to stand and watch forever if he'd not heard a voice behind him whisper, "Quite a gathering you're playing host to, Lord Eden," and he turned to see Andrew Rhoades's smiling face.

In spite of the fact that he'd only known the man for a few short weeks, he was very fond of him, and delighted that they shared a mutual love for John. "I'm afraid I don't feel very lordlike," Richard murmured good-naturedly.

"Nonetheless, that's what you are." Andrew smiled. "Come. Let's see if between the two of us we can't dry up some of those tears before the courtyard is flooded."

As they stepped toward John and Aggie Fletcher, Richard noticed the little group standing in front of one of the carriages move forward. At that moment John spied

Andrew, embraced him warmly and turned immediately to the women waiting behind him.

Still hanging back, Richard took loving note of John's face, excited, joyous, as though he were playing out a scene in reality that had lived too long only in his imagination. As he motioned for the group to come closer, his expression became suddenly solemn, as though aware of the responsibility of his position and how important it was that he do it right, bringing together all these diverse elements of his life.

Gratefully Richard observed that there was no formal receiving line. He saw John calling for him to step forward first, and as he did so, he felt John's arm around his shoulders and saw that he was being led forward to meet first a lovely woman clad in a dark blue silk traveling suit and a feathered bonnet on her head. Richard was certain that he had never seen a warmer, more open face, her dark blue eyes laughing, her cheeks flushed with excitement.

She came steadily forward, and John grasped her hand and drew her nearer, and said simply, "Elizabeth, this is Richard."

She bobbed her head, then to Richard's surprise leaned forward and kissed him lightly on the cheek. "Thank you for welcoming us to Eden," she said softly.

Feeling a blush, Richard did well to nod, then with relief he saw John guiding her on to Mary and Aggie and then old Clara, each of them the recipient of her warm embrace. She paused before Jennifer and seemed to look even more closely at those dead features, then drew her into a loving embrace, whispering, "Let's spend hours talking of Edward and Daniel," and Richard saw a dazzling smile on Jennifer's face, the first he'd seen in ever so long.

Then he looked back to see John leading the dark woman and the little boy forward. Indian was Richard's guess, though in coloring only, for both were garbed in elegantly tailored Western clothes, the woman's gown bright yellow as though to contrast her dark beauty.

"Dhari," John said quietly, his voice filled with deep affection. "And Aslam," he added, propelling the little boy forward, who with manly authority extended his hand and pronounced in flawless English, "It is my great pleasure, Lord Eden."

Surprised by the aplomb in one so young, Richard accepted the hand and noticed the book clasped beneath the boy's arm. "You're a reader, I see." He smiled.

"Oh, yes, sir," the boy replied seriously. "John has told me so much about the Eden library. I look forward to seeing it."

"And you shall," Richard assured him, grateful that he'd put his foot down when Aggie had once suggested that they sell the books.

He looked back up to Dhari and started to say something and noticed that John had directed her to Aggie and Mary and Clara. Well, later. There would be ample time for talk later, and again he felt a surge of excitement at the thought that these fascinating and exotic people would be here for a while, hopefully forever. Oh, how the Banqueting Hall would ring with good talk.

Finally he saw John extend his hand to the last lady, who looked more like a young girl, her cameo face framed by a bonnet of pink silk which matched her gown, while in her arms she lovingly stroked the big gray cat, who seemed unperturbed by the excitement.

"Richard, I would like for you to meet my wife, Mrs. John Murrey Eden, Lady Lila Harrington."

Wife! The simple announcement seemed to attract the attention of all those listening. But if the young lady was aware that she was the center of attention, she gave no indication of it, and now holding the cat under one arm, she reached into her drawstring purse and withdrew a small nosegay of yellow flowers. Carefully she pulled one delicate blossom loose and handed it to Richard.

"The first heartsease of spring." She smiled. "For you. I found a cluster of them in the woods the day before we left. I clipped a few roots as well, thinking to plant them at Eden. Does Eden have a garden?"

Her voice was so extraordinarily musical, her manner so ethereal that Richard felt himself struggling as though out of a trance just to respond, "Yes . . . well, no . . . what

I mean is, we had a garden once, but I'm afraid it's in sore need of attention."

"Then I shall attend to it." The young lady smiled. "I have a way with flowers," she added, ducking her head modestly.

With everything, Richard thought, completely captivated. Then John was introducing Lord Harrington, whose face still bore a look of surprise at his surroundings. "I too am grateful for your hospitality, Lord Eden," the man said with obvious sincerity, "and to John for rescuing me from a very large and lonely Hall."

Richard shook his hand warmly. "I suspect, Lord Harrington, that you and I might enjoy comparing tales of large empty halls."

The man laughed openly. "A questionable sport generally, though harmless, I suppose, when surrounded by those one loves."

Richard agreed and felt an instant bond with the tall graying man whose face bore the marks of a private crucible.

After the introductions had been completed, after Lila had presented one and all with a sprig of yellow heartsease, after Andrew had given brief instructions to the stewards concerning the dispersing of trunks, old Aggie, her eyes still glistening, took the steps and announced in a full and raucous voice, "There's a table spread inside. I've given it me best efforts for the better part of the last five days, and if there's one faltering appetite, I'll take it as a personal insult, I will."

She lifted her voice louder then, to the large crew of workmen standing about in the courtyard. "You gentlemen, too," she shouted. "If you're going to do the work, you're goin' to eat proper, and old Aggie promises you that."

All at once a hearty cheer went up from the men, and as all rushed toward the steps, Richard caught a fleeting glimpse of John, his arm about Dhari's waist, his hand clasping Lila's, his head turning in all directions, a look of joy on his face which transformed his countenance. There was the true Lord of Eden Castle, Richard thought, wishing that he could bestow the title upon him.

Then Richard too was swept up in the onward rush, and he vowed not to think anymore, at least for a while, and gave himself wholly to the sounds of life, to the shouts and laughter, the sparkling eyes and open arms, to the human faces reflecting what God intended them to reflect: joy, love, peace. . . .

For over an hour the crowds thronged about Aggie's table, a masterpiece of plain country cooking: golden Cornish pastries done to a turn, richly browned Scotch eggs, pyramids of summer fruit and large squares of spicy gingerbread.

Richard ate as he had never eaten before, as did everyone else. Feeling more at home in his role of observer rather than participant, he kept to the edge of the crowd, laughing openly at little Aslam chasing the gray cat through the forest of legs, the mountainous man named Alex Aldwell who received goodhearted jeers each time he returned to the table, then a thunderous round of applause as he planted a warm kiss on Aggie's face, the entire company warming to each other in a delightful fashion.

While Richard was looking out over this colorful throng, he saw John break away and walk slowly in the opposite direction, heading for the dark privacy of the far arcade which encircled the Great Hall.

Pleased, Richard started after him. He'd hoped to find him alone for a moment, to express his deep gratitude in a private and unhurried fashion. He held his position a moment to see if anyone would follow after him. And when none did, Richard skirted the crowd, moving across the Great Hall to the far arcade, where he saw John standing alone staring at the closed door of the small library.

Richard paused, trying to organize his thoughts. Perhaps this wasn't the best time after all. He seemed very preoccupied, staring at that closed door.

"John?" he called softly, trying to enter his silence as gracefully as possible.

When still the man did not turn, Richard stepped closer until he was at his side, on the verge of speaking again until he saw his face, an expression so vastly different from the one Richard had observed outside that it might have been another man, a stranger deep in mourning who somehow had wandered into this hall of festivity and celebration.

Though John was dry-eyed, Richard recognized the look of grief. "What is it?" he asked, longing to be of comfort.

Still no response, not immediately, though a few moments later he heard a whispered inquiry, "When did she . . . die?"

In the semidarkness of the interior corridor, Richard stepped closer, mystified by the question. "When did . . . ?"

It came again, louder, as though he'd waited too long for an answer. "When did . . . Harriet die?" he asked, never lifting his eyes from the library door.

Then it was clear, though Richard was aware of a heavy burden settling over him. How to explain what he, after ten years, still did not understand. "She is not dead, John," he commenced slowly, and was prepared to go on. But that tortured face lifted from the door and turned on Richard, the grief there mingling with incredible shock.

"Not dead?"

"No," Richard went on, praying briefly for the courage to describe the tragedy with which he'd lived for so long.

When he finished speaking, he made the mistake of looking back at John's face.

"And," Richard went on, with effort, "she has never left her chambers since."

John stepped toward him. "Is . . . this true?" he demanded.

"I swear it," Richard replied.

"But . . . food? How . . . ?"

"Only Peggy is permitted to enter the chamber, once a day, late at night, bearing a tray. She performs simple duties and claims that no words have ever been exchanged between them, as though my mother has forced her to a vow of silence. Over the years, Peggy seems to have absorbed the silence of the room and has become as silent herself. She serves my mother as maid and keeper and guards her imprisonment as zealously as though she were the warden."

Richard closed his eyes. How much it still hurt. "As for the rest of us," he went on, "our entreaties ceased years ago when it became clear that she desired neither our company nor our solace. And whatever you may think, John, you mustn't fault our efforts. We tried, all of us. Oh, God, how we tried to penetrate that silence. But clearly she has set a penance for herself, and in order to serve it, that door must remain closed. It has never opened to any of us, and it never will."

Again Richard turned away. It was not easy resurrecting such pain. Over the years they all had grown accustomed to it, the deep silence coming from the self-made prison. How often he'd spoken to God about it, begging for understanding. How could a human being endure such isolation, an isolation made even more incredible by the reality of her blindness. Though he'd never received an answer, God had been generous enough to give him the courage to endure, and looking back at John's stunned face, he wished that he could provide him with the same gift.

Then John seemed to rouse himself out of his state of shock. He grabbed Richard's arm. "Take me to her," he commanded.

Everything in Richard revolted. "No, John, it will serve no purpose. I beg you, leave her alone."

"Take me to her," John commanded again. Apparently realizing that he needed no guidance, that he knew the way to the third-floor chambers, he started out of the arcade at a run, ignoring Richard's final plea to, "Leave her alone, John!"

Then Richard was running after him. As he started up the central staircase, he saw John a flight ahead of him, his boots sending back an echo in the reverberating stillness of the upper regions of the castle.

It wasn't until they both were standing at the end of the third-floor corridor that Richard caught up with him, both breathing heavily from their sprint, John's eyes focused on the door at the far end of the passage.

"Please, John, I beg you," Richard tried again. "It will

serve no purpose except to break your own heart. Please . . ."

But John started slowly down the corridor, his step not faltering until he stood before the door, his hands examining it, his arms lifting to the high corners, clearly studying its unique construction, one smooth solid block of impenetrable English oak, reinforced at the center with a sheet of metal, no exterior doorknob, or bolt, or hinge, fitted tightly into the door frame.

"It can't be breached," Richard whispered.

But if John heard, he gave no indication of it, and now his hands were pressed against the door in another mood. No longer inspecting, they were moving in a caressing motion. Richard saw him lean against it, his voice scarcely audible as he whispered, "Harriet . . ."

Richard turned away, all the frustration and pain that the closed door had caused him in the past rising up before him. He walked to one of the near windows and looked down into the inner courtyard, at the workmen removing their equipment from the backs of the wagons, artisan's tools which spoke of reconstruction and the future. What a sharp contrast, that scene below, to the one behind him.

"Harriet, please . . ." he heard John begging. "It's . . . John," he whispered. "I've . . . come home . . ."

Richard looked back and saw him still pressed against the door, his hands moving out in circles, as though trying to reach through to the woman within.

"Harriet, please let me come in," John went on. "I've so much to tell you. So much has happened . . ."

Richard saw him turn his head to one side as though he were listening to the silence. Still John spoke on, as Richard had done so many times before, thinking that if he continued to speak, he might say something that would make a difference.

Again Richard turned back to the window and closed his eyes. He had hoped to postpone this grim encounter. It did not belong to this day of joyous reunion. "Please, John," he begged from the window.

But still he talked on to the unresponding door, his voice rising into a new urgency. "I have a wife now,

Harriet," he said. "I want you to meet her. You will love her, I know, and I've brought others with me as well. Can you hear them, Harriet? They're all below in the Great Hall. Please let me . . ."

All at once he crumpled softly against the door, as though at last aware of the futility of what he was doing.

Richard saw the small collapse and moved to his side. "Come," he begged, "please come away. It serves no purpose to torture yourself so. I put myself through the same agony for years."

With his hand on John's shoulder, he saw him avert his eyes. "If weeping would open the door, John," Richard said quietly, "it would have swung open long ago. Come," he urged, and at last succeeded in turning him about, wondering how long it would take that normally strong face to recover.

They had taken about five hesitant steps back down the corridor when Richard first heard it, a sound so slight as to be barely perceptible, then growing louder, a curious metallic sound, as though . . .

John heard it as well, and looked sharply back, as though the door had spoken to him. He broke away from Richard's support, both men focused rigidly on the door, on the sound, growing louder, as though someone with great effort was slowly sliding the bolt.

So intense was his focus that Richard felt his eyes blur. Had he imagined it? Had they both imagined it? All at once the noise ceased, and in the silence he looked at John, saw him standing rigidly as though he were afraid to move.

Then Richard heard a new sound, the creaking of hinges, and with held breath he witnessed a miracle, the door beginning to open, ever so slowly, an inch at a time, then stopping abruptly, revealing only a thin black crack.

Lazarus . . .

John stepped forward, throwing back one command. "Leave us," he whispered. "Leave us," he repeated.

Readily and joyfully Richard obliged, walking backward for a few steps, still not absolutely certain that he was to believe what he was seeing, that solitary crack growing no larger, but large enough, a miraculous signal that the prisoner was weary of her prison.

At the far end of the corridor, Richard looked back and saw John, his head bowed, as though he knew he was facing the most incomprehensible ordeal of his life.

Coming from the Great Hall below, Richard could hear the distant laughter, new bonds of friendship being formed, the artisans eagerly discussing changes and renovations, all sounds of a new dawn, the long dark winter over.

Again he looked back down the corridor, aware that he shouldn't be watching, but watching anyway, that sense of intimacy increasing along with the peculiar weight of hesitancy which seemed to be pressing against John.

Go to her, Richard prayed. *In God's name, go to her.* If anyone could draw her out of her prison, it would be John.

He looked down the corridor, felt the tension of waiting increasing, spreading.

Go to her, he prayed fiercely.

John lifted his head; one hand reached out.

Then he went in. . . .

Popular Romances from
BALLANTINE

Bestsellers from BALLANTINE